THE DARK COIL
DAMNATION

THE DARK COIL
DAMNATION

BLACK LIBRARY

A BLACK LIBRARY PUBLICATION

'Out Caste' first published digitally in 2012.
'A Sanctuary of Wyrms' first published in *Xenos Hunters* in 2012.
Fire Caste first published in 2013.
'Fire and Ice' first published in *Shas'o* in 2015.
'Vanguard' first published digitally as 'Adeptus Mechanicus: Vanguard' in 2015.
'Cast a Hungry Shadow' first published digitally in 2016.
Cult of the Spiral Dawn first published as *Genestaler Cults* in 2016.
'The Greater Evil' first published digitally in 2017.
'Altar of Maws' first published digitally in 2023.
This edition published in Great Britain in 2025 by
Black Library, Games Workshop Ltd., Willow Road,
Nottingham, NG7 2WS, UK.

Represented by: Games Workshop Limited – Irish branch,
Unit 3, Lower Liffey Street, Dublin 1,
D01 K199, Ireland.

10 9 8 7 6 5 4 3 2 1

Produced by Games Workshop in Nottingham.
Cover illustration by Jodie Muir.

A CIP record for this book is available from the British Library.

ISBN 13: 978-1-83609-000-7

See Black Library on the internet at

blacklibrary.com

Find out more about Games Workshop
and the worlds of Warhammer at

warhammer.com

Printed and bound in the UK.

It is the 41st millennium. For more than a hundred centuries the Emperor has sat immobile on the Golden Throne of Earth. He is the master of mankind by the will of the gods, and master of a million worlds by the might of his inexhaustible armies. He is a rotting carcass writhing invisibly with power from the Dark Age of Technology. He is the Carrion Lord of the Imperium for whom a thousand souls are sacrificed every day, so that he may never truly die.

Yet even in his deathless state, the Emperor continues his eternal vigilance. Mighty battlefleets cross the daemon-infested miasma of the warp, the only route between distant stars, their way lit by the Astronomican, the psychic manifestation of the Emperor's will. Vast armies give battle in His name on uncounted worlds. Greatest amongst his soldiers are the Adeptus Astartes, the Space Marines, bioengineered super-warriors. Their comrades in arms are legion: the Astra Militarum and countless planetary defence forces, the ever-vigilant Inquisition and the tech-priests of the Adeptus Mechanicus to name only a few. But for all their multitudes, they are barely enough to hold off the ever-present threat from aliens, heretics, mutants – and worse.

To be a man in such times is to be one amongst untold billions. It is to live in the cruellest and most bloody regime imaginable. These are the tales of those times. Forget the power of technology and science, for so much has been forgotten, never to be re-learned. Forget the promise of progress and understanding, for in the grim dark future there is only war. There is no peace amongst the stars, only an eternity of carnage and slaughter, and the laughter of thirsting gods.

CONTENTS

THE GREATER EVIL

*'Evil grows from within, not without. It is a disharmony of the self,
not the shadow of some elusive, predatory other.'*

– The Yasu'caor

– THE FIRST CIRCLE –
OUTSIDE

*No matter how often Voyle relives it, the end always begins the same way.
A deep clang reverberates through the airlock as the* Sable Star's *boarding
umbilical latches on to the derelict ship. Voyle checks the air tank strapped
to the back of the trooper beside him, then turns so his comrade can return
the gesture. The routine is mirrored by every member of the squad with practised swiftness. They have run through it twice already, yet nobody hesitates.
Nobody complains. A Void Breacher's life hangs by the integrity of his tank
as much as his weapons.*

*'Squad Indigo is bloodtight,' Voyle reports into his helmet vox when the
ritual is complete. 'Repeat, bloodtight.'*

*'Bloodtight confirmed, Indigo,' Lieutenant Joliffe acknowledges from the
bridge, unable to hide the tension in his voice. Captain Bester took his own
life fourteen days ago. Nobody knows why, but they all sense Joliffe isn't
ready to lead the company – not on this warp-cursed patrol. Voyle has considered seizing command. No one would stand in his way, least of all Joliffe,
but then the burden of choice would be his to carry. No, it is better to live or
die with clean hands.*

'Commence breach,' Joliffe orders. 'Emperor walk with you, Indigo.'

*With a hydraulic hiss the external hatch slides into its recess, revealing the
metal tube of the umbilical. Most of the strip lumens running its length have
failed and those that still work flicker fitfully. The company's five-month tour
of the Damocles perimeter has taken a heavy toll on both supplies and men,
including both its enginseers. The* Sable Star *was just three days out from
Kliest when it found the intruder, silent and powerless, yet perfectly intact.
Its markings designate it as the* Halvorsen, *but though the massive derelict
is evidently Imperial in origin, they can find no record of it. That is not unusual, for numberless ships ply the vast tracts of the Imperium and countless*

more have been lost over the millennia. Factoring in the contortions of the warp, the derelict might be decades or even centuries old. It is a cumbersome hulk devoid of guns or advanced sensor arrays – probably a civilian cargo freighter and certainly no match for a warship like the Sable Star, *but that is little reassurance for the men tasked with boarding it. With derelicts it is what lies within that matters, for the void crawls with phantoms seeking the solace of metal or flesh.*

Let it rot, *Voyle wants to say.* Better yet, blast it back into the warp!

But instead he says what he always says: 'Acknowledged, crossing commences.' And enters the umbilical. He is a Void Breacher. This is what the Astra Militarum has trained him for.

They lied to us! *Voyle yells at his former self, but it is a silent cry, for if the ghosts of the past are without eyes, so those of the future are without voice.*

The Void Breachers' magnetised boots clatter on the corrugated decking as they advance along the narrow tunnel one by one, their helmet lights slicing back and forth. The concertinaed tube creaks and shudders around them as it strains to keep the ships conjoined, the living to the dead. Despite their sealed carapace armour and therma-padding, the cold is gnawing at them within seconds and their movements grow sluggish before they are halfway across. The rasping exhalations from their helmets are like steam in the frigid air, forcing them to wipe their visors clean after each respiration, lest breath becomes blinding frost.

Voyle halts as his light finds the derelict's access hatch. The metal is dark and pitted, contrasting starkly with the gleaming umbilical clamps that encircle it. One glance tells him the locking mechanism is hopelessly corroded.

'Cut us a door, Hoenig,' he orders, moving aside as the squad's specialist steps forward. He watches as the trooper engraves a glowing oval around the hatch with a las-cutter. The tool's power pack whines and Voyle wills it to fail, knowing it won't. It never does. The nightmare won't allow it.

'Done, Breach Sergeant,' Hoenig says, then shoves the hatch. With a screech of harrowed metal it crashes into the darkness beyond. As the reverberations subside, Voyle levels his meltagun and steps through.

His own shriek wrenched him back from the brink.

But I've already fallen, Voyle thought wildly as he surged to his feet. *There's no coming back...*

The nightmare fractured and fell away in sluggish fragments, revealing a large windowless chamber. Its walls were tessellated with hexagonal panels that glowed softly, washing the space in subdued blue light. Voyle stood at its centre, his bare feet tangled in a silvery blanket. He tore himself free and spun around, trying to make sense of things.

Where–

He froze as he caught sight of something watching him from one of the walls.

Black eyes gleaming with a hunger colder than the void...

The sound that rose in his throat was somewhere between a scream, a snarl and a sigh, born of fear and loathing and... *longing?* Voyle stifled it as the predator dissolved into a human form. A woman. She was crouched in a recess in the opposite wall where a hexagonal panel had retracted, her eyes glinting in the gloom as she appraised him. Her face was tattooed with concentric rings, the first shearing through her forehead, cheeks and chin, the second encircling her eyes and mouth and the third set directly between her eyes. Voyle knew she bore a fourth and final ring, but its lines were invisible, for it embraced the mind.

'Unity,' Voyle breathed, naming the symbol... and remembering. The woman's tattoos mirrored those on his own face. With that recollection the rest flooded back and he scanned the chamber quickly, but the other serenity cells were still sealed. Only the woman, who always slept with hers open, had been roused by his nightmare and she wouldn't say anything to the others.

'Forgive me, sister,' Voyle said. 'I was walking old roads.'

Her expression gave nothing away. Sometimes she seemed as inscrutable as their liberators. Though they had been comrades since Voyle's emancipation from the Imperium almost five ago, they had exchanged few words. Other than her name – Erzul – he knew little about her save her loyalty to the cause and her talents as a pathfinder. But that was fine by Voyle. He wasn't much inclined to talk about his own past either. Remembering was bad enough. Dreaming even worse...

Why now? he wondered, reluctantly considering the old nightmare. It hadn't troubled him in years – not since he'd mastered the mantras of self-sublimation during his induction. He'd almost convinced himself it was a false memory, as his instructors had encouraged.

Almost.

Voyle rubbed the old scar under his chin. It was itching furiously, as if inflamed by the sting of the past. He wasn't going to sleep again this cycle. Maybe the sour-sweet tranquillity wafers the liberators issued their auxiliaries were losing their potency.

I should report it, Voyle brooded, knowing he wouldn't. He trusted the liberators of course, but his weakness shamed him. Void dammit, he should have taken a cell. At least that way he'd have kept his nightmares to himself. He was a big man, broad-shouldered and a head taller than anyone else in his squad, let alone the liberators, but that wasn't why he shunned the serenity cells. If his commander had demanded it, he would have squeezed into one of the hexagonal coffins, but the Stormlight had not pressed the issue. That wasn't his way.

'It is your shadow to burn,' the xenos had said, identifying his subordinate's dread with an acuity that would have confounded the Imperial officers Voyle had served under. 'You alone can light the fire.'

But the ship was already five days into its voyage and that fire remained unlit. Every sleep cycle Voyle had bedded down at the centre of the chamber, ignoring the questioning looks of his squad as they clambered into their cells.

It doesn't matter, he thought as he pulled his boots on. His loathing of tight spaces was only a whisper of the shadow that stalked him.

'I'll be in the Fire Grounds,' he told Erzul as he stepped towards a wall. It split open at his approach, revealing a brightly lit corridor. Nothing could hide in that crisp, sane light.

Void black eyes.

Why now? Voyle asked again. A new life and purpose hadn't dispelled the shadow. It had simply lain dormant. Waiting for him to wake up.

The Seeker faced the maelstrom of swirling, prismatic mist with his back straight and his staff extended horizontally before him at eye level. Its lifeless metal was untarnished by the farrago of colours assaulting him so he kept his gaze locked upon it, using its truth to filter out the lies. He had diffused his breathing to a low susurration, each exhalation extending across several minutes, yet encompassing no more than eleven heartbeats. His master had attained seven beats in the ritual of the *arhat'karra*, but Aun'el Kyuhai knew he would never match such serenity. Nor would he ever ascend beyond his current station in the Ethereal caste's hierarchy. That knowledge brought neither resentment nor sadness, for he had cast aside all desire save service to the Tau'va . All else was as illusory as the storm that raged around him.

And behind illusions prowled beasts...

They came for him together, springing from the mist in perfect synchronicity, one from behind, the other from his left, which they had identified as his weaker side. Traditionally their kind attacked in a cacophony of squawks and hoots, yet this pair came in silence, denying their prey any warning.

They are learning, Kyuhai approved. He spun to his left, thrusting his staff towards the dark shape flanking him, but it sprang away into the fog like a gangling acrobat. He felt a rush of air at his back as the other assailant's blade hacked through the space he had occupied a moment earlier. The ferocity of the swing committed the attacker for a second too long, chaining it to the impotent arc as Kyuhai whirled his staff over his shoulder. It was a blind strike, but the displaced air had told him all he needed to know. When he entered the *arhat'karra*, every moment stretched into many and every whisper shouted.

'Ka'vash!' he pronounced as his staff brushed his opponent's throat. Had the weapon's blades been extended it would have been a killing blow. Before his foe could offer the ritual response, the second beast lunged from the fog, its cranial quills erect with rage. Beady, deep-set eyes glared at him from either side of a prognathous, serrated beak. The creature was naked save for a leather tabard and its sinewy form was riddled with tribal tattoos and piercings. This time it didn't attack in silence.

Rukh expects defeat, Kyuhai recognised as he swept his staff around to meet the avian warrior's scimitar. *When Zeljukh falls, Rukh always falls with her.*

The creature struck in a whirlwind frenzy that would have overwhelmed a lesser foe, yet none of its blows passed the gliding, almost languid parries of Kyuhai's staff. To the Seeker the onslaught was akin to an infant's tantrum, but he allowed it to run its course. Perhaps it would be instructive.

Once again anger blinds Rukh, Kyuhai gauged as he blocked. He was disappointed, but unsurprised, for they had played out this scene many times before.

It was Zeljukh who ended the hopeless duel, bringing her bonded mate to heel with a derisory tirade of hoots and clicks. With a squawk of frustration, Rukh threw his scimitar aside and proffered his neck.

'*Ka'vash,*' Kyuhai said, gently tapping the creature's throat. 'End simulation.'

The swirling fog vanished instantly, revealing the ochre coloured expanse of the Fire Grounds. The *Whispering Hand*'s training bay was divided into six sectors, some housing demi-sentient sparring machines, others devoted to low-tech challenges like climbing frames or ropes. Kyuhai and his opponents stood in the simulation arena, where a large saucer-like machine hovered overhead, its underside bristling with sensors and projectors that tracked their movements. This late in the ship's sleep cycle the bay was almost empty, yet Kyuhai and his companions were not quite alone. A human was training on the far side of the bay – the big man who led the expedition's second gue'vesa support team. Their paths had crossed here before while their fellow travellers slept, but they had never spoken.

'Reflect upon this defeat,' Kyuhai told the avian warriors. 'Leave me.'

The pair inscribed the symbol of Unity with their claws then loped towards the climbing arena, where they would continue training until he summoned them. Once they would have berated each other for their defeat, but they were past such foolishness. He had brought them that far at least.

'*Your honour guard is formidable, exalted one,*' the expedition's ranking Fire Warrior had observed when Kyuhai had come aboard the ship. '*The kroot are fierce allies.*'

'*I am a Seeker, Shas'el Akuryo. I have no honour guard,*' Kyuhai had replied. '*Rukh and Zeljukh are simply companions on my path.*'

Many of Kyuhai's fellow t'au were repelled by the avian auxiliaries, but he had detected only respect in the Fire Warrior's voice. Though Akuryo and he were of the same rank within their respective castes, the Ethereals were elevated above all others, creating a gulf of authority between them. Had the Seeker commanded it, Akuryo would have taken his own life without hesitation. Such blind faith had troubled Kyuhai when he had first stepped onto his path, but he had soon learnt that it was not blind at all, for his caste was the living embodiment of the *Tau'va.*

'We rule to serve,' he said, echoing the words of his former master.

The sounds of combat drew him from his reflection. While his mind had wandered, his body had followed its own path, carrying him to the arena where the big gue'la was duelling with a pair of drones. The saucer-like machines buzzed around the man, harassing him with low intensity lasers as he whirled about, blocking their beams with the mirror shields strapped to his wrists. His only method of retaliation was to reflect the lasers back at their source, but only a direct hit on an emitter would disable a drone, while three strikes to his torso would end the bout. Judging by their tenacity the machines had been set to maximum aggression – a challenge even for seasoned Fire Warriors. Though the man moved with a speed that belied his bulk, it was apparent that his ambition exceeded his ability.

Like Rukh, he fights in the expectation of defeat, Kyuhai judged.

He anticipated the gue'la would meet failure with a curse, but when it came he simply said, 'Start over.'

'Hold,' Kyuhai interjected and the drones froze.

The gue'la turned, surprised, then bowed his head. 'I didn't mean to intrude...' He faltered, evidently unsure of the correct form of address. 'Lord,' he ventured. He spoke in a hoarse growl, as if his throat was damaged.

'Seeker,' Kyuhai corrected. His sharp eyes scanned the identity disc on the man's tunic. 'And the intrusion is mine, Gue'vesa'ui Voyle.'

'I am honoured, Seeker.'

Even by the standards of his species, with their jutting snouts and curled ears, Voyle was ugly. Like all the expedition's gue'vesa, he was shaven-headed and his skin was stained blue to mirror his liberators' complexion, but such contrivances couldn't soften the brutish cast of his features. His eyes were set deep in a craggy, scar-crossed wasteland that terminated in a slab-like jaw. It was a strange canvass to bear the concentric rings of Unity, yet also an eloquent one, for if such a damaged being could be redeemed then surely there was hope for the rest of its species. To the Seeker's mind the gue'la were infinitely more dangerous than honest savages like the kroot, but equally their *potential* was far greater.

'They are an ancient race, crooked with the malignancies of age,' Kyuhai's master had taught, *'and yet the aeons have not diminished their passion. In time they will either become our most ardent allies or our most dire foes.'*

'You fought with skill, but chose your battle without wisdom,' Kyuhai said. 'To overextend oneself is to welcome defeat.'

'I stand corrected, Seeker. My thoughts were clouded.'

'Sleep evades you?'

'I don't like what it brings. Or where it takes me.' The man rubbed at his neck and Kyuhai spotted a pale scar under his jaw. It was circular, almost like another ring of Unity. 'There are things... things I thought I was done with.'

'Are you having doubts, gue'vesa'ui?'

'Doubts?' Voyle looked up sharply, evidently surprised. 'No, no doubts... I want to see the Imperium burn, Seeker.'

'That may not serve the Greater Good. Our mission here in the Damocles Gulf is peaceful. We may yet find common cause with the people of your Imperium.'

'It's not *my* Imperium, Seeker,' Voyle said, his expression hardening. 'It never was.'

There it is, Kyuhai saw, *the potential for terrible light and darkness.*

'That is why awakened minds like yours must strive to reclaim it for the Greater Good,' he said.

Voyle didn't answer, but the denial in his eyes was apparent.

He is correct, Kyuhai reflected. *His species yearns for strife. There will be no accord with their Imperium. And yet we must attempt it, even if it only delays the inevitable. This is an inopportune time for war. When it comes it must be of our choosing, not the enemy's.*

A melodious sequence of chimes reverberated through the bay, announcing the dawn cycle.

'We will talk again, Gue'vesa'ui Voyle,' Kyuhai said, studying the man's face. 'Think upon my words.'

As the Seeker turned and strode towards the door he felt the man's shadow-wracked eyes following him.

'Review transmission Fai'sahl-359,' Por'el Adibh commanded.

The data drone embedded in the glassy table before her burbled and its dome erupted with a corona of pixels, illuminating the dimly lit conclave chamber where the embassy's leaders had gathered at her request. The iridescent particles flickered then resolved into a diminutive figure floating above the drone in a rigid lotus position. The hololithic avatar's fine features and high-collared robes identified him as a member of the t'au Water caste, like Adibh herself.

'I bear greetings in the name of the Greater Good,' the avatar announced in a mellifluous baritone. 'I am Por'vre Dalyth Fai'sahl, first emissary of the eighth branch of the Whispertide Concordance, entrusted with the enlightenment of the nineteenth parallel of the Damocles Gulf, designated the Yuxa system.

'Please forgive the excessive interval since my last communication, but my expedition has been beset by grievous travails and many of my associates have passed into the Deep Silence. Yuxa is a troubled region where the dominion of the gue'la Imperium has grown profoundly frayed. Such disorder is fertile soil for anarchy and violence, yet also for opportunity, for as the storm spawns ruin so ruination foreshadows fresh hope. And in hope there is Unity.'

You were never one for succinctness, Fai'sahl, Adibh reflected. Her colleague had always leaned towards the flamboyant, and not only in his rhetoric. It was why she had rejected his many proposals for a pairing, despite his comeliness – and also, she suspected, why she had advanced beyond him in their caste's hierarchy. Yet despite Fai'sahl's limitations his disappearance had saddened her. How like him to confound her assumptions and reappear, seemingly alive and well.

'Know that our sacrifice has not been without purpose,' Fai'sahl's image was saying, his nasal slits dilated with pride. 'Under my auspices, Yuxa's dominant gue'la faction, the Illumismatic Order of the Ever-Turning Cog, has embraced the Greater Good with formidable conviction! Though I have dedicated my life to the dissemination of the Tau'va among the ignorant, I have never witnessed an ideological metamorphosis to rival the one that blossoms here. Indeed, I believe the key to the spiritual redemption of this vexatious species – perhaps even the unravelling of its barbaric Imperium – may lie here in the Yuxa system!

'Regrettably, however, this efflorescence of reason is imperilled by recidivist elements and technological impediments beyond my capacity to salve. My gue'la associates have prepared a report of our predicament that I have appended to this transmission for your elucidation. Esteemed colleagues, I urge you to despatch a relief mission to Yuxa without delay. It would be a betrayal of our exalted commission if this promising light were extinguished in its infancy.

'Spatial coordinates and supporting specifications follow.'

The hololith flickered out and the lights rose, revealing the others seated around the conclave table. Adibh and Fio'vre Daukh, the expedition's senior engineer, had already seen the recording, but for the pair of Fire Warriors it was the first time. The older one's weathered face wore its customary disapproval for all non-military matters. Even by the standards of her caste, Shas'vre Bhoral was a dour creature, but doubtless she hadn't been chosen for her intellect. She was a tightly focussed weapon, nothing more. It was the officer sitting beside her who mattered to Adibh.

'The recording is genuine?' Shas'el Akuryo asked.

'It was encoded with gue'la equipment, but the identity ciphers are correct,' Adibh replied. 'Moreover, Por'vre Fai'sahl and I are former colleagues. It is certainly him.'

'His manner is... singular.' Akuryo's brow furrowed slightly to indicate *the-irony-that-anticipates-derision*. For a Fire Warrior he was unusually expressive, Adibh thought, even handsome in a coarse way. More importantly he was perceptive. His gue'vesa troops, to whom he was nothing less than a hero, had named him Stormlight for his stalwart guidance in both war and peace.

'How long has this emissary been missing?' Akuryo asked.

'Prior to this transmission our last contact with Fai'sahl's embassy was almost three spatial years ago,' Adibh said. 'They were presumed lost and the Yuxa system was designated non-viable.'

'The matter was not investigated?'

'As you are aware, the Whispertide Concordance is only an exploratory venture into the Damocles Gulf – a bridgehead to the gue'la. Our resources are limited.'

'His sudden reappearance troubles me,' Akuryo said, cutting to the crux of the matter.

'Naturally. That is why you are here, shas'el.'

'Then why have I been allowed only Bhoral and two gue'vesa support teams to protect you, por'el?'

'It was the High Ambassador's decree.' Adibh extended her hands, palms upward. 'We walk the path of the Open Hand. An excessive military presence might be misconstrued and opportunities of the kind Fai'sahl describes cannot be squandered.'

'Then you believe his story?'

'That is for our revered Seeker to determine,' Adibh said. 'My purpose is to facilitate a fruitful discourse.'

'As yours is to watch over us, Stormlight,' a quiet voice said behind her. 'I have no doubt you will both perform your duties admirably.'

Adibh turned and saw the Seeker standing in the entrance of the conclave chamber, his arms crossed in a posture of tranquil authority. He was attired in plain grey robes cinched at the waist by a black sash. As always, a deep cowl pooled his features in shadow, obscuring his eyes. His honour staff was clipped to a simple harness on his back.

How long has he been there? Adibh wondered as a thrill of devotion surged through her. It was rumoured that Seekers could pass unseen among the other castes and Kyuhai had done nothing to dispel that notion. Formally known as *yasu'aun* – 'the-finders-of-the-truth-that-hides' – Seekers were solitary mystics who wandered the T'au Empire, following paths only the Ethereal caste could comprehend. Sometimes they would attach themselves to an expedition, appearing unexpectedly, but always welcome, for their presence was a great honour. Though Adibh was officially still the mission's leader the *reality* of that had changed the moment Kyuhai had joined them, yet she felt no acrimony towards him. In her most introspective moments that equanimity sometimes troubled her, but the unease would never crystallise.

'We shall not fail you, Seeker,' Akuryo vowed, clearly as awed by the mystic as Adibh.

'Nor I you, Stormlight,' Kyuhai replied. He turned to Adibh. 'Por'el, when we reach Yuxa you will conduct our negotiations.'

'Under your auspices of course, Seeker.'

'You misunderstand, por'el. You will lead the embassy alone. I will observe, unobserved. The unseen eye sees further.'

'Then you suspect a trap, Seeker?' Akuryo asked intently.

'That is my path.'

When the next sleep cycle came round Voyle climbed into a serenity cell. The last thing he saw as the hatch slid shut was Erzul watching him from the cubicle in the opposite wall. Fighting down his nausea, Voyle extinguished the light.

'It's nothing,' he whispered.

But it didn't *feel* like nothing. Not at all. His heart was pounding as the memories surged up with almost physical force. Darkness and the stench of stale promethium...

Then he is inside the other *coffin again – the empty fuel silo he has crawled into and welded shut with Hoenig's las-cutter. His ear is pressed against the slick metal, listening for the abominations that have slaughtered the boarding party. Hoenig is slumped against him in the tight space, his breath coming in ragged, bubbling gasps as he bleeds out. The specialist trooper's left arm has been torn off at the shoulder, along with most of his face, yet oblivion eludes him. His surviving eye roves about, as if seeking answers to questions he can't understand, let alone ask. Voyle knows he should give his comrade mercy, but then he will be the last of them and he isn't ready for that yet.*

'I can't,' he says.

Hoenig's questing eye fixes upon him, mutely condemning, then darkens to black.

'Face your fear or it will consume you.'

Voyle recoils and slips further into the nightmare, back to the moment when it truly begins.

'Proceed,' Kyuhai commanded.

'Subject: Voyle, Ulver. Species: Gue'la, male,' the data drone answered in its sexless, perfectly modulated voice. 'Age: thirty-six biological years. Height...'

'Omit somatic data,' Kyuhai interrupted. 'Proceed to biographic.'

'Yes, Seeker,' the drone replied. 'Former Astra Militarum trooper, Eleventh Exordio Void Breachers...'

Alone in the conclave chamber, Kyuhai listened as the drone related Voyle's history. He didn't know what he was looking for, but he was certain he would *recognise* it when he found it. In time that recognition would blossom into understanding, but it was an ambiguous process, driven by intuition rather than intellect. A Seeker perceived connections and anomalous elements – be they events, objects or individuals – as an artist of the Water caste perceived the rhythm of colours, words or melodies. Like that artist, Kyuhai's calling was to create harmony, but his canvass was spiritual rather than aesthetic.

'Subject Voyle was subsequently promoted to the rank of Breach Sergeant and assigned to patrol duties along the perimeter of the Damocles Gulf,' the data drone was saying. 'His first tour...'

His eyes closed and arms folded, Kyuhai let the story wash over him. Thus far nothing in Voyle's service record had struck the discordant note he was waiting for. The man's career was competent, but unexceptional. Grey. Yet *something* had drawn him to Voyle, just as it had drawn him to this mission when so many others had vied for his attention.

Who are you, Ulver Voyle? Kyuhai mused. *Why do you matter?*

Though Voyle has fallen only minutes further into his nightmare's past it is enough to resurrect his comrades and the delusion of order. The squad has travelled far in search of the dead ship's bridge, for if there are any answers to be found they will surely be there. Unexpectedly the derelict is still pressurised, though its atmosphere is stale and none of the troopers have opened their visors. They don't trust this place enough to taste its air.

'How much further, Hoenig?' Voyle hears himself ask.

Whole again, the specialist trooper consults his scanner. The glowing map on its readout is only an approximation of the hulk's layout derived from similar vessels, but Hoenig has a talent for navigating on the fly.

'Another deck up, Breach Sergeant,' he replies. 'Should be an access ladder three or four junctions ahead.'

But Voyle, both past and present, isn't listening anymore. Did something move in the intersecting corridor he just passed? He steps back and illuminates the passageway. Its length is choked with a snarl of pipes and corroded machinery that spin strange shadows from his light. That constricted abattoir of junk isn't somewhere he wants to go, but he has to be certain, so he steps into its maw.

'Don't!' Voyle present yells silently into his past.

With a wet hiss a pile of debris uncoils before him, extending long arms that end in hook-like talons. A moment later a second pair unfurls beneath the first, but these taper into long-fingered hands that look almost delicate. The creature's gangling form is sheathed in chitinous blue plates that bulge into a carapace of bones over its chest and shoulders. Though its posture is hunched its bestial head is level with Voyle's own – so close he can see its mauve flesh pulsating.

It was waiting for me, *he understands.*

Voyle's meltagun is trained on the thing's ribcage, but his trigger finger has turned to stone, along with his legs and throat, all held rigid by its gaze. Its eyes are a lustreless black, yet the hunger in them is unmistakable. Unassailable... even beautiful in its purity...

Now one of Voyle's hands moves, rising to the seal of his visor. He gasps as the derelict's freezing air hits him, but it is not enough to snap him free of those mesmerising eyes.

'Breach Sergeant?' *someone calls behind him as the creature's jaws distend and a rigid tongue extrudes, dripping viscous ichor. The organ is thorn-tipped and pregnant with promise.*

'Burn it!' *Voyle bellows at himself as he raises his head and offers his throat.*

Perhaps his warning rends time, space and logic to stir his former self to action. Perhaps it is nothing more than a shock reflex. Either way, when the beast's tongue pierces his flesh he squeezes the trigger. As cold corruption courses into his bloodstream a blast of purifying heat incinerates the thing's torso. Its tongue is wrenched free as it falls, but Voyle feels no pain through the numbness in his neck. He snaps his visor shut as gunfire erupts in the corridor behind him.

'Xenos!' *somebody shouts.*

In the pandemonium that follows the first attack Voyle can't tell how many of the abominations there are, but within seconds his squad is fighting for its life as the things assail it from all sides. Soon three troopers are lost and the fight has become flight. Reaching the sanctuary of the Sable Star *is their only hope, but the rout has transformed the corridors into a maze and Hoenig's scanner has been lost along with the arm that carried it. Voyle wields his heavy gun one-handed as he supports the wounded man. They are both drenched in the blood pumping from the raw stump of Hoenig's shoulder, yet the specialist is still conscious – still their best chance of finding a way out.*

The seven survivors become six then five then only four as claws yank troopers into dark recesses or the pipes above.

'Sable Star!' *Voyle shouts into his helmet vox, but the only reply is a hiss of static. The squad left a string of comms relays in its wake to maintain contact with the ship, but the rout has carried them far from that path.*

'Take... right,' *Hoenig gasps as they reach another junction.*

Abruptly the vox crackles into life: '–status, Squad Indigo? I repeat...'

'Lieutenant!' *Voyle interrupts.* 'We're under attack. Taking heavy casualties.'

'Confirmed,' *the acting commander replies.* 'What are you up against, Breach Sergeant?'

'Unknown xenos... Don't know how many. We need a support team now!'

There is a long pause: 'I am disengaging the umbilical.'

'Wait...'

'I can't allow the *Sable Star* to be compromised.' *Lieutenant Joliffe's voice is walking a knife-edge of panic now.*

'Listen to me, we're...'

'Emperor protect you, Breach Sergeant.' *The vox goes dead.*

Voyle curses him as the trooper ahead is pulled through the floor by something unseen. He sends an incinerating blast into the torn ground as he steps past, virtually dragging Hoenig now. Moments later a plangent metallic scraping echoes through the corridor. Every Void Breacher knows that sound.

'That was the umbilical!' Thorsten yells from somewhere behind.

We were almost there, *Voyle realises bitterly. 'Keep moving,' he orders as he staggers on, going nowhere now, but too angry to stop.*

Soon Thorsten is also gone and only Voyle and the wounded specialist remain. Hoenig has passed out, but he's still breathing and Voyle won't leave him behind even if it makes no difference anymore. As he wanders the labyrinth he senses the black-eyed xenos watching him from the shadows, inexplicably reticent now his comrades are dead. Are they toying with him? No... Voyle is strangely certain that cruelty isn't in their nature. Stranger still, he can't bring himself to hate them. Whatever else they are, the creatures are honest in their desires. The beauty he glimpsed in his first encounter wasn't entirely false. Besides, he has no hatred left to spare for them.

'We were so close,' he rasps, thinking of Joliffe. Dimly he recalls Breacher protocol – even recognises that the lieutenant was right *– but rage drowns such reasonable nonsense. 'So... damn... close.'*

The corridors reverberate with a deep, distant pounding and Voyle realises the Sable Star *has opened fire on the dead ship. He doubts its depleted weapons can destroy the colossal vessel, but the outer sections will certainly be depressurised. Even if the ship survives he might not.*

'I'm dead anyway,' Voyle hisses. But his body denies it. And suddenly – fiercely – he realises he wants to keep it that way. His fury demands it. That and something colder.

Shortly afterwards he finds the fuel silos.

'Five spatial years ago subject Voyle was recovered from an abandoned vessel found in the ninth Damocles parallel,' the data drone said. 'The report specifies he had been adrift for three months following an encounter with hostile life forms of an unknown nature. No trace of these aggressors was found, however evidence...'

Kyuhai was listening intently now. According to the report Voyle had displayed remarkable resilience, both physical and mental, in the face of his ordeal.

'On site examination concluded that...'

'Hold,' Kyuhai said sharply. 'Repeat previous segment.'

Voyle clawed his way out of the nightmare like a panicked corpse from its grave, but the taste of rotten flesh in his mouth wasn't his own. He had finally remembered the last, worst part of the horror – the part his liberators had supressed during his induction. Only they weren't liberators at all. Not for him. How could they be when he was knee-deep in damnation?

Gut-deep.

'It was evident that the subject had sustained himself by cannibalising a dead comrade,' the drone repeated.

Cannibalism? Kyuhai thought. The practice was not unknown among some species – indeed it was revered by the kroot – but among the gue'la it was regarded as extremely deviant behaviour.

'The matter was not noted as a cause for concern?' he asked.

'The presiding Ethereal, Aun'vre Kto'kovo, deemed it within acceptable parameters of gue'la degeneracy.'

'Proceed,' Kyuhai said, supressing a rare flicker of irritation. Even among his own caste there were too many who dismissed the gue'la as primitives.

'Following screening and remedial therapy, the subject was inducted into the Kir'qath auxiliary academy on Sa'cea sept, where he demonstrated exceptional aptitude aligned with a robust commitment to the Tau'va. His initial posting...'

Five years of faultless service to the Greater Good followed, with Voyle fighting on various battlegrounds at the fringes of the empire. The Seeker listened to it all, though he was certain he had already found the key to Voyle's anomaly. Now he had to make sense of it – and decide whether Ulver Voyle was an asset or a liability.

'No,' Voyle rasped, over and over, but no matter how often he repeated it, the truth would not be denied. As the days of his confinement had stretched into untold weeks, his soul had narrowed towards nothingness. Starved of hope for retribution, even his rage had dimmed, yet his body had fought on. Somewhere blood deep – much deeper than he could see – it had been unwilling to die. When his suit's rations were exhausted he'd scavenged from the corpse beside him in the silo, and then when its supplies were also gone...

Voyle retched and slammed a fist against his sleeping cell.

'What am I?' he snarled into the darkness within.

And for the first time the darkness answered, but its voice came from without.

– THE SECOND CIRCLE –
THRESHOLD

The Yuxa system had eleven planets, but only two harboured life – Phaedra, a fungus infested water world, and Scitalyss, a bloated gas giant whose outer layers swarmed with phantasmal aeriform vermin. It was to the second of these that the *Whispering Hand* was bound, though its destination was not the planet itself, but the lesser leviathan suspended in its anaemic exosphere.

From a distance the structure appeared to be a dark blemish against Scitalyss' ochre and russet swirl, but as the vessel drew closer the mote grew spiny and misshapen, like a tumour in metastasis. Closer still it resolved into a sprawl of interconnected metal modules of varying size and shape. A monolithic spindle rose from the centre of the tangle, towering over the other structures and trailing titanic extraction pipes into the world below. The spindle's cog-like tiers shimmered with lights as they revolved, but further from the centre the expanse grew dark and the domes of its component modules were cracked open to the void, as though they had been wracked by some terrible violence.

Though the sprawl was artificial it was still a cancer, for its growth had long ago become rampant and perverse, twisted out of any semblance of order by the countless masters who had presided over it. Most had begun their stewardship in sobriety, but few had ended that way, for despite the intent of its architects, discord ran deep in this place. Whether it was the influence of the baleful giant it leeched upon or the consequence of some intrinsic flaw, the skyhive was *tainted*, its history saturated in strife. And yet it had endured across millennia, grudgingly paying its tithes to the Imperium and never quite embracing a heresy that would have invited retaliation. There were myriad such cancers growing in the cracks of the Imperium, but few as furtive.

The place had acquired many names, some truer than others. Its formal designation was Scitalyss-Altus, but its current masters had ennobled it as the Unfolding Nexus, however to the millions who eked out a living in its corroded avenues it was simply the Rat's Cradle.

I do not like it, Por'el Adibh decided, *not at all.*

The skyhive rotated slowly above the conclave table, its tangled lineaments reproduced in perfect holographic fidelity. Its presence felt like a taint upon the room. Upon *her*...

Taint? Adibh dismissed the notion. Such irrationality had corroded the collective psyche of the gue'la. It had no place in the thinking of a t'au.

'Your thoughts, shas'el?' she asked.

'It is dangerous,' Akuryo replied. He stood on the opposite side of the table, his form distorted by the hologram.

'I concur,' Adibh said, 'yet we must proceed with the mission.'

They were alone in the conclave chamber. Her first impressions of the Fire Warrior had proved correct and over the passing days she had come to value his counsel, even to regard him as a friend. After the artifice of the Whispertide Congress his directness was bracing.

'Why?' Akuryo asked. 'Why are we taking this risk, por'el? *The true reason.*'

'Because the High Ambassador has decreed it,' she replied. 'The Yuxa system interests him.' She raised a hand to stem his next question. 'I do not know why. Por'o Seishin keeps his own counsel, but we must trust his judgement.'

'He is young,' Akuryo said flatly.

'He is *gifted*,' Adibh corrected, thinking of her idealistic, driven superior. 'Exceptionally so... The empire recognises and rewards talent.'

Akuryo was silent for a moment, brooding. 'It is fortunate that a Seeker walks beside us on this path,' he said finally. 'We are due to dock in nine hours. I must go, por'el.'

'Why Bhoral?' Adibh asked as he turned to go.

'I do not understand?'

'Why did you choose Shas'vre Bhoral as your aide?' The question had nagged at her for some time. At first she had assumed the warriors were old comrades, perhaps even Ta'lissera bonded, but she had seen no warmth between them. Indeed, Akuryo seemed closer to his gue'vesa than to his fellow Fire Warrior.

'I did *not* choose her,' he said stiffly. 'She was assigned to me for the mission.'

Do you trust her? Adibh wanted to ask, but that was absurd. 'Thank you, shas'el,' she said instead. 'See to your troops.'

When he was gone she returned her attention to the hologram. She wasn't sure why she had asked the question or why Akuryo's answer troubled her. In fact, the closer they drew to their objective the less certain she was of anything.

Alone in the darkness of his serenity cell, Ulver Voyle listened to the Voice. It had grown stronger over the past few days, swelling from a subliminal murmur to an evanescent whispering, yet its *words* still eluded him.

'What are you trying to tell me?' he hissed.

– THE THIRD CIRCLE –
INSIDE

Por'el Adibh's nostril slits dilated with disgust as she stepped onto the ship's disembarkation ramp and the acid stench of the skyhive hit her. She imagined a broken machine leaking the black sludge that powered so much of the Imperium's technology. Quelling her nausea, she studied the immense expanse of the hanger bay as she descended, her data drone hovering above her head like a domed halo. The walls of the cavernous chamber were corroded and slick with filth, its floor knotted with trailing pipes and discarded tools. Dozens of sub-human labourers toiled among the labyrinth of machinery, their bodies crudely fused to metal limbs, their eyes as vacant as their minds. It had always puzzled Adibh that the Imperium embraced such atrocities while condemning the elegant drones of the T'au Empire.

So much of their suffering is self-inflicted, she mused.

'Noteworthy,' Fio'vre Daukh declared beside her. Adibh didn't know whether the stocky engineer was referring to the odour or some obscure detail only he could see, but she had learnt not enquire after such remarks; Daukh's concept of *noteworthy* rarely converged with anyone else's. He had found much of note during their approach to the hive, while Adibh had seen only decrepitude. Why had Fai'sahl led them to this floating sewer city?

Akuryo and another armoured figure were waiting for her at the foot of the ramp. They had donned their helmets so their faces were hidden behind flat, sensor-studded visors that gave them an impassive machine-like aspect. Akuryo's mottled crimson armour bore a five-armed sunburst on its breastplate – personal colours and heraldry granted to him when he'd earned his rank. In contrast, his companion's uniform was the stark, unadorned white of the Whispertide Concordance.

'Your gue'vesa understand there is to be no violence, shas'el?' Adibh asked, indicating the human soldiers lined up on either side of the ramp. Both the support teams were present, the troops' rifles slung over their shoulders as they crouched in the stance of watchful-repose. They wore lighter variants of the Fire Warriors' armour, retaining the breastplates and shoulder pads, but lacking the contoured plates that sheathed their superiors' limbs. Their helmets were fitted with tinted lenses that covered their eyes, but left their faces bare.

'The Stormlit know their duty,' Akuryo replied, referring to his troops as an extension of himself. It was a great honour and several of the gue'vesa puffed out their chests at his words.

'I have faith in *your* faith,' Adibh acknowledged, then appraised the warrior beside Akuryo. The deception was flawless. Despite the armour and helmet, she had expected to *feel* something, but all she sensed was what her eyes told her: this was just another Fire Warrior. It was as if the Seeker had somehow constricted his spirit when he had donned the armour.

He has become what he seems *to be,* she thought.

There was a pneumatic hiss as the hanger's hatch split down the centre and retracted to either side, spilling bright light into the chamber.

'And so we begin,' Adibh murmured as a robed figure entered.

His vision enhanced by the sensors of his borrowed helmet, Kyuhai studied the newcomer as it approached. Though it was swathed in a hooded purple mantle there were subtle qualities of posture and gait that spoke volumes to his refined sensibilities.

'Por'vre Fai'sahl,' Adibh declared when the stranger stopped before them.

She saw it too, Kyuhai realised, impressed. Few outside the Ethereal caste were so perceptive.

'You know me too well, old friend,' the newcomer said, pushing back its hood to reveal the familiar face of the missing emissary. He smiled and stretched out his arms to encompass the others. 'On behalf of the Order of the Ever-Turning Cog, I offer you welcome to the Unfolding Nexus, a new born engine of reason among the benighted gue'la!'

Kyuhai was perplexed. On the hololith Fai'sahl had appeared pompous – superficial even – but in person he was almost *electric*, as though an avid vitality burned within him.

'It has been too many years since we last conversed, Por'vre Adibh,' the emissary continued warmly, turning back to Adibh.

'Por'*el*,' she corrected. 'I was elevated shortly after your disappearance.'

'My apologies, *por'el*.' Fai'sahl bowed his head. 'It pleases me that your talents have been recognised.' Smoothly, he reached out and grasped her hands. It was a brazen gesture that breached all etiquette and Adibh stiffened visibly.

'I have so much to share with you,' Fai'sahl said, his eyes bright. 'This gue'la relic harbours many wonders that may advance the Greater Good.'

'You came alone, emissary?' Akuryo asked bluntly.

Fai'sahl turned to the Fire Warrior, his smile unwavering. 'No, but we thought it best that you were greeted by one who is known to you.'

'But I do *not* know you.' Akuryo indicated the iron talisman hanging from the emissary's neck – a four-toothed cog embossed with the double-loop of infinity. 'Nor do I recognise the sept you now speak for.'

'I bear the Cog Eternal as a mark of *respect*,' Fai'sahl said. His smile remained, but the warmth had slipped from his eyes.

'Your message indicated urgency, por'vre,' Adibh interjected, extricating her hands. 'I would like to meet these remarkable gue'la you have uncovered.'

'Of course, por'el...' Fai'sahl's gaze swept over the party. 'Your embassy was not accompanied by an exalted one?'

'Unfortunately they are few and the needs of the empire many,' Adibh replied.

Kyuhai studied Fai'sahl's face, expecting relief or disappointment, but there was nothing.

I cannot read him, he realised. *How can that be?*

On impulse he glanced at the gue'vesa troops, searching for Voyle. The big man stood at the front of his team, his expression distant, as if his attention was elsewhere. Though they had talked occasionally during the remainder of the voyage Kyuhai was no closer to deciphering the man's significance. And yet he did not doubt it.

'*Chance is a myth perpetuated by those who only see what seems to be,*' Kyuhai's master had taught. '*A Seeker looks beneath the lies and finds the lines that bind. And where they have become twisted or frayed, he follows, for his path is to mend when he can or excise when he cannot.*'

It was the first axiom of the *Yasu'caor,* the philosophy by which a Seeker served the Greater Good.

My path has led me true, Kyuhai judged, returning his attention to Fai'sahl's smiling, empty face. *Nothing is what it seems here.*

'Support Team One, the ship is under your watch. Be vigilant!' Akuryo commanded as he strode towards the hanger doors. 'Team Two, with me!'

Voyle shook his head, trying to break free of the Voice that haunted – *or hunted?* – him.

'Gue'vesa'ui?' someone said behind him. He turned and stared at the expectant faces of... *Who were they?*

'Voyle, the shas'el calls us!' a hatchet-faced woman snapped.

Erzul, he remembered and the rest followed.

'Move out,' he ordered. 'Go!'

Am I losing my mind? Voyle wondered as he followed his squad. Somehow the prospect troubled him less than any of the alternatives he could imagine.

Three vehicles waited outside the spaceport. Two were open-topped trucks, the third a massive armoured car emblazoned with the sigil of the Ever-Turning Cog. A group of robed figures watched over them, their long-barrelled rifles levelled at the surrounding buildings. More were stationed along the segmented wall that encircled the spaceport like a metal serpent. Floodlights illuminated the perimeter, but beyond their reach everything was swathed in gloom. Voyle looked up and counted less than a dozen lights in the iron sky of the dome. He knew each was a vast,

burning globe, but it would take *hundreds* to illuminate a city-sized territory like this one.

This whole region is dying, he guessed, remembering the many dark modules
he'd seen from space.

As the party approached the vehicles Voyle saw the guards' purple robes
were embroidered with the concentric rings of Unity, but the bronze masks
they wore under their hoods were less reassuring, for they were fashioned
to resemble something more insect than man, with jutting compound jaws
and bulbous, multi-faceted lenses.

'Watchmen of the Second Rotation,' the t'au emissary explained. 'They
are here for your protection.'

'Protection from what?' the Stormlight demanded.

'Regrettably the Order's enlightenment is not entirely unopposed. A
few dissident factions remain active in the outer districts, but they are as
inchoate as they are ignorant,' Fai'sahl said dismissively. 'The spaceport is
under the Order's jurisdiction, but to reach the Alpha Axis we must trav-
erse a... troubled... region.'

'I advise against proceeding, por'el,' the Stormlight warned Adibh. 'Let
their leaders meet us here.'

With a whir of gyros one of the guards marched towards them, its footsteps
reverberating under its weight. It was taller and more powerfully built than
its fellows, its chest encased in a slab-like breastplate. In place of a hood it
wore a backswept helmet with a vertically slit visor that pulsed with blue
light. An augmetic arm extended from its right shoulder, dwarfing the limb
below and terminating in a three-fingered claw. Alongside that monstrous
appendage the watchman's ornate rifle looked almost delicate.

'My designation is Aiode-Alpha, Warden Prime,' the warrior said in a
pristine, but lifeless female voice. 'Your security is my primary directive.
Please board the transports.' It rapped a gauntlet against its breastplate.
'For the Greatest Good.'

'There is no cause for concern,' Fai'sahl urged. 'The Warden is the Order's
preeminent guardian.'

'Be advised that I have made provisions for our safety,' Adibh warned
him. 'My ship expects to receive a coded data-burst from my drone every
hour. Any breach of this will be construed as a hostile act.'

'I am familiar with first contact protocol,' Fai'sahl said gently, 'but
this is *not* a first contact. I assure you, the Order's offer of friendship
is sincere.'

'As is the Empire's,' Adibh parried, 'but the Open Hand must be firm of
grip. You will respect my precautions, por'vre.'

'Naturally, por'el.' Fai'sahl bowed.

Adibh turned to Akuryo. 'We will proceed.'

The gue'vesa climbed into the back of a truck while Fai'sahl ushered the
t'au into the armoured car. The watchmen boarded the second truck, lining
up along its sides in regimented ranks with the Warden at their centre. Voyle
gripped the guardrail as his vehicle surged forward and took its place at
the rear of the convoy, with the other truck leading and the car shielded

between them. Once they were underway his troops began to talk, eager to weigh up their strange hosts, but he silenced them.

'Stay sharp,' he ordered, unslinging his pulse rifle. 'Trust nothing.'

'How far?' Akuryo asked. He hadn't removed his helmet and its sensors glowed in the dingy cabin of the armoured car. Adibh suspected he would have preferred to travel with his troops, but was unwilling to leave her side.

'The Axis is five zones distant. A journey of many hours,' Fai'sahl answered from the seat opposite them. 'Regrettably our only functioning port is on the hive's outskirts. That is one of the limitations we hope to rectify with your aid.'

'Fio'vre Daukh will make a full assessment of your requirements,' Adibh said, keeping her tone neutral.

'My team stands ready to assist you,' Daukh concurred earnestly, though his eyes didn't leave the car's window slit. Doubtless he saw much of note outside. 'I predict there is considerable work ahead of us.'

'The Order's resources will be placed at your disposal, honoured fio'vre,' Fai'sahl promised. 'Together we shall achieve great things.'

'Assuming we reach an accord,' Adibh cautioned, sounding querulous even to herself. In the cramped cabin Fai'sahl's presence was almost overpowering.

'We shall, por'el. When we reach the Axis you will understand everything.' Fai'sahl smiled and Adibh felt a rush of unwelcome affection for him. No, it was simpler than that – more primal.

How he has changed, she mused. *He looks younger than he–*

Bright light flashed into her face, breaking the fascination. Abruptly Fai'sahl was gone and a hollowed out, predatory *thing* sat in his place, appraising her with hungry eyes.

'Forgive me, por'el,' the Seeker said from the seat beside the apparition. He extinguished his helmet light – and with it the horror. 'I fear my helm has developed an error.'

'See that you correct it, Fire Warrior,' Adibh replied, surprised that her terror hadn't reached her voice. Perhaps it was because *shame* eclipsed the fear. The Seeker had seen her desire...

No! The desire was not mine, she thought angrily, willing Kyuhai to see *that.*

'Are you well, my friend?' Fai'sahl asked, his face furrowing with concern.

'Perfectly well,' Adibh said. It was the most profound lie she had ever told.

The twilight district passed in a blur of crooked tenements, their growth stunted by the confines of the iron sky. Some had been reduced to scorched husks, while others had collapsed into rubble. Citizens haunted the squalor like flesh-bound ghosts, either alone or in small groups, often huddled around open fires. All were emaciated and grey, their bodies as wasted as their world. Most ignored the convoy, but a few watched it pass with empty eyes. Sometimes squads of purple robed watchmen moved among them, their weapons swivelling about as they patrolled. Once the vehicles swerved around a towering bipedal automaton with a warrior sitting astride it. The machine stomped through the streets, rocking back-and-forth to its own graceless rhythm as its searchlight scoured the hovels.

This is a warzone, Voyle judged, *or the tail end of one. Occupied territory.*

They had been travelling for almost an hour when the road narrowed and carried them into a stretch of gutted manufactories. The vehicles slowed to a halt and Voyle heard a clamour from somewhere up ahead – presumably the watchmen disembarking.

'Erzul, take a look,' he ordered. The pathfinder nodded and clambered onto the truck's cabin.

'Something on the road ahead,' she said. 'Looks like another truck, but–'

She threw herself flat as a barrage of gunfire erupted from the ruins to their right. One of the gue'vesa snapped backwards and fell as a bullet punched into his face. Another ricocheted off Voyle's helmet.

'Stay low and return fire!' Voyle shouted, ducking as bullets battered the vehicle's sides. There was a chorus of electronic chimes as his troops activated their pulse rifles, followed by the sibilant whine of plasma bolts when they opened fire.

Voyle raised his head and scanned the ruins through his rifle's scope, weaving about until he locked onto a figure lurking behind a broken window. His weapon pinged as he increased the magnification and drew his target into sharper focus. It was a man in ragged grey fatigues, his head protected by a rusty iron helmet painted with a stylized 'M'. An archaic rebreather mask covered his mouth, its tubes snaking over his shoulders into a bulky backpack. Above the mask his eyes were bloodshot wounds in a pallid face riddled with scars and sores. He appeared to be in the terminal stages of some flesh-eating pestilence, yet he stood straight, unbowed by his bulky stubber gun.

This lot look worse than ours, Voyle decided sourly, lining up on the attacker's face.

Before he could fire there was a voltaic crackle and a streak of light flayed his mark like an electric whip. The man convulsed as current played about him, igniting his clothes and charring his flesh. Voyle turned and saw the Warden marching across the building's rubble-strewn courtyard with her watchmen following in a wide arc. Venting an electronic ululation, she seized a chunk of debris with her claw and hurled it at a crouching enemy. Simultaneously her rifle's glassy barrel glowed blue and spat another jagged bolt into the ruins. Without slowing their stride, her troops fired a volley of explosive rounds in perfect synchronicity, every bullet finding a different foe.

'They're fighting as one,' Voyle murmured, studying their lethal combat symmetry. He felt calm now, as if the skirmish had elevated him above his private damnation. The Voice was still there, oozing around the battlefield like an auricular spirit of war, but it almost made sense now.

Can they hear it too? Voyle wondered hazily as he slipped into harmony with the Order's enforcers, becoming another cog in a precision killing machine, aiming and firing and executing the raiders without hesitation.

Bullets exploded around the advancing watchmen, frequently tearing through their robes and ricocheting off the armour beneath. The Warden appeared impervious, but occasionally one of her cohorts would jerk or stumble as a bullet penetrated its armour. One fell to its knees with a shattered leg, but continued to fire as its comrades marched on. Another took a round in the throat and toppled over.

'They don't lack courage!' one of the gue'vesa yelled.

Maybe, Voyle thought, stirring from his combat reverie. *Or maybe they just don't know any better.*

'No heroics,' he cautioned. 'This isn't our fight.'

And they don't need us anyway, he gauged. The ambush was already faltering under the Warden's counterattack. Whoever the raiders – or rebels? – were, they were woefully outclassed by the Order's troops, but they were fighting to the bitter end.

This wasn't a chance attack. The poor bastards threw everything they had at it. Why?

As the Warden reached the building a raider threw a grenade from the window above. She seared him with lightning and lashed out with her claw, snatching the grenade from the air and hurling it back, but it detonated a few metres above her. She staggered under the concussion, her augmetic arm whipping about as she fought for balance.

What...?

Voyle's rifle pinged repeatedly as he zoomed in on her whirling limb. The explosion had torn away a patch of its armour, revealing not raw machinery but what looked like more plating, though it was rounded and dark blue in colour. Almost organic...

Like insect chitin.

Voyle froze, staring down his scope as the Warden recovered and stomped into the building, leaving him zoomed in on nothing but memories.

Void black eyes, holding him transfixed as the predator uncoils to embrace him...

'*Status report, Two?*' his helmet's communicator hissed. The Stormlight.

'One gue'vesa dead, one lightly wounded,' Voyle answered automatically. 'Situation under control, shas'el.'

'*Acknowledged, Two. Hold your position.*'

As the last of the watchmen entered the building Voyle made up his mind.

'Cover me,' he ordered his squad and vaulted from the truck. Keeping his eyes on the injured watchman who'd been left behind, he sprinted to its fallen comrade. The warrior lay flat on its face, motionless.

What do you expect to find? Voyle asked himself as he knelt by the body.

A cold and thirsty poison awakening in his blood and watching the world through his eyes...

He heaved the warrior onto its back and a *third* arm slid free from its robes. Like the Warden's 'augmetic', it was encased in segmented iron plates, but it ended in a scythe-like blade that was unmistakably *bone*.

'Mutants,' Voyle spat, feeling his gorge rise.

He appraised the gaping wound in the warrior's throat. A large calibre round had torn right through it, almost decapitating the creature. Nothing human could have survived such trauma, but did that mean anything here?

As he reached for its mask the subterranean swirl of the Voice surged into sudden clarity: '*No...*'

Voyle froze. That denial was the first meaningful word it had said to him – perhaps even the first time it had been truly *aware* of him.

'You were never talking to me, were you?' Voyle whispered, following a tenebrous intuition. 'I was only ever listening in.'

'*No.*' The prohibition was more forceful now, yet it held no sway over him.

'What don't you want me to see?' Voyle challenged. 'Why–'

A bullet drilled into the ground by his feet. He turned and saw the kneeling watchman had levelled its rifle at him.

'They're yours, aren't they?' Voyle said to the Voice. 'All of them.'

'*Go... now...*' it breathed. Now it had the key to his head it was learning fast. Did that mean it would start pulling *his* strings soon?

'No,' Voyle snarled back and activated his helmet's transmitter. 'Erzul, wounded watchman to my right. Take it out.'

A bright bolt lanced across the courtyard and erased the warrior's head in a burst of plasma.

She didn't hesitate, Voyle thought with grim satisfaction. *I might be losing my mind, but my squad still trusts me.*

Ignoring the Voice, he pulled the dead watchman's mask aside. And froze.

Watching and waiting for the moment when he can claim another to feed the hunger that can never be sated...

Voyle switched his transmitter to the squad-wide channel. 'Seize the vehicles,' he ordered. 'The watchmen are hostile. Take them down.'

He looked up and saw the Warden emerging from the building, doubtless summoned by her unseen master. Her helmet swung about, its visor slit pulsing with blue light as she scanned the battleground.

What's under there? Voyle wondered, glancing back at the corpse. Its face was a travesty of humanity, with deeply recessed eyes and rubbery, mauve-hued skin. A chitinous ridge ran from its forehead to the bridge of its nose, beneath which its face erupted into a nest of pink tendrils. Many of them were still twitching, as if animated by a life of their own.

The Voice was gnawing at Voyle's mind now, but he shut it out, sensing that every word it spoke would sink another root into his soul, like one of the corpse's undying tendrils.

'I'm not yours,' he rasped as the gue'vesa opened fire on the watchmen.

'*Seize the vehicles,*' Voyle's voice hissed inside Kyuhai's helmet.

The Seeker acted without conscious thought, moving before the command had even concluded. The tone of Voyle's *first word* was enough to tell him that the wheel of possibilities had turned, carrying them from diplomacy into conflict. The cause and consequences could be assessed later. For now only action mattered.

'Do not be alarmed,' Fai'sahl was saying beside him, responding to the muffled sounds of battle. 'The watchmen will–'

Kyuhai's armoured elbow slammed into the side of his head. As the emissary slumped over, the Seeker leapt up and surged towards the driver. The man turned and Kyuhai's fist hammered between his eyes, throwing him against the wheel with stunning force. Fai'sahl had called the pale, hairless creature a timekeeper of the Fourth Rotation. Had he been one of the armoured warriors Kyuhai wouldn't have risked holding back, but for now killing was best avoided.

'*The watchmen are hostile,*' Voyle's warning continued as Kyuhai hauled the unconscious driver from his seat and took his place. '*Take them down.*'

'What is happening, Seeker?' Adibh asked, shocked by the sudden violence.

'We are betrayed,' Akuryo answered flatly, activating his pulse rifle. He had also heard the message, but his reaction had inevitably trailed behind Kyuhai's.

'See to your men, Stormlight,' the Seeker commanded, assessing the controls. The car appeared to be standard gue'la technology – rudimentary, but robust. 'We must return to the ship immediately.'

'Understood.' Akuryo opened the hatch and leapt out, slamming it closed behind him.

'How may I serve?' Adibh asked. Once again Kyuhai was impressed with her. She had adjusted quickly.

'Search the emissary for weapons then alert the ship, por'el,' he said. 'The status code is *mal'caor*. Fio'vre, see to the driver.'

'Yes, aun'el,' they chorused.

What have you done, Voyle? Kyuhai wondered as he gunned the engine into life.

Voyle raced for the vehicles, weaving between piles of rubble as plasma bolts swept overhead and solid rounds exploded around him. Sometimes a whiplash of electricity crackled past, but he sensed that the Warden was only trying to slow him.

'You want me alive,' Voyle muttered between breaths, addressing the Voice. 'You want to know... how I work... or why I don't.'

Up ahead both the armoured car and the rearmost truck had begun to reverse along the road. Erzul and two other gue'vesa crouched in the truck's back, exchanging fire with the watchmen. Unlike the raiders' antiquated guns their pulse rifles punched through the mutants' armour with ease, forcing them to stay in cover or die. Even the tank-like Warden had retreated behind a wall. Suddenly Voyle felt a ferocious pride in his xenos liberators. In a galaxy drowning in corruption they were surely the best – perhaps the only – hope.

'*Gue'vesa'ui, be swift!*' the Stormlight transmitted.

Voyle saw Akuryo leading the rest of his team against the lead truck. The Warden had left a pair of watchmen behind and they had taken cover behind the driver's cabin, one on either side, where they held his comrades back with alternating volleys. Two gue'vesa were already down and Voyle cursed as another was blasted from her feet as she tried to flank the mutants.

'Unity!' he growled and swerved towards them, sighting down his rifle as he charged. It was a precision weapon, ill-suited to such assaults, but he knew its rhythms better than his own mind and his third shot brushed the nearest watchman's hood, setting it alight. The fourth bored a molten crater into its chest as it turned, throwing it backwards. An obscene hissing bubbled from behind its flame-wreathed mask as it tried to level its rifle at him. With a roar of loathing, Voyle barrelled into it, sending it crashing into its comrade. The impact threw him to the ground, but he kept firing, riddling the entangled watchmen with plasma bolts. He didn't stop, not even when they fell – then fell still. His hatred was too deep. Too hungry...

*And the hunger gazes back at him from the void it has carved out in his soul. And then it speaks, for it has a Voice: '***Voyle...***'*

'Voyle!' someone shouted, hauling him up. He stifled a snarl as he recognised the Stormlight.

'We must go!' his commander snapped.

'The truck...'

'No time! More enemies come.' The Fire Warrior jabbed his rifle at the road ahead. A bipedal walker was striding through the wreckage of the vehicle that had blocked the convoy's path. It was similar to the one Voyle had spotted earlier, but its saddle was fitted with a massive cannon. The gun's spinning barrel was still smoking from the destruction it had just wreaked on the obstruction.

'Move, Voyle!'

They sprinted after the retreating vehicles, following the surviving soldier who had accompanied Akuryo. Both the captured vehicles had picked up speed now, but they were still hobbled by their inability to turn on the narrow road. As the fleeing trio drew level with the car a bolt of electricity struck the gue'vesa, throwing him against the vehicle. Voyle leapt over the charred corpse that rebounded into his path and glanced over his shoulder. The Warden was marching across the rubble in pursuit, flanked by her surviving watchmen. Worse still, the strider was bearing down on the car with frightening speed, its cannon spinning up to fire. Moments later a storm of high-velocity rounds rained down on its prey.

We're done, Voyle realised, ducking as ricochets whistled past him.

Suddenly the car thrust forward, its engine roaring as it accelerated towards its hunter. The strider lurched off the road, but the vehicle veered after it, its iron-shod tires clattering over the debris. There was a thunderous crash as it rammed the automaton. The strider's legs buckled and its saddle plunged forward, sliding along the car's roof and ploughing a deep fissure in its wake. Voyle and Akuryo dived aside as the wreckage hurtled past them, still bearing its stiff-backed rider and cannon. The gun detonated when it hit the road, vomiting a fireball into the dark sky.

'Sacred Throne,' Voyle growled, dredging up the old Imperial curse as the car whirled out of control and overturned. It spun about on its roof, shedding armour as it screeched along the ground. Caught in its path, the Warden was swept up and ground down, along with the watchmen flanking her. Finally the car's momentum gave out, leaving it wedged halfway up a mound of rubble.

'*The Seeker!*' Akuryo yelled over the transmitter. He was already on his feet and racing towards the wreckage.

'Rouse yourself, por'el,' the Seeker commanded, his calm voice cutting through the cacophony that lingered in Adibh's ears. Ignoring the protests of her battered body, she uncurled from the foetal huddle she'd adopted and rolled to her knees. Kyuhai's sensor-studded faceplate loomed into view, appraising her.

'You are fortunate,' the Seeker pronounced. 'Did you send the signal?'

'I... yes...' Adibh said, struggling for focus. 'Just before... before...'

'Then come, we cannot linger here.' Kyuhai turned away, ducking under the seats that hung from the inverted roof like stalactites. Through the smoke-filled gloom Adibh saw that the others had been much less fortunate. Fai'sahl lay beside her, a spar of metal jutting from his chest. Daukh was on the cabin's far side, slumped against the hatch, the top of his head mashed into a ragged crown of blood and bone. The timekeeper was sprawled brokenly across the drive panel, his robes smouldering.

'Tread carefully,' Kyuhai cautioned as he stepped over the gaping fissure running through the floor. Choking on the smoke, Adibh moved to follow. As she climbed over Fai'sahl's body his eyes opened.

'Adibh... what...?' His words splintered into a blood-flecked cough and he clutched at her. She took his hand instinctively, gripping it as spasms rippled through his body. The predator she'd glimpsed earlier was gone, along with its baleful magnetism.

In death he is only himself, she sensed.

'The emissary still lives!' she shouted to Kyuhai.

'His injury is mortal,' the Seeker replied. 'You cannot help him.' Reaching the hatch, he heaved Daukh aside and tugged at the opening lever, but it wouldn't budge.

As the emissary's convulsions subsided Adibh leaned in close. 'The Cog Eternal,' she urged. 'What is it? The truth, Fai'sahl.'

'Told you... truth,' he wheezed as his eyes clouded. 'Greatest... good...' His head fell back, revealing a circular scar under his chin.

'That is a lie,' Adibh said sadly. 'But I don't believe it is yours, old friend.'

She released Fai'sahl's hand and crawled towards the Seeker. As she approached the fissure an electronic burbling sounded from somewhere below. *Her drone.* She leant over the rift's lip and reached down, expecting to touch the ground, but there was nothing. The car must have come to rest above a cavity. She stretched further and her fingers brushed smooth metal.

'Seeker, I–'

A cold blue light flared into life below, dazzling her. She jerked away, but something seized her wrist in a vicelike grip.

'Do not be alarmed,' a sterile voice boomed. 'Your security is my primary directive.'

Adibh shrieked as the Warden yanked her through the fissure.

* * *

'Watchmen. Heading this way, shas'el,' Voyle warned as a group of robed figures appeared on the road ahead.

'You must delay them,' Akuryo ordered.

'Yes, shas'el.' What else was there to say? They could not abandon an Ethereal. After the crash they'd climbed to the stranded car, where the Fire Warrior was wrestling with the hatch while Voyle covered the road. It hadn't taken long for more of the Order's troops to arrive, but as they drew closer he saw there was something new among them – something much larger. He sighted down his scope and grimaced. The hulking figure was swathed in the customary purple robes, but it was almost twice the height of its fellows. A bulbous helmet encased its head and shoulders, locked into place by heavy chains that criss-crossed its chest. Its visor was carved into the likeness of a cog, with a single lens at the centre and smoking censers affixed to each tooth. The giant's right arm split at the elbow, spawning a pair of armoured tentacles that were wrapped around the haft of a massive industrial hammer. Its right arm was a weapon in its own right, bulging into a serrated claw that dragged along the ground behind it.

They've given up on hiding their secrets, Voyle thought, targeting the cog-faced hulk. As his plasma bolts seared its helmet the giant swung its hammer up to protect its lens, almost as if it had read his mind. Moving like clockwork, the watchmen raised their rifles and retaliated with a volley of bullets, then stepped aside, opening a path for their champion.

I can't put that thing down, Voyle realised as the behemoth broke into a lumbering charge. *This is where I die.*

'Then lower your weapon... and live,' the Voice suggested, slithering into his thoughts like a shameful secret. It spoke fluently now, its words redolent with sombre authority. Voyle couldn't remember why he had ever questioned it.

'Because you were lost, child.'

There was a metallic creak behind him. Voyle turned unsteadily and saw Kyuhai emerge from the vehicle.

'I will assist the others, Seeker,' Akuryo said, his voice seeming to come from some distant, meaningless place.

'They are gone,' Kyuhai said.

'Por'el Adibh...'

'All of them, Stormlight.'

The Ethereal turned to Voyle, as if to speak. Instead he *moved*, whipping a metal tube from his belt and whirling it towards the dazed man. It elongated from both ends as it swept through the air, its telescoped segments snapping free with a staccato burst of clicks. In the heartbeat it took to complete its arc it had become a staff. It struck Voyle's helmet and threw him off balance. As he fell against the vehicle he saw the Seeker twirl the weapon back then thrust it forward – into the visor of the giant that had climbed up behind Voyle while the Voice held sway. The blunt tip shattered the mutant's cyclopean lens and drove through to whatever lay below.

'Mont'ka!' the Seeker shouted and the behemoth shuddered as the staff's blades sprang free inside its skull. Kyuhai twisted the weapon then wrenched it free, tearing away the creature's visor, along with most of its face. As the giant toppled backwards Voyle glimpsed a protean morass of tendrils and broken bones inside its helm. Kyuhai leapt back into cover as the watchmen answered their champion's death with a salvo of bullets.

'Your actions have invited great danger, gue'vesa'ui,' he said to Voyle.

'Yes, Seeker,' Voyle answered, lowering his head. 'I–'

'Later.' Kyuhai whirled his staff and it contracted back into a tube. 'We must go.'

'Support team, your status?' Akuryo transmitted as they retreated down the mound with Voyle bringing up the rear.

'The truck is clear,' Erzul replied. *'Do you need us, shas'el?'*

'Negative. We are en-route to you now.'

The Voice almost had me, Voyle thought as he followed the two xenos.

'Child, you must–'

'No!' Voyle hissed, biting his lip until he drew blood. 'Get out... of my head.' But now that it had tasted his soul he knew it never would.

– THE INVISIBLE CIRCLE –
UNITY

Shas'vre Bhoral triggered the jetpack of her Crisis battlesuit and launched herself into the air, arcing high above the spaceport. Ensconced within the control cocoon of the hulking machine, protected by multiple layers of angular nanocrystal armour, she felt invulnerable. It had been many years since her duties had called upon her to wear the battlesuit in combat, but the old discipline had returned the instant she'd activated the machine and its sensors had interfaced with her nervous system, transforming her into a towering bipedal tank.

It has been too long, she thought fiercely.

As she neared the city's dome she cut her thrusters and plunged back towards the spaceport, confident in her armour's durability. She came down hard, pulverising an enemy warrior under her massive piston-like legs and sending tremors through the ground. Triggering the flamethrower attached to her suit's right arm she spun at the waist, washing the dead guard's comrades in a whooshing arc of fire. Their robes were scorched away in seconds, revealing the misshapen forms beneath.

These are not common gue'la, Bhoral judged as one of the burning figures flailed at her with a scythe-like claw. *A mutant strain perhaps?*

She stomped over their charred corpses and fired a fusillade of plasma bolts with her secondary weapon, targeting the guards on the far side of the roof. A squadron of gun drones swept by overhead, their path guided by her battlesuit's tactical system. The ship had carried eighty of the saucer-like machines and Bhoral had activated them all when she had received the Seeker's signal.

Mal'caor.

The word meant 'spider', but the *code* signified 'a-great-peril-awakened'. The protocol for the situation was clear: ensure the ship's safety at all costs.

Accordingly Bhoral had launched a surprise attack on the port's guards immediately, but they had reacted with uncanny swiftness and a total lack of fear.

'They fight like machines,' Bhoral observed as a pair of three-armed deviants broke cover and charged towards her. One sported a muscular tentacle, the other a chitinous appendage that ended in a snapping pincer. They were bigger and better armoured than the others she had encountered, their heads protected by sealed helmets bearing ribbed crests.

'For... Greatest... Good!' they hissed, their words slurring as if their mouths weren't shaped for speech.

Before Bhoral could fire, a lanky avian figure sprang past her and raced to meet the mutants with a hooting cry. The Fire Warrior clicked her tongue with irritation as she recognised the kroot carnivore, though she had no idea *which* of the two it was. She had fought alongside the pair in service to the exalted Kyuhai for many years, yet she still couldn't tell them apart.

'The Yasu'caor forges strange bonds,' the Seeker had instructed when she had joined his circle, 'but it is their very strangeness that makes them strong.'

Bhoral's suit chimed a warning as something landed on its blocky shoulders. A moment later the second kroot vaulted from its perch to join the fray. The carnivores whirled about the mutants in a feral dance – hacking, stabbing and feinting with their broad-bladed machetes then leaping away, always one step ahead of the ungainly mutants. Bhoral did not doubt the outcome of the contest, but her allies' *frivolity* irked her.

'The Seeker has taught you well,' she observed, 'but you remain beasts.'

She felt a twinge of pain as an explosive slug dented her battlesuit's left arm. It was a sympathetic sensation generated by the suit's cocoon, sharp enough to bind her to the machine, but not enough to distract her. Her sensors pinpointed the aggressor in moments – a sniper crouched on a tower to her left. An evaluation of the enemy's capabilities flashed across her awareness, relayed by her battlesuit's tactical system. The threat was minimal so she dispatched a pair of drones to eradicate it and continued her advance, leaving the frenzied kroot to their game.

The last of the guards had taken cover behind a cluster of machinery. Drones buzzed about them, kept at bay by the defenders' disciplined volleys. Bhoral strode towards their position, pinning them down with a hail of plasma bolts as she approached. When she was in range she scoured their shelter with fire.

'Disharmony portends dissolution,' she decreed, quoting the *Yasu'caor* as her enemies burned. She rotated her battlesuit, scanning the rooftop. The fighting was over. Even the kroot had finished their foes, though they were still hacking away at the corpses, jabbering at one-another as they tried to make sense of their outlandish victims. The Seeker had forbidden them from eating the dead, but their fascination could not be completely curtailed.

'Forward perimeter is secure, shas'vre,' a voice reported on her transmission link – Hurrell, the leader of the first gue'vesa support team. Something was playing havoc with their communications systems and the signal was badly distorted.

'Confirmed, gue'vesa'ui,' Bhoral replied.

'I have three dead and three more wounded, shas'vre. Permission to evacuate them to the ship.'

'Denied. Remain at your post.'

'Baumann is in bad shape...'

'I will despatch a salvation team to your position.' Bhoral cut the link. The casualties were significant, but she didn't share the Stormlight's sentimentality towards the human auxiliaries. She was more concerned by the number of drones she'd lost; her strategic display recorded thirty-nine damaged or destroyed. When enemy reinforcements arrived the situation would rapidly become untenable.

She switched her transmitter to long-range.

'Seeker?' Predictably she was met by the howling electronic whine that had flooded the channel shortly after the fighting commenced. Coming to a decision, Bhoral stomped back to the kroot. They looked up from their butchery as she loomed over them.

'Bad meat,' one of them grunted, holding up a glistening tentacle.

'*Eee-veel*,' its companion added sagely.

'Enter the city,' Bhoral commanded, speaking slowly. 'Find our master.'

The carnivores exchanged a glance then sprang up and sprinted away.

It is almost as if they already know where he is, Bhoral mused. And maybe they did. She had reluctantly accepted that the savages' bond with the Seeker was tighter – or perhaps *deeper* – than her own.

Her battlesuit's strategic display bleeped as another drone's signature went dark. She frowned as the rest of its squadron followed in rapid succession. Somewhere in the spaceport the enemy was still active. Bhoral checked the squadron's last known location and hissed through her teeth. *The hanger bay...*

The truck rumbled along the dark streets, its headlights boring a tunnel through the gloom. Voyle was driving, with Erzul beside him; if anyone could retrace their outbound journey it was the squad's pathfinder. The rest of the survivors were crouched in the back, their rifles levelled over the sides. The district was deserted, its citizen-slaves presumably banished to their hovels, but an expectant watchfulness pervaded the streets. Every one of the fugitives could sense it, t'au and human alike, but none as keenly as the Seeker.

The dissonance here runs deep, Kyuhai reflected, *yet I have learnt nothing. Voyle sprang the trap too soon.*

But was that really true? The threads of ambivalent fate had woven Ulver Voyle into this tangle. There was no reasoning behind it, for the firmament of reality was blind, but there was a *rhythm* to it. It was a Seeker's path to listen and learn then tune the composition to serve the Greater Good, conducting events by intuition alone. And Kyuhai's instincts had urged him to trust this broken gue'la. Perhaps Voyle had not sprung the trap too soon, but just in time.

'Seeker, a question...' the Fire Warrior crouched beside him began hesitantly.

'Speak your mind, Stormlight,' Kyuhai urged.

'You are quite certain that Por'el Adibh was dead?'

'I could not save her,' Kyuhai said. *I could not attempt it.*

He had seen Adibh fall into the fissure – had even stepped forward to help her – then stopped when he'd heard the soulless voice booming from the rift and understood what lay beneath the wrecked car. The risk had been too great.

'Her loss will not be without purpose,' he promised.

'As you say, Seeker.' But there was no conviction in Akuryo's voice.

Kyuhai could not share the Fire Warrior's sorrow. Like love, hate and the myriad other shades of emotion that elevated or degraded his kin, sadness was a conceit he had transcended. That was what it meant to be *yasu'aun.*

'The void within stands vigil against the void without,' Kyuhai whispered to the lost city.

'Take the right,' Erzul instructed as the truck approached another junction.

She was always the best of us, Voyle thought, obeying. *She should have been our gue'vesa'ui. Maybe the others would still be alive then.*

'You led them to ruin,' the Voice agreed. *'Because you are lost.'*

It hadn't let up throughout the escape, cajoling one moment then threatening the next, but mostly just wearing him down. The worst part was that he *needed* it now.

'As I need you, *Ulver. As do your kindred in the Cog Eternal.'*

'Why did you shoot the watchman?' Voyle asked Erzul, trying to shut out his blessed tormentor. 'Back at the manufactory when I ordered it – why did you obey?'

'Because you are the gue'vesa'ui,' Erzul answered without hesitation.

'You trust me?'

'Should I not?'

'Not at all.'

'I'll warn you when to stop,' Voyle said seriously.

'Why *did* you order it?' Erzul asked.

'Because they're monsters.'

'The Imperium damns everything but itself as a monster,' the Voice observed.

'Sometimes that's true.'

'I don't understand,' Erzul said.

'Sometimes the monsters are real.'

'Then you are a monster too, Ulver Voyle.'

'I know it.' He spat, remembering the taste of rotten flesh. 'What are you?' He sensed he shouldn't encourage the entity, but he had to know.

'A traveller who became a god in service to a greater god. My children revere me as the Animus-Alpha.'

'Why can I hear you?'

'We share the same divine, star-spawned seed, though you are not of my blood. That is why you were invisible to me for so long.'

'Voyle,' Erzul said, eyeing him warily, 'you're not making any sense.'

'What do you want with me?' he pressed, ignoring her.

'I offer you freedom, Ulver. Your masters have deceived you.'

'That's a lie.'

'They are not liberators, but oppressors.'

'They... saved me.'

'They gelded you, body and soul. Have you felt any desire save obedience since they took you?'

'It's for the Greater Good,' Voyle muttered, remembering the endless mantras of self-sublimation and the contentment the tranquillity wafers had brought. 'Unity.'

'Slavery!' the Animus-Alpha corrected. And as Voyle recognised its truth, the invisible god slipped past his guard.

'Turn left!' Erzul snapped.

He turned right.

'Voyle! What are–' His left hand thrust out and grabbed her hair. Her instincts had always been razor sharp and she reacted quickly, snatching her combat knife free and swinging it towards him in the same motion. If he'd hesitated even a moment it might have been enough. But he didn't hesitate. Before the blade could connect he rammed her face into the dashboard.

No! Voyle tried to scream, but he no longer had a mouth. It belonged to the Voice now.

Bhoral's burst cannon vented smoke as it spewed plasma bolts at the four-armed abominations infesting the hanger bay. The creatures zigzagged between banks of machinery as they circled her, their sinuous forms hunched into an insect-like scuttle. Their bodies were sheathed in blue chitin that flared into spines at their joints and along the ridge of their bulbous skulls. In place of jaws their faces trailed thorn-tipped tentacles that whipped about as the creatures moved.

Drones skimmed around the beasts, chattering electronically as they harried them with bursts of plasma, but the machines were falling faster than their prey, their rigid minds confounded by their enemies' erratic movements. Bhoral hissed as another of the flying discs was yanked from the air and shredded. The beasts' claws were improbably strong. Even her battlesuit's armour wouldn't last long against a prolonged attack.

There are too many, Bhoral judged, immolating an abomination with a spurt of fire as it veered towards her. Her flamethrower's ammunition gauge chimed a warning. The weapon had already been running low when she'd entered the hanger and engaged the infiltrators. There had been seven when she'd arrived, but more had crawled from the ducts lining the walls, arriving faster than she could cull them. She had summoned all her forces, but they had turned up sporadically, never giving her the numbers to mount a concerted counterattack. Hurrell's gue'vesa team had been overwhelmed within seconds of their arrival. The drones had fared better because of their mobility, but less than twenty remained now and the chitinous onslaught hadn't faltered. The battle couldn't be won.

'Kor'vre Ubor'ka,' Bhoral transmitted to the ship's flight deck. 'Withdraw the *Whispering Hand* immediately. The Concordance must be alerted to this treachery.'

'*I cannot abandon the exalted one,*' the pilot protested.

'We must assume he is lost.' Bhoral abhorred the words, but Kyuhai had made her duty clear. 'The ship will be overrun if you delay. Authorisation cypher follows.' She sent the code as her cannon finally overheated and fell silent.

'*I understand, Shas'vre. Signal me when you are on board.*'

'That is not an option. Go!'

Bhoral kept the beasts at bay with brief bursts from her flamethrower as the docking clamps disengaged and released the slumbering ship. Before their echoes had faded the vessel's engines rumbled into life, sending tremors through the chamber.

'Come then,' Bhoral whispered as her flamethrower ran dry. The tentacled abominations surged forward, vaulting over one-another in their eagerness to reach her. She clubbed the first one aside with a clumsy swing of her cannon and rammed her flamethrower into the face of the next, shattering its skull. Then they were upon her, hissing as they raked at her armour. Within seconds her battlesuit's damage indicator was flashing red in countless places. She ignored it, knowing there was nothing more to be done. Chanting a mantra of certitude, she stood motionless. Waiting.

The hanger's massive external doors slid open behind her, unleashing a shriek of void-wracked air. A heartbeat later Bhoral was wrenched into the emptiness beyond, trailing a string of chitinous horrors. As she whirled about in the vacuum she glimpsed the departing glow of the *Whispering Hand*'s engines.

'The circle closes,' she said and overloaded her battlesuit's power core. For a brief moment she burned brighter than the engines.

I didn't warn Erzul, Voyle thought bitterly, remembering his promise to the pathfinder. He sat stiffly in his chair, his hands steering the truck of their own accord. He couldn't even turn his head to check if the woman slumped beside him was still breathing. His comrades hadn't seen the violence that had transpired in the cabin, nor could they know the treachery playing out now.

I've betrayed them all.

'No, you have saved them, Ulver. Along with yourself.' The voice was his, but the words were not.

You lied to me, Voyle accused, struggling to break free. *Where are you taking us?*

'You shall all be enlightened, but the Ethereal among you is of singular importance.'

The Seeker... How...?

'What you know, I now know, child.'

Shame washed over Voyle in a corrosive wave, scouring him of all the hopes and hates that had bedevilled him since his long fall began. Finally all that remained was a bleak yearning for nothingness.

'It is your shadow to burn,' the Stormlight had advised. *'Only you can light the fire.'*

Hesitantly at first, then with growing conviction, Voyle began to recite the nineteenth mantra of self-sublimation. *The-Winter-That-Rises-Within* focussed on attaining a state of perfect stillness, conditioning its aspirants to slow their breathing and lock their muscles rigid as they purged their minds of desire. Voyle had always been drawn to its oblique words and the ephemeral oblivion they offered.

Emptiness unwound blinds the light that binds unseen.

He repeated the spiralling phrase over-and-over, speaking with his mind until his body listened... and *remembered*. Like creeping frost his grip on the wheel tightened then froze, locking the truck to its current path. From somewhere far away he heard his own voice calling to him, wheedling then reasoning then railing, becoming ever more strident as the road ahead curved yet the vehicle didn't follow.

None of it mattered. None of it was real.

But the deceiver was blind to such truths, and in its turmoil its control frayed. The lapse was brief, but it was enough for Voyle to stamp down on the accelerator.

Emptiness unwound...

With a roar the truck leapt forward, its frame rattling as its wheels left the road.

...blinds the light...

The usurper fled his mind as the building ahead rushed towards the windscreen.

...that binds unseen.

'Bloodtight,' Voyle sighed, closing his eyes.

Kyuhai hit the ground hard, but his armour absorbed the worst of the impact. He rolled with the fall and swept to his feet. For a moment he stood motionless, gazing inward to assess his body. There was some damage, but nothing significant. As in the recent crash, his armour and training had served him well, though he would not welcome a *third* such incident any time soon. He scanned the surrounding buildings but saw nobody. Up ahead the wrecked truck was still blazing, its death throes casting a red haze over the street.

'Your truth dies with you, Ulver Voyle,' Kyuhai said, then turned his attention to the living. Akuryo knelt nearby, wrestling with his helmet. Its dome was cracked and sparks flickered behind its shattered lenses. One of the gue'vesa lay further along the road, his neck twisted at a strange angle. None of the others had jumped from the speeding vehicle in time.

'How will we reach the ship?' Akuryo asked, finally tearing his helmet free.

'We cannot,' the Ethereal replied. 'It is too late. Either the ship is gone or it is in the enemy's hands now.'

'Then only vengeance remains to us,' the Fire Warrior said bitterly, throwing his ruined helmet aside.

'Vengeance is immaterial. No, we shall keep to the shadows and learn our enemy's truth.'

'To what purpose, Seeker?' Akuryo rose to his feet unsteadily. His scalp was scorched and bleeding.

'To destroy it.' Kyuhai sliced the air with his right hand, indicating *an-outcome-already-proven.* 'It must be done. Of this I am certain.'

'With respect... we are but two.'

'We will find others. I suspect this broken world harbours many secrets, shas'el.' Kyuhai allowed himself the ghost of a smile, though it passed unseen beneath his helm. 'And we are four.'

Akuryo swung round as a rangy avian figure dropped down beside him, landing in a feral crouch. A moment later a second one leapt from the roof behind to join it.

'For Greater Good!' the kroot carnivores growled together.

– THE SPIRAL –
OBLIVION

Por'el Adibh opened her eyes as the door of her chamber opened. A t'au stood in the doorway – a female of the Water caste like herself, but much younger and clad in the purple robes Adibh had come to loathe.

'So Fai'sahl was not the last of his embassy,' Adibh observed, rising from her chair.

'Eleven of us remain,' the newcomer replied. She shared the malignant vigour that Fai'sahl had projected, though her aura was less pronounced. 'I am Por'ui Beyaal. Por'vre Fai'sahl was my bonded mate.'

'His death was difficult,' Adibh said flatly.

'His death served the Greatest Good,' Beyaal said without a trace of sorrow. 'I trust your injuries have been attended to, Por'el?'

'You know they have, traitor.' Several days had passed since the Order's minions had recovered her from the wrecked vehicle, along with the monstrous warrior that had seized her. Since then she had been confined to this room and her questions had gone unanswered. 'You are aware that your attack on my embassy will be construed as an act of war,' she challenged.

'*You* attacked *us*,' Beyaal demurred serenely. 'Without provocation.'

'I do not accept that, but I advise you to release me without delay.' Adibh softened her tone. 'Perhaps an accord may yet be reached.'

'That is our aspiration.' Beyaal extended her hands, palms upward. 'The Cog Eternal has embraced the Greatest Good. It has always sought an *alliance* with the T'au Empire.'

'Then release me.'

'As you wish.' Beyaal bowed her head. 'Please follow me, Por'el.'

Adibh didn't move. 'You agree?' she asked doubtfully.

'The Animus-Alpha will address all your concerns,' Beyaal assured her.

'Who?'

'He is the First Architect of the Cog Eternal, but many of us have come to see him as a father. I believe you shall too.'

Adibh's eyes narrowed as she spotted something lurking in the passageway behind Beyaal.

'Your pardon, Por'el,' Beyaal said, catching her glance. 'I wanted to introduce my son, Geb'rah.' She called over her shoulder. 'Enter, child! There is nothing to fear.'

A squat figure shambled in, its heavyset form swaddled in robes. Lovingly Beyaal pulled its hood back and smiled at her prisoner.

Adibh stared, aghast, struggling to make sense of the infant's face.

'He is but three *tau'cyr*,' Beyaal crooned, 'but children grow swiftly here.'

As the hybrid thing grinned at her through a veil of tendrils Adibh's composure finally unravelled and a dark thought flashed through her mind: *Perhaps the xenophobia of the gue'la is not a sickness, but a strength.*

FIRE CASTE

DRAMATIS PERSONAE

The Phaedran Commissariat

Holt Iverson	Veteran Commissar
Lomax	High Commissar
Ysabel Reve	Commissar Cadet

The Arkan Confederates

Ensor Cutler	Colonel, 1st Company
Skjoldis 'Lady Raven'	Sanctioned Psyker/ Norland Witch
'Mister Frost'	The Colour Bearer/ Norland *Weraldur*
Elias Waite	Major, 2nd Company
Jon Milton Machen	Captain, 3rd Company
Ambrose Templeton	Captain, 4th Company
Hardin Vendrake	Captain, Silverstorm Sentinel Cavalry
Pericles Quint	Lieutenant, Silverstorm Sentinel Cavalry
Beauregard Van Hal	Silverstorm Sentinel Cavalry
Willis Calhoun	Sergeant, Dustsnake Squad
Claiborne Roach	Greyback Trooper, Dustsnake Squad
Gordy Boone	Greyback Trooper, Dustsnake Squad
Kletus Modine	Greyback Trooper, Dustsnake Squad
Jakob Dix	Greyback Trooper, Dustsnake Squad
Obadiah Pope	Greyback Trooper, Dustsnake Squad
Audie Joyce	Greencap Rookie, Dustsnake Squad
Cort Toomy	Greyback Sniper, Dustsnake Squad
Jaques Valance	Scout, 3rd Company

The Lethean Penitents

Yosiv Gurdjief	Penitent Confessor
Vyodor Karjalan	Admiral
Zemyon Rudyk	Penitent Commissar Cadet
Csanad Vaskó	Corsair Zabaton

The 33rd Verzante Skyshadows

Jaime Hernandez Garrido	Pilot
Guido Gonzalo Ortega	Co-Pilot

The Verzante Konquistadores

Ricardo Alvarez — Corporal

Cristobal Olim — Aristocrat Officer

The Unquiet Dead

Nathaniel Bierce — Commissar, deceased

Detlef Niemand — Commissar, deceased

Number 27 — Unknown Soldier, deceased

The Tau

Shas'el Aabal — Fire Warrior Commander

Shas'ui Jhi'kaara — Pathfinder

Por'o Dal'yth Seishin — Water Caste Ambassador

PROLOGUE

Dolorosa Topaz – Thunderground?

And so we come to it. Well I'll tell you what I know, but be warned that my mind may wander. The fever has a hold on me once again and I'm freezing and burning up by turns. As I write I can see my phantoms stalking from the emerald shadows, staking their claim on the sins of my past. My phantoms? Oh, there are three, standing shoulder to shoulder in mute condemnation of my failings. To the right is Old Man Bierce, inhumanly tall in his spotless black storm coat, pinning me with that raptor's glare. To the left is Commissar Niemand, pale and shrunken with the revelation of his own eternally unravelling entrails, trapped forever in the moment when I turned my back on him. And at the centre, always at the centre, stands Number 27, her three immaculate, dead eyes the greatest misery and mystery of them all.

Fever dreams or visions? I doubt it matters. Whatever they are, they've come to bear witness when I walk my Thunderground. No, don't concern yourself with the expression. It's just an old myth from my home world. We Arkan are a strange breed and there are some things even the schola progenium couldn't drum out of me. The Imperium took me away from my home long ago, but it couldn't take my home away from me. Sometimes blood runs deeper than faith.

But that's not what I wanted to tell you about. The Thunderground has called to me and if I don't return, and it falls to you to take my place, you'll need facts. You'll need to understand the true nature of your enemy. Most importantly you'll need to understand that you face a twofold beast.

First there's the foe you've travelled across the stars to destroy: an unholy coalition of rebels and aliens who'll butcher your men with anything from a bow to a burst cannon. The tau are behind it all of course. You've read the Tactica manuals so you'll already know how these xenos operate. On this world they call their movement 'the Concordance,' but don't dignify them with the name. You'll find the same old pattern of infiltration and corruption, so just call them blueskin bastards and purge them as best you can.

Their leader calls himself Commander Wintertide – an irony on a planet where winter is just a myth – but then Wintertide himself sometimes seems little more than a myth. He casts a long shadow, but you'll never actually see him. Well, I plan to put his myth to the test. If it can be done I'm going to find him and kill him.

But let me tell you about your other enemy, the spirit killer who'll steal away your troops before they even face the rebels. For men like you and I, pledged to put the steel in their spines and the fire in their hearts, She's the true enemy here. Of course I'm talking of Phaedra Herself, this cesspit planet we've come to liberate or conquer or cleanse. Sometimes I forget which it is. It's been a long war.

Phaedra: too lazy to be a death world, too bitter to be anything else. While She can't muster the riot of murderous beasts or geological torments of a true death world, you mustn't underestimate Her. She'll do Her killing slowly – stealthy but steady. And yes, I do mean 'She'. All the troops know it, although High Command denies it. Survive long enough and you'll know it too. Just as you'll know She's corrupt to Her mouldering, waterlogged core, no matter what the Ecclesiarchy assessors say. You'll know it in the mist and the rain and the creeping damp that will be your constant companions here, but most of all you'll know it in Her jungles.

You see, you've come to a water world and found a grey-green hell like no other. The oceans of Phaedra are choked with islands and in turn the islands are overrun with a wildfire cancer of vegetation – a morass of stinking kelp, strangling vines and towering fungal cathedrals. Worse still, the islands themselves are alive. Just look beneath the waterline and you'll see them breathing and pulsing. The biologis tech-priests say it's some kind of coral – a minor, mindless blasphemy of xenos diversity. They say there's no taint to it, but I've heard the bitter blood music beating through this world and I say they're fools.

And so you've had your warning and my duty to you is done. Time is pressing and I must make my final preparations. Didn't I tell you there's a storm coming? It won't be one of Phaedra's killer typhoons, but it'll be a big one all the same. I can taste it in the angry, electric air. And they can taste it too, the rats hiding in the skins of my charges and turning brave men sour. My charges? Oh, they were called the Verzante Konquistadores back when they were still a regiment unbroken by Phaedra's wiles. Now they're little more than relics left to rot. Not unlike myself. Perhaps that's why fate has led me to them. And perhaps that's why I still care enough to try and save them. They were never the finest troops in the Imperial Guard, but they're not beyond redemption even now.

There are seven in particular whose struggles have been piteous and an eighth beyond pity. I've watched them teeter on the brink of heresy, held back by some last vestige of honour or faith or perhaps simple fear. But now the storm will kindle an unholy fire in their hearts and give them that final push. I have to be there for them.

You are right – I have been weak. Doubtless my old mentor Bierce would tell me an example was required long ago, but I'm as broken as everything else in this meat-grinder war. I've not had the courage to administer the Emperor's Justice since the debacle of Indigo Gorge and Number 27. Perhaps if I'd had Bierce's fire or Niemand's ice and was a finer exemplar of our special brotherhood, things would be different now and these Guardsmen wouldn't have strayed so far, but Bierce and Niemand are long dead and I'm the last one left to hold the line.

The traitors think I'm fever-blind, but I've caught their sly whispers and know the truth of it. Tonight they'll run and I'll be waiting.

– Iverson's Journal

It was never truly dark in the Mire. By day the jealous canopy of the trees strangled the sunlight into a trickle, drowning the jungle in murk. By night the swarming fungi awoke, flooding the grottos and glades with biolumi-nescence, transforming the morass into a pungent wonderland. It was a world of rival twilights, but still the ghosts came out at night.

They bled from the tangled skein of the jungle and hovered furtively at the edge of the clearing. There were seven, every one an emaciated shadow in rotting fatigues. In the bilious light their khaki uniforms were a patchwork purple and their eyes seemed to glitter with indigo fire. Crouching at the tree line they scanned the clearing, battered lasrifles flitting about warily. With a flick of the wrist from the leader they dissolved into two teams and fanned out along the perimeter. Motionless, the leader kept watch on the ruin crouched at the centre of the glade.

The rain had turned hard and heavy, battering through the vault of the jungle and raising streamers of mist, but the pale dome of the temple glowed through the murk. It was typical of the indigenous architecture. Deprived of stone, the ancient Phaedrans had carved their buildings from coral, imbuing them with a globular, organic look that was repellent to Imperial eyes. The central cupola had collapsed and the walls were honeycombed with fissures, but there was no trace of the weeds or creeper vines that preyed on more wholesome relics. A circle of barren ground radiated from the temple, holding the jungle at bay for some ten metres or so. It was a pat-tern played out by a myriad dead temples across the planet. The mystery fascinated the Mechanicus priests, but to Ignatz Cabeza it was just another sign of this world's fundamental *wrongness*.

The sergeant was a wiry cadaver of a man, his features moulded into a death mask by a paste of grey mud. His eyes gleamed in the hollows of the camouflage, the irises iridescent with the bloom of a Glory fugue, but Cabeza was no degenerate. He reviled most of Phaedra's fungal narcotics, but the Glory was different, its spores granting that razorwire sharpness a warrior sometimes found in the heat of battle. Of course the Glory was forbidden, but deep in the Mire, far from the vigilant eyes of the priests and commissars, a man made his own laws. Uneasily his thoughts drifted to Iverson, the wreck of a commissar who'd joined his regiment a month back. The man had presided over the remnants of the 6th Tempest like a carrion bird shadowing a dying man. And of course the 6th *was* dying.

The fall of Cabeza's regiment was a slow burning shame in his heart. They were Verzante, Konquistadores of the Galleon Meridian, Guardsmen of the God-Emperor and they had exulted in this campaign! Whipped into a fervour by Aguilla de Caravajal, the holy Water Dragon of the 6th Tempest, they had joined the crusade to Phaedra joyfully, eager to brand their name upon this heathen world. Instead they had drowned in its filth.

How long had it been? Three years? Four? Caravajal himself had fallen in the second year, raving and incontinent with blood, unravelled from within by a borefly infestation. Inevitably the regiment had unravelled in his wake, a thousand proud Konquistadores fading to a few hundred shadows. Tactically marginal, they had been shunted off to this worthless island crawling with xenos-tainted savages. Dolorosa Topaz – a backwater corner of the war where victory was as impossible as it was irrelevant. And here they were forgotten. *Almost.*

Long months after their exile began, an Imperial gunboat had appeared on the horizon. The Verzante gathered on the shore and Velasquez, the veteran capitán who'd held them together by sheer force of will, dared to make a show of hope, but the boat had carried neither reinforcements nor supplies, just a scarecrow in black.

There had been no mistaking the figure standing in the prow of the approaching boat. Strikingly tall and straight in his leather storm coat, his square-jawed face shadowed by a high peaked cap, he was a commissar cut in the classic mould. Watching him, Cabeza had shuddered. Though the 6th had lost both its disciplinary officers long ago, they'd left him with plenty of scars to remember them by. Not that he held it against them. He'd been a rowdy dog until the commissars had whipped him into shape. Luckily he'd been a quick learner, unlike his clan brother Greko, who'd wound up hanging by his heels in the parade ground as an example to the new recruits. After that they'd *all* been quick learners. And so Cabeza had wondered what this new tyrant would teach them.

But when the commissar stepped from the boat Cabeza had seen the truth of him. The newcomer's cap was tattered and his leather coat was more grey than black, its edges encrusted with a rime of mould. Up close he'd been pallid and unshaven, his grey hair hanging well below the shoulders. He was probably no more than forty-five, but already old with something that cut deeper than age. Worse still was the telltale lattice of a spidervine burn inscribed into his face. Only a blind man or a man too ignorant to see could have taken such a wound. Perhaps it had happened a lifetime ago, back in the commissar's first tour of the Mire, but to Cabeza the scar still marked him out as a fool.

Phaedra has no mercy for fools...

The newcomer's faded blue eyes had skimmed the Konquistadores briefly.

Distant. Disinterested. 'Iverson,' he'd said. Then he'd stalked past them to claim a tent.

Commissar Iverson's tenure continued as it had begun. Aloof and indifferent, he had kept to his tent or wandered the jungle alone, scribbling away in his battered leather journal. Sometimes he talked to himself or to something in the shadows only he could see. Like a man possessed. And maybe he was. Cabeza had seen stranger things in his time. In any case Iverson had caught the fever in his second week and hadn't left his tent since. He was just another wreck among so many. An irrelevance... Cabeza had believed it until he'd glimpsed the commissar watching the camp from the shadows of his tent. And recently he'd caught Iverson's fever-bright eyes looking directly at him. *Almost as if he knew the treachery in Ignatz Cabeza's heart...*

Something battered through the foliage behind the sergeant. He scowled as the sour-sweet stench of zoma juice hit him. Zoma! Now there was a true high road to oblivion, exactly the kind of fool's glow that Cabeza despised. Almost as much as he despised the man who lumbered up alongside him. Cristobal Olim had rubbed the camouflage away from his pasty face, leaving it luminous in the fungal light.

'I told you to wait, señor,' Cabeza hissed.

'It's raining. The water was pooling in my boots,' there was a strident whine to Olim's voice that set Cabeza's teeth on edge. The few he still had left. 'Besides you've found our objective, sergeant!' Olim stepped forward and peered at the temple, his eyes bleary with zoma. 'Oh yes, you've most definitely found it. I knew my faith in you wasn't misplaced!'

Olim took another step forward and stumbled, his feet skittering on the rain-slick coral. Cabeza let him fall, keeping his attention on his comrades as they completed their sortie and converged across the clearing. Corporal Alvarez waved him the all clear – no threats on the periphery of the zone. That just left the temple itself. Cabeza signalled the advance.

Olim was still slithering about on the ground, whimpering as he tried to find purchase on the coral. Cabeza hauled him up with one hand, keeping his lasrifle steady with the other.

'On your feet, señor,' Cabeza said. 'I don't want to lose you.'

Olim clutched at his arm, his tone suddenly sly, 'No, you don't sergeant. You really don't. Because I'm the one they want, remember. I'm the officer here!'

Cabeza looked at him. The man's attempt at cunning was pathetic. Although the Mire had sucked the meat out of him Olim still looked fat. How was that even possible? Staring at that saggy sponge of a face, with its bulging eyes and delicate, zoma-stained lips, Cabeza felt an almost physical need for violence. He hated Olim. They all did. The fat aristo was responsible for the massacre of Capitán Velasquez and the other commanders. He'd been the duty officer on the night when a dead-eyed native had walked into camp with tales of a rebel supply dump. Hungry for approval, Olim had led the native straight to the command tent, where the infiltrator had triggered the melta bomb wired into his guts. Velasquez and the other officers had died instantly, but in a twist of fate Olim had escaped untouched. As the only surviving officer, he'd inherited command and carried the 6th Tempest into its final death spiral. The man was a travesty.

'Why... why are you looking at me like that, sergeant?' The wheedling tone was back and Cabeza turned away before it was too late. Olim was a degenerate, but he was the one who'd made contact with the rebels. How he'd managed it was anybody's guess, but he was Cabeza's ticket out of here. Lady Justice would have to wait a little longer. After all, she'd been in no hurry to claim Olim so far.

'Sergeant... what's wrong?' Olim stuttered.

'I was just thinking what a blind bitch she is, señor,' Cabeza said darkly as he stalked away.

The others were waiting outside the temple when Cabeza arrived with Olim at his heels. The fungal light faltered just inside the portico, but the sergeant was loath to break discipline and use a torch. He hesitated, sensing the same disquiet among his men. Not much unnerved Ignatz Cabeza anymore, but by the God-Emperor he didn't want to step inside that living dead shell. He'd swept enough of the ruins in his time and knew what was waiting in there: the passage would bifurcate endlessly, the arterial branches twisting and turning as they burrowed deep into the tainted flesh of the island. Many men had disappeared inside the bowels of these things.

'Where are the rebs?' Cabeza asked.

'Not far,' Olim said. 'There will be a beacon. They said it would be just inside the doorway.' Olim pointed at the leering portico. When none of the others moved he licked his lips, stepped forward and knelt by the threshold. Hesitantly his hands explored the broken coral under the lintel, finding nothing but dust.

'Here... they said... it would be... promised me...' Pinned between the darkness ahead and the hard eyes behind, Olim became agitated, then frantic, scrabbling through the detritus, reaching deeper until...

'Yes... Yes! Here it is!' Olim glanced over his shoulder, smiling with relief. Something bright was clutched in his podgy hand. Awoken by his touch it emitted a soft, rhythmic pulse.

And Cabeza looked up.

Maybe it was a subtle disturbance of the light that drew his eyes or maybe it was pure instinct. Either way, he saw the shape unfolding on the lintel high above. It was just a swathe of shadows against the pale dome, but it turned his guts to ice. Wired on the Glory, Cabeza hurled himself backwards, firing on full auto before his conscious mind had caught up. As his violet fire ripped skyward the thing reared up and leapt from its perch. The las-beams stitched contrails of steam through the rain as they chased the bat-like shape and clipped a ragged leather wing.

And then the beast was amongst them like a black whirlwind. Two men went down instantly, slammed into the ground by the force of its leap and cushioning its landing. The attacker teetered, almost losing its balance as it struck out again. There was a sharp crackle and a third man toppled and already the thing was spinning wildly towards Alvarez. Too close to fire, the Konquistadore swung out with the butt of his rifle, but something hard and unbending blocked the blow. Again that crackle and then Alvarez was roaring in agony, his rifle slipping from nerveless fingers. His scream was cut short by a brutal jab to the throat and he fell, jerking about in violent spasms. And the thing spun to its next victim...

Staggering backwards, Cabeza tried to get a bead on its jagged, graceless dance, but the attacker was woven too deeply among his men. He understood its game. Outnumbered and outgunned it had gambled on surprise and shock. *Shock...* Abruptly he saw through the mythic flush of his narcotic fugue and recognised the baton in the attacker's hand... then recognised the raw electric crackle as Estrada collapsed in a twitching heap. *Shock maul!* And when the whirlwind swung to face him, Cabeza finally recognised it.

'Iverson,' he said.

The commissar had lost his cap and there was a smouldering tear in his coat where Cabeza's las-fire had clipped his shoulder. He was swaying and breathless, the spidervine scars livid against his chalk white face. His eyes were burning with fever... and something more. Seeing the indigo fire in his pupils, Cabeza spat.

'What the hell kind of commissar are you anyway?' he yelled.

'The wrong kind,' Iverson said. He smiled bleakly, his scars twisting into a strange new geometry.

And then Cabeza was shouldering his lasrifle and Iverson was loping towards him, one leg twisted and trailing, probably messed up by the jump. And Cabeza's finger was tightening on the trigger... and Iverson was hurling the shock maul...

Time snapped back into shape and Cabeza's world exploded into pain. The shock maul smashed the rifle from his hands and a split second later Iverson barrelled into his chest and threw him from his feet. He landed hard and the commissar crashed down on top of him, grinding him into the sharp coral. Iverson's fists pummelled down as his mad eyes bored into Cabeza.

'She won't... have... your soul...' the commissar hissed through ragged breaths. 'I won't... let you... fall!'

Finally the deserter lay still and Iverson lurched to his feet, stumbling as he retrieved his shock maul. He could feel his stomach convulsing with the fungal filth he'd consumed, but there had been no other way to ride out the fever. It was just another small heresy to add to his growing tally. Old Bierce would be turning in his grave if he hadn't already clawed his way out to haunt his protégé.

But I've done my duty. I've hauled them back from the brink... I'll...

'Take you back... all of you...' Iverson mumbled as he counted up the scattered, semi-conscious bodies. He wasn't sure how he'd manage that part of his plan yet. Seven broken men to carry back to camp... *Seven?* Where was the eighth? He turned to the temple and saw Olim crouched at the threshold. The noble's eyes were wide with terror. Iverson felt bile rising in his throat at the sight of him. Yes, this was the eighth turncoat – *the worm*, the one who'd sown the seeds of corruption amongst the rest. For this one there could be no second chance. Iverson drew his laspistol and levelled it at the cowering noble.

You'll be Number 28, he realised. *Maybe your death will exorcise Number 27.*

Number 27? Iverson saw her then, standing in the shadowed portico behind the fat man, watching him intently with her three dead eyes. Waiting to see him kill again.

'For the Emperor,' Iverson told her, trying to conceal the edge in his voice.

Something darted from the trees behind him, buzzing like an angry insect. Iverson spun round firing, but the sleek white saucer streaking towards him zipped between his snapshots, skimming high above the ground on an anti-gravity field. The disc was only about a metre in diameter, but Iverson knew that a soulless intelligence guided the machine. It was only a drone, its artificial brain no more sophisticated than a jungle predator, but the very existence of such a thing was blasphemous.

Blueskin technology is a heresy upon the face of the galaxy!

Of more immediate concern were the twin pulse carbines mounted on the underside of the drone. As the disc whirled to dodge his fire those guns rotated independently to lock on him. He dived aside as they spat a stuttering enfilade of plasma. The dive slipped into a fall, saving him from a second burst as the machine whizzed by. He rolled over and fired after it, catching it with a couple of rounds as it banked into a turn, but his shots only mottled its carapace. Chattering angrily the drone soared back towards him.

A hail of las-bolts spattered the machine from the side, knocking it off kilter and exposing its vulnerable underbelly. Careening wildly through the air, the drone raked the ground with plasma, shredding two of the unconscious Konquistadores. Someone roared in fury and fresh las-fire ripped into the saucer's belly. One of its carbines exploded, taking the other with it and spinning the machine out of control. Gushing smoke and burbling in distress it retreated, losing altitude as it limped towards the trees, but Iverson was already on his feet and charging. Leaping, he swung the shock maul down on the drone, smashing it towards the ground. It tried to rise and he struck again and again, elevated by a hatred untainted by doubt.

The machine exploded.

Iverson was thrown from his feet. Falling for what felt like forever he watched a ragged arm spiralling towards the sky, its hand still clenching a shock maul. It was awful and absurd, but suddenly he was laughing and someone else was laughing along with him. He glanced across the clearing and saw Cabeza. The cadaverous Konquistadore was on his knees, cackling through a mask of mud and blood. His lasrifle was levelled at the wrecked drone.

Cabeza didn't know why he'd thrown in with the commissar at the end. He'd already turned his back on the Imperium to sign up with the enemy in the hope of a better deal. He wouldn't be the first Guardsman to do it, nor the last, so why make a bad move now? What could Iverson offer him except more pain and maybe a quick death? Even for a commissar the man was crazy! Just look at him, lying there with his arm torn off at the elbow and laughing like it was the best joke in the Imperium. *Crazy!* Except Cabeza was laughing right along with him so maybe he was crazy too. And maybe that was all there was to it.

'For the bloody God-Emperor!' Cabeza cackled through the last of his broken teeth. Then a drone soared down behind him and his chest erupted in a superheated geyser of flesh and blood. Looking down at the sizzling cavity in his chest he frowned, thinking a full-grown mirewyrm could swim right through there. It was a miracle his torso was still holding things together.

But then it wasn't.

As Cabeza's corpse collapsed inwards like a slaughterhouse of cards the second drone flashed past, homing in on Iverson. Biting down on the sudden agony of his ruined arm, he rolled to his knees. His laspistol was gone, lost somewhere in the fall. It wouldn't have stopped the machine, but it would have given him a stand. Hadn't Bierce taught him that a stand was all that mattered in the final accounting?

But hadn't he stopped believing that long ago?

And if he'd stopped believing it, why was he still fighting? Maybe because Bierce was standing at the edge of the clearing, hands clasped behind his back in that parade ground rigor, watching and judging his pupil until the bitter end.

The drone swept past and began to circle him, chattering and chirping as two more descended to join its dance. The machines seemed to grow more alert and aware in numbers, almost as if they were parts of a collective mind coming together. Maybe it was just a delusion, but Iverson could have sworn there was real anger in that mind. He'd destroyed one of its components and it wanted revenge. And so the drones were playing with him, *enjoying* his hopeless, one-armed struggle against the coral, mocking his determination to die on his feet. He could almost taste their hatred. Wasn't that why the Imperium shunned such technology? Didn't the Ecclesiarchy preach that thinking machines loathed the living and would ultimately turn on their creators? Mankind had learned that hard truth to its cost long ago, but the blueskin race was still reckless with youth. Perhaps that would be its downfall. As the drones circled him Iverson took comfort in the thought.

The machine chatter rose to a higher pitch and he steeled himself for death, but abruptly the drones fell silent and drifted back a few paces. To Iverson's eyes they looked reluctant and sullen, like angry dogs leashed by their masters. And as the dogs withdrew, the masters emerged.

They crept from the trees in a low crouch, their stubby carbines sweeping from side to side as they advanced, hugging the coral with a bone-deep distrust of open ground. There were five, lightly armoured in mottled black breastplates and rubberised fatigues. Their long helmets arched over their shoulders, giving them a vaguely crustacean look, the strangeness heightened by the crystal sensors embedded in their otherwise blank faceplates. Iverson recognised them at once: pathfinders, the scouts of the tau race.

Despite their hunched postures the warriors were swift and graceful, fanning out to surround him with the perfect co-ordination of bonded hunters. Slipping on the coral yet again, Iverson abandoned dignity and faced them on his knees. He could see Bierce lurking at the periphery of his vision, demanding some final caustic rhetoric from his protégé, but Iverson had nothing to say. Glaring at the pathfinders, he noticed one of them was quite different to its companions – shorter and slighter of build, the set of its shoulders subtly wrong. The only one with hooves... Iverson's eyes narrowed as the truth hit him: the odd-one-out was the genuine article.

Under that loathsome xenos armour all the others are human!

The lone alien stepped forward and dropped to its haunches, bringing its impassive crystal lenses level with his face. There was a crimson slash running along the spine of its helmet, identifying it as the leader, but Iverson was drawn to another mark – a deep crack running from its crown to the chin of its faceplate. The damage had been patched up, but the rippled scar of a chainsword was unmistakeable to a commissar.

'Your face,' he breathed. 'Show me.' The warrior tilted its head quizzically at the challenge. 'Or are you afraid?'

'Be watchful, shas'ui.' It was one of the traitors, his voice surprisingly crisp through his sealed helmet. 'This one is of the commissar caste. Even wounded this one will not yield.'

The studied formality of the traitor's words disgusted Iverson, particularly the way he'd spoken that unclean xenos rank, '*shas'ui*', with such reverence. These traitors weren't just mercenaries or cowards looking for a way out – they were true believers.

The shas'ui considered Iverson for a moment, then it began to unclip its helmet, its four-fingered hands nimble as they uncoupled the power feed and flicked an array of seals. Throughout the ritual its cluster of crystal eyes remained fixed on him, unwavering until the helmet was swept away and he saw the face of his enemy.

Even for an alien it was ugly. Its leathery blue-grey skin was tinged with yellow and pockmarked with insect bites. A rash of boils ran from its neck to cluster around a topknot of greasy black hair, but its most startling feature was the ruination left by the chainsword. A deep rift had been carved into the right side of its face, running from scalp to jaw, mirroring the crack in its helmet. It was an old wound, but still hideous. A bionic sensor glittered from the scabrous mess where its eye had been and the whole jaw had been replaced with a carved prosthetic. The remaining eye, black and lustreless, regarded the commissar inscrutably. For all its mutilated strangeness the creature was recognisably female. She was the first tau Iverson had seen up close and whatever he'd expected it wasn't this filthy, disfigured veteran.

You're even uglier than me. It was such an absurd, irrelevant thought that he almost laughed out loud.

'*Ko'miz'ar.*' The word sounded unfamiliar on the creature's lips, but he sensed it had faced his kind before... and had the scar to show for it. '*Ko'miz'ar...*' It was an accusation ripe with hatred.

'Once and forever,' Iverson answered, denying the lie and refusing to meet Bierce's gaze. The old raven was standing amongst the traitors now, his thirst for judgement blinding him to the irony. High above, the sky rumbled, pregnant with the storm... and Niemand's shade shuffled up beside Bierce, haggard with his curse. A moment later lightning lashed the canopy into emerald fire and there was a knife in the alien's hand, tearing towards Iverson's eye... *for an eye...* flashing... so bright and swift... *But don't the blueskins despise close combat?* Then a new pain as the blade impaled the hand he'd thrown up to ward off the blow... *Not this blueskin. It wants to taste my pain... Share its pain...* A stabbing agony as the blade punched through his palm and out the other side, the gleaming tip stopping just short of his eye... *Black xenos eye, glaring with a rage so like my own.*

Then they were at the eye of the storm, transfixed by a pure harmony of hate as the blueskin pushed on the knife and Iverson pushed back, neither of them willing to break the perfect ritual of the struggle. Iverson grinned savagely into that foul, ruined face and saw its eye widen... *grinning right back at me!* And then Number 27 knelt down beside him, serene and oh so dead, and every moment bled into eternity as Iverson rose towards his Thunderground.

ACT I

DESCENT

CHAPTER ONE

The Mire, unknown

The alien has cheated me of my Thunderground. One moment we were pinned in a deadlock of hate by its knife, the next... treachery! A twist of agony and then that blade was tearing up through my hand and slashing back down into my face. It took an eye for an eye and left a scar for a scar, but mocked me with my life.

I awoke on this little atoll, stranded Emperor knows where. The traitors had bandaged my wounds, pumped me full of xenos drugs and left me with a week's worth of supplies. They'd also left me the bloody relic of my severed arm, but the real insult was the pamphlet they'd stuffed into my pocket. 'Winter's Tide' it's called, named after the slippery tyrant who leads them on this world.

Yes, of course I read it. One must know one's enemy after all. Besides, it might have offered up some clue to Wintertide himself, but all I found was a diatribe extolling the so-called Greater Good, the blasphemous philosophy that binds the blueskin empire together. The threat was implicit in every line, so polite it was almost an apology of malice: 'Join us, or else.'

Emperor damn them! They thought I was finished, but I'm not alone here. My trinity of ghosts is with me and together we will endure. There is such strength in hatred. But of course you already know that. We are of a kind are we not? That's why I've kept on writing with the wreck of a hand remaining to me. So you'll understand. So you'll be ready. But first we have to get out of the Mire...

Bleeding ectoplasm from the stump of an arm, Niemand gestures defiantly and tells me we'll be found soon, but sometimes it seems that this limbo has been forever and everything else was just a dream. Bierce always censured me for thinking too much, but out here there's nothing else to do. Besides, it's a flaw that runs blood deep, another shadow of my Arkan heritage that the schola couldn't exorcise.

You know, lately my thoughts keep turning back to Providence, the home I left so long ago. I think of the frozen Norland rifts and the blistering hell of the Badlands, the white marble colonnades of Capitol Bastion and the gabled mansions of Old Yethsemane.

I think of the pioneers and the patricians, the machinists and the savages, all the clans and cartels and tribes, forever at each other's throats but forever Arkan. They came late to the Emperor's Light and they didn't come quietly.

Sometimes I wonder what became of them all...

– Iverson's Journal

Following its ordeal in the warp, the transport ship was slumbering at low power, recovering its strength and resolve for the return journey. Its passage to Phaedra had almost ended in catastrophe and now there was hell to pay. While the ship's tech-priests worked frantically to salve its pain and the captain whipped his crew back into shape – and in one case into death – the passengers on Q-deck were left in ignorance. To the Navy men the Imperial Guard were little more than cattle with guns.

After the crisis a junior lieutenant had descended from the bridge to brief the regiment's officers, talking patronisingly of power outages and fluctuations in the Geller field – meaningless words that said nothing of the horror that had overtaken the eleven men billeted in Dorm 31 when the warp had seeped into the ship. Colonel Cutler had broken his nose and sent him blubbering back up to the bridge. After that the Guardsmen had heard no more.

All things considered, Major Elias Waite had to admit it was a bad start to the regiment's first campaign away from home. The 19th Arkan Confederates had travelled a long way from Providence, but they had a lot further to go in their hearts before this new life made any sense to them. Having passed his seventieth year, Waite doubted he'd be travelling the whole way with them. He was still technically their second-in-command, but he knew many of the officers regarded him as a spent force, and since the horror in Dorm 31 he'd begun to wonder if they were right. By the Emperor, he was tired of it all...

As he navigated the murky labyrinth of Q-deck, his lantern painting strange shadows across his path, he couldn't shake the feeling that the walls were just a thin line between life and the void. His path was carrying him along the skin of the ship, where the membrane seemed tense and fragile, ready to dissolve from one step to the next. His mind told him this wasn't so, but his blood told him otherwise and he was sure every man and woman in the regiment felt the same way. The Arkan simply weren't bred for deep space.

Well plenty of folks aren't, Waite chided himself, *but most learn to live with it. We'll just have to learn the trick along with the rest of them. We're true Guardsmen now and space is part of the job.*

The Imperium of man was a troubled giant and it was a Guardsman's lot to be shuffled back and forth across the galaxy as duty called. Besides, few Imperial forces had been as fortunate as the Arkan regiments, who'd fought all their wars at home for so long.

But were we really so lucky? Waite wondered.

Long ago, someone very wise and very bleak had remarked that civil wars were the worst kind. After the madness that had ravaged his home world, turning parish against parish and brother against brother, Waite wouldn't argue. The rebels had called it Independence, the brave old Union of Seven Stars reborn brighter and better than before. How the fools had rallied to their 'March of Freedom' – croppers and collarmen, hicks and gentry, even some of the savage tribes, banding together to throw off the shackles of Imperial tyranny.

Eleven years of blood and betrayal!

Suddenly Waite was breathing hard and there were tears in his eyes. It was the sheer waste of it all that hurt so much. What chance had the separatists ever had? Even if they'd won – and they'd come pretty damn close at Yethsemane Falls – well, what then? How could one planet have hoped to stand against the juggernaut of the Imperium? Fortunately it had never come to that. The price of victory had been high, but the Arkan faithful had put their own house in order before the wrath of the Imperium had come crashing down on their world.

'And now here we are, a billion leagues from home, come to do it all over again to some other poor fools,' Waite told the darkness. 'Emperor-damned rebels...'

There was to be no rest for the loyalists of Providence. With the civil war finally over, the surviving Arkan regiments had been thrown into the lottery of galactic deployment and scattered across space on the whims of some distant, inscrutable strategy. For the 19th Confederates that whim had led to a backwater subsector on the Eastern Fringe of the Imperium and a world called Phaedra.

Well, as the Emperor wills it, Waite decided wearily.

Realising he'd come to a standstill, he spat and got himself moving again. He wasn't usually a man prone to introspection. In his youth he'd been a traveller, wandering the high sierras and rift valleys of the frozen north, taking his chances as a trapper and a prospector, but always careful to play fair with the Norland tribes. They were a moody folk, not much inclined to trust a stranger (more inclined to spit and gut him if the truth be told), but he'd won them over. The fact was he'd always liked people and thirty years in the Guard hadn't changed that. True, he was old now, his face a brown leather walnut and his hair a fond memory of better days, but he'd kept his muscles and could still swing a sabre with the best of them. Damn, but he had to shake off this oppression. It was clinging to him like a leech...

Like the abomination Trooper Norliss had become in Dorm 31. Like the broken things they'd put to the sword in that blighted town back home. Like the tolling of the daemon bell hanging at the town's rotten heart. Waite had prayed never to hear those soul-jangling chimes again, but they had followed the regiment across the stars. Or maybe they had always been there, waiting in the warp for fools to listen. Whatever the truth of it, the daemon bell had tolled again inside Dorm 31.

Ringing in Trooper Norliss's changes...

But no, he mustn't go there. These were not memories to dwell upon at the best of times and certainly not in this gloomy mausoleum. Unconsciously Waite's fingers brushed the aquila symbol hanging from his neck. He was vaguely surprised to find that he had reached his destination. The viewing gallery was a grand atrium of fluted marble pillars and delicate murals, but in the dim emergency lighting it looked forbidding. He saw stars twinkling through the immense window in the outer wall, promising something brighter than this shadow-haunted concourse. Two figures were framed against the void, one very still, the other almost manic as it stalked back and forth, gesticulating with sharp, angry motions. Waite heard the murmur of their conversation, but the words escaped him. It was just as he'd expected: the colonel was with his witch again.

With a sigh Waite entered. Something loomed from behind a pillar and he leapt back, his hand reaching for his sabre before he recognised the giant. The man's face was pale against a cascade of ebony braids, his eyes canted above high cheekbones. He had a feral look that sat strangely with the smart cut of his grey Confederate uniform, almost like a wolf in man's clothing.

Waite cursed himself for a skittish fool. He should have expected the Norland giant. Wherever the witch went, her *weraldur* followed. The warrior had been ritually bonded to her when she'd first manifested the wyrd as a young child. As tradition demanded, he had waited patiently while his charge had made the long journey on the Black Ships to be tested for any trace of taint. If she had been found wanting and failed to return to Providence within a span of seven years that same tradition would have demanded his ritual suicide. Their fates were bound tightly in life, tighter still in death. He was her guardian and potential executioner. The double-headed axe strapped to his back was consecrated to grant the Mercy if his charge fell to the warp. Unsurprisingly the *weraldur* path was one of the few Norland traditions the Imperium had actively encouraged.

'The God-Emperor's blessings upon you, Mister Frost,' Waite said, feeling uncomfortable with the title. To call a strapping Norland warrior 'Mister' or one of their fierce, mysterious women 'Lady' was absurd, but after the war the Imperial witch hunters had come down hard on all the Outlander folk. Although many of the tribes had fought alongside the loyalists, the fanatics had campaigned to 'civilise' them all. The first things they'd stolen were their old tribal names. Take away a Norlander's name and you were halfway to owning his soul. It was the kind of logic that appealed to a witch hunter.

Waite tried a smile. 'Your vigilance commends you, *weraldur*, but I've words for the colonel.' He made to step past the giant, but the Norlander blocked him again. The major's expression turned hard and he raised his voice: 'I'm here on the God-Emperor's business, so step aside.'

He wasn't expecting a reply. The giant was a mute, his tongue removed during his bonding to the witch, but the confusion in his eyes was answer enough. Waite's brand of down-to-earth piety was well liked by the troops and since Preacher Hawthorne's death he'd served as the regiment's surrogate priest – which gave him a hold over this devout savage.

'Stand aside in His name, *weraldur*!' Waite boomed theatrically.

Frost frowned, trying to weigh up his divided loyalties. Suddenly he cocked his head, as if listening to a secret voice. The talk by the window had ceased and the silhouettes were watching them. Queasily Waite realised he'd been right about that secret voice. The witch was talking to her guardian, brushing his mind with hers. A moment later the giant stepped aside.

'Well now, I'll be damned if I recall asking for visitors,' a voice bellowed across the gallery, flush with anger and easy authority, 'but someone's here so I guess I must be damned or just plain stupid.'

'Never stupid, colonel!' Waite called back. 'And not damned yet if I've any say in it.'

Silence. Then laughter, deep and bitter and laced with something Waite didn't much care for.

'Get your scrawny arse over here, old man. There's something I want you to see.' Now there was genuine humour in the voice and Waite shook his head, already sure he wouldn't find the words to challenge his commander.

The witch drew back as Waite approached, hiding her face in the dark arch of her cowl. The colonel was still pacing across the stars, his back rigid with tension, his left hand clenching and unclenching ferociously, the right locked to the hilt of his sabre. His wide-brimmed hat was slung over his back, bouncing about as he stalked back and forth. He hadn't cleaned up since the horror in Dorm 31 and his rawhide jacket was still blotched with black stains. There was a gash in his right leg where a thorny tendril had whipped past his guard, but Waite knew it was useless telling him to see a medic. These days it was useless telling Ensor Cutler anything. These days he only had ears for the witch.

'Take a look outside, Elias,' Cutler said without breaking the fierce rhythm of his pacing.

Waite peered through the glass. The grey-green swathe of a planet curved away beneath them, looking mottled and moist, like a colossal fungal puff-ball. *Unclean.* A ship hung on the horizon, sharing their orbit. Waite could tell it was a behemoth and a warship, its prow blunt and pugnacious, its decks encrusted with gun turrets and sensor spikes. A welter of scars pitted the hull, culminating in a deep furrow carved across its midriff where something had almost sliced the ship in half. The fissure showed no signs of repair and Waite suspected any attempt to move the vessel would seal its destruction. The leviathan had taken a mortal wound and this planet would be its grave. If it weren't for the lights glittering in its portholes he'd have wagered the ship was already dead. He squinted, trying to decipher the faded tattoo of its name.

'The *Requiem of Virtue*,' Cutler said, as if reading his mind. 'Damn strange name for a warship.' Abruptly he stopped pacing and sized up the vessel. 'I don't trust it, Elias. And I trust that filthy planet even less.'

Waite hesitated, unsure whether the colonel expected an answer. He prided himself on reading the hearts of men, but Cutler had become increasingly mercurial over the last couple of years. Since Trinity and its bell. By Providence, that daemon-haunted town had cast a long shadow over the regiment.

'Zebasteyn. Estevano. Kircher.' Cutler chewed through the words one by one, evidently not much liking the taste.

'I don't follow your drift, colonel...'

'Another name I don't trust. Kircher's the Imperial Commander here – our lord and master until this war's done.' Cutler nodded towards the ship. 'Man runs the whole show from up there, hiding away in that floating hulk, keeping his boots squeaky clean while he throws good men after bad, pulling the strings and watching the chips fall. Calls himself the 'Sky Marshall', whatever the Hells that's supposed to mean! Is he army? Navy? Maybe even an Inquisition lackey...' He shook his head. 'I don't trust any of it. This war is *old*, Elias. It makes our little uprising look like a backyard tussle.'

When he got angry, Cutler always slipped into his Yethsemane drawl. Like Waite, he wasn't a product of the aristocratic academies that churned out most of the Arkan officer class. He was a patrician, but his family had been knee-deep in debt, so young Ensor Cutler had signed up with the Dust Rangers, a rough-and-ready cavalry outfit. While other officers had studied strategic theory at Point Tempest, Cutler had made his name hunting feral greenskins in the Badlands. The rawhide jacket he wore in lieu of the regulation grey was a legacy of those wild days, its tassels woven with greenskin tusks and finger bones. That coat had raised a few eyebrows when Cutler had finally received his commission from the Capitol, but he'd refused to discard it. It was the kind of thing that made him who he was – the kind of thing that got him into trouble. Inevitably the Old Guard had clipped his wings, only granting him his colonel's stars when the war was over and they could pack him off into space.

'It don't smell right, Elias,' Cutler was suddenly glaring at Waite, his eyes bright, his lips drawn back into a snarl. Looking at that fierce, leonine face, with its shoulder-length mane and tangled beard, Waite sensed this tarnished nobleman was more savage than any Norland tribesman. But it was the *whiteness* that unnerved him the most.

Cutler wasn't yet fifty but his hair was dead white from scalp to beard. Before Trinity there hadn't been a white hair on his head. That town had changed so much about him, but the whiteness was its most visible mark. Waite wondered if Cutler knew his men had nicknamed him 'the Whitecrow'. And if he knew, did he even care?

Suddenly Waite was sure time was running out for all of them. He had to find the words to get through to this man who'd once been his friend. He had to know what Cutler had found inside the mouldering temple at Trinity's heart. Waite had been by his side when they'd purged the town, but only the witch and her guardian had faced the source of the cancer with him. Only they had *seen* the daemon bell.

Why did I let him talk me into staying behind? Why didn't I insist on going in there with him? But in his secret, guilty heart Elias Waite knew that nothing could have made him walk into that desecrated shrine.

'The bastards promised me a full sitrep once we made orbit,' Cutler stormed on. 'Campaign records and troop dispositions, field maps and recon reports... Some Emperor-damned orientation! And then they send me that!' He jabbed a finger at a crumpled sheet of parchment on the floor. 'One damn page!'

Waite bent to retrieve the document but Cutler waved him back. 'Leave it. You'll hear it all soon enough, but don't hold your breath.'

Suddenly Cutler frowned and glanced at the witch, his eyes narrowing as she whispered into his mind. The intimacy of it made Waite's skin crawl. Lady Raven, the men called her, and unlike her warden's childish name, hers felt *right*. His distrust for her came from the gut. She was a psyker, a mutant cursed with heightened psychic potential that made her a living, breathing time bomb of corruption. Yes, she had survived the tests that culled all but the strongest of her kind and been sanctioned to practise her craft in the Imperium's name, but you could never be sure with a witch. To Waite's mind a sanctioned psyker was just a rubber-stamped monster. How could Ensor allow her to touch his mind? And was there any truth to the whispers about them? She always kept her face hidden, as was the way of the Norland women, but it was rumoured that she was beautiful.

'Ensor...' Waite began, realising he hadn't used his comrade's first name in almost a year. Suddenly he was sure he had the words to get through to him. 'Ensor, we have to talk about Trinity. How did that thing in Dorm 31 know...'

But the colonel waved him to silence, his attention on the witch. Finally he nodded and straightened up, rubbing his unruly beard.

'I have to go clean up, Elias. We'll be making planetfall in a couple of hours and the men deserve better than this. I'll see you at the assembly old man.' Cutler stalked away, trailed by the witch and her guardian. Alone in the dark, Elias Waite realised he had lost the words again.

'Word is Norliss went void crazy and chopped 'em up while they was sleeping. Chowed down on 'em too.' Kletus Modine licked his lips suggestively. In the dancing pilot light of his flamer he looked like a leering gargoyle. Not that the hulking, barrel-chested pyrotrooper was a pretty sight in any light. With his brutal potato head and bright red crest of hair, he was an archetypal Badlander and Dustsnake squad was his natural home.

The squad was hunkered down in a corner of the hangar bay, chewing over the fat as soldiers always did before deployment. There were near on eight hundred troops scattered around the cavernous chamber, clustered up in squads around their lanterns, creating pockets of light in the gloom. The emergency strips were running, but their thin red haze was somehow worse than the darkness. Everyone was jumpy after what had happened in Dorm 31 three days back, although nobody knew exactly what *had* happened. Nobody except the officers and they weren't talking. Sure, Verne Loomis had seen it too, but he wasn't doing much talking either these days.

'He ate 'em?' Boone's eyes were wide in his broad bumpkin's face.

'Down to the bone,' Modine affirmed. 'Colonel put a lid on them boys pretty quick too. Took a flamer in there and torched the lot of 'em. Didn't want us greyback grunts seeing what Norliss gone and done.'

'Figures.' Dix nodded sagely, always quick to back his hero. Another Badlander, he was a scrawny doppelganger of Modine, right down to the jutting crest of red hair.

'But that don't add up, brothers.' The voice came from beyond the lantern's pool of radiance, outside the Dustsnake inner circle.

'You say something back there, greencap?' Modine snarled over his shoulder.

'Just been thinking is all.' The speaker ambled into the light, seemingly oblivious to the hostility. He was almost painfully young, but taller than Modine by a head and built like a grox. His straw-blond hair was neatly cropped, his uniform pressed and pristine. The green trim of his flat-topped cap and tunic identified him as a raw recruit, just as the book of liturgies hanging from his belt marked him as a devoted student of the Imperial Gospel.

Audie Joyce was a misfit in this squad of veteran scum. He'd joined them just before they'd left Providence and Modine would have chewed him up and spat him out if the sarge hadn't been looking out for him. There was talk the old goat had had a thing going with Joyce's ma back home, might even be his pa, but not even Boone was stupid enough to ask bullet-head Calhoun about something like that.

Frowning, Joyce continued, 'I mean it weren't just his squad. Norliss killed the commissar too. And *he* sure weren't sleeping.' Gravely the boy made the sign of the aquila. 'No, brothers, the commissar's chainsword was buzzing with the Emperor's own wrath when he walked into that chamber of iniquity. And he didn't go in alone neither.'

'The greencap's got a point, boys,' came another voice from the shadows, even further from the inner circle, mocking and low. 'Ain't no way one crazy man could've taken down the commissar, especially not with old Whitecrow along for the ride.'

It was true and they all knew it. Every one of them had been there when the horror had kicked off. It was the noise that had drawn them – a deep, irregular chiming that had run through the walls and shaken their teeth like a quake from hell. There had been no ignoring it so they'd gone looking and wound up outside Dorm 31 just as Verne Loomis had come crawling out. He'd slammed the hatch shut then folded in on himself like he was all broken up inside. The crazy look on his face had stopped their curiosity dead. Modine had hit the alarm. Nobody had gone for the door.

That was when the lights had died, leaving everyone standing around in the dark fiddling with their rifles as they listened to all the tearing and chewing and screaming going on behind that hatch. Maybe if the sarge had been with them it would have gone down differently, but he'd been up in the mess hall playing cards with the other NCOs. They'd all been kind of glad about that.

The colonel had arrived in double time, almost like he'd known what was going to happen. And maybe he had, because the witch and her watchdog had been with him and she'd probably seen it like she saw everything else. Then Major Waite and Commissar Brody had turned up and the five of them had gone inside, locking the hatch shut behind them. Five of the regiment's finest against one crazy man.

After that there'd been a lot more tearing and swearing, then a hellfire snarling that was more animal than man, but like no animal the Arkan had ever heard. And then the voices had started up and that had been the worst part. They oozed through the steel hatch, sounding like a whole chorus of corpses drowning in an ocean of maggots, laughing and gibbering as they

sang the same words over and over, round and round: '*Trinity in embers…
Trinity remembers…*'

Somewhere along the way they'd heard the commissar shrieking like no
commissar was ever meant to. That had gone on forever and the greybacks
had wondered how there could be so much screaming inside one man, but
finally there'd been silence. After a while the hatch had opened and the
slayers had come marching out. All except Commissar Brody. Every one of
them was splattered with blood and some kind of black slime that reeked
like a corpse pit. The witch had been shaking under her robe and Major
Waite was watching her like a hawk, almost like he was afraid of her. And
then the colonel had grabbed a flamer and gone right back inside. Afterwards he'd sealed the hatch shut and turned Dorm 31 into a tomb for nine
men. Nine men and maybe something more than a man…

'It weren't no crazy greyback the Whitecrow torched,' the voice from the
shadows continued. 'You gotta think bigger, man. Uglier.'

Modine snatched up a lantern and lumbered over to the speaker. The
man was sitting cross-legged with his back against the wall, his eyes on the
gnarled bone flute he was carving in the dark. The same flute he'd been carving every day of their journey through the warp.

'We talking uglier than you, *Mister* Roach?' Modine growled, angry that
his safe little lie was unravelling. Scared of the truth.

Roach kept on carving, unmoved by the tired old insult. His hatchet face
had the bloodless complexion of a Norlander, but his hair was bright red.
'Roach' had been his father's name – a solid Badlands moniker – but his
mother had been a Norlander. It was a long story with a short, sharp end that
had left him an outsider wherever he went. There'd been plenty of hurt and
heartache, but after the war he'd decided he didn't much care either way.

'Ain't you heard?' Roach said. 'There's things in the warp just waiting to
find a way inside a man's head and outside into the world.'

'We don't buy that Hellfire crap in the Badlands,' Modine sneered. 'All
that spook talk's just to keep the Outlanders in their place! Course, a breed
like you…'

'You saying you don't believe in daemons, Brother Modine?' Suddenly
Joyce was standing beside Modine, his earnest face troubled. 'Or you saying
you don't believe in the God-Emperor's Holy Gospel?'

'Now wait, that ain't what I meant…' Modine spluttered, not exactly sure
what he *had* meant. He glanced at his comrades for support, but even Dix
had looked away. Only Boone grinned back at him, too dumb to pick up
on the tension. Modine could feel the intensity of the rookie's gaze, like
he was some jumped up witch hunter angling for a burning. 'Look, I was
just saying…'

'What Trooper Modine was saying is he's so dense the Emperor's light
bends right on round him,' Willis Calhoun barked, marching out of the
shadows.

The sergeant was a short, stocky veteran in his fifties whose bullet head
seemed to shoot straight from his shoulders, hairless and almost pointed
at the tip. Most men in the regiment towered over him, but there was a

pent up ferocity in that compact frame that even the apes in Dustsnake wouldn't cross.

Calhoun strode over to the pyrotrooper and glared up into his face. 'See, Trooper Modine here is a piece of deep-fried grox crap, but he'd still lick the rust off the Emperor's holy throne. Ain't that right, Trooper Modine?'

'Every golden spot, sir!' Modine bellowed, staring into infinity.

'Damn straight!' Calhoun nodded. 'Right, playtime's over you righteous maggots. I've got our drop-ship designation, so haul your sorry arses!'

The sergeant sized up his nine charges as they grabbed their gear. They were rough scum all right – the troublemakers and meatheads who'd sunk to the underbelly of the regiment, picking up charges the way heroes chased after medals, but they were his scum and they could pack a helluva punch in a tussle.

Young Joyce was still frowning as he went past. The sergeant shook his head. The last thing he needed was for the boy to start acting like a green-horn commissar. He'd told Maude the regiment was no place for him, but she'd argued and wailed until he'd sworn to take Audie under his wing. Willis Calhoun wasn't scared of any man, but Emperor's Blood, that woman could nag! If only the boy hadn't turned out so damn *holy*! He'd have to have a word with the young fool before he got himself killed. Teach him some basics. Faith wasn't optional in the Imperium, but some men believed a whole lot harder than others.

'You said you'd talk to him. You assured me he'd come to his senses.' As he spoke, Captain Hardin Vendrake kept his eyes on the Silverstorm Cavalry, alert to the slightest misstep amongst the mechanical steeds. So far his riders were keeping things together, guiding their walkers onto the waiting drop-ship with precise, elegant steps. Even Leonora was doing just fine and she was frankly the worst Sentinel rider Vendrake had ever known. He wouldn't have kept her on if her other talents hadn't been quite so exceptional...

Vendrake suppressed a smile as he addressed his fellow officer again. 'I admit I'm disappointed. Sir,' Vendrake finished pointedly.

'Don't question my judgement, captain,' Elias Waite said irritably. 'After Trinity, Ensor Cutler deserves our faith.'

'Does he?' Vendrake asked. 'Frankly I still don't know why we burned that old town to the ground.'

'Because it needed the burning!' Waite snarled. He knew Vendrake didn't like to talk about Trinity. The town had shaken the man up badly, but he was too proud to admit it. Or maybe it just didn't fit in with his neat little worldview. Seeing the unease on Vendrake's face, Waite calmed himself and tried again: 'By Providence, you were *there*, man! You saw the sickness with your own eyes.'

'Frankly I'm not sure what I saw,' Vendrake said, growing agitated, 'perhaps some kind of mass delusion... We were all half-starved and frozen when we stumbled on that place.' He waved the subject away. 'Besides, Trinity isn't the issue here.'

Waite shook his head in disgust. He despised true patricians like Hardin Vendrake, men bred with an unflappable faith in their own excellence. With his chiselled jaw and aquiline nose the captain had the look of a war poster hero, the kind of man who'd seen thousands of comrades die but never suffered anything worse than a tasteful scar. Vendrake actually had that scar, a tidy little line along his left cheek that had always gone down a storm with the ladies. But despite his rakish façade and wilful blindness, the man was no fool and Waite didn't need him for an enemy.

'Look, I'd trust Ensor Cutler with my soul,' Waite insisted, trying to believe it himself.

'And what about the witch?' Vendrake said, cutting to the chase. He smiled at the major's hesitation. 'Personally I don't give a damn who the old man cavorts with, but this is hurting the reputation of the 19th and I won't stand for that.'

'I'll talk to him after we make planetfall. You've got my word on it,' Waite said coldly and marched away.

'I'm just thinking of the regiment,' Vendrake called after him. He winced as Leonora's Sentinel slipped on the boarding ramp and she struggled to regain her balance, the clawed feet of her machine scrabbling on the metal. It looked like she was going to topple when Van Hal nosed his steed in and nudged her back to stability. Vendrake nodded his approval. A fine pilot and a gentleman was Beauregard Van Hal. A fellow made of the right stuff.

Still, he couldn't entirely blame Leonora for the error. He'd kept his riders on their toes but they'd only had a couple of months to play with the modified machines. Unfortunately there had been no choice about that. The colonel had warned him they would be fighting in swampland, where the Arkan-pattern 'hooves' of the Sentinels would be a liability. The heavy, flat pads were designed to race across the open plains and savannahs of Providence, but on Phaedra the design would mire the machines in no time, which would be fatal if they came under fire. Sentinels were light hunter-killers that relied on speed and agility to stalk their prey. While they might intimidate an infantryman, it didn't take much to penetrate their armour. Cutler had even hinted that Vendrake's force might have to sit this one out, but the captain was damned if he'd let that happen. The Silver-storm Cavalry was a bastion of nobility amongst the 19th and it would have its share of the glory!

Determined, Vendrake had sequestered the ship's forge and holed himself up with the regimental tech-priests to crack the problem. During the voyage they had replaced the Providence-pattern hooves with wide, splayed claws that distributed the weight of the machines more evenly and enabled a limited gripping action. Their research revealed that this was actually the prevalent model on many worlds of the Imperium. While extreme divergence from the sacred construction templates was deemed heretical by the Mechanicus priests, modest alterations were permitted, if not exactly encouraged.

Poring over reports of customisation throughout the Imperium, Vendrake had been drawn to the Drop Sentinels of the Elysian regiments. Fitted with grav-chutes, such machines were capable of diving directly into battle from airborne transports. Fired up by the tactical possibilities, he had resolved to win that capability for Silverstorm. At first the tech-priests had hesitated over such a radical deviation, but he had soon cajoled them into it. Under their soulless augmetics Arkan blood still ran through their veins and they hadn't lost the old thirst for invention. Lacking access to grav-tech they had opted for single-use jump packs and retro stabilisers, granting the Sentinels limited manoeuvrability during a drop.

Once the project had caught their imagination, the cogboys had pursued it with almost human passion. After that it had been a small matter to push them a little further with the modifications to his own steed, *Silver Bullet*. And over the months *a little further* had stretched the abilities of his Sentinel far beyond the norm. Bristling with directional thrusters and gyro-stabilisers, it was capable of swift contortions and great leaps that filled Vendrake with fierce joy whenever he trained in the hangar bay. The fact that some would have deemed his Sentinel a new *kind* of machine altogether – and likely denounced it as an abomination – cut no ice with the captain. He had lost himself wilfully in the challenge of forging the perfect steed. It was the kind of problem that made sense to him, unlike old Waite's obsession with that vile town…

No, he wouldn't think of that. The things he had seen there were impossible and impossible things could not be. He was a gentleman of Providence – a rational man. He wouldn't buy the propaganda the Imperium used to terrorise its ignorant rabble into submission.

Like many Arkan patricians Vendrake was no great believer in the Emperor's Light. After all, He hadn't shed much light on Old Providence. Just two centuries ago, blithely unaware of the approaching Imperium, Vendrake's ancestors had revelled in the new-found glories of steel and steam. It had been a time of unfettered innovation, with the Grand Machinists churning out new wonders every day. The Senate had declared the old gods dead and the Seven Hells mere fables. Men were free to explore a puzzle box universe where everything was possible and nothing was forbidden. Then the warships of the Imperium had arrived and crushed the dream, but the grand families had never forgotten their past.

Maybe that's why we keep on making the same mistakes, Vendrake mused. *Maybe that's why we keep on rebelling. The fools amongst us anyway…*

A klaxon buzzed and he saw the colonel stride into the hangar. Vendrake had to admit the old man had got his act together. His hair was tied back into a neat ponytail and he'd trimmed that scruffy beard. It looked like he'd finally washed too. The captain nodded approvingly, but then he caught sight of the witch trailing Cutler like a second shadow. Her giant watchdog was carrying the regimental banner, unfurled and resplendent. Vendrake's heart soared at the sight of the ram's skull and crossed sabres overlaid on the Seven Stars of the Confederation. It was good to see Old Fury awake again, even if it was in the hands of a savage.

The trio marched wordlessly through the silent ranks of the Arkan and stopped at the centre of the hangar. Suddenly Cutler let out a ferocious howl and leapt onto a crate, his agility belying his years. He held out a fist and the savage threw him the banner. The colonel caught it with a flourish and spun about, brandishing the flag above his troops as they gathered round.

'Seven Stars for Old Fury!' Cutler bellowed.

'Seven Furies for the Stars!' The men bellowed back.

'For Providence and Imperium!' Cutler roared, completing the regimental canticle. Then he led them through the litany again and again, binding them together with those glorious words, defying the horrors they'd come through and the ones still ahead. And despite himself, Hardin Vendrake shouted along with the rest of them, his heart soaring. This was the Ensor Cutler of old, the man whose audacity had won the day at Yethsemane Falls and turned him into a living legend! And then it was done and Cutler became the Whitecrow again. Vendrake could almost see the bitterness seeping back into the man as Trinity exerted its curse.

There is no curse, Vendrake told himself. *Cutler's intellect is weak. That's why the horror is eating him alive, but I won't fall for it.*

'I won't lie to you, Arkan.' Cutler's voice was flat with suppressed rage. 'And I won't dress things up nice and pretty either. You and me, we've come too far for that.' There were murmurs from the crowd, agreement and unease in equal measure.

Damn it all, Vendrake thought, *we're so far from home even the memories are stale. This isn't the time for truth. Give them some hope, man!*

'So I'm just going to tell you what I know,' Cutler continued, 'but frankly that's not a whole lot.' He touched a switch on his belt and a murky sphere flickered into life beside him. 'Gentlemen – and all you Badlander scum too – meet the Lady Phaedra.' The hologram was blocky and riddled with distortion, but the planet's essential ugliness still bled through.

I don't want to breathe Her air, Vendrake realised with sudden conviction. The intensity of the instinct disturbed him. It was entirely irrational.

'Pretty name for a rat's arse of a planet,' Cutler growled. 'She's got swamps, rain and a thousand dirty ways to kill you. Gentlemen, you're going to hate her like the Hells, but I've got something else you're going to hate even more.'

He threw another switch and the planet morphed into a disembodied alien head. Its skull was hairless save for a braided topknot that looked fibrous and fleshy. The face was a flat wedge from brow to chin, bevelled with deeply recessed cheeks that gave it a vaguely cadaverous look. Its mouth was a lipless slit and there was nothing resembling a nose.

'What is it, sir?' asked Templeton, the quietly intense commander of the 4th Company as he peered at the hologram through thick round spectacles.

'That, Captain Templeton, is a tau,' Cutler said. 'Take a long, hard look because it's the reason you've been dragged halfway across the galaxy to this mud-ball. Seems these xenos have themselves a jumped-up little empire of their own and our Lady Phaedra is sat right between Them and Us. She's a worthless harlot, but we can't let her go and neither can the tau.' Cutler chuckled, the sound low and harsh. 'There's a whole subsector's worth of pain just waiting to happen if she falls. I guess the tau see it that way too.'

'These tau boys, what have we got on 'em, colonel?' Major Waite growled.

'I'm told they're big on guns and tech, but not so fond of getting up-close-and-personal.' Seeing that Waite expected more, Cutler shook his head ruefully. 'That's all I've got, Elias.'

'What about numbers? Mechanised divisions or air support?' Under his bushy eyebrows Waite was frowning ferociously.

'I can give you rebels – a whole planet full of them. They call themselves the *Saathlaa*. As far as I can tell, Phaedra was a pre-Imperial colony much like home, but unlike us the Saathlaa were dead in the water by the time the Imperium came along. Whatever civilisation they ever had was long gone.'

'Savages,' Captain Machen sneered. The 3rd Company commander was notorious for his loathing of the Outland tribes back home. 'We cross half the hellfired galaxy and we still can't escape their stench!'

'Degenerates,' Cutler corrected, 'but that didn't stop them turning on the Imperium when the xenos came along. I'd guess these tau boys are sneakier than the greenskin vermin we're used to back home.'

'What's the game plan, colonel?' Waite again.

'Seems we'll be touching down on what's called a Poseidon-class battle-ship.' Cutler snorted. 'Which is a fancy way of saying a damn big boat. We're talking the old kind here – the kind that sails on water, not across the stars. From there we'll be joining up with a push on a chain of islands that go by the name of Dolorosa. Some kind of rebel stronghold...'

'How long, colonel?' Vendrake interjected. 'Exactly how long has this war been going on?'

'Sharp as ever, Captain Vendrake.' Cutler rubbed the bridge of his nose wearily. 'Like I said, I won't lie to you. Gentlemen, the Imperium and the Tau Empire have been fighting over Phaedra for near on fifty years.'

There was a long silence as the men thought it through. Then a murmur began, rising to a hubbub of disorder as the reality sank in. The explosive crack of a bolt pistol put a stop to it.

'Much obliged, Elias.' Cutler nodded appreciatively to Waite as the veteran holstered his sidearm. Vendrake could see the colonel gathering strength, dredging up every drop of his faded myth. Uncannily he seemed to be looking every man in the eye, talking to each soldier as if he were an old, personal comrade. 'Arkan, I expect better from you...'

Abruptly a klaxon began to wail. The main lights flickered on and Cutler glimpsed the hangar chief signalling to him. It was time to go, but he wasn't finished yet.

'In fact I expect the best!' Cutler shouted over the noise. 'It's what you've always given me and it's what you're going to give me now. Do that and I'll get you through this mess! Now move out and make Providence proud, Arkan!'

He knew they had no cheers left in them and he didn't much blame them, but at least they'd get on the drop-ships. Right now he couldn't ask for more.

CHAPTER TWO

The Sisyphus, Argonaut-class battle cruiser

A recon patrol found me wandering along the shallows of the Qalaqexi River, almost a hundred kilometres from the Verzante outpost on Dolorosa Topaz. The captain here tells me I was half-starved and delirious, raving about holy ghosts and unholy traitors. He also tells me I was carrying the maggot-riddled ruin of my own right arm, decayed beyond any hope of repair. Of course I had no such delusions, but I do not tell him this. I carried my arm out of the Mire because I refused to leave any part of myself to Her, but I do not tell him that either. Just as I do not tell him that I still see my ghosts, though I am no longer half-starved nor delirious. And I certainly do not tell him how holy they are. He would not understand these things. Such truths are only for you and me.

Instead I tell him about the traitors who are nothing but dead men running. I tell him about the fall of the Verzante Konquistadores and the encroachment of the blueskins into Dolorosa Topaz. I tell him that I have been following Commander Wintertide's trail and must not falter now. I tell him that I am a commissar and he must offer me his every assistance.

Instead he contacts Lomax, who is the High Commissar of the Dolorosa Campaign and my direct superior. And of course Lomax recalls me to Antigone base. The captain tells me she has concerns.

– Iverson's Journal

Abel... whispered the hollow voice.

'Abel...' she echoed, the name slithering from the immaterium onto her lips.

'Skjoldis?' It was the Whitecrow, urgent and angry, calling her back from the Whispersea. He was the only one amongst the blind folk who knew her true name. 'Skjoldis, snap out of it, woman!'

Abel seeks...

'...seeks the Counterweight,' she finished.

Her eyes flicked open and she saw the Whitecrow leaning over her, frowning ferociously. Over his shoulder she could see her *weraldur*, watching her with that special sharpness that always turned her blood to ice. The Mercy was still slung across his back, but his right hand was on the haft, poised to wrench the axe free in a heartbeat.

Is it my time? Am I poisoned?

Dispassionately she turned her gaze inwards and explored the secret hunting grounds of her soul, sifting through seething rift valleys of frustration and turning over spiny stones of despair, questing for the spoor of corruption. She had sensed no poison in the speaker called Abel, but the serpents could be so very sly–

'Raven!' The insult snapped her back into *annatta*, the shadow maze the blind ones called reality. In the maze she appeared to be lying on a cold marble surface under starlight that was even colder.

'Be still, Whitecrow.' Her voice was raw with the strain of the wyrd. 'There is no poison in me.' The tension in him subsided, but his stormy grey eyes continued to search her face.

My face? Open to the stars!

Her veil was gone, leaving her face vulnerable to the soul serpents waiting between the stars. Once they knew her face they could shape themselves into a mirror of her soul and seep inside. Her instincts screamed out against the violation and she reached for her hood, but the Whitecrow caught her wrist.

'Who in the Seven Hells is Abel?' he demanded.

It was the first time Cutler had seen her face in anything but the dim glow of an oil lamp. In the starlight he was struck anew by the mysterious confluence of her features. She certainly wasn't beautiful in any conventional sense. Her skin was like faded parchment stretched tight over a skull that was too narrow, accentuating her sharp cheekbones and lending her a carved, half-starved fragility. A gossamer tracery of tattoos wound from her temples to encircle her vivid green eyes before tapering into the bloodless bow of her lips.

Noticing Cutler's fascination she snapped her wrist free and pulled up the cowl, hiding her face in shadow... from shadows. Her eyes glared accusingly at him. 'You gave me your oath you would not touch the veil, Whitecrow.' The bitterness in her voice made him blanch.

'And I kept it,' he said. 'You took the thing off yourself, woman.'

Her eyes widened and she glanced at her *weraldur*. The giant nodded, a hint of hurt creeping into his flat eyes. She knew it was true; while there was life in him he would not allow anyone to violate the veil. Not even the Whitecrow.

What happened to me? Skjoldis wondered as she recognised the gloomy vault of the viewing gallery. She rose and the marble-clad window onto the void drew her gaze like a beacon. *Is it really a window... or a mirror?*

'What's going on, Skjoldis?' Cutler's voice had softened, but she didn't need to touch his mind to read the doubt in him. It stung like a betrayal.

'I am not *tainted*,' she said. It was the Imperium's word for the soul poisoning. 'Is that not enough for you, Whitecrow?'

'No, that's not enough.' He sounded tired as he scooped up her discarded veil and joined her. 'Even from you Skjoldis, that's not nearly enough.'

'Don't you mean, *especially* from me,' she said bitterly as she took the veil. If the soul serpents were watching it was already too late, but the garment was part of her identity. A truer friend than her own face could ever be.

Because my face is an open wound to my soul...

Cutler regarded the witch in silence as she covered her face. The wyrd had come over her in the hangar bay just after the second drop-ship had flown. He'd been chatting with Elias Waite when Skjoldis had started moaning. Feeling a sudden charge in the air he'd glanced round and seen her walking away with her watchdog at her heels. That had set Elias off, but Cutler hadn't let him make a fuss. He still felt guilty about the hurt on the old man's face when he'd ordered him to shut up and ship out.

I'll make it up to you, old friend, Cutler swore. We'll talk soon and I'll tell you whatever it is you need to know.

He'd left Waite and followed Skjoldis to the viewing gallery, a place that had always fascinated and repelled her. There she'd stood staring into space with her hands touching the glass, whispering nonsense and ignoring his entreaties. He'd sensed the wyrd gathering strength around her, creeping through the chamber like static electric frost and turning the air to ice. And suddenly she'd cast away her precious veil and pressed her face up against the glass, almost as if she'd been trying to push herself through into the void.

Can she hear the daemon bell? Cutler had wondered bleakly.

His hand had drifted to his sabre, compelled by a gut-deep dread of psychic corruption. The *weraldur* had mirrored the action, preparing to fulfil his most sacred duty. Had she fallen? Would she turn and leer at them with a grin that tore her face in two? Would she look like the thing Norliss had become in Dorm 31? Or would she be like the broken ghouls they'd slaughtered back home in that doomed town? *Would she be worse?*

But then the wyrd had receded and Skjoldis had fallen to the floor like a meat puppet whose strings had been cut. Drawing closer, Cutler had heard those last enigmatic words about 'Abel' and a 'counterweight'. Every instinct told him not to let the mystery go, but it would have to wait.

'We have to go, Skjoldis,' Cutler said, but she wasn't listening. Her eyes had slipped past the yellow crescent of the planet and fixed on the ancient corpse ship. And suddenly she remembered it all.

None of them noticed Hardin Vendrake watching from the shadows.

It was the stench that hit Roach first, a heady brew of the sea and the grave, like rotten fish vomited up by a corpse. A heartbeat later the heat came crowding in, thick and liquid, clinging to him like an oily second skin. He thought he'd beaten heat long ago, but this wasn't like the slow burn of the Badlands. The drop-ship hatch had only just opened and he was already drenched in sweat.

I'm never going to be clean again, he realised.

'Quit dreaming and shift your arse outta my way, breed!' Modine snarled over his shoulder. Roach glanced back at the men clustered in the drop-ship behind him. Their faces looked as grey as their fatigues. They could all smell the sickness waiting out there. All except Modine, who couldn't smell anything through the promethium tar clogging his nostrils. The ape didn't know how lucky he was.

'What you got, Snake Eyes?' Toomy asked, speaking for the whole squad. Roach might be a half-breed, but he was also their scout and they trusted his instincts. Probably because he *was* a half-breed...

They want something dark and wise from me, a touch of the Norland wyrd to ground their fears. And so I'm Snake Eyes now, the squad's totem against the unknown, but later on, when they're all sat around the fire together, I'll just be the breed again. At least Modine always says it like it is. Well to the Hells with 'em all!

Without a word Roach turned back to the hatch. The exit ramp had lowered then stuck midway, but it was only a couple of metres to the ground so he swung himself over the lip and jumped. He landed with catlike grace on the deck below, but almost slipped on the slime coating the corroded plates.

In this heat maybe even metal has to sweat, he thought with disgust.

He heard Modine swearing above him and smiled coldly. Getting off was going to be a bitch for the pyrotrooper with that bulky flamer strapped to his back. Still, Roach was the squad's eyes and he didn't want any of them breaking their necks on his watch, not even Modine, so he called back a warning as he scanned the terrain.

True to the colonel's words, the drop-ship had touched down on the deck of a ship, but Cutler's 'damn big boat' didn't come close to the reality. Roach had served on his share of steamboats back home, but this monster was nothing like those brave old vessels. It defied belief that anything so vast could even float. He guessed the landing strip alone was some thousand metres long and maybe five hundred across, the space sliced into a grid of landing pads and fuelling stations, all connected by a web of pipes and cables. Ugly barnacles of machinery clung to the deck and a crane sprouted from the starboard side like a gallows for giants. He squinted at its outstretched arm. By the Seven Hells, there *were* bodies hanging up there! Not giants, just ordinary men – dozens of them. It was hard to be sure at this distance, but it looked like they'd been skinned.

Uneasily Roach tore his eyes away from the crane and took in the rest of the ship. Sternwards the deck erupted into a sprawl of metal blocks and conning towers that loomed over the strip like a cast-iron fortress. The keep had been daubed with a crude rendition of the Imperial aquila, the double-headed eagle snarling savagely. The bow was dominated by the ship's main gun, a mounted cannon that looked big enough to punch a hole in a starship. The monster was bolted to the deck by rivets the size of a man and tended by a whole squad of scarlet-uniformed troops. Psalms from the Imperial canticles ran the length of the barrel, the white paint livid against the black metal. Along the port and starboard sides smaller emplacements jutted from the battlements, manned by more men in scarlet. The troops were too far away for Roach to get a good look at them, but he sensed they were ignoring the newcomers.

The clarion call of a bugle drew his attention to another drop-ship further along the deck. He guessed it had touched down a few minutes earlier because its passengers were already disembarked and standing to attention. They were Captain Templeton's 4th Company and he could see the man himself strutting back and forth like he was on the parade ground. The captain's dress uniform was sagging in the wet heat, making him look like a drowned peacock, but Roach had to give him credit for trying. Templeton wasn't nearly as stupid as he looked and he wasn't a total bastard like 'Ironbones' Machen, Roach's own company commander.

The Dustsnakes had once been part of the 10th Company, but that was back in the days before Yethsemane Falls, when the regiment still had almost two thousand men to its name. After that carnage the Dustsnakes were the *only* part of the 10th Company. It had been a similar story throughout the regiment and Cutler had been forced to reshuffle the survivors into four functional units, each numbering around two hundred men. Unfortunately the Dustsnakes had wound up at the arse end of the reformed 3rd, under Jon Milton Machen, a man who believed Norlanders and Badlanders were just two strains of the same plague. It was yet another piece in the cosmic puzzle that proved life, the immaterium and the Emperor all had it in for Mister Claiborne Roach.

'Fire from the sky!' Modine roared and slammed down beside him with a meaty thud. He had all the grace of a dead grox, but to Roach's surprise the pyrotrooper didn't stumble.

'Almost squashed you under my boots like a 'roach, Roach!' Modine said with a sneer that was oddly half-hearted.

'Make some space down there you brain-dead sons o' bitches!' Sergeant Calhoun bellowed from above. As the two greybacks obeyed, more hatches clanged open along the ship and the rest of 3rd Company began to disembark. Sourly Roach noted that *their* exit ramps hadn't jammed.

He saw Captain Machen stomping onto the deck at the head of his command squad. In his Thundersuit the man looked like a vast iron crab that had reared up to walk on its hind legs. Under its elegantly moulded carapace the suit was an industrial masterwork of spinning cogs and pistons that clattered and hissed in perfect harmony, almost drowning out the stirring chords of 'Providence Endures' booming from its brass shoulder speakers. A heavy stubber was fixed to one ironclad paw, the ammo belt coiling into a fluted dispenser on the back, while the other ended in a massive drill inscribed with the 'Testament of the Founding Fathers'. The captain's crew-cut head was visible through the thick glass porthole of his baroque helmet. He was still wearing his wide-brimmed officer's hat and there was a fat cigarillo rammed between his jaws, but even he wasn't quite crazy enough to light it in there.

Roach wasn't impressed by the spectacle. The antique fighting suit was a legacy of Old Providence, a cherished heirloom passed down generations of the captain's blueblood family. Sure, there was no denying its toughness – after all, the thing was closer to a tank than a suit of regular power armour – but it was unpredictable and hideously difficult to maintain – not to mention noisy as all the Hells! To the scout's way of thinking such relics were more effective as status symbols than practical tools of war.

Which probably suits that son-of-a-bitch Machen just fine...

Jon Milton Machen was the spiritual father of the Steamblood Zouaves, a cross-company brotherhood of mechanised nobles who revered the Emperor in His aspect as the Machine God. There were eighteen of them in the regiment, all patricians with the wealth to maintain a fighting suit. They saw themselves as questing knights, free to align themselves with whichever unit had the most need. Each Zouave possessed a unique, customised suit, but they were mostly variants of the smaller Stormsuit template and none of them possessed anything like Machen's monstrosity. Modine had once joked that the captain was compensating for inadequacies elsewhere. It was the only time Roach had laughed along with the pyrotrooper.

He glanced across at Modine, surprised the big man was sticking alongside him. In the green light the Badlander's face looked bestial, but his eyes were filled with wonder as they took in this ugly new world.

'You still with us, Snakeburn?' Roach asked.

'The sky's full of blood,' Modine muttered. Roach saw he was right: there was nothing like a natural cloud in the blotchy canopy, but it was woven with threads that looked just like the thin blue vessels in a man's arm. Or like that stinking cheese the aristos liked so much – the kind that was all wormy with fungus. As he looked at them, those threads seemed to twitch and it began to rain – a sticky, slow motion drizzle that clung like glue.

It's more dribble than drizzle, Roach thought. *Like the sky is drooling over us.*

'It ain't natural.' Modine seemed mesmerised by the rainfall.

'Different world, different rules,' Roach said, unsure of the Badlander's mood. 'We just got to learn how it works, man.'

Modine looked at him, frowning. Then he spat in disgust and found safe ground. 'Yeah, like you'd know shit about it, breed.'

'Aw no, don't you be doing that!' Dix yelped behind them. They turned just in time to see young Audie Joyce standing in the hatch, heaving up his guts over the scrawny Badlander below.

'You greencap rookie piece of crap! You total frakwit!' Dix shrieked as he fumbled for his lasrifle. Modine stalked back and swung him round.

'Easy, Jakob,' the pyrotrooper said. 'Boy didn't mean nothing by it.'

'The greencap trash gone and puked over me, Klete!' Dix yelled. With the vomit dripping down his long nose, his scraggy face would have been funny if wasn't burning with hate. 'I'm gonna...'

'You want Calhoun to put you down like a crazy rhinehorn bull?'

'But he *puked* on me Klete,' Dix whined, sounding petulant now. When all was said and done, Jakob Dix had always been yellow.

Roach had lost interest in the argument, his attention diverted by the strange party emerging from the battleship's metal fortress. Three of them were dressed in the distinctive storm coats of commissars while two others wore the red robes of tech-priests. They were flanked by a contingent of troops armoured in glossy crimson plate and tall, conical helmets. He didn't recognise the bulky guns the soldiers were carrying, but each was linked to a shoulder-slung power core and he guessed they'd pack more punch than a regular lasrifle. Trailing along behind the rest was a whole procession of Ecclesiarchy types. He counted six zealots with wild hair and jutting beards. All wore filthy rags and vests of chainmail that must have been hell in the heat. Several dozen flagellants loped along beside them, their scarred bodies almost naked below their peaked hoods. The whole troop was chanting and wailing something high and mighty from the Imperial Gospel. To Roach they looked even crazier than the puritans back home.

That's one heck of a welcoming party, he thought uneasily.

A glint from one of the conning towers caught his eye. There was someone up there. The figure was silhouetted against the sky and Roach couldn't make out any details, but he was sure it was watching them – any scout worth his salt would recognise the flash of magnocular glasses in an instant. He was reaching for his hunting scope when the company bugler blared the assembly and Calhoun yelled at him to get into formation. It was only as he rushed to obey that he realised why the watcher had unsettled him so much: something about its shape had been *wrong...*

'Have you prayed for me, Gurdjief?' The voice fluttered fitfully, little more than a dry rattle. The speaker lowered his magnoculars as the sharp-eyed newblood on the deck below hurried back to his squad. There were so many of them this time. Surely some would serve.

'I always pray for you, my lord.' The confessor's rich baritone was a stark contrast to the watcher's brittle rasp, but then everything about Yosiv Gurdjief was a world away from the blighted creature he revered. Despite his shabby robes the priest looked like a heroic statue given life, a sculpture of coiled steel turned to muscle through the alchemy of faith. His black hair fell below his waist and obscured his face behind a filthy curtain, yet for all his wildness his features had the arrogant cast of a noble. Taller than most men, Gurdjief towered over his stunted master.

'Then why is there no end to this pain?' the ruined man asked.

'Pain is a blessing. Through suffering we share in His eternal sacrifice and draw closer to the light of His wrath.'

A withered claw shot out and clasped Gurdjief's wrist.

'Then why do you not share this blessing, priest?' the wreck snarled.

Gurdjief could feel the spiny nodules in the man's palm digging into his skin, but he was unmoved. This was an old ritual between them and they both knew he was immune to the fungal leprosy. Most men were. Phaedra was a world of a thousand blights, yet Her foulest pestilence was also Her most selective, capable of infecting less than one in a thousand. In Gurdjief's eyes Admiral Vyodor Karjalan had been exalted.

'I am unworthy, Vyodor,' Gurdjief breathed, twisting his wrist to grasp that ruined claw, just as he twisted his words to grasp the admiral's name and seal their friendship. 'But you have served Him for almost two centuries across countless worlds. You have earned this benediction.'

'And what of Bihari and Javorkai and all the other peasants who were *blessed* with this filth?' The admiral sneered, recalling the dozen mariners who had shared his curse. 'What of Natalja? She was just a girl. How did *she* earn your precious gift, priest?'

'Do not question Him, Vyodor.' Gurdjief's mournful eyes were suddenly bright with wrath and compassion. 'We cannot know what secret hero-isms our brothers and sisters performed in His name. Their glory is lost...'

'Their lives are lost!' The screech tore a cloud of spores from the admi-ral's desiccated throat, triggering a spasm that sent him reeling against the balcony. Gurdjief breathed deeply of the blight as he watched his master's rapture. The man's misery was truly inspiring. Under his misshapen great-coat every inch of Vyodor's flesh was covered in fungal swellings. Some had ripened to calloused spines that threatened to tear through the fabric, while others clustered in bloated, pulsating reefs. The infestation had rooted itself deep in the man's bones, contorting his skeleton into a new shape. Without the regular blood transfusions devised by the ship's tech-priests his joints would calcify and render him immobile. Gradually the transformation would accelerate, the fungus reshaping its host's flesh while nurturing and preserving the brain with hideous intimacy. Gurdjief knew this to be true for he had catalogued the process in other hosts. Indeed he had witnessed the final, magnificent torment...

'Natalja... is dead,' the admiral wheezed, drained by his rage. The priest grasped his hands, willing him the strength to rejoice in his suffering.

'She died a saint in the Emperor's eyes,' Gurdjief insisted, glossing over the lie. He had not granted Vyodor's daughter the Emperor's Mercy as he'd promised, but he had not allowed her the transfusions either. Despite her screams and curses he had forced the girl to face her destiny, even con-secrating a chapel to her in the bowels of the ship. They had been secret lovers once and he had felt an obligation to enlighten her. Over the years she had bloated and blossomed to fill the chamber like a sacred cancer until she *was* the chapel. Whenever Gurdjief felt doubt rising in him, whispering that his faith might have taken a dark twist, he would descend to Natalja's sanctum and steady himself with the purity of her torment. Her eyes were still so very beautiful...

'Then perhaps I should die too,' the admiral taunted. 'Perhaps I should make a clean end of it.' He stared down at the vertiginous drop from the tower. 'I could do it now.' But they both knew it was a lie. Admiral Vyodor Karjalan had lived too long to embrace death, no matter how hideous life had become.

There was a rumble overhead and they looked up as a third drop-ship swooped over the tower and descended towards the landing strip.

'What if none of them have the right blood, Yosiv?' Karjalan asked. Only those who were susceptible to the blight were viable for the transfusions and the admiral's supply was running perilously low.

'It will be as the Emperor wills it, Vyodor,' the confessor said. 'But now I must join my brethren for the consecration of the newbloods.'

'Indeed, priest.' The admiral's twisted form seemed to straighten at the call of duty. 'I have received word from General Oleaus at Dolorosa Breach. The 81st Encinerada have been routed and the Iwujii Jungle Sharks are pinned down a league into the Mire. The push is faltering.'

The confessor nodded, unsurprised. The push was *always* faltering. The Imperial drive to subjugate the Dolorosa continent was the oldest, most bitter campaign on Phaedra and the cost in lives was immeasurable. The region was a vast tangle of islands riddled with waterways and infested by some of the worst jungles on the planet. It was also the heartland of countless Saathlaa guerrillas and their xenos puppet masters. It was even rumoured that Wintertide, the tau commander, lurked somewhere at the heart of the continent.

'Oleaus needs more men in the Mire. We cannot lose momentum now.' Karjalan's eyes were bright points of passion in the dark morass of his face.

Sometimes Gurdjief pitied his friend's petty dreams of victory, but perhaps they were a mercy. If they gave Vyodor the strength to endure then so be it. For the confessor there were no mercies left. He had ventured too deep into the Mire and seen too much to deny the truth of things. By any sane reckoning the archipelago was the worst kind of no-man's-land imaginable, but Gurdjief had abandoned sanity long ago and seen the horror behind the horror. Unlike his master he understood that the Emperor had not cast them into this hell to find victory.

The Lethean Mariners had come to Phaedra fresh from the glorious Purgation of Sylphsea, where Vyodor Karjalan had prosecuted a masterful campaign against the Aoi brood armada. It had been a magnificent triumph marred only by the loss of the Imperial Governor's son, a young hothead who had sailed his cruiser into the jaws of a brood submaniple. There had been no saving him so Karjalan had fired the main gun on the lot of them, making the boy's death count for something. Unfortunately the Governor hadn't seen it that way and their next posting had been this dead-end war. Despite the insult, Karjalan had been confident of breaking the Dolorosa stalemate and winning absolution. Back then he was still an unbreakable commander of men who had never known defeat. Back then Gurdjief was still a naïve young soldier with no thoughts of entering the priesthood.

Back then was more than a decade ago.

'I want these Arkan dandies on the transport boats within the hour, priest,' Karjalan said. 'They have the look of toy soldiers, but perhaps there is fire in their hearts.'

'As you say, my lord.' Gurdjief bowed and turned away.

'But save me the true bloods,' Karjalan whispered, watching the troops on the deck with bleak, hungry eyes.

The drop-ship shuddered as it dipped into the viscous soup of the planet's atmosphere. Strapped into flight couches along the cramped tunnel of the cabin, the Arkan avoided each other's eyes. Most of them were Burning Eagles, the elite 1st Company of the regiment. Unlike the regular Confederates they wore navy blue jumpsuits padded with dark leather. The standard flat-topped foraging caps were replaced with fluted bronze helmets, their visors sculpted into the visage of a ferocious raptor. The imagery was more than a conceit: the Eagles were paratroopers, trained to fight as they rappelled or dived from the sky, but they weren't riding an Arkan steam dirigible now and their disquiet hung in the air like a psychic smog. Captain Vendrake wondered if the witch could taste it more keenly than the rest of them.

He was watching her out of the corner of his eye. She was sitting further along the cabin, squeezed between her watchdog and the colonel, unreadable in the swathes of her midnight blue robe. Behind her veil she might be grinning at their naiveté. Or changing…

Just like the damned of Trinity.

Angrily he thrust the thought aside. He hadn't been able to shake the memory of that confounded town since his argument with Waite. If he didn't get a grip he'd end up as mad as the Whitecrow. He had to put the past and its daemons – real or otherwise – behind him and focus on the clear and present danger amongst them. The witch was the issue here! The sight of her face in the viewing gallery had unnerved him. He'd seen no beauty or grace there, only a bitter weariness that wasn't quite human. Perhaps she had a place in the regiment as a weapon, but if so she was the kind of weapon that could backfire on its wielder like an overloaded plasma gun. Certainly she had no place as the consort to the regimental commander. He stared at the colonel sitting so arrogantly beside his pet hag. How could such a soldier fall so far?

'We're all behind you, Hardin,' Lieutenant Quint whispered into his ear. 'Just say the word and we'll back you to the blasted hilt.'

'Back me how exactly?' Vendrake asked, turning to the man sitting beside him. Quint's earnest expression sagged with hurt. Silverstorm's second officer had once been considered quite dashing, but he'd let himself run to fat.

'Oh come now, Hardin,' Quint wheedled. 'We've all seen you scheming away with old Waite.'

Vendrake shook his head sourly. Pericles Quint was a vaguely competent rider, but he was also a total idiot. Like most of Silverstorm he was a patrician, but his lineage was on a different order of magnitude. Hailing from one of the Founding Families, he was the wealthiest man in the regiment, with a dozen titles to either side of his name. The only mystery about him was why he hadn't jumped ship back on Providence.

'Scheming is a vulgar sort of word, lieutenant,' Vendrake said. 'Not the sort of word a gentleman of Providence would care to associate himself with.'

Quint began to bluster, but Vendrake had already turned back to Cutler. He knew that Silverstorm would back him if he moved against the colonel, but the key players would be the company commanders. If they stood with him the whole regiment would fall into step. The Norland-hater Machen was already champing at the bit about the witch so he'd play along for sure, but Templeton was a strange bird and Waite was still fiercely loyal to his old friend.

Unexpectedly Cutler looked up and met Vendrake's gaze, his expression stony. The captain's mouth went dry. Had the witch sensed him spying in the viewing gallery? Had she plucked the treason from his mind and informed on him? How could he defend against something so insidious?

Suddenly the colonel's attention snapped to his vox-operator. The elderly greyback was sat opposite Cutler, too far away for Vendrake to hear over the rumble of the engines, but he saw the man fiddling with his vox-set, growing frantic as Cutler harangued him. Others in the cabin began to notice the commotion.

What in the Seven Hells is going on? Vendrake wondered.

Then Cutler howled. It was a sustained bellow of rage that made Vendrake's hackles rise. No sane man would make a sound like that...

The colonel's face was twisted with wrath and his muscles bulged against his harness, fighting straps he could have simply unbuckled. With a final effort he broke free and surged to his feet. Convinced his commander had finally snapped, Vendrake reached for his sidearm.

He's like a man possessed!

Then Cutler reeled to an abrupt standstill and swung round to stare at the witch. Long moments passed, then Vendrake saw his face twitch as the mania drained out of him, leaving a residue of cold fury.

She's leashed him in like a mad dog. Vendrake was repelled by the insight.

The colonel breathed deeply and seemed to grow taller as he glared around the cabin. 'Confederates, I've just received word from the ground.' Cutler paused, playing his old trick, addressing them all, yet seeming to speak to every man individually. 'Major Waite is dead and we have all been played for fools.'

With that the colonel drew his pistol and stalked towards the cockpit.

The boat crested an angry wave, tilting almost vertically as it crashed back down into the churning ocean. Sour spray cascaded over the gunwales and splashed the men huddled on the metal benches within. The water looked like curdled milk, yellow and blotchy with a glutinous algal scum that reeked of sewage. The stench had been bad enough up on the battleship, but down in the seething cesspit sea it was almost unbearable.

Another wave wrenched the boat and Toomy lolled senselessly against Roach's shoulder. The man's head looked like one enormous bruise above his vomit-encrusted beard. Absently the scout pushed the unconscious sniper aside and continued carving his bone flute, seemingly oblivious to the angry sea. Sat across from him, Dix gagged and threw up again, not even bothering to target the greencap this time. Wedged beside him, gripping the safety rail so hard it hurt, Audie Joyce felt his own guts heaving in sympathy, but he was all out of puke. Most of the men in the boat were. Over the last hour almost everyone had added to the rancid soup swimming around the bottom of the boat, even Sergeant Calhoun.

It had scared the Hells out of Joyce seeing Uncle Sergeant Calhoun retching like that. He'd always thought the old man was a rock – immovable and invulnerable, but he'd been the first to pay his dues to the sea. Only the half-breed had managed to hold it all in, but Joyce figured that must be down to his Norland blood. The savages were tainted so maybe they liked keeping the puke inside them. That made sense, didn't it? He clung onto the thought because nothing else made much sense anymore...

Major Waite was dead. Joyce had seen it happen and he still didn't believe it. The Confederates had been lined up for inspection when the major's drop-ship had touched down with the 2nd Company. Everyone had watched proudly as the Old Man had marched over to meet the welcoming party from the battleship. But then there'd been a lot of arguing and another holy man had come down from the iron castle and joined in. Joyce could tell the newcomer was *really* important because he was taller than anybody he'd ever seen in his life. At first the boy had wondered if the man might even be a Space Marine, but he wasn't wearing the sacred armour he'd seen in all the paintings so Joyce had decided he was probably a saint instead. Later he'd heard the sailors call the man Confessor Gurdy-Jeff, which sounded like a pretty holy name to him.

As a child Joyce had once seen Deacon Jericho give a sermon and thought him the holiest man alive, but Confessor Gurdy-Jeff made Providence's senior witch hunter look like a common street preacher. Despite the stink of this heathen world Joyce had felt his heart soar at the thought of fighting alongside a hero like that, but for some reason Major Waite had kept arguing with the saint, shaking his head and waving angrily, like he'd been told to jump into a fire or something. Joyce hadn't understood him at all – if Confessor Gurdy-Jeff had asked *him* to jump into a fire he'd have leapt without a second thought, content in the knowledge that he was doing the God-Emperor's work.

Worried that Major Waite would make the Arkan look like heretics to these holy folk, Joyce had grown angry. The saint must have been angry too, because suddenly he'd quit talking and jabbed a hand into the major's face, the fingers straight and pointed as knives. Some of the others weren't sure what had happened, but Joyce had seen the major's eyes pop. The Old Man had fallen to his knees with blood running through his hands. He'd squealed like a stuck hog until the saint had brought that holy fist chopping down onto his neck so hard that Joyce swore he'd heard the snap. Sergeant Hickox, who'd been with the major forever, had tried to pull a gun then, but the three commissars from the battleship had been faster and he'd gone down in a storm of las-bolts. Then Lieutenant Pettifer had tried to step in and they'd just shot him too. They hadn't stopped shooting until all three bodies were sizzling and smoking like boomerfish on a griddle.

After that everybody had gone real quiet, just standing there like the sky was raining frogs, the way that Deacon Jericho always said it would if folk didn't do right by the God-Emperor. Then some of the others had gone for their guns, but Captain Machen had shouted them down and across the deck Captain Templeton had done the same. That was when Joyce had noticed how the gun turrets on both sides of the deck had spun right round to cover the Confederates. If it had come to a scrap those big guns would have minced them up in no time.

Joyce wasn't too sure about what had happened next, but Captain Templeton had gone over to the saint and started gabbing away, all nice and peaceable like. Joyce hadn't caught any words but he figured they must have straightened things out because suddenly the priests in chainmail had been everywhere, rushing around and blessing the Arkan with some mighty fine words. Their cog priests had followed, sticking needles into folk, taking blood and checking it in a machine that one had growing right out of his gut.

Cog priests had always made Joyce queasy. With their strange machine bits and messed up metal faces no two were ever the same, but all were as ugly as sin, even the pair who served the regiment. The Arkan called their cog priests 'professors' because that's what their kind had been called before the Imperium came to Providence, but the name didn't make them any better. Professor Mordecai's face looked like a steam engine had tunnelled through it and got stuck halfway, but Professor Chaney was even worse. Under his hood there was nothing but a windmill of mirrors that reflected a man's face right back at him in a thousand different shapes and sizes, all spinning and whirling like a silver twister. They both made Joyce's skin crawl, but since they were *priests* he guessed they must be all right. He still hadn't got that part of the Imperial Gospel figured out...

'Why do we call them priests?' Joyce wondered out loud. 'The professors I mean, how come they're priests too?'

Everyone in the stinking, heaving boat looked at him like he was snakebite crazy. He remembered that his brothers didn't worry about the Gospel as much as he did, which was kind of sad and probably bad too.

'Only thing I want to know about those coghogs is why they took Klete,' Dix said, wiping the puke from his lips. There was a dazed look in his eyes that had nothing to do with his messed up guts. Joyce guessed he must be missing his friend and knew he'd feel the same way if the cog priests had taken Uncle Sergeant Calhoun instead of Brother Modine. Something bad had shown up in Modine's blood and the priests had said he'd need 'noculating' against the sickness in the jungle. They'd promised to give him back but none of the others had really believed it and Brother Modine had looked real scared. For a while Joyce had thought he might even put up a fight, but in the end he'd just chucked down his flamer, told them to find her a good home and gone quietly. The cog priests had marched him off, along with a couple of boys from the 2nd Company.

'Why'd they have to go and pick Klete?' Dix moaned again.

'Maybe those sailor boys were running short of fresh meat,' Roach taunted. 'Plenty of meat on good old Klete...'

'Shut your trap, breed,' Dix snarled. The snarl turned into another gut heaving retch as the boat bucked violently. Toomy lolled against Roach again and blood oozed from his broken mouth as he groaned wetly.

'I'm just saying...' Roach shoved Toomy away. 'If you wanted meat for your larder you could do a lot worse than Kletus Modine.'

'Knock it off, both you maggots!' Calhoun snapped, but there was no fire in it. Joyce had never seen the sergeant looking so tired, but then he'd never seen the sergeant looking tired at all. Hunched down on the metal bench with Modine's flamer cradled in his lap like a lost dog, Willis Calhoun looked *old*.

Although he was only a greencap and this was his first time in the fire, Joyce was pretty sure wars didn't usually go like this. He wasn't sure about much else though – like why they were on this boat and where it was taking them. Things had happened so fast after the cog priests had done their tests. The sailors in red had herded them onto the boats hanging alongside the battleship like big metal boxes, corralling them fifty to a boat like cattle in a stockade. One wall of each box had been tilted down into a gangway, waiting for them to get on board, then snapping shut like a trap afterwards.

There'd been a sailor waiting inside, sitting up front in a little cabin while everyone else was left out in the rain. He'd turned and welcomed them with a grin like a hungry landshark, but there was an aquila branded into his forehead so Joyce guessed he must be all right. Speaking with a voice like broken glass, the sailor had ordered them to sit with their backs straight and grip the safety rails, warning them to keep their jaws shut unless they wanted to bite off their tongues. The man had laughed at that last part like it was the greatest joke ever told and Joyce had decided maybe he wasn't all right after all.

One of the Steamblood Zouaves had boarded the boat alongside them, clanking onto the deck like a clockwork god. He was too big for the benches and too proud to listen to the grubby sailor anyhow, so he just stood in the aisle, looking grand. Joyce wasn't sure if the Steambloods were *properly* holy, but they did look mighty fine and he was glad to have one along for the ride.

And then the sailor had pulled a lever and sent the boat plunging down into the sea. Joyce's guts had rushed up into his mouth and his butt had surged off the bench. Scared half to death, he'd gripped the safety rail and forced himself back down, fighting for his life against the freefall. Just then the Zouave had come careening down the aisle, all out of control. He caught Toomy's head with an iron boot as he flew past and it was a miracle he hadn't kicked it clean off! There were no miracles left for the knight though. Joyce had seen his eyes through his visor as he flew past and they were wide with a surprise that was bigger than fear. And then he was gone, tumbling over the stern gunwale like a scrap metal bird. They'd heard him splash into the ocean a heartbeat behind the boat, but nobody had tried to do anything. Even a greencap like Joyce knew the iron man must have sunk like a stone. Only the sailor had reacted, giggling hysterically like he'd played a fantastic joke on the new boys.

Nope, nothing made sense anymore.

Bobbing about in a puke-filled box on a sea of sewage, Joyce remembered the knight's eyes and wondered if everyone looked that way when they were about to die. The thought made him uneasy so he prayed instead. He prayed for the soul of the lost knight who'd died without honour or glory. He prayed for poor Brother Toomy who was looking really bad right now and he prayed for Brother Modine who'd looked so scared when the cog priests had taken him away. But most of all he prayed that doing the God-Emperor's work was going to get a whole lot more glorious than this. And somewhere along the way it seemed to him that the God-Emperor answered.

CHAPTER THREE

Imperial Seabase Antigone, the Sargaatha Sea

I've been on this creaking, ocean-straddling base for over a month now, healing up while I wait on High Commissar Lomax. She's never liked me and I doubt my unauthorised sojourn in the wilderness will have improved her opinion much. She'll want answers, but where do I begin? How can I explain the path that led me to those Verzante deserters when I don't understand it myself? How can I make her believe I was on the trail of Commander Wintertide when I'm not sure I believe it myself? Perhaps she'll have me shot. Or more likely she'll just do it herself.

But no, I've been given a new eye and a new arm so execution won't be on her agenda. Did I say 'new'? In truth both the augmetics are ancient, doubtless salvaged from one corpse after another. The hand is a tarnished metal gauntlet that grinds whenever I flex the fingers and locks up unless I keep it lubricated, but the optic is worse. It's like an iron spike rammed into my eye socket – a hollow iron spike with an angry wasp trapped inside it. Not that I'd give a damn if it worked properly, but sometimes things flicker or flare and suddenly I'll see the world through a hash of snow or broken down into a crude mosaic of reality. And sometimes I'll see things that aren't there at all. It's just as well I've learned to recognise true ghosts.

Take Niemand for example. He has stood vigil at the foot of my bed throughout my time in the infirmary, invisible to the medics and orderlies, but occasionally glimpsed by the worst of the wounded. A few days ago they wheeled in a man who looked like a heap of raw meat and I saw him staring at my revenant in abject terror. Doubtless the dying man thought the shade had come for his soul. He could not know that Niemand cares only for me.

Detlef Niemand is the least of my three ghosts, yet his hate runs the deepest. He was always a cold bastard, the kind of man who brought nothing but malice to the Commissariat. I once believed that our kind were exemplars of the Imperium, unflinching in the face of death and faithful to a fault. How else could we be trusted with the power of life and death over our charges?

'We have to be the best of the best, Iverson,' my mentor Bierce used to say, knowing full well that few of us ever were. Even so, Niemand was amongst the worst of the worst. He was assigned to me on my first tour of the Mire and although he was just a cadet back then, I could see the darkness hiding behind his pale, colourless eyes. He was morbidly proud of the six executions he'd already made and took every opportunity to regale me with the details. I loathed him from the start and never understood why he was so reverent of me, a twenty-year veteran with a paltry ten executions to my name. When he finally earned the scarlet and took his own commission his departure was like a shadow lifting from my soul.

The next time our paths crossed we were equals: joint commissars serving with the 12th Galantai Ghurkas in the kroot-infested tributaries of Dolorosa Magenta. By then Niemand had tallied almost two hundred executions, taking a life for even the slightest misdemeanour amongst his charges.

'Iverson, you think too much,' he chided whenever I confronted him, echoing Bierce's old admonitions. 'You and I are engines of the God-Emperor's will, unshackled from the doubts and passions that enslave lesser men. Hesitation can be our only crime!'

That icy façade never fooled me for an instant. I could see how much he enjoyed the killing. That was why I left him to the kroot. How did it happen? We were lost deep in the Mire when he took a wound to the gut – a solid slug that tore him right open. He pleaded with me to carry him out or make a clean end of it. Instead I shot off both his hands so he couldn't do it himself. As I walked away I remember him begging and cursing and then finally screaming when the xenos found him. You see the kroot are particularly foul lapdogs of the blueskins. They are avian carnivores that delight in tearing their enemies apart and eating their flesh. And not always in that order...

I suppose Niemand's return was inevitable, but I underestimated his poison. One way or another he damned me. After he came back I grew increasingly careless with the final resort, almost trebling my executions in the space of two years and thinking nothing of it. Thinking nothing much at all in fact, until Indigo Gorge and Number 27, the girl with the eyes of a saint. After that everything changed.

– Iverson's Journal

'But you can't come in here!' the young drop-ship pilot blustered, his eyes agog at the antique autopistol in the intruder's hand. 'The shipboard regulations are quite unequivocal about–'

'Nothing's ever unequivocal son, except the man pointing a gun in your face,' said the white-haired madman who had burst into the cockpit. 'And maybe the Emperor's word, though I'm none too sure about that one right now.'

'Besides, the man is already here, Jaime,' the co-pilot observed languidly. 'And I'd wager he'll not be going away any time soon.'

Colonel Cutler turned from the youth in the pilot's chair to the much older man lounging in the seat beside him. The co-pilot's thinning grey hair was tied back into a drooping ponytail, giving him the air of a faded rake. His mahogany skin was deeply seamed and the bags under his eyes mirrored the sagging sack of his gut. Cutler guessed he was well past sixty and looked every day of it.

'Your name, sir?' the colonel asked, unable to decipher the letters on the rogue's crumpled jumpsuit.

'That would be Ortega, señor.' The co-pilot's cadence was almost theatrical, the voice of a man who enjoyed talk for talk's own sake. 'Guido Gonzalo Ortega, pilot third class and falling, 33rd Verzante Skyshadows, indentured unto the glorious 6th Tempest in service to his Holiness the esteemed Water Dragon Aguilla de Carajaval, may his exalted bones bless this pestilential snake pit unto eternity.'

'That is heresy, Ortega!' his comrade protested stridently. 'The Water Dragon is doing the Emperor's work in the Mire, cleansing the savage and purging the xenos.'

'The Water Dragon drowned in his own blood and vomit years ago, boy.' There was an unexpected bitterness in Ortega's tone. 'Along with every one of the poor fools he dragged into the Mire with him. No, we Skyshadows are the last of the 6th Tempest, Jaime.'

'You will address me by my full rank, sub-pilot Ortega!'

'Son, why don't you just fly the ship and leave the talking to us oldsters,' Cutler said, waving his pistol at Jaime.

Indignantly the pilot returned his attention to the helm and swore at the blinking red light that indicated yet another clogged engine filter. The drop-ship was submerged in the effluvium of the Strangle Zone, Phaedra's miserable excuse for a cloud layer. Flying through the dense strata of floating fungal detritus was dirty work, but dropping below the smog was far more dangerous. The fleet had lost countless birds to enemy 'sky snipers' – high altitude drones armed with lethal rail guns.

With expert fingers the pilot flicked a sequence of switches and flushed the filter. The red light winked out and he sighed with relief. It was Ortega's job to supervise the filters, but the fool couldn't be trusted with anything these days. Jaime had reported his laxity many times, but the Sky Corps was so short of airmen that Ortega had escaped with a demotion. More importantly the report had earned Jaime Hernandez Garrido the silver badge of the Skywatch, an honour awarded only to men of impeccable loyalty. Garrido wore the winged eye on his lapel with pride, relishing Ortega's dislike of it. Unfortunately the old goat's retribution had been a vigorous campaign of flatulence that had turned the cockpit into a toxic no-man's-land to rival the smog outside. With any luck Ortega's luck would run out soon and Jaime would be assigned someone younger and more devoted. It was the natural order of things. There was no room for broken relics in a holy war.

The metal gangway crashed down onto the shore and Ambrose Templeton, captain of the 4th Company, lurched from the boat. Still reeling from the boiling embrace of the sea he stood blinking on the ramp, trying to make sense of the chaos that was the beach. Searching for words...

Blind, bound and broken heartless, dancing eyeless to a symphony of sorrows.

Templeton had written those words on the killing fields of Yethsemane Falls, scrawling them feverishly into a notebook with blood-slick hands, diverting the horror to the page before it could drown his sanity. Beneath his gaudy finery the captain was a grey man, sallow faced and balding, but beneath the grey he was a riot of restless words. Before the Providence uprisings he'd been an assiduous historian of warfare, poring over the strategies of the past to inform the tactics of the future. The discipline had served him well during the conflict and the scholar had become a fine officer. And in time the fine officer had become a fair poet. After Yethsemane, Templeton had come to see the materiel cost of war as material for his own epic, his 'Canticle of Crows'...

Carrion hawks, circling in strident contemplation of man's fathomless loss...

Lieutenant Thone staggered from the boat behind Templeton and slipped, sending them both tumbling to the beach. The captain thrust his hands out to catch his fall and felt them punch through something soft and brittle that exploded into a cloud of liquid fetor. Choking and spluttering, he found himself straddling a fleshy fungus that looked like a crude parody of a man. Then he saw the dull eyes staring up at him from the violet balloon of its face... Saw the distended jaws rammed open by the gnarled toadstool erupting from within... Saw the gleaming dog tags engraved into its bloated neck. By a small miracle his spectacles hadn't slipped loose and he could even read the name of the fungus: *Falmer, C.A., Corporal.* Templeton squinted in confusion, trying to make sense of it, hunting for a metaphor...

...Like bittersweet flowers of boundary, the dead shall bloom and the blossoms shall devour those that linger at the threshold...

And then he saw Falmer's skin rippling and quaking and he felt something nipping at his hands inside the ribcage. Nearby Thone was screaming and Templeton felt an echo welling up inside himself. If he let that scream out he knew it would never end, so he tried to drown it with more...

...words to snare and bury and deny all the sins that...

'On your feet Kapitan Bloodbait!' The voice was guttural and thick with the accent of the battleship crew. Lethean, Templeton recalled through his rising panic.

The speaker grabbed him by the collar and hauled him to his feet, tearing his hands free of the corpse in an eruption that spattered his glasses with ichor. He tried to wipe the slime away, but his hands were knocked aside and someone began to brush him down urgently. Through a liquid haze he could see dozens of pale, coin-sized grubs being swept from his sleeves. The vermin were all shells and pincers and thorny tendrils, something between a crab and a jellyfish. Several clung stubbornly to his hands, fighting to burrow into his flesh, but his rescuer tore them off with practised efficiency.

'The dead, they are full with the skrabs.' The Lethean laughed harshly. 'Mostly they only bite, but is not good to be bleeding inside a meatbag!'

Behind the voice Templeton could hear his men cursing as they deployed to the beach. Lieutenant Thone was still shrieking like a madman and Sergeant Brennan was bawling at him to stand still. Lubin, his vox-operator was praying in a breathless staccato rhythm. Behind the familiar voices he could hear distant shouts and cries punctuated by the clatter of Steambloods and a shrill blare of whistles.

'Is done,' said the Lethean. 'Welcome to the Dolorosa Breach, Kapitan Bloodbait.'

Wiping the slime from his glasses, Templeton peered at his saviour and groaned inside. Another damnable commissar! This planet was crawling with them!

Under a quagmire of scars and sores the fellow looked too young for the role, but there was no mistaking his black storm coat and high-peaked cap, though both were threadbare. Like the commissars on the battleship he'd woven razorwire into the blue band of his cap and epaulettes, ornamenting his faith with the promise of pain. Pinned to his lapel alongside the traditional Imperial aquila was an unusual silver icon: a diamond-shaped eye framed with angular wings. Templeton had never seen anything like it, but every regiment had its own traditions and the ram's skull of the 19th probably looked equally peculiar to this commissar.

'I am the Commissar Cadet Zemyon Rudyk of the Lethean mariner corps,' the youth announced, gesticulating fiercely to punctuate his words. The brass whistle hanging from his cap bobbed about in accompaniment.

Before Templeton could answer, Thone lurched towards him, clutching at his coat with beseeching hands. The lieutenant was still screaming and Templeton caught a glimpse of his eyes glittering through a writhing crustacean carpet. To his horror Templeton realised the man was covered in the creeping, clawing skrabs. Instinctively he reached out to help, but Rudyk shoved him aside and launched a brutal kick at Thone, sending the hapless officer reeling to the ground. A moment later the commissar's autopistol barked and silenced the screams.

'Was too late for that one, yes?' Rudyk grinned at Templeton, exposing blackened teeth that had been filed to sharp points. 'And the Emperor, he condemns.'

Templeton recognised the phrase from the Lethean battleship. The savage confessor had uttered the same words after he'd murdered poor Elias Waite. That injustice was still burning a hole in Templeton's heart, but the recriminations would have to wait. Back there on the battleship capitulation had been their only option. It had been a crisis for all of them, but only Templeton had grasped the extent of the confessor's madness and seen his regiment's peril. Just like the hellfire puritans back home, the Letheans had turned the sharp, cleansing blade of the Imperial Gospel into something twisted. There could be no reasoning with such men.

Once again, Templeton thanked Providence he'd been able to vox a warning to the colonel during their sea crossing. What Cutler would do with the warning was anybody's guess, but at least he wouldn't be coming in blind. Even so, Templeton sensed that nothing could prepare a newcomer for this world. There was a sickness here that ran deeper than the stench and the vermin, a malaise that could rot away a man's very soul. But there was also inspiration here. Gazing across the open graveyard of the beach, Templeton felt his soul ignite with imagery for his dark saga. Where the sea of sewage ended, the sea of decay began, drowning the shore in a swathe of death. Corpses were strewn everywhere...

...deposited in geological sediments of corruption, the bleached skeletons of the first wave buried beneath the suppurating efflorescence of the last...

'Kapitan Bloodbait!' The commissar snapped at him, misreading Templeton's awe for fear. 'The Emperor, He demands the courage!'

Templeton turned to him, the wonder in his eyes magnified by his thick glasses. 'Or else the Emperor condemns?'

'Is so, yes,' Rudyk agreed. 'Now get your newbloods off beach before the skrabs eats them all!' He gave Templeton a comradely slap on the shoulder and jerked the whistle to his lips.

Sergeant Calhoun heard another shrill whistle blast and yelled at his squad to shift their arses. There were at least three of the snakebite commissars prowling the shore, pouncing on the new arrivals as they spilled from the boats, bawling and cussing at the muddled men. He'd already seen two grey-backs and an officer gunned down and he was damned if he'd lose anyone to the bloodthirsty blackcoats. Boone lumbered past with Toomy slung over his broad shoulders. Catching a glimpse of the broken man's bloody scalp, Calhoun swore viciously. It was a helluva thing to lose their sniper before the bullets had even started to fly.

'It just gets better and better don't it, sarge?' called Roach as he sped past, dancing nimbly between the corpses.

Calhoun shook his head, taking it all in. The beach was a screwed up hell-hole, but when all was said and done things could have been much worse. It looked like the 19th had arrived on the tail end of the *really* bad stuff, after the fighting had already moved inland. This coastline had already been captured and the corpses choking its shores had paid the price. There was no telling how long it had taken and how many waves of men it had cost. For all he knew the beach might have been won and lost over and over again across the course of this decades old war. That grim thought turned his mind back to the boy. Why had he let Maude talk him into bringing young Audie along? And where was he anyway?

Everyone was off the boats now and racing towards the distant tree line, but he hadn't seen the greencap go past. Stubbornly he refused to acknowledge his anxiety. Despite what Maude had said he wasn't convinced the boy was his. The kid seemed too creed-struck to be a genuine Calhoun. Even so, he couldn't deny his relief when Joyce emerged from the boat. The boy paused on the ramp, gazing at the shore with a faraway look.

'What in the Seven Hells are you doing back there, greencap?' Calhoun hollered.

Joyce turned his distant eyes on him and Calhoun saw something almost furtive in his expression. Then the boy leapt to the shore and saluted smartly. 'Just checking something out, Sergeant Calhoun, sir,' he said.

Calhoun was about to question him further when Dix started shrieking.

'Looks like Brother Dix is in need of salvation, sir.' Joyce pointed further up the beach and Calhoun grimaced. Too damn right Brother Dix was in need of salvation! The rangy Badlander was struggling frantically to free his foot from the clinging carcass he'd trodden in. Cursing, Calhoun stalked over and hauled the idiot out of the rotten mire.

'Get it together, greyback!' Calhoun bellowed. 'I'm not pulling your grox feet out of every meatbag on this beach!'

'It ain't right sarge!' Dix wailed. 'It ain't right to just leave 'em here like trash. Thousands of 'em gone to feed the 'shrooms and the grubs like meat candy and...' The words bubbled out in a manic stream that told Calhoun the man was heading for the edge.

'I'll feed you to 'em right now if you don't can it!' Calhoun slapped Dix across the face. Hard. The greyback stared at him stupidly and Calhoun slapped him again, catching him as he stumbled. 'Are we done here, Trooper Dix?'

Dix nodded uncertainly, still snivelling. Calhoun snorted and thrust Modine's flamer towards him, but the Badlander jerked away as if he was being offered a venomous snake.

'He'd want you to have it,' Calhoun said stiffly. 'You going to dishonour the man, trooper?'

'No sarge, you got it all wrong.' There was a pleading look in Dix's eyes. 'See Klete, he'll be back real soon, just like them cogboys promised. I ain't touching his girl!'

'I'll take her, sergeant,' Joyce said, startling Calhoun. He hadn't seen the boy come up alongside him. 'I did some practising with burners in basic and they told me I got a gift for it. I always loved the sacred burnings back home. There's a holiness in fire you can't get from a bolt or a bullet.'

That serene glaze was back in the boy's eyes and Calhoun found himself feeling oddly uneasy. 'You still with us, boy?' he asked gruffly, feeling awkward.

'I'm just fine, sergeant.' Joyce reached for the flamer and Calhoun found himself handing it over. The greencap slung the bulky fuel canister over his shoulder and smiled happily. 'And Lady Hellfire's going to be just fine too.'

Captain Jon Milton Machen loped up the beach, the pistons of his colossal Thundersuit bellowing and wheezing furiously in the heat. The machine armour was a cantankerous old monster, but he knew it would never fail him. Like Machen himself, it was too full of bile and spite to lie down and die. Too hungry for war!

Prentiss and Wade kept pace with him on either flank, leaping over the corpses in their lighter Stormsuits while Machen simply waded through them, pounding the dead into pulp beneath his iron boots. He'd lost contact with Gledhill and Ashe but the rest of the Zouaves had signed in on the intra-suit vox. They were scattered along the beach, supporting the Arkan infantry like hard points in a tapestry of soft meat. His iron knights!

He surged past the blackened husk of a tank, catching sight of the yawning cavity in its hull. It was just one of countless broken hulks littering the beach. He'd clocked dozens of Chimera transports and Hellhound tanks, even a couple of heavier machines he didn't recognise, all shredded into scrap metal in mute testament to the power of the enemy munitions. There was no clue to the identity of the tank killers, but he knew that even a glancing shot from one of those mystery guns would obliterate his armour in an instant. The thought made him uncomfortable and he suddenly felt vulnerable out on the open coral. He didn't fear death, but he wouldn't welcome a fool's end!

Finally he saw the jungle looming over the coral dunes. The tangled wall of foliage looked like it had been dredged up from the sea bed and left to rot in the sun. Wherever he looked he saw stems and stalks and bladders and tendrils, puffed up with a fleshy, unclean vitality that sickened him and urged him to burn and burn. Lovingly he stroked the trigger of his flamer...

And a screaming torrent of fire lanced up from behind the dunes, immolating a cluster of cancerous trees. A moment later a second stream leapt up alongside the first, then another and another, uniting into a blazing, cleansing wave that surged through the jungle. It was as if the Emperor himself had granted Machen's desire to burn.

Puzzled, the captain crested a final dune and saw the base. The Letheans had only offered a cursory briefing on the battleship, but they'd mentioned Dolorosa Breach. It was the only Imperial base on the southern archipelago, a rag tag camp manned by the remnants of several decimated regiments. There were at least twenty Hellhound tanks down there, stretched out along the tree line, their inferno cannons shrouded in steam as they cooled down. Scattered among the flame tanks were dozens of Chimeras and a pair of Leman Russ Vanquishers. Machen scowled at their slipshod formations: they were spaced almost randomly and some weren't even facing the jungle. Behind the mechanised perimeter things looked even worse.

The outpost was a sprawling shanty town of tents and makeshift huts that had obviously grown without any central or defensive planning. There were at least a thousand men bustling about the camp, but there was no cohesion or discipline to them. The troops were clustered up in their original regiments, still bound – and doubtless divided – by their old allegiances. Their uniforms spanned countless traditions, ranging from simple khaki fatigues to faded velvet finery to rusting suits of armour. Machen even spotted a gaggle of dark-skinned warriors galloping along the perimeter on horseback, whooping manically as they raced each other between the flames. To the captain's rigorous eye it was absolute bloody chaos.

By the Golden Throne, the Dustsnakes will fit right in with this rabble! Machen thought grimly.

'Do we go in, sir?' Wade voxed, his disgust mirroring Machen's own.

The captain had stopped on the dune and the rest of his company were catching up and fanning out on either side of him, awaiting his orders. Further along he saw young Lieutenant Grayburn leading the 2nd Company towards the outpost, while that dreamer Templeton lagged halfway up the beach with the 4th. And there was still no word from the colonel and his vaunted Burning Eagles. Doubtless the old man was still fooling around with his Norlander witch while his regiment was thrown to the wolves, leaving Jon Milton Machen to pick up the pieces.

The Hellhounds roared again and their stubby inferno cannons doused the jungle in a fresh wave of fire. Watching that filthy tangle burn, Machen grinned and boosted the output of his shoulder speakers, assaulting the dunes with a riot of martial chords. This war was a mess, but it would offer countless opportunities for a man who cared only for vengeance.

'Of course we're going in!' Machen bellowed. 'We didn't cross the damned stars to rust away on this Throne-forsaken hill!'

'No colonel, what you must understand about Phaedra is that there are countless spiders caught in Her web alongside the flies like us,' the portly co-pilot, Guido Ortega, observed sagely. 'They've been weaving their own little traps within the greater trap for decades, building petty fiefdoms in hell. For instance, take this Admiral Karjalan – the Sea Spider we call him...'

Keeping his eyes on the control panel, Jaime Garrido frowned. Ortega was still gabbling away to the crazed Guard officer as if they were old comrades reunited across a gulf of lost years, waxing lyrical about his conspiracy theories and picking holes in their sacred crusade. With mounting fury Garrido touched the silver icon on his lapel, praying for guidance. The shuttle was coasting through a relatively clean pocket of air right now and the turbulence had died down. With the Emperor's grace the ship's machine spirit could be trusted to coast along untended for a minute or so. If Garrido moved swiftly...

'Diseased you say?' the colonel was asking.

'So the rumours go,' Ortega paused for effect. 'Naturally the admiral keeps himself locked away in the high towers of his accursed warship, hiding away like one of those bloodsucking monsters from the old myths. Nobody has actually seen the man in years save for his priests. Ah, but they're a grim crowd! The Lethean Penitents they call themselves. I tell you señor, those bastards will crucify you as soon as look at you!'

'Would I be right in thinking you're not a devout man, Guido Ortega?' Cutler asked.

'On the contrary señor, I would cast my soul into the warpsea for the God-Emperor!' Ortega protested. 'But these Penitents are a perversion of the Imperial creed. They have made a virtue of malice, a sanctity of suffering...'

'And what about the Sky Marshall?' Cutler cut through the man's increasingly purple rhetoric. 'Seems to me he's sleeping on the job up there in orbit...'

'Sky Marshall Zebasteyn Kircher is a hero of the Imperium!' Garrido snarled, spinning to face them. There was a stubby service pistol in his hand. Cutler dived aside as the youth fired. A round whizzed past his face and another tore through the shoulder of his jacket, but the third was completely off. As the bullets ricocheted wildly around the confined space a distant, coldly professional part of the colonel's mind observed that Garrido was an appalling shot. Then Cutler was on his knees, levelling his own pistol, but Guido Ortega was already on top of the young pilot, wrestling for the weapon like an angry old bear. Garrido was spitting and snarling furiously, but like his aim, his muscles weren't much to speak of and he couldn't shift Ortega's bulk. The co-pilot smacked the youth's trigger hand against the control panel, mashing it against the sharp edges until the gun slipped free. As Garrido howled in pain Ortega head-butted him full in the face. Once. Twice. After the third crack the youth slumped senselessly into his chair.

The burst of strength drained out of the co-pilot and he slumped against the helm, breathing hard. His sweaty face was spattered with blood from his comrade's pulverised nose. Slowly at first, then with increasing violence, the ship began to shake.

'Ortega!' Cutler growled.

The Verzante threw him a dazed look as the shuttle groaned and the cockpit canted sharply downward. Ortega swore and crashed down into his seat. His hands darted over the controls like birds of prey as he struggled to rein in the vessel's neglected machine spirit.

'Padre de Imperios...' Ortega breathed as the turbulence finally subsided and the world steadied around them. His eyes were fixed rigidly ahead.

'You still with me, flyboy?' Cutler asked.

'That was... a very long time coming,' Ortega said through harsh gasps.

'Feels good, doesn't it?'

'And what exactly is it that I'm feeling so good about?'

Cutler stared at him for a long moment, suddenly unsure himself. Then he sighed, dredging up a soul-deep weariness that made him seem much older than Ortega. Instead of answering he hauled the unconscious pilot to the floor and sank into his place, gazing at the nebulous fog swirling past the windows and seeing nothing. Ortega lost himself in the old, trusted task of steering the ship while he waited for an answer. His rasping breaths had slowed by the time Cutler replied.

'Tell me Guido Ortega, would you have the balls to fly this tug into a hot zone?'

'I might say that I could do it with my eyes closed and my hands bound,' Ortega said. 'But that would be a manifest exaggeration.'

'I guess I'm going to take that as a yes,' Cutler said. 'Which is just as well, because we won't be stopping off on the Spider Admiral's boat.'

'I'm not sure that I follow you, señor.'

'Does a place called Dolorosa Breach mean anything to you?' Cutler was watching him with bright, angry eyes.

'Nothing that I like,' Ortega said carefully.

'Well that makes two of us, sir.' Cutler nodded. 'But I'm not asking you to like it. I'm just telling you to take me there.'

* * *

Keeping his eyes on their guide, Captain Templeton slashed a path through another snarl of creepers with his sabre and swatted hopelessly at the swarming flies. The vermin had hit the Arkan in a furious, biting wall the moment they had entered the jungle, then harried them every step of the way like tiny winged daemons. Nothing seemed to deter them and some of the men had already given up the fight, but their sly bites made the captain's skin crawl and he kept slapping at them stubbornly. The Phaedran veterans probably had some kind of repellent for the vermin, but if so they hadn't offered it to the newcomers. They hadn't offered much of *anything* except a rapid passage into the Hells.

There had been little respite at the ramshackle base called Dolorosa Breach. Templeton's company had been met by a patrol of slovenly sentries and waved on to the tree line where a craggy-faced officer had been overseeing all the new arrivals. The crew-cut ogre had ridiculed their tardy landing and 'dandy boy' uniforms, gloating that they wouldn't last a day in the Mire, but he'd soon grown bored, almost as if the newcomers weren't worthy of his wit. Without bothering to offer his name or rank, the brute had launched into a mission profile that was so thin on detail it would snap from a sharp glance. In short – and there was no long – their orders were to reinforce a push on an ancient temple complex some three kilometres inland. Designated 'the Shell', the necropolis was thought to serve as the primary rebel base for the region. The attack had begun three days ago and there were at least two other Imperial forces involved, but the composition, disposition and current status of those forces was unknown. Intelligence on the enemy seemed equally threadbare to Templeton: they would be facing a small contingent of tau, probably a few xenos mercenaries and a whole heap of 'fish'.

'Fish?' Templeton had asked, trying to ignore the furious itching in his left hand where the skrabs had bitten him.

'Yeah, Fish. The indigenous scum.' The officer had pointed to a band of gangly figures in grey jumpsuits slouched by the perimeter. Templeton had assumed they were simply bedraggled Guardsmen, but that mistake hadn't stood up to closer scrutiny. The Phaedrans – or Saathlaa as Cutler had called them in his briefing – were clearly of human stock, but their degeneracy was obvious. There was nothing overtly wrong about them, but nothing that was quite *right* either. All were at least a head shorter than an average man, but their stature was further diminished by their spindly bowlegs and hunched posture. Their faces were uniformly broad, flat and brutish, with widely spaced goggle eyes and fat, rubbery lips.

'Fish. You see it, right?' The officer had grinned and Templeton had reluctantly agreed that yes, he did indeed see it. In fact the degeneracy had unsettled him deeply.

Is the human bloodline really so open to corruption? Templeton had wondered. *And if so, might our entire race not sink back into the primordial slime with the passing of ignorant aeons?*

'Webbed fingers too,' the brutish officer had continued. 'Personally I'd cleanse the lot of 'em, but apparently they just about pass muster for human. Well, they're ugly scum, but they've got their uses. The ones who didn't rebel are almost pitifully loyal, probably because they know the rest will skin 'em alive if we lose the war. And they make damn fine guides.' He pointed to the gang by the trees again. 'These boys call themselves *askari*. I guess that means "scout" in Fishspeak.'

After three hours trekking through the Mire, Templeton had come to share the officer's faith in the *askaris*' jungle craft. The native assigned to his platoon had led them through the jungle with swift, knowing steps, steering them around impenetrable clusters of vegetation and creeper infested fissures. They were travelling a clotted, broken land that conjured up visions of a vast weed-choked regicide board where the light and dark squares corresponded to vitality and decay. Aware that one misstep in this tangled disharmony of life and death could prove fatal, the captain found himself growing more grateful for their guide the deeper they went. For all his degeneracy the native was their lifeline in this maze.

Occasionally the *askari* would bring them to a halt with a raised hand and drop to his haunches, sniffing suspiciously at the ground like an animal, then nod and scurry on. Often he would stop to peer at a glistening fungal tree or a swarming curtain of creepers, keeping his distance as he searched for some obscure telltale clue. Then he would either hurry past or urge his charges back with sharp gestures. On one occasion he had fled from something on the path ahead, frantically shooing the platoon away. As he retreated, Templeton had caught a glimpse of a titanic violet bloom leering at him from the clearing ahead and shuddered at its gently undulating mantle of tendrils, both fascinated and repelled. He hoped the other platoons had been gifted equally talented guides.

Their force was spread out, advancing through the jungle in a loose wedge of twelve platoons, each numbering around fifty men. The platoons of the 2nd Company had taken the centre, while those of the 3rd and 4th had fanned out on either flank. They had entered the jungle in a much tighter formation, but the labyrinth of trees had played havoc with that plan and the teams had soon lost sight of each other. Although they maintained vox contact, nobody really knew where they were anymore and Templeton could only pray that they were all going in the same direction.

The wiry *askari* guide raised his hand and the greybacks of Dustsnake and Hawksbill squads crowded up alongside him, peering into the murk. A few paces ahead the ground dipped sharply and the jungle dissolved into a mist-wreathed swamp. The water was strangled by a tangle of mangrove-like trees, but those weren't the only things choking the swamp. There were bodies everywhere, floating languidly with their limbs splayed like broken dolls. Some were so riddled with arrows that they looked like human pincushions, while others were shockingly charred and sundered, evidently the victims of powerful energy weapons. Although the corpses were crawling with flies and leeches, they were obviously still fresh.

'Must be at least a hundred of 'em down there.' Sergeant Calhoun had to raise his voice over the buzzing feeding frenzy of the vermin. 'Looks like the poor bastards never even saw it coming.'

'The Jungle Sharks,' Lieutenant Sandefur said sombrely. The tall, square-jawed veteran had been given overall command of the two squads and Calhoun figured that was just fine. Sandefur might be an academy boy with a pole rammed up his backside but he was actually a half-decent soldier. By Willis Calhoun's reckoning that was a pretty good result for an officer.

'Aren't those the boys we're meant to be linking up with?' Calhoun asked.

'Indeed, but let's not be in a rush to link up with them now, eh sergeant,' Sandefur said with grim humour. He shot a questioning look at their guide and the Saathlaa nodded, indicating that their path lay through the corpse-choked swamp.

'Well now, don't the Emperor just love his greybacks today,' Roach muttered, drawing a frown from the lieutenant.

'It isn't a question of love, Dustsnake,' Sandefur said. Then he spotted the scout's tassels hanging from Roach's cap and smiled. 'Care to take point with our swampy friend, scout?'

'And here I was thinking you'd never ask, lieutenant.' Roach tipped his cap and grinned sourly at their *askari* guide. 'You and me, we're going make a fine team, *Mister* Fish.'

To his surprise the native grinned right back at him.

'Do you smell that?' Valance asked. The black-bearded scout had stopped, sniffing suspiciously at the smog rising from the marshland.

Machen couldn't smell anything through his sealed helmet, but he trusted the ex-trapper's instincts. Unusually for a scout, Jaques Valance was a barrel-chested bear of man, but he could move as silently as any Norland tracker. Rumour had it he'd learned his craft smuggling skins past the feral ork tribes.

'What do you have, scout?' the captain growled, scanning the skeletal trees for a target. The damnable mist was filtering everything into a soft focus blur.

'Don't know captain, but it's something new.' Valance was frowning as he tried to make sense of the odour. 'Smells like milk that's turned sour... and something else, something sharp. Maybe blackroot or...'

'We've lost the Fish!' someone shouted from up ahead.

'Prentiss, Wade, with me,' Machen called on the intra-suit vox. He tore his iron boots free of the clinging sludge and clanked towards the unseen speaker with his brother Zouaves on either flank. For the last hour or so his platoon had been up to their ankles in mud and over their heads in smog. The stuff rose from the ground in thick streamers, transforming the vegetation into a ghostly graveyard parody of the jungle. Everything looked withered and desiccated here.

Even by the standards of this arsewipe planet this region is ugly! Machen reflected gloomily.

'Hill and Baukham are gone too!' There was an edge of panic in the point man's voice as the Zouaves stomped up alongside him with Valance at their heels.

'They were there a moment ago!' The greyback pointed ahead. 'Just past those trees...'

Machen signalled to Valance and the scout advanced cautiously. He stopped by the suspect cluster of trees, his sharp eyes picking out a residue of black slime splattered across the trunks. Gingerly he sniffed the stuff and gagged at the stench. Catching a glint of metal, he dropped to his knees and ran his fingers over the bark, wincing as something drew blood. Squinting, he saw the trunk was riddled with a web of tiny, razor sharp metal filaments.

'I've found...' A soft hiss came from the smog ahead and Valance froze. A moment later the hiss was followed by a low, wet rattle. The scout rose and backed away, his eyes never straying from the mist ahead.

'There's something out there,' he breathed. 'Something more than an animal.'

'Form up around me, greybacks,' Machen commanded, stoking up the old fury in his gut like a loyal friend. If the Hells were going to break loose then Jon Milton Machen was ready to oblige them.

Templeton had lost his bearings hours ago, but their guide clearly knew his business so he had immersed himself in the nightmare trek, hoping to embrace the living dead phantasmagoria of the jungle. It offered such a wealth of allusions to a refined spirit, such potential for metaphor and wordplay... Yet try as he might the words eluded him, lost in the smog of pain that had slowly seeped across his mind. It was the bites of course, some infection he'd caught from those damnable corpse crabs back on the beach. His left hand had been throbbing for hours now, summoning up a fever that was turning his thoughts to sludge.

The captain paused to catch his breath, letting the others march past as he unwound his makeshift bandage and inspected the wounds. His whole hand had swollen up and he could see a tracery of purple lines weaving up his wrist. Once again he cursed himself for letting the bites go untended at the outpost, but they'd seemed so trivial back then. Besides, he hadn't wanted to look weak in front of Machen. His fellow captain already had precious little respect for him.

Something whirred by overhead with a sonorous, buzzing drone. Templeton glanced up and caught a shape flitting between the treetops, dark and jagged against the emerald canopy. It was gone in the blink of an eye, but he was left with the impression of something thorny and misshapen, like a huge insect...

The Lord of Flies, chitinous monarch of sickening skies.

'One helluva big bug that, eh sir?' Sergeant Brennan said, disturbing Templeton's vague inspiration. Brennan was a cheery, pragmatic bruiser who might have been the captain's polar opposite. 'Seen half a dozen of 'em fly past in the last hour. Don't much like the look of 'em.'

'The Mire is full with the xenos filth, yes,' Commissar Cadet Rudyk interjected as he came up alongside them. Much to Templeton's irritation the youth had fastened onto his squad. 'Here all animal and all plant is tainted. One day we burn them all, but it is not today.'

Rudyk marched past and Templeton saw that the back of his storm coat was riddled with bullet holes. The young cadet wasn't the first man to wear that coat and probably wouldn't be the last. In all likelihood commissars didn't last very long on Phaedra.

Another of the giant insects flittered by overhead, punctuating its flight with a rhythmic medley of twitters and chirps. Its strange song drew a chorus of replies from a dozen unseen companions. Through his growing delirium Templeton felt something nagging at him. Something about that song...

'You all right, sir?' Brennan asked, peering at the captain's pallid, glistening face.

'Just a touch of heatstroke, sergeant.' Templeton smiled weakly, unsure why he was hiding the truth. 'Best get on. We don't want to fall behind in this maze.'

But as they went deeper into the Mire, Templeton found his eyes returning to the canopy, watching the treetops for a flash of chitin.

CHAPTER FOUR

Imperial Seabase Antigone, the Sargaatha Sea

I was discharged from the infirmary two weeks ago, yet High Commissar Lomax still hasn't summoned me. Doubtless she's engaged with more pressing matters than an errant commissar, but sometimes I can't help thinking she's playing games. I have occupied my reprieve by exploring the abandoned lower tiers of this rusting old sea platform, delving through the flooded under-chambers as I try to straighten out my story. Any lie will do, so long as it convinces Lomax of the one truth that matters: I am going to kill Commander Wintertide.

Number 27 accompanies me on my wanderings, a mute reminder of Indigo Gorge, where my quest began nine months and an eternity ago. Indigo Gorge. In twenty years of soldiering across more worlds than I care to recall I've never seen the likes of that killing ground. We were dying in droves, wading upriver through the red corpse paste of our fallen as the flickering lances of the blueskin guns sliced down from the escarpments high above. They had the cover, the range and the elevation. What good was faith against that? And what possible purpose did my twenty-seventh execution serve? If that murder had somehow turned the rout, well what then? Another thousand lost, probably more, yet we'd have been no closer to victory. But Niemand's shade was with me that day, filling my heart with ice, so when the charge faltered and my charges fled, I didn't hesitate to take the shot. There was no calculation in my choice – the sacrifice was just another fleeing shape amongst so many. A coward. Expendable. Execrable.

I'd still believe it if I hadn't seen her eyes, but as she fell she rolled over and I caught her gaze. Her features were made strange by the distorting waters, stranger still by the perfect geometry of the third eye my bullet had punched through her skull. She couldn't have been more than eighteen, a plain girl already haggard with the rigours of life in the Guard, but as she slipped into the water and out of life she looked right at me and I caught the last flicker of something that I can only call holy.

And so Number 27 became the third member of my shadow

triumvirate, but while Bierce and Niemand despise me, her gaze
burns with a terrible pity that is so much worse. It is for her that I
will kill Wintertide and end this meat grinder war.

– Iverson's Journal

The men of Dustsnake were wading waist deep through the curdled soup of
the swamp, their rifles held over their heads to keep out the muck and their
mouths shut to keep out the flies. Together with the Hawksbill greybacks
they followed their guide through the morass with silent determination.
All except Boone.

The burly Badlander was cussing and splashing about, angrily chewing
up insects as he tried to dislodge the razor-toothed thing that had latched
onto his boot. Toomy was still slung across his shoulders, a dead weight
that sometimes burbled and groaned, but showed no other sign of reco-
very. A couple of the others had offered to take a stint carrying him, but
Boone had refused. The sniper had always been good to him, never calling
him a groxbrain and even letting him win a few hands of cards now and
again. Sergeant Calhoun had wanted to leave the injured man behind at
the outpost, but Boone hadn't liked the looks of that place and eventually
old bullet-head had backed off. The big man had it all worked out. Even if
Toomy didn't get better, it would be fine because then Boone wouldn't be
the dumbest greyback in the squad anymore. This was probably the deepest
insight of his life and it had made him intensely happy. Despite the heat and
the flies he'd carried his burden with a big smile, sure that life was finally
on the up. And then the eel thing had started biting at his boots. It spoiled
the last few minutes of Gordy Boone's vague life.

When the end came Calhoun was shouting at him to shut the Hells up
and Roach was turning to offer a gem of sarcastic wisdom. And then something slapped Boone right in the eye. For a moment he was angry and then
he was hurt and then he wasn't anything anymore except a slab of dead
meat toppling into the water. Toomy splashed down beside him, groaning
reflexively at the shock.

Roach grinned, thinking the big groxbrain had slipped. And then he saw
the black spine sticking out of Boone's right eye as he sank below the scum.
Something whickered past Roach's ear and a Hawksbill greyback gurgled,
clutching at the arrow sprouting from his throat. In another heartbeat the
air was alive with a hail of arrows and men were screaming and falling all
around him. Their native guide dived below the water and Roach followed,
screwing his eyes shut against the filth. Above him the surface popped with
impacts and he felt something scrape his shoulder. Desperately he forced
himself down to the silt bed and swam, blindly hunting for cover.

'Get into the mangroves!' Calhoun yelled, ignoring the arrow jutting from
his shoulder as he surged through the mire towards a clump of trees. Cully
and Pope splashed along beside him, firing wild volleys of las-fire at the

shadows dancing in the mist. They could see Lieutenant Sandefur leading a gaggle of Hawksbill men to a mound of fallen trees, his sabre raised and his pistol flaring, sending heroic, hopeless bursts into the mist.

The three men crashed down into cover and found Dix already there, struggling to jam his wiry frame into the cavern of gnarled roots. To Calhoun's disgust he was whimpering Kletus Modine's name over and over like a child begging for its mother.

'They're coming at us from all sides,' one-eyed Cully snarled, frantically trying to train his lasrifle everywhere at once as the Saathlaa guerrillas tightened their circle. The naked warriors dissolved out of the mist like hunched ghosts, fired their arrows with guttural whoops and then faded away to reload.

'Get in as deep as you can!' Calhoun shouted, his eyes hunting for the boy as he snapped the shaft in his shoulder and crawled into the tangle. He breathed a sigh of relief as he caught sight of Joyce crouched in the hollow bole of a tree across from him. This was the greencap's first real tussle but he didn't look scared. In fact there was a big grin on his face that made Calhoun proud and uneasy at the same time.

Dix squealed as a huge spider flopped down onto his face from the rotten hollows of the mangrove. It gripped his head like a pair of skeletal hands, all bony legs and hard ridges and far too many eyes. Calhoun ripped it away and threw it aside. It took Dix's nose with it, leaving a gushing crater in the middle of his face. Swearing in disgust, Calhoun pumped the scrabbling spider full of las-bolts and turned to the others.

'We've got to start dishing the pain back at 'em!' Calhoun yelled, trying to blot out Dix's screeching. 'They can't get at us under here, but we've got to hold 'em back!'

One of the giant insects swooped low, hooked its clawed feet into a man's back and tore him shrieking from the ground. Surging back into the tree-tops it let go, turning its victim into a shrieking, flailing manikin. Captain Templeton leapt back as the man crashed into the mulch at his feet, broken but still breathing. Blood gurgled from the wreck's ruptured throat as it tried to beg for help and Templeton fell to his knees, his hands fluttering helplessly over the broken pile as it gasped for words that wouldn't come. Templeton understood. The words wouldn't come for him either.

Commissar Cadet Rudyk charged past him, leafing frenetically through a battered Tactica manual with one hand as he snapped off shots with the other. Somewhere nearby Sergeant Brennan was shouting and the vox-operator was screaming into his crackling set and a Steamblood Zouave had triggered his shoulder speakers, flooding the glade with bombastic music. And men were swearing and fighting and dying all around Ambrose Templeton.

The captain shook his head and slapped himself hard in the face, trying to dislodge the clouds in his skull. The attack had come so suddenly. His platoon had just entered a wide forest glade when a battle had flared up somewhere in the distance. In that moment the insects had surged down from above, almost as if they were obeying a prearranged signal...

And damn it all, they were! And I knew it was coming all along! I knew they were talking to each other!

Yet again Captain Machen heard the ghost rattle from the mist. Then again on their left flank... their right... from behind...

'Whatever it is, there's more than one,' Valance whispered.

'Let's flush the craven scum out,' Wade said over the intra-suit vox, his patrician tones filled with contempt.

'Wait. Let them come to us,' Machen hissed. 'They're hungry for it.'

He had the platoon formed up in a tight phalanx that bristled with lasrifles on every front, reinforced by the three armoured Zouaves and their heavy stubbers at equidistant points. It was a textbook defence that Machen had favoured against feral greenskins and Outlanders back home on Providence, but his patience was wearing thin. They could all hear the muffled sounds of distant las-fire as the other platoons engaged the enemy, winning glory while Jon Milton Machen just sat here.

Suddenly something clacked and whirred in the fog, like a machine slowly winding up. Two more machines chugged alive in response.

'Sir, might I suggest...' Prentiss began, but his voice was disintegrated in a screeching cacophony as a storm of metal erupted from the mist, tearing into the phalanx from three sides.

Sergeant Calhoun grinned as another primeval guerrilla leapt from the mist – right into the sights of his lasrifle. Before the Saathlaa could loose his arrow the sergeant lanced him through the eye and flicked the barrel across to another savage. Cully and Pope were wedged between the roots on either side of him, backing him up with short, sharp bursts, but he'd given up on Dix. The injured Badlander had huddled up into a foetal ball, whimpering pitifully as he clutched at his ruined face.

The ambush had cost them nearly half their number, but the survivors were pulling things back. Lieutenant Sandefur had set up a decent firing perimeter with half a dozen greybacks, targeting the rebels with precise, disciplined volleys.

These savages have spirit and cunning, but bows and arrows are no match for Arkan fire! Calhoun thought fiercely.

A bolt of energy streaked from the mist and tore through a tree sheltering a lone greyback, sundering his chest into charred chunks of meat. Calhoun's confident grin faded.

'What in the Hells was that?' Pope hissed.

'That was us fragged,' Cully answered as a second killing bolt sizzled out of the jungle. And Calhoun had to admit he was probably right.

Something buzzed behind Templeton. He lurched round and stared blearily into a face out of nightmares. It looked like an insane three-tiered pyramid of compound eyes built on a plinth of mandibles. Long, tapering antennae flared out from either side of the conical head, tilted sharply towards its prey as it closed in.

Despite his peril, Templeton was fascinated by the monstrous warrior, almost hypnotised by the quicksilver blur of its wings. The thing was craggily bipedal, but any resemblance to humanity ended there. Its double-jointed legs ended in massive talons and its body was a patchwork exoskeleton of hard plates and vicious barbs. Strangest of all, the insect was carrying a gun. As it levelled the weapon he saw the blur of its wings flitter and oscillate, modulating their rhythm. The crystalline prong in the gun barrel shimmered, resonating in harmony with the droning, almost as if the wing case was calibrating the gun and...

Sergeant Brennan bowled into Templeton and threw him aside. Spinning, he sent a volley of las-fire into the insect's face, incinerating two tiers of eyes. The creature chittered in pain and pulled away, its wings beating furiously as it soared towards the canopy. Brennan spun after it, tracking its path with a stream of las-fire that flared off its tough exoskeleton. With icy calm he adjusted his aim and ripped through the delicate web of its wings. Twittering furiously the thing crashed headlong into a tree and plunged to the ground. A band of baying, vengeful greybacks were on it in seconds, hacking and stabbing with their bayonets.

'We have to find cover!' Brennan yelled, hauling Templeton to his feet.

A ripple of energy pulsed down from above and struck the sergeant, unravelling his atoms in a frothing crimson spiral. A moment later, all that remained of Brennan was the hand gripping Templeton's greatcoat. The captain glanced up as Brennan's killer streaked towards him with outstretched talons. He ducked frantically and the insect swept over his head, whipping him with a trailing claw that shredded his hat and sent him reeling. Off balance, he sent a salvo of wild las-rounds after it and drew his sabre, hunting the sky.

Watch the skies, the fangs of their eyes, weeping chittering chitin rain...

Only the three Zouaves had weathered the razor blade storm. Wave after wave of metal filaments had bombarded Machen's phalanx, the tiny threads shredding flesh and bone but only scratching the solid Steamblood carapaces. The attack left them standing over the mangled wreckage of their comrades like knights in an abattoir. Incredibly a few of the butchered carcasses were still alive, moaning and wailing as they bled out from a thousand cuts.

'Both of you stand absolutely still,' Machen whispered over the vox.

'I don't understand...' Wade voxed back.

'Quietly!' Machen hissed. 'We're sealed up tight but let's not play with fire. Now just do as I say unless you want to die!'

'By your command,' Wade whispered formally.

'Prentiss?' Machen said. 'Prentiss, did you get that?'

There was no reply from the third Zouave, but Machen couldn't risk checking on him. He had to ignore the wounded too. They were probably beyond help, but that didn't make it any easier.

'Sir, what in the Hells just happened to us?' Wade's voice sounded strained and Machen guessed some of the filaments had got through his armour, probably slipping in at the joints.

'Loxatl,' Machen said bleakly. The moment the attack had come he'd recognised the weapon and realised the folly of bunching his men up.

'What are those lizard trash doing here?' Wade hissed incredulously.

'What they're always doing – killing for pay. It seems these tau bastards like to hide behind mercenaries.'

I've travelled so far only to find the same old vermin waiting for me, Machen thought bitterly. *And why should I be surprised when that has always been the way of things?*

Long ago an old preacher had thrown him a scrap of wisdom that hit him with the force of absolute truth: 'Wherever you go, there you are.' It was a bleak truth, because wherever Machen went, horror went too. Why would Phaedra be any different? Besides, the loxatl were naturals for this filthy planet and its filthier war: amphibians and mercenaries who fought for the highest bidder, just as they'd fought for the rebels back on Providence.

'I can't see anything out there,' Wade said. 'What are we going to do?'

'We'll wait.'

'But they'll tear us apart!'

'I've faced these scum before. They're virtually blind on land. They rely on smell and taste to find their prey.'

There was a long pause as Wade considered this.

'Our armour...'

'Exactly. We're sealed. If we stand perfectly still the bastards won't even know we're here.'

'Sir... I'm bleeding. Rather badly as it happens.'

'And so are fifty other souls, lieutenant. Just stand still and the lox won't sniff you out from the crowd.'

'But the wounded...'

'Will draw the lox out. These scum may kill for pay, but they *like* the killing.'

'You want to use the wounded as bait?' Wade sounded appalled.

'I want to give them vengeance, man!' Machen struggled to keep his voice down as the fury welled up. He crushed it with an effort. 'The lox won't leave anyone alive, but they'll want to enjoy the killing. If we wait they'll come to us...'

Another bolt of superheated energy sizzled across the swamp, tearing a chunk out of Lieutenant Sandefur's cover, but Calhoun's eyes were on his boy. Joyce had slipped quietly into the water and lay floating on the surface, playing dead. Calhoun had seen him emptying some of the promethium from his flamer's fuel canister and wondered what he'd been playing at. Well it was obvious now, but Calhoun didn't like it any better. The air in the tank was keeping Joyce buoyant as he paddled slowly towards one of the lethal snipers. To a careless observer he would pass for another floating corpse, but it was a hell of a risk. Calhoun ground his teeth in frustration.

As he bobbed towards the Emperor's foes Audie Joyce was thinking of the saint from the battleship. How proud that wonderful, terrible giant would be of him now! Like the saint, he had passed beyond fear and doubt. The epiphany had come to him during the terrible sea crossing, born from the fate of the Zouave knight who'd been thrown overboard. Joyce hadn't been able to shake the look of surprise in the knight's eyes and the more he'd thought about it the angrier he'd become at the sailor who'd doomed him. That was why he'd crept back to the cabin after the boat had landed. The sailor had grinned impudently, but he'd soon stopped grinning when Audie had put his big hands round his throat. He'd watched the man's eyes goggle with shock as he squeezed and squeezed, confirming his intuition that men were always surprised when death came for them.

That vengeance had felt pure. *Holy*. Like the saint, Audie Joyce had done the Emperor's work with his bare hands, but now he had a flamer and there was more work ahead.

'Aim for their wings!' Templeton yelled, trying to make sense of the chaos around him. His greybacks were dashing about, firing frantically into the air or diving to avoid the deadly beams. Several of them had fallen to their knees, risking death for a better shot at their speeding tormentors. Their remaining Steamblood knight had locked his armoured legs, transforming himself into a sturdy firing platform. His massive heavy stubber was blazing away, raking the canopy with a steady stream of high velocity rounds and spilling out a cascade of spent shells. Martial music blared from his shoulder speakers in accompaniment to his amplified bellowing. The man's comrade had fallen in the first flyby, atomised by a concentrated lattice of beams, and the surviving knight wanted payback.

As Templeton watched, the Zouave snagged a flier from the air and the greybacks yelled triumphantly. Like a mob, they charged towards the tumbling ruin of chitin and Templeton charged with them, suddenly eager for blood. Commissar Cadet Rudyk got there first, yelping with hatred as he rammed the barrel of his pistol between the creature's twitching mandibles and emptied his clip on full auto. His eyes were bright as he looked up at Templeton and grinned. He shook open the Tactica manual clutched in his other hand, revealing the page he'd marked with a finger. Templeton glimpsed a crude sketch of the insect warriors.

'Is the *vespid* we face, yes! Ves-pid Sting-wing!' The youth explained, brandishing the manual triumphantly. 'Is vassal race for the tau, you see? For scout and assault. Is very quick and is very agile.'

'We have to... find cover...' Templeton muttered blearily, seeing two grinning cadet commissars.

'Maybe we find the kroot here too!' Rudyk said, licking his lips at the prospect.

The loxatl slithered from the mist with sly, sinuous movements, crawling with its belly to the ground on four clawed legs. It paused and sniffed at the air with flaring nostrils, sifting through the scent of carnage for a threat.

Watching the beast from the corner of his eye, Machen's finger caressed the trigger of his heavy stubber. The loxatl aroused an almost primal revulsion in him, its serpentine form somehow embodying the worst aspects of *otherness.* Its head was a flat, snakelike torpedo that bristled with teeth under the slits of pale, almost sightless eyes. Black saliva drooled from its maw as it flicked its snout back and forth, tasting the air with a questing tongue. Its languid movements were mirrored by the stubby flechette blaster attached to its back. Mounted inside a synapse-linked augmetic cradle, the gun responded directly to the creature's thoughts, allowing it to track prey without encumbering its claws. Machen heard the weapon clack and whirr as it spun about, lingering on the men who still breathed amongst the pile of bodies.

'Sir, one of the bastards has just crawled right into my sights,' Wade voxed from somewhere behind him. 'Request permission to open fire.'

'Wait. That's only two. There's still one more out there,' Machen said.

'Sir, I'm bleeding...'

'I said wait. We'll only get one chance at this.'

Motionless, Machen kept his eyes on his own loxatl. He couldn't see the one approaching Wade or risk looking around for the third, but he sensed it watching and waiting. It was more cautious than its brethren, probably the brood leader, old and canny with the wisdom of countless hunts. Even so, once its packmates started killing the wounded it wouldn't be able to hold back...

Roach felt a gentle tug at his shoulder. Gasping for breath, he surfaced amongst a bed of tall reeds. The Saathlaa scout was waiting for him, crouched low with only his neck showing above the waterline. Instinctively Roach followed his lead. The *askari* had guided him through their desperate underwater flight with occasional prods or tugs, always signalling when it was safe to come up for air. Apparently the native had no problems seeing in the murky water with those big, fish-like eyes of his. The greyback guessed he was lucky his guide had taken a liking to him, but the native's impulsive loyalty made him uncomfortable. Claiborne Roach wasn't much used to anyone looking out for him.

He heard an electronic burble as something scudded over the water towards their position. With an urgent wave the *askari* dived again. As Roach followed he saw the shadow of a disc flitting by overhead. He heard several more of the things whiz past, their machine chattering dampened by the water.

It felt like an age before the native pulled him back to the surface. The cacophony of battle raging across the swamp had intensified with the arrival of the flying discs. Peering cautiously through the reeds, Roach saw them whirling around his embattled comrades, sometimes skimming low over the water, sometimes flitting amongst the treetops. They were only about a metre in diameter and looked kind of ridiculous to Roach, but the twin guns fixed to their undersides were no joke. Fortunately their aim was poor when they were on the move, only stabilising when they came to a hovering halt. Each time one of the discs attempted that, the Arkan defenders tore it apart with concentrated fire, but it was a dangerous game.

And then there were the snipers. Roach had counted three of them, scattered about the swamp, hidden deep in the mist. Their rate of fire was slow, but the power of their weapons far exceeded anything the Arkan infantry carried, slicing through flesh or solid bark with equal ease. The sneaky bastards had already picked off four greybacks. Unless something was done about them this skirmish was going to end badly.

'We're running out of time,' Roach whispered to the *askari*.

Keeping low in the water, the native gestured to a clump of mangroves some twenty metres away. Roach waited and a moment later a bolt of energy whooshed from the hideout.

'Nice work, Mister Fish,' Roach smiled, winning a lopsided grin from the *askari*. 'Okay, let's take him down.'

They dived again.

'Tell the colonel... tell him we've been thrown to the wolves,' Templeton rasped through a raw tunnel of pain.

'I'll do my best, sir,' Lubin muttered as he fiddled with his vox-set, 'but I can't promise you anything.'

The pessimism was an old ritual between them, but the skinny little man was the best vox-operator in the regiment and Templeton had personally financed his long-range comms set. It was the kind of foresight that had served him well in the past.

'Kapitan Bloodbait, we must advance, yes!' Rudyk snapped at him. 'A Guardsman, he must go forward always! The Emperor, he...'

'He condemns. Yes... I do recall...' Templeton said, quite sure that the Emperor had already condemned *him*. His infected hand had swollen monstrously under the bandages, pumping the skrab poison through his whole body, but mercifully his head had cleared a little. He scanned the jungle uncertainly, trying to work things through. His platoon was sheltering under the drooping canopy of a huge toadstool, crouched behind a bed of smaller fungi. The stingwings had broken off their attack, but there were other enemies out there.

'We need... to regroup... find the others...'

'And together we go forward, yes!' Rudyk said, slapping his hands.

'Yes,' said Templeton, thinking no.

Machen was staring at the scouting loxatl, willing it to signal the 'all clear' to its wary brood leader.

'Sir, I've got a clean shot!' Wade's voice buzzed eagerly over the vox.

Abruptly Machen's loxatl reared up onto its hind legs and cocked its head, gurgling that liquid rattle deep in its throat. Somewhere behind the captain its companion responded. Machen cursed Wade, sure the beasts had detected the muffled vibrations of his voice.

'Sir, don't you think–'

'Keep quiet you fool.'

Suddenly the loxatl leapt, streaking through the air almost too fast for the eye to follow. It landed on Machen's towering Thundersuit with a wet thud. One of its claws scrabbled against his domed helmet and a milky white eye peered blindly through the porthole of his visor. He froze.

Perhaps it thinks I'm a tree. A strange tree to be sure, but then this Emperor forsaken jungle is full of strange trees. If Wade can just keep his mouth shut for...

'It's almost on top of me!' Wade buzzed.

The dead eye widened and the loxatl hissed. As it tried to spring away the captain's iron-clad arms shot out and caught it in a vice-like grip, crushing its flechette harness like matchwood. Its claws raked desperately against his armour and its jaws snapped at his faceplate, but it couldn't penetrate the carapace. He squeezed hard, grinding the beast against his cuirass until its attack turned to a frantic escape attempt. Behind him he heard Wade open fire on his own lizard, but he had no attention to spare. The lox in his grasp was writhing and contorting like a snake, its oily skin so slick he could barely hang on to it. But he did hold on, grimly tightening his grip as he paid back the horror eating him up from inside.

The horror that could never be paid back...

Machen had once thought he'd lost the capacity for horror on the killing fields of Yethsemane, but he had been wrong. Returning home after the war he'd found horror waiting for him like an old friend in the smouldering ruins of his estate. Valens Parish was far behind the loyalist lines, but horror had rushed ahead of his homecoming to give him a hero's welcome in the charred bodies of his wife and daughters. One of the estate's slaves had seen it happen: the killers had been stragglers heading back home, leaderless and drunk on victory. Badlanders. Loyalists.

The captain had strung up the slave for surviving when his family had died, then tracked down and executed the murderers with the same fussy precision he directed towards troop movements and munitions supplies. Afterwards he'd screamed until he had nothing left inside but hate. Then, with nowhere else to go he'd returned to the 19th. His family had been avenged, but vengeance was greedy.

And vengeance wasn't choosy...

Something snapped in the loxatl's back and a froth of mucous erupted from its jaws, spattering Machen's faceplate. For a moment the beast jerked about spasmodically, then fell still. With a triumphant howl the captain cast the broken carcass aside.

There was an angry hiss from the mist and a hail of flechettes sliced towards him and clattered harmlessly across his armour. Snarling, he returned the gesture with a burst from his heavy stubber, raking the fog as his unseen attacker bounded away.

'Wade, did you kill yours?' Machen shouted into the vox.

'I hit it!' Wade replied excitedly.

'Did you *kill* it, man?'

'I... I'm not sure. It was so damnably fast, sir.'

Machen swore and stomped over to the Zouave, who was tracking his weapon uncertainly across the smog.

'I did hit it! It's bleeding out all over the place!' Wade pointed to a trail of black slime that disappeared into the mist. From somewhere beyond they heard a ragged growl as something dragged itself through the mulch.

'You have to hound a killer down and finish him!' Machen snarled, storming into the mist after the blood trail.

He found the second loxatl crawling painfully towards a stagnant pool. It swung on him with a defiant hiss, its mangled flechette blaster clicking impotently. The creature's left forearm and half its face had been torn away by Wade's salvo, but it still lunged at him, snapping feebly with its shattered jaws. He batted it to the ground and crushed its skull beneath an iron boot.

Just one more and this game is over, Machen thought hungrily.

Roach and his guide surfaced quietly some ten metres behind the sniper's hideout. There were three guerrillas hunkered down in the bushes. To his surprise the sniper himself was a native, almost naked under a thick paste of grey mud. Incongruously the Saathlaa's head was encased in a sleek, backswept helmet fitted with a crystalline optical sensor. The warrior was a bizarre amalgam of the primeval and the hi-tech, but there was no mistaking his skill with the oversized rifle he cradled. He handled the heretical weapon with a tenderness that bordered on worship, whispering to it and stroking the barrel each time he took a shot.

In a way, the other two guerrillas were even more surprising. Both were true humans and undoubtedly professional soldiers. They wore open-faced helmets and loose black fatigues augmented with cuirasses and shoulder pads. The armour looked like it was moulded from some kind of hard plastek and had a rounded, alien aesthetic.

Alien. Yes, it was the xenos that Roach had expected to find here. The *true* enemy, not more savages and these human traitors. Some part of him had wanted to bring pain to the tau themselves, to get some payback for poor dumb Boone and the others. From somewhere across the swamp he heard the unmistakable whoosh of a flamer and the three guerrillas began to argue furiously, the humans harassing their Saathlaa sniper to switch targets fast.

Well, whoever they are, they're still the enemy, Roach decided.

Signalling to the *askari* beside him, he sighted along his rifle and took the shot. The gun fizzled impotently, something inside it wrecked by the drenching it had taken. He grimaced as the native sniper cocked his head at the sound and began to turn. The *askari* leapt up and flicked something from his hand. A dagger-like thorn slapped into the sniper's chest and sent him crashing back into the mesh of creepers he'd been lurking in.

The two human traitors swung round and Roach dived forward, ducking under their first snapshots. Desperately he jabbed the barrel of his rifle into one man's eye and sent him reeling, but the other smashed the butt of his own weapon into Roach's face. Stumbling drunkenly he saw the *askari* cannoning into his attacker and heard the splash as they hit the water hard. The first soldier was lurching about, clutching at his ruined eye with one hand and trying to level his rifle with the other. Fighting the concussion, Roach lurched along with him and saw the dead sniper entangled in the creepers. He snatched the big thorn from the corpse's chest and staggered into the half-blind solider, batting away the man's rifle and ramming the makeshift dagger into his remaining eye.

And then it was all too much and the world spun out from under his feet and came crashing down.

Audie Joyce felt the Emperor's wrath pulsing through his veins as he incinerated the xenos-loving heretics. Their hideout was a blistering wire-frame inferno and he could see the rebels flailing about in there like charcoal skeletons. One of them dived into the water in a cascade of steam, but Audie could tell it was too late for him. A couple of savages leapt out of the jungle to his right and he swung the cleansing stream of fire over to greet them, grinning as they flared up.

Everything had gone to plan, just as he knew it would. Even the heathen discs had missed him as he paddled towards the sniper's nest. When he had leapt up and unleashed the holy fire he'd caught a flash of surprised eyes in the foliage and smiled at his growing wisdom.

'Get into cover you greencap idiot!'

Joyce swung round at that familiar voice and saw Uncle Sergeant Calhoun charging towards him in slow motion, struggling through the treacle of the swamp. His lasrifle was spitting fire as he advanced, chasing the discs that were racing ahead of him towards Joyce. He caught one and sent it spinning and smoking into the water. The others chattered furiously and whipped round, soaring back towards the veteran. Roaring like a madman, Calhoun emptied his clip at the advancing discs, standing his ground as return fire from a dozen guns stitched the water around him into steam.

As Joyce stormed back towards his hero he saw other greybacks leap out of cover to support Calhoun and draw some of the heat. Everyone was shooting and dashing about now, all caution thrown to the wind as the Arkan chased the Thunderground in their souls. Three of the discs went down in flames, three others swept past leaving a couple of Arkan dead. The surviving sniper claimed another victim, but several greybacks clocked his position and raced towards him, heedless of the risk.

Joyce heard the clamour of martial music as a Steamblood knight waded in from their left flank at the head of another Arkan squad, its heavy stubber blazing away at the rebels fleeing before it. Arrows pinged off his armour from all sides and the beleaguered Arkan cheered mightily. As if in retaliation, a kind of madness seemed to wash over the Saathlaa and they charged out of the mist, whooping wildly as they cast aside their bows and bore down on the Arkan with coral-tipped spears and clubs.

'Engage the savages!' Lieutenant Sandefur shouted, his sabre flashing through the putrid gloom as he surged towards the guerrillas.

Joyce heard someone hollering angrily at the Saathlaa to stay put and cursing them for brainless savages. Guessing he was hearing the enemy leader, he veered off towards the voice. A guerrilla leapt at him, jabbing with a spear and spitting like a venomous toad. He blocked with his flamer and answered with a burst of purifying fire. One of the machine discs whipped past, coming so close it almost knocked him off balance. He sent a stream of flames after it and turned it into a fireball. It flittered about blindly and splashed a couple of rebels with burning promethium before crashing into a tree. Joyce howled along with the savages.

This was glory!

Machen was creaking about and firing randomly into the mist, acting as bait while Wade watched over him silently. If the final loxatl went for the captain it would offer him a brief target. It wasn't a bad plan, but the brood leader was cunning and Wade was nowhere near silent enough. The creature had already figured out that it faced two enemies, so it ignored the obvious lure and homed in on the muted clicks and whirrs from the smaller metal warrior.

It was crawling stealthily through the heap of fallen Arkan, intent on Wade's back when one of the bodies surged up from below and ripped open its belly. The creature squealed in pain and peppered Wade's carapace with flechettes as Valance tore his hunting knife up through its body. Desperate to throw off its attacker, the creature flipped over onto its back, but the scout hung on, driving the knife in again and again. Driven by the loxatl's pain reflexes, the blaster strapped to its back continued to fire, shredding its hide before exploding in a hail of white-hot shards. It was over, but Valance continued to hack into the corpse until Machen pulled him away. The scout's eyes were glazed with hatred as he wiped his knife clean. He was panting hard, exhausted by the struggle.

'I ducked down... behind you... when they hit us,' Valance gasped.

'It was well done, scout. I shall put you forward for a commendation,' Machen said, entirely serious.

Six other greybacks had survived the loxatl ambush, but two of those were beyond help. Solemnly Machen gave them the Emperor's Mercy. As he'd suspected, the third Zouave was also dead. There must have been a flaw in Prentiss's faceplate because the flechettes had shattered the reinforced glass. Inside the confines of his helmet the man's skull had been liquefied, but his rigid exoskeleton had kept him standing. The suit would probably remain that way for decades after Phaedra had devoured the soft flesh inside its shell. Machen wasn't sure how he felt about that.

'What's the game plan, sir?' Wade asked. The edge of pain in his voice was more pronounced now and Machen guessed he was bleeding badly. Unless he got the man to a medic soon he would lose both his wingmen today.

'We find the others,' Machen said and looked at Valance. 'Can you do it, scout?'

Sheathing his knife, Valance surveyed the fogbound jungle. Somewhere in the distance he could still hear the sounds of gunfire.

'This place hasn't got anything on the Methuselah Swamplands back home,' Valance lied. 'Sure I can do it, sir.'

'Then lead the way man,' Machen growled. 'There's Arkan blood being spilt out there!'

* * *

Joyce saw Willis Calhoun die. It was a bad death, clumsy and pointless. The sergeant took a spear in the groin from a dying guerrilla floundering in the water beside him and reeled backwards, right into the fire of a passing disc. It tore him clean in two.

The boy went cold as part of him died with his unspoken guardian. He wasn't exactly sure what he'd lost, but he thought it might have been the *best* part of him. Then he heard the guerrilla leader shouting again, still hidden but very close now. Like a drowning man grasping for a line, Joyce gripped the barrel of his flamer and gritted his teeth as the red-hot metal stoked up his rage. Then he was on the move again, fighting through the rebel scum like a man possessed.

He heard the leader snapping at someone who replied in calm, oddly accented tones. Something about that second voice made his hackles rise and he snarled as he fought his way towards the unseen pair. He found them lurking behind a curtain of fronds, hunched down over one of the killer discs. The saucer was hovering at waist height, its casing bristling with sensor spikes and blocky modules of alien machinery. Joyce guessed it was carrying some kind of comms array, maybe even the control device for all the other discs. A warrior in strange armour had his head down in the array while a burly man in combat fatigues watched impatiently. Going by their bickering Joyce was sure they were officers.

Grinning like a skull, he tore through the fronds and levelled his flamer. The rebels looked up and Joyce felt a thrill of horror as he recognised the flat wedge of the machine operator's face – *black eyes, no pupils and no nose*. He'd seen the holo-pict of a tau but it hadn't prepared him for the unclean reality of the xenos.

He froze up.

Watching Joyce with steady brown eyes, the human officer raised a placatory hand and spoke. 'Son, you don't want to do this.' There was a tired wisdom in the man's voice that reminded Joyce of Uncle Sergeant Calhoun. 'Whatever they've been telling you, it's all lies,' the officer continued. 'You don't have to throw your life away for–'

Joyce squeezed the trigger hard and lit them both up like greasy candles. The traitor stopped talking and started screaming. The screaming didn't last long but Joyce kept on burning until the flamer had run dry. He was sweating with something that had nothing to do with heat and everything to do with hate.

'You're both insane!' Jaime Garrido wailed through broken teeth. The young pilot was kicking about on the cockpit floor, struggling against the cords that bound him. 'Ortega, you know the regulations! We don't fly over enemy territory!'

Cutler and the co-pilot ignored him. Ortega's attention was riveted to the controls as he made his descent. Moments later the ship dropped out of the Strangle Zone and the dense smog outside the window segued into the grey-green blur of the Mire rushing by below.

'If there are any sky snipers up here we're dead,' Ortega breathed.

'There won't be,' Cutler said. 'If I've read them right, the tau won't waste that kind of tech where it's doing no good.'

'And how, precisely, would shooting down an Imperial drop-ship do the tau no good?' Ortega asked with a raised eyebrow.

'You say nobody's flown over this stretch in years, right?'

'Indeed, the Dolorosa archipelago is a no-fly zone, by direct order of the Sky Marshall himself.'

'You ever wonder why the man would give an order like that?' Cutler asked with a frown, sensing yet another mystery. He put it aside, filing it away with all the other unanswered questions for the moment. 'Anyway, the tau will have shifted the snipers somewhere useful.'

'With respect, you are guessing, señor.'

'Call it tactical gambling, friend.'

Cutler's personal vox-bead buzzed and Vendrake's voice piped into his ear.

'The Silverstorm Cavalry is locked and loaded, colonel.' The Sentinel officer sounded strained.

'We'll be going in hot, captain. If any of your riders aren't up to the job I want them to sit it out. That blonde gal of yours...'

'We're all good to go,' Vendrake snapped and signed off.

Cutler frowned, knowing there was going to be trouble from that quarter sooner or later. Probably sooner.

'We'll be over the Shell any minute now,' Ortega said, sweating profusely. 'That whelp Garrido is right, señor. This is utter madness.'

'Maybe so, but that's just the way I like it.'

With a shudder Ortega noticed the colonel was grinning like a white wolf.

The Shell was an apt name for the rebel base. It was a hollow, twisted city of temples dedicated to forgotten gods who had stopped listening eons ago. Presiding over a vast swathe of barren ground, the necropolis spiralled out in a coral web of melted ziggurats and globular rotundas. It was a gestalt leviathan, every structure bound to the whole by arterial, rubble-clogged colonnades and soaring, flanged walkways. Age clung to the dead city like a veneer of dust, mocking the alien vehicle gliding gracefully through its streets.

The sleek hover tank was a creature of the future, arrogant with youth. The smooth contours of its glossy black carapace shrugged off the dirt and the rain, defying any blemish to its dignity. Its dorsal engine nacelles were massive, but they propelled the tank along in near silence, keeping it suspended just above the street. The prow curved gently towards the ground, splaying out into broad fins on either side, each one emblazoned with the mark of Commander Wintertide: a white circle containing a geometric black snowflake. Mounted alongside each mark was the distinctive disc of a dormant drone, but the tank's main weapon was the fearsome rotary cannon protruding from beneath its nose. Commissar Cadet Rudyk would have identified the vehicle as a Devilfish, the primary troop transport of the tau race.

The tank halted as a deep rumble rolled over the necropolis, approaching like distant thunder. The twin drones rose from their mounts and spun about, burbling uncertainly as they assessed the disturbance. Somewhere an alarm began to chime. Moments later the warning was echoed throughout the city. And then the alarms were drowned out by a thunderous roar as an Imperial drop-ship swept in low over the rooftops, shaking the coral structures. The ship was gone in seconds, storming towards the heart of the necropolis. Chattering furiously the drones zipped back to the tank and it accelerated away in pursuit.

Squads of Concordance soldiers were racing through the streets, some on foot, others crammed into open-topped hover transports. There were no native guerrillas amongst them. These troops were all professional soldiers equipped with moulded flak-plate and stocky pulse carbines. They were gue'vesa janissaries, humans who had forsworn their old vows and pledged allegiance to the Tau Empire. They were something more than mercenaries, something less than respected allies.

The Devilfish overtook the transports, negotiating the twists and turns of the streets with breathtaking precision. A couple of T-shaped skimmers flipped out of a side street and buzzed past like enraged hornets. The open-topped Piranhas were rapid response scouting vehicles, each carrying a pair of tau Fire Warriors. The helmets of their hunched riders blended into the contours of their vehicles, melding tau and machine into a single blur as they surged ahead.

The Devilfish caught up with its speedier brethren as it swung into a wide plaza and braked to a frictionless halt. A circular hatch slid open and a slender tau warrior in rubberised grey fatigues and black plate slipped from the interior. Her head was enclosed in a battered helmet, the matt black scored with the twin honours of the crimson stripe and an old chainsword scar. As her gue'vesa neophytes fanned out behind her, the veteran watched the invading drop-ship from behind a veil of sensor lenses.

A hail of ordnance raked the intruder from all sides as it dipped towards the plaza. Angry drones flittered around it, peppering its hull with small-arms fire while janissaries scorched it with heavy weapons from distant rooftop emplacements. The pilot fought to keep his vessel steady amidst the firestorm, hovering some fifty metres above the ground. There was a collective hiss and hatches swung open along the length of the ship, spewing out guide ropes. A moment later soldiers in bronze helmets rappelled towards the ground, firing lasrifles one-handed at the janissaries who rushed to meet them. Both the Piranhas raced into the fray, but the scarred veteran held her pathfinders back, unwilling to commit.

With a pneumatic shriek the ship's cargo hatch burst open and a wing-less metal bird leapt towards the plaza. The jump pack fitted to its casing burned brightly, fighting to cushion the bird's fall. Even so, the invader's claws hit the ground with a crash that cracked open the brittle coral, but its reverse-jointed legs absorbed the impact. With barely a pause the machine hopped forwards, racing to intercept the Piranhas as a second walker made the jump. The tau skimmers spat fire and the bird replied with a storm of bullets from its rotary autocannon. One of the Piranhas was shredded but the other strafed away in a blur of speed.

Sentinels. The veteran scowled behind her faceplate, recognising the invading machines. Her anger grew as the drop-ship hovered about with surprising agility, deploying men and machines across the plaza. One of the Sentinels landed badly and lost a leg in a tremendous snap of metal. Crippled, the bird hopped about frantically, then toppled over, pulverising a couple of invaders. The gue'vesa neophytes cheered, then cheered again as a pair of solid projectiles lanced into the drop-ship from across the plaza. The missiles struck with such force that the ship was sent spinning, pitching a waiting Sentinel into an explosive nosedive and sending several invaders tumbling from their ropes.

Recognising the devastating power of a rail gun, the veteran squinted, triggering her optics to zoom in on the armoured giant lumbering into the fray. Like all tau battlesuits it was an elegant construct of interlocking plates and modular, geodesic blocks mounted on massive piston-like legs. Its boxy, lens-encrusted helmet looked small in proportion to its body, but the veteran knew the 'head' was just a sculpted housing for the suit's sensor array. The tau pilot was safely encased within the heavily armoured chest cavity, linked to the machine by a neural interface that afforded an intimacy the crude gue'la technology could never match.

Amongst the warrior caste of the Tau Empire it was considered a great honour to command a battlesuit. The veteran had earned the right long ago, but she had chosen to remain a pathfinder. She knew that many of her Fire Warrior comrades thought her disfigurement had made her insane, but they were wrong. The injury had defined her place in the *Tau'va* and made her whole. Had she not found her true name through her scars?

Jhi'kaara – the broken mirror.

The others found her choice unsettling, just as they found her fascination with knives repellent. Perhaps that was why she had been left to rot in this remote enclave.

'What are your orders shas'ui?' one of her neophytes asked, calling her by her caste and rank. It was the proper form of address from a gue'vesa janissary.

Intent upon the battle, she did not answer. The battlesuit was tracking the drop-ship with the twin-linked rail guns mounted on its broad shoulders. The angular cannons jutted out like blunt tusks, projecting so far it seemed a miracle they didn't imbalance the machine. Of course Jhi'kaara knew the real miracles were the anti-gravity stabilisers supporting the cannons, and like every miracle of her people they were not really miracles at all, but the fruits of vigorous technology. Unlike the stunted, superstitious gue'la, the tau exulted in innovation. Insane or not, she was certain that the future belonged to her race.

But not this city. Not today.

Even as the Broadside battlesuit fired again she knew it was too late and this battle was lost. Most of their force was deployed in the jungle, leaving only a token garrison within the city – no more than twenty Fire Warriors and two hundred gue'vesa janissaries. The Broadside was their only battlesuit, her Devilfish their only tank. It would have been enough if the silk-tongued

Water Caste had been true to their word, but despite their assurances the invaders had attacked from the sky.

The second Piranha burst into flames and Jhi'kaara felt the rage building inside her, but beneath the rage there was a fierce joy. *Today everything has changed,* she realised. The Imperials had violated the Invisible Accord so painstakingly arranged by the Water Caste. Once word of this treachery spread amongst the Fire Caste all the talk of 'shadow treaties' and 'long games' would end and the warriors would be free to fight this war unfettered. Once again Jhi'kaara saw her path on the *Tau'va*. She would be the one to carry the good news to her comrades.

With a flick of the hand she ordered her neophytes back on board the Devilfish. As she followed, she glanced over shoulder and saw the lone battlesuit torn apart by a trio of Sentinels.

'Your sacrifice will further the Greater Good,' she promised. 'I swear it.'

CHAPTER FIVE

Imperial Seabase Antigone, the Sargaatha Sea

High Commissar Lomax has finally summoned me, but I still have no answers for her. I cannot explain, excuse or justify my actions with anything but results. Only Wintertide's death will exonerate my desertion.

And there you have it. I've finally accepted the word that is anathema to our kind. Desertion. Old Bierce glares at me as I make the confession at last, but you must understand that it wasn't fear or faithlessness that drove me into the wilderness after the massacre at Indigo Gorge. I swear to you that it was duty.

Unfortunately Bierce will never accept that. His suffering is on my hands and words will never sway him. He has been my judge for too long, watching and hating and waiting for my fall with the bitterness of the betrayed...

What? No, of course I didn't kill him! I loved the old man as a father, albeit a harsh and humourless father who never had a kind word to say. He raised me to terrorise and take the lives of lesser men, but I understood his calling – our calling – and I was always loyal. Yes, even when I betrayed him.

It was complicated. You see I'd just completed my apprenticeship and earned the scarlet. I was impatient to escape the old man's shadow and make my own name, but he insisted that I accompany him on one final campaign. It was an inglorious affair – yet another petty uprising, yet another wretched world too angry to know better. Fool that I was, I thought I'd seen it all before.

Well, we crushed the rebels soon enough, but the pacification dragged on forever and I grew restless, eager for enemies worthy of the name. My arrogance blinded me to the assassin. Oh, I saw him all right – a ragged little bag of bones shambling towards Bierce – but all I saw was a filthy street urchin hunting for scraps, not a child soldier chasing martyrdom. I certainly didn't see the needle gun concealed under his rags. None of us ever figured out how such vermin came by so rare and precious a weapon. Maybe one of the rebel leaders kitted him out in a last ditch bid for revenge or maybe he found it in the ruins of the aristo palace. Either way he was true to the whims of hate. He died in a hail of fire a heartbeat after he struck, but that was a heartbeat too late.

My second betrayal came a week later. Bierce wouldn't die you see. The neurotoxin in his bloodstream was cruel, twisting him into a mute, misshapen tangle of pain, but taking its time with the killing. The medicus warned me he might last for months. Emperor forgive me, I just couldn't abide it.

I remember retching at the stench when I walked into the old man's room. He looked like a living corpse. As I drew my pistol he stared at me, silently urging me on. I pointed the gun right into his face... and froze. His eyes hardened with contempt, dismissing my struggle, already certain that I lacked the courage to pull the trigger. Because of that contempt I'll never know if it was love or hate that stayed my hand. Perhaps I've never really known the difference and maybe that's a mercy in a galaxy where there can only be war.

And so I fled Bierce and that nameless world, but his shade came after me, following me across the stars. Over the decades I did my duty in one dead-end war after another, fiercely proclaiming the Emperor's glory but feeling nothing inside. And eventually the spiral ended on Phaedra. After that there was nowhere left to run and the old man finally caught up with me.

My first shadow has never talked. His contempt has no need of words. Well, I must trust that Wintertide's death will satisfy him and lay all three of my ghosts to rest. Until then I dare not die.

But now I must answer the High Commissar's summons.

– Iverson's Journal

Night crept furtively through the jungle. As the sunlight slithered away an unseen orchestra struck up a symphony to greet the fungal dawn. Listening to the croaking, chirping cacophony, Ambrose Templeton thought the transformation both hideous and beautiful. He was in a strangely mellow mood. With nightfall, his fever had subsided to a rhythmic pounding deep inside his head...

Like a seismic migraine seething in my psyche, teething through the tectonic plates of my skull...

He cast the words aside and tried to focus on the task at hand, knowing the reprieve wouldn't last long. What was it he had to do? Ah yes... the perimeter. He was going to do the rounds one last time.

Keeping his head low, the captain crawled painfully along the inner rim of the caldera where his forces had dug in. The depression was almost two metres deep and totally devoid of vegetation, a paradoxical dead zone in the jungle. Templeton suspected the atrophy had something to do with the strange building coiled up like an alabaster snake at the heart of the crater. There was a brooding, expectant quality about the ruin that called to him,

promising answers to questions he'd never thought to ask and wasn't sure
he even understood...

*Beckoning with the secret wisdom of murder-tainted aeons, tempting saints
and sinners alike to enter the eye of the needle-storm that unstitched time...*

'Care for some recaff, sir?' Templeton jumped at the voice, blinking rapidly
as he tried to make sense of the steaming mug in the speaker's hand.

'What?' he managed vaguely.

'There's a dram of firewater in there too.' The man's uniform was caked in
dried mud. 'No disrespect to you captain, but you look like you could use
it,' the greyback continued. 'We've only the one small keg between us, but
I figured you'd earned it, seeing as you pulled us out of that swamp and all.'

Unsure whether the fellow was being impudent or genuinely hospitable,
Templeton mustered a wan smile and accepted the drink. He'd never been
adept at bantering with the rank and file.

'My thanks, trooper...'

'Roach, sir.'

'Quite so,' Templeton muttered. 'My thanks to you, Trooper Roach.'

Sipping the drink, Templeton regarded the men hunkered down around
Roach. They were a peculiar bunch of ruffians to be sure. One was a boy
with the eyes of a zealot who cradled his flamer like a holy relic. Another
just sat staring into space from a face that was one big bruise. A third was
rubbing obsessively at the raw crater where his nose had been. Strangest
of all was the native guide wearing a flat-topped Confederate cap. Seeing
Templeton's quizzical look, Roach nodded towards the savage.

'Mister Fish here saved my skin, so I figured I'd sign him up to the squad
for keeps,' Roach said. 'It's not like there's many of us left.'

'Quite so,' Templeton repeated, unsure what else to say.

'Strange sort of nights they got round here, don't you think, captain?'

'Indeed. One would venture to speculate that the indigenous fungi are
equipped with a metabolic...' Seeing the blank look on the greyback's face,
Templeton trailed off. 'Yes, a strange sort of night indeed,' he finished lamely.

After that they drank their laced recaff in awkward silence. Templeton
found the brew unpalatably bitter, but he finished it gamely, thinking it
was the right thing to do. He had no idea what else to say so he just handed
back the mug and moved on with his inspection.

The greybacks were crouched below the rim of the caldera, manning the
improvised battlements against the jungle. There were almost two hundred
men in the crater, including nine armoured Zouaves. Templeton hoped
there were more survivors out there, but these were all his search had
turned up.

After the vespid stingwings had retreated he had set about consolidating
the scattered greybacks, methodically tracking down the other platoons. It
had been a desperate, embattled search, but his force had grown steadily.
Despite the savagery of the ambush the Confederates had given a decent
account of themselves and weathered the storm. The Saathlaa guerrillas
were numerous and slippery, but they were a poorly armed rabble, prone
to panicked routs and suicidal charges. Templeton suspected they were

afflicted by a racial insanity that made them unstable in the heat of battle. Doubtless it was a consequence of their degeneracy.

Unfortunately there were other, more dangerous foes in the jungle. The vespid stingwings had continued to harass his forces, but they had become cautious, keeping to the treetops and picking off stragglers with sneaky hit-and-run attacks. Reading aloud from his Tactica manual, the late Commissar Cadet Rudyk had explained that the stingwings were considered elite shock troops, prized by the tau for their mobility and speed. Thankfully there hadn't been very many of them in this benighted region.

The squadrons of flying discs – gun drones, Rudyk had called them – were much more numerous. Worryingly, the Tactica manual implied that the drones were just the tip of the tau war machine. The young morale officer had shown Templeton sketches of outlandish battlesuits and hover tanks, chattering on about 'Crisis Suits' and 'Broadsides' and 'Hammerheads' with a morbid enthusiasm that had done very little for the captain's morale. He prayed that his men wouldn't encounter anything like that after he was gone.

The fever was resurfacing with renewed vigour now, threatening a skull-bursting eruption and Templeton pushed on before it was too late. He was exhausted by the time he reached Machen's position. The Zouave captain stood watch like a crude iron statue, unable to crouch down in his massive carapace. His head and shoulders were out in the open, making him an easy target for one of the lethal guerrilla snipers, but he'd refused to remove his armour.

The man is stubborn to his miserable core, Templeton thought. *He hasn't even bothered to clean the blood off his gauntlet. Commissar Cadet Rudyk's blood...*

'Captain Machen,' he began uncertainly.

'It had to be done,' Machen snapped. 'The murderous runt was going to kill you. And after you, how many more until he got his way?'

Templeton knew he was right. There had been no alternative. Once the Arkan had regrouped in the caldera, Rudyk had railed at them to push on with the attack, growing furious when Templeton had tried to argue. Finally the cadet had drawn his gun. The captain had hoped it wouldn't come to that, all the time knowing it would. Even so, he couldn't help feeling sorry for the boy. Despite his black storm coat, Rudyk was just a brutalised youth with too much responsibility and too little sense. Templeton had wanted to try reasoning with him again, but Machen had simply stomped in, bearing down on the cadet like a tank on legs. The boy had opened fire instantly, backing away with wide eyes as the auto rounds ricocheted off the heavy carapace. He'd tried for Machen's visor, but couldn't crack the reinforced glass. Then he'd tripped. Scrabbling backwards he'd yelled for assistance, but the greybacks had stood by with stony faces, remembering what Rudyk's comrades had done to Major Waite. Then Machen had reached down and grasped the cadet's head in a massive gauntlet.

'The Emperor con–' Rudyk had begun as Machen squeezed.

Templeton didn't want to remember the sound Rudyk's head had made.

Instead he addressed the sombre giant: 'I wanted to thank you, Machen. For saving my life.' *Even if you've only delayed matters...*

'Enough Arkan blood has been spilled today.' Machen's voice sounded hollow inside the cavern of his helmet. Templeton realised his faceplate was open. Did the man have a death wish? Well, perhaps he did... He recalled that Machen's platoon had been hit hard in the ambush. A man like Machen would take that personally.

'I really must speak with you, Machen.'

'Later. I am standing vigil for my men.'

'It's my arm you see...'

'Go away, Templeton.'

Well, I believe I shall. And I'll probably be gone for quite some time.

Templeton hesitated a moment longer, but suddenly getting through to Machen didn't seem so important anymore. Gingerly he rubbed at his wounded arm and felt something slithering wetly under the bandages. It took him a moment to realise the movement was actually under his *skin*. He sighed, too tired for disgust and too wise to the inevitable to care any longer. He had done his duty by his men as best he could. Machen would have to take up the mantle now. His only regret was that he'd never complete his beloved 'Canticle of Crows'. Through the rising fever he could hear the spectral ruin calling to him again, whispering of veiled paths between the stars...

...winding like glistening ribbons of misbegotten hope through the hearts and minds of dead dreamers, hastening their flight as they sleep down the slope of nightmare...

Tentatively at first, then with growing conviction, Templeton crept towards the waiting ruin.

Much later, Machen saw the tip of a fungal tower topple as something tore a path through the jungle beyond the caldera.

'What do you think it is?' the greyback beside him whispered nervously.

Machen ignored him, intent on the unseen metal beast trampling through the jungle. There was something familiar about that grinding, clanking rhythm. On an impulse he flicked his shoulder speakers into life, flooding the night with the bombast of Providence. The man beside him almost jumped out of his skin. Moments later everyone in the caldera was dashing about frantically. Someone hammered on his armour, pleading with him to shut the noise down, but he paid no heed.

It didn't take long for the machine to find them. Machen allowed himself a cheerless smile as the Arkan Sentinel burst through the trees. It prowled restlessly around the caldera, dazzling the men with a questing searchlight, then skittered back to face the Zouave captain. There was a hiss of pneumatic pistons as the walker powered down and sank back onto its haunches. A moment later the cockpit swung open and the pilot leaned out.

'Well met, Captain Machen!' Lieutenant Quint hollered, his fat face beaming with delight at his discovery. 'Would you and your men care to join us for a spot of dinner at the Shell?'

It was only when they abandoned the caldera that Machen realised Templeton was missing. A hurried search uncovered the man's prized notebook by the entrance of the ruined temple. The dusty steps of the portico were scuffed with footprints, but the trail petered out just beyond the inner threshold. They called for him, but there was no answer from the dark chamber. It was almost as if Captain Ambrose Phillips Templeton had walked right out of the world.

Skjoldis saw her *weraldur* drop into a rigid fighting stance. She froze, watching his silhouette through the canvas of the tent, but a moment later he relaxed and resumed his vigil outside her quarters. She knew he was nervous in this tainted place. Her guardian didn't possess the wyrd, but any Norlander could sense the wrongness of the ancient city slumbering around them. She had warned the Whitecrow against camping within its precincts, but he had been stubborn. His men had bled hard to capture the city and he wouldn't abandon it so quickly.

With a sigh Skjoldis returned to her divination. Kneeling on the raw coral she muttered the Emperor's name and cast the sacred whisperbones, watching as they scattered in the thrall of gravity, then leapt up and danced in the name of something even older. Her eyes narrowed as the carved fragments flipped and spun about, clacking restlessly like dead men's teeth in a hollow skull, unable to find peace.

'So what do your trinkets have to say, Raven?' Cutler sneered from the recesses of the habtent.

Intent on her reading, Skjoldis ignored the insult. The Whitecrow always used her mock-name when she cast the whisperbones – the Emperor's Bones they were called these days. It was his way of dealing with the elder traditions of her wyrd. Besides, he'd been drinking, swigging down his precious firewater like their supply was endless.

'Raven, I asked you...'

'The whisperbones say everything and so they tell me nothing,' she snapped, troubled by the fretful runes.

'Are you finally admitting you're a charlatan, woman?' Cutler chuckled.

She scooped up the bones and looked at him with distaste. He was slumped on a trestle bed, staring up into the darkness with his arms crossed behind his head. His jacket lay crumpled on the ground, alongside several empty bottles. When he was like this, drunk on firewater and self-pity, she almost despised him.

But he has just lost his closest friend, she chided herself. Although Elias Waite had always distrusted her, the old man had been like a brother to the Whitecrow. Ashamed of her impatience she tried to explain.

'The bones sail the whispertides of a world, but where there are no words, they can find no harbour.'

'Or maybe this world's just talking crap!'

'Yes, that is also a possibility.'

'Or just talking too fast for your old bones to keep up.'

'I am serious, Whitecrow. There is something very wrong here.'

'Are you going to tell me this is a *bad* place, Raven?' Suddenly the drunken slur was gone and he was razor sharp with sarcasm. 'Because I already figured that out for myself.'

'I am telling you that this world is poisonous.'

He laughed bitterly in the darkness. 'Every world is poisonous, woman. You just have to peel back the skin and you'll find the teeth waiting for you.'

She knew he was thinking of Trinity again, the backwater hovel that had gone to the Hells while nobody was watching. It had made him hers, but only because it had broken something in his soul.

'On some worlds the poison can be rooted out and bled dry,' she said. 'On others it has run too deep and spread too far. Here it has become one with the weave and weft of the world.'

'High Command says there's no taint here.'

'They say whatever suits their purpose.'

'And what do you think that is?' He turned towards her, his eyes gleaming yellow in the shadows. 'Because I sure don't see it. All I see is waste and plain murder. You know, I think those bastards *wanted* to throw my men away today.'

She understood his anger, but she had no answers for him.

'Your plan worked,' she said instead.

It was true. His bold assault on the rebel base had been a magnificent success. Once the battle in the plaza was won the enemy resistance had crumbled rapidly. The Whitecrow himself had cornered the rebel commander on the steps of a towering ziggurat. It had been an unsettling encounter. Countless years in the waterlogged jungle had shrivelled the rebel officer, making him look ancient inside his glossy xenos-forged armour. His head had protruded from the plastek gorget like a shrunken prune, yet his eyes had been clear and strangely placid as the Arkan surrounded him. When the Whitecrow had demanded his surrender he had simply smiled and tapped the snowflake tattoo on his forehead. Then he'd raised his rifle and died, falling to a hail of Arkan fire that never touched his smile. The serenity on his dead face still intrigued Skjoldis. What truth had carried him so far beyond fear?

'My plan worked because they didn't expect any trouble from above,' Cutler said, breaking her train of thought. 'I knew it in my gut, but why in the Hells would the tau be so sure of it?'

'Does it matter?'

He stared at her as if she were a fool. Before she could say anything more he leapt to his feet and began to pace, running his hands through his unruly white mane.

'They mothballed us you know,' he growled, 'those armchair generals back home. All that fine talk of sending us to the stars to win glory for Providence – that was all poison honey. They just wanted us gone!' He paused, thinking it through. 'They wanted *me* gone. It was never about the 19th. It was always about me.'

'Whitecrow, this is empty talk...'

'They sent my men to the Hells for my sins. Because of that damned town.'

Skjoldis wondered how much longer she could hold the fractures inside him together. Would this world finish what Trinity had begun?

'Back in space,' Cutler murmured, 'that thing from the warp that took Norliss in Dorm 31... How did it know me?'

Skjoldis sighed, knowing this conversation had been inevitable. 'The Whispersea, which you call the warp, flows through all things, Whitecrow. It reflects time and space in an infinity of shadow consequences and dim possibilities. Most of them are too tenuous and misshapen to prosper, but no whisper is ever lost and sometimes a predator will listen. The serpents – the daemons – thrive on our doubts and desires. It is their way into our world.'

She saw him struggling to understand, a plain-speaking man whose world of absolutes had been swept away by something impossible yet undeniable. He was too stubborn to accept the truth, but too honest to deny it. Such men often drowned in the Whispersea. It was why he needed her.

'That doesn't explain it,' he insisted. 'That thing in Dorm 31 looked right at me and laughed! It *recognised* me.'

'And then we killed it. That is our purpose.'

'I can feel it watching me all the time, you know. Like it's looking for a way inside. Just like it got into Norliss and all those poor damned fools at Trinity.' He sounded brittle now. 'Am I cursed, Skjoldis?'

She laughed. It was a hoarse, broken cackle that set her own teeth on edge.

'Of course you are cursed, Whitecrow!' Seeing his bleak expression she stifled the laugh. 'You are cursed and that is why you must not fail in your duty.'

'And what exactly is my duty on this sewer world?'

She regarded him thoughtfully, weighing up his mood.

'What is it, woman?' he pressed.

'Do you recall my... trance... in the chamber of stars?'

'Too damn right I recall it.' His eyes narrowed suspiciously.

'Then perhaps it is time that I told you of Abel.'

Captain Hardin Vendrake was bone weary, but sleep wouldn't come so he just kept on riding, haunting the coral avenues of the necropolis like a lost soul. At each junction he would pivot his Sentinel at the waist and pierce the gloomy side streets with his searchlight, weighing up its prospects on a whim. Sometimes he would whip past and sometimes he would take the new branch, navigating the maze as the mood took him. He'd told his men he was going out on patrol, but they'd all known it was a lie. He was riding to stay ahead of the guilt.

Leonora was dead. The leap from the drop-ship had proven beyond her limited abilities and she'd snapped her Sentinel's leg clean off. He hadn't seen her fall, but he'd heard her terrified cries over the vox as she fought for balance. She'd been calling for him, but he'd been too busy chasing a tau skimmer to pay any attention.

Too angry with her for screwing up again...

He'd found her in the mangled cockpit of her walker. Under those long blonde tresses her head had been twisted right round, dangling from a neck turned to jelly. There were two men dead under her machine, crushed and broken by her fall. Pericles Quint had played the bleeding heart card, sucking up to him as always, but the rest of Silverstorm had kept quiet and avoided his eyes. They all knew it was his fault. Leonora had never been cavalry material, but he'd kept her on anyway. She'd been terrified of the jump, but too proud to back out. And he'd let her go ahead and try.

Knowing all along she wouldn't make it...

Havardy was dead too, his steed blasted right out of the drop-ship by the tau battlesuit. His blood wasn't on Vendrake's hands, but he'd been a talented rider and his loss weakened Silverstorm. There were only ten of them left now. But despite the lost Sentinels, Vendrake had to admit that Cutler's gamble had paid off. The drop-ship had taken a beating, but the pilot had made a remarkable crash landing, saving all hands on board. Afterwards the 1st Company had taken the city with surprisingly few casualties. Unfortunately the same couldn't be said for the rest of the regiment.

With the city secured, Cutler had tasked Silverstorm with tracking down their missing comrades. Determined to cover as much ground as possible before nightfall, Vendrake had scattered his Sentinels through the jungle. At first they'd only found stragglers – men so exhausted they could barely walk. The survivors told of ambushes and xenos abominations. One battered Zouave knight, almost delirious with terror, raved about a swarm of avian monsters that had hounded his platoon from the trees, pouncing on men and tearing them to shreds. He swore the beasts had devoured the flesh of the slain. But despite the grim evidence of slaughter, Silverstorm had met no opposition. It was as if the enemy had melted away when their city fell.

The Sentinels had drifted back to the city one by one, bearing too many horror stories and too few survivors. To Vendrake's surprise, Pericles Quint had been the last to return, sauntering back to camp in his gaudily decorated machine long after nightfall. Behind him was a train of weary survivors, including an unusually subdued Captain Machen. By the sorry standards of the day it was a triumph and Quint had preened in the glow of Cutler's praise. The look on his fat face had–

Vendrake jumped as something clanged against the canopy of his Sentinel. Uneasily he swung about and angled backwards, raking the rooftops with his searchlight. Fat drops of water swarmed down the bright beam, clattering angrily against his windshield. Just moments ago he'd have sworn the rain was little more than a faint drizzle. Cursing, he flicked on his wipers and leaned forward, trying to pierce the murk. The rain-blurred buildings seemed to shrink back from his beam, recoiling from the light like startled creatures of the deep sea. Of course it was only a trick of light and shadow.

Get a grip man. It was just a splinter of debris that hit you. This place has probably been falling down forever. The rebels have fled. There's nothing alive in this tomb but us. Somehow the thought didn't reassure him.

His vox crackled, breaking the almost hypnotic drumming of the rain. 'Vendrake,' he acknowledged.

The only response was a babble of static. He tried again with the same result. Growing irritated he killed the noise and got moving. The downpour had taken the edge off the heat, turning his cabin cold and clammy.

Suddenly he was eager to get back to camp, but the poor visibility restricted him to a cautious crawl. At this rate he wouldn't be back before dawn.

The vox hissed again. He scowled and snapped it to send: 'Vendrake here. Who in the Seven bloody Hells is this?' More static. 'Quint, is that you? Look, I'm in no mood for games.'

There was a barely audible sigh, like something washed up on a tide of white noise. He leaned towards the vox, frowning in concentration as he strained to filter out the static. It sounded like someone was breathing on the other end, harsh and irregular. As if they'd forgotten how...

'Who is this?' he whispered.

'*Belle du Morte* signing in.' The voice was as brittle as dry leaves in the wind, so fragile he might almost have imagined it.

But I didn't imagine it.

Suddenly Vendrake was racing away at breakneck speed, all thoughts of caution crushed by the need to escape those haunted streets.

'*Belle du Morte*' had been Leonora's call sign.

As a bobbing trio of will-o'-the-wisps approached through the downpour, Audie Joyce pushed himself deeper into the shadows of the colonnade, holding his breath until the lanterns had faded away. He wasn't sure why he was hiding from the patrol, but he figured they'd start asking him questions – like what he was doing out here in the rain when he could be huddled up inside a habtent. He didn't want to answer questions right now. He just wanted to be left alone with the Emperor.

Screwing his eyes shut he carried on talking to Him, praying hard and fast. It was the only way to stop the tears. If he let them fall they'd drown him and he couldn't let that happen, not when the Emperor was counting on him. Uncle Sergeant Calhoun was gone and Audie's ma would be mad at him for letting that happen. She'd never understand that the old man was with the Emperor now, fighting dead heretics forever and watching over Audie to make sure he kept sending them his way. That was how things worked: the living and the dead were all part of one big justice grinder, with the Emperor right up there as the Chief Grinder. Audie still wasn't sure if *He* was living or dead, but guessed He might be both. The Emperor was complicated like that.

The greencap heard laughter from the habtent nearby and grimaced. How could the Dustsnakes be celebrating when they'd just lost their sergeant? Audie had expected the squad to pray together through the night, but after they'd reached the heathen city the men had started up with the drinking and the cards, acting like nothing bad had happened. Roach had even tried to rope him into it...

'We're just paying our respects to the sarge and blowing off steam,' the half-breed had said. 'If you don't roll with the punches they'll break you in half, boy.'

For a moment Audie had almost believed him, but then the native freak who'd become so pally with Roach had offered him a drink – some kind of filthy local brew that would probably turn him into a 'shroom. Seeing that moony, fish-eyed face grinning at him from under a decent Arkan cap, Audie had exploded. Snarling like a prairie lizard, he'd shoved the mutie right off his feet and stormed out of the tent.

Listening to their laughter, he decided the Dustsnakes were too stupid to know they were finished. There were only seven of them left and that included Toomy, who was worse than useless. The medics didn't think the sniper would ever recover from the head injury he'd taken in the boat. It made Audie mad that a brainwreck like that had survived the ambush when Uncle Sergeant Calhoun had died. He'd felt sorry for Toomy once, but now he hated him. Just like he hated all the Dustsnakes – hated them for their easy laughter and dirty jokes and all their little blasphemies. He was pretty sure Saint Gurdy-Jeff would call them heretics. Suddenly he wondered how the saint was doing.

Confessor Yosiv Gurdjief entered the Shell at dawn. The rain had finally subsided, leaving the ruins swathed in a halo of mist that writhed around his chugging gunboat. He had sailed up the great Qalaqexi River and entered the city via its central canal. Standing in the armoured prow of the boat he watched the ruins seep past like titanic, fossilised anemones, rising then falling back into the smog. This was his first visit to the dead city, but he remembered the river well, for he had travelled its treacherous paths long ago.

It was said that a man could cross the entire continent along the Qalaqexi, but Gurdjief doubted many men would complete such a journey, for deeper inland the river frayed into a tangle of tributaries that could lead a traveller in circles forever. They called that labyrinth the Dolorosa Coil. Gurdjief had once entered the Coil and returned, but he often wondered if he had ever truly escaped.

Sailing through the mist-shrouded dawn, his mind drifted back to that delirious voyage. It had been the Letheans' first year on Phaedra and Admiral Karjalan had requested volunteers to reconnoitre the wilderness behind enemy lines. It was dangerous work, but Gurdjief had been a fresh-faced lieutenant eager to make his mark. Posing as a lone pilgrim in search of enlightenment he had ingratiated himself amongst a tribe of nomads called the Nirrhoda. Even by the standards of Phaedra they had been degenerates, but they had embraced his lies and allowed him to join their wanderings along the Qalaqexi. And in time his cover story had become a perfect truth, for deep in the Coil all thoughts of spying and war had sloughed away like fading dreams until nothing had mattered but his quest for the God-Emperor's Truth.

Time flowed strangely in that grey-green limbo. He recalled years of soul-grinding despair punctuated by fleeting moments of ecstasy. He had explored lost valleys haunted by colossal, primordial beasts and wandered the sunken ruins of pre-human civilisations that made the Shell seem a modern metropolis. Deep in the coral heart of the planet he had duelled and debated with daemons, never quite knowing whether they were real or delusions and not even sure there was a difference.

Strangest of all, he had once encountered a lone tau warrior wandering the jungle in a hulking battlesuit. Judging by the cracks riddling its tarnished ceramic plates the armour had seen better days, but it was easily capable of annihilating Gurdjief, so he had offered no hostility. Instead he had tried to make sense of the mystery. The suit was painted a mottled crimson, a colour at odds with Wintertide's stark whites and midnight blacks. Gurdjief had no idea what faction the alien belonged to, but the five-flanged sunburst adorning its breastplate looked like personal heraldry, identifying its wearer as a warrior of distinction.

They had talked like fellow pilgrims, sharing tales and striving to map the impossible geometries of the Coil. The xenos was a soldier like himself, lost in time and place but still true to the mission that had led him into the wilderness. He had been vague about that mission, but so far as Gurdjief could make out he was hunting a band of traitors he called 'The Canker Eaters'.

'The savages turned on us and slaughtered my comrades,' the warrior said. 'They devoured our flesh.'

'Yet you survived?'

'I... Yes... I survived. It must be so,' but the xenos had seemed uncertain.

When Gurdjief had politely enquired about his caste, already knowing he must be a Fire Warrior, the tau had become confused. Finally he had answered 'Smoke'. Gurdjief had sensed no lie even though he knew the tau only had five castes and 'Smoke' was not one of them. They had parted without incident, neither friends nor foes, which had been a mystery in itself. Afterwards he realised that the enigmatic warrior had offered neither his name nor his rank.

Decades later, Gurdjief had returned from the Coil and found he'd been away less than a year. He could offer Admiral Karjalan neither maps nor news of the enemy. Instead he bore the seeds of revelation, together with other, stranger seeds that soon took root in the admiral's own flesh – voracious fungal spores he had carried unwittingly from the heart of the Coil. When Gurdjief's beloved Natalja also ripened with the blight he had first despaired, then rejoiced at her suffering. And so his creed had gradually taken shape. Mankind was born damned and redemption could only be achieved through divine suffering in the God-Emperor's name.

'The renegades, they are watching us,' said the commissar beside Gurdjief, drawing him back to the present. 'I have seen them spying from the ruins and scurrying away like rats.'

'They know they have strayed and must face the Emperor's judgement,' the confessor said sadly.

'The Emperor, He condemns,' the commissar offered devoutly.

Yes He does, Gurdjief agreed. *And today He will condemn this rogue colonel – this Ensor Cutler.*

The Arkan commander had spurned the *Puissance* and cheated its admiral of precious donors, sending poor Vyodor into an apoplexy of rage. That insult had been injury enough, but Cutler's victory at the Shell had sent ripples of discord all the way up to the Sky Marshall himself. In truth Gurdjief cared nothing for the Marshall's arcane schemes, but he had threatened Vyodor with removal unless the Arkan were brought to heel. That was something Gurdjief would not tolerate. Nothing must interfere with his master's sacred pilgrimage of torment.

An example will have to be made of this heretic, Cutler. Something particularly enduring...

As the canal wound into a rubble-strewn plaza a spectral army dissolved out of the mist: Arkan, hundreds of them, lined up along the banks like lost souls waiting for passage out of limbo. Most were haggard, pale-faced ghosts in grey, but a few wore those ridiculous clockwork suits that Vyodor had laughed at. Gurdjief also counted several Sentinel walkers towering over the crowd, tracking his boat with an array of heavy weapons.

'I do not like the look of these heathens,' murmured the commissar. 'Have a care my lord confessor. I have only fifty men with me.'

Gurdjief ignored him. His eyes had fixed upon a tall officer standing in the front ranks. The man's white mane lent him an ancient yet paradoxically ageless quality, a duality of faded dignity and savage vigour. He could almost taste the hatred pent up inside that apparition. A sane man would have sailed away, but Confessor Yosiv Gurdjief simply smiled, knowing he had found his quarry.

Cutler waited in silence as the robed giant leapt ashore and stalked towards him, smiling like a shark behind a morass of black hair. A skeletal commissar followed, flanked by a squad of soldiers in crimson flak-plate. Though the Letheans were heavily outnumbered and outgunned he saw no trace of fear on their vicious, tattooed faces.

'That's the maniac who did for Elias,' Machen hissed. The armoured Zouave stood behind the colonel, reined in like a thunderstorm in an iron cage. By Providence, Cutler knew how the man felt!

Whitecrow, we walk a narrow path! You must cloak your heart in ice–

Angrily Cutler shoved Skjoldis out of his mind and saw her flinch beside him. He had no patience for the witch woman's anxieties now, not with Elias's murderer standing right in front of him.

'You are Colonel Ensor Cutler.' It wasn't a question and the priest didn't wait for an answer. 'I am Confessor Yosiv Gurdjief, First Herald of the Emperor's Justice for the Dolorosa continent. You will come with me.'

'Where are my men?' Cutler asked.

Gurdjief looked at him blankly. He obviously had no idea what Cutler was talking about.

'Elroy Griffin, Grayson Hawtin and Kletus Modine,' Cutler snapped. 'Your cog priests took them away. I want them back.'

The confessor was taken aback. This fool had lost almost half his regiment, yet he was concerned about three peasants.

'They are dead, colonel,' he lied. Gurdjief expected some kind of outburst, but Cutler said nothing, almost as if he had expected the answer. 'Regrettably they succumbed to Phaedra's pestilence,' Gurdjief continued smoothly. 'As you have doubtless witnessed, this is a blighted world!'

'That it is, sir.'

Gurdjief waited, but Cutler said nothing more. Determined to seize control of the encounter, the confessor spread his hands in a gesture of openness.

'Colonel, your recent actions have caused some... consternation. Nevertheless you have won a great victory here. If you will accompany me back to the *Puissance* I can assure you a fair penitence.'

'I see.'

Another long silence. Gurdjief felt his patience fraying and he hardened his voice. 'Surely your men have suffered enough, colonel.'

'Elias Waite,' Cutler said. His eyes looked cold and dead.

'I don't follow you...'

Cutler moved like a whirlwind, wrenching his sabre from its scabbard and lunging forward in one fluid motion that tore Gurdjief's confusion into bright agony. The confessor looked down and saw the blade buried in his abdomen. Fascinated, he watched as his robes blossomed crimson around the wound.

'For Elias Waite,' Cutler said, plunging the sabre deeper. 'And all the others.'

Gurdjief gasped as the blade ripped through his back, bringing him closer to the white-haired renegade until their faces were only inches apart. He saw that the colonel's eyes were no longer cold and dead. In fact they seemed to be on fire, blazing from the man's skull like twin suns. Abruptly the confessor wondered if this was another delirium. The pain seemed so real, but perhaps he was still lost in the grey-green eternity of the Coil.

How could I hope She would ever let me go?

The sudden cacophony of battle exploded around him, but it seemed muffled and distant. Unimportant. The world had narrowed to the scope of the terrible, agonising blade that bound him to the monstrous colonel.

'Is this a dream?' Gurdjief asked.

The apparition appeared to give it some thought.

'I guess you'll know if you ever wake up,' it replied.

Then Cutler thrust the priest away, ripping his sabre free in a welter of blood. Gurdjief tottered backwards, mouthing wordlessly as he tried to break out of the nightmare before it killed him.

It cannot end here. I have walked the tainted heart of this world and wrestled with daemons and seen the secret clockwork bones of reality.

But perhaps all those raptures had been mere delusions and he himself nothing more than a madman. His feet stumbled on empty air and he toppled over into the canal. As he sank into the fecund embrace of the Qalaqexi, Yosiv Gurdjief wondered if he would indeed wake up.

The skirmish was almost over when Vendrake's Sentinel raced into the plaza, but the insanity was still burning fiercely. The captain clattered to a halt as he saw the last couple of Lethean soldiers die, blasted from the deck of their gunboat by a barrage of high velocity rounds from Silverstorm. Swarming along the banks of the canal, the greybacks roared and fired a victorious salvo into the air.

With an oath, Vendrake swung open the canopy of his machine and leapt to the ground. His legs almost buckled under him, rebelling after long hours in the cramped cockpit. His hellish journey through the city streets had lasted all night. The web of ruins had seemed to close in around him, every junction leading onto another and another, but never offering a way out. And somewhere in that maze he'd heard another Sentinel behind him, racing at a speed that should have been impossible for something so battered and broken.

Nothing is impossible or inviolable, Vendrake realised as he watched the chaos on the shore. *There are no rules and there never were. There is no sense or sanity to any of it. Waite was right. I just didn't see it until I came here. I wouldn't see it...*

A black-bearded ruffian crashed into him, howling like a savage. The captain threw him aside and pushed his way through the throng like a man fighting to reach his own execution. All around him, greybacks rushed about, whooping and jeering, some of them spraying dead Letheans with las-fire, scattering and burning the corpses like ragdolls. Vendrake heard himself railing at them, but his own words were lost to him, stifled by the shadows of the past.

It's like Trinity all over again, Vendrake realised as long-buried memories came flooding back. *The sickness in our souls rising up to make monsters of us all...*

He saw Cutler and Machen through the riot. They were standing over a broken commissar who was struggling feebly, trying to rise to feet that were no longer there. Cutler was leering down at the man with a bestial grin that turned Vendrake's blood to ice. Machen was little better; through his open faceplate the Zouave's jaws were frozen in a rictus of hate, transforming his face into a grinning skull. Only the witch seemed troubled by the madness, fluttering desperately around Cutler while her giant *weraldur* loomed over her, shielding her from the crowd. Unexpectedly her green eyes locked onto Vendrake's and she screamed into his mind: *You have to stop this!*

He was stung by the insult as much as the invasion. Of course he had to stop it! *I can't stop it. There's no turning back.* Forcing down the doubts, he barrelled his way through to the officers.

'Enough!' Vendrake yelled, shoving Cutler away from the commissar. 'By Providence, that's enough! We're Arkan, not warp-tainted animals!'

Not like the damned souls of Trinity!

Cutler swung to face him, snarling as he raised his sabre. Vendrake recoiled from the fury in the colonel's eyes, but stood his ground over the injured man and glared back, willing the madman to back down. And then a stronger will than Vendrake's joined the struggle and Cutler faltered, his face contorting as he wrestled against the invader. This time Vendrake was grateful for the witch woman's intervention, but it was a hard-fought battle. He could see her physically quaking with the effort to calm her charge. As she tightened her grip the humidity in the air froze around them and fell in a sprinkling of ice crystals. And then Cutler's sabre clattered to the ground and he looked at Vendrake with dazed eyes, like a man waking from a nightmare.

'Seven Furies for the Stars...' Cutler murmured.

Move! The witch lashed Vendrake's mind, throwing him aside as a las-bolt streaked towards him from the ground. He spun round and saw the mutilated commissar aiming a laspistol at him.

'The Emperor con–' Machen cut the Lethean commissar short with a merciless stomp.

'That's becoming a habit,' he said balefully.

As the skirmish died down, Roach felt Audie Joyce sagging in his grip. He nodded to Mister Fish and they released the greencap. The boy fell to his knees, crying like a big, broken child. *Which is pretty much what he is*, Roach figured. Still, Joyce was old enough to get himself killed if he didn't get his act together. The kid had gone wild when Cutler had gutted the crazy priest, screaming about heresy and murder. It had taken two of them to hold him down.

'Glory Days!' Dix yelled. Roach grimaced as the rangy Badlander sauntered back from the riverbank, grinning like an idiot. 'Reckon I just got me a piece of my Thunderground, boys!'

Roach spat in disgust. The skirmish had been a massacre – fifty men torn apart by nearly five hundred, including nine Sentinels! The Letheans hadn't lasted a minute. Roach had no love for the murderous bastards, but he hadn't wanted any part of it.

'What you looking at me like that for, breed?' Dix growled.

'I ain't looking at you no-how, Dixie. You ain't never been a pretty sight and I sure don't have the stomach for the new you.'

He turned his back on the mutilated Badlander.

'Don't you walk away from me, breed!' Dix pulled a knife and charged, just as Roach knew he would. The scout spun, catching Dix full in the face with a kick that sent him lurching backwards. If he'd still had a nose, it would be a ruin now.

'You really want to walk your Thunderground, man?' Roach snarled as he waded into the stunned Badlander with a flurry of punches. 'Then you got to look a whole lot harder. You got to *bleed* for your Thunderground, Dixie!'

The rest of Dustsnake looked on impassively as Roach battered the man, throwing all of the horror and pain of the past day into it. When Dix went down the scout waited, then kicked him as he tried to get up. He turned away, then thought better of it and kicked him some more, just to be sure. He noticed Mister Fish staring at him with wide, troubled eyes and felt oddly ashamed.

'Hey don't worry about it,' he said. 'Me and Dixie there, we go way back.'

'There is no going back,' Machen said with finality.

'But that priest murdered Major Waite!' Lieutenant Quint insisted. 'Surely if we were to explain what really happened...'

'What happened is we killed a ranking member of the Ecclesiarchy and his entourage,' Machen said. 'This is the Imperium, not the Capitol judiciary back home. Justice is irrelevant.'

'You sound almost happy about that, Jon,' Vendrake said, knowing that Machen loathed being called by his first name.

'I am merely stating the facts, *Hardin*,' Machen spat back.

'Or maybe the life of a renegade sounds just dandy to you...'

'We are not renegades!' Cutler shouted, his voice echoing hollowly around the amphitheatre. The meeting had been running for almost an hour, but it was the first time he had spoken. Now he eyed the seven men gathered around him, sizing each of them up in turn. They were standing in a loose circle, debating on their feet in the old Arkan manner: the last surviving officers of the 19th Confederates.

'The men we fought in this city, *they* were renegades,' Cutler went on, 'or more precisely, turncoats. They were Guard gone bad, gentlemen.'

'But do we know that for sure, sir?' Quint asked. 'What I mean is, these tau chaps seem to have quite the propensity for mercenaries.'

'We found meat tags on the bodies – regimental insignia,' Lieutenant Hood interjected. He was a Burning Eagle, curt and efficient to a fault. 'According to the tags every one of those men belonged to the 77th Oberai Redeemers.'

'And they still fought as a functioning unit,' Cutler said. 'The whole sorry regiment's probably deserted to the enemy.'

'If they got the kind of reception we did, I wouldn't blame them!' Lieutenant Grayburn blurted out.

'Wouldn't you, lieutenant?' Cutler looked at the young officer who had stepped up to fill Waite's shoes. 'Well that's worth knowing, because personally I despise them.'

Grayburn reddened and began to bluster, but Cutler waved away his protests.

'No, Grayburn, I'm not gunning for you. You did a fine job out there with the 2nd and I know you're mad after what happened to the major, but mad won't get us through this mess.'

Vendrake tried to reconcile this scrupulous, charismatic leader with the savage he'd seen scant hours earlier. It was almost as if the rage had purged Cutler, leaving him stronger and sharper than before.

Maybe that's how he deals with the truth, Vendrake thought uneasily. On the back of that intuition came another, more disquieting one. *I'm going to need a solution of my own for that particular problem, because I won't be able to bury Trinity again. Leonora won't let me...*

'Gentlemen, something stinks to High Terra about this set-up,' the colonel was saying. He had begun to pace, as if chasing an idea that wouldn't quite crystallise. 'I don't know what the Sky Marshall's game is, but it has cost us near on three hundred men and I'm done playing.' He stopped at the centre of the circle and looked up sharply. 'But we are not the 77th Oberai. We are the 19th Arkan and the 19th Arkan are not and never will be renegades nor traitors.'

Impulsively Vendrake decided to test the man: 'I doubt the Imperium would agree with you, *Whitecrow*.'

Cutler froze at his words. The assembled officers eyed each other uneasily. None of them had ever used the colonel's mock-name to his face. But when he looked at Vendrake, Cutler's expression was calm, even faintly amused.

'I fear you're likely right,' he said. 'And that's why we're going to have to play this the hard way.'

Jakob Dix drifted away from the bustle in the plaza, looking for some space before the regiment moved out. Night had fallen and the greybacks were almost done breaking camp. They'd loaded up the captured Lethean gunboat, along with some transport ships left behind by the rebels. It was going to be a squeeze, but the colonel figured they had enough boats to float everyone upriver. Dix didn't know *why* they were going upriver and he didn't much care, which was pretty much how he felt about most things. So long as there was drink and cards and maybe some gals along the way, Jakob Dix just did what he was told, but he sure did miss old Klete Modine. Things had taken a nosedive since his buddy had gone – 'Bullethead' Calhoun had bought the farm, Dix had lost his nose and now the breed had all the Dustsnakes ganging up on him. Worst of all, the squad was almost out of firewater.

Dix stopped as he saw Joyce mooning about on the banks of the canal. The big greencap was sitting on his haunches and staring into the water like it was full of gold dust. The Badlander grinned, seeing an opportunity for a little fun. If he just crept up quietly and shoved...

'Don't worry, Brother Dix, you'll get your payback,' Joyce said without turning. Dix stopped a couple of feet away, caught off guard by the strangeness in the greencap's voice.

'I weren't going to do nothing,' he said guiltily, not sure why he was making excuses to a lousy rookie.

'But you will,' Joyce said fervently. 'If you embrace His light you'll do great things, brother. Down among the Dustsnakes, you and me, we're like candles in the wind. That's why they hate us. That's why the breed beat up on you.'

'Well that weren't hate exactly,' Dix said, confused by the way this was all going. 'We just do things rough in the Dustsnakes is all.'

'*It were hate!*' Joyce snapped and turned to look at him. The boy's eyes seemed to glitter in the darkness. 'They hate you because you tried to do what's right.'

'I... did...' Dix said uncertainly.

'You and me, we were the only ones who tried to save the saint when the heathens turned on him,' Joyce said bitterly.

'We did?' It slowly dawned on Dix that Joyce had got things mixed up. The kid thought he'd run into the skirmish to fight *for* the crazy confessor, not shoot up dead Letheans. A dim instinct told Dix it was probably best to let things be.

'The heretics held me down and you had to fight for the saint alone,' the boy's voice quavered with emotion. He rose to his feet and grasped the Badlander's hands.

'You couldn't save him, Brother Dix, but don't you be despairing none. The Emperor, He don't let His chosen die easy.' Joyce nodded at the canal. 'The saint, he's only sleeping down there. I been talking to him and I tell you he's going to come back some day. And he won't forget what you done.'

'He won't?' Dix licked his lips, peering uneasily at the murky waters.

'Ain't nothing ever lost in the Emperor's eyes, but until that day comes, lesser men got to carry the burden.' Joyce was staring at the Badlander with the intensity of a hunting cobrahawk. 'You and me, Brother Dix, we got to be like Space Marines among the sheep.'

'Space Marines,' Dix said with wonder, imagining himself in the awesome armour of the Emperor's finest. Even with his face all messed up he reckoned that would win him plenty of gals. Real Space Marines probably had to fight the ladies off every night!

'That's right, brother,' Joyce urged. 'It's going to be a long, dark road out of the Hells, but we got to lead our folk true, 'coz if we don't...' He paused and Dix found himself hanging onto his words, mesmerised by the boy's intensity. 'Well, the Emperor condemns, Brother Dix. He sure does condemn.'

ACT 2

COIL

CHAPTER SIX

Imperial Seabase Antigone, the Sargaatha Sea

There are Arkan on Phaedra! They have been here nearly seven months and I never knew – an entire regiment of my kinfolk, or whatever's left of them, lost in the hell of the Dolorosa Coil. And they have gone rogue... But no, you are right. I am getting ahead of myself.

From the beginning then...

My meeting with High Commissar Lomax was perplexing and I am still trying to weigh up the implications as I prepare for my departure. The news about the Arkan was the most surprising part of it, but everything about our encounter was unexpected. Except for her dislike of me of course. Some things never change. But her contempt aside, Lomax had changed. She was already old when she arrived on Phaedra, but she had always carried the years with a grim ferocity that seemed to elevate her into something ageless. Like my mentor Bierce, this compact, dark-skinned woman with the close-cropped iron hair had once seemed the epitome of our unbreakable kind, but Phaedra had finally worn her down...

– Iverson's Journal

The haggard ghost who met Iverson in the windswept watchtower of the Antigone was not yet broken, but she was close. Lomax had shed so much weight that her greatcoat hung loosely from her bony shoulders, dragging across the floor like a sloughed skin as she prowled the confines of the tower. The whole time they talked she kept moving, flitting from corner to corner like a condemned prisoner looking for a way out. But if there was fear in her, Iverson sensed it was the fear of dying before her work was done. Even at the end, Lomax was a creature of duty.

She never questioned him about his desertion. It was almost as if she knew that pursuing the matter would oblige her to take his life. He didn't understand her mercy until he realised it was no mercy at all, but necessity. Despite her long-standing dislike, Lomax trusted him.

'You and I are relics, Holt Iverson,' she said. 'Between the two of us we've given more years to the Emperor than any ten of Phaedra's so-called commissars taken together, and I'm not talking about the snot-nosed cadets the Sky Marshall sends me these days! He chooses them himself, you know – draws them from the regiments he favours and orders me to train them up. Oh they're brutal enough, but it takes more than muscle and spite to wear the black. These idiots get themselves killed almost as fast as I can send them into the field! I haven't had a genuine graduate of the schola progenium in years. You're a bloody mess, Holt Iverson, and you brood like a Space Marine on downtime, but you're the closest thing I've got to a real commissar on this side of the planet. On Phaedra we're a dying breed.'

That was one reason why she had chosen him for the task ahead. The other was his heritage. Although he had been little more than a child when Bierce took him from Providence, Holt Iverson was still Arkan and the High Commissar's problem was with his kinfolk. And so he listened as she told him the story of a wayward regiment who had been thrown to the wolves and lived through it to become the wolves in turn.

Naturally she didn't put it quite like that – she was a High Commissar after all – but she made it easy for him to read between the lines. Besides, they both knew the reputation of Admiral Vyodor Karjalan and his hellish battleship. The admiral wasn't nicknamed the Sea Spider for nothing, but like so much else on Phaedra, his rot had been allowed to fester and spread. By the Seven Hells, Iverson was proud of the way his kinfolk had escaped the Spider's web!

'Their commander is called Ensor Cutler,' Lomax explained. 'He's the kind of man some would call a maverick hero. I don't share that view. As you know, I have little patience with... unpredictability.' She threw him a pointed glance. 'However, neither am I inclined to trust that old monster Karjalan at his word.'

Iverson was surprised by her frankness. Karjalan was a favourite of the Sky Marshall, a paragon of his stagnant regime and not a man to cross lightly. On other worlds, under other overlords, a High Commissar would have removed a cancer like Karjalan long ago, but this was Phaedra and the Sky Marshall's word was the only law. It seemed Lomax was growing reckless in her twilight.

'Colonel Cutler has led his men into the Dolorosa Coil,' she said. 'They're operating deep inside enemy territory, well beyond our advance...'

'Our advance?' Iverson snapped. 'There's been no advance into Dolorosa for years. All we do is shuffle back and forth along the same lines, winning and losing the same beaches, pushing just so far upriver before being pushed back. The whole campaign is a travesty!'

Lomax looked at him sharply and Iverson thought he'd gone too far, but her eyes were sly and calculating. Suddenly he realised she agreed with every word he'd said. She was quietly crossing a line of her own, which was why they were meeting in this remote tower rather than the confines of her office. Nothing about this encounter was quite what it seemed.

'The intelligence I've received has been sketchy at best,' she went on, 'but it seems that Cutler has spent the last seven months turning his regiment into a Titan-sized thorn in the enemy's backside. His renegades have been waylaying rebel patrols and supply convoys, sabotaging comms relays, even raiding small outposts.'

'He's loyal,' Iverson said firmly. 'Despite whatever those degenerates on the *Puissance* did to his regiment, the man is still fighting for us.'

'Or for himself,' Lomax said. 'Either way, he's stirred up a vespid's nest amongst High Command. They say the Sky Marshall has come down on Karjalan like a virus bomb, even threatened to sink his little empire unless he ends Cutler's spree.'

'Ends it? The first real incursion we've made into Dolorosa since this Emperor-forsaken war started and the Marshall wants to end it? That's insanity.'

Again Lomax threw him that sly look: 'Sky Marshall Kircher is not insane, Iverson.' There was something telling about the way she said it, almost as if the denial was a condemnation, but she moved on before he could dwell on it.

'As you'd expect, Karjalan has sent kill teams after Cutler, but the Letheans are little more than sledgehammer zealots. I doubt any of them got anywhere near the renegades. Certainly none of them ever made it out of the Coil. The Sky Marshall has demanded another approach. We need something with more finesse.'

'Surely you're not signing up to this debacle, Lomax?'

'*High. Commissar. Lomax.* As always, you forget yourself, Iverson. It's a failing that may do worse than kill you one day. And no, I am not signing up to any debacle. I am however, tasking you with tracking down our rogue colonel.'

'You want me to kill Cutler because he's actually hurting the enemy?' Iverson was aghast.

'I want you to test Colonel Ensor Cutler before the Emperor's Justice,' Lomax said, emphasising the words with steely precision. 'And then I expect you to do your duty.'

Mission Log – Day 1 – The Sargaatha Sea: Beginning an End?

Finally I am away, bound for Dolorosa Vermillion, the western archipelago where my errant kinsmen made their landfall seven months ago. There's no telling how deep into the Mire they've travelled, especially if they're following the tangle of the Qalaqexi River, but it's my best starting point. I'll follow in their footsteps and trust in the Emperor's providence. I have to believe that such a thing still exists.

Regardless, it's good to be out on the open sea again, even if that sea is more like an open sewer than a sane ocean. It'll be a long crawl in this transport tug – a rusty crate that's as worn as the war itself – but at least I'm free of the Antigone. There's a slow doom creeping up on the old sea base that's drawn closer during my absence. Or maybe it was just Lomax getting to me. That brittle, sly-eyed raven was like a harbinger of my own doom. You see, at the end she entrusted me with more than the fate of a rogue regiment...

'There's something else,' she told me.

And then she gave me a dossier sealed with a scarlet ribbon. She offered no explanations or instructions, but as I took it I understood that she was passing on a curse. Can one more really make any difference to me? How many times can a man be damned?

Day 2 – The Sargaatha Sea: The Fall of the 19th?

No, I've not touched the scarlet dossier. There are other, more prosaic documents that require my attention first. I have a whole heap of reports on the Arkan 19th and their role in the civil war back home. I never knew there'd been another Arkan uprising, but I won't say I'm surprised. We're a reckless, restless folk and this Ensor Cutler reads like the worst of us – an arrogant glory hunter who leads his men on little more than a wing and a prayer. It's no wonder that his record is such a patchwork mess of distinction and notoriety. The deepest mystery here is why he fought for the Imperium instead of the rebels. But no, that's not entirely true. There is another mystery – something that doesn't quite fit with his fast and loose, yet always heroic exploits: the massacre of a backwater town called Trinity. I haven't found the details yet, but my gut tells me it matters. I must dig deeper. Lomax's scarlet dossier will have to wait.

Day 3 – The Sargaatha Sea: A Fourth Shadow

Lomax didn't warn me about my shadow. No, I'm not talking about my dead shadows – my ghosts appear to have taken their leave of me for the present – but the living, breathing spy who has attached herself to me. Commissar Cadet Ysabel Reve caught up with us this morning, ferried in by a speeding sea skimmer. The first thing I noticed about the girl was her height. She can't have been much past twenty, but she was almost a head taller than me and I'm taller than most. Everything about her was hard and brutally efficient, from her lean, muscle-plated build to her square-jawed face and shaven scalp. Her storm coat and boots glistened with polish, complementing the bright silver pin of the Sky Marshall's chosen. By Providence, the girl was even carrying a gold-plated autopistol!

I didn't believe any of it for a moment...

– Iverson's Journal

'Yes, I'm sure you're a first-class shot, Reve, but that won't be nearly enough in the Mire.' Iverson shook his head. 'This isn't going to be a routine patrol. I won't be able to look out for you, girl.'

And I don't want to be looking over my shoulder for you.

'I have done three stints on Dolorosa Azure,' the girl said in a clipped, guttural accent he couldn't quite place. 'I will pull my weight, sir.'

Iverson didn't doubt it. The band of her cap might be blue, but this woman was no raw cadet. He wasn't even convinced she was a commissar. That pristine storm coat and fancy autopistol were a façade to lull him into thinking she was green, but he'd learnt never to trust the obvious. A person's story was written in their eyes and Ysabel Reve's were flat and cold. They told an assassin's tale.

She's not here to learn from me or watch my back. She's here to finish the job if I can't. Or stab me in the back if I won't. But who sent her?

'Look, does Lomax know about this?' Iverson said.

'Indeed yes, the High Commissar approved my appointment personally, sir.'

'I see. Well, we're only three days out of Antigone,' Iverson said with a shrug. 'I'll get her on the vox to confirm that. For your sake, you understand.'

'I am sorry, sir. Did you not receive the news?'

'I have no idea what you're talking about, cadet.'

'Sir, High Commissar Lomax is dead.'

Iverson stared at her.

'She died the day after you sailed, sir. I assumed you knew.'

'How did she die?' he asked flatly.

'She fell from the watchtower, sir. The medicae believe she died instantly.' Reve lowered her eyes. 'I am sorry. I know that you and she were friends.'

'Friends...'

'Yes, the High Commissar always spoke highly of you, sir. In the training sessions.'

Did she really? Somehow I doubt that, Reve.

'They say it was suicide.' The girl hesitated and Iverson could see she was thinking, weighing him up. 'I am sorry, sir,' she repeated finally.

Once again, Reve, I rather doubt that.

Day 4 – The Sargaatha Sea: The Scarlet Testament

I am troubled by Lomax's death. We were never friends but she was a constant in this changing-changeless morass. She was true to her vows to the Emperor and utterly unswerving in her duty. And at the end she chose to trust me.

I must make the time to study the papers she passed into my care... But no, that is sheer prevarication! Time has nothing to do with it! This damnably slow tug has given me all the time I could possibly need, but I cannot bring myself to break the scarlet seal of that dossier. I can feel it bulging with documents and picts, almost certainly hiding the truths that killed her. I know my duty, yet I hesitate. Why?

Where are my ghosts when I need their counsel?

Day 7 – The Sargaatha Sea: Shadowplays

We are due to rendezvous with the Puissance tomorrow. Her

reputation precedes her, but this will be the first time I actually set foot on that grim old battleship. Apparently Admiral Karjalan wants to brief me personally. I suspect I'm his last hope of staving off the Sky Marshall's displeasure so he'll offer me the best he has. That will be a gunboat and a platoon of his finest men, probably the infamous Penitent Corsairs. From what I've heard about those zealots they're just about the last troops I'd want along on a mission like this. I have enough to worry about with Cadet Ysabel bloody Reve looking over my shoulder all the time. That girl's playing a sharper game than I first gave her credit for...

– Iverson's Journal

'Commissar Iverson, may I speak with you? Off the record?'

'You're a commissar, Reve.' *Aren't you?* 'You know nothing's ever off the record.' He glared at her. 'Especially something you want off the record. Out with it.'

'Very well,' she steeled herself visibly. *Overacting again...* 'I do not believe the High Commissar killed herself, sir.'

'You don't?' Iverson was surprised.

'Sir, High Commissar Lomax was a true hero of the Imperium,' Reve said passionately. Iverson was impressed – the girl sounded genuinely upset. 'She had too much steel in her soul to take the easy way out.'

'What are you getting at, cadet?'

Reve hesitated before looking him straight in the eye.

'Sir, I believe she had enemies amongst High Command. I believe she might have discovered something. Something damaging.'

'That's a very serious allegation, Cadet Reve,' Iverson said, watching her closely. 'What do you think she was on to?'

'I was hoping...' She paused, returning his intense scrutiny – *Testing me as I am testing her* – 'I was hoping that she might have told you, sir.'

He had to admit she was good. If she hadn't overplayed her hand with that spotless uniform and ridiculous sidearm he might even have believed her.

'Why would you think that, Cadet Reve?'

'Because she trusted you, sir.'

'Perhaps not as much as you think,' Iverson said. 'Look, I've got nothing for you, cadet. Lomax was old and worn to the soul with this filthy planet. Maybe it was just plain suicide.' He turned away from her. 'Despite what you've been led to believe, none of us are unbreakable. Sometimes things are simply what they seem.'

But not you, Ysabel Reve, most definitely not you...

Day 8 – The Puissance: Death Ship

If ever a ship was tainted, it is this ancient Lethean ironclad. I'm no damned psyker but I sensed it the moment I saw her on the horizon, rising like an iron canker on a sea of sludge, vast and dark and spiteful as the Seven Hells. They say the Puissance hasn't moved in over a decade – not since old Karjalan took ill and disappeared from sight – and I have no reason to doubt that.

The water around the ship was encrusted with a rime of glutinous algal scum. Thick tendrils of the stuff had climbed the hull, twining round the corroded battlements and binding the vessel to its floating grave. The morbid tribulation continued on the deck, where corpses hung from the ship's crane, some of them still fresh, others little more than skeletons. And wherever we wandered I saw the metal glistening with a patina of slime, something excreted rather than acquired, almost as if the iron marrow of the vessel itself was polluted.

By Providence, even the Mire feels pure beside the Puissance! It appals me to tarry here, but Karjalan was unable to see us until after nightfall due to a shipboard crisis. It seems that a prisoner broke free of the brig shortly after our arrival. I wonder at the man who could manage it and cause the Letheans such vexation. And I admit that I wish him well in his flight from this charnel ship. Whoever he is and whatever he has done, his crime cannot be greater than Karjalan's own.

As I prepare to meet the admiral, one thought gnaws at me: if the web is so foul, then how much worse the Spider?

– Iverson's Journal

'Forgive the theatrics, Commissar Iverson, but I fear I am not the man I used to be,' the voice warbled from the darkness, sounding desiccated and damp in the same breath. 'But despite Her depredations, Phaedra has not yet worn away my vanity.'

Iverson peered across the chamber, trying to pierce the gloom, but the speaker hadn't put his trust in shadows alone. A silk screen had been drawn across the furthest recesses of the room, turning the man into a vague silhouette. He could make out little more than a hunched shape swaddled in heavy blankets. Occasionally its arms would wave about loosely, stick thin and oddly frayed, but it was impossible to gauge its height or build. For all he could tell, Admiral Vyodor Karjalan looked exactly as he sounded: a mummified corpse bloated on congealed blood.

Shaking off the unwelcome image, Iverson tried to focus on the admiral's words, but his thoughts came slow and muddy. The humidity in Karjalan's chamber was worse than anything he'd experienced in the Mire, almost like a hydroponic hothouse. The air was hazy with the bittersweet reek of incense, but the smoke couldn't quite disguise a deeper stench – the promise of something ripe with decay.

The soporific effect was heightened by the rhythmic gurgle-hiss of an arcane life support array in the far corner. Two Lethean priests attended the machine while a Penitent Corsair in scarlet plate stood watch. A muddle of pipes sprouted from the array like questing, industrial creepers. Some trailed away behind the admiral's screen, while others coiled around a body lying on a pallet nearby, its waxy flesh pierced by a lattice of needles. Iverson could see the victim's blood being siphoned away into that greedy snarl of pipes.

'I trust my medication does not disturb you?' Karjalan wheezed, seeming to read the commissar's mind.

'I'm long past being troubled by anything I see,' Iverson lied. He couldn't help taking some satisfaction in Cadet Reve's pallor. Perhaps the assassin wasn't quite as cold as he'd first imagined.

'Nevertheless, I am grateful for your indulgence, commissar.' The admiral chuckled and his silhouette jerked fitfully. 'I occasionally toy with making an end of things, but my service to the Emperor prohibits it. And my beloved Letheans would be lost without me. Indeed, they vie with one another to offer up their blood that I may live.'

'Admiral, I am hoping to set out at first light,' Iverson said, struggling to pull his thoughts into order. 'I'll be needing a gunboat and...'

'Do you find my conversation so tiresome, commissar?' Karjalan hissed. 'Are you bored with me so soon, *Arkan*?'

Iverson ignored Reve's sidelong warning glance and forged on.

'Admiral, I'm here on the Emperor's business...'

'As am I! Have you not heard of the Lethean Revelation, commissar?'

'I've given it little thought.'

'Ah, but you must! You see the Emperor condemns!' Karjalan cackled wetly. 'And I am holy! So damnably holy it hurts!' Abruptly his humour dried up. 'Your kinfolk have done me a grave insult and a graver injury, Holt Iverson. Tell me; are all the men of Arkan such savages?'

Iverson hesitated, taken aback by the insult. To his surprise Reve spoke up: 'My Lord Admiral, Commissar Iverson has often told me of the shame he feels over the conduct of the Arkan 19th. His blood ties have made the matter personal for him.'

'The matter is *personal* for me also,' Karjalan said. 'These Arkan scum slaughtered fifty of my Letheans in cold blood, together with a man who was like a brother to me!'

'Confessor Yosiv Gurdjief,' Reve said with a nod. 'His murder was a heinous crime against the Ecclesiarchy...'

'It was a crime against *me*!' Karjalan shrieked, splattering the screen with ichor.

'Sir, I assure you that Commissar Iverson takes this matter...'

'Be silent you soulless bitch! Does your precious master have no voice of his own? Where's your tongue now, eh, Iverson? Won't you speak up for your backwater brothers? Don't you have the courage to–'

There was a wet pop and Karjalan's voice disintegrated into a ragged cough. His form heaved and something raked the curtain spasmodically. One of his attendant priests flitted urgently behind the screen.

'My Blessed Lord, you must not excite yourself so–'

The priest's admonishment was choked off as something lashed out and seized him by the throat. Horrified, Iverson and Reve watched the priest's silhouette shudder to its knees, twitching frantically. The other two attendants watched the mayhem with something like rapture on their faces.

'This is monstrous,' Reve whispered, beginning to rise.

Iverson caught her wrist, then her eyes, holding both in an iron grip.

'This is Phaedra,' he said.

They heard something rip violently behind the curtain and more fluid splattered the fabric. This time it was dark and viscous.

Day 9 – The Sargaatha Sea: Penance and Pain

We sailed from the Puissance at dawn, but my relief at escaping that tainted ship is tempered by shame. The reality of the Sea Spider proved to be much worse than the darkest rumours: Karjalan is an abomination in body and soul. Duty demands that I take his life, yet duty also demands that I keep my own for now. Duty delights in making a man dance on hot coals! But I digress...

Once Karjalan was done with feasting his reason returned and he remembered that I was his last hope of tracking down the rogues. With ill grace he granted my request for a Triton-pattern transport – an amphibious gunboat capable of negotiating both land and water. They are fine vessels and woefully rare on Phaedra. If we had more such vehicles we might have won this war long ago. I am beginning to wonder if that is why we have so few...

In typical Lethean fashion my craft is called the Penance and Pain. I won't deny that it is a fitting name.

– Iverson's Journal

'I do not trust them,' Reve growled, indicating the troops in scarlet plate prowling the deck below. 'They are the creatures of a debased heretic.'

'A heretic who thinks he's a martyr to the Emperor,' Iverson said. 'Look, it's not a question of trust, cadet. This ship is Lethean. I had to take her crew. Besides, we couldn't sail her alone.'

They were standing together on the upper deck, watching the Penitent Corsairs lumber about their duties with brutish determination. There were eight of the hulking zealots on board, every one a tattooed, shaven-headed thug bristling with devotional charms and totems. To Iverson they looked more like steroid-boosted hive gangers than professional soldiers, but their equipment belied it. All of them wore sculpted body armour with jagged shoulder plates and conical helmets that flanged into fins at the sides, giving them a distinctly marine look. In place of regular issue lasguns they sported high-powered hellguns connected to fluted, shell-like backpacks.

In a more sober regiment Iverson guessed the Corsairs would be classed as storm troopers, but these elites had a propensity for fevered prayer and self-flagellation. Fortunately they went about the business of war as if the Emperor Himself was breathing down their backs, never slacking on patrol and manning the gun emplacements to port and starboard as if they were holy shrines.

The more mundane matters of sailing and maintaining the craft fell to the lowly Penitent Mariners. Iverson wasn't sure how many of the scraggy ratings they had on board, but he guessed there must be at least twenty. They were all filthy, tangle-haired ruffians who revered the Corsairs as holy knights. In turn those worthies treated them as slaves, regularly brutalising and beating them. It was a tried and tested dynamic that Iverson had seen countless times over. It could be as strong as folded steel or as brittle as rotten timber.

'How can they believe that abomination serves the God-Emperor?' Reve sneered.

'Karjalan believes it himself,' Iverson said, regarding her curiously. 'Besides, he's a creature of the Sky Marshall. Isn't that enough for you?'

Reve looked at him sharply: 'It is not, sir.'

'That mark you're wearing says otherwise.'

'This?' She jabbed at the silver icon on her lapel, understanding dawning on her face. 'This is why you do not trust me?'

'I didn't say that, Cadet Reve.'

'You did not have to,' she glared at him with what looked like real bitterness. 'The Skywatch is nothing to me, but with respect sir, you are a *starblood*.'

'What in the Seven Hells are you talking about, cadet?'

'Commissar, you were sent to Phaedra from... from somewhere else,' Reve gestured vaguely towards the sky. 'You arrived with rank and honours, but I was born in the mud and blood of this war – just another Guard brat among thousands. This is the only world I have known. There is no schola progenium here, only the Skywatch Academies. They are the only path to advancement for my kind.'

'But you trained under Lomax?'

'Only because I am of the Skywatch!' With a snort she ripped the badge from her lapel. 'But if they murdered the High Commissar I want no part of them.'

'Be careful, Reve.'

'I am done being careful.' She flipped the badge overboard with an indifferent flick and stalked away, leaving Iverson frowning at her back.

You almost had me there, but you overcooked it again at the end, girl.

His frown turned to a sour smile as he noticed Bierce standing vigil at the prow of the ship. The old revenant had his back to Iverson, intent on the dismal coastline of Dolorosa Vermillion rising on the horizon. Seven long months ago the Arkan 19th had landed on those shores and disappeared into Hell.

And wherever you've gone, brothers, be sure that I'll follow.

Iverson's grin faded as he realised his augmetic hand had jammed up, locking his grip to the railing.

Day 10 – Vermillion Sound: The Broken Man
I have returned to the Mire and my ghosts have returned to me, creeping back one by one, as I always knew they would. It is only

right and proper, for Commander Wintertide still lives and my penance is not yet done. Fortunately their restoration has blessed me with a strange clarity. I am now certain that this hunt for my rogue kinsmen is part of my greater quest. It cannot be coincidence that our threads have crossed the stars to interweave in the Dolorosa Coil. Somehow Ensor Cutler will be the key to my salvation. Somehow he will open the door to Wintertide.

Yet despite my conviction I cannot put Lomax's death – her murder – from my mind. I believe the High Commissar knew her enemies were closing in and the scarlet dossier is her last testament against them. If I don't accept it she may yet rise and make my trio of ghosts into four. I have welcomed my shades back, but I will not countenance another on my conscience. No, it's time to face her will.

I have the dossier beside me, but I cannot seem to rally my thoughts. With nightfall the mouldy reek of the Mire has become almost overpowering in the confines of my cabin...

– Iverson's Journal

Iverson paused, his pen hovering over the page as he listened for the sound. A moment later it came again – a low, ragged rasp, like a man struggling for breath. He turned slowly, his hand slipping towards his holster as he squinted into the murk of the cabin. The lantern perched on his desk cast a flickering aura that merely taunted the gloom. Iverson rose to his feet and raised the lamp over his head, trying to throw back the crowding shadows. There was something lurking at the threshold to his small washroom.

'You ain't got no call for the shooter,' the intruder said. Its voice was little more than a hoarse croak, but the accent was unmistakeable, even though Iverson hadn't heard that thick burr in decades. *Arkan.*

'Show yourself,' Iverson demanded.

'Not a problem, but I got to warn you, I ain't a pretty sight, brother.' The shape shook with something between a chuckle and cough, sounding uncannily like the infested admiral. Suddenly Iverson recognised the rancid ordure wafting from the shape – it was the same stench that had permeated Karjalan's chambers.

'You're no brother to me,' Iverson said.

'I heard you talking up on deck,' the shape drawled wetly. 'I can tell you've been gone a while, but you ain't lost your Providence twang. You're Arkan. In this hellhole that makes us brothers.' With that the speaker stepped from the shadows. He was a massive, craggy-faced brute, naked save for a filthy medical smock. His mottled skin hung from his bones in sagging wattles, as if his flesh had been sucked dry.

'The name's Modine, Private third class, 19th Arkan Confederates,' the intruder said. 'And I could sure use a drink if you've got anything going.'

* * *

Day 11 – The Shell and Dolorosa Breach: The Sleeping Front

We sailed through the Shell at dawn. The coral maze was deserted, long abandoned by the Imperial forces that had followed in Cutler's footsteps. The men of Dolorosa Breach had occupied the necropolis for less than a week before evacuating to the saner, safer horrors of the Mire. We found them a couple of leagues upriver, entrenched in a sprawling tract of burned jungle. Cadet Reve was dismayed by the chaos, but the ragtag army was no worse than I'd expected. Thanks to Cutler's efforts our advance has staggered a little further inland, only to falter into stagnation once more. I suspect they haven't moved in months.

We stopped off for supplies and I took the opportunity to requisition fatigues and a flamer for the fugitive who crept into my quarters last night. I'm not entirely sure what to make of Private Kletus Modine and his escape from the Puissance, but he was right about one thing – we are both Arkan and I cannot surrender him to the Sea Spider. Besides, after the horrors I witnessed on board that death ship I have no reason to doubt his story.

For the record, Modine told me he was the last survivor of three troopers taken by force and bled dry to curb the admiral's disease. I won't elaborate on the lurid details of his torment and escape, but it seems he got wind of our arrival and made a break for it, surprising the captors who thought him comatose. He's brazen to the point of insubordination and tests my patience relentlessly, almost as if he's daring me to shoot him, but I won't do it. There's more to Kletus Modine than meets the eye and he may yet prove to be my only ally on this journey. I have claimed a storage berth alongside my cabin for the stowaway. For the time being he will remain my secret.

Oh yes, there was one more thing: a prisoner waiting for us at the Breach...

– Iverson's Journal

'Please, you have to get me back to my squadron,' the haggard youth in the tattered jumpsuit pleaded. 'I'm a pilot, you see. And a member of the Skywatch!'

'I understand, Airman Garrido,' Iverson said coldly, 'but you'll have to give me something on the renegades if you want my help.'

'But I've told you everything I know! The scum hijacked my ship and flew us into the Shell. I swear I fought them, but that old heretic Ortega betrayed me! And then they all turned on the Letheans...'

'And you're quite certain that Cutler killed the confessor personally?'

'I saw it myself. That white-haired savage is insane. He was like a man possessed, but they were all bloody barbarians! Now please, you can't let me rot down here...'

Iverson dismissed the pilot, already convinced he knew nothing more.

Jaime Garrido had been found hiding out in the Shell, abandoned when the renegades fled upriver. The commissars of the Breach had kept him locked away in anticipation of this fleeting, fruitless interrogation.

The pilot was still pleading when Iverson walked away. For Jaime Hernandez Garrido it was the end of the road.

Day 13 – The Qalaqexi River: Modine's Blasphemy

Tonight I returned to my quarters and found Modine trawling through Lomax's testament. The scarlet ribbon lay on the floor and her precious secrets were scattered about my desk: classified troop and munitions reports, officer psych assessments, tactical maps and surveillance picts and Emperor knows what else, all passing through the grubby hands of a diseased greyback. He met my shock with a cheerful leer...

– Iverson's Journal

'You needed a push,' Modine said. 'I seen you staring at this thing like it was a ticking bomb. You was too scared to open it, but too hungry to back off. Well you've been good to me, so I figured I'd lend a hand, chief.'

The insolence washed over Iverson as he approached the muddle of papers. Now that the secrets were out their call was hypnotic, reducing Modine to a faintly irritating irrelevance.

'Of course, I ain't never been too sharp with my letters,' Modine went on, 'so I ain't got too far...'

'Leave,' Iverson interrupted, his eyes never straying from the documents. 'Aw, come on, Holt...'

Iverson spun round and Modine found himself staring down the barrel of an autopistol. The commissar's surviving eye bored into him, an open window to somewhere glacial and unforgiving. To the greyback it looked less human than its augmetic partner. Modine raised his hands slowly. 'Hey, no worries, brother.'

Iverson's face twitched with an involuntary spasm. 'Out,' he said.

Keeping his eyes on the gun, Modine nodded and backed out of the cabin. Iverson's ghosts took his place, drifting from the shadows to encircle their beacon as he sank into a chair and began to read.

Day 16 – The Qalaqexi River: The Wages of Truth

I haven't stirred from my cabin since the night Lomax's plague of truths was loosed, but there's still so much to digest. It will take weeks to sift through her catalogue of errors and inconsistencies and accounts of sheer stupidity and bloody-minded madness, but one thing is already certain: we have all been betrayed.

– Iverson's Journal

Reve was pounding at his cabin door again.

'I'm busy,' Iverson growled, rubbing at his surviving eye. The augmetic one was buzzing furiously, threatening to gnaw a hole through the back of his skull.

'Sir, you have not been on deck in days,' Reve called from behind the locked door. 'The Letheans are beginning to ask questions.'

They should be asking questions, Reve. We should all have been asking questions long ago.

Day 17 – The Qalaqexi River: Seven Stars

We are sailing through no-man's-land. The sleeping ghosts of the Shell and the Dolorosa Breach are far behind us. The hungry ghosts of the Qalaqexi Coil lie ahead. There are no Imperial forces past this point save for a few scattered jungle fighters working deep recon. We're on our own and if we run into a significant rebel detachment we'll soon be dead. But that's unlikely to happen once the great river narrows and frays into the Coil.

I've never been this far inland, but I know the stories of the infamous labyrinth. There are dozens of paths to the heart of the continent and many more to nowhere at all. If we go slow and silent and the Emperor's Grace goes with us, we might stay undetected for months. Of course logic dictates that this is a double-edged sword, for how will we in turn find our quarry? Well, my friend, this is where we must abandon logic and cleave to faith, or whatever else it is that guides us. You see, despite the odds I know that we shall find them. Or they shall find us...

– Iverson's Journal

'I want this hoisted,' Iverson said, unravelling the heavy banner. The Seven Stars of Providence glittered against its deep blue fabric, looking impossibly bright in the murky dawn light. The Lethean Mariners shuffled about, casting uneasy glances at their armoured overlords. One of the Corsairs stalked over and inspected the flag with unbridled disgust.

'The Penitents, we do not sail under false idols,' he growled.

'You're talking about the Seven Stars, the flag of my home world; a world that has stood by the God-Emperor for ten thousand years,' Iverson lied, quite certain these ignorant zealots wouldn't know any better.

'But is Lethean ship...'

'No, it's the Emperor's ship and I am His appointed servant on this holy mission. Do you question His word?'

The Corsair glared pure hatred at him, but Iverson paid him no heed. 'Hoist it,' he snapped at the Mariners. 'Now!'

As the seadogs scurried to obey, Cadet Reve raised a quizzical eyebrow.

'Before you ask, I had it commissioned back on the Antigone,' Iverson said. 'As to why, Cadet Reve... Why don't you tell me?'

'Obviously you are hoping to draw the renegades out,' she answered without hesitation. 'That was not my question, sir.'

'Then enlighten me, cadet.'

'If they do come, what will you say to them?'

'What do *you* think I should say?'

She hesitated. The game between them was growing more treacherous by the day. Finally she made a cautious move: 'That is not for me to say, sir.'

'A good answer, Reve,' Iverson said and turned his back on her.

Day 19 – The Qalaqexi River: The Mouth of the Coil

We entered the Coil at dusk. The jungle seemed to darken and close in around us as we slipped into the embrace of that primal morass. Even the Lethean thugs were unnerved by the change and I suspect there will be no end to their coarse prayers tonight. Dead Niemand, who approves of their ways, has urged me to share their worship, but I no longer believe the God-Emperor cares for such prattling. Like the Coil, my own faith has unravelled into something dark and tangled, yet I sense His hand pulling at the threads, urging me forward. I can only hope that He isn't laughing.

– Iverson's Journal

It was raining again, the heavy drops punching through the dense canopy to spatter the leather-coated commissars standing watch on the upper deck. Iverson ignored it, so Reve ignored it too, their intransigence an unspoken bond.

'What do you think we'll find in here?' she asked, eying the grey-green walls of the Mire seeping past on either side.

Vengeance, Niemand gloated.

Justice, Bierce glared.

Redemption, Number 27 beseeched.

'All or nothing,' Iverson said. *My Thunderground,* he thought.

CHAPTER SEVEN

PROVIDENCE MILITARY ARCHIVES,
CAPITOL HALL
REPORT: GF060526
STATUS: *CLASSIFIED*
FROM: Major Ranulph C. Kharter, Investigating Officer (Internal Affairs)
ATT: General Thaddeus Blackwood, Director (Internal Affairs)
REF: War Crimes – 19th Arkan – Trinity Township, Vyrmont
SUM: As per orders I have undertaken an investigation of the frontier township designated *Trinity*. Preliminary evidence supports claims the town was razed with maximum prejudice. All structures have been burned. A mass grave was discovered on the town perimeter (speculate intent of concealment) containing several hundred corpses. Despite advanced decomposition the bodies were clearly burned, but the cause of death appears to be various and violent. No evidence of significant rebel affiliations apparent.

CON: Further investigation recommended.

Note: What in the Hells did Cutler do to these poor bastards?

The bell tolled again, booming somewhere deep inside the prisoner's gut. He moaned as he felt himself slipping back into the hungry old nightmare. Awakening again...

It was long after sunset, but the blizzard had stained the night white, transforming the old town into a blur of crooked silhouettes lost in static. The gale whistled through the narrow avenues like a forlorn ghost, stirring up the snow around the intruders as they pressed on toward the town square. Every man in the squad was half-frozen and bone-weary, but if there was any welcome to be had in this backwater burg it would surely be there.

We'll find no welcome here. None that we'll be glad of anyways...

Major Ensor Cutler thrust the gloomy thought aside, irritated by the dark mood hanging over him. It was strange that victory had left him feeling so hollow, but word of the rebels' final surrender had reached the 19th late, catching the regiment deep in the Vyrmont rifts with the first frost of winter already in the air. They had been hounding Colonel Cadey's infamous Liberty Brigade and the old warhawk had led them a wild chase, fighting to the last man despite Cutler's entreaties that the war was already over. It was a shabby epitaph to a shabby war. Cadey had been a courageous foe and hunting him down like a mad dog had left Cutler feeling dispirited and dishonoured. More importantly it had left the 19th battered, exhausted and lost in the middle of nowhere with the Big Freeze bearing down on them. Hoping to outrun the winter they had marched south, but the snow had caught up within days, tormenting them like Cadey's vengeful spirit. When men began to die, Cutler had scattered the Sentinels into the wilderness to scout for shelter. He hadn't held out much hope, but two days later *Muse in Iron* had called in a discovery.

'Major, I've gone and found you a town,' Lieutenant Nevin 'Kiljak' Jaxon had voxed, his smugness loud and clear through the distortion. 'It's not much to look at, but this far north....Well, I'd say it's a miracle it's here at all.'

Cutler hadn't argued. Taking a squad of volunteers, he had forged ahead to reconnoitre the town while the regiment trailed behind with the wounded, but hope had soon turned to bitter disappointment. Their sanctuary was a ghost town. His hails had gone unanswered and the creaking timber houses they'd checked out had proven stone cold and empty. They'd found no victuals or anything else of use either.

What they had found was a bizarre, almost clinical mayhem: garments shredded to thin strips and furniture smashed to matchwood, even utensils bent out of shape. No object had escaped intact. Strangest of all, the detritus had been arranged into neat, geometrically perfect piles, forming shapes and structures that seemed redolent with meaning yet at the same time totally senseless. The junk sculptures had lured the eye and reeled in the mind with the need to *understand*. Even the memory of those deranged symbols made Cutler's head pound. And then there were the pervasive messages scrawled across the walls of every hovel, sometimes painted, sometimes carved, but always the same:

'THE BELL TOLLS, THE WORLD UNFOLDS'

'These hicks sure must've loved this damn bell of theirs,' Captain Waite had observed gruffly, but Cutler had wondered. Was it love or something darker that had inspired such devotion?

As they pushed on towards the square, his thoughts kept returning to that enigmatic bell, chewing over the mystery with growing disquiet. And then he heard it. A discordant note rumbling under the wind, so deep it was almost subliminal.

The echo of a drowned bell...

For a moment the snow whirled apart and he caught sight of a tall shadow in a wide-brimmed hat standing in the street ahead. He couldn't make out its face, but some instinct told him it was looking directly at him.

'Who goes there?' Cutler hollered over the squall, but the snow had already swept the wraith away. He strained, listening for another chime, looking for the stranger, but both were gone.

If they were ever there at all...

'What's up?' Elias Waite yelled beside him, his voice muffled by the woollen scarf wrapped around his face. Clearly the old captain hadn't noticed anything untoward. Nor had any other member of the squad for that matter.

Cutler peered warily at the shuttered windows on either side of the narrow street. They were just dark blurs through the swirling whiteness, but he imagined furtive eyes behind every one of them, watching the intruders with growing malice.

'Ensor?' Waite urged.

'Quinney,' Cutler called to the squad's vox-operator, 'any word from *Muse in Iron* yet?'

'Been trying to raise him every couple of minutes, sir,' the skinny greyback answered. He was hunched miserably under the bulky vox-set strapped to his back. 'Ain't got nothing since before sunset. Could be the storm fragging with the comms of course,' he finished doubtfully.

Cutler frowned, wondering if Jaxon had run into trouble. He had ordered the cavalryman to meet them at the edge of town, but like most Sentinel riders, 'Kiljak' was a cocksure chancer who couldn't sit still to save his hide. Besides, what did a Sentinel have to fear from a bunch of stir crazy inbreeds?

'It don't feel right, does it?' Waite said, sensing Cutler's mood. 'You know, I'm thinking maybe we ought to pass on this hand, Ensor.'

'We've a killing cold at our backs, old man,' Cutler said. 'Even if this town's dead we can hole up and wait out the storm here.'

'And what if it ain't dead, just dying?'

'I'm not losing another man to the snow, Elias.'

Although it might be a cleaner way to die than all the filthy fates waiting for us here...

Uneasily Cutler waved his squad onwards.

The prisoner stirred, his body fighting unconsciously against the restraints that bound him as his mind fought against the hooks dragging him inexorably deeper into horror...

They found *Muse in Iron* standing forlornly in the town plaza. The walker's canopy was thrown wide open but there was no sign of Jaxon. Cutler halted the squad at the edge of the square, hanging back in the cover of the street. His instincts were jangling like alarm bells and his muscles were taut with a tension he couldn't explain.

Why do I feel like I'm trussed up like a steer in a slaughterhouse?

'I see a light,' Waite said, tapping his shoulder. Cutler followed his pointing finger to a tall building that loomed over the rest like a hunchbacked giant. It was a crude edifice built from timber and brick, but it had probably pushed the ambition of this stunted town to the limit. The light was seeping through a huge, lopsided window above the portico. Something, probably the glass, had stained the glow into a polychromatic chaos that writhed like a living thing in the white noise of snow.

'Now that has to be the sorriest excuse for a temple I've ever seen,' Waite growled. Cutler saw him touch the aquila pendant hanging from his neck.

Warding off evil. In his rough-and-ready way, the captain had always been a true believer.

But it didn't save you, Elias...

An inexplicable pang of sadness hit Cutler as he looked at his old friend. He was suddenly sure that Elias Waite was long dead.

'Why you looking at me like that, Ensor?' Waite asked, but Cutler had no answer for him.

That was when someone stepped from the temple. For a moment the newcomer stood silhouetted against the rainbow light, swaying gently as if unsure of its balance, then it began to walk towards them, homing in on their position with unerring accuracy. The squad tensed up around Cutler like a gestalt animal, raising lasguns and bayonets like defensive spines to ward of a predator. Then the stranger emerged from the varicoloured haze and they recognised him.

'Jaxon!' Cutler called out.

The tall cavalryman stopped a few metres away. His finely chiselled features looked flat and lifeless without their characteristic smirk, but it was his dead white hair that turned Cutler's blood to ice. When Jaxon had departed the regiment two days ago his hair had been a deep brown.

'Lieutenant, what happened here?' Cutler pressed. 'Why did you abandon your Sentinel?'

Jaxon looked at him with eyes like painted eggs – false eyes only pretending at life. 'They gave me a choice sir,' he said in a flat monotone, every word flowing into the next without texture or inflection. 'Many choices actually so many there was really no choice at all sir.'

'Who gave you a choice?' Cutler stepped forward, wanting to shake the man, but instinctively unwilling to touch him. 'Are you talking about the townsfolk, lieutenant?'

'No the townsfolk are all gone sir.'

'Gone where? Are you saying they're all dead?'

'No not dead they're still here just gone sir.'

'You're not making any sense, man.'

'That's as it should be if you just look between the lines they'll show you how it really is sir.'

'Who are *they*?' Cutler said, taking another step towards him.

'Oh you'll see them soon sir they already see you.' Jaxon's hand came up holding a bright dagger. 'They say I have to go now.'

'Easy son, we're here to help you,' Waite said steadily.

'There is no help.' The ghost of a smile haunted Jaxon's face as he put the dagger to his own throat. 'And all the choices are lies.'

'Wait!' Cutler shouted, but it was too late. The cavalryman jerked the dagger convulsively and bright arterial blood sprayed into the blizzard. For a moment he just stood there watching his life drain away, then he looked at Cutler and his lips moved as if he wanted to say something more, but his vocal chords were gone so he just sighed and toppled. His corpse hit the snow with a sonorous clang that reverberated across the square.

Cutler stared at the corpse in confusion, unable to link that concussion of sound with the sight. Then the boom came again and he glanced up at the temple, suddenly understanding. It was the bell tolling. Calling to the damned...

And the damned came by the dozen, bursting from shadowed doorways and windows like starved rats. They were the citizens of the blighted town, broken ghouls eager to share their curse. Despite the cold, most were stripped to the waist and their flesh shone blue with the frigid kiss of hypothermia. A few carried antique firearms, but most made do with the makeshift weapons of home and hearth. They laughed and wailed in an ecstasy of misery as they bore down on the greybacks.

'Fire at will!' Cutler roared without hesitation, but the townsfolk were already on top of the squad, hacking and slashing with wild abandon.

Cutler rammed his sabre between the tines of a jabbing pitchfork and twisted, tearing the weapon from his attacker's numbed hands. The peasant glared at him, one eye burning with fury, the other brimming with merriment. His cadaverous face was a bipolar caricature, the left side twisted into a rictus of joy, the right into a snarl of hate. It reminded Cutler of the grotesque carved masks he'd seen back in the Capitol playhouses.

'Stand down!' Cutler shouted at the disarmed man.

With a sob of joy the maniac leapt forward and impaled himself on Cutler's blade, then thrust onwards, rapturously disembowelling himself as he groped for his killer. Horrified, Cutler rammed his autopistol under the man's jaw and blew away that insane flesh mask. As he struggled to withdraw his sabre an axe came chopping in from the right. Desperately he swung the impaled corpse round and caught the blow. The axe man ululated furiously, his distended face rippling like melting wax as he struck again and again, trying to break through Cutler's meat shield.

The bell tolls and the world unfolds...

Cutler caught snatches of his beleaguered squad through the chaos. He heard the boom of Waite's antique bolt pistol and the throaty roar of Sergeant Hickox's chainsword revving up. To his right he saw a burly greyback thrashing about with his bayoneted lasrifle, holding back the crazies while another knelt beside him, snapping off wild rounds into the teeming horde. To his left he saw Belknap go down, his face split wide open by a meat cleaver. His killer, a mountainous matron with a bone-white mane, waved her weapon about and howled triumphantly. Cutler put two bullets into her skull and she toppled like a felled tree.

'Give no quarter!' Cutler bellowed.

Something tugged at his arm from below, sending his pistol tumbling away. He glanced down and saw a scrawny girl child latched onto his wrist, trying to gnaw through the heavy fabric of his greatcoat. She had the face of a shrivelled crone and her eyes were sewn shut. With a cry of revulsion he pulled his arm away, but the urchin clung on and came with it, her feet kicking the air as he tried to shake her loose. The meat shield pinned to his sabre was coming apart under the axe man's blows so he let the sword go, sidestepping as the madman toppled forward under his own momentum. With his free hand he wrenched the child loose and threw her through a broken window. Then Waite was at his side, tearing into the horde with explosive bolt-rounds. It bought Cutler a moment to retrieve his sabre.

'Form up around me, Arkan!' Cutler yelled, beheading the axe man as he clambered to his knees. 'Fall back in good order!' Three men had gone down in the first onslaught, but the survivors held their nerve admirably, pulling together into a tight phalanx and covering every approach as they backed away down the street. Hickox cleared their path with his buzzing chainsword while the others kept the horde at bay with pistols and bayonets.

'What's got into these wretches?' Waite shouted as he ejected a spent clip, but the revulsion in his voice told Cutler he had already guessed the truth. While civil war had raged across their world, another, more insidious madness had taken root in this forsaken town. The soul taint had come to Providence.

A cadaverous hag leapt from a window overhead in a shatter of glass. Screeching manically she landed on Trooper Dawson's back and clung on with her scrawny legs. He thrashed about frantically as she clawed at his face, sending the man beside him skidding to the ground. Seeing an opening, the horde rushed in like wolves, leaping over their dead in a frenzy of blissful bloodlust. A pitchfork nailed the fallen greyback through the back of the neck, pinning him to the snow. Another trooper hurried to fill the gap and caught a barbed pole in the gut. Dropping his weapon he clutched at the spear, his face frozen in shock. A moment later he was gone, tugged from the phalanx by his unseen assailant.

'I'm through 'em!' Hickox called from the back.

Cutler glanced round and saw the sergeant standing over a heap of slaughtered degenerates. With visibility down to a few metres there was no telling what lay in the street beyond, but it was their best chance. The defensive phalanx was disintegrating under the sheer weight of the horde and once the crazies got in amongst them it would be over.

'Disengage!' Cutler bellowed. 'Withdraw at speed!'

Run... It was a bitter order to give, but the alternative was suicide and they had to live through this. The cancer they had stumbled upon here must not be allowed to spread.

'Move yourselves!' Cutler slashed about in a wide arc as the surviving greybacks raced past Hickox. Waite was still at his side, firing two-handed to control the violent bucking of his bolt pistol.

'Just like Yethsemane Falls, eh Ensor!' Waite growled, knowing full well this was nothing like that honest bloodbath. Fearing it might be something infinitely worse.

'Get clear!' Sergeant Hickox yelled behind them as he threw a grenade over their heads. Cutler saw it fall among the throng and felt the concussion at his back as he spun and ran, pushing Waite along in front of him. The frag grenade tore through the close-packed townsfolk like a shredding wind, throwing mangled bodies into the air and bowling others from their feet. It didn't stem the tide for more than a few heartbeats, but it was enough for the battered platoon to vanish into the blizzard.

As they raced through the streets, Cutler heard the frustrated howls of the cheated ghouls loping after them. Trooper Dawson was just ahead with the hag still clinging to his shoulders like a crazed jockey. He kept flailing at her as he ran, protecting his bleeding face but unable to dislodge her. Cutler caught up with him and swept away her head with a surgical slash of his sabre, but her legs remained locked tight. Abruptly Dawson giggled and threw him a broken look. One of his eyes had been gouged out and the other was wide with madness. Then the big greyback whirled around and ran back the way they had come, ignoring Cutler's shouts. He made to follow, but Waite pulled him back.

'He's gone, Ensor!'

A shutter flew open alongside the squad and a shotgun flared in the darkness beyond. The vox-set on Quinney's back exploded, sending him sprawling into the snow. Waite put a burst of fire through the window while Cutler stooped to haul the injured man over his shoulders. Then they were running again, storming through the town gates with hell on their heels. A wooden sign flashed past. It was wormy with rot, but the crudely carved words were still legible:

'WELCOME TO TRINITY – Pop. 487'

Not any more, Cutler thought grimly.
Not on either count.

The prisoner awoke to the sound of his own ragged laughter. Blinded by the sudden brightness he felt himself falling again. This time he held on, pushing away oblivion as he struggled with the straps binding him to the high-backed chair. Finally the glare resolved itself into a padded cell and he remembered that he was still...

...dreaming.

There was an alien staring at him through a shimmering force barrier. Its face was a wizened wedge of faded blue, unmistakably ancient, but its eyes were bright with fascination.

'Welcome, Colonel Ensor Cutler,' the xenos said in perfect Gothic. 'I am Por'o Dal'yth Seishin of the Wintertide Concordance and it is my sincere aspiration that you and I shall walk in friendship.'

CHAPTER EIGHT

Day 44 – The Coil: Adrift
Reve is right. We are completely lost.

– Iverson's Journal

'If you do not know your place in the Tau'va, you do not know yourself. And if you do not know yourself you have no place at all.'

– Winter's Tide

Claiborne Roach battered his way through another wall of clinging fronds and burst into the clearing beyond. His breath came in short, ragged gasps now, trying to keep time with his hammering heart. The rain thundered down in an angry barrage, churning the soil into treacherous mulch, but he didn't dare slow his breakneck pace. His pursuers were too close. He could hear them crashing through the foliage and calling to each other, no more than thirty paces at his back. He'd cut the chase fine, but sometimes a man had to play for all or nothing.

With a whine of displaced air a tau drone shot by overhead and spun to scope him. He threw the hovering disc a grin as he raced forward, flashing past the coral corpse at the centre of the clearing. The ruin was little more than a broken stub, but it was enough to sterilise almost twenty square metres of jungle. And it was more than enough for his plan.

He heard a triumphant shout as the first of the Concordance janissaries broke into the clearing and spotted him. Fine beams of markerlight lanced around him as he hurtled towards the trees ahead. Dredging up a last burst of speed he dived for cover, ducking under the lattice of violet fire that swept after him. Rolling to his knees, he tore his carbine free and swung round, but it was already over.

As the janissaries raced past the ruin, Roach's comrades rose from behind the coral and unleashed an enfilade of their own markerlight into their backs. The hunters' weapons deactivated in a bleeping tide of mock kills, taking them out of the game in quick succession. Their leader swore and threw down his dead carbine as Roach ambled back from the foliage to join his victorious cluster. Mister Fish met him with a grin and they slapped hands like old gang buddies. And truth to tell, the Saathlaa guide *was* the closest thing Roach had had to a friend in years. The *askari* had told him his real name once, but 'Mister Fish' had already stuck and the native didn't seem to mind it. Life would be a whole heap easier if more folk just went with the flow like the Fish, Roach reckoned.

'That was well done, Friend Roach,' Ricardo Alvarez, the leader of their cluster declared. 'Your skill in the field almost compensates for your doubts about the *Tau'va*.'

'Doubts keep a man sharp,' Roach quipped.

'*Kauyon*,' someone said behind them, speaking in an inflectionless electronic monotone. They turned and Roach squinted, hunting for their hidden observer. He nodded in satisfaction as he spotted a vaguely humanoid shimmer lurking at the edge of the clearing. The translucent shape looked like it had been sculpted out of thin air by the rain; in other conditions the tau stealth suit would have been almost invisible.

'You honour us, Shas'ui Jhi'kaara,' Alvarez said with a bow, acknowledging the tau's compliment. *Kauyon*, which loosely translated as 'the Patient Hunter' was one of the two fundamental philosophies of the tau art of war. It was an approach dedicated to stealth and cunning, stressing the use of a lure to entrap the enemy.

'It was a passable execution of the principle, but you risked much,' the rain-shadow continued. 'If your foe had fielded pathfinders the ruse would have failed.'

'They were cocky,' Roach said. 'I knew they'd fall for it.'

The shape flickered then blurred into solidity, revealing a compact black battlesuit with a hefty burst cannon attached to its right arm. To Roach the xenos looked like a bulkier, better armoured Fire Warrior rather than a stealth operative, but as with all things tau its advantage lay with techno-wizardry. Although there was no arguing with the effectiveness of the suit's integrated distortion field, Roach didn't regard it as *real* scout-craft.

'And you, Janissary Roach,' the tau said, 'were you not equally... *cocky*?'

Recalling the grin he'd flashed the observer drone, Roach shrugged affably. 'Like I said, I know my business, *shaz-wee*,' he answered, stumbling over the alien honorific.

'You are gifted with spirit, but crippled by arrogance,' the tau observed.

'It's not like that,' Roach said, surprised he cared enough to argue.

Staring into that inscrutable, crystal-studded faceplate, he found himself wondering what Jhi'kaara actually looked like. Alvarez had said their officer was female, but that angular armour and toneless vox-coder gave nothing away. Nevertheless something about the alien's manner told Roach that Jhi'kaara was indeed a she. She could sure be bitchy as hell when the mood took her, which was all too often. Whatever else she might be under all that plate, the lady was certainly one angry xenos.

'You will either live long or die quickly, Janissary Roach,' Jhi'kaara concluded before amplifying her voice to address the rival clusters. 'This exercise is ended. We will return to the Diadem.'

And then she was gone.

Alvarez slapped Roach on the back and grinned, 'I think our shas'ui likes you, Friend Roach!'

The Cuttlefish troop transport nosed its way through the clinging smog, skimming just above the surface of the lake. Its whirring anti-grav rotors barely stirred the turgid expanse of water.

Dead water, Roach thought. Mister Fish had told him the place was called *Amrythaa*, which meant 'Wellspring of Life', but Roach guessed things must have changed a whole lot since the ancient Saathlaa had done their naming. The great lake was virtually an inland ocean, but its size didn't make it any less dead. Or any less rank...

Roach hawked and spat over the side of the vessel, adding a dram of black saliva to the ooze. The stench rising from the water was bad enough, but what really got to him was the smog. It hung over the entire valley, dusting the vegetation with soot and congealing into thick scum on the water's surface. The stuff got everywhere, making skin itch and throats burn, but there was no escaping it during the crossing. The tau had issued them all with rebreathers, but the cheap masks clogged up fast, making them worse than useless. Only the real arse-kissers persevered with them, always keen to suck up to their alien masters.

Of course those masters don't share our misery, Roach observed sourly, glancing at the armoured xenos standing at the prow of the skimmer. Doubtless Jhi'kaara's helmet was equipped with a proper filtration system, unlike the mass-produced junk doled out to the human grunts. Still, at least she showed her charges a little respect, unlike the rest of the blueskins on the Diadem.

The Diadem. Now there was another screwed-up, highfaluting name for a place. Guido Ortega had explained that 'diadem' was a fancy word for 'crown', but there was nothing regal about the Mechanicus monument that crowned the dead lake. In fact the massive refinery was just about the ugliest thing Roach had ever set eyes on. Hidden deep within the Coil, the rig dated back to Phaedra's first pacification, making it almost a thousand years old.

And it sure as the Hells looks its age...

Roach could see the relic looming out of the smog now, towering over the lake on a frame of stilts and pipes like a colossal jellyfish cast in iron and rockrete. Its mantle was a puzzle-box of manufactories and hab-tenements that bristled with chimney stacks and coolant towers, all bound together in a web of pipes and catwalks. The visible section was as big as a town, but Roach knew the monster's tendrils ran deep beneath the water, piercing the silt lakebed and burrowing into the living coral like an industrial vampire. Down there they were busily sucking the blood out of the planet and pumping it back up to the distilleries to be sifted and refined into promethium. In return the engine threw out waste on an epic scale, flooding the valley with toxic slag and smoke.

No wonder Lady Phaedra hates us so much, Roach thought. *We've been ripping out Her guts for centuries. Compared to us the tau are just gnats. Even if they have stolen our thunder here...*

As they drew closer to the monster he heard its heart pounding – a deep, hungry beat that rippled through his blood and set his teeth chattering. Like the smoke, the rhythm was at its most painful out in the open where there was no cover. Soon enough the vomiting began, running through the janissaries like a tide of nausea, with poor Ortega suffering the worst of it. Roach saw the elderly Verzante hugging the side of the boat, looking shockingly grey and drawn. The once portly pilot had slimmed down and toughened up since he'd thrown in with the Arkan, but he was just too old for this kind of punishment. Roach decided he'd talk to Alvarez about letting him sit out Jhi'kaara's endless games. Rumour had it she was looking to recruit a batch of trainee pathfinders, but Ortega was never going to make the grade, so why push him? Besides, if the old man's heart gave out Roach's own plans would be well and truly fragged.

Suddenly a wave of dazzling light cut through the smog, casting the world into a negative image of itself. The janissaries shielded their eyes, but the beam passed by in seconds, swept away as the titanic lamp continued its steady rotation. Mounted in the apex of the Diadem, the great beacon was like a tireless eye that watched over the lake for approaching enemies. Uneasily Roach wondered if the sentinel could see right through him. As if to confirm his anxieties, the transport was swathed in light again as the floodlights of a Devilfish punched through the mist. Roach found himself holding his breath as the hover tank pulled up alongside them and disgorged an inquisitive drone. Jhi'kaara's own drone rose to greet it with a burst of machine chatter and the guardian slinked away satisfied.

It's just routine, Roach chided himself. *I should be used to it by now.*

He had been at the Diadem nearly a month now and was no stranger to this journey, but it still unsettled him. He'd counted at least six Devilfish prowling the lake, their patrol intersected by darting Piranha skimmers and twittering squadrons of gun drones. A heavier tank lurked by the feet of the rig, tracking their approach with a massive turret-mounted ion cannon. Alvarez had told him the Hammerhead was a tank killer, a variant on the standard Devilfish that sacrificed transport capacity to pack more punch. Eyeing that big gun, Roach guessed even a glancing hit would take out a Sentinel. The xenos were taking no chances here.

I've never seen so many blueskins in one place, he mused. *Maybe it's just the promethium they're after or maybe it's something more, but this old rig is important to them. It might even be their HQ in the Coil...*

The transport glided into the nest of piers splayed around the refinery like lazy tentacles and nosed its way towards an empty berth. Hulking, heavily armoured combat servitors patrolled the promenade, gliding back and forth on elegantly moulded anti-gravity skirts. Their heads were little more than nubs of dead meat protruding from iron torsos, hanging between their massive shoulder pads like dried fruit. Roach shuddered at the sight of their sightless, milk-white eyes. By any yardstick that counted, servitors were dead men, mind-wiped and melded with machines to serve as soulless thralls to the Imperium.

Except these walking corpses aren't even walking and they sure don't serve the Imperium no more...

While all servitors were mongrels of man and machine, these creatures were tri-part hybrids, twisted a notch further away from humanity by the touch of xenos-tech. The smooth contours of their anti-gravity skirts betrayed their alien origin, along with the burst cannons welded to their right arms and the drone antennae jutting from their skulls. Those high-tech plumes linked the dead men into the Diadem's security array, granting them an eerie sharpness that sickened Roach more than all the other violations heaped upon them. Sometimes he'd swear there was real hatred burning behind those cataract-encrusted eyes...

If the tau are so bloody enlightened, why didn't they scrap these poor bastards when they set up shop here instead of joining in with the fun?

But Roach already knew the answer to that one. His time among the Concordance had taught him plenty about the tau mindset. While many races fastened onto grand notions like honour, glory or righteous hate, the tau simply got on with the job of winning. For all their fine talk of the Greater Good they were hard-nosed pragmatists: a race of materialists who saw the world as an ornery, but essentially logical, place that could be chipped, whittled and sometimes just plain hammered into shape. More to the point, they hated waste and loved tinkering, hence the fate of the augmented zombies they'd 'inherited' at the Diadem.

Although technically the zombies don't belong to the tau, Roach reflected. *I guess the cogboys are still pulling their strings.*

The servitors weren't the only relics on the rig. There were a whole bunch of Mechanicus priests here, including a full-blown magos, backed up by an army of tech-guard – Alvarez called them '*skitarii*.' These augmented heavies were the rig's permanent garrison, as opposed to the janissary clusters who just passed through for training. At first Roach had been surprised to find the skitarii were all drawn from native Saathlaa stock, but given the age of the Diadem it made perfect sense. The original off-world soldiers would have died out long ago, forcing the priests to recruit – or more likely enslave – replacements locally.

Of course the priests themselves were a different matter. Such men had the knowledge to make themselves virtually immortal, although the price they paid might make them unrecognisable as men. After centuries of augmetic butchery there was no telling what Magos Kaul and his cronies were hiding under their flowing red robes, but Roach doubted it would be anything he'd call human.

I still don't know what the deal is with this place. What have the cogboys been doing here for all these centuries? Were they stranded after the first pacification lost steam or did they want *to stay? And what about now? Are they working alongside the tau or are they just glorified slaves like the rest of us?*

As he hauled himself up onto the pier, Roach realised he was still a long way off cracking the Diadem's secret. Probably he never would.

'Subject 11 persists in obfuscating my endeavours to establish a rapport, habitually retreating behind a barrier of atavistic hostility.' Por'o Dal'yth

Seishin paused to gather his thoughts, steepling his fingers in an oddly human gesture. 'He presents a most perplexing, yet compelling paradox.'

Perched cross-legged on the padded dome of a floating throne drone, the tau Water Caste ambassador had the look of a mystic immersed in some profound meditation. His emaciated body was swathed in an azure robe of shimmering silk that flared into a rigid, high-backed collar to frame his hairless skull. Although his face was little more than a wedge of bone wrapped in grey parchment, his black eyes shone with vigour. At eighty-three he was an ancient, his lifespan extended well beyond the natural limits of his species thanks to Magos Kaul's juvenat techniques. Doubtless some of his more orthodox colleagues would disapprove of such artificial longevity, but O'Seishin knew it was all for the Greater Good. He had entered the Fi'drash conundrum at its inception and would see the matter through to its logical conclusion. However, if everything proceeded according to plan that would be a very long time coming.

'As I have posited previously, the gue'la are afflicted by a racial predilection towards extreme psychoses,' he continued. 'I would further postulate that the fungal pathogens contaminating this planet's atmosphere might induce a psychotropic response in emotionally charged individuals...'

There was a chime at the chamber door and O'Seishin sighed. 'Suspend recording,' he ordered his attendant data drone. 'Come.'

The scarred warrior who entered offered only the hint of a bow. It was a slight from one of her rank; she was a veteran of the Fire Caste, but he had attained the pinnacle of his own. While tau society attached no stigma to those of lower rank, experience was to be respected and obeyed. In the absence of a ranking Fire Warrior he was her superior.

'You summoned me, O'Seishin,' Jhi'kaara said, using his personal name with impudent familiarity.

'That is so, shas'ui,' O'Seishin answered, countering her disrespect with perfect courtesy. 'Regrettably your request for reassignment to front line service has been denied. It seems your most excellent mentoring of the gue'vesa neophytes precludes it. Your talents are too valuable to place in jeopardy.'

And you are best placed precisely where I can see you, he thought.

'I am a warrior,' she said bitterly. 'I was born to fight.'

'Correction: you were born to fight for the Greater Good,' O'Seishin said smoothly. 'And for the time being the Greater Good requires you to forge capable janissaries.' His nostrils flared in the tau approximation of a smile. 'I do however have some good news for you. Your achievements here have been recognised by the shas'el and he has approved your promotion to the rank of shas'vre.'

'What of my request to meet with the shas'el?' There wasn't a trace of gratitude in her tone. O'Seishin frowned, finally becoming exasperated by her insolence.

'It is in process,' he said, 'but the acting commander is burdened by manifold and onerous responsibilities. Be assured that he will summon you in due course.'

'It has been many *rotaa* since I reported the gue'la's treachery at the Shell,' Jhi'kaara urged. 'I swore an oath of consequence to my comrades when they died.'

'Shas'el Aabal has been informed of your concerns. In the meantime I have requested an XV8 battlesuit for you, shas'vre.'

'That is unnecessary–' she began.

'*It is necessary,*' he snapped. 'According to the records you are battlesuit trained and you are now the ranking Fire Warrior here. You must be prepared for any eventuality.' He glanced at the chronolog on his data drone: his session with Subject 11 was due shortly. 'Regrettably I must excuse myself, shas'vre. I am also burdened with multifarious responsibilities in service of the Greater Good.'

'No, friend Roach, you're still not getting it. The Greater Good, it don't work that way,' Alvarez urged. 'It's something new, man. Something better than the lies the aristos and the padres been telling us since forever.'

'I see that, but grunts like you and me, we still don't matter none,' Roach said. 'Sure, these tau boys treat us decent enough – a whole lot better than the patricians did back home – but that don't mean they *care* about us.'

'They gave me back my voice, Friend.' Alvarez tapped his scarred neck. It was an old wound and a favourite parable of the Verzante deserter. 'I told you how that crazy commissar busted me up real bad, right? So why did the tau put me back together if I don't matter?'

There were murmurs of agreement from the other Concordance janissaries gathered in the dormitory. Mister Fish looked uneasy and Ortega threw Roach a warning glance, but he ignored them both, too irritated to back down.

'They fixed you up because you're a good soldier,' he insisted. 'You're *useful* to them, but you're still just a cog in the Big Machine, just like you was back in the Imperium.'

'No, we're talking a whole different *kind* of machine here, Friend Roach,' Alvarez said. 'Sure I'm a cog, but so are the Fire Warriors and the Water Speakers – even the Ethereals themselves. See, we're all in this together, everyone doing their bit for the Greater Good. And we're in it because we believe, not because some crazy *pendejo* in black leather is holding a gun to our heads.'

'And they don't judge a man by his blood,' Estrada piped up, nodding meaningfully at an obese Verzante slumped on a bunk. 'Else fat Olim over there would still be calling all the shots.'

'That's right!' Alvarez was nodding furiously. 'The tau reward a man by what he can do, not the clan he's born into.'

'But that don't go for the tau themselves,' Roach said triumphantly. Seeing their blank faces he pressed on. 'I mean for *them* it all comes down to how they're born, right? A tau that's born a warrior won't get to build anything and one that's born a builder won't get to fight, no matter how angry he gets. Every caste is a prison they can't ever escape.'

'Why would a warrior want to build anything?' Estrada seemed genuinely confused.

'The newcomer is implying that your logic is flawed, Señor Estrada,' the pariah, Olim observed languidly. 'He is actually rather bright for a peasant.'

'You say something back there, aristo?' Estrada snarled, rounding on the fallen nobleman. Olim cringed, instinctively shielding the bruised potato of his face.

'Be easy, Friend Estrada,' Alvarez restrained his comrade. 'Friend Olim already knows his place in the *Tau'va*.' He flashed a benign smile at the cowering noble. 'The latrines will need cleaning before you start your shift in the comms tower. Don't disappoint me now, Friend Olim.'

Olim scurried away like a plump mouse, keeping his distance from the others as Alvarez turned his smile on Roach: 'As for you, Friend Roach, you're still new to our cluster and have a way to go, but you got to open up your mind...'

'That's what I keep telling him,' Ortega said, ambling over with a conciliatory smile. 'But will he listen?' He gave Roach a pointed glare and the scout shrugged helplessly. Ortega had indeed warned him repeatedly against baiting their fellow janissaries, but Roach still kept walking into the same old arguments. The crazy thing was he *liked* Alvarez and the rest of them. Sometimes he even caught himself thinking there might actually be something to their whole Greater Good deal.

'We must make allowances,' Ortega continued. 'I fear these Arkan churls don't have the wit and wisdom of Verzante Seabloods like you or I, Friend Alvarez.'

'That's no excuse, Friend Ortega. Just look at his kinsman over there.' Alvarez indicated another neophyte whose face was buried in a laminated copy of *Winter's Tide*. 'He's picking up the path real quick. Isn't that so, Friend?'

The reader looked up and his disfigured face broke into a gap-toothed grin: 'For the Greater Good,' Jakob Dix drawled. 'Damn straight.'

'It ain't right,' Audie Joyce growled over the inter-suit vox. 'We've been watching these xenos-loving heretics near on a month now, but we're still skulking in the hills like jackals. This ain't what the God-Emperor forged us for!'

There was a crackling chorus of assent from the other Zouave knights hidden along the ridge. They were spread out in a loose line overlooking the smog-choked lake far below, keeping watch on the activity around the rebel base. All they could see of the refinery itself was the slow gyration of its beacon light, but their vantage point took in the connecting waterways, revealing a restless flow of ships back and forth between the lake and the rest of the Coil.

'We've found the heart of the cancer, brothers!' Joyce went on fervently. 'How long must we wait to burn it out?'

Captain Machen frowned, once again regretting the arrogant greencap's promotion to the Zouave brotherhood. 'We'll wait as long as it takes, boy,' he said. 'The colonel will send word when it's time.'

'No disrespect intended sir, but he's probably skrabmeat by now,' Joyce said.

'Ensor Cutler is alive. If he was dead *she* would know.'

'And you'd trust the word of a Norland witch, captain?' Machen blanched at the scorn in the youth's voice. 'emperor's Blood, she might even be working for the blueskins!'

Once again the Zouaves lent Joyce their support and Machen gritted his teeth, biting clean through his unlit cigar. The boy had only been among the Steamblood Brotherhood five months, yet the old guard was rallying around him as if he was some kind of hero. Joyce's meteoric rise had exceeded Machen's worst fears about opening up the brotherhood to commoners, but there had been no choice.

During their first weeks on Phaedra the Arkan had been hit hard by the planet's more insidious taints. Fever and fungal infections had swept through their ranks like wildfire, laying almost everyone low. Thirty-three men had never recovered, including two of Machen's Zouaves, leaving him with eleven warsuits and just nine nobles to wear them. Forced to recruit from the common greybacks, he had been determined to find the best.

Unfortunately the *very* best had proven to be a rookie from Dustsnake squad whose passion for the Imperial creed bordered on stupidity. His comrades had taken to calling Joyce 'the Preacher' and most were only half-joking. The youth's brand of hellfire rhetoric was backed up by true grit, winning him plenty of admirers, while his apparent immunity to Phaedra's ailments had sealed his status as a rising regimental legend. Machen, who still suffered from a dozen disorders, detested him with the malice of a fading alpha wolf. If the boy hadn't been so damnably talented he would have weeded him out long ago, but his instinct for the iron was uncanny. Within weeks of his initiation Joyce had been throwing his armour around like a veteran. A month later he'd surpassed the lesser knights. After that it had been too late to expel him.

'The Emperor has blessed our flesh with iron and our hearts with fire,' Joyce was ranting. 'I won't hang my fate on the ravings of a barbarian witch!'

'That's enough, boy!' Machen snapped, furious to be defending the woman, who he personally despised. 'The colonel trusts her and she's led us true so far. We've no cause to doubt her now.' He could almost taste the friction on the vox-band, but Joyce had just enough sense to shut up. Wrestling down his irritation Machen levelled his voice. 'We're the steel backbone of the 19th, not a pack of greencap hotheads fired up by the Gospel. We've got our orders and we'll stand by them. If we throw that away we're nothing but renegades.'

'He's back,' Valance's voice crackled into his ear over a secure channel. 'Just got into camp this minute, captain.'

Machen acknowledged the scout and stalked away, leaving Wade in command. His old wingman was the only Zouave who hadn't bought into the boy preacher's mystique – the only one who was still loyal to the old order. Stomping down the other side of the ridge he wondered how things had become so hellfired complicated. How had he ended up backing Ensor bloody Cutler and speaking up for his Norland whore? The Machen of old would have been champing at the bit to turn the tables on them both and make a play for command. In truth he'd have shared the boy's eagerness to take the battle into the valley. What had changed?

Ringing in the changes, like a cawing, clawing canticle of crows heralding damnation valley, where dead men come to cast the die…

Machen snorted at the words that had slithered into his head like leeches. The Seven Hells take Ambrose Templeton and his confounded ramblings! Machen supposed it was guilt that had prompted him to keep the notebook left behind by the vanished captain. They had never been friends – far from it in fact – but there was no denying that Templeton had proved to be an able leader on their first day in this hell, yet Machen had turned his back on him.

Go away, he'd said when the man had asked for help. And Templeton had. That was why Machen had begun to read his notebook and somehow never stopped. He always got lost somewhere around the halfway mark, where the tale turned slippery, its meaning contorting upon itself and forcing him to go back and reread from the start. Over and over again…

Am I haunted by a dead man's unfinished tale?

The thought made him shudder inside his carapace. Whatever the truth of it, Templeton's doomed epic had wormed its way into his soul, leaving him riddled with doubt. These days his thoughts kept drifting back to his lost wife and daughters, dragging him down to a horror that rage alone could no longer tame. Once again he swore to burn the treacherous book, knowing full well he never would.

'The risk is too great,' the witch insisted, her eyes boring into Vendrake like viridian suns. 'The forces arrayed against us at the Diadem are many and grievous. We cannot squander the Sentinels on this venture of yours.'

Exasperated, Vendrake threw himself down onto the stool opposite her. Skjoldis saw that his hand shook as he wiped the sweat from his sallow, stubble-smeared face. It was sweltering hot in the cramped cabin, but the Sentinel captain was used to such things.

What he isn't used to is being on the wrong side, she reflected. *Even if he understands that the wrong side is actually the right side.*

The regiment's self-imposed exile had been difficult on all of them, but Hardin Vendrake had taken it harder than most. For all his rakish posturing he was an idealist and idealists had further to fall. Certainly the ragged apparition slumped across from her was a far cry from the dashing patrician officer of old. With his unruly hair strangled up in a red bandana he looked more like a feral jungle fighter than a graduate of the Capitol Academy.

Especially with that indigo stain in his eyes…

'Captain, I have asked you to abstain from the Glory,' she said. 'The fungus carries a taint.'

'And I've told *you* the Glory keeps me sharp,' he shot back with a sickly grin. The tension between them had eased after she saved his life back at the Shell. Sometimes she even felt they were drifting towards a brittle friendship, but he still didn't trust her.

And why should he when the Whitecrow and I have kept our secrets so close? We should have told him about Abel long ago. He deserves the truth.

'When did you last sleep?' Skjoldis asked.

'Look, I'm touched by your concern witch, but that's not why I came to see you.' Vendrake leaned forward, glaring right into her face. 'We have to bail this commissar out.'

'If you save him he will almost certainly turn on you,' Skjoldis said with a sigh. 'Such men are not renowned for their forbearance, captain.'

'But he's flying the Seven Stars. And he has the look of an Arkan. I think he wants to talk.'

'Or he plans to trick you.'

'It's a chance we have to take,' Vendrake urged. 'We've been playing Cutler's game almost nine months now, wandering around the Coil like pawns on a regicide board, chasing after a redemption only the two of you seem to understand...'

'And I have promised you that the endgame is in sight.'

'That's not enough anymore!' he snarled, showing stained teeth. Drawn by the captain's anger, Mister Frost loomed out of the shadows behind him. Skjoldis shook her head and her hulking guardian faded away, but Vendrake had caught the movement. Since their exile he had grown almost preternaturally sensitive to the slightest movement at his back, almost as if he were afraid something was creeping up on him. Or *galloping* up on him, she sensed in a frisson of psychic empathy.

He still blames himself for the death of his protégé.

'You must calm yourself, captain,' Skjoldis said with a peculiar sense of déjà vu. Did a streak of madness run through every Arkan officer? Was it her doom to play nursemaid to one tortured patrician after another?

'The men are running out of hope, witch.'

'And you believe that a commissar can give them hope?'

'I believe he can give them *legitimacy*,' Vendrake hissed. Seeing her scorn he slumped back and closed his eyes, hovering at the edge of exhaustion.

She waited.

'Beauregard Van Hal,' he said in a whisper. 'You won't know the name because he keeps himself to himself, but he's probably my finest rider. Might not have a whole lot going on up there,' Vendrake tapped his temple, 'but he's loyal to a fault and born to the cavalry.'

'I do not follow your meaning.'

He silenced her with a weary hand. 'The other day Van Hal asked me why we were fighting the rebels when it was the Imperium who wanted our hides. He was wondering why we didn't just sign up with the tau like all the other sorry dregs who've been screwed over in this mess. You know what I said?' He opened his eyes and looked at her with a terrible blankness. 'I didn't say a damn thing.'

'Vendrake, you need to be patient. The Diadem is what we've been searching for. Once the colonel sends word...'

'It'll be too late,' he shook his head. 'No, woman, we need something *now*. Maybe you're right and this commissar will prove to be another bloody zealot, but he's the only shot we have.'

* * *

Still brooding, Machen strode back into camp. Brushing off the sentries' half-hearted calls for a password he wove through the sprawl of habtents, making for the flotilla of ships moored along the riverbank. They were a miserable sight: most of the stolen gunboats and transports were little more than rust-bitten shells on their last legs. Much like the regiment itself, he mused grimly. There were some three hundred and fifty men gathered here, virtually all that remained of the eight hundred who had left Providence a lifetime ago. These Arkan were survivors, but they were also ghosts...

Crooked shadows lost on the crow road from Despair to Delirium...

Angrily Machen shook Templeton out of his skull, struggling to focus on the facts, but tone and texture kept slipping back in, hinting at meanings he didn't need – or want – to see. Every one of the greybacks was lean to the point of starvation, with bloodshot eyes that either blinked too much or didn't blink at all...

Facing oblivion with a twitch or a stare, souls laid bare to the empty one-way mirrors of fate and fortune squandered...

Most were suffering from multiple afflictions – foot rot or gutrot, mire fever or swamp burn, greyscale rash or splinterskin... The roll call of Phaedra's petty torments was as endless as the windings of the Coil, but misery was the only constant amongst the troops. Only the proud Burning Eagles of the 1st Company still had the look of a coherent unit. Their bronze raptor helms and para-armour had withstood the rigours of the Mire while the uniforms of the common soldiers had sloughed away, forcing each man to improvise his apparel as best he could. Many had scavenged synthetic fatigues or flak armour from dead janissaries, stubbornly scrubbing away the rebel insignia. A few had gone further and salvaged fragments of tau armour. Although the xenos breastplates were too small for a man, the pauldrons and tessellated greaves were serviceable. Even the helmets could be made to fit with a little work. Cully, the one-eyed rogue from Dustsnake squad, appeared to be on a mission to rebuild himself as a patchwork Fire Warrior. The veteran had a knack for tech and had even got some of the targeting optics in his pilfered helmet working. Many such opportunists had also adopted the lighter, punchier carbines of the janissaries, with Cully sporting a prized rail rifle.

The more devout men shunned such heretical gear and stuck with their sturdy Providence-pattern lasrifles. Following the example of their *askari* guides they had woven rough garments from animal skins and vines that made them look wilder than the savages back home. But despite the tangle of xenos and native junk, every man wore scraps of his Arkan heritage: a threadbare jacket here, crimson-striped breeches there... polished rhineskin belts and harnesses... flat-topped kepi caps bearing the ram's skull icon of the Confederacy, carved from bone as was the regimental custom...

Pirates! We look like Throne-forsaken pirates, Machen reflected miserably.

'He's with the witch,' Valance said, interrupting the captain's reverie. Machen snorted, irritated that the scout had crept up on him. It was uncanny how such a big man could move so quietly. Nevertheless, the scout was one of the few greybacks he still trusted.

'Stormed into camp in an all-fired hurry,' Valance continued. 'Went straight to her. It ain't seemly, especially with her being the colonel's lady and all.'

Machen nodded inside his helmet, recognising the Sentinel standing beside Cutler's command boat. Vendrake had been gone nearly two days, shadowing the idiot commissar who had followed them into the Coil. He didn't understand his fellow captain's obsession with their pursuer and he didn't much care, but it was intolerable that he'd gone gallivanting off into the jungle when so much was at stake. They had put their differences aside in Cutler's absence, working together to keep the regiment afloat, but Vendrake's vices had eaten away his brains. It was time to have things out with the degenerate.

As Despair sows Delirium so Delirium sows Discord...

'Shut the Hells up you dead bastard!' Machen snarled. Ignoring Valance's quizzical look he marched towards the command boat.

'Our plan hangs on a knife edge of synchronicity,' Skjoldis insisted. 'What if he calls and your Sentinels are not here, Vendrake?'

'So ask him,' the captain said. 'I know you can do it. It's how you've coordinated things since they took him.'

'It is not so simple. He is no psyker. At this distance it is difficult to touch his mind – and painful for him. We have agreed times...'

'Well, that's too bad because the commissar's time is running out. The man is sailing right into the bloody Meatlocker,' Vendrake hissed. 'Do you have any idea what's waiting for him there?'

'I–'

'Vendrake!' Machen bawled from the shore. 'Vendrake, get your fungus-addled arse off that boat! We need to talk!'

Skjoldis glanced towards the cabin door, but Vendrake gripped her wrist urgently.

'Ask him!'

Subject 11 groaned and began to shudder, struggling against the restraints that bound him to the chair. His eyes were screwed tight shut in a face wracked by an agony of concentration. Alarmed by the seizure, Por'o Dal'yth Seishin skimmed backwards on his throne drone. Although a force barrier separated him from his prisoner, the ambassador had not lived so long without exalting prudence.

'*Do it...*' the prisoner hissed. A crimson trickle oozed from his right nostril. 'Go get him.' Suddenly his head snapped backwards and he looked directly at O'Seishin, his eyes gleaming with sly malice.

'Trinity remembers!' he roared in a savage croak. Then he slumped lifelessly in his chair. O'Seishin watched the man uncertainly, but he didn't stir. Cautiously the ambassador hovered back to the barrier.

'Do you require medical assistance?' the tau asked. The prisoner's eyes flicked open and gazed at him through a tangle of white hair. 'Your meaning eluded me,' O'Seishin pressed, debating whether to retreat again. 'Who was it you wished me to get?'

'I was just thinking out loud,' the exhausted man wheezed, straightening up with an effort. 'Us humans, we do that sometimes. Especially the crazy ones.'

'Our assessments would indicate that your cognitive faculties are unimpaired,' O'Seishin said. 'You do however exhibit symptoms of severe personality disorder, perhaps even latent schizophrenia...'

'Glad to know it,' the prisoner snorted.

'Indeed, knowing oneself is the first and final step to enlightenment, my friend.'

'I'm no friend to you, blueskin.'

'I concede that this is so, yet I aspire to overcome our differences, Ensor Cutler,' O'Seishin said.

'You know, you talk real fancy for a xenos pen-pusher, Si.'

'My thanks, it is the calling I was born to.'

Cutler chuckled, the sound low and mocking.

'You believe I do not understand sarcasm, Ensor Cutler?' The tau's nostrils flared in amusement. 'You are mistaken. I am of the Water Caste and as I have previously stated, communication is my calling.' O'Seishin paused, then finished more haltingly: 'You-son-of-a-bitch.'

This time Cutler's laugh was genuine.

'But you...' the tau said, leaning forward on his floating perch. 'You choose to communicate in the manner of an obtuse barbarian, which you most assuredly are not. Why do you persist in this fabrication?'

'Full of questions today aren't we, Si?'

'It is–'

'Your calling! Yeah I already got that part,' Cutler said. 'Look, why don't you just send in the *bad* xenos and get started on the needles and shockwires or whatever it is you blueskins use to get answers, because I've got nothing to say to you.'

'There are no bad agents of the Greater Good,' O'Seishin replied primly. 'Such would be a contradiction.'

'Well, what about Wintertide then?' Cutler suggested. 'Why don't you send in the big chief and maybe I'll talk to him, one soldier to another.'

'Perhaps I am Commander Wintertide.'

'And I'm the Sky Marshall.' Abruptly Cutler cast off his brash mask and was all business. 'Why are we talking, Por'o Dal'yth Seishin?'

The tau considered the question. This was his eleventh interview with the renegade commander, yet they were no closer to a rapport. He reviewed the facts once again: Cutler had been captured almost a month ago, betrayed by a squad of his own men who had grown weary of their piratical existence. For nearly two weeks he had raved in his cell like a savage, throwing himself against the force barrier and refusing food until O'Seishin had indeed doubted his sanity. Then, seemingly from one moment to the next, he had become deadly calm. After that O'Seishin had begun the interviews and the duel for Cutler's mind had begun.

'Look, I don't know where my men are or what they're up to,' Cutler said. 'And I if did, I sure as Hells wouldn't pass it on to you.'

'Your comrades are irrelevant,' the tau murmured, still lost in thought. 'Since your capture they have caused us no tribulation. We have concluded that their spirit is broken.'

'Then you're fools.'

You'll need strong men who haven't forgotten how to think, O'Seishin recalled the Sky Marshall telling him. Forget the zealots who'll die before they dream a new thought, or the fickle rabble who'll follow anything that promises change, then hanker after another change and another, until they've got nowhere left to go. Such folk are the fodder of humanity and all you'll build with them is a paper castle. But win the heart and mind of a man like Ensor Cutler and you'll have a true hero by your side. And where such men lead others will follow.

'What do you want from me, xenos?' Cutler urged.

O'Seishin's nostrils twitched in a wry smile. 'I want you to do what is right, Ensor Cutler.'

Skjoldis frowned as she watched Vendrake's taskforce depart. The regiment could ill afford to lose any of the precious machines. Despite the devotion of the tech-priests the Sentinels were dying, worn down by the Mire. The remaining eight were running on little more than cannibalised parts and prayer. Risking them on this fool's errand was insane, yet she couldn't find it in herself to blame Vendrake.

Tell me the truth about Trinity, the cavalry captain had urged once again. Tell me what really happened there?

The doubts eating him alive had been seeded long ago, but they had lain dormant, waiting for the right catalyst. Skjoldis didn't know if that catalyst had been his lost protégé or Phaedra Herself, but Vendrake was on the brink of madness. He deserved the truth – about Trinity and about Abel. She would have relented if Machen hadn't started hammering at the door, demanding his own answers.

The Zouave captain was still storming about the camp now, angry at Vendrake's snub and frightened by something else. Skjoldis supposed she should talk to him, but she was too weary. Weary and terribly afraid for the Whitecrow...

He has been alone with his daemons too long.

Her telepathic contact had taken the colonel by surprise and for a few brief moments his soul had been unguarded. In those moments she had looked below the surface and his daemons had looked right back and grinned.

Cutler was awoken by an ungodly shriek. Alarmed, he reached for his sabre, then realised the sound was only the wind whistling through the eves of the rickety old barn. The blizzard was still raging, threatening to tear down the shack where the platoon's survivors had gone to ground after their flight. They were on the outskirts of the tainted town, watching the road for the trailing bulk of the regiment and praying the crazed citizens wouldn't show up first. The tension in the draft-riddled shack was electric: every one of the greybacks here would have chosen the sane perils of wind and snow over the horrors just a stone's throw away, but Cutler had ordered them to sit tight.

'What's up, Ensor?' Waite asked. The seams in his walnut face were etched deeper by concern. 'For a moment there it looked like you weren't at home.'

'I was just thinking,' Cutler murmured.

Of doing what's right...

'We have to go back,' he said, his voice growing stronger as reality firmed up around him. 'We can't let this stand.'

'Ensor, that town is warp-touched,' the captain protested. 'Listen, Fort Garriot can't be much more than three days march from here. We can call this mess in from there and let the witch hunters deal with these degenerates. It's what they're trained for.'

'Providence can't carry this kind of shame, especially not after the uprisings,' Cutler said. 'We're in the Inquisition's bad books already.'

'You really think they'd get involved?'

'Make no mistake about it, those planet-murdering bastards are watching us like hawks.' Cutler shook his head grimly. 'They've let us put our own house in order so far, but if word gets out that we're not just ornery, but *tainted* with it...'

'But this is just one misbegotten slum in the boondocks!'

'Maybe that's how the fall always starts.' Cutler sighed. 'We can't take the chance, Elias. It was providence that led us here and it's for Providence that we'll return.'

'I see 'em!' Sergeant Hickox called from the upper floor. 'Our boys is coming up the road now!' There were brittle cheers from the other survivors gathered in the barn.

'I need to talk to the witch,' Cutler said, running a hand through his glossy black hair. 'Maybe she can give us an angle on this mess. Then we have to go back.' He squeezed his comrade's shoulder. 'It ends here, old friend. With us.'

CHAPTER NINE

Day 63 – The Coil: The Scarlet Dossier

Are we nearing the heart of the Coil or just sailing in circles? It is impossible to tell when nothing changes from one day to the next save the diminishing measure of our supplies. The only certainty is this grey-green limbo and the river running through it. That and the black joke the Sky Marshall has worked on us all.

I've finished studying Lomax's Scarlet Dossier and it's all there, the whole sorry debacle of this war mapped out in a damning geometry of incompetence, negligence and sheer madness. Every shred of evidence was annotated with the High Commissar's spidery scrawl and focussed into a sharp truth. Taken individually each folly might be dismissed as mere misfortune, but seen together they spelled out nothing less than wilful betrayal.

Consider the High Command of the Phaedran War Group. We are cursed with witless tyrants like General 'Ironfoot' Mroffel, who convinced himself that tanks could float and sent an armoured battalion to a watery grave; or aristocratic buffoons like Count Ghilles de Zhegal, who dallies with war like a colour-blind regicide player, confusing blueskins with greenskins and gunboats for gunships. And then there are the madmen like Vyodor Karjalan and Ao-Oleaus (who is known as the Clockwork Butcher for the obsessive timing of his doomed sallies). Of course the Imperium harbours many such fools and monsters in its darker corners, but here they have been nurtured to strangle any hope of victory stillborn.

And then there is the record of perverse strategic decisions that range from the anomalous to the outrageous. Why the blanket embargos on long-range shelling and flights across enemy territory? Why the preferred requisitioning of tanks over amphibious vehicles? And why was the offer of a brigade of Catachan Jungle Fighters turned down when such men were surely born to tame the Mire? Why... why... why? Question upon question, error upon error and every one of them spiralling back up to the Sky Marshall himself.

For years Lomax had been surreptitiously collating and cross-referencing Zebasteyn Kircher's follies, building a case she knew

*she'd never live to make. That's why she passed the torch on to me,
the only person on Phaedra she still trusted. And that's why she
sent me into the Mire after my kinfolk. They were never meant to
be my quarry. They were meant to be my allies.*

– Iverson's Journal

'You know your problem, Holt? You think too fragging much,' Modine pronounced sagely. He laughed at the baleful glare Iverson threw him. 'What?
You got that look again, like you seen a spook or something?'

'Just answer my question, greyback,' Iverson said, trying not to gag on
the stench wafting from the diseased man. Modine's condition had worsened steadily over the weeks and his makeshift cabin reeked of decay. In
the gloom his face had the look of a crude coral sculpture and his fatigues
bulged with something that wasn't quite muscle anymore.

'You saying you don't like hanging out with old Klete no more?' Modine
said with feigned hurt. 'You ain't stopped by to see me in days, Holt.'

'I need to know if Cutler will hear me out,' Iverson pressed.

'Well it ain't like I ever knew the colonel personal like,' Modine said. 'The
big boys never hung out with grunts like me.'

'But is he an honourable man?'

'From what I seen of him I reckon *he'd* say so.' Modine shrugged. 'Look,
if he thinks you're straight up he'll likely back you, especially if you can
clear his name.' He peered at Iverson suspiciously. 'Are you on the level
about that part, Holt? You really going to wipe the slate clean for the 19th?'

'I have that authority,' Iverson said, the lies coming easily these days, 'but
redemption has a price.'

'And what about me?' Modine said with sudden vehemence. 'Are you
going to yank that sick frak Karjalan outta his web and haul him over the
coals for what he done to me?'

'It's complicated...'

'Yeah, that's what I figured,' Modine spat.

'It's complicated, but yes. You have my word on it,' Iverson said, determined that this would be no lie. 'Vyodor Karjalan is a heretic and I'll see
that he faces the Emperor's Justice for his crimes.'

*Along with all the other monsters that have stalled this war and wasted
so many Imperial lives.*

Modine held his gaze for a long moment. Finally he nodded. 'Well then,
me and Lady Hellfire's sweet daughter over there...' he pointed at the flamer
Iverson had requisitioned for him, 'we've got your back all the way.'

Day 65 – The Coil: Modine's Folly

*Despite my warnings Modine got careless this morning. I was
on the upper deck with Cadet Reve when a commotion broke out
down below. Recognising the stowaway's furious shouts I guessed
what must have happened, but it was too late to stop it. We arrived*

just as he was dragged up top by a mob of Letheans. He was put-
ting up one hell of a fight, kicking and punching like a cornered
beast, but there were too many of them. They must have taken him
by surprise, catching him before he'd been able to go for his flamer.
I watched as the Letheans threw him to the deck and surrounded
him like jackals, jeering and taunting and cursing him for a
mutant freak. In the emerald light he certainly looked the part: his
gnarled skin had a reptilian cast and his body seemed to seethe
and contort beneath their blows. I admit I almost let them finish
their work, but then I caught Modine's tormented eyes and I knew.
If I stood by he would come back...

– Iverson's Journal

'That's enough,' Iverson said. He yanked a Mariner aside and stepped inside the vicious circle. 'I said enough! This man works for me!'

Almost as one, the Letheans went quiet, fixing him with hostile stares that ranged from the sullen to the outraged. Cadet Reve looked as angry as the rest.

'What is this you say?' Csanad Vaskó demanded. The shaven-headed brute was the Lethean's 'zabaton', a warrior priest they revered and feared in equal measure. He was also the man who had confronted Iverson over the matter of the Arkan flag, an affront he had never forgiven. His rage was a palpable, poisonous charge in the air.

'Private Modine is a specialist assigned to me for this mission,' Iverson said. 'Due to his affliction I requested that he remain in isolation until we reach our target.'

'He is touched by the hand of Kaosz,' Vaskó growled. 'Must be burned.'

'You are mistaken,' Iverson said, wondering at the fanatic's blindness to his own leader. Then again, Karjalan kept himself hidden from all but his most dedicated servants. Vaskó and his crew probably had no idea that they served a monster.

'Perhaps the zabaton has a point,' Reve spoke up. 'This individual is evidently tainted, sir.'

'Is so. The Emperor condemns!' Vaskó insisted.

'And don't He just love doing it,' Modine wheezed from the floor. His cackle turned to a cry as the zabaton sent him reeling with a kick to the ribs.

Iverson drew his autopistol slowly, letting them taste the ritual as he levelled it at Vaskó. 'I have already cautioned you once against obstructing the Emperor's will,' he said. There were angry murmurs from the gathered Letheans, but the zabaton himself didn't even blink. 'This will be my final warning.'

Don't make me shoot you. Your dogs will tear me apart if I do it.

'A good death bring a man closer to God-Emperor,' Vaskó said coldly.

'And is this such a good death?' Iverson asked.

'Better than the one you get if you kill me.'

'Sir, this is not a sound tactical...' Reve's words were shredded by a terri-fied scream from above. She whirled to stare at the upper deck, along with most of the Letheans. Only Iverson and Vaskó remained frozen, each man tacitly challenging the other to break first.

'Janosz!' One of the Mariners yelled as the scream was cut short. He headed for the stairway, but Reve shoved him aside and took the steps by twos. Iverson whirled away from the standoff and stalked after her.

'To your stations, seadogs!' Vaskó bellowed as he followed with a pair of Corsairs. 'The Emperor calls!'

They found a broken lasrifle by the ladder to the crow's nest, but the lookout was gone. Muttering angrily in his native tongue Vaskó started to climb, but Iverson yanked him down. The zabaton snarled at him, baring black teeth. The commissar didn't remove his hand.

'Whatever took him could still be up there,' Iverson said levelly, nod-ding at the arboreal snarl overhead. Some of the fronds were trailing right through the crow's nest as the ship drifted along. The zabaton shook him off and glared at the canopy.

'You think was plant took him?' Vaskó asked.

'It could have been anything. There's no telling in the Coil, but the crow's nest is off limits for now. And we need a team up here day and night. At least one Corsair among them.'

Vaskó nodded and headed for the steps, but Iverson called after him: 'Private Modine falls under my authority, zabaton.' The man froze. 'Is that understood?'

Vaskó turned and appraised Iverson with a frown.

'Very well, is so,' he answered softly, 'but understand this, commissar. If you prove false, I make new flag from your hide.'

Day 66 – The Coil: Canker Eaters

Sometimes I think I'm dead to horror, but then some new abom-ination steps up to the challenge and shoves the truth down my throat: horror can never be sated and no man will ever be allowed his fill. There is always more and worse to come.

– Iverson's Journal

The ship bucked violently and Iverson staggered, almost losing his grip on the iron handrail. With a curse he hauled himself along the cramped corri-dors of the lower deck, reeling about like a drunk as the world tossed and turned around him. Water was gushing through the ceiling and swilling around the floor, almost ankle deep. He threw open the hatch to the main deck and a volley of hard rain hit him like gunfire. Still drowsy with sleep, he tried to make sense of the chaos.

Are we under attack?

It was long after nightfall, but there was no trace of the jungle's pervasive bioluminescence. In the dim glow of the emergency lights he saw Mariners scurrying about with torches and buckets, harried by their Corsair overlords. Beyond the gunwales there was nothing but inky blackness.

'Why are the engines dead?' Iverson yelled over the gale.

'Seems the river's jammed up just ahead,' Modine called back. He was slouching beneath an awning by the steps, nursing his flamer protectively. 'And this fraggin' squall sure ain't helping none!'

'I told you to keep out of sight.'

'Hey, I'm just keeping an eye on things for you, Holt.'

A flash of lightning lit the deck and Iverson caught sight of Vaskó up in the wheelhouse. The zealot was cracking his ritual whip and bellowing orders. Old Bierce stood beside him with his hands clasped behind his back, brooding over the mayhem. He caught Iverson's eye and shook his head.

I don't like it any better than you do, old man, Iverson thought as he struggled across the heaving deck. The spray coming over the sides was flooding the ship almost as fast as the Letheans could bail it out. Why in the Hells weren't the pumps working? He hadn't come this far to drown in the Qalaqexi...

Iverson froze on the steps to the wheelhouse as he caught sight of the threatening shapes surrounding the ship. They loomed out of the gloom like spongy, malformed giants. Then a searchlight flashed across them and he relaxed, recognising the lumpy Saathlaa igloos. Like the natives themselves, the buildings were degenerate and slovenly, just simple timber frames caked in dried mud and thatched with broad leaves. These primitive hovels were an order of magnitude removed from the coral edifices of the ancient Phaedrans.

'Is Fish village,' Vaskó called from the wheelhouse. 'River runs through it, but there is wall ahead!'

Iverson joined him and peered through the rain-smeared glass of the cabin. Following the wide beam of the ship's forward searchlight he saw a dam straddling the river about twenty metres ahead. Although crudely woven from timber and creepers, the thing was at least three metres thick and twice that in height. One of the ship's scout boats bobbed about in the churning river alongside the dam, crewed by a gang of Letheans. The Corsair leading the party kept watch while his Mariners hacked away at the barrier with machetes and axes. It was a brave, but futile endeavour, especially in the storm.

'Can't you just punch through it with the main gun?' Iverson asked, indicating the lascannon at the prow.

'Can,' Vaskó said, 'but power cells very low. Only six, maybe seven shots left. Do not want waste, no?'

'Seven shots?' Iverson was outraged. 'But we haven't even fired the bloody thing! Why would the cells be drained?'

'Is Phaedra,' Vaskó said with a shrug, as if that explained everything. Unfortunately Iverson knew it did.

'We should back up and take another branch,' a voice said at his shoulder. He turned and saw Reve standing beside him, frowning at the barrier. To his surprise he realised he had almost missed his fourth shadow. 'This smells like a trap.'

'But this place just stinking Fish nest!' Vaskó bridled. 'Is nothing here my Corsairs cannot kill dead, girl.'

'Maybe so, but Cadet Reve is right,' Iverson said. 'We can take another path.' *After all, we're not really going anywhere.* 'Get those men back on board, zabaton.'

'We only need to weaken wall, then we push through it easy!' Vaskó insisted, unwilling to back down yet again.

'Zabaton...'

Something whipped out of the storm and shattered the forward searchlight, plunging the men by the barrier into sudden darkness. Down in the prow the Mariners operating the light yelled and scrabbled about for a replacement.

'Bring more lights!' Vaskó shouted into the ship's loudhailer.

A shrill howl ululated through the gale. Out by the barrier a Mariner lit up a torch. Iverson saw him perched atop the dam, frantically chasing shadows with his beam while his comrades fumbled about for their own lights.

'Pull them back,' Iverson ordered.

'Is just Fish!' Vaskó said stubbornly.

A rangy shadow leapt from the gloom and swept the light-bearing Mariner from his perch. As he splashed into the water the night rushed back in like a hungry ghost and the screams began. They were riddled with bestial snarls and strange, warbling cries that made Iverson's hackles rise. He had hoped never to hear those sounds again.

'Those aren't Fish,' Iverson hissed.

Crimson laser light slashed through the darkness as the stranded Corsair opened up with his hellgun, then a flash of lightning threw the tableau into stark relief, revealing stooped, predatory shapes slinking amongst the Letheans. A heartbeat later it was pitch dark again and the Corsair stopped firing.

'Forward!' Vaskó shouted to the helmsman. 'To battle stations, seadogs!' he yelled into the loudhailer.

The Mariners reacted with swift discipline, casting aside buckets and unslinging lasguns as they rushed to their posts. The Corsairs stalked among them like armoured gods of war, chanting prayers as they powered up their hellguns. The forward searchlight flared back into life and pinned the dam in bright light, but the work team was gone.

'The engine awakens, my zabaton,' the helmsman said.

As the ship chugged forward something slammed down onto the cabin roof. They glanced up as clawed feet scrabbled about for purchase. Vaskó fired without hesitation, his superheated hellbolts punching through the metal ceiling as if it were paper. The unseen boarder yelped and a tangle of bony legs toppled past the window.

'Zabaton, turn this tug around now!' Iverson ordered.

And then the predators were everywhere. Propelled by powerful, reverse-jointed legs they bounded from the rooftops of the village and soared over the gunwales. One landed by the wheelhouse steps. It came down on all fours and skittered off balance on the rain-slick metal. Although its sleekly muscled form was canine its rapid, jerky movements suggested an avian metabolism. Its grey flesh was leathery and hairless, but a ruff of sharp quills jutted from the back of its neck.

'Is that a dog?' Reve breathed from the doorway.

At the sound of her voice the creature's head snapped round on a sinuous neck. They caught a glimpse of slanted eyes above a curved, razor blade beak evolved for rending and tearing. The thing hooted – a strange sound somewhere between a bark and a squawk – and pounced straight for the wheelhouse.

Iverson shouldered Reve aside and thrust out his augmetic arm. The hound's jaws clamped shut on the metal, but its momentum sent him crashing back into the petrified helmsman and they both went down under its bulk.

'*Ördög kutja!*' Vaskó cursed in his native tongue, unslinging his hellgun.

As the beast's claws tore at his coat Iverson clenched his trapped hand around its tongue and squeezed. The hound tossed its head about furiously, spattering him with drool as it tried to get at the soft flesh beyond his augmetic. The carrion stench wafting from its maw made him dizzy with nausea, but he held on, tightening his grip. Up close he could see the monster's flesh was covered in suppurating lesions and tangled fungal nodules. Phaedra had claimed the beast as Her own.

'Kill it!' Iverson roared at the others.

Vaskó was at his side first. The zealot jammed his rifle up against the monster's midriff and opened fire. It squawked in agony and sent him flying with a flailing claw, but the hellgun had virtually torn it in half and its strength was fading fast. A carefully placed shot from Reve punctured an eye. A second tore open its skull and it lay still.

'The Emperor condemns!' Vaskó bellowed as he raced out into the storm, eager to spill more blood in his god's name.

'By the Throne, what are they?' Reve asked as Iverson pulled himself up.

'Kroot hounds,' the commissar said bleakly. 'And where there are hounds the handlers won't be far away. We have to get out of here.'

Down on the storm-lashed deck Modine stood with his legs splayed wide for balance. His flamer coughed as he gunned it into life. He spun as one of the dog-things leapt for him, its beak slick with gore from a butchered Mariner. He batted it aside with the bulky weapon and sent it crashing against the guardrail in a snapping, snarling tangle. It was on its feet again in an instant, howling with raw malice. Modine howled right back and torched it. The monster's challenge turned to a squeal and the pyrotrooper cackled, revelling in the mayhem. He was being eaten alive by some kind of mutie mushroom and everyone he'd ever known was probably dead, but by the Hells life could still be good!

He saw a Corsair crawling along with a hound straddling his back. Its jaws were locked around the man's head, trying to crack his helmet like an iron egg. Whistling softly, Modine bathed its quills in a delicate wash of flames and it let go with a yowl of pain. As it spun to face him he rammed his flamer between its jaws and cooked its brains. Breathing in the scent of burning flesh, he looked around the deck eagerly, but all the hounds were dead and the fight was done.

It seemed the Corsairs had enjoyed the tussle as much as he had. They were all chanting some kind of hallelujah to the God-Emperor with big, cheesy grins on their faces. Even the idiot who'd nearly had his head chewed off was singing along. The Corsairs might be Throne junkies, but Modine had to admit they weren't short of guts. The Mariners had guts too, but mostly they were the wrong kind – red and raw and littered about the deck like off-cuts in a slaughterhouse. Nope, things hadn't gone down well for the deck monkeys. Without the hellguns and armour of their masters they'd been easy meat for the dogs and Modine guessed more than half were done for. Well, the runts had been just as quick to beat up on him as the heavies so he wasn't going to shed any tears for them.

'You fight well for mutant scum,' said the Corsair he had saved.

'That wasn't no fight,' Modine drawled. 'That was just playing around.'

Mangled Helmet grinned, flashing teeth studded with shiny gemstones.

Someone wailed in the wind, long and lost and full of pain. Everyone on the deck heard it, but it was the zabaton who spoke: 'Is Zsolt. The Fish scum have taken him.' The zealot's tattooed face was a devil mask of fury. 'They mock us, brothers!'

'It's not the Fish who took your man,' Iverson said from the wheelhouse steps. 'There's something far worse out there.' He indicated the shanty-town stretched out along the river. 'Something we don't want to tangle with right now.'

'I will not abandon a brother Corsair,' Vaskó said coldly.

'He's already dead...' The cry came again, putting the lie to Iverson's words. 'It's a trap,' he urged, but the zabaton was already turning away, shouting orders at his surviving comrades.

'Zabaton, the mission comes first!'

The zealot whirled on Iverson. 'Then you must shoot me, Holt Iverson,' he snarled, 'because this time I will not yield.'

Seeing his hate-glazed eyes, Iverson didn't doubt it for a moment.

'But I should go with you, sir,' Reve insisted. 'You will need backup out there.'

'That's Modine's job,' Iverson said. They were talking up in the wheel-house while Vaskó prepped his search party on the deck below. 'Besides, I'll need backup right here. Our zabaton insists on taking all the Corsairs with him. Someone needs to watch the fort while we're gone. If we lose the ship we're finished.'

'Are you saying you trust me, commissar?'

'Are you saying I shouldn't, cadet?'

She gave him a wintry smile and he almost returned it. Their cat-and-mouse game was almost playing itself these days.

'Anyway, if I'm right and there's a kroot war band waiting for us in that village...' He gave her a pointed look. 'Well, let's just say this would be a very bad time to let me down, cadet.'

'So what's the deal with you and the ice maiden?' Modine whispered as they crept amongst the huddle of Saathlaa igloos.

'I don't believe I take your meaning, greyback,' Iverson said, his eyes dancing over the huts. They were dilapidated and mangy with rot, their walls puckered like the skin of spoiled fruit. Decay hung over the shanty-town like a mantle.

'Aw, come on Holt. You can't fool an old dog like Klete Modine,' the pyro-trooper said with a leer. 'I seen the way you two is always gabbing away together.'

'Are you telling me you're jealous, Modine?' Iverson said. 'I remember what they used to say back home: never trust a Badlander at your back.'

Modine sniggered. 'Did you just crack a joke on me, Holt? You know, back in...' His words trailed off as the missing Corsair cried out again.

Vaskó called a halt, trying to get a bearing on the sound. It was much closer now, but between the darkness and the storm the settlement was proving a nightmare to navigate. The zabaton was growing increasingly agitated, but to his credit he hadn't suggested splitting the search party up.

We're already too few, Iverson thought, glancing over his comrades. *Seven bloody-minded zealots, four terrified seadogs, one degenerate Badlander and a faded commissar. Not exactly the stuff that legends are made of.*

'It came from that way,' Modine said, jabbing a stubby finger to his left.

Vaskó scowled at him. 'You think I do not know this?'

'So what's the hold-up then, boss?'

'There is no path, fool!'

'Sure there is,' Modine said, obviously enjoying himself. 'You just got to think creative is all.' With that he kicked out at a neighbouring igloo. His foot went through the wall as if it were matchwood, shaking the entire struc-ture. Another couple of kicks brought the barrier tumbling down. They saw that the splintered wooden frame was riddled with ropey grey fibres that glistened like maggots in the rain. Iverson was repelled: the igloo was just a husk, sucked dry by the insidious fungus. The entire village was probably infested with the filthy stuff. Suddenly he was glad of the hard rain. In any other conditions the air would be ripe with spores.

'See, us Badlander boys, we like to make our own way in the world,' Modine said with a grin.

After that any attempt at stealth seemed irrelevant and the pyrotrooper led the way, whistling cheerily as he bulldozed a path towards the siren cries. While the others stepped over the tainted debris gingerly, he seemed to revel in it. Iverson guessed that infection wasn't a big worry for Kletus Modine anymore...

He's already halfway to being Phaedra's, even if he doesn't know it yet. Then again, maybe he knows it perfectly well and this little rampage is a kind of payback.

They found their quarry in a big roundhouse that was built to a grander scale than the igloos. The place might have been a chieftain's hall in better days, but those days were long gone. As they crowded inside their torches sliced the shadows into flickering wedges of horror.

'Hellfire...' Modine breathed, his cockiness draining out of him like life-blood.

The lost Corsair was dangling from the ceiling by his feet, swaying gently back and forth. The other missing Letheans were hanging beside him, along with Janosz, the Mariner who had been snatched from the crow's nest the day before. Janosz was already bloated with decay, but while the others were fresher they were just as dead, including the Corsair. Every one of them had a ragged red tear in his chest where his heart had been ripped out.

'I'd say this jaunt is looking like a really bad idea right about now,' Modine growled.

The roundhouse was an ossuary. The floor was littered with the relics of death – cracked skulls, yawning ribcages and an unrecognisable muddle of lesser bones, all heaped together in casual desecration. A fur of grey mould shrouded everything, clinging to the walls and hanging from the ceiling in thick cobwebs. Tendrils of the fungus wove through the chamber like shrivelled snakes, coiling around the bones and insinuating themselves into eye sockets.

There are enough pieces here to build a hundred skeletons, Iverson estimated grimly. *And enough skeletons to repopulate a whole village with the dead...*

There were other bones caught up in the foetid skein: smaller, more delicate and darker of hue. The xenos skulls were devoid of the gaping nostrils and grinning teeth that gave humanity its last laugh in death, but then the tau were an altogether more sober species. Not that sobriety had done them much good here.

Fragments of tau armour and guns were buried amongst the bones like treasures in a defiled tomb, but the most wondrous relic had been given pride of place. Tethered to a coral totem piercing the heart of the ossuary was a towering suit of alien armour. Trussed up and defaced with primitive scrawls, the Crisis battlesuit had the look of a fallen star god. Under a patina of mould its plates were a mottled crimson and Iverson could still make out its heraldry – a five-flanged sunburst. He didn't recognise the symbol, but something told him that this dead warrior predated Commander Winter-tide's rule. It was *old*, perhaps older than the war itself.

Who were you and what brought you to this doom?

Whatever the truth, the warrior's fate had been a grim one. The armour's breastplate had been cracked wide open, revealing the hero within. His skeleton was still intact, suspended almost tenderly in a cradle of fungal threads. There was something fleshy and infinitely unclean blossoming within his ruptured ribcage.

Phaedra loathes us all as equals. Human and tau, we're both just intrud-ers to Her. Nothing but meat to be corrupted and devoured and turned...

Uneasily Iverson wondered what terrible alchemy Phaedra had worked on the kroot who haunted this village. The savage creatures believed they could steal the strength of an enemy by devouring its flesh. It seemed a far-fetched idea, but the kroot bloodline was known to be fluid and unpredictable. By all accounts the kroot hounds were a dead-end branch of the race that had overspecialised in hunting to the detriment of all else. Had their doom resulted from their choice of prey? And if that were true, what would happen to a kroot war band that glutted itself on tainted flesh? The flesh of a degenerate Saathlaa tribe for example...

Canker Eaters.

The name sprang into Iverson's mind with the clarity of a true vision. Suddenly he was sure that his guess about this place was correct: the village had fallen to the kroot and the kroot had in turn fallen to Phaedra.

And then the monsters had turned on their tau overlords and slaughtered them too.

'Burn it,' Iverson hissed at Modine. 'Burn it all.'

'Wait!' Vaskó said as the pyrotrooper raised his flamer. 'We cannot leave Zsolt in this tomb!'

'He's gone, zabaton,' Iverson said tightly. His head was pounding. 'And we have to be gone too. This place isn't a tomb. It's a larder.'

They wait for the flesh to putrefy before they feed...

The butchered Corsair wailed again. Everyone stared at the mutilated corpse. Its mouth was gummed up with clotted blood. Another cry came, soft and mocking this time, drawing their eyes upwards.

There was a xenos perched precariously at the tip of the totem. The creature was sitting back on its haunches, gripping the coral with clawed feet like a bird of prey. Its leathery skin was hairless, but a cascade of fungal coils sprouted from its throat and shoulders, draping the beast in a fibrous, fleshy cloak. The creature's limbs rippled with sinewy muscles and Iverson knew it would tower over most men when standing erect. Like the hounds it was evidently a predator, but the eyes shining above its flat beak regarded the intruders with sly amusement. Instinctively Iverson knew it was a leader – a *shaper*, the kroot called them.

The xenos tilted its head to one side in an unmistakably avian gesture and spoke in a near perfect imitation of the commissar's voice: '*This place isn't a tomb. It's a lardeeeeer!*' The words trailed off into squawking laughter and a crest of quills flared out behind the beast's head in mockery. Recognising the deception, Iverson felt rage rising within him like a living thing. Or a long dead thing butchered by this foul species...

Suddenly Detlef Niemand was at his shoulder. 'Cleanse the xenos!' the mutilated commissar demanded, jabbing at the shaper with a raw stump.

Iverson and Vaskó opened fire at the same time, but both were too slow. Dodging ahead of their attacks with unnatural speed, the creature back-flipped from its perch and latched onto the ceiling with its talons. Chased by their fire it skittered away upside-down and disappeared among the rafters.

'Bring this charnel house down, Modine!' Iverson shouted.

The pyrotrooper's flamer burst into life, bathing the roundhouse in angry red light. A moment later a tide of purifying fire drenched the unclean bones. Iverson added his own salvo, punching round after round into the chest cavity of the infested battlesuit, ripping apart the fruiting body pulsing within. The dangling corpses of the Letheans dropped into the bonfire and Modine brushed them gently with promethium.

'Burn bitch, burn...' the diseased man muttered repeatedly and Iverson knew he was cursing Phaedra Herself.

The conflagration soon took on a life of its own and the intruders backed away. Except for Modine. The pyrotrooper kept up a steady stream of fire and hate, seemingly untroubled by the advancing flames. His ruined face looked rapturous.

'We're done here, soldier,' Iverson called, but the man paid him no heed. 'Modine, we're done!'

There was a warbling cry from outside, followed by a chorus of angry hoots and squeals, then a thunderous squawk that sounded mercifully distant.

'Time to go!' Iverson yelled. For a moment he thought Modine planned on burning alive, but the Badlander nodded and turned his back on the inferno. Outside, the raindrops sizzled and popped against his cooling flamer like insects lured into an electric trap.

'Damn, that felt good,' Modine said.

'*Felt good...gooood...gooooood!*' His voice yodelled back from above.

They looked up and saw the shaper framed against the roiling sky, leering at them from the roof of the roundhouse. Its words spiralled up into a high war cry. A Corsair answered with a gurgling shriek as a spearhead erupted from his chest in a shower of blood and shattered flak plate. A kroot warrior sprang up behind him, hooting victoriously. It lifted the impaled man effortlessly by the haft of its spear and flung him over its shoulder. More of the monsters dived from the rooftops, landing amongst the away team like twisted angels of death. One ripped away a Mariner's face with its talons as it came down. Another was torn to ribbons by Vaskó's hellgun before it even touched the ground.

'Purge the unclean!' the zabaton roared. He leapt into the fray like a whirling dervish, lashing about with his whip as he fired his rifle one-handed.

'Sounds like a plan!' Modine hollered cheerily. He flicked his flamer back into life as Iverson backhanded a charging kroot with his metal fist. The xenos reeled away and Modine sent a chaser of flames after it, turning it into a wailing, flailing pyre of steam. The Badlander arched backwards, catching another savage in midair then spinning to intercept a pair of loping kroot hounds.

The booming squawk came again, much closer now.

'Fall back to the river!' Iverson shouted, ignoring dead Niemand's scowl.

This isn't worth dying for, he thought fiercely. *Only Wintertide matters. Wintertide and maybe the Sky Marshall. If there's still any difference between the two.*

Standing watch in the wheelhouse, Ysabel Reve saw the fire start up. It was only an orange smear against the darkness, but she knew it was the beginning. Scant seconds later her prediction was confirmed by the rattle of hellguns and the distant, desperate cries of dying men. It was the moment she had been waiting for.

'Lower the treads,' she said. 'We're going in.'

'Commissar, this we cannot do!' Gergo, the lanky helmsman protested.

'This is an amphibious vehicle is it not?' Reve said, giving him a withering look. 'We shall prove this.'

'But is not so easy, commissar,' Gergo whined, gesticulating vaguely. 'The machine spirit of the ship, it need *much* reverence for such big work.'

'We will revere it later. Right now you will do as I ask or I shall kill you.'

Gergo decided the machine spirit could wait after all.

'Fall back!' Iverson shouted as the Mariner beside him went down under a slavering kroot hound.

'A zabaton does not run!' Vaskó called back. The aquila tattooed across his face seemed to writhe with a life of its own in the dancing light of the inferno.

'*Ruuuuun!*' the shaper keened as it thudded down behind him.

Vaskó ducked the slash of its serrated knife and whirled into a low spinning kick, but the xenos hopped over his counter-attack and hacked downwards. The Lethean swung his rifle up into a two-handed block that shattered both weapons and threw him to the ground. As the shaper reached for him Iverson charged forwards, pumping rounds into the alien's chest as he came. The creature's spongy mantle absorbed the bullets, but the impact sent it careening backwards. With inhuman reflexes it twisted the imbalance to its advantage, flipping onto its back and kicking out with both talons like a spring-loaded trap. The blow took Iverson in the chest with the force of a pneumatic sledgehammer and hurled him through the building opposite. He hit the ground so hard a wave of oblivion came rushing in.

'On your feet!' Niemand sneered, reeling the fallen commissar back from the brink. In the darkness he was a jagged electric spectre haunting the green snow of Iverson's augmetic vision. 'For Emperor and Imperium!' Niemand demanded. For Hate and Vengeance, he meant, but right now either pair was just fine by Iverson.

He sat up, fighting the agony of his bruised ribs. Through the rent he'd made in the igloo he saw the shaper lift the struggling form of Vaskó above its head. It flicked its head round and looked right at the commissar, finding him unerringly in the darkness. Iverson couldn't read its expression, but he knew it was grinning in whatever way a kroot might grin. Then it hooted with mirth and cast its prize into the blazing roundhouse.

'Purge the xenos!' Iverson roared, stumbling back outside. The shaper waited for him, its mouldy quills rippling with excitement.

'*Purge the xenooooos...*' The alien's mimicry turned into a yowl of surprise as a cord lashed out and wrapped around its throat. Iverson's eyes snapped to the blazing roundhouse. A burning man swayed at the threshold like a damned soul teetering at the gates of hell. Before the shaper could move, Vaskó sent a full charge rippling along his smouldering shockwhip. The kroot jerked about in a nerve-shredding, muscle-twitching spasm and gibbered in agony. Its quills blistered and its eyeballs exploded into blood-streaked geysers of steam. As his muscles melted away Vaskó lurched backwards, hauling his catch into the inferno after him. Niemand howled with rapture and spread his stunted arms wide.

'Like the man said, the Emperor condemns,' Modine smirked as he staggered up alongside Iverson. The big man was bleeding badly, but there was a madcap grin on his face. 'And sometimes He even gets it right!'

Then they were running, backtracking along the path of destruction Modine had ploughed on their way in. Only three Corsairs and one Mariner had survived the assault and Iverson himself was in bad shape. Bierce was waiting for him at every turn, his expression thunderous with disapproval, but Iverson paid him no heed.

It's duty that drives me to flight old man.

The kroot were relentless in their pursuit, taunting their prey with hoots and squawks as they sprang between the rooftops like manic acrobats. Iverson guessed they were enjoying the hunt too much to make a quick end of it.

Wintertide must die... Kircher must answer for his crimes...

The Corsair in the lead skidded to a halt and stumbled back with a frantic yell. Over his shoulder Iverson saw a hulking shape loping towards them on all fours, using its massive forearms to propel itself along like a hunched ape. Its head was a pugnacious caricature of a kroot, dominated by a slab-jawed beak jutting from beneath beady black eyes. A kroot warrior was perched between its shoulders, looking impossibly fragile beside its mount. Iverson had never seen one of the giants before, but he recognised it from the Tactica briefings. Like the hounds, the krootox was a dead-end branch of the kroot evolutionary tree. The creatures were dim-witted brutes, but their prodigious strength and resilience made them melee monsters on the battlefield. During his stint in the kroot-infested hell of Dolorosa Magenta he had been regaled with horror stories of the beasts. One veteran had sworn blind he'd seen a krootox tear a battle tank apart with its bare hands. Right now the commissar wasn't inclined to doubt him.

'Back up!' Iverson shouted, but the path behind them was swarming with kroot hounds.

'Keep 'em off me!' Modine snarled at the Corsairs behind him. As Mangled Helmet and his comrade raked the hounds with gunfire, Modine slammed a fist through the neighbouring igloo. Something lunged at him through the gap and he replied with a brief spurt of promethium. There was a howl from inside and a blazing kroot burst through the wall, groping blindly for him. He clubbed it aside and lashed out with a kick that sent it spinning into the baying hounds.

'Go! Go!' Iverson barked, firing vainly at the oncoming krootox as the others swept into the igloo. A heartbeat later he ducked under a lunging fist as the giant stampeded past. Moving too quickly to break its charge, it crashed headlong into the hounds and scattered them like yelping ninepins. Iverson saw that its hide was blotched with a lurid patchwork of toadstools and tendrils. The rider hung limp and shrivelled between its shoulder blades, seemingly welded to its mount in a cancerous saddle. The kroot turned at the waist, peering at him with cloudy white eyes.

This is Phaedra's heartland, Iverson realised. *The restless blood of the kroot was easy prey for Her here.*

Braying with frustration, the krootox swung round and Iverson hurried after the others. Modine was already breaking into the next igloo when he caught up. Somewhere in the medley of wind, rain and thunder Iverson thought he heard another, deeper rumbling. He listened, trying to make sense of the sound, but then the hovel behind them collapsed as the krootox waded in after them and the rumble wasn't important anymore.

'Clear!' Modine said as he peered through the rent he'd made.

Everyone dived through into the darkness and raced for the far side. The surviving Mariner shrieked as a sinewy arm shot down from above and hooked him by the scruff of the neck. Iverson glimpsed terrified eyes and wildly kicking legs, then the man was gone, yanked through a hole in the roof. Mangled Helmet sent a blind salvo after him, more in the hope of granting him a quick release than catching his attacker.

'Keep moving!' Iverson shouted. He heard more krootox bellowing nearby, sniffing them out in the ramshackle maze. Bierce was waiting on the roof outside, his hand extended in mute accusation. A kroot leapt right through the phantom and Iverson almost laughed as he blasted the xenos out of the air.

'Clear!' Modine called again as he tore open the next hut.

Halfway across the hovel one of the Corsairs tripped and clattered to the ground. Iverson turned to haul him up when their pursuer came barrelling through the wall. The commissar stumbled back as the beast lunged forward and snatched up the fallen Lethean. The man cursed in his native tongue as the krootox dangled him upside down and peered at him with dim curiosity. It rattled him about and pecked experimentally at his helmet, irritated by the noises he was making. The Corsair was still trying to level his hellgun when it grew bored and chewed off his head. It tossed the corpse aside, rose on its haunches and roared at Iverson. The challenge was cut short when a metal leviathan stormed over the hut and ground the beast into oblivion. Iverson dived back as a lethal wall of spinning wheels and churning treads passed just inches from his face.

'Reve!' Iverson shouted, but the gunboat's clatter drowned him out as it rolled past. He saw its hull was swaddled in enormous caterpillar tracks that suspended the deck high above the ground, transforming the gunboat into a gargantuan tank. The sponson-mounted autocannons on either side were blazing away, deterring attacks, but with only a skeleton crew the *Penance and Pain* was appallingly vulnerable.

She's heading for the fire at the roundhouse, he guessed.

'Back this way!' Iverson called to his companions as he hurried after the gunboat. It was moving fast, but not so fast a running man couldn't catch it. *Even a man with a chest like broken glass...*

Iverson's breath was coming in harsh gasps now and his mashed ribs threatened to crush his lungs, but he pushed on. He shouted until he was hoarse, even though he knew the gunboat crew high above couldn't possibly hear him.

Wintertide... Kircher... Wintertide... Kircher... The names chased each other round Iverson's skull in a whirling mantra of loathing. He was riding high on hate the way some men soared on combat stimms. He felt a brief pang for the Glory he'd used against the Verzante deserters – so long ago now – but the narcotic was a tainted blessing. *Her blessing.* Hate was pure.

...Wintertide...

He looked back and saw his comrades behind him. There was a second krootox bounding after them, even bigger than the first. Blanking it out, Iverson locked his eyes on the receding stern of the boat and saw Bierce up there. The old man had his back to him, turning away in contempt as salvation raced away.

... Kircher...

Mangled Helmet hurtled past Iverson, twirling something around his head as he ran. The Corsair cast the grapple with a skill forged through years of ship-to-ship combat and it sailed over the gunwales like a guided missile and caught. The racing vessel yanked him forward violently, but he kept his balance and soared ahead. A moment later he was abseiling up the hull in leaps and bounds. Iverson heard the krootox squawking in fury at his escape.

...Wintertide... We just need to stay ahead a little longer...Kircher...

He glanced over his shoulder and saw the beast thrust itself into the air like a vaulting ape.

'Down!' he shouted, diving into the mud. Modine fell to his knees instantly, but the remaining Corsair made the mistake of looking back. The krootox tore through him like a cannonball, almost shearing him in half. It crashed down onto the path ahead, a rampaging barrier between its prey and the gunboat. The impact snapped its atrophied rider off at the waist like a dried twig, but the brute was unperturbed.

Phaedra is its true rider now, Iverson thought as he raised his pistol. There was nothing left now except the last stand. *Where are you Bierce? You should be here to see this, you old vulture!*

The krootox loomed over him, shrugging off the small calibre rounds like insect bites. Its beak snapped open as it reached out... and exploded into flames. Iverson dodged away from the squawking inferno as Modine advanced with his flamer. He was singing a bawdy Badlands ballad as he drove the beast back with a stream of fire.

'...and Lady Soozie, she ain't never looked so fine...' He winked at Iverson. His flamer sputtered and ran dry. 'Well shit...'

The krootox charged him like a raging bull. Its hide was a charred ruin that hissed and smoked in the rain, but the fire hadn't reached its muscles. A pile-driver punch sent Modine toppling to the ground. He kicked out but the brute caught him by the ankles and hoisted him into the air. Iverson opened fire as it began to whirl its catch round, but the bullets only irritated it further. At the corner of his eye he saw the gunboat brake to a halt and begin to crawl back.

Too late...

With a primal bellow the krootox smacked Modine against the ground like a human whip. The first impact shattered every bone in his body. The second left him hanging in its fist like a rag doll. By the time his legs came off he was a shapeless liquid ruin.

Too bad...

Iverson was already staggering for the gunboat when the beast came after him. He saw Mangled Helmet up on the deck, hollering for more speed. Reve appeared beside him, watching the chase through her magnoculars.

Too far... Wintertide... Too slow... Kircher...

He heard the krootox stomping just behind him. Felt its hot breath at his back. Felt his own breath tearing through him like razorwire. Some impulse told him to duck and he rolled away just as a claw swept over his head... and kept rolling as the beast pounded the ground with its fists, just one step behind him.

Winter...tide... Kir...cher...

Iverson's blind roll brought him up against something solid. He looked up and saw a metal giant towering over him. The thunder of the Sentinel's autocannon was deafening as it tore the krootox into steaming chunks of meat. The machine swivelled smoothly at the waist and raked the rooftops, obliterating a cluster of charging kroot. A second Sentinel clanked up alongside it, spewing fire from a gun that dwarfed Modine's flamer. Iverson froze as he recognised the Seven Stars stencilled across its barrel.

By Providence, they've found me!

After it was over and the town was silent, Iverson went looking for Modine. The Badlander's body was gone, but the rain hadn't quite erased the blood-smeared trail he'd left behind when he crawled away. Iverson followed it to a small hut at the edge of town and found his quarry curled up in the shadows like a shredded slug. The man was legless and liquescent, but hideously alive. For all its ravages, Modine's disease had turned him into one tough son-of-a-bitch.

'How are you doing, greyback?' Iverson asked from the threshold.

'I've had better days,' the Badlander wheezed through broken teeth. 'You here to give me the Emperor's Mercy then, Holt?'

'Do you want it?' Iverson asked, reaching for his pistol.

Modine shook his head. 'Nah, He ain't exactly been good to me so far. Why start now?'

'You know I should grant it anyway.'

'Sure, but you won't. Not unless I ask. And I ain't asking.' The Badlander chuckled wetly. 'Sorry chief, I ain't going to make it that easy for you.'

'Duty was never meant to be easy.'

Modine spat a gob of blood-flecked saliva. 'You toast all them freaks?'

'Most of them, but there will be survivors. There's no telling how many.'

'Well, I'll take my chances.' Modine raised a blubbery paw and grinned. 'Besides, they might even see me as kin now.'

'Why in the Hells would you want to live like this, man?'

Modine gave it some thought, then nodded slowly. 'I've never been much of a believer, Holt. The way I see it, when you're gone, you're done and there ain't nothing more.' He chuckled again. 'Anything's got to be better than that, right?'

'You're wrong, Modine.'

'Maybe so, but if it's all the same by you, I'll see this through.'

'What are you going to do?'

Modine shrugged vaguely. 'I guess I'll just sit here a while. See how things go.'

How things grow...

Iverson shook his head and turned away, but Modine stopped him with a sharp gesture. 'You won't forget what you promised me about that bastard Karjalan will you? You gave me your word back there, brother.'

'I did,' Iverson said.

'Well then, I reckon that's good enough for me.' Modine threw him a languid salute. 'I'll see you around, Holt.'

'I hope not.' Iverson walked out, leaving Kletus Modine to Phaedra. He suspected She wouldn't keep him waiting long.

CHAPTER TEN

Day 67 – The Coil: A Silver Storm

My search is almost at an end. The Confederates came to our aid at the eleventh hour and we purged the kroot as brothers-in-arms. And by the Emperor the purging felt good! I've been chasing shadows for so long that I'd almost forgotten the taste of an honest battle. I admit there was little glory in it, but if Phaedra has taught me anything it's the value of truth over glory. This foe needed killing and my new-found allies obliged with thunder in their hearts!

True to their name the Sentinels of the 19th descended upon the kroot like a silver storm. There were only nine, but every one was a titan wrought in miniature. My kinfolk have always had an affinity for fighting machines, but these riders surpassed the old tales. Riders? Surely that does them an injustice, for each man's mastery of his machine was so perfect it moved like an extension of his own body. They raced and spun about with an agility that I never imagined possible for such hulking machines. We prowled the town together, burning the tainted igloos and cleansing the savages in droves. Only one Sentinel fell, its legs torn from under it by a dying krootox.

Just one loss, yet even one was too many when they were already so few...

– Iverson's Journal

Dawn was breaking over the village when Iverson returned from his tryst with Modine. He found the Arkan cavalrymen gathered around the fallen Sentinel, cutting their dead comrade from the wreckage with a dignity that belied their ragged appearance. Reve stood at the edge of the circle, aloof and watchful as ever.

'Modine?' she asked as Iverson approached.

'Gone,' he said. He nodded a greeting to the Sentinel commander. 'I believe we owe you our lives.'

'We'll take Boulter with us. Burn him downriver,' the man answered obliquely. 'There's not much of him left, but I won't leave one of my riders here.' He glared at Iverson as if expecting an objection.

He blames me for the death of his comrade, Iverson thought. *Or he blames himself for making one of his own pay for my salvation. Either way, he's wondering if I'll be worth the price.*

'Are you Cutler?' Reve asked the officer bluntly.

The man looked up from the wreckage with a scowl: 'Do you see any stars on my chest, lady?'

'I see no insignia of any kind,' Reve replied, glancing pointedly at the rider's fur-trimmed flying jacket. The garment was a gentleman's affectation, expensive and flamboyant, but it had weathered Phaedra better than its wearer. Haggard and wolfish, the man looked like a pirate dressed up in his victim's finery, yet there was a faded arrogance about him that betrayed his blue blood. There was blue in his eyes too – the lurid indigo stigma of a Glory addict.

'I may be a Throne-forsaken renegade, but I'm not Ensor bloody Cutler,' the commander said. 'The name's Vendrake.' He straightened up. 'Captain, 19th Arkan Confederates.' He made it sound like a challenge.

'Iverson,' the commissar said. 'And this is Cadet Reve. We've been looking for you – all of you – for quite some time.'

'Maybe we didn't want to be found.'

But that's a lie, Iverson thought. *After all, you came to us, Captain Vendrake.*

'That's unfortunate,' he said, 'because I'm here on the Emperor's business.'

Vendrake's eyes narrowed. 'And what would that be, commissar?'

Iverson hesitated. If he misread Vendrake these men would kill him where he stood. 'That would be justice, Captain Vendrake.' His words hung in the air like a whiplash waiting to fall. At the corner of his eye he saw Reve's hand inching towards her pistol. *Surely you're not such a fool, girl?*

Finally a sour smile touched Vendrake's lips.

'Justice?' He sighed with what might have been relief. 'Well then, say your piece and be done with it, commissar.'

Day 68 – The Coil: A Barbed Alliance

'You're no renegade, Hardin Vendrake,' I told him, 'and neither is the 19th.' They were simple words, but true – the right words for the moment.

Of course words won't be enough to win these men over, but they broke the ice and Vendrake agreed to take me to Cutler. For all his hostile bravado I believe it's what he intended all along, so why the games? I sense there's more than brinkmanship going on here. It's almost as if Vendrake wants me to judge him. There's an edge of darkness to the man that runs deeper than his devotion to the Glory. Dead Niemand believes he is insane and I'm inclined to agree, but he's the only lead I have. Besides, he tells me his comrades are just two days upriver so I'll have my answers soon enough.

– *Iverson's Journal*

'You won't like what you find, commissar,' Vendrake said. In the violet fungal light his features had a ghoulish cast. Iverson couldn't quite tell if he was grinning or not. 'Actually I think you'll want to shoot the lot of us.'

'Perhaps,' Iverson said, regarding the riders hunkered down around him on the banks of the river. Their Sentinels loomed over them like a second circle of judges. It was the first night of their journey together and the unspoken trial was in session once again. 'Do *you* think I should shoot you, Captain Vendrake?'

'Does it matter what I think?'

'Maybe not, but tell me anyway.'

'Well then...' Now Vendrake *was* grinning. 'What I think is this: we're not what you'd call heroes of the Imperium anymore. Not heroes of any stripe or colour in fact.'

'But you've been fighting the enemy,' Iverson said.

'Because they're here to fight.'

'The enemy will always be here to fight. It's the way of things.'

Vendrake snorted and took another swig from his canteen. He'd been working his way through it all night and Iverson guessed it wasn't filled with water.

'Sir, if I may?' The speaker was Silverstorm's second officer, Pericles Quint. 'Despite Captain Vendrake's misgivings, please rest assured that the 19th has not strayed from its tradition of courage and honour. We have harassed the rebels at every opportunity...'

'Oh quit whining, Quinto!' Vendrake snapped. He obviously despised his subordinate and Iverson could see why. Clear-eyed and clean-cut, Quint was his captain's opposite, the epitome of an Arkan noble confident of his place in the scheme of things. According to Vendrake the man had once been overweight, but there wasn't a trace of fat on him now. While Phaedra had sucked the vigour out of Vendrake, She had seemingly whipped Quint into shape.

'It needs to be said, sir.' To the commissar's trained ear there was the faintest tremor in Quint's voice. 'We have stayed true to Providence and the Imperium.'

There were murmurs of assent from the other riders and Iverson wondered if Quint was angling for a power play. If so, Vendrake seemed blind to the threat. Or perhaps he just didn't care.

'Do you really think an Imperial commissar will give a damn for anything you have to say, Quinto?' Vendrake scoffed.

He's speaking to Quint, but I'm the one he's really asking, Iverson realised. *Why are you so eager to be condemned, Captain Vendrake?*

'Tell us about Cutler,' Reve interjected. 'Is he at your camp?'

Vendrake squinted at her. 'You seem mighty keen to meet the Whitecrow, lady. Now why would that be?'

'He is your leader, is he not?' Reve said.

But is he your target, Reve? Iverson wondered.

'Colonel Cutler is...' Quint began.

'Quite dead,' Vendrake interrupted. Reve stared at him and he laughed,

210

PETER FEHERVARI

a harsh, humourless bark. Nobody joined in. 'No, don't worry girl, I'm just messing with you. As far as I know the Whitecrow is still breathing, but some things can wait. In fact *this*...' he swept his arm across the gathering, 'this can all wait. Let's see what the Raven makes of you.'

'The Raven?' Reve asked.

'Oh don't worry cadet, you're going to love her!' Vendrake hauled himself up. 'She's always full of questions too.' He turned towards his Sentinel. Out in the Mire all the riders slept in their machines. 'I'll see you at dawn.'

'Why don't you tell us about Trinity first, captain?' Iverson's words struck Vendrake like cold water. When he turned his grin was gone.

'What?'

'Trinity,' Iverson said. 'It's on the regimental records – a backwater town razed by the 19th. If I recall correctly it happened right at the tail end of the war.'

'What of it?'

'There were questions. A military tribunal.' Iverson was watching Vendrake closely. 'I thought it might be important.'

The captain swayed, looking unsteady on his feet. His men were silent. Even Pericles Quint kept his mouth shut.

'Captain?' Iverson pressed.

'That town died *after* the war, commissar,' Vendrake said. He paused, thinking about it. 'Or maybe long before. I'm still not sure which it was.'

'And was it important?'

'No,' Vendrake looked at him with eyes like broken windows into Hell. 'No, it wasn't important.'

But Iverson saw the lie. For Hardin Vendrake, Trinity was the most important thing of all.

'He is sick and almost certainly tainted,' Reve said when they were back aboard the *Penitence and Pain*.

'Perhaps,' Iverson said, 'but Vendrake is our only lead.'

'Why do you always retreat to "perhaps" or "maybe", sir?' She sounded exasperated. 'Doubt and you will falter, falter and you will fall.' It was a quotation from the Commissariat Primer.

Does that mean you're the real thing, Reve? Iverson wondered. *Or have you just done your homework? And does it matter either way?*

'Sometimes "maybe" is the best we can do, cadet. Sometimes there's no knowing the truth.'

She was indignant. 'Then we *act* regardless. Hesitation is a greater crime than error.' Another quotation. 'Your pardon, but you think too much for a commissar, sir.'

He was silent for a long time. 'Yes,' he replied finally and realised he meant it. 'Yes, I fear you're right.'

'Then you agree? You will act?'

'I believe I must,' he said sadly. 'Goodnight to you, Cadet Reve.'

* * *

That night, like most nights, Hardin Vendrake dreamt of murdering the town that was already dead. And yet again the nightmare began the same way.

His Sentinels reached the outskirts of Trinity at the head of an unravelling grey snake that stretched back almost a kilometre. Most of the men were so dazed with cold and starvation they could barely walk, let alone hold a formation together. The last of the Chimera sleds had given out four days ago, the last of the horses a day later. After that it had fallen to the Sentinels to haul along the wounded carts. It was an inglorious task that they rotated dutifully, but fuel had run as dry as blood by the time they reached the town.

Vendrake felt his heart leap at the sight. It almost made him forget the cold. He'd killed his Sentinel's heater days ago to save on power and the cabin had turned into an icebox. He was swathed in furs like a barbaric mummy, but his fingerless mittens left his hands vulnerable and the tips were blue with cold. Like any rider worth his salt he wouldn't sacrifice dexterity for comfort, but he guessed frostbite was just a hair's-breadth away. But the town was closer.

Then Vendrake spotted the major waiting by the side of the road like a grim gatekeeper and knew something was wrong. Of course Cutler wasn't the Whitecrow back then. His hair was still coal-black and he didn't wear misery like a mantle, but his fate was already closing in.

'Level the town, captain,' Cutler called over the wind. 'Bring it down and burn it.'

'Burn it...' Vendrake echoed hollowly.

'Except for the temple. Leave that to me.'

'And the people?' He was too tired for shock.

'Burn them too.'

'I don't understand.' And he was too tired to try.

'That's for the best, captain.'

Vendrake hesitated just once. 'Is this right?' he asked. But he must have been too tired to care, because he didn't remember Cutler's answer. Didn't even remember if Cutler had answered at all. What he did remember was leading the cavalry into Trinity and putting the town to the sword. And when the locals fell upon them, hacking at their metal steeds with axes and hatchets and even lesser weapons, he put them to the sword too. He was numb to their fury. The cold had made him invulnerable to doubt.

His invulnerability lasted until a putty-faced maniac leapt onto his steed from a collapsing rooftop. The attacker howled in futile outrage as he battered at the Sentinel's canopy, then pressed his molten features against the windshield. Pressed so hard it began to come apart.

Which, the face or the windshield?

Lost somewhere between the dream and the cold, Vendrake couldn't tell where flesh ended and glass began. He only knew he mustn't let that furious dissolution reach him. Desperately he tried to shake his attacker loose but the degenerate hung on like a leech, his wild eyes glaring hate and hope like dark-bright beacons in a whirlpool of vitreous flesh. And then the windshield began to bulge inwards...

'*Belle du Morte* signing in,' the vox crackled suddenly.

At those words the world ran down like a failing machine. The sounds of battle distended and faded to silence. The face outside/inside his windshield congealed into stillness, becoming a tortured sculpture framed against the frozen flames devouring the town.

'Leonora,' Vendrake croaked, dimly aware that this was a new twist on the nightmare. Something he hadn't seen before.

'Another night, another murdered town,' sang the voice of his dead protégé and lover. 'Tell me, which slaughter felt better, Hardin?'

'It had to be done,' he said. He was vaguely sure that was true. Hadn't someone important once said so? Cutler perhaps. Or maybe poor dead Elias Waite...

'That's not what I asked, Hardin.'

'You can't be here, Leonora. You joined us after the war ended. You weren't ever here.'

'But *you're* here. And that's all that matters, dear Hardin.'

'I don't understand,' Vendrake said. He couldn't take his eyes off the monstrosity carved into the windshield. There was hatred frozen in its eyes like an insect trapped in amber. It was a voracious, crawling thing, eager to escape so it could make a nest of his skull. 'I don't understand...' he repeated in a whisper.

'That's because you're trying too hard, Hardin.' The dead voice giggled at the chance alliteration. 'It's like staring at the sun. Look right at it and you'll go blind, but catch it in the corner of your eye and you'll see the truth of things.'

'And what's that?'

'That you were blind all along and always will be!' Her laugh was like the swish of rotting velvet. 'The world is broken and there's no fixing it. The puzzle makes no sense and nonsense is our only hope.'

'You're not... Leonora.' He struggled to string the thoughts together, let alone the words. His hand fumbled for the service pistol taped to the dashboard.

'Don't be cruel, Hardin!' she chided. 'But no matter, you'll know me when we meet.'

'You're... lying.' His hand closed on the gun.

'Of course... I'm not!' She giggled again. 'Either way, I'm coming for you. Perhaps it was true love after all...'

He tore the pistol free and levelled it between the mad eyes petrified inside his windshield.

'Oh, you don't want to do that!' she exclaimed. 'Do you?'

Vendrake had no idea, but he did it anyway.

The two Sentinel riders keeping watch by the riverbank heard the pitiful shrieks coming from Vendrake's machine, but neither spoke up or moved to intervene. They were used to their captain's nightmares.

Day 69 – The Coil: Dead Men Sailing
Vendrake greeted me like a manic ghost this morning, his eyes

rancid with the Glory. He didn't mention Trinity, but waking or sleeping, I know that's where he spent his night. Without his narcotic fix I doubt he could walk straight let alone pilot a Sentinel. Reve was aghast at the sight of him, but I shrugged it off. There was a time when I would have berated or pitied his addiction, perhaps even shot him for it, but such things do not matter anymore. If Vendrake needs the Glory to lead me to Ensor Cutler then so be it. And lead he does...

The Sentinels guide my ship from the riverbank, flitting through the dark tangle of vegetation like bright shadows, navigating the weft and weave of the Coil without hesitation. Their riders have learnt to see hidden paths where lesser men – or men less damned – would see only chaos. And so we follow, sailing the Coil in a floating tomb, our numbers diminished and our supplies almost gone...

– Iverson's Journal

Standing on the upper deck, watching the Mire drift by, Iverson caught sight of Bierce waiting at the river's bend. The phantom's finger was still jutting out in accusation. He was implacable and immovable, but the Sentinels waded through him as if he wasn't even there.

'You saw his eyes this morning,' Reve insisted. 'He is a degenerate.'

'Captain Vendrake will keep his word,' Iverson said.

'But he cannot be trusted.' She was whispering even though they were alone.

'You said the same thing about the Letheans. You're not the trusting type are you, cadet?'

'And you are?'

No, Ysabel Reve, I am not. But I've grown lax.

Before he could answer there was a heavy clanking on the steps below and the surviving Corsair climbed up to join them. He had discarded his mangled helmet after the battle, revealing a head like a craggy moon daubed with paint. His tattooed face was brutish, yet his pale green eyes were penetrating, suggesting a shrewd cunning. Iverson wasn't sure if that was going to be a problem, but so far the man had fallen into line and the Mariners had followed.

'Milosz's wounds claimed him this morning,' the Corsair said in surprisingly fluent Gothic. 'And Bencé will die before sunset. Six seadogs survive to serve.'

'This is a big ship. Can they keep it running?' Iverson asked.

'They are bred to sail,' the Lethean answered. 'They will be enough.'

The ship rounded a bend and Iverson watched Bierce drift by once again. He turned to face the Lethean. 'You understand that they are *your* men now, Corsair?'

The Lethean shrugged, seeming neither proud nor perturbed.

'And you are *my* man.' Iverson made it a statement.

'As you say, commissar,' the Corsair said flatly.

'I didn't get your name, soldier.'

'I am Tás Zsombor, tethered blood-brine of Underlocker 5.'

'You're proud of your lineage?'

'I am shamed. The Underlockers are sunken prisons where the scum of Lethea are cast down to brawl and drown and die,' Zsombor grinned like a shark, displaying his gem-studded teeth. 'But like all Corsairs I fought my way up to the land and the light.'

'To redemption?'

'To penitence and pain,' Zsombor growled. 'There is no redemption, commissar. There is only holy torment. Have you not heard the Lethean Revelation? The Emperor condemns.'

Iverson made no reply. Bierce was waiting for him at the next bend in the river.

Day 70 – The Coil: Redemption and Damnation

Vendrake says we will reach the Arkan camp tonight. I admit I am eager to meet Ensor Cutler at last. Whatever he has become, I am certain he will bring me a step closer to Wintertide and my salvation. Unlike the Letheans I will not accept that redemption is impossible. I'll willingly suffer and die for the God-Emperor, but I won't believe it's for nothing. Surely there must be a purpose to the misery we endure in His name?

But before I redeem myself I must fall a little further.

There's one final loose end to tie up before I reach Cutler. I've been putting it off because I've never been quite certain of my suspicions. By Providence, I'm still not certain, but with Cutler so close I can hesitate no longer. Too much hangs in the balance for doubt. Reve was right – I must act. And may the God-Emperor forgive me if I am wrong...

– Iverson's Journal

Reve hacked through another curtain of creepers with her machete and pushed through into a narrow glade. The clearing was hemmed in on all sides by gargantuan toadstools whose caps melded into a knotted, mucilaginous canopy high above. Violet light drizzled down from the gills, transforming the space into a pocket nightscape.

'Surely this is far enough,' Reve said, scowling at the pale things scuttling amidst the fleshy rafters. 'We have been walking almost an hour, sir.'

'You're right,' Iverson said behind her. 'This place is as good as any.'

Something in his tone made her turn and she saw the pistol in his hand. It was levelled at her head. Iverson watched her face flit through a range of emotions until it settled on plain annoyance.

'You promised me the truth,' she said quietly.

Yes, I did, Reve...

Around midday Iverson had ordered a halt to their journey. Offering Vendrake no explanation for the delay, he'd asked Reve to follow him into the jungle. A little later he'd told her she'd earned the truth, but the truth was too dangerous to risk around the others. Later still he'd fallen behind and let her take the lead. And so they'd finally stumbled upon this twilight glade.

It seems a fitting place for our shadow play to end, Ysabel Reve.

'So you have decided not to trust me,' she challenged.

'I think you're working for the Sky Marshall,' he said.

'I am not.' There was no trace of fear in her voice. He had expected nothing less of her.

'You appeared out of nowhere and claimed Lomax sent you when I know she didn't. You pretended to be green when you were anything but and you've stuck to me like my own shadow, always prying for secrets.' He shook his head. 'You're a spy and an assassin, Ysabel Reve.'

'Then why did I come for you at the tainted village?'

'Because you needed me to reach Cutler.'

'You are wrong.'

'I might be,' he admitted sadly, 'but *you* were right: mistakes are smaller sins than doubts. I can't take the chance you'll kill Cutler.' The emotion slipped from his voice. 'Give me a reason not to shoot you.'

She sighed and opened her hands, palms upwards. 'High Commissar Lomax was my mother.'

'Too contrived. You can do better than that, Reve.'

'She kept my existence secret and trained me personally. I was raised to be her weapon against the Sky Marshall. I hate Zebasteyn Kircher more than you ever can. That bastard murdered my mother.'

'It's a good story.'

'It is a true story.'

'I don't believe it.' Iverson shook his head. 'I think *you* murdered Lomax. She was on to the Sky Marshall's game and you were sent to silence her, just as you'll silence anyone who threatens him.'

Reve sighed. 'Your mentor was correct. You are a fool, Holt Iverson.'

'What are you talking about?'

'I am talking about Commissar Nathaniel Bierce, the hero you betrayed in your youth. He was like a father to you, was he not?' She nodded, acknowledging the surprise on his face. 'Yes, I have seen your record, but that is the least of it.'

'You're not making any sense, Reve.'

'Then listen to me. Bierce never stopped looking for you. He followed your trail across the galaxy, but when he finally found you on Phaedra and saw what you had become he turned his back on you. I believe this was three or four years ago.'

'That's impossible. Nathaniel Bierce was murdered decades ago on a planet you've never even heard of.' The guilt tasted fresh on Iverson's tongue. 'An assassin got to him with a xenos neurotoxin – something the medicae couldn't begin to fight. I saw him die.'

And I've seen him dead every day of our journey through the Coil. In fact he's here now, hovering just over your shoulder. Turn around and maybe you'll see him too, Reve!

'You did *not* see Bierce die,' Reve said. 'You left him to rot, but he survived.' She gave him an icy smile – the first he'd ever seen on her face. 'The neurotoxin destroyed his flesh, but the Commissariat decreed his mind worthy of preservation so they gave him a new body. I never met him, but my mother thought him a remarkable man. Although *man* was no longer quite the right word for him.'

'You're lying, Reve.'

'Then how do I know all this?'

'Because the Sky Marshall has given you half-truths to work with.' He could feel the rage uncoiling in his chest like a burning snake aching to strike. He looked past her and met Bierce's eyes.

She's right of course. You were like a father to me, old man. And I'm sorry. I've never stopped being bloody sorry...

Iverson forced his gaze back to Reve. 'You're lying,' he repeated hollowly.

'Then shoot me.'

'Do it!' dead Niemand hissed in his ear. 'The bitch is playing mind games with you!'

Iverson's finger was tightening on the trigger when he saw Number 27. His third revenant was watching him from across the glade. Unlike her companions she was a rare and precious curse and weeks had passed since her last visitation. As always, she filled him with ineffable sorrow.

What do you want here? What are you trying to tell me?

Following his eye line, Reve glanced over her shoulder. She looked right through Bierce and saw nothing. She turned back to him, frowning. Iverson could almost hear her mind working, calculating her chances.

Yes, I'm distracted, Reve. Make a move! Force my hand and prove me right!

But Reve made no move. Doubtless she suspected a trick.

So be it, girl.

Iverson stepped back, widening the distance between them. Slowly he lowered his pistol and eased it back into its holster, but his hand hovered over the weapon.

'Back on Providence we have many old myths and customs,' he said. 'Most wouldn't make any sense to an off-worlder and truth to tell, many don't make much sense to me either.' He shook his head ruefully. 'But there's one I don't doubt. It dates right back to the first colonies and runs like firewater in the blood of every Arkan, noble and savage alike. We call it the Thunderground.'

Iverson noticed Bierce nodding in rare approval. The old vulture was Providence born. He was the one who'd taught Iverson the traditions and tales of their home world, weaving them into the Imperial creed with masterful logic.

'The Thunderground is a secret place waiting inside every one of us,' Iverson said. 'It's the needle in the eye in of the storm that's life, the testing point that'll make or break you in the God-Emperor's eyes. You'll only walk it once, but that walk will be forever. There's no turning back and no second chances so you'd better walk with fire in your heart and steel in your spine.'

'You sound more like a wordsmith than a commissar,' Reve said, sounding uncertain for the first time.

'All good commissars are wordsmiths, Reve. Words are our business as much as guns. When we get them right, our charges face death willingly.'

'Then you still believe you're a good commissar?'

He smiled bleakly. 'I know I'm a poor wordsmith.'

'Are you trying to tell me this is your Thunderground, Iverson?'

'No, Ysabel Reve, I'm telling you it's yours.'

The fingers of his augmetic hand twitched reflexively, but its human partner stayed rigid and perfectly poised over his holstered pistol.

'Go for your gun, Reve.'

Very slowly, very deliberately she raised her hands. 'No.'

'Then I'll kill you where you stand, assassin.'

'I will not humour your delusions of honour, Iverson.' She sounded angry now. 'I will not give you that comfort. If you kill me it is on you alone.'

They remained frozen for a long time, locked in a stalemate while Iverson sought his bearings amongst his ghosts. Like a sailor navigating by black stars he floundered between Niemand's spite and Bierce's contempt and the dead girl's strange compassion, but in the end it was simple weariness that decided him.

'Throw aside your gun,' he said. She obeyed gingerly, careful not to offer any hint of a threat. He nodded. 'If you try to follow me I'll kill you.'

'I understand,' Reve said. As he turned to go she called after him. 'Iverson! You do realise you are insane, don't you?'

He stopped and looked back at his ghosts, lingering on Bierce. If she'd told the truth he was being haunted by the shade of a man who still lived. Was that worse than being haunted by the dead? He found he had no answers.

'Do you think it makes a difference?' he asked, but Reve had no answers either, so he turned away.

Have I just stepped back from the brink?

'She's going for her gun!' Niemand yelled.

Iverson swung round and his pistol seemed to leap into his hand with a will of its own. Number 27 rose up before him, her hands outstretched as if to beseech him or ward him off, but he was already firing. The bullets ripped through her in a splatter of ectoplasm and found Reve. She was standing motionless and...

What gun? I see no gun!

The first round punched through her right eye, the second and third sheared away half her face. Horribly she was still alive when she hit the ground.

'Reve!' Iverson knelt over her, already knowing there was nothing to be done. 'Ysabel, listen to me...'

Her surviving eye rolled in its socket, hunting for him. 'Ivaah...ssaah...' Her shattered jaw mangled the words into wet nonsense as she clutched at him. 'Yah... baahh...staaahh...' With a last shudder she was gone.

Iverson looked up at Niemand. The ghost was staring at the corpse avariciously.

'Why did you do it?' Iverson asked.

'It was the only way to be sure, Holt,' the dead commissar gloated.

Iverson opened fire on full auto and sundered the phantom into whirling ribbons of ectoplasm. His pistol clicked on an empty chamber and he slotted in a new clip mechanically. He kept on firing, going through clip after clip until the spectral gobbets had faded into nothing.

He never saw Detlef Niemand again.

'Where did your lady friend get to?' Vendrake asked when Iverson returned.

'She's gone,' Iverson said.

Just like Modine, he thought, knowing full well it wasn't. Unlike Kletus Modine, Ysabel Reve would certainly be coming back.

ACT 3
ASCENT

CHAPTER ELEVEN

PROVIDENCE MILITARY ARCHIVES,
CAPITOL HALL
REPORT: GF067357
STATUS: *CLASSIFIED*
FROM: General Thaddeus Blackwood, Director (Internal Affairs)
ATT: Major Ranulph C. Kharter, Investigating Officer (Internal Affairs)
REF: War Crimes – 19th Arkan – Trinity Township, Vyrmont
SUM: Be advised that this town has been designated a *rebel affiliate*. While
the ruthlessness of Major Cutler's purge is regrettable, such incidents are
inevitable in times of war.

CON: You are ordered to desist all investigations of the Trinity site forth-
with. The 19th Confederates will be disciplined by Internal Affairs in due
course. This matter is *closed*.

Note: I want Cutler and the 19th gone within the month. Give the man his
stars and ship him off-world. He did what needed doing, but he's a hothead
and too unpredictable to trust with a secret like this. If the Inquisition gets
wind of Trinity the consequences for Providence are unthinkable.

'You are an anomaly on Phaedra, Ensor Cutler,' Por'o Dal'yth Seishin
observed from the pulpit of his throne drone, 'but you have always been
an anomaly, have you not? Most especially to your superiors.'

The white haired prisoner behind the force barrier snorted. 'You're not
telling me anything I don't already know, blueskin.'

'But I am offering you an opportunity you cannot deny,' the tau ambassador urged. 'Unlike your Imperium, the Tau Empire embraces creative
leadership. A man such as yourself could be an invaluable asset to us.'

'Then let's see your cards.' Cutler leaned forward on his stool, his expression sly. He had grown lean and wolfish during his incarceration. 'Come
clean with me, Si. What's your game on Phaedra?'

O'Seishin steepled his fingers, contemplating the question. This was his
twenty-fifth 'interview' with Subject 11, yet the man's stubbornness was
undiminished. Perhaps it was time to twist the blade a little deeper.

'Phaedra is worthless,' O'Seishin declared. 'It is a sinkhole for a war the
Tau Empire has no intention of winning. The conflict serves the Greater
Good where victory would not.'

'You're telling me the war is a sham?' Cutler said bitterly.

'Not so. The fighting is genuine, but there is no heart in it. A single company of your vaunted Space Marines would take this world within a week, a few regiments of seasoned Guardsmen within a year, but your Imperium *chooses* to send only the dregs of its military – the incompetent, the broken or the deranged – soldiers who have lost the will to win or the faith to care.'

'That sounds to me like a slur on the 19th,' Cutler snarled.

O'Seishin raised a placating hand. 'As I stated previously, anomalies sometimes slip through the net.'

'Real soldiers, you mean?' Cutler shook his head. 'No, I don't buy it. Why would the Imperium play to lose?'

'It does not play to lose. Like ourselves, it simply does not play to win.'

'Why fight a war nobody wants to win?'

O'Seishin twisted his face into an approximation of a human smile. He had been practising the manoeuvre rigorously and thought it rather good. 'I have a different question for you, Ensor Cutler. *Who* is your Imperium fighting on Phaedra?'

'I don't follow you.'

'Consider the facts. The Saathlaa indigenes are numerous, but primitive and militarily insignificant. Our mercenary auxiliaries are effective, but few. As to my own kind...' O'Seishin extended his hands, palms upwards. 'How many tau have you encountered on Phaedra, Ensor Cutler?'

'I'd say one too many, Si.'

'Then you are privileged, because I doubt there are more than two thousand of my kind remaining on the entire planet. Contrast that with nearly one hundred thousand of your Guardsmen.' O'Seishin paused to let the numbers sink in. 'I ask you again: who is the Imperium fighting on Phaedra?'

'Turncoats,' Cutler said bleakly, 'but the scale you're talking about...'

'Has been precisely balanced,' O'Seishin finished smoothly. 'Over the decades we have stripped back our own troops as yours have swelled our ranks. Your Imperium casts its people into oblivion and we offer them hope. You have been fighting each other, Ensor Cutler.'

'This really is just a game to you, isn't it?'

'On the contrary,' O'Seishin demurred, 'our purpose is serious and our message sincere. Phaedra is a feasibility study – a microcosm of a future happening as we speak. While your Imperium is diverted by this inconsequential war, our agents – *human agents* – are waging the true war beyond this gateway world, winning the hearts and minds of the subsector. Everywhere they go they find discontent and a desire for something better. Your species is not as unified as your Imperium pretends, my friend.'

'And you've got all the answers?'

'Not all,' O'Seishin admitted, 'but many. For example, the psychic malaise that plagues your race – you call it "the Chaos" I believe – this condition does not afflict the tau.'

Cutler stiffened visibly. 'It doesn't afflict you because you blueskins don't have souls.'

'Then perhaps the price of owning a soul is too high,' O'Seishin said seriously. 'I have more facts for you, Ensor Cutler. Your species is hardy, but riddled with the maladies of age. Mine is vigorous, but prone to the follies of youth. Separately we are vulnerable, but together we could become unbreakable. The tau are not your enemy.'

The ambassador sat back, awaiting the inevitable sarcasm, but Cutler was silent, his eyes glazed with thought. Surprised, O'Seishin pressed on.

'Phaedra is a sacrifice for the Greater Good of both our races, Ensor Cutler. In your heart you know your Imperium is in its death throes. Do not die with it. Do not let your men die *for* it.'

The haunted look on the prisoner's face was almost pitiful. In that moment O'Seishin was quite certain the gue'la were a doomed species. He leaned forward eagerly, sensing victory.

'Tell me, Ensor Cutler, does the name "Abel" mean anything to you?'

The blizzard had returned with a vengeance, but the fire raging through the murdered town had pushed the temperature right up. Skjoldis, the witch woman, remembered that she had been sweating inside her heavy robes that night. And suddenly the sweat was there.

Trinity burns cold...

She sighed, reluctant to walk this memory yet again, but once the nightmare began it always ran its course. Resigned, she picked her way across the field of charred limbs jutting from the snow, making for the hated temple that waited across the square. Her *weraldur* was at her back, his axe unsheathed lest some stray cultist had survived the massacre to threaten her. She recalled that a chasm-faced maniac was due to rise from the snow when they were halfway across the plaza and pointed him out to her guardian in good time. The cultist was duly despatched. Her *weraldur* would have caught him anyway, but the warning speeded matters along.

The Whitecrow and old Elias Waite were waiting for her by the heavy oak doors of the temple. Three squads of the regiment's finest were lined up alongside them, covering the entrance with lasrifles and bayonets while a pair of Sentinels prowled about, swivelling and tilting restlessly at the waist to scope the building. The rainbow light blazing from the stained glass window above transformed them all into torn shadows, insubstantial and fragile.

Which is nothing less than the truth, Skjoldis mused.

'You summoned me, Ensor Cutler,' she said, playing her part in the past once more.

'That I did, Mistress Raven.' It was the first time he had looked her in the eye, though he'd watched her covertly often enough, thinking she hadn't seen it. From the day she joined the regiment he'd been drawn to her strangeness, but sanity had kept him away. Now, in this twisted town she was irresistible. Inevitable.

He pointed towards the coruscating light streaming from the window above. 'As our sanctioned shaman, it occurred to me you might have some insights into this matter, lady.'

'The Great Wyrm has poisoned this place,' she answered. 'You were wise to clip its wings, but the heart of the beast still beats. You must find it and destroy it.'

'Well, I don't expect the finding will be troublesome,' Cutler said with forced lightness, 'but as to the other part...' He threw her a defiant grin. 'That might prove interesting.'

'I will come with you,' she said.

Did I ever have a choice or was the past as fated as this dream is now?

'I'll be glad to have you along, Raven.'

'That is not my name, Ensor Cutler.'

He nodded, weighing that up. 'Then perhaps you'll give me a better one when this is done, but right now...' Cutler turned to face the temple. 'I've a snake to crush under my boot.'

'Now hold fire there, Ensor!' Waite protested. 'I say we torch this heathen nest like the rest of the town. We ain't got no call to go in there...'

'I'm afraid we do,' Cutler said. 'Burning won't be enough, Elias. We have to be sure.' He glanced at Skjoldis, seeking her approval for the first time. 'Am I right, lady?'

'You are correct,' she said. 'If the evil slips away it will take root elsewhere.'

'Since when did her word hold any sway with you, Ensor?' Waite looked at his friend askance. 'She's a witch in a town gone to the Hells with sorcery. For all we know the taint might be inside her too!'

'That's enough!' Cutler snapped, then his tone softened as he recognised the fear in his friend's eyes. 'I'm not asking you to come with us, Elias.'

'Now Ensor, you know that ain't what I meant...' But the relief in the old man's voice gave him away. He was almost sick with terror, just like the greybacks facing the temple. They were all veterans of untold carnage, but the horror haunting this town was worse than any flesh and blood enemy. They all sensed that a man risked losing much more than his life in Trinity.

'You know I'll back you to the hilt,' Waite finished weakly.

'Of course, old friend, but I need you right here, watching our backs in case anything gets past us.' Cutler turned to Skjoldis. 'Any idea what we're dealing with here?'

She sighed and spoke the litany of the nightmare: 'The Great Wyrm has many hues and poisons, Ensor Cutler. Some will turn hearts sour with black passions or rose-scented deliriums. Others will twist the mind with impossible despair or desperate possibility. Rage and lust, anguish and ambition, all are playthings of the Wyrm at the Heart of the World, but all corrupt the soul equally and warp the body like putty in the hands of a lunatic child.'

She saw him grasping for mockery or humour – anything to blunt the peril of her words. 'So tell me the really bad news?' he wanted to say, but her cold gaze wouldn't allow him the mercy.

The Great Wyrm is not a thing to be mocked, Ensor Cutler. Will you ever learn that lesson, I wonder?

And then the daemon bell chimed once again and any hope of levity was gone. Terror congealed amongst the soldiers like bad blood. Skjoldis knew every one of them was praying he wouldn't be called upon to enter that desecrated temple. She also knew they had nothing to fear on that count because the burden had always fallen on Cutler, herself and her *weraldur* alone and always would.

'Psyker,' a voice buzzed in the wind, bone dry and impossibly distant. 'Are you there?'

The words sent a ripple of discord through the world. The swirling snow flickered into static and the memory of Trinity was swept away, carrying the men and the town back to limbo. Skjoldis sighed as a jagged shape twitched out of the chaos.

'Hello Abel,' she said.

Standing rigid on the riverbank like a rusting statue in his Zouave armour, Audie Joyce watched the returning Sentinels shepherd a gunboat into camp. A tall figure loomed at its prow, so still he might have been a statue himself. Though the newcomer's peaked cap was missing there could be no mistaking his calling. This was the commissar Captain Vendrake had gone chasing after.

'He's got a face to raise the Hells,' Audie Joyce muttered into the turgid waters where the murdered saint slept. He knew that Gurdy-Jeff had endured beyond death, as true heroes of the Imperium always did. The saint had followed his killers into the Coil, drifting along the silt bed and touching their dreams, but only Audie had been found worthy of his blessing. That blessing had carried him from green cap to knighthood and there was no telling where the path would end.

Blood... for... the God-Emperor...

'You say something, preacher?' a fellow Zouave asked over the vox.

Realising he'd left his armour's vox-channel open, Joyce smiled. For all their airs and graces, the Zouaves hung on his every word. The day was fast approaching when Audie would replace that fossil Machen at the head of the brotherhood. Sure, there weren't a whole lot of them left now, but it would still be a fine thing. The Emperor and Uncle Calhoun would be mighty proud of him.

'Penance just sailed into camp, brothers,' Joyce broadcast, reading the gunboat's insignia, 'and Pain won't be far behind.'

'What is this madness?' the shape hissed, oscillating wildly as it struggled to find a form in limbo. 'Where are you, psyker?'

'I am dreaming, Abel,' Skjoldis answered, 'and you are intruding.'

The spectre considered her reply. 'This is how you dream?'

Abel's confusion was telling. He – if indeed Abel was a *he* – did not possess the wyrd. He had little understanding of the immaterium and even less interest. His presence in her mind was facilitated by an astropath, a human relay station trained to channel telepathic messages across the void. The astropath's name had been eroded away by that corrosive flow of information long ago, along with everything else that had once made him human. He was a powerful psyker, yet he was also nothing. His mind was like a bright light shinning from an empty shell.

Abel was a remote ghost inside that shell, a shadow presence beyond

Skjoldis's reach. She had often extended covert feelers through the astro-path, hoping to taste Abel's mind, but had always met a blank. It was as if Abel had no psychic presence whatsoever. Forced to fall back on intuition, she had constructed a picture from his words alone, but that had proved equally frustrating. Abel did not talk like anyone she had ever encountered. His cadence was skewed and his expression stilted, his thoughts seem-ingly shaped by tactics and logistics alone, as if war was his sole concern.

'You are not welcome here,' Skjoldis said.

'I require the Counterweight,' Abel stated, dismissing the dream state as irrelevant, along with her reproach. 'The Pendulum must fall upon the Crown.'

She frowned. Abel's fondness for code words and allusions irritated her more than his coldness. 'That is impossible,' she replied. 'Our force has become divided.'

'Divided? How so? Why so?' he snapped. 'I instructed that you maintain cohesion of your assets at all times.'

Skjoldis bridled at his contempt. 'Our situation here is volatile. There is disquiet amongst the officers. We have been waiting too long...'

'And the waiting is over. A convoy of newly sworn janissaries is inbound for the Crown. They are due in three days time. I will divert them to your position.'

'We are not ready.'

'Another opportunity will not arise for many... months, psyker.'

'Give me a week.'

'I may not have a week,' Abel said. 'My position has become precarious. Certain of my agents have been exposed.'

'Will they betray you? Do they know your identity?'

'*Nobody* knows my identity,' Abel said. 'Not even this husk of a telepath who carries my voice.'

'Then why are you so frightened?'

'I am not frightened,' Abel hissed, displaying rare passion, 'but the Water Caste are subtle and clever. That ancient monster O'Seishin is getting too close.'

'Then why did you lure him to the Diadem?'

'To make him vulnerable! He is the true engineer of this stalemate and he is the key to ending it.'

'What of Wintertide and the Sky Marshall?'

The shape flickered, but said nothing.

'Who are you, Abel?' Skjoldis asked.

'You're a bloody fool, Vendrake!' Machen snarled, stomping forward as his fellow captain leapt from his Sentinel. 'You've brought a snake right into our camp!' He thrust an ironclad paw towards the scarred man watching from the gunboat. 'He'll betray us the first chance he gets.'

There were murmurs of assent from the greybacks crowding the riverbank.

'He's a commissar, but he's Providence born!' Vendrake shouted over the growing hubbub. 'He'll give us a fair hearing!' But there was no con-viction in his voice.

'We murdered an Imperial confessor and his retinue!' Machen mocked. 'There's no going back from that!'

The greybacks roared their support and closed in on the gunboat like jackals.

'You're right,' the commissar called as he stepped onto the gangplank. 'There is no going back.' He didn't shout, yet his voice cut through the mob, snuffing out the clamour like a chill wind. None of them would meet his searching, glacial gaze. Even Machen looked away, blinking furiously.

The commissar nodded with infinite weariness, as if he had seen it all before. 'This far down the road to Hell you can only go forward.'

'Who are you, Abel?' Skjoldis repeated firmly. 'If you want my help you will tell me.'

'I have already answered this,' Abel said finally.

That was true, even if his answer had been a lie.

Abel professed to be a senior naval officer aboard the Sky Marshall's battleship, a man with connections that ran right to the nerve-centre of Kircher's inner cadre. He also claimed to lead a covert resistance movement dedicated to exposing the 'Phaedran Lie'. He was playing a long and dangerous game that required staunch allies and perfect timing. With access to the records of all inbound regiments, Abel had been quick to spot the potential of the 19th Arkan.

'You do not belong here,' Abel had said during that first, fleeting psychic contact in orbit almost a year ago. 'Your regiment has been betrayed.'

After the Arkan fled into the wilderness Abel had approached Skjoldis every night, wooing her with tantalising nuggets of information that offered a glimmer of hope. Finally she had told the Whitecrow and ever the gambler, he had taken a chance on Abel.

'What do we have to lose?' he'd said.

And so they'd listened and Abel's counsel had proven sound. He had outlined rebel patrol routes and supply lines, guided them to ammunition dumps and outposts, even revealed passwords that changed on a daily basis, always keeping them one step ahead of the enemy. But over the months his advice had grown more elaborate, his strategies bolder, and somewhere along the way their goal had changed from survival to striking back at the Sky Marshall.

You were right Hardin Vendrake, Skjoldis mused. *The regiment is being moved about like a piece on a regicide board, but the Whitecrow and I were never the players.*

'Tell me you hate them,' Skjoldis demanded. 'Tell me you hate the Sky Marshall and his puppet masters.'

Make me believe it...

She sharpened her senses to a razorwire edge, eager to taste every nuance of Abel's answer. It came without hesitation: 'I despise them.'

'Skjoldis!' called another voice. Then again and again...

An insistent pounding reverberated through the dream. Briefly she wondered if it was the daemon bell chiming from lost Trinity. Then she heard her *weraldur* bellow and her eyes flicked open. Dazed, she saw her guardian striding towards the cabin door just as it was flung open. Vendrake stood at the threshold, looking half-dead and all damned, but it was the face over his shoulder that tore her fully awake. One of its eyes was a lustreless black sun, the other a corroded augmetic rammed through the eye socket. Both were bound in a lattice of scars that glowed like seams of magma beneath parchment skin.

Worst of all, she recognised that face.

'He asked us to follow him into the heart of darkness,' Audie Joyce whispered to the still waters of the river. 'And then he promised he'd bring us out the other side if we had the guts for it.'

The Zouave was alone on the riverbank. While his comrades chewed over the commissar's revelations in noisy clusters he was communing with the drowned saint.

'He told us the Sky Marshall had broken faith with the Emperor and turned xenos lover,' Joyce went on. 'Told us the blueskins have been playing the Guard for fools, turning good men bad and chewing up the ones who stood tall.' He sighed. 'It's a helluva thing if it's true.'

Joyce glanced at the command boat moored further along the riverbank. The commissar had gone in there to talk with the witch. With a bit of luck he might even shoot her.

'The name's Iverson,' the dead man said, watching Skjoldis from across the table. His eyes were no longer monstrous – the left was a faded blue, the right a failing augmetic – and his scars no longer burned, but their geometry was unchanged. That tortured lattice held her gaze like a cage.

He looks younger, but it is him, Skjoldis decided. *And he is not dead.*

'It's an old wound,' he said, misunderstanding her fascination. 'Razorvine. I walked right into the bloody stuff. Strange to think it, but I was green to Phaedra once.' He smiled with bleak humour, distorting the mesh. She saw many things caught up in that net: determination and despair, broken faith and unbreakable hate, courage and the fear that courage was only a lie, murders old and new... but not a trace of recognition.

He does not know me. But how can that be? And how can he be younger?

'It was a lifetime ago,' he said.

She caught her breath, misunderstanding his statement.

'But are you still a fool?' Machen mocked from the doorway. 'It seems to me you must be, walking into a den of renegades.'

'I'm not here to judge you,' Iverson said, keeping his eyes on Skjoldis.

He does not know me, but he senses I am the authority here, she realised.

'You really expect us to believe that prattle about a pardon?' Machen snorted.

'No, I don't expect *you* to believe it, captain,' Iverson said. 'There'll be no pardon for any of us, but it's what your men needed to hear.'

Machen snorted. 'Then why would we help you?'

'Because we've all been betrayed,' Iverson said. 'And because we want the same thing.'

'Justice,' Vendrake said quietly. He was slouched in a chair, but his eyes were bright.

'To the Hells with justice!' Machen spat. 'I want to see those bastards burn!'

'Then let me help you,' Iverson said, talking to them all, but speaking to the witch. 'Trust me.'

I do, Skjoldis discovered to her surprise. *Against all sense and sanity, I do trust you, Iverson. Whatever you were in the past, you are untainted now.*

And finally, with the relief of one who has carried a burden too long, she told them about Abel and the Counterweight.

'The pendulum falls...' Verne Loomis stuttered. 'Three days... We have... three days...' His nose erupted in a welter of blood and his eyeballs rolled, showing the whites. Roach caught him before he hit the ground.

'Easy Verne,' the scout whispered, setting the trembling man down gently. 'We hear you. You just rest up now.'

Roach felt bad for his fellow greyback. Loomis hadn't been right in the head since he'd walked in on the warp-spawned nightmare in Dorm 31, way back in space. That horror had turned him into a wall-eyed scarecrow that saw things that nobody else could see. Sometimes those things made him giggle and sometimes they made him cry like a baby, but lately they mostly made him scream.

'It hurts,' Loomis moaned. 'Every time she talks to me it's like she turns my head inside out.'

'I know, but you done real good and she's gone now,' Roach said.

Unfortunately for Loomis his experience had left him sensitive to the wyrd, so he'd drawn the short straw of 'talking' to the witch long distance. He was the Arkan infiltrators' psychic vox-receiver and it was burning him out.

'Whenever she does it *they* can see me,' Loomis grabbed Roach's wrist in a vicelike claw. 'They can see right inside of me and I know they want to come in.'

Roach turned to the others. 'He can't take much more.'

'He won't need to,' said Klint Sandefur curtly. 'He's done his duty. The rest is down to us.'

The blandly handsome Arkan lieutenant cast a steely eye over the men gathered in the empty silo. They were deep in the bowels of the Diadem, well below the waterline. It was about as remote as they could get on the rebel refinery, but nowhere was really safe. They only gathered when Loomis got twitchy, which meant the witch had something to say.

'You all heard Loomis. We don't have much time,' Sandefur continued. He was the leader of the eight-man infiltration team who had 'betrayed' their colonel and signed up with the rebels. Roach couldn't fault his smarts, but he was a cold bastard and too heavy on the Creed by a long shot.

'Redemption Day is coming and I don't want any mistakes,' Sandefur finished sternly.

'Can't come soon enough for me, lieutenant.' Jakob Dix drawled. 'Another month hanging out with these xenos lovers and I'll start buying into their Greater Crud!'

'You do and I'll shoot you myself, Trooper Dix,' Sandefur said without a trace of humour. 'We've been sleeping with the enemy near on five months now. This isn't the time to fall for them.'

The man thinks he's the Whitecrow in waiting, Roach decided. He stifled a scowl as he weighed up his comrades. Mister Fish wore his usual serene smile, unmoved by Loomis's news. Dix was grinning like a ghoul in a graveyard and his buddy Tuggs was smirking along with him, showing buckteeth big enough to stop a bolt-round. The black crags of Pope's face were unreadable in the shadows, but then they were pretty much that way in any light. Guido Ortega's expression was only too easy to read. His eyes were wide and he was biting his flabby lips nervously. Roach guessed the Verzante pilot had given up on Sandefur's 'Redemption Day' ever coming and probably hadn't lost much sleep over it. Thinking it over, Roach realised he felt much the same way himself.

The rebs have treated us pretty good, he admitted. *Better than the Guard ever did. Even the blueskins ain't so bad once you get used to them...*

'I know this has been tough on all of you,' Sandefur was saying. 'We're soldiers, not filthy spies, but you'll get the chance for some payback.' He turned to Roach. 'You're certain you can breach the Eye, scout?'

'No problem,' Roach answered with a nod. 'See, we got this blueblood chump in our gang, name of Olim. He's got a regular shift up there. Man's the platoon punch-bag and I've become his best pal in the whole world. He'll get me in for a look-see.'

'Do you have a problem with that, Mister Roach?' Sandefur asked, catching the scout's sour tone.

'No sir, I'm just dandy,' Roach said, 'but things could get messy in there.'

'Nothing we can't clean up!' Dix quipped, raising a guffaw from Tuggs.

'Well let's make sure you've got the right tools for the job.' Sandefur turned to the dark skinned greyback. 'Pope, did you secure the devices?'

'I got 'em right here.' Pope, who'd wangled a stint guarding the tech-priests' arms laboratorium, slapped the satchel on his shoulder. 'Swiped four of 'em. Couldn't risk no more. The cogboys watch their new toys like hawks.'

'Four it is then,' Sandefur said crisply. 'That's one per man taking a shot at the Eye. Pass them round, greyback.'

Pope pulled out a bundle of glassy, needle-like daggers with bulbous hilts and handed them over to the men chosen to strike at the comms centre: Roach, Fish, Dix and Tuggs. The two Badlanders eyed the fragile weapons dubiously.

'What d'you expect me to do with this here toothpick, lieutenant?' Dix snorted. 'It ain't fit to slice an owlskunk's hide. Won't do spit against an iron-plated zombie!'

'You got that wrong, Dixie,' Pope drawled. 'I seen these pigstickers being tested out. One jab'll put down the biggest of the cogboys' freaks.'

'And one jab is all you'll get,' Sandefur warned. 'We got the word on this gear from the colonel's source. They're brand-new tech, something the cogboys have cooked up with their blueskin pals...' He trailed off, looking uneasy at the blasphemy he was describing.

'It ain't right messing with stuff like that,' Dix said, sniffing his blade suspiciously. Tuggs nodded in vigorous agreement.

'Look, I won't pretend I like it any better than you,' Sandefur snapped, 'but we'll be turning the heretics' weapons against them. And you'll need every edge you can get in the Eye.'

'Go on,' Roach encouraged, genuinely curious now. 'Tell us what these things do.'

Sandefur straightened and nodded. 'Those blades are mods of EMP tech. They'll hit a target with an electromagnetic pulse that'll fry its machine spirit, but one charge is all they pack, so choose wisely.'

'We'll make 'em count,' Roach promised.

'See that you do, Dustsnake,' Sandefur said. 'Right, we're done here. You all know your parts, so let's make Providence and the Emperor proud.'

'It is done,' Skjoldis said. 'They have heard me.' She sank back into her chair, drained by her efforts.

'Good work,' Iverson said. He turned to the two captains. 'Brief your men then do it all over again. Hammer the plan home until they're breathing it. There will be no second chances. And find me a chainsword.'

They left without a word. All the words had already been said, all the arguments fought to a standstill. After Skjoldis's revelation Machen had raged and Vendrake had laughed, but Iverson had stuck to questions until the questions had become tactics and Abel's plan had become their plan.

He knows it is our only chance, Skjoldis observed. *He saw that from the beginning and embraced it with the fatalism of a drowning man.*

'Do you trust this Abel?' Iverson asked. He had asked before, but now they were alone he wanted the truth.

'No,' she said, 'but I trust his hatred for the Sky Marshall.'

He nodded, holding her gaze. 'Have we met before, witch?'

She froze, half expecting his scars to ignite with hellfire, but his expression was simply puzzled.

'That is not possible,' she answered cautiously. 'You said you were taken from Providence as a boy, while I have been away scarcely a year.'

'I know, but the look on your face when you first saw me...' Iverson faltered and she glimpsed something barbed shift beneath the black ice of his soul.

'I was sleeping,' she said. 'You walked in on a nightmare.'

'I see,' he said, but he obviously didn't.

And I hope you never do, Holt Iverson.

CHAPTER TWELVE

The Last Day: Counterweight

The witch knew me. Her veil couldn't hide the recognition in her eyes. Perhaps it was a consequence of her wyrd, some remote viewing or precognitive vision, yet neither would explain her dread of me. But I've no time to dwell on this mystery. Despite Raven's strangeness I must trust her as she trusts her shadowy benefactor, Abel. They are both enemies of my enemy and perhaps that's the best that friends can be in Hell. Besides, Abel's plan offers our only chance of ending this heresy.

Abel. He claims he's been building a network of dissidents for years, fomenting discord and preparing for a day of reckoning. Well, that day is today. In nine hours mutiny will break out on the Sky Marshall's battleship. The resistance doesn't have the muscle to take the ship, but that's where we come in. Abel calls us his 'Counterweight' – the secret weapon that will swing the balance of power. His mutiny will open a window for us to reach the Sky Marshall and end this. But first we have to get into space.

There aren't many ways off Phaedra, but the Diadem offers one of the few. The old refinery has its own shuttle, a rickety tanker used to ferry promethium into orbit. With its silos emptied the tug will easily take half a regiment – not a comfortable ride, but a short one at least. Unfortunately the Diadem is one of the most heavily defended enemy bastions on the entire planet. We can't hope to capture it, so we'll have to get in and out before the rebels know what's hit them. Once the assault begins there can be no hesitation and no mercy. We push on until the job is done – or until we're done.

Three hours from now a convoy of Concordance janissaries will pass through a choke point in the river, a narrow fjord overlooked by an escarpment...

– Iverson's Journal

Howling with blissful rage, Audie Joyce leapt from the cliff top and plummeted towards the stalled convoy far below. The four ships looked like toys overrun with swarming ants. The gunboat in the lead was a blazing ruin and its three charges, all cumbersome hover barges, were in disarray. Rebel janissaries scurried about the decks, tormented by hidden snipers and heavy fire from the Sentinels lining the ridge. Iverson's gunboat was steaming up behind the convoy, packed with greybacks. Machen was clinging to the prow like an iron barnacle, excluded from the sky dive by his massive Thundersuit.

This glory is mine to lead, the young preacher thought.

'Flay the xenos lovers, brothers!' he shouted. As the ships raced closer he opened up with his heavy stubber, heralding his path with a hail of bullets. Plunging through the air alongside him, his fellow Zouaves followed suit and stitched the rebels with high velocity rounds. Together they were a coterie of armoured angels, falling into fiery atonement.

A beam of incandescent light flared up from an emplacement below and struck the man to Joyce's right, detonating him in a whirling nova of blood and steel. The preacher knight cursed, feeling the loss of his brother like a physical blow. He swivelled his aim and tore apart the rebels manning the lethal rail gun before it could fire again.

A flock of small saucers rose from the convoy to meet them, tilting awkwardly as they tried to aim their underslung weaponry towards the sky. Joyce whooped as he smashed through the strata of drones, scattering them like broken spinning tops.

'Thrusters!' he ordered, triggering the repulsion jet on his back. The Stormsuits didn't carry true jetpacks, but the single use rockets were enough to cushion their fall. As the Zouaves slowed, a stray blast from a drone ripped through another knight's rocket pack. Trailing puffs of steam he shot past Joyce and hit the leading barge like a missile, pulverising a gaggle of rebels and punching right through the deck. A second later the ship quaked as the human bomb ruptured something vital in its guts. Black smoke poured from the rent as Joyce crashed down into chaos. Grinning fiercely he fired up the buzz saws attached to his wrists and tore into the rebels, hacking a blind path through the choking, flailing mob. His heart soared as blood spattered his armour, lending it a crimson sheen.

'Blood for the God-Emperor!' the preacher bellowed, saying the words aloud for the first time.

'We're done here, Silverstorm,' Vendrake called into the vox. The Zouaves were down and Iverson's ship was seconds away from the convoy. 'You know the drill. Head for the rendezvous point, double time.'

Yanking levers expertly, he hauled his Sentinel away from the precipice and spun about. Up ahead the escarpment dipped sharply into the jungle, but Vendrake charged down the incline as if damnation was on his tail. And maybe she was. Lady Damnation, chasing him down in a rust-bitten Sentinel that reeked of the burial pit and ran on unclean truths.

I'm coming for you, my love, he heard her sing again, closer now, always closer. Vendrake's Glory-fired eyes tracked every dip and snarl in his path like violet lasers, triggering live wire reflexes that bound him to his machine.

He'd given Iverson his word he wouldn't use the Glory today, knowing all along that his word was worthless.

I lost my honour at Trinity. I just didn't know it until I got to Phaedra.

As his gunboat bore down on the rearmost barge Iverson thumbed the activation stud of a borrowed chainsword. Angry tremors reverberated up through his metal fist, falling into harmony with the martial beats pounding from Machen's shoulder speakers. While his comrades crouched in cover the Zouave captain stood tall at the prow, suppressing the rebels with a constant stream of fire. He was like a tank and an orchestra combined, his music vying with the chatter of his heavy stubber. Sporadic ripostes flared back from the barge and scorched his iron hide, but he paid them no heed.

'Now!' Machen called, silencing his gun. His comrades surged to their feet and Zsombor, the last Corsair, cast his grappling hook. A wave of other grapples followed, launching from the gunboat like a shoal of barbed worms. They snarled in the gunwales of the barge and bound the ships a moment before they collided. There was a bone jarring impact and the greybacks roared furiously, eager for the fight.

'For Providence and the Imperium!' Iverson shouted as he leapt over the narrow divide. His kinsmen followed like grey wolves, their lasrifles bristling with bayonets. They landed amongst a rabble of surprised janissaries who'd been crouching in cover. Before the rebels could level their guns Iverson was in close, slashing and stabbing and thinking of Reve.

She was a traitor... He sawed through an officer's breastplate... *She would have turned on us...* Felt the teeth chew into the ribs beneath... *She'll answer me...* Thrust through the turncoat's back, ripping away the face of the man behind... *When she comes back...* Yanked the blade free... *Why hasn't she come back?*

A withering fusillade rained down on the brawling mob, slicing indiscriminately through greybacks and janissaries alike. Iverson spun and saw a band of armoured xenos warriors perched on the upper deck. There were six of them, three kneeling and three standing behind, formed up in a classic defensive line. They fired their pulse rifles in disciplined, alternating bursts, cooperating to maintain an unbroken barrage. Iverson's bile rose at the sight of their backswept helmets and impassive lens-studded faceplates. Fire Warriors – the true enemy.

'Machen!' he yelled into his vox-bead. 'Upper deck – take them down!'

The Zouave acknowledged with a hail of bullets, but none found their mark. The air around the xenos squad crackled and scattered the rounds like sparking confetti. Iverson swore as he noticed a peculiar, tetrahedral machine hovering above the warriors. The thing must be some kind of shield drone, upgraded so it could throw a barrier around an entire squad.

There's no second guessing blueskin tech, Iverson thought bitterly. *It moves too fast for us.*

Machen threw up a gauntlet to protect his faceplate as the tau retaliated with a volley of pulse rounds. Even his tank-like Thundersuit could not withstand such punishment for long, so Machen launched himself across the divide and crashed down onto the barge. With his head bowed like a raging bull he charged the xenos squad, scattering soldiers of both camps while the Fire Warriors tracked him smoothly, chewing deep craters into his armour. His left knee guard ruptured and spurted steam, but he was moving too fast to stop. He smashed into the wall of the upper deck with a concussion that shook the whole barge and sent one of the tau tumbling towards him. He batted it overboard with his stubber and plunged the whirring bit of his drill attachment into the wall, tearing through the metal like paper.

'Wait! We need the ship!' Iverson shouted into his vox-bead, but Machen paid no heed. Cursing, the commissar fought his way towards him, hacking down rebels and shouldering aside greybacks. The battle was raging across the entire deck now, but the turncoats had little heart for it and were going down fast.

They don't know what's hit them, Iverson reflected grimly. *This deep inside the Coil they thought they were safe.*

With a shriek of tortured metal the upper deck lurched and canted downwards, spilling four of the tau from their perch. Machen caught one on his drill and stamped down on the others. The impaled alien spun about on the drill like a broken doll as its chest was liquidised. A moment later it whirled away in two pieces, trailing streamers of gore. The last Fire Warrior clung to the deck above, scrabbling for purchase. Machen tore him down and slung him to the mob. A dozen bayonets pierced the xenos before it could rise.

'We need the damn ship!' Iverson bawled into Machen's faceplate as he came up alongside.

The captain grinned, his face glistening with sweat behind the glass. 'And you have it!'

It was true. The fighting was over. Most of the rebels were dead and the survivors were on their knees with their hands over their heads.

'Move on to the second ship,' Iverson ordered.

'What about them?' Lieutenant Grayburn asked, indicating the prisoners. Bierce was standing by his side, watching his protégé expectantly. Iverson threw him a curt nod. 'Kill them,' he said.

'Please...' The rebel's plea was torn into a wet gurgle by Joyce's buzzsaws. His head spun away and his body slipped to its knees, offering up a fountain of blood. Joyce leaned forward, breathing deeply as he bathed his armour in the sacrificial spray.

'What in the Hells are you doing, boy?' Wade said as he marched out of the smoke. 'We're not bloody savages!'

Dripping gore, Joyce regarded his fellow Zouave. Wade was Machen's creature and an unbeliever to the core, but still... The boy hesitated, biting his lip uncertainly. Then he remembered how the saint had purged old Elias Waite and knew he had to be strong.

'You're a disgrace to the brotherhood,' Wade went on. 'When Captain Machen hears–'

Joyce thrust a buzzsaw into his fellow knight's visor. The glass shattered and Wade jerked about as his skull was bisected at the eye line. The preacher tugged his blade free and the heretic toppled over with a heavy clang.

'The Emperor condemns,' Joyce whispered reverently. He heard the other Zouaves approaching and turned to greet them as they emerged from the smoke. Together they had turned the barge into a floating abattoir.

But it won't float much longer, Joyce realised as another explosion rocked the deck. 'We need to move on,' he said. 'Brother Ellis gut-shot this tug good and proper when he came down.'

'The lieutenant...' Lascelles began, pointing at Wade's body.

'He died for the God-Emperor,' Joyce said. 'His penance is all done now.' None of them questioned him.

The Last Day: Lake Amrythaa

The convoy is ours, what's left of it anyway. We lost one of the barges and that fool Machen almost wrecked another, so I've decided to take the Triton along. We need the capacity and the firepower. It's a gamble, but if Abel's clearance codes are good I doubt the rebels will question it. Certainly the codes have worked so far. We cancelled the convoy's distress calls and the rebels bought it. Of course they might be bluffing, hoping to lure us into a trap, but we'll have to take that chance.

We picked up the Sentinels an hour ago. Vendrake's burning Glory again, but at least he's got his squad running like clockwork, which is more than I can say for the Zouaves. There's an unspoken power struggle going on amongst them that makes me uneasy. I hope Machen can hold them together a little longer because we're going to need his knights on the Diadem. My kinsmen fought well this morning, but there's no telling what's waiting for them on that old rig. We're coming up on Lake Amrythaa now...

– Iverson's Journal

The witch opened her eyes. 'It has begun,' she said. 'Abel has made his play and cast the Sky Marshall's dominion into disorder.'

'What about our infiltrators?' Iverson asked. He was standing at the port-hole of his cabin, staring out at the mist wreathed lake.

'I have sent the signal. They will move within the hour.'

'Then we're set.' He shoved a battered journal into his pocket and turned. As she unravelled from her lotus position on the floor he stepped over to help her rise, but she flinched away.

'Why are you so afraid of me?' he asked.

Her green eyes narrowed. 'Now is not the time to talk of it.'

'It might be the only time we'll get.'

She got up stiffly. 'Do not go home, commissar.'

'What?'

'You must never return to Providence,' she urged.

'And how in the Hells would I ever manage such a thing?'

Perhaps only *through the Hells,* Skjoldis realised with a flash of insight. She shivered and backed towards the cabin door.

'You should seek a clean death today, Iverson,' she said gravely.

'Don't play games with me, witch.' Suddenly he seemed every inch the Imperial commissar. 'You're hiding something.'

'Your shadows are real, Iverson.' She turned then hesitated at the threshold. 'Even if they are not what you think they are.'

The blood drained from his face. 'What are you talking about?'

But she was already gone.

The door of the holding cell slid open and Ambassador O'Seishin glided in on his throne drone. As always, the prisoner was waiting for him behind the force barrier, his expression watchful.

'You asked to see me,' O'Seishin said, concealing the eagerness in his voice. He was certain the moment had finally come. The prisoner was going to turn.

'Here's how it's going to go down,' Cutler said. 'You give me the truth and I'll give you Abel.'

The doors of the turbolift hissed open and Cristobal Olim ushered his charges out into a dimly lit corridor. There wasn't much call for illumination on the upper levels of the Diadem; they were the domain of the tech-priests and their augmented servants, none of whom required light to see. Only a handful of rebel janissaries had any business up here: men with the aptitude to assist the tau engineers who monitored the Eye.

'Are you quite certain this is a good idea, Friend Roach?' Olim asked yet again. 'The Eye is the nerve centre of the Diadem and access is highly restricted. This information you have uncovered... perhaps I could pass it on to the tech-priests...'

Roach shook his head regretfully. 'That's real decent of you, Cristo, but it's ugly news. Trust me, you don't want to be the man telling it.'

And I don't want to be the man doing this, Roach thought bitterly. He felt like he'd signed up to a one-way voyage on a sinking ship.

Olim licked his lips nervously. 'Perhaps you are right. I would not wish to endanger my imminent elevation to the Eye.'

'Exactly!' Roach gave the chubby janissary a slap on the back. 'I just hope you won't forget your friends when you move on.'

Like I've forgotten Alvarez and Estrada and all the others in my cluster...

'A nobleman never neglects his allies,' Olim preened, 'but my talents would be wasted in the Mire. I am a master conjoiner of communications.'

A halfway-decent vox-operator, Roach translated. Olim wasn't the dumbest blueblood he'd ever met, but he was mighty close. He was also so full of himself it was a miracle he didn't burst open at the seams. Someone with serious muscle had been pulling strings to get Olim a shift up in the Eye while keeping his feet down among the grunts – where he needed a buddy like Roach to look out for him. It was all part of The Plan.

And this is where The Plan really kicks in...

The infiltrators had received the go ahead from the witch a couple of hours ago and Roach had gone to Olim with 'The Story', saying he'd found out something so big they had to take it straight to the Eye. The rig's control room was located at its crown, right under the beacon tower. The whole level was locked down with security codes and patrolled by combat servitors, but Olim had the clearance. Whoever his mysterious backer was, he was certainly a major player.

I'd lay odds of ten-to-one we're talking the same *player who's backing the Whitecrow,* Roach guessed. *Whoever that sneaky son-of-a-bitch is, he's in deep.*

'You're doing the right thing here, Cristo,' he said cheerily, swallowing his own doubts. 'It might even speed up your promotion, but if you're worried I can always go through First Friend Alvarez.'

'No, no... that won't be necessary! But must these other gentlemen really accompany us?' Olim indicated Roach's three companions. 'Even one of you is a frightful breach of protocol.'

'I hear you, but they're part of the story,' Roach said. Dix and Tuggs nodded vigorously. Mister Fish smiled.

'Very well,' Olim said, sounding as if the weight of the war was on his shoulders, 'but I do hope this story of yours is a good one.'

'Hey, you got nothing to worry about, fatboy,' Dix said with a chuckle. 'It's gonna blow things wide open!'

'I have already told you the truth about the war,' O'Seishin said.

'Then tell me about Wintertide,' Cutler urged. 'If I'm going to sign up to your army I'll want to meet the general.'

O'Seishin's nostrils dilated in a smirk. 'You *have* met him, Ensor Cutler. Many times.'

'You.' Cutler nodded, unsurprised. 'You're Wintertide.'

'There is no Wintertide,' O'Seishin corrected. 'A mythical figurehead is infinitely more versatile than the reality could ever be. Wintertide is nowhere, so the enemy believes he is everywhere. Wintertide is nothing, so the enemy believes he is everything they fear.'

'But you're the man pulling the strings?'

'Following the lamentable fall of our revered Ethereal, Aun O'Hamaan, the honour of supreme administration has been mine, yes.'

'I thought war was Fire Warrior business.'

'Phaedra shall herald a new way of war that lies beyond the faculties of the Fire Caste,' O'Seishin crowed. 'The true craft of war lies in conquering your opponent without engaging him in battle.'

'You're telling me you're not up to the fight?'

'The Tau Empire is potent, but its enemies are legion. We cannot prosper through force of arms alone.'

'Like I said before, this is all a game to you.'

'Perhaps,' O'Seishin conceded, 'but if so, it is the noblest game of all.'

Olim brought his party to a halt outside a sealed metal hatch embossed with a stylised eye. The reinforced plasteel looked solid enough to stop a lascannon at close range. Nervously, the nobleman raised a podgy hand to the keypad by the door.

'Hold-up a moment, Friends,' said a familiar voice behind them. They turned and saw Ricardo Alvarez step from the shadows.

He's been following us all along, Roach realised with a start.

'Ah... Cluster Leader Alvarez,' Olim stuttered. 'I was just assisting...'

'Shut up, aristo.' The janissary commander's gaze bored into Roach. 'What's going on here, Friend Roach?'

Roach stared back dumbly, as if betrayal had strangled his words.

'Give me a good reason not to call this in, Claiborne,' Alvarez said quietly.

He's giving us a chance, Roach realised. *Maybe I can still turn this around...*

'I got plenty,' Dix blurted out. His friendly grin never slipped as he opened fire. Alvarez was thrown against the wall, leaking smoke from his scorched chest. An alarm blared into life before his corpse hit the ground.

The wail of the klaxon startled O'Seishin so badly he almost slipped from his perch. Flustered, he activated his drone's data array and began scouring for information.

'I'll save you the bother,' Cutler said. 'That will be our friend Abel.'

A moment later the muffled cacophony of gunfire exploded in the corridor outside. O'Seishin glanced up anxiously, but his fingers continued to flutter across his data array, as if with a life of their own. The door slid open and a pair of janissaries entered.

'Your report,' the ambassador demanded.

'Counterweight,' one of the newcomers said. He tapped a switch on the wall and the force barrier imprisoning Cutler vanished.

'Impeccable timing, Lieutenant Sandefur,' Cutler said as he loped forward. He threw O'Seishin a wolfish grin and yanked him from his throne. 'See, you're not the only player in this game, Si.'

Shas'vre Jhi'kaara was meditating in her quarters when the klaxon sounded. The tau veteran rose nimbly from her unity mat and activated her comms band.

'Fire Watch, status report?' she demanded.

'Unspecified security breach in the Watchtower, shas'vre,' the clipped voice of a Fire Warrior answered. 'Shas'ui Obihara's squad is en route now.'

Jhi'kaara paused, considering. A genuine breach in the eyrie of the tech-priests was doubtful. How could an enemy have penetrated to the highest levels of the Diadem? The duty officer had come to the same conclusion. 'I suspect a system error, shas'vre,' he ventured.

She frowned, knowing he was almost certainly correct. Despite the tech-priests devotions the refinery was in a state of decay and system errors were not uncommon. And yet...

'Prime the Crisis team,' she ordered.

'I don't understand,' Olim blubbered as Dix loomed over him.

'Open the door,' the Badlander said, 'or I'll open you.'

The terrified nobleman punched a code into the keypad and the hatch swivelled open with a whirr of hydraulics. A hulking combat servitor glided into their path from the chamber beyond, its bionic arms extended to cover them with a pair of burst cannons. Dix shoved Olim into its arms as Mister Fish leapt forward and rammed his EMP dagger between its jaws. The heretical blade pulsed and fried the cyborg's lobotomised brain with a surge of current. As the servitor jerked backwards Mister Fish vaulted onto its shoulders and opened fire on the surprised rebels beyond.

'Go!' Dix shouted as he stormed into the cavernous chamber. He and Tuggs blazed away with their carbines, gleefully mowing down charging skitarii guards and fleeing operators while Roach swung back to cover the corridor.

Chattering manically, the EMP scarred combat servitor began to whirl about on its hover skirt. Its arms flailed out and spat plasma around the room. Mister Fish leapt from its shoulders and Olim was flung away, catching several bursts of fire as he tumbled. Each one gouged a burning crater into his flesh and propelled him another step, keeping him on his feet by sheer kinetic force. When his corpse finally hit the ground it was little more than a charred husk.

'Hellfire, Dix! We needed him!' Roach yelled as he peered at the hatch mechanism. 'We got to lock this place down!'

'He had it coming,' Dix chuckled as he hurled a frag grenade across the chamber.

Roach's gaze drifted out to the access corridor and found Alvarez's corpse. The deserter's eyes were wide with the shock of betrayal and sudden death and they were staring straight at Claiborne Roach. The scout fought down the urge to go back and close them.

It won't make any difference. All my chances are used up. There's no getting off this ride now, even if it takes me all the way to the Hells.

The only thing going for the transport shuttle was its size, Guido Ortega decided as he approached the landing pad. To his pilot's eye the ship was a blocky, brutal monstrosity that looked like it had been patched up so many times there was nothing of the original left over. Still, he had no doubt it would fly well enough. The tech-priests might be blind to aesthetics, but they'd keep their precious machines ticking over.

He flinched as a squad of janissaries rushed past him. The whole rig was on alert now and the alarm was drawing security away from the outer platforms. Heading in the opposite direction, Ortega kept his pace swift and confident, trying to look like a man on official business. Unfortunately Verne Loomis wasn't doing so well. Ortega glanced back at his comrade and frowned at his blanched face and bloodshot eyes. The scraggy greyback had always been a strange one, but his last communion with the witch had really pushed him over the edge. He was muttering to himself as he jogged along at Ortega's heels, his lips twisting around the words as if they were broken glass. Ortega couldn't make out what he was saying and didn't want to know.

'You must get a grip, Señor Loomis,' he said as they reached the landing pad. 'With the alarm ringing the sentries will be watchful.'

Loomis gawped, showing black stubs of teeth. Neither of his skewed eyes met the pilot's gaze. 'Then they hear the bell too?' he asked eagerly. A trickle of drool oozed from his lips.

Ortega grimaced, wondering why he'd let Sandefur pair him up with this cretin. If Loomis was the only backup they could spare then Ortega would have preferred to do this alone. The fellow made him physically nauseous.

'Please follow my lead up there,' he said, indicating the landing pad. Loomis nodded vaguely, bobbing his head up and down like a skull on a rubber stalk.

'It's an all-fired grox shoot!' Dix hollered as the last of the skitarii fell. There hadn't been many guards in the Eye and surprise had given the attackers an edge.

'They're coming up the corridor now!' Roach shouted from the hatch.

'So shut the fragging door, breed!' Dix called back cheerily. He and Tuggs were on the far side of the chamber now, chasing down the last of the operators. 'Hey, we got us some blueskins back here!'

A fusillade of plasma hissed down the corridor towards Roach. He ducked back from the threshold and peered at the strange sigils on the keypad, trying to make sense of it. More fire sizzled past him and he heard the hum of an approaching combat servitor. Crouched by the doorway across from him, Mister Fish frowned and gestured urgently.

'I know, man!' Roach snapped. 'I'm on it...'

To the Hells with this crap! He slammed his fist into the keypad and the hatch swung shut. That was usually the way with security – get things wrong and stuff just shut down. At least until somebody came along with the right codes...

'We've got to move fast...' Roach trailed off as he saw a pair of tech-priests sweep from a shadowed recess on the far side of the room. They glided across the floor like wraiths, their faces and limbs lost in billowing swathes of crimson fabric. Roach knew there was no telling what was under those robes. Some tech-priests were just human relics kept alive by augmetic implants, but others were souped-up killing machines packed full of nasty surprises. Something told him the Diadem's priests weren't going to be the easy kind.

'Take out the cogboys!' Roach shouted as he opened fire. Moving in perfect harmony the wraiths leapt away from his volley and latched onto the ceiling like shrouded bugs. As they scuttled overhead he caught a glimpse of chitinous metal tendrils swarming amongst the red robes.

'What you talking about?' Tuggs called as he gunned down a cowering blueskin tech. 'I don't see no–'

One of the priests dropped from above and engulfed him in a red swathe. His scream was cut short by a churning, cracking cacophony that made Roach's hair stand on end. Scant seconds later Tuggs was spewed out in a dozen glistening pieces. Some of them hit Dix, who'd been standing right beside him. With a snarl of hate the Badlander yanked his EMP dagger from his belt and plunged it into the priest. There was an electronic howl and the cyborg's robes erupted into a forest of spines as its tendrils went rigid with terminal shock. Caught in the priest's death throes, Dix was impaled a dozen times over.

Overhead, the second tech-priest raced towards Roach and Mister Fish, dodging past the frantic bursts of their carbines. Desperately the scout dived for the deranged combat servitor and swung a plasma-spitting arm towards the priest. As it leapt towards him three bursts found their mark and brought it crashing down in flames. The smouldering robes were still squirming with life when Roach and Mister Fish unloaded their carbines into it.

'Well, I guess that could have gone down a lot worse,' Roach said. His Saathlaa friend raised a quizzical eyebrow, for once unable to muster a smile. Roach figured he was finally getting cynical.

The landing pad was a massive platform built from moulded rockrete. Spiderwebs of scaffolding and fat metal feeder pipes formed a wall around it, broken by a ramp wide enough to take a tank. Ortega felt horribly vulnerable as he marched up the slope and the 'comrade' at his back wasn't helping his nerves at all. He could hear Loomis babbling away behind him, giggling occasionally, as if at some private joke. Pushing the idiot from his mind, Ortega waved at the janissaries waiting by the shuttle. There were six of them, all young and fired up by the distant alarm.

'How goes it, Friends?' he greeted them jovially.

'What's with th'alert?' the eldest janissary said in a low, liquid cant. Like his comrades, his swarthy face was riddled with tattoos and scars, betraying his ganger origins.

'They didn't tell you about the drill?' Ortega asked, feigning surprise.

'Didn't say no-t'ing to us, grandpa.'

'Well, take it from me, it's just an exercise.' Ortega stepped towards the cargo ramp, but the leader blocked his path.

'Where you t'ink you going, oldster?'

'Evidently they didn't tell you about us either!' Ortega sighed with exaggerated weariness. 'We're cover crew for–'

The janissary shoved him back. 'You t'ink we dumb fraks jus' 'cause we don't talk fancy like–' His lips were still moving when his head spun through the air, hacked clean off by Loomis's machete.

Snarling like a wolf the rangy greyback laid into the other janissaries, moving so fast Ortega could barely follow his lethal jig of chops and swipes. Half the men were dead before they knew what hit them, the other half died seconds after, their faces twisted with terror. Loomis was left standing over a pile of butchered corpses. He had his back to Ortega, but the pilot could tell he was shaking badly.

'Loomis...' the words dried up in Ortega's mouth as the maniac's head swung round to look at him. The pilot was sure a man's neck shouldn't swivel so far.

'They wasn't going to let us in,' Loomis said hoarsely. His eyes gleamed with delight. And they weren't skewed anymore.

'No...' Ortega agreed uncertainly.

'I guess we ought to stash 'em.' Loomis pointed at the cargo hatch.

'Yes...' But suddenly Guido Ortega was quite certain he didn't want to enter that dark space with Verne Loomis. In fact it was the very last thing in the world he wanted to do.

Jakob Dix was a mess. Skewered on the dead tech-priest's rigid, razor-sharp tendrils, he hung suspended in the air like a bug caught in a pincushion. Roach couldn't work out how he was still breathing.

'Wreck whatever you can,' Roach ordered Mister Fish. The Saathlaa nodded and hurried over to the nearest console while Roach stepped into Dix's field of vision. The Badlander's surviving eye rolled to fix on him. He gurgled around the spine piercing his throat, his breath coming in raw, wet rasps. Roach raised his carbine and Dix nodded, almost imperceptibly. Then Roach remembered Ricardo Alvarez and all the others Dix had killed so cheerily.

'Hey, you saying you're okay, man?' Roach said, slinging his carbine over his shoulder. Dix's eye widened and he groaned, pleading incoherently. Roach nodded. 'Well it's your call. You just hang in there then, brother.'

He turned away – just in time to see a blueskin engineer creeping up on him. Clad in a plain grey body stocking it was shorter and stouter than the Fire Warriors he'd seen, with a square-jawed face and big, workman's hands. *Big hands holding a laser cutter...* Roach flung himself aside as the xenos lunged at him. It was an awkward attack with a device intended as a tool rather than a weapon, but the beam was lethal at close range. He screamed as it sheared through his right hip and thigh, slicing and cauterising the flesh in the same instant. As he fell, the engineer loomed over him and jabbed at his face with the cutter. Desperately Roach lashed out and caught its wrist, knocking the beam off course. The tau hissed through its nostrils, its flat face puckered with hatred as it fought for control of the tool. Despite its size, the xenos was surprisingly strong, while Roach was in bad shape. The laser inched towards his head...

I thought these Earth Caste boys weren't meant to be fighters!

The engineer's head disappeared in a spray of purple mist. Roach threw the corpse aside as Mister Fish knelt beside him.

'You took your time,' Roach chided, then grinned at the Saathlaa's hurt expression. 'Hey, I'm just kidding, friend.'

Gingerly he examined his wounded leg and found there wasn't much of it left. When the Fish tried to haul him up, Roach shook him off.

'No, I ain't going nowhere. You finish up and get out if you can.' His comrade hesitated and Roach slapped him on the shoulder. 'They'll be through the hatch any time now. Go!'

The Fish nodded and rose. Roach watched him blast away at the remaining control panels, finishing up the job they'd come to do. He was pretty sure the rig's comms array would be down long enough for the 19th to make orbit without the Sky Marshall getting wind of things. Despite his doubts and the screaming pain in his leg, the thought felt good. This wasn't the path he'd have chosen, but at least he'd seen it through. He felt consciousness slipping away and hauled himself back with a brutal effort.

'You done enough,' he called to the Fish. 'Get out of here!'

His friend nodded and hurried over to the turbolift that served the beacon tower. Their exit strategy had always been hazy, Roach remembered. Just like his head was now... Something about abseiling down the outside of the tower...

Mister Fish paused at the lift doors and threw him a crisp salute. 'For Phaedra and the Imperium,' he said in perfect Gothic, grinning at Roach's incredulous expression. Then he was gone.

'Well sh–' Roach's words were cut short as the entrance hatch whooshed open and the first combat servitor glided in. Its cataract-filled eyes locked on him unerringly and it chattered something in harsh, nonsensical scrapcode.

'Yeah... and you too...' Roach answered with a grin. Offering up a prayer to a God-Emperor he didn't believe in, the scout drew his EMP dagger and prepared to walk his Thunderground. He figured it might be something worth seeing.

CHAPTER THIRTEEN

The Last Day: Diadem

Our convoy is almost halfway to the centre of the dead lake. I can't see the refinery yet, but its beacon light slices through the smog every minute or so, throwing the predatory shapes around us into stark brilliance. Devilfish and Piranhas – the tau vehicles could not have been more aptly named. They shadow us relentlessly, scenting for the blood of deceit. Though our passwords have been given and accepted I sense they do not trust us. Soon we shall fight. It is only a question of when. Bierce nods his agreement. Whatever he is, we are in concord now.

– Iverson's Journal

Up in the gunboat's wheelhouse Iverson saw the Diadem rise through the mist like a titanic, scrap-metal octopus. The old rig was screeching – a wail of klaxons that told him the infiltrators had made their move. Some of them would be dead by now, perhaps all of them. Maybe they'd done what needed doing and maybe they hadn't. Either way, the Arkan were committed.

Wintertide will die. The Sky Marshall will die. Together we'll stand. Together they'll fall.

Iverson glanced to either side, appraising the captured transports chugging along beside the Triton. Both were badly battered and wouldn't take much more punishment. He'd packed as many men onto his own ship as possible, but the gunboat wasn't built for transport so most of the force was on the barges.

'How much further, Iverson?' Machen called over the vox. There was a strain in his voice that went beyond impatience.

'Not far,' Iverson replied. 'We're through the first wave of checkpoints. Maintain vox silence until I signal you, captain.'

Machen signed off with a grunt. Nominally he was in command of one barge, Vendrake the other, but neither captain was in a position to offer much leadership since both were sealed up inside their machines, playing dead along with the rest of the Arkan armour. Dispersed across the convoy, the Sentinels and Zouaves were powered down and sheathed in tarpaulin, as if in storage. It was a gamble, but the tau drones would have sniffed them out if they'd hidden below decks, so they'd hidden in plain sight instead. Likewise, the infantry were wearing the insignia of dead janissaries, giving them the appearance of rough and ready new recruits. The tau had bought the deception so far, but Iverson could almost taste their suspicion.

The blueskins don't know how to trust their instincts, Iverson decided. *They're too orderly and rational to go with a gut feeling. Maybe that will be the death of them.*

A Devilfish pulled up alongside the Triton and disgorged a pair of drones. The saucers flitted over to the gunboat and began to sniff inquisitively around the deck. It was the third search since they'd entered the lake.

But their instincts are screaming.

Machen felt like he was locked inside an iron coffin with a rabid dog chewing at his leg. The wound left by the Fire Warriors hadn't impaired his control of the Thundersuit, but the pain was shockingly insistent. For all he knew the limb might be gone from the knee down. Perhaps he was bleeding out inside his suit and he'd be dead before the battle even began. Hadn't something like that almost killed Wade once? Yes, a loxatl flechette to the femoral artery... in that ambush, so long ago now... but Wade had survived... only it hadn't made much difference in the end, because he was dead now. Daniel Wade, the last of *his* Zouaves. Machen would be damned if he didn't reap a measure of vengeance for the man.

Damned if you do or don't. Die if you will or won't. All's one in the love of hate...

'Get out of my head, Templeton!' Machen snarled, knowing full well the lost captain would shadow him to the end.

Vendrake sat in the lightless cockpit of his Sentinel with his eyes wide open. The darkness was preferable to the things he might see if he closed them. He'd taken another draught of the Glory and the need for action pulsed through his veins like liquid fire. He should have waited until the battle started, but this vigil in the dark had seemed intolerable without the drug. The nightmares were too close now. *She* was too close.

She isn't real. It's just this damned planet playing with my head – something in the air or the water. I know I'm not the only one who's haunted...

But he'd glimpsed Leonora's Sentinel stalking his barge from the riverbank, keeping to the shadows but never falling far behind. Perhaps he'd be safe on the lake. Surely she couldn't follow him onto the water without a ship?

She can't follow me anywhere because she's dead! But if she's dead how will water stop her? The thoughts spiralled around in his head, reason chasing away superstition, superstition chasing away reason. *Perhaps that's the curse of the Providence-born, he decided. We all think too bloody much.*

The waters around the convoy were seething with tau hover tanks and speeders now. Iverson could feel Bierce glaring at his back, urging him to commit. Almost unconsciously he reached for the ship's loudhailer.

'Wait,' the witch said at his shoulder. 'We must get closer.'

'The sentries are getting jumpy,' Iverson said. 'We have to strike before they do.' He noticed her eyes were locked on the rig and guessed she was thinking of Cutler. Vendrake had said that there was something between them.

'Wait a little longer,' she urged.

The convoy was about five hundred metres from the rig now. Iverson saw platoons of augmented skitarii warriors lined up along the iron promenade of the pier.

Waiting for us.

'Just a little closer...'

Somewhere nearby a buzz saw roared into life.

'What the...?' Iverson's face was thunderous as he yanked down the alarm lever and yelled into the loudhailer, 'Go! The Counterweight is go!'

Audie Joyce knew he was meant to hold fire until the commissar gave the order, but he'd waited and waited and nothing had come and all the while the xenos tanks had circled the Triton like big, angry fish. The drone had been the last straw; it had circled him suspiciously, then stopped right in front of his hidden visor, trying to get a look inside. That was when the Emperor's righteous rage had lit Joyce up – and it must have lit up his armour too, because the next moment his buzz saws were screaming and the drone was falling out of the air in two pieces. Then the alarm went off and he heard the commissar hollering over the hailer, telling them the fight was on, so Joyce reckoned he'd done the right thing after all.

'Man the sides!' Lieutenant Hood bellowed and the greybacks surged to the gunwales, blazing away with carbines and pulse rifles. They couldn't dent the tanks so they targeted the drones, swatting them from the air like flies. A moment later the ship's autocannons opened up on either side and battered the tau skimmers with armour piercing rounds. A Devilfish crumpled and a couple of Piranhas whirled away in flames. And then the lake caught fire. The scum of crude promethium coating the water sizzled and popped as it burned, turning grey smog to black smoke.

'Rebreathers!' Hood shouted. Choking men fumbled for their masks as the air turned caustic.

'Wake and burn, brothers!' Joyce voxed, knowing full well his knights were already powering up. He sang them a canticle of faith as he leapt to a firing platform and let rip with his heavy stubber. Behind him a Sentinel whirred into life and hopped over to the port side, firing intermittent bolts of energy from its lascannon. Its rate of fire was almost painfully slow, but the heavy weapon compensated with its sheer stopping power. Through the smoke Joyce saw a similar pattern playing out on the barges to either side of the gunboat, but the tau skimmers had been wary and many swept away untouched. Joyce longed to launch himself into the molten lake and give chase.

Yea, though I walk upon the Lake Infernal, my flesh shall not wither if my soul burns in His name!

He steadied himself as the Triton surged forward, steaming for the refinery at full tilt. It shamed Joyce to let the tau sentries go, but the plan was to stop for nothing until they reached the shuttle.

'Watch out to port!' someone yelled as a Devilfish darted up alongside the Triton. Spinning to face its prey, it strafed along sideways with its rotary gun blazing. Men screamed as they were raked from the gunwales. A blast grazed the edge of Joyce's shoulder pauldron and almost threw him from his perch. Cursing, he returned fire but his gun barely scratched the tank's white patina. As if irritated by the affront, it swivelled to target him. As its burst cannon spun up the Sentinel loomed over Joyce and spat incandescent light. The bolt from its lascannon punched through the Devilfish's nose and hurled it backwards. Long seconds later a second bolt struck an engine nacelle and the tank exploded.

'Stormchaser – second kill confirmed – Devilfish,' Vendrake's vox reported crisply. The captain nodded, recognising Beauregard Van Hal's call sign. It seemed Silverstorm's ace rider was already surging ahead in the kill stakes. Most cavalrymen lived for these fleeting, frantic moments when the world was distilled to the purity of the hunt.

Even a cesspit world like Phaedra...

Vendrake spotted a trio of T-shaped Piranhas bearing down on his barge. He skittered his Sentinel over to the stern and met them with a storm of bullets. The skimmer in the centre took the brunt of it and burst open, but its companions banked away to either side and kept coming, weaving a madcap pattern through his fire. Vendrake grinned and answered with a near random spray that clipped the skimmer to his left. It spun out of control and capsized, spilling both its riders into the burning water. He shredded them as he swerved after the remaining Piranha. It was dangerously close now.

'It's going for our engines!' someone yelled. Salvos of lighter gunfire erupted from the barge as greybacks crowded around Vendrake and sniped at the open-topped skimmer. Abruptly the Piranha abandoned its manoeuvring and sped straight for them, buzzing like a giant mosquito. Vendrake nailed the pilots in seconds, already knowing he was too late.

It has been too late for too long, if not forever...

To Vendrake's Glory-fried eyes time seemed to stretch taught, pinning the incoming Piranha just metres from its target, strung like an arrow in a bowstring of flames. And suddenly he knew he'd seen all this before, the same lethal hues painted across a different canvas – frozen flames and fate staring at him through his windshield.

'*Belle du Morte* signing in,' Leonora's spiteful voice sang from the vox.

Then the arrow was released and the skimmer smashed into the barge like a missile.

'Vendrake's in trouble,' Machen called over the vox. His voice sounded strained, as if he were struggling to stay awake.

'Confirmed,' Iverson said, watching the barge to starboard shake and stall. Within seconds Vendrake's ship had faded into the mist, left behind by its speeding companions.

'We cannot abandon them,' the witch said quietly.

'I'm going back,' Machen said. His ship was already turning about.

Iverson hesitated. Bierce shook his head. 'Negative,' Iverson ordered. 'We press on for the rig.'

'To the Hells with you, Iverson.' Machen cut the line.

Another explosion rippled through Vendrake's barge. This time the whole ship heaved, as if in the throes of a violent seizure. With a creak of tortured metal the stern plummeted towards the lake, sending scrabbling, screaming greybacks tumbling into the burning water. They burst into flames the moment they touched the lake, almost as if they'd combusted from within. Vendrake dug his Sentinel's claws into the deck and arched backwards, struggling for balance on the sheer slope. A third explosion rocked the barge and more men slid towards the brink. A lucky few found handholds on his machine's legs. Then a fellow Sentinel lurched over the lip, almost dislodging him.

Now we're only six, a distant, clinical part of Vendrake counted. *And Arness is on this tug too, somewhere up front. Once the ship goes down we'll be four. And I won't be one of them.*

With a throaty roar, Machen's barge pulled up alongside the dying ship and fired a barrage of grappling hooks. Desperate men abandoned their handholds and leapt for the lifelines. Coughing and cursing, they fought their way across the sloping deck towards the rescue ship. A Zouave who'd wedged himself behind a fuel pipe rocketed over with a greyback under each arm. Arness's Sentinel hopped across with men clinging to its cockpit. Balanced precariously over the lake, Vendrake didn't dare move, didn't see how he *could* move without falling.

'*Belle du Morte*, killed in action,' a sinuous voice whispered from his vox. '*Your* inaction, dear Hardin.'

Vendrake tried to blank her out. His entire body was taut with the effort of keeping his mount steady. He had never felt more at one with his machine.

'It's almost time, my love,' the wraith said.

'What do you want from me, you dead bitch?' Vendrake snarled, feeling his grip on sanity slipping along with his grip on the deck.

'Why, Hardin, that's no way to talk to a lady!' A broken glass giggle, then a death rattle sigh. 'I just want us to be together. Forever...'

He saw her dissolve from the smoke and come skittering across the fiery lake like a herald out of the Hells. Her Sentinel's hide was scorched black and encrusted with coral spines that flickered with unholy current.

'There's so much to see, Hardin. You just have to open your eyes.' Rainbow light oozed from her cockpit like prismatic pus, leaving swirling streamers of corruption in its wake.

'You aren't Leonora,' he hissed through gritted teeth. 'You aren't anything.'

'Then what does that make you, my love?'

'I...'

A trio of tau tanks stormed from the smog and swept the apparition away. Suddenly Leonora's challenge didn't matter anymore because Vendrake's focus had narrowed to another, more pressing question.

How do I stop them?

Two of the tanks were Devilfish, but the third was something much worse. It was built around the same sleek chassis, but sported a massive turret-mounted cannon that turned Vendrake's blood to ice. He'd never encountered one before, but he'd heard the descriptions: the third attacker was a Hammerhead, the main battle tank of the Tau Empire.

A couple of shots from that monster cannon will sink Machen's tug before he knows what's hit him.

Suddenly Vendrake saw the aliens' plan with dreadful clarity. They could have finished his dying barge in seconds, but they'd been patient and used it to lure the others back into a trap. Wedged against the sinking barge, Machen's vessel was appallingly vulnerable. Vendrake's mind whirled, soaring on Glory as he sifted and discarded tactics, tearing through options in split seconds, hunting for an answer before it was too late. And somewhere in the desperate alchemy of Glory and guilt he found his answer.

I am the Silverstorm.

Vendrake let go and vaulted from the sloping deck. At the height of his arc he ignited his undercarriage thrusters and set the leap on fire. Pushing his customised machine to its limits he soared across the lake to intercept the leading Devilfish. It was an insane, outrageous move that was almost heretical in its abuse of the machine's tortured spirit, but then the machine itself was a heretical construct, twisted far beyond the sane limits of the Sentinel pattern by his obsessive tinkering. It was something more than a Sentinel, just as Vendrake himself had become something more than a man in this moment when the world had become something less than real.

This is my Thunderground.

His Sentinel came down hard on the tank, cracking its carapace and sending it into a wild spin. Calculating trajectories in a blur, Vendrake leapt across to its neighbour with his talons extended and his autocannon blazing. The landing raked deep grooves into the second Devilfish's canopy and the bullets tore it wide open. And then Vendrake was leaping again.

This is my redemption.

Intent on Machen's barge, the Hammerhead never saw him coming. Its gun was powering up to fire when the Sentinel slammed down onto its barrel. The ion cannon exploded like a miniature sun, disintegrating the tank's canopy and the Sentinel's legs. Vendrake's burning cockpit was hurled into the air like a rocket. Thrust back into his couch by the propulsion, Vendrake watched the sickening clouds soaring towards him. His body was burning and his mind was almost burned out.

Maybe I'll see the stars, he thought fleetingly. *Maybe I'll escape Phaedra after all.*

'There is no escape, my love,' Leonora said, sounding peculiarly wistful. He could no longer tell if she was speaking through the vox or inside his head. 'But don't despair, Hardin. I'll always be with you.'

And then he jackknifed in the air and plummeted back towards the lake. *I'm a silver bullet that's going to punch right through to the heart of this sick world.* Vendrake grinned. *Who knows, I might even kill the bitch.*

Spilling cascades of water, Iverson's gunboat surged from the lake and rolled onto the refinery pier. Combat servitors and skitarii were scattered or crushed as they tried to mount a defence against the armoured leviathan; more were mown down by the Triton's guns and the greybacks crouched behind its walls. The lascannon at the prow flared and rendered a chattering defence turret down to molten slag. The weapon was fully charged and eager to kill, its spirit restored to health by the ministrations of the Arkan tech-priests. It fired again, disintegrating a trio of skitarii as the gunboat rolled up the pier like a mobile fortress.

Iverson surveyed the scene from the wheelhouse, trying to marry up the reality of the rig with Abel's painstakingly transcribed maps. Up close, his first impression of an industrial octopus was reinforced. The Diadem was a city-sized sprawl built on a mosaic of interlocking platforms that were packed with manufactories, silos and hab-blocks linked by a network of roads and tunnels. The centre was occupied by the octopus's mantle, a cyclopean tower block crowned by the beacon light. A cascade of pipes and scaffolding splayed from the mantle like tentacles and enfolded the other buildings. Looking at that covetous tower, Iverson sensed the rig was somehow alive and even dimly aware of their presence.

'We have to get off this thing before it wakes up,' someone whispered at his ear. Iverson turned, half expecting Reve, but finding only the witch. He could feel the anger radiating from her in waves.

'I hope Abel's directions are as good as his codes,' he said. Their informer had plotted their path to the shuttle pad with meticulous care. It lay some two kilometres into the sprawl and the idea was to run the rig's gauntlet before it closed its grip.

'You should not have left the others behind,' she said coldly.

'I had no choice. We had to hit the pier hard and fast.' He activated the loud-hailer. 'All armoured personnel disembark and assume flanking positions.'

'Armoured personnel,' she mocked. 'A handful of Sentinels and Zouaves! That's all we have left now.'

Something snapped inside him and he rounded on her. 'I don't know what your game is, but I won't tolerate insubordination during a combat operation.'

Standing beside her, Bierce nodded fierce approval.

'Do you intend to shoot me too, Holt Iverson?' she challenged.

Shoot you... too? How do you know about Reve?

Looking down, he saw his hand had strayed to his holster.

'Commissar,' Machen called over the vox, 'we're coming in now. I saved as many as I could.' The captain sounded worse than before, his voice a barely audible croak.

Iverson glanced out the window and saw Machen's barge pulling up alongside the pier. 'You disobeyed a direct order, captain.'

'Vendrake is dead,' Machen said. 'So are half the men who sailed with him.'

'Deploy around the Triton. We have to get moving.'

'Confirmed,' Machen said tightly over the vox. 'And Iverson – when this is done I'm going to kill you.'

'What do you hope to achieve with this insanity?' O'Seishin asked as Cutler's team crossed the deserted shuttle pad. The tau ambassador was back on his floating throne drone, but Obadiah Pope was right beside him with a carbine wedged discreetly into the small of his back. Most of the Diadem's forces had been drawn to the Watchtower and the handful of janissaries they'd encountered along the way hadn't questioned the ambassador and his 'retinue'.

'Just hang in there and you'll get the picture soon enough, Si,' Cutler said.

'emperor's blood!' Lieutenant Sandefur exclaimed from up front.

The party halted, staring at the scene ahead. There was indeed blood, a great deal of it, but Cutler doubted any of it belonged to the Emperor. It was pooled around the shuttle's cargo hatch in a semi-congealed swathe, black with swarming flies. A severed hand protruded from the ooze, its fingers extended almost apologetically. The shuttle's ramp was extended into the filth like a questing tongue, its length smeared with trails of blood.

'What in the Hells happened here?' Sandefur was pale with shock. Violence was nothing new to any of them, but there was an obscene quality to this carnage that went beyond honest killing. Almost a miasma...

It's back, Cutler sensed. Drawing his sabre, he stepped onto the ramp.

'I will not enter there,' O'Seishin said. He tried to pull back from the ship, but Pope shoved him forward. 'Ensor Cutler, I cannot!' the alien implored.

Cutler scowled at him. All the ambassador's arrogance had dissolved away, leaving behind an ancient, frightened relic.

'You can and you will,' Cutler said. 'You think you've got us gue'la monkeys worked out, don't you, Si? Well then, this is something you've just got to see.'

'Taking heavy fire!' Dryden shouted over the vox. 'Coming in from all sides!'

Lieutenant Pericles Quint peered through the windshield at his fellow rider. Fifty metres down the road ahead, Dryden's Sentinel was dancing about frantically, tormented by bright bursts of energy. Every strike bit deep into the machine's armour and drew a gush of smoke.

'I... I don't see them,' Quint blustered, hunting about for the attackers. The energy bursts seemed to be coming out of thin air. 'Initiate firing pattern Wolf 359...'

'Pull back!' Beauregard Van Hal cut in. 'Do it now, Dry!'

'I've lost my–' Dryden's Sentinel exploded with shocking suddenness.

'Dryden?' Quint asked dully, staring at the burning wreckage.

'Suppression fire, full auto,' Van Hal ordered. 'Purge the street.'

'But there's nothing...' Quint's whine was drowned in a barrage of gunfire as the other Sentinels followed Van Hal's lead. Almost against his will, the lieutenant followed suit. They battered the empty street ahead with bullets and las-fire for a full thirty seconds before Van Hal called a halt.

'You've got us shooting at ghosts,' Quint snapped, trying to regain the upper hand in the squadron. Now that Vendrake was gone, he was Silverstorm's commanding officer and Van Hal had no business undermining him.

'Not ghosts,' the veteran rider said, striding forward. 'But maybe something close.'

'What are you talking about, man?'

'They moved fast, but we got one.' Van Hal hopped over to a broken shape lying by the side of the road. It was a tau warrior in bulky black armour. The broken carapace was still phasing in and out of visibility erratically. 'It's some kind of cloaking system,' Van Hal said. 'Typical blueskin trickery.'

'What's the hold-up?' Iverson voxed. 'We've got a whole battalion of skitarii on our tails back here!'

The Sentinel squad had forged ahead, scouting out the path for the Triton and the infantry. It was dirty, dangerous work and they'd already lost Rees to a skitarii ambush. With Dryden gone they were down to just four machines.

'Bit of a tussle with the blueskins,' Quint said, 'but don't you worry, I've nailed them, commissar!'

'There'll be more,' Van Hal said. 'They were working as a squad.'

'Then perhaps you should take point,' Quint huffed, 'seeing as your eyes are so blasted sharp!'

'That man's an idiot,' Iverson snarled and flicked the vox over to Machen's channel. 'What's your status, captain?'

'We're holding, but there are hundreds of them now.' Machen's reply was framed by a relentless wash of gunfire. 'They've come crawling out of every bloody service tunnel along the way.'

The surviving Zouaves were arrayed around the Triton, supporting the beleaguered infantry. At first resistance had been light and they'd made good speed, but then the Diadem had started to wake up and its guardians had massed around the intruders like antibodies. Iverson checked Abel's map: the shuttle pad was just a couple of blocks away, but the advance was in danger of stalling.

The infantry are too slow. We need to run for the shuttle.

Iverson wasn't sure if the thought was his or Bierce's... or perhaps even Reve's. His augmetic eye was playing up badly now, the electric wasp inside flittering about and painting sparks across his vision. He glanced down at the deck. There were some fifty greybacks manning the walls of the ship. Would they be enough?

'Don't do it,' the witch cautioned. 'Don't leave them behind again.'

But the mission is all that matters...

Machen mowed down another pair of charging skitarii. The Mechanicus warriors died as silently as they fought, their pallid Saathlaa faces untouched by pain or fear when they fell. All were clad in the same rust-red flak armour, but they sported a riot of customised augmetics. He saw glowing optics, bionic arms flush with blades, even spring-loaded legs, but every warrior moved with the same implacable purpose, as if controlled by an overarching mind. That mind had already ground down a score of greybacks on the road to the shuttle. There were less than a hundred men left on the ground now, every one of them battered and bleeding. Without the Zouaves they would have been overrun in minutes.

We forged our path in the blood and bones of our fallen, erecting squalid mortuary markers along the Crow Road...

'Shut up!' Machen screamed, berating the agony in his leg as much as the ghost in his head. 'Let me think for a moment, Templeton!'

A squat skitarii warrior with piston-like legs sprang from the crowd, its arms extended to batter him with twin pneumatic hammers. Machen caught it on his drill, but the dying cyborg cracked him over the helmet so hard his visor shattered. Shards of glass licked his eyeballs like sandpaper. Half blind, he cast the corpse away and parried a jabbing blade. And suddenly he was vomiting inside his armour, his whole body wracked by spasms of agony. Phaedra's air was crowded with a billion tiny killers and he'd left the wound in his leg untreated too long.

'Make way!' Iverson yelled over the loudhailer and suddenly the Triton was rolling backwards. The Confederates leapt aside as it gathered speed and ploughed into the pursuing ranks of skitarii, steamrollering scores of the slow-moving cyborgs into a paste of meat and metal.

'Purge them, brothers!' Machen heard the boy preacher bellow.

With a cacophony of buzz saws and chainblades, Joyce and his Zouaves charged after the gunboat and tore into the skitarii stragglers who had escaped the onslaught. Squinting through a haze of blood the captain followed like a battered tank, trying in vain to blot out Templeton's end-less saga.

And then the bell tolled thirteen and we knew all our granite-carved victories were but scribbles in the sands of time.

Cutler's torch found the words first:

'THE BELL TOLLS'

The phrase was smeared in blood above the gaping bulkhead to Silo Chamber 3. A headless corpse lay across the threshold with its arms folded neatly across its belly. Its wayward head was propped up inside the splayed ribcage, blood-shot eyes staring up at the colonel in mute outrage.

I guess you won't be flying us out of here after all, Señor Ortega, Cutler thought grimly as he recognised the corpse. *Which means none of us are getting off this mud ball. But that was a problem for later.*

Cutler shone his torch into the dark space beyond. The silo stank of pro-methium and blood, but all he could see was the blood and its sundered containers. Something had turned the chamber into an abattoir, garnish-ing it with a display of ragged limbs and yawning torsos, all bedecked with glistening streamers of entrails. There was a deranged order to the car-nage, everything positioned and angled *just so*, the hideous parts hinting at some infinitely more hideous whole. It was a pattern Cutler had seen twice before, first in the hovels of Trinity, wrought in broken junk, then in Dorm 31, rendered in flesh.

'Who did this?' Sandefur asked weakly. He looked like he was going to be sick.

Loomis, Cutler decided. *It will be Loomis this time.*

'Nothing human,' Cutler answered. 'We have to kill it.'

They entered the silo one by one, with Pope taking the rear, still shepherding the tau ambassador. O'Seishin was almost apoplectic with terror, his deep-set eyes whirling about the butchery as if afraid to settle anywhere. He was muttering a mantra in his native tongue, speaking so fast he was almost tripping over his own words.

Welcome to our 'psychic malaise' you smug bastard, Cutler thought as he pushed on into the chamber. It was a hollow cylinder, about ten metres in diameter with a sloping ceiling that pinched into an intake duct high above their heads. He played his light around the aperture, but found nothing. Apart from the duct and the grilled vents in the floor the silo was featureless. There was nowhere to hide.

But you're in here somewhere. I can feel you...

A cackle came from behind them, fluid and feral and rancid with hate, then an awful cacophony of voices: '*Trinity in embers...*'

They whirled round and saw the daemon. It was plastered against the wall above the doorway with its arms splayed wide and its ebony talons buried in the metal. It wore Loomis's face like a flesh mask stretched across something *other*, but the bulging, terror-struck eyes were still his. His naked body had bulked out with muscles that rippled and writhed with a life of their own, as if searching for their true form. But worst of all were the faces. There were dozens of them suffocating under his skin, all screaming and snarling for a way out.

'*Trinity remembers!*' shrieked the faces drowning in Loomis's flesh.

Pope reacted first, but the daemon was faster. As the greyback raised his carbine it launched itself from the wall and landed right in front of him. Its jaws gaped impossibly wide, tearing the remnants of Loomis's face in half. A pink, leech-like maw surged forward and engulfed the horrified greyback's head before he could fire. The monster arched backwards at the waist with bone-snapping violence and hauled Pope into the air, swallowing him down to the waist. His flailing legs smacked O'Seishin from his perch and sent his drone spinning away. There was a violent burp and Pope was gone, compressed to a writhing bulge in the daemon's belly.

'Kill it!' Cutler roared and leapt forward with his sabre. A claw flashed out with inhuman speed and caught the blade mid-swing. The colonel fought to free it as that hungry, lamprey maw twisted to face him.

'Down!' Sandefur yelled, opening fire with his carbine. Cutler threw himself prone as the energy bolts seared across the chamber. The daemon screeched in pain and swung to face the new threat, letting Cutler's sabre clatter to the ground. The lieutenant was down on one knee, firing in rapid bursts that gouged smoking pits into the horror's churning flesh. The daemon belched and its entire body heaved as if wracked by a massive spasm.

'Look out!' Cutler yelled, but it was too late. The daemon spat Pope back out and the half-dissolved cadaver thudded into Sandefur, throwing him to the ground and spattering him with corrosive juices. He screamed, trying to throw the corpse off, but Pope's bony arms locked around his neck, animated by some hideous un-life. The corpse's mouth yawned wide and vomited into Sandefur's face. The lieutenant's shrieks trailed into ragged chokes as his flesh was eaten away by the smoking bile.

Cutler rammed his retrieved sabre into the daemon's belly and twisted. The beast roared in pain and lashed out, throwing him clear across the chamber. He hit the wall hard and sagged to the ground, blood spewing from deep gashes across his chest. Through a haze of pain he watched the abomination rear up towards its full height. It seemed to be uncoiling from within itself, erupting from the possessed man in a ravenous slurry of eyes and maws and tongues that blinked and gnawed and screamed their way into reality.

'*He's coming home,*' the drowned faces chorused. '*And you didn't kill him, Whitecrow. You never killed him!*'

'What are you?' Cutler groaned through gritted teeth as he felt consciousness slipping away.

'*What are we?*' The faces cackled in disharmony. '*We are Trinity!*'

Then they laughed like a winter wind, and through the wind Cutler heard the tolling of a bell. *The bell.*

And then he was back in the blighted town again, entering the heart of its darkness with the witch and her *weraldur*, who everyone called Mister Frost and whose true name was known only to her. They walked into the chapel of rainbow light and found the daemon bell hanging from a chain into nowhere. It was a black iron monstrosity tarnished by a cancer of coral nodules that pulsed with unholy vitality. The cone was easily big enough to accommodate several standing men, but Cutler doubted any man would last long if he attempted such a thing, for its mouth was the wellspring of the toxic light.

'What is it?' Cutler asked as he had asked so many times before.

'A rift into the Whispersea,' Skjoldis gave her eternal answer, 'a gateway to the warp. The taint flows from it like blood from an open wound.'

It's warp-forged, but it carries the blight of Phaedra, Cutler realised. And this was a new truth, something he hadn't known back then. *Someone's brought Phaedra to Providence...*

And then the bell tolled again and the world shimmered and twitched and the dark man was standing before them. His greatcoat seemed impossibly black in that place of many colours and his bowed head was swathed in the shadows of a wide-brimmed hat. He was taller than any man had a right to be, but agonisingly thin with it, as if every fibre of his body had been stretched to the breaking point, attenuating him into *otherness.*

'All the worlds unfold into one,' the stranger said, 'and so all the stains of corruption become one strain.' Its voice was an ephemeral whisper that rode the streamers of light. 'You know, it's taken forever and a day to find you, Colonel Ensor Cutler. So long I've almost forgotten why I ever came looking.'

'How in the Hells do you know my name?' Cutler challenged, taking a step forward. 'Who are you?'

The stranger looked up, casting the shadows from its face. Its bloodless skin was incised with a lattice of smouldering, smoking scars that framed inhuman eyes: one was a dead black orb, the other a burning augmetic. It smiled and the seams of magma running through its flesh were routed into a fresh configuration. Reality seemed to shiver and shimmer before the new order.

'Me?' the stranger said. 'I'm just a man who found his way back home.'

And then the world exploded in a flash of pure white light.

CHAPTER FOURTEEN

The Last Day: The Shuttle Pad
The skitarii horde is broken for the time being, but the respite cost us heavily. We lost almost half our infantry in the struggle, together with a pair of Zouave knights. We must be gone from here before the tech-guard masses again, as they surely will. The Sentinel scouts are coming up on the shuttle pad now...

– Iverson's Journal

'What do you mean you're not sure, Quint?' Iverson growled into the vox. 'Either you've found evidence of a skirmish or you haven't. Which is it?'

'Quite so, commissar, quite so,' Quint blustered. 'Indeed, *something* most certainly happened here, but it's...'

'Put Van Hal on the line.'

'Sir, I don't see...'

'Van Hal here,' the veteran broke in. 'We've got blood outside the shuttle – lots of it – but no bodies. Quint's right. Something's very wrong here.'

'Maybe Cutler's team hid the bodies,' Iverson suggested.

'Then they left Seven Hells of a mess behind,' Van Hal said. 'No, it doesn't add up.'

'And there's no sign of our infiltrators?' Iverson frowned. Without Cutler's pilot nobody was going anywhere.

'If they're here, they're inside the shuttle. Want me to check it out?'

'No, secure the pad and wait. We're only a block away.' Iverson cut the link and turned to the witch. To his surprise she was sitting cross-legged on the floor with her eyes closed. That was when he realised how cold the wheelhouse had grown despite the heat outside. The scrawny Lethean helmsman had noticed it too and was staring at the woman in abject terror.

'Is witchcraft,' the Mariner muttered in his broken Gothic. 'She carries the taint!'

'Keep your eyes on the road!' Iverson snapped. 'She is the Emperor's servant.' *At least I think she is.* Either way, he knew where her mind was wandering. *I just hope you find him alive...*

* * *

'Whitecrow!' the voice said again, growing more insistent. 'You must wake up!'

Skjoldis? Cutler stirred, struggling against the white oblivion that had swallowed him. *Is that you?* His eyes flicked open. He was still in the temple, but the unholy light was gone, leaving behind a washed-out façade of the reality. A jagged chasm yawned beneath the spot where the daemon bell had hung. The bell itself was gone, along with its master.

We fought, the dark man and I, Cutler remembered. *At least it felt like fighting.* He rose and hobbled over to the rift. It was an infinitely black gash in the greyscale murk of the temple. To fall in there would be to fall forever.

'Open your eyes, Whitecrow!' the voice nagged again.

I have, he thought. *Haven't I?*

'Skjoldis?' he said it aloud this time. 'We were wrong. We were wrong all along.'

More memories... Skjoldis with her arms spread wide, struggling to stem the tide of ghosts that came flooding from the bell in the dark man's wake. There were so many – angry ghosts and bitter ghosts and mournful ghosts – phantoms in every shade of misery and malice, all drawn to the dark man like moths to an unholy flame. He lured them with promises of redemption or vengeance or simple silence that radiated from him like black light. And while Skjoldis held them back with incantations and imprecations, Cutler duelled with their master, though they did not fight with guns or blades. He couldn't recall the way of it, but he knew his soul hung on the outcome, and perhaps the soul of his world too, so he fought with everything that he was, but in the end it was the *weraldur* who ended it. With an honest swing of his axe he sundered the chain suspending the bell and tore down the gate, casting out the dark man and his congregation.

But they never fell back into the Hells. They simply fell somewhere else.

'He's still on Providence,' Cutler said. 'We didn't kill him.'

'I know,' she sighed. 'I've always suspected it.'

'Then why didn't you tell me, woman?' he asked bitterly. 'Why didn't you tell me the bastard had us beat?'

'Because it was the best we could do, but it would not have been enough for you, Whitecrow.'

'The best we could do was lose him?' Cutler was staring into the rift as if he might jump. 'He'll come back, Skjoldis. Maybe he's the one sending the daemon after me.'

'The daemon was spawned by the death agonies of Trinity's damned.' She stood before him now, a hovering, hazy spectre. 'It shadows you through the warp because you are its father in murder, Whitecrow. It was your command that purged Trinity and conceived its malice.'

'And what am I supposed to do about it?'

'The only thing you can do: you fight.' She sighed, a long, soul-weary exhalation. 'Sometimes there is nothing more to be done. But now you must wake up...'

...Before it is too late.

Cutler opened his eyes. Again. He was back in the charnel house of Silo 3, slumped against the wall where the daemon had thrown him. *The daemon!* His eyes roved about frantically, but found nothing. *Why would it spare me?* Then he saw its legs. They were kneeling amongst the corpses, as if in prayer. Smoke was still pouring from the charred ridge of its waist and above the waist there was nothing at all.

What in the Hells? Cutler tried to rise and pain hit him in a raw red wave that almost washed him back to oblivion. He looked down and saw the shredded ruin of his jacket. Gingerly he pulled aside the rags and grimaced at the gouges in his chest. The daemon's slash had cut deep.

You have to get up, Whitecrow! Skjoldis urged.

'And do what, woman?' Cutler said. 'Our flyboy's dead. We're not going anywhere.'

A contemplative silence, then: *Is his head intact? Yes... I see from your thoughts it is.*

'His head? What's the poor bastard's head got to do with anything?

Bring it to the cockpit, Whitecrow. There may be a way.

He struggled to his feet, too exhausted to argue. His comrades were dead. Sandefur's skull had been hollowed out by the daemonic bile and what was left of Pope wasn't even recognisable as a man. O'Seishin was gone. Blackened shards of his throne drone were scattered around the chamber, a couple of them embedded in the metal walls like blades.

It was his drone that killed the daemon, Cutler realised. *There must have been a bomb built into it and O'Seishin triggered it when the beast went for him. But where's the sly son-of-a-bitch got to?*

He found the ambassador halfway down the access corridor. The ancient tau was breathing in ragged gasps as he pulled himself along, dragging his spindly legs behind him like dead things. He looked up in abject terror when the colonel loomed over him.

'Now where do you think you're going, Si?' Cutler chided.

'I was wrong,' the tau whispered, staring at the severed head hanging from the colonel's belt. 'We cannot work in concord. Your species is sick.'

'Well, I won't argue it.' Cutler bent painfully and heaved his quarry up and over his shoulders. 'But you and me, we're going to see this through together.'

'Then Cutler's alive?' Iverson asked as the witch got to her feet.

'He is dying,' she answered in a brittle monotone. 'We are running out of time.'

'I understand,' he said. 'We're coming up on the shuttle now.' He saw the Sentinels stalking about on the pad ahead, restless and distrustful of the lull. He appraised the witch thoughtfully.

I have to know. Whatever it is she's hiding about me, I have to know.

'Tell me,' he said quietly, certain she wouldn't mistake his meaning.

She didn't meet his eyes, but he could feel her coming to a decision. 'Iverson...'

Something hit the Triton so hard the whole world seemed to quake. There was an ear-splitting boom and a shriek of tortured metal. A bloom of orange fire spewed from the prow, detonating the lascannon and immolating everyone up front.

'Down!' Iverson yelled, throwing himself across the witch. The cabin windows exploded inwards, shredding the bewildered helmsman instantly. Fragments of glass and charred meat rained down on Iverson's back as he covered the witch.

Get up!

Iverson's greatcoat was smouldering as he rose to his knees. Bierce stood over him with his hands clasped behind his back, untouched by the fire storm.

War is the only truth, your will to fight the only virtue.

The witch's guardian burst through the door. His face went dark with fury as he took in the carnage. With a broken cry he hauled Iverson off his charge and lifted her in his arms.

'She's all right,' Iverson wheezed, coughing on the acrid smoke. 'Just dazed.'

That was when he heard the clamour from the deck below. He swung the door open and stared into a scene of abject chaos. The greybacks were milling about in disarray, trying to escape a searing hail of energy bolts that seemed to come out of nowhere. Men were going down fast, picked off by the unseen assailants amongst them.

'Follow their fire!' Iverson yelled, then ducked back inside as a burst of fire leapt towards him.

'They're on board!' someone in the crowd yelled. 'They're up here with us!'

'I don't see nothing!' old Cully swore. He was kneeling with the stock of his bulky rail rifle wedged into the crook of his shoulder. 'There ain't nothing here!' A bolt scorched away his left ear and he yelped, firing off a wild shot.

'Form up in your firing teams!' Lieutenant Grayburn was bawling from the stern. 'We need to establish–' Cully's hypervelocity slug punched through his breastplate and exploded out of his back, almost decapitating the man behind. Grayburn staggered back, his lips working soundlessly, then toppled over the gunwales. Cully never even saw it happen. He had dropped his rifle and was on his knees, clawing at his ruined ear. Someone snatched up the weapon.

Cort Toomy sighted down the long barrel of the xenos rifle and felt the old instincts kick in. The sniper had never recovered from the head wound he'd suffered on their first day in the Mire... so long ago... It was a kick, he remembered, from a knight... on a boat. After that the world had gone dim, like somebody had turned out the lights in his head, so he'd just tagged along with the other guys and done what he was told, never talking or even thinking much. Everyone figured he'd be dead within a week, but here he was, almost at the end of the road, still breathing when so many others were scrab meat. And now he knew why. A lopsided smile lit up his slack features as he felt the thrum of the rifle in his hands. This gun felt *right*.

'We got work to do, Eloise,' he told the rifle, marvelling at the sound of his own voice. He couldn't recall why he always called his guns Eloise, but he knew he always had, every one of them. Now he cradled her lovingly, careless of his own safety as he read the pattern of enemy fire, tracing the lethal threads back to their source, chasing a target...

Got you! The attacker was almost invisible, just a man-like shimmer on the starboard firing platform, but the flaring aperture of its gun was a beacon to the sniper. Toomy took the shot.

Iverson saw a burst of bright static through the crowd. A heartbeat later a headless body in bulky carapace armour toppled from one of the firing platforms, fizzling in and out of sight as its infiltration system went haywire.

Stealth suits, Iverson realised. Hadn't Van Hal mentioned running into them earlier? Alongside their invisibility the tau infiltrators were equipped with jetpacks so the Triton's open deck was an easy target for them. He scoured the deck for the others. According to reports their cloaking systems weren't *quite* perfect.

Where are you?

And then he had them – a pair of humanoid shapes, one crouching on the stern engine housing, the other on the port firing platform. The light seemed to slip around them, leaving behind colourless, quicksilver shadows that flickered wildly in the green-tinged field of his augmetic eye. Irritated, Iverson blocked the bionic with a hand and squinted with his good eye – and the shadows were gone.

It's the eye. Something about it lets me see them. Maybe there's more to this relic than I thought. Once again he wondered how many others had carried the optic before him. The thing was *old*. But this was no time for idle speculation. Men were dying out there. Firing up his chainsaw, he leapt to the deck below.

The Triton was a wreck. It was stalled some two hundred metres from the shuttle pad, its prow burning ferociously. To Machen it sounded like bedlam had broken out on the deck above, but that wasn't his battle. His heart pounded in fitful spurts as he raced across the platform housing the shuttle pad. His body was rotting inside his carapace, just as his mind was rotting inside his skull, one eaten by microscopic vermin, the other by a dead poet's deliriums.

Weak meat inside an iron skin, kindred fates twinned too late...

The fever had him in its grip now and he was shivering and burning up all at once, but that didn't matter anymore. Nothing mattered except the fury that promised his Thunderground.

Racing fate for the final hour, chasing hate before hate turns sour...

He was loping towards the armoured giant that had killed the gunboat. The Broadside battlesuit had stepped into their path from a silo up ahead and fired its twin rail guns before anyone could react. That one shot had demolished the Triton's frontal armour as if it were the lightest flak plate. Squads of Fire Warriors had struck simultaneously, materialising from access tunnels and silos around the platform. There weren't many – no more than twenty or thirty troops – but they were lethal at long range. The surviving greybacks were crouched under the gunboat's treads, fighting back furiously, but the Fire Warriors' accuracy was terrifying. Once again, the Zouaves would have to turn back the tide.

'Engage them!' the boy preacher had commanded and the knights had obeyed without question, splitting up to charge the scattered aliens. Machen had gone straight for the Broadside and it had swivelled to face him, tracking him with those massive tank-killing cannons. As he closed in he stared into the impassive sensor cluster that passed for its face, trying to read the pilot's mind.

Burning rage before rage runs cold...

A pencil-thin ray of light touched Purcell when he was halfway to his foes. A moment later the Zouave was lit up with spectral blue light. As if following some unspoken edict, a dozen Fire Warriors focussed their attacks on the knight, pounding him with deadly accuracy. His archaic Stormsuit buckled under the barrage in seconds and he clattered to the ground. The marker light moved on from the melted wreckage, seeking another target.

Audie Joyce watched it happen from the other side of the square, where he was hacking apart a quartet of Fire Warriors. The tau were pathetically fragile in melee and there was no glory in killing them, but when he saw Purcell die he knew that was wrong. Cleansing the xenos – any xenos – was an Emperor-given gift!

Scowling, he followed the questing ray back to its source and spied a lightly armoured alien perched on a rooftop. The warrior's helmet bulged with enhanced optics and sensors that identified him as some kind of spotter. He was directing the marker light across the battlefield with a telescopic device in his hands. Joyce levelled his heavy stubber... and saw the ray drift towards Machen.

When every colour is just another shade of damnation...

Machen dodged a heartbeat before the battlesuit's rail guns fired. The killing bolts screamed past him, as if furious at his escape. He laughed triumphantly but heard only a brittle, dead man's cackle. It was only when he tried to fire that he noticed his gun was missing, along with his left arm. One of the hypervelocity slugs had sheared off the limb at the shoulder and he hadn't even noticed. He found he didn't care. One arm would suffice for his vengeance.

And the final fires have fallen into ash...

He ducked low and death streaked over his head, leaving twin contrails in its wake. Then he was upon his foe. Shuddering with rage and fever, he thrust his drill into the battlesuit's chest. His entire body vibrated as the screeching bit bored through layers of tough carapace. It was agony, but he embraced it gladly.

And all hope's awash insensate fate...

The battlesuit's rail guns flailed about as the pilot tried to bring them to bear on an enemy that was too close. It tottered backwards, but Machen followed mercilessly, digging ever deeper as his own body tore itself apart in sympathy. Abruptly the drill surged forward, breaking through the final strata of plates into blood and bone. Machen held it there for several seconds, liquidising the xenos within, longing for the rapture and finding nothing.

'Are you my Thunderground?' he wheezed at the dead xenos, knowing it was not. He staggered back, leaving the suit standing mute witness to his failure. 'Templeton, if you know so much, then tell me...' his voice broke into a spasm of blood-flecked coughs, 'tell me what I need to do!'

Then heed the bell that tolls the end of always.

Dimly, Machen wondered why his fever had turned the world bright blue. Then the marker light fluttered through his broken visor and came to rest between his eyes, almost like a benediction.

For always was never a promise.

'Is this my–'

Joyce smiled wistfully as a score of pulse rounds hammered into Machen's visor. The captain's monstrous Thundersuit shuddered under the barrage, but did not fall.

'And yea, the old and the faithless were found wanting,' the boy preacher said, reciting truths the dead saint had shared with him. 'And the Emperor withdrew from them His grace and raised up the righteous so that they might carve His word across the galaxy in blood and fire!'

Then the murder light flitted away from Machen's iron tomb and Joyce opened fire, obliterating the spotter on the rooftop. Giving thanks to his god, he raced towards the nearest cluster of Fire Warriors. Doing the Emperor's work was good!

Shas'vre Jhi'kaara watched the battle unfold from a manufactory rooftop. She knew her comrades were impatient, but she waited until the Sentinels had charged into the fray before giving the order: 'Crisis team enable strike pattern Aoi'kais.'

Jhi'kaara launched herself into the air and rocketed towards the platform below, the blocky bulk of her battlesuit looking like some experimental flying machine. Her armoured companions, Kaorin and Asu'kai streaked after her on either flank, exhibiting a grace that humbled her own.

They despise my elevation to the Crisis team, Jhi'kaara thought.

The pair of veterans *were* the Diadem's Crisis team. They had served together for years and were Ta'lissera bonded, which made them closer than siblings. Jhi'kaara herself had never taken the warrior's oath of communion; the scars within and without had left her an outsider among her own kind, yet O'Seishin had elevated her over these bonded veterans. It was wrong, not least because the battlesuit didn't *feel* right to her. While she was familiar with the technology, it had been many years since she'd worn a Crisis battlesuit into combat. She knew she was no match for her subordinates and they knew it too.

O'Seishin, your power games have made a mockery of our ways, she thought bitterly. *The Water Caste has no reverence for the traditions.*

The canker had set in decades ago, when the Ethereal assigned to Phae-dra, Aun'o Hamaan had been lost, along with Shas'o Gheza, the commander of the Fire Warriors. As the most senior tau left on the planet, O'Seishin had assumed command and never relinquished it. For years Jhi'kaara had expected replacements from the Ethereal or Fire Castes to come, but nobody had and she'd finally accepted nobody would. Without a spiritual or martial figurehead the war had stagnated into something she no longer understood.

But here and now, I have a purity of purpose, Jhi'kaara decided. *Today my life or death shall serve the Greater Good. Whatever that is...*

That final dark thought disturbed her, but the time for thinking was done. Their fusion guns blazing, the battlesuits swooped on the Sentinels.

Van Hal was the only one who saw the attack coming, although 'saw' wasn't really the word for it. It was more the 'sense' of a shadow falling across the skin of his Sentinel. There was no logic to it, but the cavalryman had long ago learned that logic had nothing to do with survival. He didn't think, he just acted, swerving his machine aside so violently a lesser rider would have tripped. A barrage of powerful fusion blasts raked the air in his wake and chewed deep fissures into the metal floor. Arness's Sentinel took the full brunt of a parallel salvo and its cockpit exploded violently. The headless walker stumbled on a few paces before crashing to the ground. Mister Silver got lucky – his assailant, seemingly less skilled than its comrades, missed him completely. Quint hadn't been targeted at all. Doubtless the attackers had identified him as the poorest of the cavalrymen.

'Battlesuits,' Van Hal voxed, knowing it in his guts before the machines even touched the ground. Their splayed feet and piston-like legs absorbed the impact gracefully, but the one in the centre stumbled a little. *You sir, don't know your mount!* Van Hal observed wryly.

'I see fusion blasters and flamers!' Mister Silver yelled. He was a young Norlander who'd been drafted into Silverstorm as a mascot, but his talents had shone through and the captain himself had financed his walker. The move had riled the die-hard patricians like Quint, but Van Hal was proud to share the field with Silver.

'Pull back to the Triton!' Quint yelled and raced for the stranded gun-boat. It was a fatal error. While Van Hal and Silver careered about in evasive loops, dancing through the battlesuits' sustained fire, Quint peeled away in a straight line. One of the suits spun and lanced his legs out from under him with derisory precision. His Sentinel toppled forward and the cockpit snapped off at the waist as it crashed to the ground. They heard Quint squealing in terror as his cabin skidded along like a runaway train. The squeals turned to screams as the wreckage caught fire.

Van Hal cut the lieutenant's vox-feed and weighed up his enemies as he danced around them. The blocky battlesuits had landed in a neat delta formation with the poorest pilot in the centre, presumably in command. 'Focus fire left,' he ordered.

The Sentinels spun violently at the waist and fired synchronously. Both made magnificent shots despite their wild evasive dance. Van Hal's lascannon took the Crisis battlesuit on the left square in the chest and Silver's autocannon battered its legs from under it.

'Split-kill: Battlesuit!' Van Hal called.

And just like that Kaorin was gone, all her years of training reduced to nothing. Jhi'kaara felt no grief, only a cold regret that they had underestimated these foes. With those perfect killing shots the surviving riders had proved themselves to be masters of their machines.

Which I am not...

She noticed that Asu'kai was hunting his comrade's killers furiously, his judgement clouded by the passion of her loss. His fire wasn't even coming close to the cavorting Sentinels. Any moment now they would turn and kill again...

I will not die so easily and I will not die a fool!

Jhi'kaara drew deep of the bitterness in her heart, struggling to bond with her unfamiliar machine. She chose a foe and focussed, studying his erratic manoeuvres, willing herself to find a pattern. And suddenly she had it.

Van Hal knew he was dead the moment he committed to attack the berserk battlesuit. It was the wrong target. The other one, the one that had missed them from the air and stumbled when it landed, *that one* was going to kill him. He saw it in a subtle shift of the machine's stance and weaponry and in the way its sensors locked onto him like they could see right into his soul. It had woken up to the game.

Stormchaser: 213 kills and counting.

There was no way out, so he completed his strike and blew apart the battlesuit on the right. A moment later the survivor hit him at precisely the right angle, just as he'd known it would. Van Hal didn't even try to dodge.

Stormchaser: 214 kills and we're all done.

Jhi'kaara growled with the joy of her kill, drinking in the burning Sentinel to feed her hate. Doubtless the Ethereals would not approve of such feelings, but the Ethereals had deserted them so what did it matter anymore? Perhaps the mystics were wrong about the Greater Good. If hate could bring such focus – such power – then perhaps it was the true path.

I will slay the gue'la and I will keep slaying them until they are nothing but dust and bitter memories!

She swung to track the remaining Sentinel. It was circling her warily, frightened by the loss of its brother. The rider was skilful – even more skilful than the one she had slain – but she could tell he didn't believe it and his uncertainty would be his undoing.

'Purge the blueskin plague!' a voice bellowed behind her.

With an agonised whine something crunched into her back plate. She lurched round and flailed out with her fusion blaster, but her attacker deflected the swipe with a spiky vambrace. He was wearing a baroque iron battlesuit that was the antithesis of her sleek, minimalist machine. The armour was spattered with blood and daubed with crude sigils that marked him out as a barbarian even by the standards of the gue'la.

'Look upon their heresies and reap!' the savage boomed through an amplifier as he pressed his attack, swinging the whirling buzz saws jutting from his wrists in wide, alternating arcs. Jhi'kaara blocked with the fusion blaster and felt the housing buckle. She could not bring her guns to bear. He was in too close...

If I am broken then I am stronger for it!

Snarling, she angled her flamer towards the ground and unleashed a deluge of fire. With a whoosh of tortured air the backwash surged up and engulfed them both. Warning indicators flashed across her vision, but she kept the stream flowing, confident her battlesuit would outlast her foe's relic.

Your species are the plague! Your time is done!

Joyce's armour was warming up like an oven, drenching him in sweat. He could hear the machine's archaic cooling systems wheezing and clattering as they struggled to dissipate the heat from the tau's flamer. Through the conflagration he saw the sensor module that served as his enemy's head regarding him with glacial detachment. He knew that detachment was a lie: the xenos inside the suit hated him, just as he hated it. It was how things were meant to be.

There isn't room for us both, not in all the Heavens and Hells of infinite space.

As his skin began to blister, Joyce swung at the battlesuit in a frenzy that drowned his pain. The xenos stood its ground, spewing fire and parrying clumsily with the fusion blaster clipped to its left arm. Finally the flames penetrated the gun's cracked housing and it exploded with a violence that tore away the battlesuit's arm and flung Joyce from the inferno.

'Hang back and I'll nail the bastard!' Mister Silver called over the vox, lining up his Sentinel for a shot, but Joyce paid no heed. Howling a psalm of castigation he threw himself back into the fray, but the respite had given his foe the chance to level its flamer...

Though you burn my flesh, my spirit shall not waver!

He took the full force of the fire head on. His armour whined in protest as its cooling systems overloaded and gave out. The breastplate turned red hot, scorching the flesh from his ribs and setting his skin alight. Joyce chewed up the pain and spat it out as sacred fury. With a burst of his rockets he leapt onto the Crisis battlesuit's broad shoulders and sawed into its stubby head. The machine clattered about, trying to dislodge him, but he sank a blade into its shoulder and clung on while he hacked away with the other.

'I am His will and His word made manifest!' Joyce sang joyfully as his flesh bubbled inside its iron skin. 'I am the blade of His wrath...' The battlesuit's head came loose in a tangle of fizzing wires and he flung it aside. 'And I am the shield of His scorn!'

And then they were rocketing into the sky, propelled by the Crisis battlesuit's jetpack. With its sensor module gone the machine was flying blind, but it bucked and spun about as the pilot tried to dislodge him. Joyce hung on like a limpet, chopping away with his free hand, hunting for the tainted xenos flesh inside the shell. Something ruptured between the suit's shoulders and a cascade of small detonations rippled through it. Then the jetpack exploded with a sudden, terrible concussion that catapulted Joyce away like a kite caught in a tornado. Spiralling head-over-heels through the air, he glimpsed his nemesis plummeting towards the shuttle pad.

'Blood for the God-Emperor!' the preacher thundered, thinking how proud the saint and the Emperor and his old ma would be right now. As his momentum died and he began to fall he ignited his own rocket pack. The battered machinery squawked in protest, chugging impotently as it tried to engage. He cursed and thumped the ornery thing. It exploded like a krak grenade and Audie Joyce rained down from the sky in a thousand broiling pieces.

Jhi'kaara lay broken and blind inside the ruin of her Crisis battlesuit. The fall had shattered every bone in her body, but her hatred was undimmed, burning dark-bright at the core of her being, calling her back from the bliss of nothingness like a beacon.

I will... not... let go...

A crack of light appeared in the black vault above, almost painfully bright after the darkness, then the suit's chest plate was heaved away and the light became a flood. She tried to avert her gaze, but her neck wouldn't obey. A wrinkled gue'la appeared against the sky and peered down at her with a wolfish grin. He was missing an eye and an ear and most of his teeth.

'Hey, we got a blueskin alive in here!' he called to his unseen comrades. He licked his lips as he appraised her facial bionics. 'You got some real fancy gear going on there, sister,' he purred, 'and old Cully, he's what you'd call a collector, see.' A dagger appeared in his hand and he leaned inside. 'Hold still now, gal!'

He yelped with surprise as someone wrenched him away, then another face appeared above Jhi'kaara. All the gue'la looked alike to her, but this one wore scars like no other. Though it had been many *rotaa* since their encounter in the Mire she recognised him with shocking clarity.

'*Ko'miz'ar,*' she wheezed. His lattice of scars contorted and she knew he recognised her too. '*Ko'miz'ar...*'

'There's no such thing as chance, is there?' he said quietly. 'Or if there is, it's broken beyond repair.' She stared at him, uncertain of his meaning. Without a lexical module in play her grasp of the gue'la tongue was limited at best.

'Commissar!' someone called. 'Everyone's on board, sir. We're good to go!'

For the first time Jhi'kaara noticed the impatient rumble of the shuttle's engines. They hadn't seemed important before and they still didn't seem important to the scarred man. All his attention was on her.

'You should have killed me,' he told her, 'back when you had the chance.'

'Kill you...' she hissed, understanding this and trying to rise to it. 'Will... kill...'

'Yes. I think you're one of the few who still could.' He paused, as if puzzled by his own words. 'Next time perhaps.' And then he was gone.

Shortly afterwards the shuttle's rumble burst into brief, explosive thunder, then that too was gone and Jhi'kaara was alone with her hatred.

CHAPTER FIFTEEN

The Last Day: The Shuttle

Phaedra is behind us. She clung to our shuttle like a spurned lover when we ascended, fighting our escape every step of the way. I believe I felt the precise moment when we broke free of Her atmosphere into the clean void of space. I don't know what's waiting for us on the Sky Marshall's ship, but at least we won't die in Her embrace.

There's a mystery to our escape because I'm not sure who's actually flying the ship. I thought our pilot was dead or missing, but the witch assured me he was waiting up in the cockpit with Cutler. The edge in her voice told me this was neither quite the truth nor a lie, but something I shouldn't pursue. By tacit agreement I stayed in the cargo hold when she headed up to the cockpit with her bodyguard. Shortly afterwards we were in the air. For now that is enough.

We're due to dock with the Requiem of Virtue within the hour, but we won't last long if Abel's revolt has faltered. Truth to tell, we're not going to be much of a counterweight to the Sky Marshall's security forces. Our passage through the Diadem has left us battered and diminished.

Three Zouaves survived intact, but they're all shell-shocked by the loss of their leader, whoever that really was. I don't know if they're grieving for their captain or their adopted preacher, but I'll have to drum some spirit into them before we dock. Then there's the Norland cavalryman, 'Silver.' He's a skilled rider, but his Sentinel won't be much use to us on a battleship. Besides these four I have just sixty-three men left, ranging from fine soldiers to near vagabonds like the scum who tried to loot the Crisis battlesuit. The only officer amongst them is Lieutenant Hood, a dour veteran who's led the elite Burning Eagles for nearly a decade. He's a good man to have along, even if most of his Eagles have fallen.

There is another matter I must record. A scout called Valance found something in one of the silo chambers...

– Iverson's Journal

'I figured you'd want to see it, commissar,' the black-bearded man said, 'so I came straight to you.'

He's too big to be a scout, Iverson reflected vaguely. His mind was trying to defer the carnage his eyes were sending its way. The precision mutilation in the silo defied comprehension, but it wasn't the horror that disturbed him so much as the sense that somewhere deep down he *did* comprehend it. It was nothing more than the tenebrous hint of an intuition, yet he couldn't shake it.

I know, or rather I will *know what this madness means.*

'You did the right thing, scout.' Iverson slammed the silo hatch shut. 'Not a word of this to anyone else, you understand?'

'Whatever you say, sir.' Valance hesitated, looking troubled. Iverson could tell he wasn't a man much used to fear, but this... The scout spread his hands helplessly. 'What happened here, commissar?'

'The tau are degenerates,' Iverson said levelly. 'Don't let their superior airs and graces and all their techno heresies deceive you.'

'You're saying the blueskins did this?'

'Who else?' Iverson didn't intend it as a question, but it came out like one. Valance nodded, obviously unconvinced.

Which makes two of us, Iverson thought grimly.

'This is wrong,' O'Seishin said. It was the most direct thing Cutler had ever heard him say. The ambassador was huddled in a corner, shivering in the frigid electric air of the cockpit.

'Sometimes a few small wrongs can make a great big right,' Cutler drawled from the co-pilot's couch. His face was pale and drawn with the pain of the tainted wounds, but he'd managed to staunch the bleeding for the moment. 'Didn't your precious *Tau'va* ever teach you that, Si?'

'You think this is a *small wrong*?' the xenos hissed.

'I think we need to fly this Emperor-forsaken tug!' Cutler snapped, his bravado melting away in a moment. 'Now shut up and let the lady work.'

Cutler didn't believe his own bluster for a second. Watching the woman beside him he knew this was one 'Great Big Wrong' and then some. Skjoldis's hands were flitting expertly over the flight controls, but the eyes behind her veil were not her own. The dead pilot, Guido Ortega was in there, flying the shuttle while the witch steered him away from the memory of his recent death. Skjoldis's roving green eyes watched her body working from the sockets of Ortega's severed head, which was perched on the drive bay like a grisly totem.

Necromancy, the foulest of magicks...

Cutler recoiled from the truth of the woman. He'd come to accept and even respect her wyrd, but this was something darker and infinitely more dangerous than her scrying and telepathy. Something tainted.

'His spirit still lingers here,' Skjoldis had said, cradling Ortega's head in her hands and staring into his murder-stricken eyes. 'A bad death can chain a soul for days or years or even forever. We are fortunate – his death was very bad.'

Despite their long separation she'd offered Cutler no greeting. He'd watched her prepare the ritual and strap herself into the pilot's couch without a glance in his direction. Afterwards she'd appraised his wounds sombrely and spoken without meeting his eyes.

'The daemon's wrath has cut deep,' she'd said, as if he didn't know it already. 'Your wounds will not heal, Ensor Cutler.' Afterwards she'd relayed Abel's final instructions, barely leaving him time to think, let alone speak. Then without a word of warning she'd entered the trance and this new horror had begun.

She got us into space, Cutler told himself, *and she'll get us to Zebasteyn bloody Kircher. She knows what she's doing.* But he knew it wasn't that simple. Sorcery of this kind had consequences. *She was frightened. That's why she wouldn't look me in the eye. She thought I'd stop her.*

Cutler leaned towards the witch, but a restraining hand pulled him back. The *weraldur*, Frost, was looming over them both. The giant shook his head, though his watchful eyes never left his mistress. That was when Cutler noticed that Skjoldis's veil had slipped free, offering up her delicate, desiccated face to the stars.

Only it didn't slip. She's opened herself up to the warp.

Remembering her terror of the stars, Cutler tried to heave himself out of the couch, but Frost held him down.

It's too late, Cutler realised. *She's already committed. Whatever the price...*

Standing by a filthy porthole, Iverson watched the hulking battleship blot out the stars as the shuttle drew closer. The *Requiem of Virtue*: the name was redolent with irony, like almost every other name he'd encountered on his journey.

Nothing is chance or else chance is broken. The thought came to him again, trailing another: why hadn't he killed the scarred Fire Warrior on the landing pad? Yes, she had spared him once, but her act had been a mockery rather than a mercy. *And who's to say mine wasn't?* It was a pity Reve wasn't around to discuss the matter. She might have been a traitor and an assassin, but she'd had a logical mind.

Why hasn't she come back?

The battleship's hangar bay yawned ahead, black as an unanswerable question.

A clang reverberated through the shuttle as it touched down. The witch slid back in her couch with a shuddering sigh that seemed to ripple through her entire body.

'Skjoldis?' Cutler asked. 'Are you done?' He tried to get up, but the *weraldur* would not loosen his grip. 'Get your hands off me, man! Can't you see she needs my help?'

'Kill... it...' The psyker's voice was little more than a shrivelled exhalation. Cutler gawped at her convulsing body. She was breathing in harsh, rapid gasps, but her lips hadn't moved.

'I don't understand...'

'Kill it!' she hissed with sudden ferocity. Cutler looked round and met her outcast eyes, still glittering in Ortega's severed head. They were wide with horror and desperation. 'The pilot was not... the only one... who lingered here...' she croaked through dead lips.

She can't get back inside her body, Cutler realised with horror, *because something else is in there now.*

'We see you, Whitecrow!' a hateful chorus wheezed beside him. He swung round to the pilot's seat just as Skjoldis opened her eyes and looked right at him.

Black eyes leaking noxious rainbow light...

'We taste you!' A rictus grin tore the corners her mouth and the hairline fissures ran through her porcelain skin like fault lines, mirroring her tracery of tattoos. She raised an accusing hand and the fingers split open like over-ripe fruit, revealing black iron barbs. *'We will be you!'*

The *weraldur* howled with gut-wrenching grief and hefted his axe... and hesitated, staring at his mistress with tortured eyes.

'Kjordal!' Skjoldis shrieked from her dead prison. 'Do not betray me at the last!'

A new resolve hardened the giant's features, but it was too late. Cackling gleefully, the proto-daemon lashed out with razor blade claws and tore his throat open. The *weraldur* tottered on his feet, struggling to do his duty as his life gushed away. Inch by painful inch he raised the axe... and the abomination struck again, punching through his chest with splayed talons and digging deep, gouging and tearing. The giant screamed wordlessly as it wrenched his heart out in a welter of blood and bone. The weapon slipped from his numbed fingers and he pitched over.

Kjordal, Cutler thought feverishly. *His name was Kjordal...*

He dived aside as a claw slashed spastically across his couch. Laughing and chanting its endless litany of malice, the seething monstrosity tore free of its restraints. Cutler heard O'Seishin whimpering and Skjoldis screaming from the drive bay: 'Kill it before it grows too strong!'

How many times? How many times does the damned thing have to die? But Cutler already knew the answer, because the 'damned thing' was part of him. *It'll keep coming back as long as I live.*

His fingers found the haft of Kjordal's axe and the killing purity of the weapon thrilled through his body like wildfire. The daemon reared over him, dripping blood from the heart crammed into its lamprey maw, its swarming eyes weeping chromatic Chaos. *Laughing at me!* With a feral howl, Cutler swung from the ground and lopped off a leg at the knee. The beast screeched and toppled over, flailing out with its iron talons as it fell. Desperately he rammed the weapon's haft into its face and surged to his feet. The daemon reached after him, its arms dislocating and attenuating like thorny tentacles as it called his name.

You won't take me – not today, not ever! Cutler swore as he brought the axe chopping down with the full weight of his body and soul.

Iverson's vox-bead buzzed and someone spoke into his ear: 'Commissar.'

'Colonel,' Iverson answered, recognising the voice though he'd never spoken to the man before. It was a powerful voice used to command, but it was tight with pain. 'You've been a difficult man to find.'

There was a long pause, as if Cutler was disturbed by his words, then: 'I guess that's just the way it had to be, commissar.'

'I don't doubt it.' Iverson searched for something else to say to the man he'd been tracking for so long. 'Colonel—'

'Commissar,' Cutler interrupted. 'We don't have much time. Here's what you've got to do.' He told Iverson the last part of Abel's plan.

'Do you trust him?' Iverson asked afterwards.

'Like the Hells I do,' Cutler snorted. And then he explained his own plan.

The Last Day: The Requiem of Virtue

I believe this will be my final entry. We have infiltrated the Sky Marshall's eyrie and the remainder of my forces are assembled. My forces? No, that's not quite correct because I've returned command of the 19th to Colonel Ensor Cutler. He will lead them on their final mission, as is his right. Besides, our paths must diverge here. It's strange that Cutler and I shall part without ever meeting, but he's been delayed in the cockpit – 'attending to a personal matter' – and I can wait no longer. Neither of us is likely to survive this endeavour, yet I sense that Cutler and I will meet someday.

I shall conceal this journal on the shuttle. If I fail to do my duty today I trust you will find it and learn from my mistakes. I don't know your name, your rank or even your calling, yet you have followed me this far so I believe you must be true. Whoever you are, I hope you are a better soldier than I.

– Iverson's Journal

'Counterweight,' Iverson said to the trio waiting for him in the hangar bay. Two of them wore padded flak jackets over blue jumpsuits and were armed with stubby shotguns. Their uniforms marked them as naval security officers, but both had torn away the Sky Marshall's insignia. The third was a cadaverous ancient swathed in a jade habit that arched up into a cowl. His milky white eyes were almost luminous in the shadowed recess of his hood. He was blind, yet Iverson knew he could see further and deeper than any normal man. This was almost certainly Abel's astropath.

'You the 'sar?' the female officer growled in coarse Gothic. Her severe face was topped by a spiky, no-nonsense crewcut and her bare arms were corded with muscles. She was short but there was no mistaking her hard-bitten competence.

'Commissar Iverson,' he said and peered at her badge. 'Officer Privitera?'

'You don't look the part,' she said dubiously.

I know it, girl. His peaked cap was long gone and his greatcoat had turned a stale grey that matched his lank hair – hair he hadn't cut since he'd departed the Antigone months ago. It hadn't seemed important.

'He is the Blade,' the hooded ancient said in a surprisingly resonant voice.

'Well that don't make no odds to me, astro.' Privitera scowled as she watched the Confederates disembarking from the shuttle. 'It's the muscle I'm after and I ain't seeing much of that right now.'

'These men have walked through the Seven Hells for your uprising,' Iverson said coldly. 'You will show them the respect they deserve.'

Privitera didn't flinch. 'Listen up 'sar, I've got people dying all over this fraggin' ship 'cause Abel told me the cavalry was on the way. He promised me an army.'

'So you've seen Abel?' Iverson asked with sudden interest.

'Me?' she snorted. 'Nobody gets to *see* Abel, except maybe his pet freak over there,' she jabbed a thumb at the astropath, 'and he ain't got no eyes.'

'But you trust him?' Always that same question, as if the answer could make any difference so late in the game.

'Abel makes things happen. He's in so deep he can pull all the right strings and get people synced up. Our movement wasn't worth spit 'til he showed up.' She slung her shotgun over a shoulder. 'Look, I gotta shift, man. We nearly had the bridge cracked when a whole heap o' blueskins showed up.'

'He is the Blade,' repeated the astropath. 'He must come with me now.'

'Why didn't you want me to meet Iverson?' Cutler asked as he wiped the *weraldur*'s axe clean of daemonic ichor. The melee had reopened his wounds and he was running on raw willpower.

Because you would have tried to kill him, said the voice in his head, *and that is not possible, but he might have killed us.*

Us? Of course Skjoldis was right. She was a part of him now, her soul woven into the fabric of his own. After he'd killed the daemon she'd asked him to open up his mind and let her in. He hadn't hesitated for a moment. Without her guidance he was lost.

Cutler sighed and popped a couple of Furies. He hated using the combat stimms, but they were cleaner than Phaedra's narcotics and he wasn't going to last another hour without them.

'Why would I try to kill the commissar?' he asked.

Later. We must go now, Whitecrow. Your men are waiting for you.

A chorus of cheers greeted Ensor Cutler when he stepped from the shuttle. The honest joy of his men stopped him in his tracks. With O'Seishin slung across his shoulders and the axe in his hands he probably looked like some kind of barbarian king, but that didn't deter the Confederates. As they cheered him, Cutler felt a sadness bordering on despair. So many were gone and so few were left. What had happened to Vendrake and Machen and that promising young officer, Grayburn?

I did this, he realised. I brought the 19th to ruin.

Whitecrow, this is not the time for self-recrimination, urged Skjoldis. *Tell them what they need to hear. Let them believe in you.*

'Look, this is all real touching,' a woman in security officer's gear growled, 'but can we cut to the chase. My guys are dying up on A-Deck.'

Cutler looked at her with strange, mismatched eyes – one grey, the other green – and nodded. 'I think we can turn things round for you, officer.'

'And how d'you figure that exactly?' she challenged. 'The blueskins have got the bridge locked down.'

'Maybe so, but I've got one very special blueskin right here.' Cutler flung O'Seishin to the ground and grinned. 'Gentlemen – and lady – I'd like you to meet Commander Wintertide.'

Iverson had been following his eerie guide for almost an hour. Despite his blindness the astropath never hesitated or stumbled as he negotiated the vast, multi-tiered labyrinth of the battleship. Iverson had lost his bearings, but he sensed they were travelling into the bowels of the craft. Along the way he sometimes heard distant shouts and gunshots, but nobody crossed their path.

'Where are you taking me?' Iverson asked as they turned down another gloomy corridor.

'You are the Blade,' the astropath intoned. 'I am taking you to the Sky Marshall.'

'I understand that, but why would he be down here? Surely his place is on the bridge?'

'The bridge flies the ship and the ship does not fly,' his guide explained as if he were talking to a fool.

'But the engines must be fuelled and functional to maintain orbit,' Iverson pressed. 'So the ship *could* fly.'

'The ship does not fly,' the astropath repeated, letting Iverson's logic wash over him.

He's not wired to think, Iverson decided. *He's only a messenger. But he'd better be wrong about the ship.*

The doors of the turbolift slid open and Cutler's team swept into the corridor beyond. O'Seishin was strapped to the colonel's back, piggybacking like a withered child. Privitera was waiting with the forward team and a band of armsmen.

'Welcome to A-Deck,' she said. 'We're actually about midway up the ship, but this is officer country and "Deck 112" didn't cut it for 'em.'

'And the bridge?' Cutler asked as the turbolift descended for the next group.

'Up front, a few blocks along, but there's only one way in and it's crawling with blueskins. We've held on to this sector, but they've got the bridge access sewn up tight.'

'Show me.'

'Right, but stay sharp,' she said. 'The blueskins have got drones working the vents and those floaters pack a helluva punch.' As she turned away Cutler swallowed another Fury. He was already over the limit with the stimms, but that was the least of his worries right now.

'You all right, sir?' Valance asked, tagging along beside him.

'Never better, scout,' Cutler said as the angry glow lit up his blood. 'Let's go get us a bridge!'

Control the bridge and you control the ship, he reflected as he followed Privitera. It was the age-old logic of shipboard mutinies. The uprising had gravitated here like a force of nature, but it was just a distraction from Abel's real target. Cutler wondered how the armswoman would feel if she knew the truth. *She's just another pawn like all the rest of us sorry bastards...*

Along the way they passed scores of rebels. There were men and women from every strata of the ship's society: armoured security troops leading studious looking adepts, smartly dressed naval ratings paired with filthy galley dogs, even a tech-priest leading a trio of combat servitors, but shamefully no officers at all. According to Privitera nearly half the ship had risen up against the Sky Marshall and his xenos allies – far more than the rebels had anticipated. Cutler read the dissenters' faces as he swept by, clocking anger and fear, determination and desperation. And always hate.

Our loathing of the xenos runs deep. Kircher might have glossed over it for years, maybe even decades to keep his corrupt little empire ticking along, but the hatred was always there under the surface, waiting for this moment of truth.

To his surprise he wasn't sure how he felt about that truth. Trinity had shaken his faith in many things, including humanity's divine right to rule the stars, but that didn't make the tau any better. For all his fine talk of the Greater Good, O'Seishin was just another conniving son-of-a-bitch selling another flavour of oppression.

Better our evil empire than theirs...

'Hey, slow up!' Privitera cautioned as they came to a wide cross-junction. 'This cuts onto the main access corridor and trust me, you don't want to step out there.'

There were rebels positioned on either side of the junction, all well-armed and alert, doubtless the best of Privitera's men. There were also bodies – lots of them, scattered about in the random contortions of violent death. Most of them were human, but it was impossible to tell whether they'd been rebels or loyalists.

And of course the rebels are *the loyalists here,* Cutler mused with black humour. *Civil wars always play havoc with the rules.*

'Valance,' he said and signalled the scout forward.

The scout nodded and knelt by the junction. He fished a small mirror from his pouch and clipped it to the barrel of his lasrifle. Cautiously he angled the gun round the wall, reading the reflection with narrowed eyes.

'The whole corridor's packed with xenos soldiers,' Valance said. 'I've got at least fifty Fire Warriors and a Crisis battlesuit. Plenty of drones too.'

'Grenades?' Cutler suggested.

'You think we didn't try that?' Privitera gave him a dirty look. 'The blueskins know the game, man. They're too far back.'

'She's right,' Valance said. 'They've got the range and the firepower. Probably packing some shield drones too, just for insurance.'

'And there's no other way in?' Cutler asked the rebel leader.

'We tried the vents, but they're crawling with drones. I lost some good men that way.' Privitera shrugged. 'No man, there ain't no way in except through here.'

Cutler nodded and jabbed a thumb at the tau strapped to his back. 'Well then, I guess it's time to play Commander Wintertide.'

Iverson knew he was getting close to his quarry now. The dingy, corroded decrepitude of the lower deck had given way to pristine white corridors fashioned from some kind of moulded plastic that hummed softly and emitted its own light. This remote sector of the ship had been remodelled from the ground up by the tau, creating a secret world within the battleship.

How long has this been going on? Iverson wondered. *When did Kircher sell out the Imperium? Five years? Ten? Twenty? How long have we been fighting for a lie on Phaedra?*

The scale of the betrayal was appalling and Iverson felt his fury catch fire with absolute conviction. It had been too long since he'd felt such pure contempt. Whatever else was true or false, right or wrong, one thing was certain: the Sky Marshall had cast countless lives into the meat grinder of this sham war. He had to die.

And I'll be the one to do it. This is what my life has been leading up to. This will be my redemption.

He wondered where Bierce had disappeared to; he hadn't seen the old ghost since he'd left Phaedra. It was almost as if his mentor had served his purpose.

'We are here,' the astropath said, coming to a stop outside an iris-like door.

Iverson stared at the sealed hatch. 'The Sky Marshall is through there?'

'Yes,' his guide said without inflection or interest.

'Where are the guards?' Iverson asked, indicating the brightly lit corridor. 'We're right in the heart of his territory, but we've seen nobody, not even a drone.'

'They are not here.' It was the most incontrovertible and pointless statement Iverson had ever heard.

'*Where* are they?' he asked through gritted teeth.

'They have been summoned to the bridge.'

'All of them?'

'Yes. Abel has arranged it.'

Iverson shook his head and turned his attention back to the hatch. 'And how do I get in there?'

'You are the Blade.' The astropath touched his palm to the sensor pad by the door and it spiralled open soundlessly. 'Abel has arranged it.' Without another word he turned and walked away.

Abel has arranged it. Why do I like that less and less?

Iverson walked through the door.

'I am Por'o Dal'yth Seishin,' the ambassador called out weakly. 'You will hold your fire, warriors.'

'You heard your boss,' Cutler shouted, 'none of us want any slip ups here so just take it easy.' He stepped out into the access corridor with the ambassador on his back and a grenade in each hand, the pins already depressed. 'If we do this right we might all make it through to tomorrow.'

Scores of dispassionate lenses stared back at him above a forest of pulse rifles and carbines. The Fire Warriors were lined up along the corridor in orderly formations, the foremost ranks lying prone, the next kneeling and the last standing. Gun drones hovered and flitted over the troops like miniaturised spacecraft and right at the back, looming by the bridge door, Cutler saw the blocky shape of a Crisis battlesuit.

Valance was right, Cutler decided. *This corridor is a killing ground.*

'See, what we've got here is a stalemate.' He advanced with his hands raised, making sure the tau got a good look at the grenades. 'Ain't that right, ambassador?'

'What do you hope to achieve with this?' O'Seishin asked wearily. 'They will not let you pass, Ensor Cutler.'

'Maybe I'll talk them round. Or make them see things differently.' Cutler stopped when he reached the first rank of Fire Warriors. 'Who's in charge here?' he called.

The Crisis battlesuit stomped forward. Fire Warriors slipped aside as it advanced to loom over Cutler. It tilted at the waist and regarded him impassively with its lens-studded head.

'I am Shas'vre Zen'kais,' a toneless voice boomed from the battlesuit's chest. 'You will release Por'o Dal'yth Seishin.'

'I could do that.' Cutler seemed to give it some thought. His mind was on fire with the Furies. He'd thrown caution to the wind and swallowed another couple before making his gambit. 'But then I wouldn't get to do this.' He threw the grenades over the battlesuit and dived against its bulk with a yell: 'Counterweight!'

One grenade exploded fiercely, tearing through the second rank of Fire Warriors. The other vented a cloud of smoke that billowed out to choke the corridor.

'Counterweight!' Lieutenant Hood bellowed back at the junction. 'Go!'

The sniper, Toomy, rolled out of cover, sighting down his rail rifle as he moved. The three Zouaves followed him on either side, allowing him just enough time for a single shot.

We got to make this one count, Eloise, he purred to his gun as he fired.

The Crisis battlesuit's sensor module disintegrated in a burst of light. Toomy managed a grin before a volley of return fire incinerated his face. Then the Zouaves were storming down the corridor like a moving shield, with greybacks and rebels racing along behind them. Intermittent pulse rounds battered their armour, melting away the heavy plates with frightening speed. Several stray bolts flashed past the knights, every one claiming a life in the packed corridor. If the xenos had a chance to rally and focus their fire the Zouaves would go down in seconds and it would all be over.

While the blinded Crisis battlesuit flailed about, Cutler tore the axe from his belt and leapt for the nearest Fire Warriors. The aliens hesitated a split second, unsure what to do about the ambassador. Then their chance was gone and he was in amongst them.

'For Providence and the Seven Stars!' he bellowed, swinging the axe like a madman as O'Seishin shrieked and swayed about on his back.

More tau rushed from the smoke to join the front ranks, adding their fire to the defence as drones zipped forwards. One of the Zouaves fell, his breastplate reduced to molten slag. Another barrage tore through the gap in the advancing shield wall and mowed down dozens of charging men.

'Put your backs into it you worthless dogs!' Hood shouted. A pulse round punched into his leg, another through his shoulder. The force spun him round, but he caught himself and limped on, trailing smoke.

And then the onslaught hit the xenos line like a hammer. One of the Zouaves crashed into the Crisis battlesuit and his momentum threw them both to the ground. His comrade dashed on into the smoke, hacking about blindly with his buzz saws. The Fire Warriors in the front ranks tried to fall back, but became entangled with others rushing forward to reinforce the line. A moment later the angry tide of humanity swept over them and any hope of cohesion was gone.

'Rip out their fraggin' blue hearts!' Privitera yelled as she rammed her shotgun into a Fire Warrior's faceplate and fired.

Cutler staggered from the melee, his head swimming in its own personal mire. The lacerations in his chest had opened right up and he was bleeding badly.

You must be strong, Whitecrow, Skjoldis insisted. *We have to finish this. Iverson must not be allowed to escape.*

'I still... don't get it,' Cutler murmured, trying to hold onto consciousness. 'Why does he matter? Who is he?'

'Commissar Holt Iverson,' the Sky Marshall said. 'I take it you've come for your Thunderground.'

CHAPTER SIXTEEN

My Thunderground?

'So you're familiar with our myths?' Iverson asked, keeping his pistol levelled on the pair standing inside the brightly lit chamber. One was a tau Fire Warrior, lightly armoured and bare headed. The other was a man in a plain grey uniform.

'You really think the Thunderground is just a myth?' The man seemed surprised. 'I would have thought that you of all people would be a true believer, Holt Iverson. Haven't you chased your destiny like a bloodhound?' He offered a smile that looked sincere. 'But to answer your question – yes, I've made a point of familiarising myself with all things Arkan.'

'Because we've been a thorn in your side?'

'Because your people intrigue me.' The smile became a frown. 'You most of all, Iverson.'

'How do you know my name?'

'Oh, I know rather more than that, though I admit you didn't catch my eye until Lomax singled you out for her mission. And then of course you vanished off the radar, but your record made for interesting reading.' He spread his hands magnanimously. 'So what do you make of my nerve centre?'

'It's impressive,' Iverson admitted.

The circular chamber was not particularly large, but it was alive with information. Banks of monitors and holo-screens tiled the walls all the way to the high, conical ceiling. Iverson saw live vid-feeds, topographical maps and tactical maps, psych reports and inventories... the density of intelligence was almost overwhelming. A huge photo-realistic hologram of Phaedra hovered above a dais at the centre of the room, revolving slowly. The image crawled with brightly coloured icons representing bases and troop movements, all appended with restless statistics.

'My window upon the world below,' the man said, approaching slowly. 'The science is all tau of course. We get most of our surveillance feeds from drones, although you wouldn't recognise them if you saw them. Drone tech is outstandingly flexible and a spy drone can be smaller than the human eye.' He smiled again. 'On occasion we've actually *replaced* the human eye with a drone and left the recipient none the wiser.'

Iverson touched his own optic uneasily, but the man shook his head. 'No, don't worry. Your augmetic is clean, Iverson.'

'You are Sky Marshall Zebasteyn Kircher?' Iverson asked, gathering his thoughts. He already knew the answer, but the question had to be aired. Protocol and the moment demanded it.

'I am.' Kircher stopped a couple of metres from Iverson and straightened up. 'I take it you're here to serve the Emperor's Justice?'

Iverson regarded the man he had come to kill. He had imagined his nemesis in many shades of corruption: a seedy, silk-tongued despot sagging with depravity, his uniform ripe with garish epaulettes and empty medals. Or a haggard ghost who kept to the shadows and whispered tormented riddles, all the while secretly longing for his own doom. Or perhaps a granite-faced egomaniac cut from the true military block, his eyes burning with fervour as he declaimed his creed. The galaxy was rife with tyrants, but their cancer always seemed to follow the same old strains of self-congratulation, self-loathing or self-deception.

Yet this man is none of those things.

Kircher was broad shouldered and muscular in the manner of a middle-aged soldier accustomed to hard exercise, although Iverson knew he must be over a century old. Doubtless he had availed himself of juvenat therapies to hold back the years, but there wasn't a trace of vanity about him. His square, businesslike face was free of wrinkles, but otherwise untouched by cosmetic enhancements. His nose had been broken and set askew, like an off-kilter sundial at the centre of his face. He wasn't particularly tall, but he was straight-backed and sturdy, lending him a quietly imposing air. The dignity ran through to his uniform – a modest tunic and cap devoid of any ornaments save the silver Skywatch badge. He looked more like an NCO than the governor of a world, yet there was a pervasive, muted authority about him.

You're not what I expected, Zebasteyn Kircher.

'Why?' Iverson asked. It was a simple question that encompassed so much. Like his first question it needed asking.

Kircher didn't show a trace of fear as he stared past the barrel of Iverson's gun and looked him in the eye. 'Because it was necessary.'

'That's not good enough.'

'No? I've just confessed that I've betrayed the Imperium. Surely that's all the justification you need, *commissar*?' Iverson said nothing and Kircher nodded. 'No... no, of course it's not. For any other man of your creed it would be more than enough, but not for you, Holt Iverson. You see, you have become addicted to truth and you crave answers. Am I wrong?'

You think too much for a commissar. How many people have told me that down the years? How many of them have I failed?

'Furthermore you are incapable of denying a *manifest* truth, no matter how much it may torment you,' Kircher went on. 'I think it's your Arkan heritage showing through. For all your training and indoctrination, that troublesome, dissenting blood won't let you sleepwalk through life.'

'This isn't about me.'

'I disagree. At this particular moment in time it is *precisely* about you.' Kircher shrugged. 'After all, you're the man pointing a gun at my head. You have the power to end me if you so choose. I'd say that makes you very significant indeed.'

'Are you Abel?'

'What?' For the first time the Marshall seemed wrong-footed. He frowned, looking genuinely puzzled. 'No, I'm not Abel. Why would you think that?'

'It's the only answer that makes any sense,' Iverson said emphatically. 'Who else would have the authority to bring us this far? Who else could have cleared out the guards so I could walk right in here? Abel can only be you.'

Kircher nodded slowly. 'I see your logic and there is certainly a mystery here, but why would I assist my own assassin?'

'Because I am not your assassin – I am your judge. And you want to be judged.'

The Sky Marshall considered this, his wide-set eyes bright with thought. Finally he shook his head. 'You are mistaken, Iverson. I do not wish to be judged. I have already judged myself and continue to do so every day of my life.'

'So you think you're innocent?'

'No, not innocent, but simply necessary.' Kircher sighed. 'As I have already said, that's what this is all about – not honour or justice or any such rousing virtue – just plain necessity.'

'Betraying tens of thousands of Imperial lives was necessary?'

'To preserve hundreds of thousands, perhaps millions more? Absolutely.' Kircher waved a hand around the room, indicating the flow of information. 'The carnage on Phaedra is nothing beside the horrors to come if this war is allowed to spread across the subsector.'

'So you and your xenos friends decided to play us for fools and cap things here?' Iverson said bitterly. 'And never mind all the lives you threw into the meat grinder.'

'You still fail to grasp the wider picture, Iverson. This region is a buffer zone between two embattled giants. Neither the Imperium nor the Tau Empire can spare the resources to fight this war on a system-wide scale – not when there are so many greater threats elsewhere, but equally neither side can be seen to back down.'

'You're telling me the Imperium is party to this heresy?'

'My remit for the war came directly from the High Council of Terra,' Kircher said quietly. 'They tied my hands from the outset. I confess there was a time when that appalled me.' He searched Iverson's face. 'Don't tell me you're honestly surprised by this.'

No, I'm not surprised, Iverson realised sadly. *I'm not surprised by any of it.*

'But you decided to take things further,' he said with growing certainty.

Flanked by the two surviving Zouaves, Cutler stepped up to the bridge bulkhead. The massive hatch was sealed tight. 'Open it,' he snarled at the tau strapped to his back, 'or I'll throw you to the Hells after your lapdogs.'

'The tau do not have a concept of Hell,' O'Seishin said in a brittle voice. 'I have already explained this to you, Ensor Cutler.'

Lieutenant Hood limped up alongside them, smelling of burnt meat. 'A few of 'em slipped away in the chaos, but the corridor's ours, colonel.' He shook his head wearily. 'It cost us though.'

'Every step of this journey has cost us, Hood.' Cutler reeled against the hatch as another wave of nausea hit him. He was drenched in sweat and blood now – so much of both he couldn't tell where one ended and the other began. 'It's eaten us away... piece by piece...'

That is enough, Whitecrow! Skjoldis berated him.

'No, it's not enough. It's never going to be... nearly... enough,' he muttered through harsh gasps. Then he punched the hatch hard, drawing more blood. 'Open it!'

'You are correct,' the Sky Marshall said without hesitation. 'I took things *much* further. And I regret none of it.' He clenched his fists, as if to reinforce his thinking. 'The Imperium can't last, Iverson. It is a brutal, multi-headed leviathan forged for war, but despite the billions of souls that feed its engines, it is running down.' His voice rose with passion as he found his stride. 'Corruption and infighting have become endemic to its machinery. Ignorance and spite have become its orthodoxy. Shackled by fear, humanity tears itself apart from the inside out while it fights a thousand wars on a thousand fronts! Even the reprieve here is just a stopgap until the Imperium can spare the resources to prosecute *this* war to the full.' Kircher shook his head in disgust. 'I suspect the Imperium had a purpose once, but now it's nothing but a vicious relic.'

'What about the Emperor?' Iverson asked.

'The Emperor?' Kircher seemed surprised by the question. 'Who can say what He really stands for after all these millennia. Like His empire He might have meant something once, but now...' He snorted dismissively. 'Frankly I've had my fill of serving a corpse that won't die. Humanity needs a fresh perspective if it is to survive.'

'So you've bought into the tau and their Greater Good?' Iverson said tightly.

'I have not *bought* into anything,' Kircher snapped. 'I have *chosen* to use my intellect to find the best of all possible paths!' He calmed himself with a visible effort. 'But yes, the Greater Good has merit. It cultivates a mature humility in its followers, a rationality that puts our own fixations with honour and glory to shame. Mankind is an ancient race, yet we behave like feral infants beside the tau.' He shook his head. 'We have to grow up before the galaxy gives up on us.'

Iverson felt the electric wasp in his optic stirring awake and suddenly he remembered the most important question: 'What about Ysabel Reve?'

'Who?' The Sky Marshall seemed nonplussed.

'Commissar Cadet Ysabel Reve. Did you send her after me?'

'I don't know what you're talking about.' Kircher shook his head ruefully. 'Even I can't keep tabs on everyone. Who is Ysabel Reve?'

'She's dead,' Iverson said.

'I'm sorry,' Kircher said carefully. 'Was she was important to you?'

'I killed her.'

'And you regret this?'

'Should I?'

Kircher's eyes narrowed as he considered it. 'Was her killing necessary?'

Not right or wrong... The wasp in Iverson's skull was flitting about angrily... *Not just or unjust...* Hunting for a way out... *Merely necessary or not...*

'Is that all there is to it?' he asked hollowly.

'No, but everything else is suspect,' Kircher said, his eyes bright with conviction. 'To prosper we have to strip away the delusions of emotion and morality and work with the facts. That's the core philosophy of the Greater Good. It is a path focussed on hard reality rather than fluid ideals. A path we can build upon.'

'Why are you telling me all this?'

'Because you were right,' Kircher said with wonder, as if he had only just realised it himself. 'You *are* my judge, Iverson. I didn't seek you out, but here you are regardless – a sharp mind with a gun pointed in my face. Perhaps there's an opportunity in that.'

'You expect me to spare you?' Iverson's face twitched as the wasp burrowed through his brain, triggering strange synapses. 'You expect me to turn a blind eye to this heresy?'

'I expect you to *think*,' Kircher urged. 'Consider the horror you'll set loose if you end this stalemate.'

'I am an Imperial commissar.'

The Sky Marshall's eyes bored into him with an iron will. 'That is a lie, Holt Iverson. Whatever you are, you stopped being an Imperial commissar a long time ago.'

And I cannot deny a manifest truth.

The bridge crew didn't put up a fight. Fragile, pale-skinned men and women in smart naval uniforms, they backed away from the intruders with raised hands and lowered eyes.

'Where's the captain?' Cutler demanded. With his blood-drenched axe and rawhide jacket he knew he must look like the worst kind of pirate to them. Seeing their terrified expressions he wanted to laugh aloud, but if he did that something might break inside him before he was done here.

'I'll ask nicely one more time. After that I'll get mad.' Cutler hefted the axe meaningfully. 'Where in the Hells is the captain?'

'Kill me and millions more will die,' the Sky Marshall said. 'Justice demands it, so justice is blind.' He stepped forward so the barrel of Iverson's gun was touching his forehead. 'End this ugly lie and begin an infinitely uglier truth. Honour demands it, so honour is monstrous.'

Iverson held the gun rigid as thoughts flashed and faded across his mind like dancing fireflies. *Kill him and be damned? Spare him and be redeemed? Or is it the other way round? Redeemed or re-damned?* Where were his ghosts when he needed their counsel the most? He glanced past the Sky Marshall, searching for Bierce or Number 27 or even Niemand. Hoping for Reve... He saw the Fire Warrior. The tau hadn't moved at all during the confrontation, but he was watching them intently.

He's waiting for my choice.

And then the choice was taken away. Moving with a swiftness that belied his years, the Sky Marshall flung up an arm and caught Iverson's wrist in an iron grip. The gun fired, but Kircher had already sidestepped with the grace of a dancer. He twisted and the pistol slipped from Iverson's numbed hand. Kircher didn't pause for a moment. Using his fists like pistons he lashed out with almost inhuman speed, pummelling Iverson's face and chest. The commissar staggered back, but Kircher followed remorselessly, battering him like a threshing machine until he fell.

'I'm sorry,' the Sky Marshall said as he stepped away from his prone opponent. 'I wish I could have let you choose, but there's too much at stake to gamble on your sanity.' He was breathing hard, as if the sudden violence had drained him. 'For what it's worth, I believe you would have done the right thing, Holt Iverson.'

The Fire Warrior appeared at his shoulder, holding Iverson's pistol. Kircher acknowledged the tau with a nod. 'Kill him, shas'el.'

The xenos shot Zebasteyn Kircher through the eye.

'The captain is gone,' a skinny naval lieutenant said. 'He disappeared decades ago. He never saw eye to eye with the Sky Marshall.'

'I like the man already,' Cutler said. 'Right, forget the captain. You boys can do the job, right?'

'The job?' the lieutenant stuttered. 'What are you asking me... sir?'

'Fire up the engines. We're leaving.'

'Leaving?' The officer's eyes goggled in confusion.

'Clearing out from Phaedra,' Cutler said. 'The way I see it, this ship's a symbol of everything that's wrong here, so I'm taking the symbol away.'

'But that's impossible,' the lieutenant was outraged. 'The *Requiem of Virtue* hasn't flown since the war started.' There were murmurs of support from his fellow officers. 'You've seen the state of her. She'll probably disintegrate before we break out of orbit.'

'I'm not telling you to break out of orbit, boy. I'm telling you to break out of space,' Cutler said cheerily. 'Let's do this like we mean it, eh?'

'You want us to enter the warp?' The officer's outrage had slipped into outright terror. 'That's suicide! I don't even know if the ship's Geller fields are still functioning. Without them we'll be eaten alive!'

'You are insane, Ensor Cutler,' O'Seishin said, but there was no strength in his protest. He sounded resigned to his fate.

Gunfire exploded somewhere outside.

'The blueskins are back!' Hood yelled from the doorway. 'And they've brought along a whole brigade of Skywatch cronies!'

'Well, I guess we're done talking,' Cutler said and shot the skinny lieutenant. He grinned at the man's shocked comrades. 'Now, who can fly this hellfired ship?'

'I am disappointed in you, human,' the Fire Warrior said, standing over Iverson. 'I chose you for this task because you are a commissar. I expected you to execute the traitor on sight.'

Iverson looked up from the Sky Marshall's crumpled body and met the alien's gaze. 'Who are you?'

'I am Shas'el Aabal, acting commander of the Fire Caste on this world,' the tau said proudly. 'I am also the one you know as "Abel".'

Iverson shook his head, trying to focus. 'I was sure it was Kircher. Why would you betray your own kind?'

'I have not,' the xenos said coldly. 'I am loyal to the Greater Good, but the Water Caste have made a mockery of this war. O'Seishin's "experiment" must not succeed.' He indicated the Sky Marshall. 'The chaos you have sown here will prove your species is too dangerous to be trusted. When reports of this mutiny reach the Tau Empire this travesty will be ended.'

'You want the war to spread,' Iverson said with growing understanding.

'I want the war to be prosecuted by warriors, as was decreed by the enlightened ones,' the tau said. 'The Greater Good will not prosper through conspiracies and lies.'

Iverson chuckled, low and bitter.

'This amuses you?' the tau asked coldly.

'Don't you see the irony?' Iverson smiled sourly. 'You're a schemer too, *Abel*. Maybe the biggest schemer of them all.'

'It was...'

'Necessary?' Iverson shook his head. 'You know, I don't think you blue-skins are nearly as enlightened as you pretend to be. In fact I'd say you're much like us.' To his surprise Iverson found this casual heresy amusing.

'We are *nothing* like you, gue'la!' Abel spat. 'The *Tau'va* elevates and unites us.'

'Only when your precious Ethereals are around to keep you leashed,' Iverson mocked. 'When they're away things start to fall apart, don't they?' He frowned, intrigued by the idea. 'Why is that? What kind of a hold have the Ethereals got over the rest of you?'

'You know nothing about us.'

'And how much do you really know?' Iverson urged, following the shadowy intuition through. 'I'll wager you've actually enjoyed being free of them here.'

'Be silent.' Abel levelled the gun.

'It's a lie,' Iverson said with sudden certainty. 'The Greater Good, under all the fine talk and sparkle, it's just another lie.'

Abel fired just as the world was wrenched out from under them.

'We have to cut the engines!' a crewman yelled as the bridge quaked. 'The ship's tearing itself apart!' There were calls of agreement from his comrades so Cutler shot him, then shot the man next to him, just to be sure. The sounds of battle in the corridor were getting closer, the gunfire punctuated by desperate yells of fury and pain. Time was running out.

'Take us into the warp,' Cutler shouted. 'Or I'll put you all down!'

'We don't have a navigator.' The speaker was a tall, hairless woman in her autumn years. Unlike her comrades she seemed more angry than afraid. 'Even if the Geller field holds we'll never find our way back out of the warp.'

Perfect, Skjoldis whispered. *He must never escape.*

* * *

The quake threw Abel to the floor and sent his shot wide. The round punched through Iverson's left shoulder, but he barely registered the wound.

Cutler's done it! The thought filled him with fierce joy. *He's fired up the engines!*

Iverson surged to his feet, flooded by a reserve of strength that seemed to come out of nowhere. Tottering unsteadily he caught sight of his enemy. The xenos was lying prone, but it hadn't lost its hold on the gun. *You're no better than us, blueskin.* Fighting the tremors, he staggered towards the tau. Seeing him, it snarled and opened fire, gripping the bucking gun two-handed. Iverson threw up his metal hand to shield his face. *You're just like us!* He felt the bullets smacking into him like hammer blows as he advanced... and felt a dim pain in his legs... his gut... his chest... *You're just as lost and just as damned.* Heard the bullets pinging off the metal fist... saw the sparks as it took the punishment... *There's no way out for any of us.* Felt the scorching pain as a bullet slipped past and tore open his cheek.

'It's all a lie,' he wheezed as he fell upon the alien.

Abel had time for one last shot, then Iverson caught the autopistol in his augmetic and squeezed, crushing metal and flesh into a jagged aggregate pulp.

'Do you understand what I'm telling you?' the female officer said levelly. 'You're condemning us all to hell.' Despite her years, her eyes were a piercing blue.

Maybe that is where we belong, Skjoldis said.

'Maybe that's where we belong,' Cutler said. He found he didn't want to shoot the woman with the blue eyes. Whoever she was, she had more guts than all her comrades put together.

'There is no Hell,' O'Seishin muttered, sounding like he was trying to convince himself. 'It is just a primitive delusion.'

'Well, I guess we're going to find out together, Si.' Cutler levelled his gun at the woman he couldn't bring himself to shoot. 'Do it.'

'Your race... is dying!' Abel sneered as he wrestled hopelessly with Iverson. 'We are... the future!'

Iverson mashed his rigid augmetic eye into the tau's face and silenced its scorn. He struck again and again, ignoring the echoing agonies in his own skull as he hammered the bionic through flesh and bone.

We're all dying and there is no future. Perhaps there never was.

At last his enemy was still and Iverson slumped back, fighting for breath. Abel's final shot had pierced a lung and he could feel his chest filling up with liquid.

I'm drowning in my own blood. Perhaps I always was.

He stared at the alien's ruined features. One of its eyes had been ruptured, but the other stared back at him with lifeless spite. As he gazed into that black abyss the world seemed to stretch away from him, tearing him out of reality like a flat paper cut-out and leaving him behind at the wrong end of an infinitely extending telescope. Through its impossibly distant lens he glimpsed a seething maelstrom of rainbow light.

We've entered the warp and the Geller fields have failed and now the warp is in here with us. Perhaps it always was.

Nausea turned him inside out and he retched blood. The liquid whirled about his head in dark streamers as he slipped away from his enemy and fell backwards... and felt like he was falling forever... falling down the telescope towards that eager, prismatic oblivion.

I'm going to end here and that's for the best and there's no perhaps about it.

'You will not end here, Iverson.' The voice sounded like it had slithered from the bed of a polluted ocean, but the clipped accent was unmistakeable.

'Reve...' He closed his eyes and saw her kneeling beside him. The right side of her face was encrusted with iridescent fungi while the left was a bloodless alabaster. Pale things crawled about in the ragged cavity of her neck.

'Reve, you're wrong,' he whispered. 'You're too late. I'm already dead.'

She laughed, a low gurgle that scattered ephemeral parasites from her throat. 'That is just the beginning of the road, Holt Iverson.'

Somewhere across an immeasurable morass of space and time he heard a bell tolling and thought of home.

OUT CASTE

'A Tau chooses neither its caste nor its True Name. We are blood born to the first and borne by blood to the second, named for what we have done and might yet do. And like ourselves, our true names are not carved in stone.'

– The Tau'va

The warrior crouches in darkness, eyes locked on the softly glowing lenses of the helmet in its hands. Remembering. Seeking a name.

When I completed my training and stepped onto the Path of Fire I was summoned before the academy commander alongside my fellow shas'saal cadets for the Naming. Who better to decipher a warrior's true name than the master who has honed that living weapon? While others were honoured for their endurance, or agility, or precision with arms, I was named for my skill in reading the hearts of my comrades: J'kaara, 'the mirror'.

'You have been their shining core,' he said. 'You recognise and draw on their strength, reflecting it back threefold.'

He predicted a path of leadership, confirming what I already knew, that I was first amongst equals. Yes, there was pride, but it was hard earned, for though there is no prejudice against females under the Tau'va, few of us burn brightly on the Fire Path. I dreamt I would eclipse Shadowsun herself.

She frowns at the memory – the arrogance of impossible youth past and the price that will never pass. Sighing, she strokes her helmet with calloused fingers. It has been with her since her first, all too sweet, taste of war.

A new-forged shas'la, I embarked on my first campaign alight with a conviction that did not flicker in the cold winds of war. Our enemy was the bhe'ghaal, a race of green-skinned beasts that infested vast tracts of the galaxy and made frequent raids into tau territory. They were a brutal, ugly species that lived for war, yet made a mockery of the craft, fighting in mobs that swept about the battlefield intoxicated by their own fury. We spun circles of death around them, luring them into one trap after another, decimating them from a distance with firepower they couldn't hope to match, then falling back before they overran us with sheer numbers.

It was a flawless execution of *kauyon* that confirmed the tau mastery of war... and my own mastery of hearts, for though I did not lead by rank, my comrades followed me regardless, inspired by my example and my words. Indeed, words flowed so freely for me that our shas'ui joked that I must be a waterborn changeling!

I was beyond fear or doubt, certain of my place in the perfect geometry of the Tau'va – untouchable. And when the shas'ui fell, none were surprised that I was chosen to take his place. A veteran in my youth, I believed myself a hero. I was too young to understand that easy victories have no heroes.

She shivers as her fingers find the scar. Abhorrent. Reverent. She traces the shallow fault line from the helmet's crown to the chin. It is a mere ghost of the rift that was once there, but its truth is undiminished.

Fh'anc... Dhobos... Po'gaja... More paltry worlds and petty wars fought against inept or feeble foes, more easy victories to burnish my pride.

Oba'rai...

A small planet on the fringes of the Second Expansion, Oba'rai was uncannily beautiful, its arid plains reminiscent of revered T'au itself. It was a natural home to the people, worthy of risk.

'There are gue'la here,' our cadre shas'o told us. 'Their Imperium lays claim to this world, but their shadow has grown pale in this region, sapped by distant conflicts. If we strike swift and hard the Imperium will turn a blind eye.'

Gue'la – 'hu-maans'... They were an ancient race steeped in belligerent superstition, yet they were neither fools nor savages. I thrilled at the prospect of facing a worthy enemy at last. Perhaps I would earn the rank of shas'vre here.

The disfigured helmet gazes back at her. Challenging. Accusing. It has been crudely repaired by her own hands, functional but ugly. An artisan of the earth caste could have restored it to perfection, but perfection would have been a lie.

The gue'la colonists fought fiercely, but their technology and tactics were primitive beside our own. Only their vaunted Imperial Guard gave us pause – a single regiment who had been promised the planet as a home if they could hold it. The shas'o offered them the opportunity to surrender, but his terms were harsh and they spat in his face. The outcome troubled me because they were honourable foes, but when I mentioned these doubts to my shas'vre, he laughed.

'Do you believe the shas'o *wanted* them to surrender? This war calls for the Killing Blow, not the Open Hand – a clean sweep, not complications.'

She nods at her scarred shadow, acknowledging the moment when perfection withered and doubt blossomed – the moment when her true name became a lie.

* * *

The Guardsmen made their last stand in Oba'rai's primary city, fortifying the walls and rallying a militia of thousands, but it was an empty gesture. Our stealth teams infiltrated the bastion and destroyed their artillery with surgical precision, leaving the defenders helpless against our long-range missiles and railguns. We razed the city without losing a single warrior, yet never once during that nightmare bombardment did the Imperials attempt to surrender. My comrades derided them for fools, but I was silent.

As I expected, the shas'o decreed we would take no prisoners. Scouring the ruins would be dangerous close-quarters work, so he unleashed the kroot, our alien auxiliaries, upon the broken city. They were bloodthirsty avian predators, little better than beasts, but loyal and perfectly suited to the task. *And yet...* The thought of those savages running riot amongst fallen *warriors* reviled me. If the rumours were true, the kroot had a taste for the flesh of their enemies...

She is no longer a shining mirror, but she is still strong and she still serves the Greater Good, not because it is perfect, but because everything else is less so. Now the strength she reflects is dark and fractured, so perhaps imperfection will be her key.

Even now I cannot explain the compulsion, but I disobeyed the shas'o's edict and led my squad into the ruins, lying to them and playing on their trust, seeking something I couldn't name. A swirling miasma of black smoke transformed the city into a shadow labyrinth haunted by charred corpses and twitching things that had no business being alive. Wordlessly we killed them as we passed. It was a mercy, yet I sensed my squad tightening with reflexive revulsion and felt their unspoken question: *why?* They were my closest comrades, the ones I hoped to swear the *ta'lissera* with, yet I had carried them into this filth, rubbing their faces in a carnage we tau prefer to keep at arm's length.

Why?

As we pressed deeper, the moans of the dying echoed around us, sometimes broken by the gleeful hoots of the ravening kroot. In the city square we came upon a pack of the beasts huddled around a mound of corpses and I learnt that the rumours about our allies were true. One of them saw us and chittered, rocking back and forth on its talons, trailing red ruin from its serrated beak. Then it cocked its head and beckoned, sly and mocking, inviting us to join the feast. Two of my comrades retched inside their helmets as we backed away, stumbling in our eagerness to distance ourselves from these vile allies.

Lost in smoke and revulsion, I tripped over a corpse in a smouldering greatcoat and froze. The dead man's eyes were wide open in a face scorched to the bone - *looking right at me.* Absurdly, his high-peaked cap was still intact, its melted rim fused to his skull.

Why? I might have asked it aloud, though of what I have no idea.

The gue'la surged up with impossible, hate-driven vitality, something bright and furiously alive buzzing in his hands, sweeping towards me. I staggered back, throwing up my rifle to block the blow and it was torn asunder in a storm of tortured metal that shook my entire body. I heard my comrades' wild shouts and the burst of their carbines as the whirling chainblade kissed my helmet...

The warrior reaches up and touches the other scar, the one that can never be repaired because it cuts deeper than flesh or bone, proclaiming a darkness that was perhaps always there. Her comrades killed the ko'miz'ar a heartbeat before he killed her, but still a heartbeat too late. Afterwards, they were comrades no more and there have been none since. The flaw has made her an outcast amongst her own kind, denying her the bond of the ta'lissera, but it has also forged her into something more. Crouching in the darkness as the darkness crouches inside her, she finally names her truth: Jhi'kaara, 'the broken mirror'.

A SANCTUARY
OF WYRMS

-BEGIN RECORDING-

We walk blindly along a knife-edge slicing into oblivion. If we misstep we fall from our path. If we walk true we fall with our path. Perhaps there is a difference, but I have come to doubt it. Nevertheless, I will honour the Greater Good and allow you to draw your own conclusions from the facts.

I have little time, but even in extremis one must observe the correct protocols. That is what it means to be a tau amongst savages. Whatever else I have lost to this diseased planet, I will not lose that. Therefore know that I am Por'ui Vior'la Asharil, third-stream daughter of Clan Kherai. Though I hail from a Sept of worlds where the wisdom of the water caste is eclipsed by the ferocity of the fire caste, my family has served the Tau Empire with grace since the dawn of the first colonies. As I serve with this, my final account.

And so I shall offer you a beginning. Let it be the grey-green murk that is the perennial stuff of Fi'draah, my new world. As I stepped from my shuttle the planet seized me in a stinking, sweltering embrace and wouldn't let go. Blinking and choking in the smog, I heard harsh voices and harsher laughter; then someone thrust a filtrator mask over my face and I could breathe again.

'The first time is like drowning,' my saviour said. 'It gets better.'

I don't recall who the speaker was, but he lied: breathing this world never got any better.

'You have evidently made powerful enemies for one so young, Asharil,' the ambassador said without preamble, peering down from the cushioned pulpit of his hovering throne drone. His voice was soft, yet vibrant. It filled the spacious audience chamber like liquid silk, the weapon of a master orator. His summons had followed directly upon my arrival and I was mortified by my dishevelled state.

'I do not understand, honoured one,' I blustered, stumbling between respect and revulsion for the ancient who presided over our forces on this remote planet. O'Seishin's authority was a testament to the excellence of our caste, but he reeked of years beyond the natural span of the tau race. His flesh had aged to deep cobalt leather, barely concealing the harsh planes of his skull, but his eyes were bright.

'This is a terminal world,' he continued, 'a graveyard for broken warriors and forgotten relics like myself, not a proving ground for the hot blood of youth. Who did you offend to get yourself posted here, Asharil?' He smiled, but his eyes belied it.

'I walk the water path,' I answered, seeking the natural poise of our caste. 'My blood runs cool and silent, so that my voice may weave–' O'Seishin's snort cut me short like a physical blow.

'I am too old for wordplay, girl!' He leaned forwards and a strand of spittle escaped his lips. 'Why have you come to Fi'draah? Who sent you?'

'Honoured one...' I stammered, struggling to avert my gaze from the lethargic descent of his drool. 'Your pardon, but I requested this posting. I have made a study of the language and customs of the *humans*' – I deliberately used the gue'la word for themselves – 'and Fi'draah offers most excellent opportunities to deepen my insight.'

He appraised me with a distrust so candid it was almost conspiratorial, as if we were both willing players in a game of lies. A game that he was used to winning...

'So you wish to test yourself in the field, Asharil?' He smiled again and this time I saw humour there, though no humour I cared to share. 'Then I shall not deny you. Indeed, I believe I have a most suitable commission for you.'

I will never know why O'Seishin became my enemy in that one brief meeting, but he proved to be the least of the blights awaiting me on this world.

Of the long conflict between the Tau Empire and the gue'la Imperium for mastery of Fi'draah I shall not speak. Mysteries shroud the war like whispering smoke, but I learned little of them before O'Seishin dispatched me to oblivion. Of the planet itself I could say much, for I travelled its wilderness for almost five months, but I will content myself with a single truth: whatever you are told in your orientation, it will not prepare you for the reality of this place. To classify Fi'draah as a 'jungle world' or a 'water world' is to garb a corpse in finery and call it beautiful. Eighty per cent of its surface is drowned in viscid, lethargic oceans that blend into the sky in a perpetual cycle of evaporation and drizzle, wreathing everything in a grey-green miasma that seeps into the flesh and spirit. The continents are ragged tangles of mega-coral choked with vegetation that looks – and smells – like it has been dredged up from the depths. Stunted trees with fleshy trunks and bladder-like fronds vie with drooping tenements of fungi and titanic anemone clusters, everything strangling or straddling or simply growing upon everything else – fecundity racing decay so fast you can almost see it.

Whether Sector O-31 is the worst of Fi'draah's territories I cannot say, but it must surely rank amongst them. The gue'la call it *'the Coil'*, a name infinitely more fitting than our own sober designation, for there is nothing remotely sober about that malign wilderness. A serpentine spiral of waterlogged jungles, it is the dark heartland of Fi'draah's largest, most untamed continent. The war has left it almost untouched, but rumours haunt it like bad memories: of regiments swallowed whole before they could clash...

Of lost patrols still fighting older wars than ours... And of ancient things sleeping beneath the waters...

Naturally, I dismissed such nonsense. My task was to cast the light of reason across this enigma and 'unravel the Coil' (as O'Seishin so artfully sold it). I was to accompany Fio'vre Mutekh, a distinguished cartographer of the earth caste on his quest to map the region. Fool that I was, I believed myself honoured! It was only later, when I saw how the Coil twisted in upon itself, that I realised the absurdity of our endeavour. I have often wondered whether O'Seishin is still laughing at me.

It says much about the nature of the earth caste that Mutekh approached his impossible assignment without rancour. A robust tau in his autumn cycle, he had a pompous manner that exasperated me, but he was utterly rigorous in his work. His assistant, Xanti, was a placid *autaku* (or data tech) who spoke rarely and never met my gaze. I believe he preferred the company of his neo-sentient data drone to his fellow tau.

The fourth and final person of note was our protector and guide, Shas'ui Jhi'kaara. A fire warrior and veteran of Fi'draah, she regarded the jungle with the tender distrust of a predator who knows it is also prey, and like many alpha predators she commanded her own pack: a dozen gue'la janissaries equipped with flak-plate and pulse carbines. They were all Imperial deserters, lured from the enemy by the promise of better rations rather than ideology, and despite the trappings of our civilisation they remained barbarians. Every night they gambled, quarrelled and brawled amongst themselves, but never in Jhi'kaara's presence. Had they known I spoke their native tongue they would have guarded their words more closely. Listening in on their crude passions and superstitions, I marvelled that their stunted species had ever reached the stars.

Together we entered the Coil: earth, water, fire... and mud, travelling its strange waterways in a pair of aging Devilfish hover transports. Every few days Mutekh would spot a 'notable feature' and call a halt. Then we would spend an eternity recording some obscure geological phenomenon or ancient indigene ruin. As the cartographer updated his maps and the janissaries patrolled, the jungle would press in, watching us with a thousand hungry eyes that belonged to a single beast.

'It hates us,' Jhi'kaara said once, surprising me as I stared back at the beast. 'But it welcomes us in the expectation that we will grow careless.'

'It is just a jungle, Shas'ui,' I said, squaring up to the warrior. 'It has no thoughts.'

'You are lying, waterkin,' Jhi'kaara said. 'You see the truth, but like all your kind, you fear it.'

'My kind?' I was shocked. 'We are the *same* kind. We are both tau.'

Her face was hidden behind the impassive, lens-studded mask of her combat helmet, but I sensed her sneer.

As our expedition stretched from weeks into months I came to detest every one of my companions, but Jhi'kaara most of all. While I recognised the place of the fire caste in the Tau'va, there was a coiled violence about her that disturbed me. Perhaps it was her hideous facial scarring or her playful contempt... But no... I believe it was something deeper. Like O'Seishin, she had become tainted by this world.

Taint. Such an irrational term for a tau to use; surely one better suited to the Imperial fanatics who condemn otherness for otherness's sake? Perhaps, but lately I have come to wonder whether the fanatics may have it right.

It is time I told you of the Sanctuary of Wyrms.

'What is it?' I asked, trying to decipher the dark shape through its veil of vegetation. Squat yet vast, it rose from the centre of the island ahead, evidently a structure of some kind, but unlike any other we had encountered in the Coil. Despite the obscuring vegetation, its harsh, angular lineaments were unmistakable, suggesting an architectural brutality at odds with the flowing contours of our own aesthetics. Even at a distance it filled me with foreboding.

'The Nirrhoda did not lie,' Mutekh said, lowering his scope.

The Nirrhoda? I recalled the feral, mud-caked indigenes we had encountered some weeks back. Technically 'indigene' was a misnomer since the native Phaedrans were descended from gue'la colonists who had conquered this world millennia ago and then, in turn, been conquered by it. Squat and bowlegged, with huge glassy eyes and yawning mouths, they were primitive degenerates who wandered the wilderness in loose tribes. All were unpredictable, but the Nirrhoda clan, who followed the chaotic arrhythmia of the Coil, were notoriously belligerent. Yet Jhi'kaara had known their ways and won a parley for Mutekh, who had traded trinkets for shreds of truth about their deceitful land. One such shred had led us here.

'They certainly did not lie about the wyrmtrees,' the fire warrior observed sourly. 'That island is infested with them.'

I had taken the gentle undulation of the towering anemone-like growths encrusting the island to be a product of the wind... *Yet there was no wind...* Now I watched their swaying tendrils with fresh eyes: at the base, each was thicker than my waist, tapering to a sinuous violet tip that tilted towards us, as if tasting us on the air.

'Are they dangerous?' I asked.

'Their sting is lethal,' Jhi'kaara said fondly, 'but they grow slowly. These must be over a century old. That structure–'

'Evidently predates the war,' Mutekh interrupted with relish. 'We must evaluate this discovery thoroughly.' Something like avarice swept across his broad face, revealing another shade of taint: the hunger to *know*. 'You will clear a path please, fire warrior.'

Jhi'kaara turned the rotary cannons of our Devilfish upon the forest, shredding the rubbery growths into steaming slabs that seemed more meat than vegetable. The trees shrieked as they died, their warble sounding insidiously sentient.

'It proved a poor sanctuary,' Xanti said with peculiar sadness. I glanced at Mutekh's assistant in surprise. He shrugged, embarrassed by my attention. 'That is what the savages called this place: the Sanctuary of Wyrms.'

Then the janissaries went amongst the detritus with flame-throwers, laughing as they incinerated the flailing, orphan tendrils. One brute grew careless and a whip-like frond lashed his face as it flipped about in its death spasms. Moments later the man joined it in his own dance of death. It was the first time I saw violent death, but I was unmoved. Fi'draah had already changed me.

Unveiled, the building was almost profound in its ugliness. It was a squat, octagonal block assembled from prefabricated grey slabs that were as hard as rock. The walls tilted inwards to a flat roof that looked strong enough to withstand an aerial bombardment, suggesting the place might be a bunker of some kind. Circling it, we found no apertures or ornamentation save for a deeply recessed entrance wide enough to accommodate a tank. A metal bulkhead blocked the path, its corroded surface embossed with a stark 'I' symbol. Despite its simplicity, the sigil had an austere authority that deepened my unease.

'I am unfamiliar with this emblem,' Mutekh mused, running a hand over the raised metal. 'Your thoughts, Por'ui?'

'It looks like a gue'la rune,' I answered. 'Linguistically it translates as *'the self'*, but in this context it probably has a factional connotation.'

'So the gue'la built this place?' Xanti asked.

'Oh, I would most definitely postulate an Imperial provenance,' Mutekh said, clearly enjoying himself. 'Though it lacks the vainglorious ornamentation typical of their architecture, the configuration and construction materials are manifestly Imperial.'

'Why would there be Imperials on Fi'draah before the war?' Xanti seemed confused by the notion.

'Why *wouldn't* there be?' Mutekh proclaimed. 'Throughout the ages there have been Imperials almost *everywhere*. They are an ancient power that coveted the stars millennia before the Tau'va was revealed to us. There is no telling when they first came to this world. Or why.'

'This place has the strength of a fortress, but not the logic,' Jhi'kaara offered, speaking for the first time. 'The walls are solid, but there are no emplacements or watchtowers.'

'Perhaps they are hidden,' I suggested.

'No, remember this is a *pre-war* relic,' Mutekh chided. 'It was not constructed to keep an enemy out, but to keep a secret within.'

'What kind of secret?' Xanti asked loyally.

'The kind that was worth hiding well!' There was a glint in the cartographer's eyes at the prospect. 'The kind that is worth learning for the Greater Good.' He slapped the bulkhead. 'Open it!'

There was no obvious access mechanism, but Xanti's data drone detected a biometric scanner embedded in the bulkhead.

'For the gue'la it is a sophisticated system,' the *autaku* murmured, his face lost in the dancing holograms projected by his drone. The small saucer-like machine hovered by the hatch, interfacing the mechanism with its data-laser and mapping it into territory its master could negotiate.

'I doubt I could deceive this,' Xanti said, 'but it appears the seal has *already* been broken... and crudely reset.' He looked up with a frown. 'Someone has trespassed here before us.'

Despite the damaged seal night had fallen by the time Xanti synthesised the correct trigger. Dead cogs ground into life and the bulkhead rose, groaning at this second desecration. A sour fungal fetor seeped from the dark maw, so dense it was almost visible. Some of the janissaries chuckled as I retched and fumbled for my filtrator mask, but their faces were pale. Jhi'kaara silenced them with a sharp gesture, but I felt no gratitude. Her sealed helmet spared her the stench we suffered. Where was the equity in that?

We entered the cavernous chamber beyond in a practised formation, with Jhi'kaara's hovering gun drone taking point and the janissaries fanning out to either side. Our torch beams thrust back the darkness, but it clung to every corner and crevice like black cobwebs. The burned-out hulks of amphibious transports and machinery loomed on all sides, casting shadows across a graveyard of barrels and crates.

'The invaders closed off the escape route,' Jhi'kaara said, gauging the devastation. 'They destroyed the vehicles and sealed the exit in case anyone slipped past them.'

'Why did no one fight back?' I wondered. 'There are no bodies here.'

'A good question, waterkin.'

Across the chamber the inner hatch lay amongst the detritus, shredded and torn from its recess. Jhi'kaara knelt and ran her fingers over the wreckage. The edges were curled into serrated whorls of tortured metal.

'Chainswords,' she said.

'How can you be sure?' I asked.

'The teeth leave a pattern.' She paused and looked over her shoulder, staring right at me. 'Their mark is... unique.' It was almost a challenge.

'Unique?' As if by their own volition my eyes were drawn to the ghost of a scar running down the faceplate of her helmet, a wound that echoed the rift in her own face. And suddenly I understood why she knew these weapons so intimately.

The destruction petered out in the corridor beyond, but the sense of oppression did not. It shadowed us as we passed through one deserted chamber after another, closing in as we moved deeper into the outpost.

'Smaller teams would cover more ground,' Mutekh protested. 'Your caution is illogical, Shas'ui. This place is long dead.'

But the fire warrior would not split our force, and I was struck anew by the differences between the castes. We worked together for the Greater Good, yet our natures were discordant. Mutekh and Xanti were creatures of reason, while Jhi'kaara was pure instinct. What did that make me?

I brooded over the question as we pressed on, passing through guardrooms and storerooms, the hollow tomb of a dormitory and a mess hall where food still waited on the table, fossilised and forgotten.

'It took them unawares,' Jhi'kaara murmured, 'and it took them swiftly.'

'It?' I asked. 'You mean the invaders?'

'No...' For the first time she sounded troubled. 'No, I think this was something else.'

We found the first corpse in the communications room, propped up against the vox-console. Shrouded in heavy crimson robes, the mummified cadaver looked more machine than man. Its face was an angular bronze mask studded with sensors, seemingly riveted to the skull. A pistol was clutched in a bionic claw, the barrel shoved through the broken grille of its mouth. Its cranium had ruptured into a crown of splintered bones and circuitry.

'He shot himself before the intruders reached him,' Jhi'kaara judged.

'Or because they reached him too late,' I offered uncertainly. She glanced at me, waiting as I tested the intuition. 'He's the only one we've found. Perhaps that makes him different.'

'He was certainly different,' Xanti said eagerly. 'Judging by his extensive bionics he was a Mechanicus priest, probably an important one. Unlike ourselves, the data techs of the Imperium aspire to become one with their machines.'

The *autaku's* passion surprised me. Abruptly, I realised how little I knew about my companions. We had travelled so far together yet we were still strangers. Was it our castes that divided us, or merely our personal flaws? Uneasily, I put the question aside and concentrated on the facts.

'Perhaps he summoned the invaders,' I suggested.

Jhi'kaara considered it. 'Perhaps he did, waterkin.'

And perhaps I am not the fool you took me for, I thought.

The elevator to the lower levels had been demolished and the hatch to the stairwell was welded shut from within, but that was no obstacle to our plasma cutters. Beyond, a metal staircase wound down into darkness.

Jhi'kaara's gun drone led the way, levitating down the stairwell as we followed on the spiralling steps, its searchlight diving ahead into the abyss below. As we descended, the walls became brittle and powdery, sucked dry by silvery seams of fungus. In places the filth had erupted into cancerous fruiting bodies, but they were all desiccated husks, seemingly petrified in the moment of blossoming. The stench was dreadful and I kept my filtrator firmly in place. Mutekh and Xanti soon followed suit, but the janissaries suffered stoically, unwilling to show weakness before Jhi'kaara.

They are like dogs trying to impress their master, I thought.

At regular intervals we passed access hatches to other levels, and I realised the bulk of the outpost lay beneath the ground, like a buried mountain riddled with tunnels and caves. Some hatches were sealed, other gaped open, but we ignored them all. Exploring the entire complex would take days and none of us cared to linger here. Instead we pressed on, drawn by a collective sense that the answers we sought lay below. But when the drone's light finally found the bottom of the stairwell we froze.

'Emperor protect us!' one of the janissaries gasped, but nobody reprimanded him for his atavism.

Our path terminated in a charnel pit. Dozens of cadavers were piled up below, mangled and contorted by violent death. The walls around them were pitted with deep craters, suggesting heavy gunfire, but it was impossible tell whether it was bullets or chainswords that had cleansed these dead.

Cleansed. It is another term that sits uneasily with the Tau'va, yet it is the right term, for these creatures were *unclean.* Despite their wounds and decades of decay, it was obvious they were only superficially gue'la. Their withered flesh was stretched taut across misshapen bones, thickening to gnarled plates at the ribs and shoulder blades. Many had double-jointed legs and scythe-like appendages jutting from their wrists. Their faces were atrophied relics in elongated, almost bestial skulls, the jaws distended by hardened, stinger-tipped tongues. Some still wore shreds of clothing, but most were naked.

They shed their clothes like redundant skins when the change came over them...

'We should go back,' I said with utter conviction. For once I suspected the janissaries were with me, but to my surprise they weren't the only ones.

'Asharil is right,' Jhi'kaara said. 'This tomb is best left buried.'

Mutekh hesitated. He was as repulsed as the rest of us, but leaving a mystery unsolved was anathema to him.

'Unacceptable,' the cartographer declared. 'It is our duty to assess, quantify and record this anomaly. The Greater Good demands courage. Has yours failed you, fire warrior?'

Jhi'kaara stiffened. The tension passed through the janissaries in a sympathetic wave and I saw their weapons twitch reflexively towards the cartographer. Even Xanti noticed it, looking back and forth between the opponents with a confused expression that was almost comical. Only Mutekh seemed oblivious to his own peril.

'I will continue alone,' he pushed, 'if you are afraid...'

I thought she would kill him then. I tried to intervene, to rise to my calling and smooth over the discord, but the words slipped away before I could marshal them. Instead, Jhi'kaara found a reserve of discipline I had not credited her with.

'Fire always walks at the fore,' she said. Without another word she stepped down amongst the corpses. And sealed our fate.

We followed the intruders' trail of devastation through a maze of laboratories and workshops that soon became unrecognisable. The fungal veins riddling the walls had grown ripe here, erupting into groping, ropey strands like calcified viscera. Before it froze, the stuff had entwined itself about everything, melting the rigid Imperial architecture into soft organic shapes.

We are crawling through a diseased corpse, I thought, *but what if it's not dead, just forever dying?* I fought to suppress the absurd notion, grasping for the clarity of the Tau'va, but in this cesspit it seemed a flickering, false hope.

The blighted dead were everywhere, snarled up in the weave where they had fallen. Shredded, pulverised or charred, they had died in droves as they swarmed against the incursion, and I found myself wondering at the lethality of their slayers. What kind of creature could carve a swath through such horrors?

We found the answer in a ravaged infirmary where the invaders had suffered their first casualty. The fallen warrior was almost buried beneath a mound of mutants, but there was no mistaking his stature. Alive, he would have been almost twice my height and countless times my weight. *Could it really be?*

'Space Marines,' Jhi'kaara said with something like reverence. 'And where there is one, there will be others.'

My breath caught as she confirmed my suspicion. I had studied accounts and pictures of the Imperium's elite warriors, but they had seemed a distant, almost mythical peril. They were the stuff of nightmares, bio-engineered giants bred to be utterly merciless in the service of their dead Emperor. It was rumoured that a hundred of these monsters could conquer a world.

'What were they doing here?' I wondered, staring at the dead Space Marine in fascination. A helmet with a sharp, almost avian snout hid his features, but I could imagine the face beneath: it would be pugnacious and broad, with skin like toughened leather and a fretwork of scars and tattoos – a face not merely honed by war, but *rebuilt* for it.

Jhi'kaara gestured to the janissaries and they heaved the mutants aside, exhuming the warrior's void-black power armour. Peculiarly, his left arm looked as if it were cast in silver, its shoulder pad carved into a stylised 'I' sigil inset with a skull. More incongruous still was the bright yellow of the opposite pauldron. For all his ferocity, this warrior's grasp of aesthetics had been woeful.

'I recognise this heraldry.' Jhi'kaara tapped the angular fist inscribed on the yellow pad. 'The Imperial Fists are old foes of the Tau Empire, but this...' She indicated the silver pad. 'This I have not seen before. And the Imperial Fists wear *yellow* armour, not black.'

'Wait,' I said, 'this second symbol... Isn't it like the one we found at the entrance?'

'It *is* similar,' Mutekh said, peering at the device, 'but the inset skull is a significant deviation. There may be a connection, but careless assumptions are dangerous...'

'Does it matter?' Xanti asked. 'The gue'la fanatics are all insane. Nothing they do makes sense.'

'Know your enemy as you would know yourself,' Jhi'kaara said, doubtless quoting some fire caste credo. 'There is a mystery here.'

There was certainly no mystery about the Space Marine's death: his breastplate had been cracked open like a shell and one of the mutants had virtually crawled inside his chest as it disembowelled him.

'The Imperium sent its finest warriors to purge this crisis,' Jhi'kaara murmured thoughtfully.

'All the more reason for us to leave,' I insisted.

'No, we cannot.' She stepped away from the dead giant. 'Space Marines do not leave their fallen behind.'

'I don't see the relevance...'

'Do you not? *Think*, waterkin.'

'I...' The realisation struck me like ice water. 'You believe they failed.'

'Whatever happened here...' she said, sweeping a hand over the mutated horde, 'we must be certain it is over.'

The trail ended at the uppermost tier of a subterranean amphitheatre. Our torches struggled to make sense of the vast space, picking out details but unable to capture the whole, leaving me with the impression of a gargantuan hive woven from grey strands. Hunched in a depression at the centre of the chamber was a pale mound. Thick cords of fungus sprouted from its base, multiplying and tapering as they spread out to insinuate themselves into every surface.

As we descended, it became apparent the mutants had made their last stand here, throwing themselves between the invaders and the heart of their hive, but one-by-one the Space Marines had also fallen. The first lay two tiers down, still gripping his chain-sword though his head was missing. Like his comrade he wore black and silver power armour, but his right pauldron was completely different.

'A White Scar,' said Jhi'kaara, pointing out the crimson flash on the white pad. 'They fought honourably on Dal'yth.'

'There were Space Marines on Dal'yth?' I was appalled by the idea of the Imperium penetrating so deep into tau space.

'They almost *took* Dal'yth, waterkin.' She chuckled dryly. 'Among your caste some truths are left unspoken lest they wither your faint hearts.' Despite her words there was no malice in her voice. We had achieved an understanding of sorts, she and I. Of more concern was the possibility that my own caste had lied to me. Was that really possible? Remembering the ancient manipulator O'Seishin, I found little comfort.

As we continued our descent Jhi'kaara paused beside each of the fallen Space Marines and examined his insignia solemnly: a blue raptor against white... A white buzzsaw against black... She recognised neither of them, but she paid her respects regardless, for each had died hideously and heroically, surrounded by sundered enemies.

'Why would they bear different cadre badges?' I said, seeing how the riddle of their mismatched fraternity troubled her.

'*Cha'ptah* badges,' she corrected. 'Space Marines call their factions *Cha'ptahs*.' I frowned at her awkward pronunciation of the gue'la word *'Chapter'*. 'And to answer your question, waterkin: I do not know. This co-fraternity contradicts everything I was taught about their kind. Space Marines adhere rigidly to their own clans.'

'Perhaps they were forced to fight together,' I suggested. 'Maybe it was a penitence for some transgression. Or an honour.'

Neither theory was reassuring, especially since the dead mutants were growing more fearsome. Some bore no resemblance to the gue'la at all, looking more like the spawn of an entirely different, utterly aberrant race. A few actually dwarfed the Space Marines, their bulk covered in spiny exoskeletal plates that looked strong enough to withstand a pulse-round. All were mottled with a fur of silver-grey mould, but it was impossible to tell whether the fungus had grown upon them or from *within* them.

Abruptly Jhi'kaara stopped, gazing at one of the larger beasts. 'I know what they are,' she said quietly.

'They are mutants,' Mutekh declared, 'evidently the product of some ill-conceived Imperial dabbling...'

'They are Yhe'mokushi, beasts of the Silent Hunger,' Jhi'kaara said. The reference meant nothing to me and the others looked equally mystified. She nodded, unsurprised. 'A predatory species the Tau Empire has only recently encountered. These differ from the bioforms depicted in our orientation sessions, but diversity is in their nature. They are living weapons that can steal form as well as substance, becoming whatever suits their purpose.'

'And they are hostile to the Tau Empire?' Xanti asked uneasily.

'They are hostile to *all* life save their own. Like locusts they exist only to consume and multiply, leaving nothing but dust and shadows in their wake. It is said the Imperium has suffered greatly from their depredations.'

We were silent. Here was another ugly truth hidden in the name of the Greater Good. Over the last few months my certainties had eroded away, revealing deception, obsession and horror. *What else had been kept from me?*

Down... further down... More dead Space Marines... First a golden beast's head set against midnight-blue, then another raptor, this one red against white.

'You respect these warriors,' I said, watching Jhi'kaara carefully.

'I respect their strength, Asharil.'

But I sensed her admiration ran deeper. Jhi'kaara was an outsider amongst her own kind, closer to Fi'draah's wilderness than the wisdom of the Tau'va. She was drawn to these warriors for their brotherhood as much as their strength.

By the time we reached the lowest tier we had found eight Space Marines. The last had succumbed at the periphery of his objective, his armour pierced in a dozen places by scything claws. Bizarrely he was still standing, his body wedged on its feet by the mass of corpses pressed against it. Even amongst his brothers he was a giant, but there were other differences. While the rest had painted their left arms silver, both his arms *were* silver – or more likely some stronger metal. Each was an angular augmetic, one terminating in a slab-like fist, the other in an intricate claw whose purpose was probably manipulation rather than combat. His personal heraldry was black, its symbol a stylised white gauntlet.

'Iron Hand,' Jhi'kaara declared. 'Another old enemy.'

'These would appear to be specimen containment units,' Mutekh said, pointing out a pair of toppled glass cylinders that looked big enough to hold the largest abominations. Ropes of fungus were wrapped around them, squeezed so tight the reinforced glass had fractured.

'The fools brought the Silent Hunger to Fi'draah,' Jhi'kaara hissed. I was surprised by the fury in her voice. She sounded like her *own* world had been threatened.

'So this place was some kind of prison?' Xanti asked.

'Not a prison,' Mutekh said as he followed the web of pipes running from the cylinders to a corroded bank of consoles. 'Remember the laboratories we passed through? No, this is a research facility. The Imperials were experimenting on these creatures. Perhaps they were seeking a means of communication...'

'The Imperium does not seek communion with its enemies,' Jhi'kaara said. 'They were looking for a weapon.'

'But why here?' Xanti wondered. 'Is it just a coincidence they came to Fi'draah?'

'Many of the indigenous fungi are lethal,' Mutekh speculated. 'Perhaps they were attempting to synthesise a pathogen.'

'Then they failed,' Jhi'kaara said flatly.

'We do not know that,' Mutekh protested. 'The techniques of the gue'la are riddled with superstition, but...'

'The Yhe'mokushi strain was too strong,' I said, surprised by my own conviction. 'When the Imperials infected it... it devoured the fungus...'

Intuition, I realised. *I am neither entirely a creature of reason nor instinct, but something subtler than either.*

'It *became* the fungus,' I finished. 'And then the fungus devoured them.'

My comrades stared at me, then their eyes wandered to the infested expanse around us. Jhi'kaara broke the silence: 'Search the Space Marines,' she ordered the janissaries. 'Gather their grenades.'

'What is your intent, fire warrior?' Mutekh demanded.

'We will complete our enemy's mission.' She indicated the monolithic puffball. 'Sometimes the enemy of your enemy is the greater enemy.'

'You will do no such thing!' Mutekh was appalled. 'We must ascertain what the Imperials discovered here.' He looked to Xanti for support, but the young data tech avoided his gaze. *'Autaku!'*

'I am sorry, Fio'vre,' his assistant muttered unhappily, 'but whatever the Imperials found here... it did them no good.'

'I will search this one,' I said, heading for the nearest Space Marine.

'I trust you know what a grenade looks like, waterkin?' Jhi'kaara mocked gently. Then she was gone, heading for the upper tiers.

'Cowards,' Mutekh called after us. 'You are all betraying the Greater Good.'

No, we are serving the Greater Good, I thought fiercely. *Even if some of us have come to doubt it.*

Biting down my disgust I dragged a corpse away from my chosen warrior, intent on reaching his utility belt. That was when I noticed the hum. It was faint, but its source was unmistakable: *this Space Marine's armour was still powered.* Unsettled, I peered up at his archaic helmet. A flat visor covered the right side of his face, but the left was a tangle of bionics clustered around a jutting optical sensor. Up close he seemed more machine than man.

Iron Hand, Jhi'kaara had called this one...

'Fio'vre, wait!' The voice was Xanti's, its urgency irresistible. I glanced round and saw Mutekh standing beside the puffball, a laser scalpel in one hand and a sample container in the other.

'Wait!' I echoed, but the scalpel was already descending towards the mottled surface. 'Don't–'

The puffball exploded like a bomb.

And that's precisely what it is, I realised, *a spore bomb, dormant but not dead.*

There was no fire or fragmentation in the blast, but the concussion threw Mutekh across the tier, slamming him against the consoles with bone-breaking force. I saw his body rebound a heartbeat before everything was smothered in swirling grey smog. Clutching my mask tightly, I screwed my eyes shut and crouched, sheltering beneath the Iron Hand. The scattered janissaries cursed as the spore cloud rolled over them, then the curses turned to choked screams as their lungs drowned in filth. I heard them stumbling about as they fought to escape their torment. Someone opened fire blindly, his pulse-rounds sizzling as they ripped through the congealed air. Someone else screamed his last as a wild round struck him.

That was a mercy. The only kind remaining to these men...

I risked a glance as one of them fell to his knees alongside me. The toxic whiteout reduced him to a vague, flailing silhouette, but I could see his entire body heaving violently, as if in the grip of some bone-deep tremor.

Not bone-deep. This quake ran much deeper than that.

I heard his flesh seething as its muscles contorted into new shapes, stretching his skin taut in the struggle to contain the chaos beneath. Suddenly he screamed, spewing blood and spores as his back arched inwards at an impossible angle. The spine broke – then snapped back into a sleek, predatory curve. Vicious spikes erupted along its length, racing to catch up with his rapidly elongating cranium. His arms shot out in a welter of shredded fingers, propelled by the bone scythes surging from his wrists. He tried to scream again and his tongue burst free, thickened and barbed, like a stinger-tipped snake.

It looks like there is a wyrmtree growing inside him, I thought wildly. Any moment now, the newborn hybrid would turn and see me...

'Fio'vre! Where are you?' Xanti called as he came stumbling through the mist, his faithful drone hovering beside him. He saw me and raised a hand in relief. 'Asharil! Did you see–'

The hybrid leapt. Propelled by powerful, double-jointed legs it streaked through the air and was upon the *autaku* before he saw it coming. The bone scythes slashed down, impaling him through the shoulder blades and pinning him to the ground. His shriek was cut off as the beast's tongue shot out like a spring-loaded blade and punched through his filtrator mask. His legs kicked about spastically as it wormed its way down his throat, stinging and seeding him with spores. The abandoned data drone twittered in confusion and a scythe flailed out and sent it spinning my way. I covered my head as the saucer smashed into the Iron Hand and toppled beside me with a forlorn squawk.

The smog had thinned out, the spores settling over the chamber like softly luminescent dust. By their pallid light I saw that none of the janissaries had escaped the change. Some were still going through the final trauma, but five were racing towards a solitary figure on the topmost tier. Jhi'kaara was kneeling, tracking the approaching hybrids with her pulse rifle. She fired, but her chosen mark darted aside with shocking speed. I imagined her cursing then, angry but not afraid. *Never afraid...* She fired again, then once more in quick succession, the first shot tricking her target into the path of the second. The round struck the hybrid mid-leap, throwing it to the ground in a writhing heap. Before it could right itself a third shot sheared through its skull. A kill, but it had cost her precious time.

With a chittering yowl one of the creatures leapt onto Jhi'kaara's tier, but she ignored it, intent upon a more distant mark. Before I could shout a warning, her gun drone swooped from the shadows and lanced her aggressor with its twin-linked guns, almost tearing it in two. Whirling round, the saucer sped towards another hybrid, spitting fire, but the beast danced about in ragged avian bursts, bounding between the floor and the walls as it charged. At the last moment it rolled low and sprung up beneath the saucer, latching on to its rim. The drone spun about, firing furiously as it tried to dislodge its attacker, but the beast was too strong. I imagined the machine's primitive logic core assessing probabilities and weighing up options. It found its answer within seconds and self-destructed, incinerating the hybrid from the waist up.

I had no more time to spare for Jhi'kaara's battle. Done with its prey, Xanti's attacker sat up on its haunches, sniffing the air while its victim writhed beneath it in the throes of change. I looked around, hoping for a fallen firearm... cursing myself for refusing to carry one... desperate for a clean death...

'Power...' The voice sounded like the wheeze of a dying machine. *A machine that spoke Imperial Gothic...* I looked up and saw the impossible: the Iron Hand had inclined its head towards me, its optic glowing a dull red, like a doomed sun. Beneath that merciless blaze water turned to fire and I became a creature of instinct. Grabbing Xanti's battered drone I hauled, staggering under the weight as I raised it to the giant like an offering to some primal god. The burden was as much philosophical as physical, yet my path seemed clear.

The galaxy was tainted and taint had to be cleansed...

A metal tendril uncoiled from the warrior's helmet, swaying about like a blind snake. Then it struck, its sharpened tip drilling through the drone's casing with a whine of ruptured metal. A moment later the snake became a leech, burying itself inside the broken machine's innards and sucking it dry of power. Power to reignite its master's hatred.

Honest hatred!

I heard Xanti's assailant rise behind me, but my world had narrowed to the awakening Iron Hand. I knew my sanity had gone, unravelled by O'Seishin's lies and Fi'draah's truths. All that remained was horror and the will to face it.

For the Greater Good...

The rest was a blur. The hybrid howled behind me and its kin answered from all sides. I spun round as it leapt, its virulent tongue extended towards me. The Space Marine's fist met the beast in midair like a turbotram, punching clean through its ribcage. He cast the corpse aside as the others fell upon him in a chittering, screeching mob. There were four in all, fully transformed and almost mindless in their need to rend and tear and infect.

The first came head-on and died in a heartbeat, its skull pulverised by a pneumatic punch to the face. His armour grinding like rusted cogs, the warrior swung at the waist and grabbed another by the throat, squeezing until bone and cartilage collapsed into paste. In the same instant he rammed his manipulator claw between the jaws of a third. Its head convulsed violently as the claw became a whirling rotary blade inside its mouth. He yanked the tool free in a storm of shattered bones as the final hybrid vaulted onto his back, scythes poised to hack down. Before it could strike, a bolt of energy punched through its skull, throwing it from its perch. I glanced up and saw Jhi'kaara kneeling a few tiers above us, her rifle levelled.

Cleansed, I thought, *every one of them.*

'Asaaar...haaal...' The voice made my name sound like something dredged up from a polluted ocean. I turned as Xanti hauled himself up, using his malformed scythes like crutches. His movements were clumsy, crippled by the capricious mutation of his muscles, as if the fungus was baffled by tau physiology. His face had stretched into a death mask, the lower jaw almost touching his belly, but his eyes were unchanged, staring at me with ago-nised recognition. *Pleading...*

'Asaaar...' Xanti's barbed tongue surged towards me. The Space Marine shoved me aside, but the stinger lashed my shoulder as I fell. A terrible numbness seized my arm before I even hit the ground. Dimly I saw Jhi'kaara vault from the tier above. She raised her rifle to her shoulder and advanced on the abomination, firing as she came. She didn't stop until it was a charred ruin. Then she turned her wrath on Mutekh's broken, spore-saturated body. The cartographer never stirred beneath the barrage. Perhaps he was already dead, but I doubt Jhi'kaara cared. The last thing I saw before consciousness slipped away was the dimming red light in the Iron Hand's optic.

'Power...' he whispered. And then we both faded to black.

'You were fortunate,' Jhi'kaara said when I awoke. The numbness in my arm had faded, leaving behind a dull ache. 'Its sting did not carry the infection.'

Then by unspoken consent we fed the Iron Hand, gathering the janis-saries' weapons and power packs and offering them up to his ravenous mechadendrite. Our ritual was without sense for the enemy of our enemy was destroyed, leaving only the enemy, yet we never hesitated. We were both creatures of instinct now, bound by an imperative stronger than the Tau'va.

'How long have you waited?' I asked the giant when we were done. The Imperial Gothic came easily to my tongue. It always had.

'How...? Long...?' His voice was slurred and electronic, the syntax broken. 'Very – long...'

'How did you survive?'

He turned his optic on me, weighing me up like an iron god. Abruptly the visor covering the right side of his face slid aside. In place of flesh and bone I saw a formless grey tangle riddled with electronics and corroded rivets.

'The Flesh – betrays,' he said, though he had no lips, 'but the Machine – is faithful.'

I saw his doom then. His body had succumbed to its wounds, but his depleted augmetics had endured, cradling his consciousness as life slipped away. Half-corpse, half-machine he had stood frozen in this chamber for untold decades, burning with impotent rage as his dead flesh was consumed. Denied sleep or the deeper oblivion of death, he had watched as corruption blossomed within and without. I saw him descending into madness, then clawing his way back in the hope of redemption... then falling again. How often had that cycle repeated? And where did it stand now?

'Your mission is complete,' I said carefully, indicating the tattered spore bomb. 'We destroyed the taint.'

'You did – Not. This was – Nothing – just another Tendril – of the Corruption. I watched it grow – then grow stale – over the long – Long – long...' He faltered as his splintered mind strove for coherence. 'The Root – survives...'

He stepped towards the centre of the chamber, moving with surprising grace. We followed and saw the pit for the first time: a dark slash in the ground where the mega-fungus had bloomed. On closer inspection I saw it wasn't a pit at all, but a steeply inclined tunnel, its walls resinous with fungus, like the aperture of a titanic blood vessel. Or a stalk...

The spore bomb grew from here, I realised, *and the corruption is still down there, rooted deep in the ground.*

'The mission is – Incomplete.'

Like the Iron Hand's mission my story is incomplete, but that is of no consequence. My purpose is not to entertain you, but to warn you. Jhi'kaara will carry this log out of the Coil and ensure that it is heard and heeded. This undying tomb must be quarantined lest we fail to destroy its voracious legacy. *We?* Yes, I have chosen to accompany the Iron Hand on his final duty. I am no warrior, but I can carry grenades and we will bear many into the unclean bowels of this place. Jhi'kaara argued against it, of course, telling me it was her duty to make the final descent.

'You should bear the word and I the fire,' she said, but it could not be.

You see, I cannot return. Jhi'kaara was wrong: Xanti's sting did carry the contagion. Though his touch was fleeting I can feel the taint stirring in my blood like the promise of lies. I don't know how long I have, but I will not hide in the darkness until the blight takes me. Besides, my corruption is more than blood-deep, for I have fallen from the Tau'va. I am no longer a creature of water or fire, nor indeed of sanity, but I can still serve. I shall descend into the pit alongside my enemy and purge the unclean... For the Greater Good.

- END RECORDING -

ALTAR OF MAWS

In ages past, the Saathlaa, who are descended from this ailing world's first human colonists, consorted with many abomin-ations, both primordial and preternatural. The facts of their corruption have degraded into fables alongside their once vibrant civilisation, but such tales always bear a kernel of truth. They are a warning to the wise and a lure to those who seek darker wisdom. Few are as obscure, yet disturbing, as the myth of Krol Szaajal, the Sunken Maw, a hidden lake that reputedly served as a crucible for unspeakable rites. I never found this malign place, but I suspect its hunger persists. Once awoken, such appetites are rarely sated.

– Crossing the Mire World
The Requiem Infernal

i. Advent

The Captain stood on the bridge of the *Polyphemus*, gripping the control wheel tightly, as if braced for a storm, though no storm had ever raged here. This was his rightful, required station and he hadn't moved in a long time. He couldn't have said *how* long exactly, any more than he could recall how long his vessel had been trapped, or how many of its crew had died since the lake claimed them. Time had become as slippery as his ship's slime-coated deck. Sometimes events tilted backwards so that dead men rose to go about their duties once more – then lurched suddenly forwards, spewing out one sickly dawn after the next without a night's respite. His memories of the war his regiment had been waging across this drowned world were hazy, along with much of his past. Nothing felt certain except his divine duty and the need to endure so he could see it through.

I'll fulfil the sacrament, the Captain promised the lake, as he had done so many times before... and after. *I'll make things right.*

His burden offered more purpose than most souls ever found, though few recognised their emptiness or yearned to fill it, especially if they glimpsed the price, but he was grateful. After all, he hadn't always been a master, of this gunboat or the sacrament. The ship's former captain, a devout but shallow tyrant, was still on the bridge, woven into the far wall by the web of fungi blooming from his corpse. The cancerous tangle pulsated, wheezed and occasionally oozed strange dreams, so perhaps its host wasn't entirely dead. The Captain liked to think he'd freed his predecessor by slitting him open to new possibilities. Light radiated from the cadaver, washing the bridge in lurid hues that made the spore-saturated air shimmer. It was beautiful – a sure sign of the God-Emperor's grace.

Our lord is generous, the Captain mused, savouring the sacred reek. It was the incense of his faith, just as the lake was its altar and the Sleeper Beneath its holy spirit.

'As above, so below,' the Captain rasped, spattering the window before him with blood-flecked mucus. He watched reverently as the filth formed a fresh pattern on the glass. It was a map of this world, charting the protean flow of its waterways and the possibilities they wove. Only he could read it, of course. That was why he'd been chosen. His vision had snared the ship's crew when their first captain denied the lake's sanctity, then bound them in shared betrayal. Every one of them had planted a blade in the old heretic's heart and pledged allegiance to the new order.

'I'll set things right,' the Captain vowed aloud. The words triggered a coughing fit, and he retched a fresh configuration onto the window. His eyes narrowed as he caught sight of something unexpected in the muck – a blue mote spiralling towards the chart's centre. Was this the sign he'd glimpsed in his visions? He watched with anxious rapture, wary of disturbing the augury, then shivered as the speck completed its passage.

Finally.

The Captain ripped his hands from the wheel. They'd been there since his vigil began and rot had welded them to the rubber grip, but he scarcely felt the pain of release. Trailing strips of torn skin, he reached for the ship's vox-caster.

'All mariners, man your stations,' he broadcast. 'Our sacrament begins.'

I shall die on this world, Shas'ui Tal'hanzo predicted, gazing into the undulating grey-green limbo ahead. *For the Greater Good,* he added loyally, but with less conviction. Every time he invoked that once inviolable credo its potency diminished. The loss was imperceptible if measured in days, but there had been a great many days since he'd come to Fi'draah and his creed had become a need. He'd grown old alongside that decline, slipping past his prime while the war slithered on, seemingly without end. Sometimes, in his darkest moments, he wondered whether either side truly wanted to win.

Murmuring a mantra of self-admonishment, Tal'hanzo focused on the present. The day had decayed into dusk, its gloom deepened by the jungle's canopy. That ever-present tangle had grown denser as the river widened, as though the fat, fleshy trees to either side were tightening their grip on the sky to deny the water its liberty. Tal'hanzo's hover barge raked ripples through the milky liquid, but nothing else disturbed it, above or below.

The emptiness endures, the fire warrior gauged. His helm's sensors illuminated a scum of floating flora, but still no fauna. That was unusual. Fi'draah's

rivers typically swarmed with vermin. Their absence could signify the territory of an apex predator, but it had been like this for hours and his wariness
had waned. Besides, the gun drone piloting his barge would alert him to
any threats. The small disc-like machine was perched atop the control panel
before him, chittering softly as it navigated. It was an older model, like most
of the equipment passed down to the troops of the Wintertide Concordance, but its twin-linked carbines were more than a match for any natural
predators.

Except the small ones, Tal'hanzo thought sourly. Fi'draah's most lethal killers were tiny and patient in their predation, like the fungal strain that had
overrun several outposts during the occupation's first years, undetected
until it bore fruit. Or the splinterskin malady that shattered the mind with
pain long before it was done with the body, driving its victims to violence.
Despite the diligence of his cadre's physicians, such threats were perennial
here. It was a wonder that the enemy, hampered by primitive technology
and superstitions, could endure such depredations at all.

'Do not underestimate the gue'la,*'* Jhi'kaara had cautioned when he'd
mocked their foe. *'There is weakness in their barbarity, but also great strength.'*

Tal'hanzo glanced at the barge to his right, seeking his fellow veteran.
Like himself, Shas'ui Jhi'kaara stood at the prow of her long, open-topped
vessel, her helm's lenses glowing in the murk. Her armour's white plates
were scabbed with mould and foliage. Unlike the other fire warriors, who
washed away the filth every night, she let it accrue until a mission was complete. It didn't impair her armour's functioning and their cadre's shas'el
believed she had earned the right to hunt as she saw fit, but Tal'hanzo dis-
agreed. To his mind Jhi'kaara epitomised the spiritual malaise afflicting the
Concordance. She was a survivor, yes, but what was she surviving *for*? Her
name meant 'broken mirror', reflecting her extreme facial scarring, but he
suspected her wound ran deeper than flesh and bone. And her *connection*
with this world was troubling.

What do you see out there, broken one? he wondered. *What do you seek?*

His gaze shifted to the giant looming over Jhi'kaara. Her pet *gue'vesa* was
never far from her side. It was an ugly brute, even by the vulgar standards of
its species, its features squeezed between a heavy brow and a slab-like jaw.
O'grinn, the gue'la called such beasts. Apparently they were an uncommon
yet stable mutation of the core species, adapted to high-gravity worlds.

This breed epitomises the true nature of the gue'la, Tal'hanzo judged. His
nasal slits flared with disgust as his optics zoomed into the creature's face.
It was a female, its long black hair braided into dreadlocks entwined with
bones. The geometric snowflake symbol of the Wintertide Concordance was
carved into its forehead like a tribal marker. This was a common practice
among gue'vesa janissaries – a show of loyalty towards their benefactors –
but recently it had begun to spread among the cadre's fire warriors also. The
river of influences ran both ways on Fi'draah and, like the planet's waterways, that could lead nowhere healthy.

'We're lost, boss,' someone called out behind Tal'hanzo. He turned, already
knowing who'd spoken. It was the scrawny, red-haired prisoner in the second

row – the one who looked weaker than the others until you noticed his eyes. Tal'hanzo still struggled to decipher gue'la facial expressions, though he had lived alongside them for years, even mastering their language, yet he could read those wide-set green eyes perfectly. There was a sharpness in them that cut through the idiosyncrasies of species or culture. They reflected a mind that was fully *present*. The Tau'va called this quality *Lhaat elesh* – 'To slice with sight'. Every member of the ethereal caste possessed it, but it was rare on Fi'draah, perhaps because there were no ethereals here to nurture it. It burned bright in Jhi'kaara's surviving eye, but had dimmed in Tal'hanzo's own. He'd sensed it fading alongside his faith in this war.

'Lost, ain't we?' the prisoner pressed. An indigo spiral encircled his left eye, radiating across his cheek and tapering off at his lips, which were pierced by multiple rings. A charm hung about his neck, depicting a canine beast with a fish's tail, crudely carved from coral. It wasn't a typical Imperial icon, yet many of the prisoners sported it in some form. Tal'hanzo suspected it was a regimental badge or a memento of their home world.

'We are not lost, gue'la,' he answered, with more conviction than he felt. He had no confidence in the convoy's commanding officer, Shas'vre Ibolja. She wasn't a newcomer to Fi'draah, yet she still trusted technology over instinct.

'We've been on this river for days, like,' the sharp-eyed prisoner continued. His accent and syntax were difficult to parse, but Tal'hanzo was accustomed to such diversity – *disorder* – among the gue'la. They were an anarchic species. 'We was promised a new start, boss.'

'And you shall have it,' the veteran replied. 'If you prove worthy.'

'Eight men 'ave died on this tub already. What's left of us ain't doin' so good neither.' The prisoner's lips curled upwards, showing dirty teeth. It was an expression of warmth or humour, if Tal'hanzo remembered correctly, though neither made sense in this context. 'Look, me name's Sharkey. I'm a medicae, right. Give us a field kit and–'

'You will receive treatment at the cadre's base.'

'Hey xenos, you gonna slab us then make it quick!' another prisoner shouted, drawing supportive growls from his comrades. At least fifty of them remained, hunched along the barge in rows of four or five, their wrists locked together and static-clamped to their benches. The last of the wounded had died days ago and been thrown overboard without ceremony. It was a winnowing of the weak, but also a retribution, as the shas'el had commanded.

So it must be, Tal'hanzo judged, weighing up the rabble. These gue'la hadn't accepted the Greater Good willingly. They'd fought back when the cadre attacked their coastal fortress, albeit without much enthusiasm. The T'au Empire was merciful, but resistance couldn't go unpunished, even if it was pitiful. Hence this mission. While the cadre's main force was airlifted back to base, the prisoners would be forced to endure a gruelling water-borne voyage. Four barges were assigned to the task, escorted by a Devilfish transport and a pair of light Piranha skimmers.

'*Our foe has been routed from this region,*' the shas'el had briefed the convoy's fire warriors. '*Your journey will be long, but I anticipate minimal danger. It will chastise these savages. More importantly, it will serve as an orientation lesson for our shas'saal reinforcements.'*

Nobody had voiced what they all knew – Fi'draah was no place for novices, no matter how promising they were, and the eight shas'saal who'd recently joined the cadre were not at all promising. The youths ran the gamut of flaws from over-aggression to timidity, with a minimum of martial aptitude between them.

That is why they were sent here, Tal'hanzo guessed. *Where they won't live long enough to bring shame upon their septs.*

Two shas'saal had been assigned to each barge under a veteran's command, along with a couple of experienced gue'vesa janissaries. Tal'hanzo doubted any of them would last a year.

'Freaks!' a prisoner yelled, snapping him back into the moment. 'I heard they gelds any man what joins up with 'em. Don't like us breedin', do they!' That incited another chorus of jeers.

'D'you want to bring back an empty boat, boss?' Sharkey asked. He spoke quietly, yet his voice carried through the clamour.

I do not, Tal'hanzo admitted to himself. *The shas'el would deem that a failure.*

'See to your comrades,' he said, unlocking Sharkey's clamps with a subsonic pulse from his helm. 'Bring him a salve pack,' he ordered a janissary.

'Thanks, boss,' Sharkey said, rubbing his wrists.

'Betray my trust and you will all suffer,' Tal'hanzo warned.

'I hear you.' The medicae rose unsteadily. 'Don't worry, I ain't much of a fighter anyways. More of a...' Sharkey trailed off, his eyes growing distant.

'Gue'la?' Tal'hanzo asked. 'What is wrong?'

'I... Nothing. It's nothing.' Sharkey's fingers brushed his necklace, as though seeking comfort from its charm. 'Been off me feet too long, is all.' He smiled – *grinned?* – again. 'I'll get to it, then.'

The other prisoners had fallen silent. Satisfied, Tal'hanzo turned away. Sometimes the Open Hand was stronger than the Clenched Fist.

'So it flows,' he murmured. It took him a moment to realise the vista had changed while he was distracted. Swirls of mist were rising from the water, yet somehow the river seemed brighter and much broader. Not like a river at all, in fact...

He hissed with surprise. The trees were gone, along with the banks to either side. Gazing up, he saw open sky for the first time in days. The cloudy grey swathe looked much like the water, save for the thin light leaking through. It would be dark soon. Why did that prospect disturb him?

I am thinking like a gue'la, Tal'hanzo chided himself. *Their irrationality is a pestilence.*

He turned full circle, cycling his optical sensors through various wavelengths to pierce the murk, but found no land. There was *nothing* beyond the convoy. The four barges were still travelling two abreast, with Jhi'kaara and himself leading and Niotal and Rho'noka behind. He hadn't seen the Piranhas since noon. That was to be expected since their role was reconnaissance, but Ibolja's Devilfish had drawn too far ahead for his liking. It was just a smudge in the mist and fading fast.

I should caution her, he thought, knowing he wouldn't. She wouldn't listen anyway.

'Did you feel it, shas'ui?' someone asked beside him. It was one of the janissaries – a big, bearded man whose name he'd forgotten. Wintertide gue'vesa were issued stripped-down variants of a fire warrior's uniform, with open-faced helms and lighter armour, as befitted their inferior status. This one's eyes were wide – a common sign of fear among them.

'Feel what?' Tal'hanzo replied, irritated.

'The moment when... we...' The janissary faltered, then bowed his head. Blood dripped from his nose as he moved. 'Nothing, shas'ui.'

Nothing? Tal'hanzo wondered. The answer echoed Sharkey's. Did that signify anything? No, that was absurd. He was thinking like a gue'la again, seeing connections where none existed.

'Resume your duties, janissary,' he ordered, returning his attention to the lake. It looked endless. It might almost be an ocean.

'Bad place,' rumbled the hulking o'grinn janissary, Coraline, speaking in T'au. It was a coarse approximation of the language, but more than most gue'vesa ever managed. 'Much bad.'

Yes, Jhi'kaara agreed. There were no *good* places on Fi'draah, but some were worse than others and she feared this barren lake might be among the worst. The planet's jungles were riddled with lakes, but there shouldn't be one *here* – or anywhere near the region they were crossing. That meant they were... elsewhere.

It has happened again, she judged. *The twisting.* She had felt the moment when the convoy slipped between streams, of both water and sanity. Her mind had lagged behind her body, reluctant to follow its ignorant partner into the unknown, then snapped back into place when the strain became too great. She had experienced that fleeting, yet somehow interminable dislocation many times before, but only ever in Fi'draah's most treacherous heartlands. Had that tainted region somehow extended its reach?

To take me back?

'We have slipped,' Jhi'kaara murmured to Coraline, knowing her companion also sensed it. Many of the other gue'la would have felt it too. Their species was far more receptive to such violations of the natural order than her own people. And yet she shared their sensitivity. What did that say about *her* nature?

'Yah,' Coraline grunted. 'Is Rosa.'

Rosa. The Dolorosa Coil. It was the gue'la name for Fi'draah's heartlands, but Jhi'kaara had adopted it long ago, sensing its *rightness* for that rapacious wrong.

'Yes, that is likely, *ta'liss,*' she said. Her fellow fire warriors would be affronted to hear her use the term for a gue'la, but anything less would demean their bond. They had stumbled upon each other in the Dolorosa Coil two years ago, each the sole survivor of their unit. They'd met as enemies, wounded and worn to the core, but unwilling to surrender. Jhi'kaara's rifle was long depleted so she'd faced the giant with a knife, finally accepting death, for she could never defeat such an opponent in close combat. But instead of attacking, it had regarded her with surprisingly thoughtful eyes, then asked, 'You find way out, blue?'

We found it together, Jhi'kaara remembered. *But the Coil – Rosa – never let us go.*

Her helm's communicator chimed, announcing a nasal voice: *'Shas'ui, affirm?'*

'Affirmed, shas'vre,' Jhi'kaara replied.

'This lake is not marked on our charts,' Shas'vre Ibolja observed, sounding offended by the notion. *'Why did you not alert me to the discrepancy?'*

'I was unaware, shas'vre.'

'But you have traversed this region previously.'

'I have. Many times. There was no lake here.' Jhi'kaara waited, but Ibolja didn't reply. She pictured the convoy's leader struggling to process the contradiction. Under other circumstances it might have been amusing. Ibolja was woefully unprepared for such riddles. Since her arrival she had rarely ventured beyond the cadre's coastal bases, where Fi'draah's taint was weakest, and never into the deeper jungles. For this mission she had ensconced herself in the sealed bubble of her Devilfish, segregated from the reeking corruption outside. As if that could protect her.

You cling to a lie, shas'vre, Jhi'kaara thought sadly. *Like so many of us.* Her people would never grasp the realities of this world, or the wider terrors they implied. The t'au were too balanced. Too sane. That was why the gue'la were so dangerous. They *prospered* on insanity.

The silence dragged on.

'We have strayed from our path, shas'vre,' Jhi'kaara said finally, putting her superior out of her misery. 'We must turn the convoy around.' There was no telling whether this would work, but it was their best chance. With luck they might slip back to their former location.

'Unacceptable,' Ibolja piped primly. *'My control drone confirms we have adhered to our prescribed course. I will not squander precious time over a cartographic error. Or your oversight, shas'ui.'*

'I strongly advise–'

'We will proceed.' The communicator chimed again, ending their conversation.

'Fool,' Jhi'kaara whispered, with more weariness than anger.

'No turn back?' Coraline asked.

We could, yes. Jhi'kaara was tempted, but she knew the other barges wouldn't follow. It would mean abandoning them. Had she drifted so far from her comrades? So far from the Greater Good?

'No turn back,' she answered, mimicking her companion's cadence. 'We will push through to the far side of the lake.'

If it has one, she added silently.

ii. Consecration

Shas'la Shenjul was the first to spot the island, though she had fallen behind her fellow fire warrior. Their Piranhas' sensors had been performing erratically

since they'd reached the lake, growing worse the further they went. By the time
the island loomed out of the mist ahead, they were relying on their eyes, and
hers had always been sharper than Dal'thyr's. She cursed when the massive
landmass appeared out of nowhere, seemingly racing towards her skimmer.

'Beware!' Shenjul transmitted, veering away, then swerving again, more
sharply, as a smaller mass appeared before her – then another. Her Piranha's
anti-grav rotors churned the water into waves as she manoeuvred around
the hazards. It splashed her open-topped cabin, drenching her and speck-
ling her lenses. As she wiped them clean there was a screech of torn metal
from somewhere up ahead, followed by an explosive boom.

Dal'thyr!

Shenjul slowed her skimmer to a gentle glide and surveyed the area.
Knotted mounds jutted from the water around her, all formed from the
same dark coral. She guessed they were outgrowths of the island, encircling it like a natural minefield.

'Dal'thyr'?' she sent. White noise hissed from her helm's transceiver, along
with a sluggish pounding, so deep it was almost subliminal. The interference had
been plaguing their communicators for the past hour or so. 'Dal'thyr, affirm?'

We were foolish, Shenjul scolded herself. She and Dal'thyr were friends –
more than friends, if truth be told – but also rivals, eager to prove themselves
and rise beyond humble shas'la. Neither had been willing to return to the
convoy until they'd found a path through the lake, but that didn't excuse their
haste. The dreary, changeless expanse had tempted them to ever-greater
speeds, until they were racing like–

'Shenjul, affirm?' a voice called through the static.

'Dal'thyr! I hear you.'

'Are you safe, Shen?'

'Yes. Where are you?'

'On the island. I think...' The pain in his voice frightened her. *'I hit something... big. Our* Emperor *Ibolja will be displeased.'* He used the gue'la honorific
as a mockery. It was an old jest between them.

'I will find you,' Shenjul said. Piranhas were designed for two riders, but
the shas'el had deemed that excessive for this mission. They hadn't even
been allocated drones. 'Activate your marker beacon.'

'Too dangerous. Strong currents here.' He snorted harshly. *'Let the shas'vre
come for me... in her armoured cocoon... if she dares.'* The openness of his
contempt for their superior was worrying. It spoke of someone with nothing
to lose.

'Dal, if you are hurt–'

'Go, Shen! I shall endure... until you return.'

'Affirmed, ta'liss.' They hadn't formally sworn the Ta'lissera oath yet, but
neither doubted they would. 'I shall be swift.'

'Not too *swift,'* Dal'thyr cautioned.

It took longer to clear the reef than Shenjul anticipated. The mist had curdled
into a thick, clinging fog, forcing her to move slowly, but even so, the distance felt *wrong.* Night had fallen by the time she was back on open water,

but her relief didn't last long. She'd completely lost her bearings. She didn't even know which side of the island she was on.

It's too big, she thought, staring at the vast, mist-swathed mass. *We should have seen it.*

Putting aside her unease, she tried contacting the convoy, but nothing came back except that sluggish pounding. How far behind could the others be? Surely–

A throaty roar reverberated over the water, seemingly coming from everywhere. Shenjul rotated her skimmer, hunting for the source, but it was futile. Her lights scarcely penetrated the murk. Their anaemic beams swirled with mist, as though infested. Would they carry the contamination back to her?

Act, shas'la, Shenjul urged herself, striving to quash the irrational notion.

The roar receded into a rhythmic metallic chugging. An engine? Yes, but nothing like the harmonious machinery of her people. This was a raucous, rancorous noise. A noise that hated...

The enemy, Shenjul thought, with a stab of fear. But how could that be? This region had been pacified.

'Act,' she murmured. *Warn the others.*

A dark shape scudded from the fog to her left, hardening into an armoured vessel as it drew closer. The gunboat dwarfed her Piranha, its rivetted iron hull towering over her like a curved black wall. Motionless figures lined the deck above, their silhouettes gnarled and elongated by the mist, as though they'd been wrenched out of shape by an unsteady hand. A massive gun jutted from the vessel's prow, manned by a pair of shadows. With a groan its barrel spun into life and tilted towards her.

Act!

As Shenjul hit the accelerator a hail of bullets raked her skimmer, tearing through its chassis and detonating within. The vehicle burst into flames, spewing smoke into the mist as it spun out of control.

I am sorry, Dal, Shenjul grieved as she burned. The pain was terrible, the guilt even worse, but both were mercifully brief.

The Captain closed his eyes after the kill was confirmed, turning his mind inwards then *down*, diving and divining for the flow of echoes beneath the lake. Longing for what must follow.

Blood calls to blood!

Sure enough, as the offering's scorched flesh mingled with the waters, he felt the God-Emperor's avatar stir. Not its body – the sacrifice had been too paltry for that – but its *spirit*, straining against the shackles of unwanted sleep. Craving more. Only bloodshed could break its chains.

'You'll have it, lord,' the Captain promised, diving deeper while his vessel ploughed on above. He had mastered the trick of divining during his blessed purgatory, reclaiming a gift he'd once shunned as sinful. That was how he'd tasted the Sleeper's restless dreams, though he hadn't understood much at first, only heeded, *believing* from the start. That was surely why the Sleeper Beneath had drawn the *Polyphemus* to the lake, singling out this vessel above all others for the latent prophet on board.

'Betrayed and forsaken, drowned by doubters in darkness, then forgotten,' the Captain rasped, 'but never forgetting.' He'd dredged the prayer up from the depths, along with the fury it embodied. The words wrenched a violent spasm from his lungs as he choked out the final verse. 'Forever unforgiving, as the God-Emperor wills it!'

Even now, after untold years of service, he didn't really understand the Sleeper's nature, other than its innate holiness. And its age... Such a fearsome, soul-grinding weight of age! The dreams he'd tasted ran aeons deep, drenched in pain and righteous rage. Sometimes he glimpsed scenes from that lost era and grasped them as revelations, even though they made little sense. No matter. He didn't need to understand. Besides, he understood his role in the Sleeper's sacrament. That was enough.

'I'll make things right!' Rising back into his body, the Captain leaned forward to consult the prophecy his words had spewed onto the window, though he already knew what he'd find there. Fate couldn't – *wouldn't* – be denied. Today the God-Emperor's avatar would feast!

Shas'vre Ibolja reclined into her piloting couch and breathed deeply, trying to meditate, but it was no use. She couldn't slough off her irritation with the scarred recidivist, Jhi'kaara, who'd led her convoy astray.

'I should not be here,' the officer muttered. It was a well-worn complaint. She'd been making it since her ordeal on Fi'draah began, though she rarely voiced it aloud, and never to the other fire warriors, who might report her to the shas'el. She *had* confided in him once, shortly after her arrival.

'Are you suggesting the Empire makes mistakes, shas'vre?' her superior had asked, sounding amused. There was only one acceptable answer to that.

'No, shas'el,' Ibolja had conceded, seeing the trap, but no way to avoid it.

'Correct. You are here because it serves the Greater Good.' Then his tone had hardened. 'And because you are flawed. *Irredeemably* flawed.' The darkness in his eyes was disturbing. 'As are all who serve here.'

Those words still stung. They confirmed the rumours about Fi'draah. This was a dead-end posting in every sense. Ibolja could see the logic of that when applied to the dysfunctional relics and hotheads under her command, but her own record was *impeccable*. Well... other than the incident on Kol'hoosi, but she had settled that. Hadn't she? Regardless, she didn't belong here.

'It *was* an error,' Ibolja insisted, savouring her defiance. She was alone except for her control drone, which didn't have the capacity to care about her grievances, let alone report them. Its narrow intellect was focused on piloting her Devilfish, while updating the cadre's woefully inaccurate map. More errors!

Ibolja snorted. It felt like her convoy had been on this execrable lake for hours. Just how big could it be? Reluctantly she activated the screen above her drive console, bringing up the vessel's forward video feed. It had worsened since she'd last checked, turning the fogbound lake into a glitch-riddled abstraction. Her sensors were also playing up, reporting utter nonsense. There must be a source of interference under the lake – a massive magnetic lode perhaps? Her understanding of such things was limited. They were earth caste matters.

'Status update,' Ibolja commanded. The drone slotted into the interface berth overhead didn't reply. 'Status update!' Her voice sounded very loud in the enclosed cabin.

Dangerously loud.

Ibolja contracted her nasal slits into a frown, confused by the intuition. Suddenly she regretted travelling alone. Her transport could carry ten, but she had chosen isolation. Why?

Because you despise your companions.

That was true, but she couldn't tell whether the answer had come from within or without. It felt like someone had spoken *behind* her. Someone crouched in the gloom just beyond her monitor's lights. Someone with a taste for shadows.

Why don't you turn around and look, shas'vre?

Once again, Ibolja wasn't sure whether the thought was hers. Its mockery was familiar, yet unlike herself. As she wracked her memories, trying to identify it, she realised her drone still hadn't responded to her query. Indeed, it was completely silent. That wasn't right. Active drones emitted a constant low burble while they performed their calculations. When had that ceased?

It took an effort of will to raise her hand and touch the machine. It felt inert, its customary vibration absent. Inoperative. Then who was piloting the vehicle?

Nobody. The anxiety infusing this thought left its ownership in no doubt. Fear was alien to the shadow-thinker, except as something to be given, generously but not without a price, whilst Ibolja herself was shamefully familiar with it.

Flawed, the shas'el had judged. *Irredeemably flawed.* Suddenly Ibolja recognised that sardonic inner-outer voice. Shas'el Aabal, watching and denouncing her from the shadows.

'No,' she protested. 'I don't belong here.'

Her console's communicator chimed. The pristine sound was a lifeline back to sanity. Ibolja moaned as she grasped it, opening a channel. 'This is Shas'vre Ib–'

Static spewed from the receiver, washing over her with a force that felt physical. She gagged at the *stench* of the noise. It was foul – shockingly, *irredeemably* unclean. She tried to stem it, but her fingers wouldn't move.

You are weak, the shas'el decreed. *Unfit to serve at all.*

'No,' Ibolja protested, then shuddered as a dark shape broke through the fog on her monitor, surging forward to fill the screen. A ship. Coming for her, just as the be'gel horde had come for her on Kol'hoosi, except this time there was nowhere to run. Nobody to hide behind.

Coward.

'Yes,' Ibolja confessed, closing her eyes as her executioner opened fire.

A fiery light bloomed in the fog ahead, accompanied by an oddly ululating boom, then faded into a stain that lingered.

Ibolja!

Tal'hanzo fell into a crouch, unslinging his pulse rifle in the same motion. A glance towards the barge on his right confirmed Jhi'kaara had followed suit – or more likely *led* by a heartbeat. She was more attuned to disaster than he was.

'What was it?' the sharp-eyed prisoner, Sharkey, asked, dropping down beside him.

'My shas'vre,' Tal'hanzo replied flatly. He hadn't seen the kill – Ibolja's vessel had been lost in the fog bank ahead – but he knew the sound of a Devilfish dying. The wail of their ruptured engines was unmistakable. Almost melodic.

'Firewatch forward!' he shouted. His janissaries hurried to their preassigned posts, but the two novices stood gawping at the red haze like water caste navel-gazers.

'Wake up, shas'saal!' Tal'hanzo bellowed. 'Move!'

One of the youths stumbled in his haste, almost dropping his carbine. Tal'hanzo cast his eyes over the prisoners, wary of disorder, but they were quiet.

'They won't give you no trouble,' Sharkey said. 'Lake's got 'em spooked.' He spat overboard. 'Got me spooked too.'

I should restore his bonds, Tal'hanzo thought, then noticed something more pressing. His drone was silent. He was about to report it when his transceiver pinged.

'*My drone is down. Sensors also,*' Jhi'kaara declared on the command band, addressing all the fire warriors. '*We are under attack.*'

She leads again, Tal'hanzo brooded, surprised by his anger.

'*Switch to direct drive,*' his rival continued. '*Formation Gyoh'shu.*' The static haunting her voice couldn't diminish its authority.

'Affirmed,' Tal'hanzo replied, disengaging his drone as acknowledgements followed from the other boats, both equally distorted. Had this interference somehow disabled their drones? It seemed too subtle a weapon for the Imperium. Either way, there was nothing to be done about it. Steering one-handed, Tal'hanzo slowed his vessel as the barges behind advanced into the gap between the leaders, forming a row of four.

'*Hold position,*' Jhi'kaara ordered. '*Let the foe come to us.*' It was a sound strategy. Hover barges weren't designed for combat, so maximising their crews' firepower was wise, yet Tal'hanzo bridled at obeying.

'*Enemy vessel approaching,*' Jhi'kaara reported. A moment later Tal'hanzo heard it too – a laboured chugging, growing louder by the second.

'I can take the helm, boss,' Sharkey offered. 'Free up yer hands for the shooter.'

'You can pilot a hover barge, gue'la?'

'I know boats. All us Brine Dogs do.' Sharkey jabbed a thumb at his comrades. 'Born to 'em, we are. Besides, I've been watching this one for days.'

'So be it,' Tal'hanzo said, moving away from the console. It defied protocol, but that was the nature of things on Fi'draah. Only fools like Ibolja failed to see that. 'Hold us steady.'

'Aye, boss,' Sharkey said, taking his place.

Tal'hanzo shouldered his pulse rifle and peered along the barrel, automatically linking its sights to his helm's targeting optics, then cursed as the overlay jittered wildly.

'The old way then,' he whispered, deactivating the mechanism. His eyes were still sharp, even if they'd lost the rarer sharpness of the *Lhaat elesh*. An unexpected thrill ran through him. Perhaps he would rediscover it here.

iii. Sacrament

A starless night had fallen, yet darkness failed to follow. The lake shone with an eerie green light that bled from somewhere below. It was a seeping, *seeking* radiance that stained everything it touched, leaving no shadow undefiled. Kneeling at the prow of her boat in that sly twilight, Jhi'kaara knew she had been right about the lake. It was a diseased place, perhaps even a cyst of sorts.

A cyst with teeth. Her scar itched at the thought, stitching fire along her face and teasing phantom images from her lost eye. She had removed her helmet when its sensors failed, preferring an unfiltered view of the lake, but perhaps that was a mistake. She didn't like the toxic radiance on her skin. It was caressing her scar, as if sensing a fissure in her resolve – a wound sealed, but never truly healed. Ripe for peeling open...

No, Jhi'kaara vowed. *You will not.*

When an Imperial gunboat emerged from the fog bank a few hundred yards ahead, she was almost relieved. It was a formidable foe, but its threat was banal beside the light's malice. She'd fought ships like this before. They were lumbering weapons platforms that could hit hard and withstand heavy punishment. Their weakness was a lack of agility and tactical flexibility, with their firepower concentrated on a fixed forward cannon. T'au hover tanks could run rings around them while wearing down their armour, but that wasn't an option for her sluggish, lightly armed force.

'Open fire!' Jhi'kaara transmitted, leading by example. A barrage of bright pulse-fire erupted from the gathered barges, lancing through the murk to strike the gunboat. Nobody missed a shot, but none of their hits mattered. Nor would any that followed. Not in the time they had left. The ship was closing the distance slowly, but inexorably, confident in its invulnerability. Only Coraline's heavier weapon, a modified burst cannon, could do real damage to such a vessel, but its range was short. The giant had scavenged it from a wrecked battlesuit during their first mission together and used it to such devastating effect that their shas'el let her keep it, even commissioned a custom power harness for it.

'All units, widen formation!' Jhi'kaara ordered. 'Unfolding Fingers!' Beside her, Coraline tugged the nav-stick, nudging their barge into a sideways glide away from its neighbour. She was cradling her cannon one-handed while she steered, holding fire until the enemy was closer.

It won't be enough, Jhi'kaara judged bleakly.

'You can kill us,' she whispered to the enemy. 'Nothing more.'

But was that really true? There was a pulsating quality about the green light now, as though it was excited by the imminent carnage. She had told her comrades she'd seen its like before – a harmless emanation from an aquatic fungal field, nothing more – and they'd believed her because they wanted to, but the truth wouldn't be denied much longer. The light also wanted something. To be tasted and to taste in turn.

To feed.

This would be an unclean place to die. *Unclean?* It was a strange notion, rife with ignorance and superstition – the kind of vagary that fuelled the gue'la Imperium – yet it felt right. Dying here might not be an end, but a *beginning.* One without hope for an ending. Or for anything at all.

These abstractions danced through Jhi'kaara's mind like a shadow play, but her focus was on the enemy. She spun through the cold calculations of battle while she fired, hunting for a way to win, but it was a simple equation and the outcome was always the same. She couldn't stop this foe.

'Why they wait?' Coraline asked. 'Why no shoot back?'

'They mock us,' Jhi'kaara answered. Yes, she was sure of it. The gunboat was toying with its prey, delaying its retaliation out of spite. That fitted the hubris of the hulking vessel. The *slovenliness*. She imagined its captain staring back at her from the wheelhouse, gloating at his superiority, though his ship was a disgrace. With every passing moment its decrepitude became clearer. It was a derelict, gnarled by corrosion, neglect and untreated wounds that had festered into badges of dishonour. The raptor emblazoned on its blunt prow had lost both its heads and acquired a veil of slime, exchanging pride for degradation. It was a fitting symbol for a decaying empire.

You should be long dead, Jhi'kaara judged. *But you are too baneful to surrender.*

It was another irrational intuition, yet she couldn't shake it. Fi'draah had opened her mind to such insights and she was long past questioning them. The enemy vessel was both more and less than a machine. In some aberrant yet irrefutable sense, it was *alive.*

In death.

'Rosa,' Coraline spat, making it a curse. The giant released the nav-stick and braced herself to fire, raising her multi-barrelled cannon above the prow.

'Yes, ta'liss,' Jhi'kaara agreed. This derelict embodied the Dolorosa Coil's corruption perfectly. It was almost pitiful… *No,* there was no room for pity here! She twisted the emotion into hatred and kept firing. Every round scorched a fresh crater into the gunboat's hide, but the wounds were only skin-deep and devoid of pain. It would take too long to blast through to the restless, rusting organs powering the ship.

'You won't have me,' Jhi'kaara murmured, defying the lake, its light, and the undying hulk they'd bred to serve them. With defiance came sudden clarity and she glimpsed a way out. *But not for all of us,* she realised, gauging the gunboat's trajectory.

'Save your fire,' she told Coraline.

'Eh?' Her friend frowned, confused.

'*M'yen'kesh,* ta'liss,' Jhi'kaara said. 'The Unforeseen Blade.' She tapped her wrist-mounted grapple-launcher. 'We must bring this foe down from within.'

'Repeat order!' Tal'hanzo shouted over the interference spilling from his transceiver. A pounding had risen through the static – deep and rhythmic, like a drowned heartbeat gathering strength. It had battered Jhi'kaara's last command into gibberish. 'Repeat–'

The noise swelled in reply, reverberating around his helmet. Tal'hanzo cut the connection and looked for Jhi'kaara's barge, squinting through the green haze, but couldn't see past the intervening boats. The Imperial ship was heading directly for them. They were pulling apart, trying to force it to choose between them, but their gue'vesa steersmen weren't nearly as capable as drones.

Faster! Tal'hanzo urged, frustrated by their leaden glide. Thankfully Sharkey had coaxed some speed out of their own vessel, carrying it clear of the immediate danger. Evidently the man hadn't lied about his affinity with boats.

'We need to go, boss,' the medicae said. 'Try to lose 'em in the fog.' Despite his words he seemed unafraid. Indeed, there was a calm intensity about him as he steered.

'Wait,' Tal'hanzo ordered, trying to think. His optics were glitching and throwing up artefacts – crawling, clawing shadows that lingered in his eyes as tenaciously as that loathsome pounding echoed in his ears. Sensory ghosts that wouldn't quite fade... He shook his head, trying to clear it. Logic told him Sharkey was correct, but that didn't make him *right*. A fire warrior never abandoned his comrades.

Even if they are already lost?

As if to confirm the treacherous thought, the nearest barge whined and stalled. Its captain, Shas'la Niotal, pushed aside the man at its helm and took control, but it was too late. The prisoners on her barge were yelling as the gunboat loomed over them. Their shouts turned to screams as Niotal's panicked novices opened fire on their charges. Each shot seared through multiple bodies, leaving the blackened craters ablaze. One went wide and scorched away a janissary's face. He fired reflexively as he toppled backwards, gunning down the prisoners near him.

'Fools,' Tal'hanzo hissed, appalled by the disorder.

'We gotta go now,' Sharkey urged.

'Wait!' The fire warrior swung his rifle back and forth over the gunboat, searching for a meaningful target – something he could damage, even if it was only a sting of defiance – but there was nothing. Its crew had remained out of sight behind the iron ramparts, offering no return fire. Even the vessel's forward cannon appeared to be unmanned. The arrogance of that enraged him.

This is no battle, he thought bitterly. *It is a massacre.*

In her final moments Niotal looked directly at him. He didn't know her well enough to guess the expression she wore under her visor. Somehow that blank was worse than anything else, as though she was already nothing.

'For the Greater Good!' Tal'hanzo shouted, with more anger than conviction, raising a fist in fierce salute. Niotal was gone before she could return it. The hulk didn't so much ram her barge as wade right through it, crushing everything in its path. It was a ponderous, almost lazy annihilation that yawned across several seconds. Wailing prisoners tugged at their bonds as their executioner ground towards them, mangling metal and bone with equal indifference. One man tore his bloodied hands free a moment before he died. Another giggled manically as he went under the grinder. A clump of prisoners towards the rear were singing some kind of prayer, their faces turned towards the sky. The surviving janissary fled past them and leapt overboard, buying himself a few extra breaths before death caught up to him.

The second barge, Rho'noka's, was luckier. It had reversed as it turned so it was almost clear when the gunboat raked its side, but even that glancing contact ripped its hull open and hurled it into a wild spin. Tal'hanzo lost sight of it behind the enemy. The hulk eclipsed everything to his right as it slithered past like a predator bloated by its kill.

Bloated, but not sated.

Glaring at that black iron wall, Tal'hanzo fought for self-control and lost. With a cry he rose to his feet and opened fire again. Every shot was as impotent as the last, yet not without meaning. Not at all! His fury eclipsed the futility of his retribution, sparking a rare passion in his heart. He had never felt so at one with the element that symbolised his caste. His blood sang with its heat, threatening to set him ablaze, but he didn't care. This would be a magnificent way to die!

Rage makes monsters of us all, an inner voice cautioned, but it was too weak to douse the fire. The teachings of the Tau'va had never felt so insipid. So empty. Another voice was yelling at him from outside, exhorting him to listen, but it was weaker still, barely penetrating the fire's beat. That rhythm was leaking through his transceiver now, pounding in time to the pulsing light. Or was it the other way round?

'Burn!' the fire warrior roared as the gunboat passed him by. 'Burn!'

'We must help them!' the shas'saal shouted at Jhi'kaara, pointing at the barge to their right. The gunboat's impact had shoved it past her vessel with brutal force. It was dead in the water some thirty yards away, listing to one side, its anti-gravitic suspensors wrecked. Smoke gushed from the drive panel, where its fire warrior, Rho'noka, was slumped, stunned or dead, while his crew stumbled about in confusion.

'We will,' Jhi'kaara lied. The stricken barge would sink within minutes, carrying its prisoners with it. She'd tried transmitting a signal to unbind them, but couldn't get through the interference. The crew might survive if they swam, but she wouldn't be surprised if the stranded novices couldn't. They were a pitiful wave of recruits. The fool wasting her time was no better or worse than the rest, merely more inconvenient. Mal'na, he was called. A brash, self-absorbed hothead who saw the Tau'va as a blunt weapon. She'd overheard him bragging that he'd be called Thunderhoof someday, when the Empire recognised his talents.

'They are my friends!' Mal'na whined, obviously referring to the stranded shas'saal. His kind didn't care for aliens, allied or otherwise.

'Enough!' Jhi'kaara snapped, returning her attention to the Imperial gunboat. It was alongside her barge now, so close she could almost touch it. 'You have your orders.'

'We won't fail you, shas'ui,' her second novice answered quickly. It was the first time this one had spoken, so perhaps he had a measure of sense.

'See that you don't,' Jhi'kaara said. She didn't like leaving her boat in their care, but she needed her janissaries for the attack. Tal'hanzo hadn't confirmed her last order, so her team would likely be alone against the gunboat's crew. Maybe thirty or forty Imperials, she estimated. Poor odds, but she had Coraline, who was worth ten common gue'la.

It can be done, she told herself, watching the hulk slide past, waiting for the right moment. Surprise was the key to victory here. They must attack from the vessel's rear, where there would surely be fewer guards.

'Now!' Jhi'kaara shouted, activating her grapple-launcher. With a pneumatic whoosh its harpoon shot towards the ramparts above, trailing an almost unbreakable nanocular-threaded cord. Three more soared in its wake as her team fired in quick succession. She felt the cord go taut as its harpoon punched through metal and flicked out multiple blades, lodging itself securely.

'You won't have me,' she whispered to the lake. Bracing herself, she depressed the grapple's trigger. With whiplash speed the cord retracted into the embedded harpoon, yanking her into the air. She kicked out as she swung towards the hull, her armoured hooves hitting it with a clang, then rappelled up, letting the cord pull her. It wasn't a traditional fire caste tactic. Nor was the grapple-launcher standard equipment, but Fi'draah had demanded new ways of war and the t'au were nothing if not adaptable.

'For Gretta Gud!' Coraline rumbled as she surged past, hauling herself up by strength alone, her cannon swinging about on her back. She was too heavy for her grapple's retractor, but that didn't slow her. Jhi'kaara sensed her comrade's eagerness. Part of it was battle-lust, but the greater measure was *faith*. Coraline was a genuine convert to the Tau'va. The cadre had accepted her more warmly than her own kind ever had.

That is our greatest strength, Jhi'kaara thought with a flash of unfamiliar pride. *Not our machines.* Glancing back, she saw the janissaries weren't far behind her. Further down, her barge was receding as the gunboat glided on. Hopefully–

She frowned, noticing the water. From this height there was a distinct radius to the green glow, as though it emanated from a vast orb under the lake. The water was churning furiously within its boundaries, clearly agitated by the light.

Later, she told herself firmly. *After the fighting is done.* This mystery was irrelevant for now. It had to be.

She looked up just as Coraline clambered over the ramparts. There was no gunfire in return. A good sign. Surprise was with them. Moments later her friend reappeared and extended a hand to haul her up and over.

'My thanks, ta'liss,' Jhi'kaara whispered as she dropped into her customary defensive crouch. Sighting along her rifle, she appraised the situation. The deck was littered with broken machinery and crates, but otherwise feature-less save for the bunker-like wheelhouse towards the prow. Shadowy figures were hunched along the ramparts, keeping their heads down. It was much darker up here, away from the lake-light, so she couldn't make them out clearly, but none were nearby.

'I count at least thirty,' she murmured. Some of the Imperials were huddled together too closely to tell apart.

'Yah.' The giant grinned as she hefted her cannon. 'Easy kill.'

No, Jhi'kaara thought. Nothing on Fi'draah was ever easy. Except dying. There was a ragged, apathetic look about these Imperials, yet they unset-tled her in a way more orderly troops wouldn't have. Like their decaying vessel, they belonged to the Dolorosa Coil.

'Hold fire,' she cautioned. 'Wait for the others.'

Long seconds later the janissaries joined them, mirroring her stealthy stance. As she expected, there was no fear on their faces. Unlike her peers, Jhi'kaara hand-picked and honed the gue'vesa under her command, foster-ing a team of trusted regulars. She knew them all by name, along with their capabilities. These two, Shea and Thraft, were among her best.

'Our foes are *many*,' she whispered, implicitly censuring Coraline's bravado. 'We must cull them swiftly.' Switching to hand signals, she assigned her team firing arcs. There was no margin for error here. This had to be a perfect execu-tion of the Mont'ka doctrine, breaking the enemy with sudden, overwhelming force before it could retaliate. Maybe these wretches were as pitiful as they looked, but she didn't plan on testing that.

'Be swift and sure,' she warned. 'And trust nothing.' Even up here, away from the green glare, she could feel the lake's gaze on her. Its waters were thrashing against the hull below. Seeking her?

You won't have me, she vowed again, taking aim. 'On my signal.'

iv. Awakening

The Captain sighed with joy as he felt the last of the lake's unholy chains break, sundered by their captive's exertions. The Sleeper Beneath had fed well on the souls its prophet had sent it, growing stronger with every morsel until it was undeniable. He'd been right to withhold his ship's firepower and deliver the offerings broken, but unburned. They were more whole-some that way.

Purer.

Supernal tremors reverberated from the lake's depths, vibrating through his ship's hull and mould-riddled decks. His sigh became a wail as the wave surged up his legs and along his spine, spreading through his bloated body like a storm. He gripped the wheel as a holy seizure wracked him, rupturing organs and snapping bones into new configurations, each more profound and improbable than the last, every one bringing him a little closer to his lord. It hurt – oh, how it hurt! – but he welcomed the benediction.

It's done, he thought, staring at the dirty window where he'd deciphered the God-Emperor's will through the long years. He wanted to say it aloud, but his tongue had torn free of its roots and slithered down his throat. He could feel it grubbing about in his belly, searching for words to celebrate his victory, though he already had the best ones.

It's done!

The sound of gunfire rippled through his blessed torment, coming from the deck outside, so far away it didn't matter. His crew was dying – truly dying this time, finally and forever – but that didn't matter either. They'd fulfilled their purpose, as had this vessel. The sacrament was complete.

I've made things right!

None of his followers resisted or resented their end. Indeed, the few who could still feel anything welcomed death. He didn't begrudge them oblivion. They'd been a loyal crew.

Once I showed them the way, the prophet added, thinking of his predecessor, who was hissing and shedding fervent spores behind him. The former heretic was caught up in the ritual's consummation too, all his doubts forgiven. That pleased the Captain. Unlike his god, he'd never been a cruel man by nature, but necessity had nurtured what it needed.

So it goes, he remembered, sensing but not quite understanding the wisdom of that phrase, or where he'd heard it or why, which was the whole story of his life-in-death really. But even that didn't matter. Not to a man of faith. Besides, his own story was also coming to an end. He could feel its finality in his guts, blooming amid the putrid blood and viscera down there. That sludge was becoming uncontainable now. Like his tongue, it wanted to go its own way.

Then go, he acceded, opening his mouth. The tide rose to his invitation, as eager and unstoppable as the sleeper he'd awoken. His neck distended with pressure as he spewed his insides over the wheel and the window, along with his wayward tongue and a shoal of rotten teeth. He shuddered with the release, but it wasn't enough. Not nearly enough. The flow wouldn't stop. More and more kept coming. Surely more than he'd ever held within him...

That was when he felt it – something *vital* stuck in his throat. Something that refused to go. Its persistence was trapping him in this choking purgatory. He wouldn't be free until that last, desperate morsel of himself was vented.

Go! the Captain urged then begged then bled. His eyes bulged as his jaws gaped ever-wider, then dislocated, tearing his cheeks open. The wheel cracked in his grip and lesions appeared along his neck, leaking ichor.

Please!

With a final, desperate heave that burst his eyeballs, the prophet vomited his soul onto the glass.

The gunboat was gone, swallowed by the fog again, this time behind the barges. The water in its wake was flushed with blood, but there was no telling t'au from gue'la. Both the purple and the red were stained black by the green light, finally alike in death, but the water itself wasn't dead. Far from it. It churned with a fierce, insurgent life of its own, writhing against the tyranny of gravity as though it yearned to drown the sky.

Caught in the lake's turmoil, Tal'hanzo's barge bobbed about unsteadily, yet he remained standing, his gaze fixed on his foe's last position. He couldn't recall when he'd stopped firing, but his anger had faded with the gunboat's retreat, leaving him stranded in the afterglow of wrath.

Retreat? he wondered blearily. *Did it really retreat?* No... That wasn't right. The enemy would return to finish the survivors. Soon. He had to act before it was too late, just as Sharkey kept insisting. Tal'hanzo tried to give the order, but it wouldn't pass his lips. The noise flooding his helmet wouldn't allow it. It was the lake's song, woven from static and sighs and that insistent, insidious pounding, somehow melded into a melody of sorts.

Here... Down... Here... Down...

Tal'hanzo's gaze slipped into the water. It was gazing back at him, watching through myriad wounds in its restless skin. Each was an eye and a maw in one, wide open and rimmed with spiny, liquescent teeth that chattered, gnashed and gnawed as they strained against their own membranes. A spiral iris glared from every throat, whirling and burning with green light, like a snared nebula enraged by its cage. The wounds were numberless and limitless in size and form, forever shifting as they flowed to the beat of that unseen, all-seeing heart. Blinking with secret promises...

See... Seek... See... Seek... The words were Tal'hanzo's, but their source was not. The water, or rather the thing infesting it, was leeching on his thoughts, guiding their flow towards its will.

'This can't be,' he whispered, knowing it could, was and always had been. His fleeting, glorious fury had scorched away the dogma binding – *blinding!* – him, opening his eyes to a much older, blood-borne wisdom that even his youthful species shared, as all thinking beings must, even if they didn't recognise it. It was like the *Lhaat elesh*, but infinitely sharper. *Deeper...*

With a moan, one of the janissaries hurled himself into the swarm of maws. He turned as he fell, eyes goggling and mouth agape, as though aping the entity he'd surrendered to. It was the bearded man who'd sensed the lake's strangeness earlier on, a lifetime of lies ago. He was devoured in seconds, gnawed down to the bone and sucked clean by countless eager mouths, stripped of flesh, blood and something far more precious – something ineffable and essential that became one with his killer.

'Soul-eater,' Tal'hanzo murmured, drawing the words from that blood-deep cache the fire had exposed.

'Don't look at it!' Sharkey shouted, but it was a useless warning. How could he look away from Truth, even if it had teeth? *Especially* if it had teeth. Facing such horrors was a warrior's calling. He felt the wondrous fire warming his blood again, kindled by his fortitude.

This is the real war, Tal'hanzo sensed, seeing it as clearly as the seething abomination saw him. *The only one that matters.*

The dead janissary's bones were floating amidst the swirl, still bound into a loose structure by liquescent cords. As Tal'hanzo watched, the surrogate muscles rippled, jerking the skeleton into a fitful semblance of life. Green fire flickered in the skull's sockets, illuminating the tendrilous teeth framing them. The water heaved, propelling its puppet towards his barge, arms raised for an embrace.

See... Seek... Feed... That last thought was the true sum of the abomination's desires, Tal'hanzo sensed. All else was merely a reflection of its prey's psyche.

Feed... Feed... Feed...

A tangible foe was the spark he needed to break free of its spell. 'No,' he gasped through the lake's song. It wouldn't be silenced, so he yanked his helmet off and threw it aside. The stench of unfiltered air was worse than anything he'd ever smelled – a ripe-rotten reek so thick you could drown in it – but his anger was stronger.

'Burn!' he roared, opening fire. His first round struck the corpse-puppet's skull, shattering it in a burst of green light and steam. The rest punched through its ribcage and shoulders, tearing it apart. Denied a frame to build upon, the liquid animating it melted back into the water.

It can't reach us, Tal'hanzo realised. The ooze was all around his barge, clinging to its skirts and splashing furiously to get higher, but its prey was hovering just out of reach. Its thrashing cords sundered whenever they extended too far. Some of his prisoners were begging to be released, but many were silent, either gazing vacantly into the water or straining at their bonds to answer its call. One of the shas'saal was on her knees, hands clasped about her helmet as she rocked back and forth. The other novice was gone.

'Be vigilant!' Tal'hanzo shouted to his remaining janissary. 'The dead return.'

'Yes, shas'ui!' she answered, sounding mercifully alert. Some minds were apparently more vulnerable to the beast's lure than others.

It almost had me, Tal'hanzo admitted. That weakness repelled him more than the entity itself. With a stab of dread, he scanned the lake for the other barges. They were under attack too. The blight was everywhere, covering the water like a rash. Jhi'kaara's vessel was intact and aloft, but Rho'noka's slumped in the water, its prow completely submerged. A tide of eyes was gushing up its length, devouring everyone in its path and spawning skeletal puppets in its wake. Stripped of flesh, the dead prisoners slipped their bonds and slid into the water, flowing towards Jhi'kaara's barge. Rho'noka's surviving crew had retreated to the stern, where they were firing into the ooze, tearing steaming tunnels through it, but the wounds closed as quickly as they were created. The lake would soon be infested with corpses.

'You can't help 'em, boss,' Sharkey warned, following his gaze. 'We gotta run while we can.' Remarkably the man's calm remained unbroken.

Have you seen such horrors before, gue'la? Tal'hanzo wondered. It seemed unlikely, yet–

A glistening skeleton lunged out of the water beside him, scrabbling for a handhold. Its sleek helmet was still in place, the lenses glowing green.

With a snarl, Tal'hanzo rammed his rifle's butt into the dead novice's visor, but the corpse wouldn't let go. Liquid eyes glared at him from the ooze sheathing it. Others snapped at his gun as he slammed it down again and again, trying to dislodge the invader. Many more were slithering up their puppet's back in a distended wave, using it as a bridge to board his vessel.

That would be our end, Tal'hanzo judged. As he swung his rifle to strike again a pulse-round punched into the corpse's head, incinerating dozens of eyes, but it clung on, driven by many more.

'The arms!' Tal'hanzo shouted to the female janissary, who'd fired. 'Destroy its arms!' He backed away as more rounds lanced the invader, striking its hands with admirable accuracy. The puppet lashed out with charred stumps as it flopped back into the water, splashing its contagion over the mesmerised prisoner behind Tal'hanzo. The man shuddered as his upper body was gnawed down to the bone, but it was only a reflex spasm, devoid of emotion. Even this trauma couldn't break the abomination's grip on his mind.

'Kill it!' begged the captive beside the infested man, tugging frantically at his bonds. 'Kill–' His plea broke into a shriek as his neighbour thrust its rippling head towards him and spattered his face with slime.

With a flash of pure foresight Tal'hanzo glimpsed his vessel's doom. The blight would spread through the bound prisoners like wildfire, consuming and consummating its corruption, growing exponentially with every kill. Disaster was almost inevitable.

He fired without conscious thought, blasting away the screaming prisoner's face to stem the taint, then turned his rifle on the shuddering, half-eaten thing beside the corpse. His weapon wasn't designed for close combat and its long barrel was scarcely a handspan from his target. At this range the pulse-rounds were devastating. Every shot boiled away a large patch of water and charred the bones beneath. More gunfire blasted the puppet from behind as the janissary followed Tal'hanzo's lead.

'Burn,' the fire warrior hissed, savouring the word's honest strength. Its *purity.* He kept firing until his rifle's powercell was drained. He reloaded instinctively, but the smoking husk was completely lifeless. Cauterised.

'More coming, shas'ui!' the janissary yelled.

There were several skeletons floating towards the boat. Six... No, seven at least. Rho'noka's barge was too far away so these must be the remnants of Niotal's group. Those that were intact enough to animate.

'Go, Shar'kee,' Tal'hanzo hissed as the dead surged towards them, borne by unnatural waves. 'Go!' He had no idea *where,* or whether there was even an end to these tainted waters, but there was nothing for his team here except death.

'Aye!' the medicae said. 'I'm on it!'

As their barge accelerated away, Tal'hanzo watched Jhi'kaara's vessel recede. There was no sign of its crew and the first wave of Rho'noka's dead were clambering aboard unopposed. The mesmerised prisoners were fortunate. At least they would die without feeling terror or pain.

'So, you were broken after all, Jhi'kaara,' he murmured, picturing the scarred veteran. 'Nothing more.' He was surprised that she had succumbed to the lake's allure, and even more so by his sadness at her fate. All her brooding mystery had come to nothing in the end.

'They look like they were already dead,' Thraft observed, prodding a fallen mariner with his boot.

Long dead, Jhi'kaara judged, studying the corpse. Its skin was loose and livid with decay, even missing in places. Fungal growths had erupted all over its body, tearing through its filthy uniform. Seemingly given free rein to fruit, they had twisted the creature into a grotesque parody of its species. All the gunboat's crew were much the same.

'Easy kill,' Coraline said, but she sounded subdued, even though she was right. The mariners had been the *easiest* of kills. Most had fallen to her team's opening salvo. The few who survived had watched their executioners with pale, empty eyes, making no attempt to fight back or flee. They'd just stood there, waiting for death.

We gave them what they wanted, Jhi'kaara thought. She didn't like that conclusion at all.

'Any movement?' she called to Shea, who was further along the deck, watching the wheelhouse.

'No, shas'ui,' the janissary answered. 'Can't see nothin' through the windows, though. Dirty as the Dog-Emperor's arse.' It was a bold thing for a gue'vesa to say, even one as bitter about his former life as Shea, but he wasn't trying to impress her. No, he was trying to rally himself. Every one of them felt the sickness saturating this derelict.

We cannot linger here, Jhi'kaara decided. Her team had cleared the deck, checking the bodies for survivors, then sealed the hatches to the lower levels, where she had no intention of going. Only the wheelhouse remained, yet something about that squat iron block made her hesitate.

It's the worst of it, she sensed. *This ship's cyst.* And like the lake, it would probably have teeth.

'No worry, ta'liss,' Coraline growled, rapping her cannon pointedly. 'We all gud.'

'Yes.' Jhi'kaara placed a hand on her comrade's elbow, which was as high as she could reach. 'Let us end this.'

She split her team on either side of the wheelhouse hatch, with Coraline alone on the right. They needed the ship's controls intact, hence their tactical options were limited, but there couldn't be many enemies inside. Besides, if they were anything like the degenerates littering the deck this would be over quickly. Breaching the hatch would probably be the hardest part.

The cyst, remember, her inner voice cautioned. Yes, but what choice was there?

Reluctantly Jhi'kaara turned the handle. To her surprise it wasn't locked.

'Wintertide!' she shouted, yanking the hatch open. It obeyed with a force that tore the handle from her grip, almost breaking her wrist. A cloud of grey-green gas gushed out, hissing with the release of pent-up pressure. Jhi'kaara leapt back, skidding on the wet decking. Shea dived clear to the left, but Thraft, who was closer and slower, caught the full force of the emission, as did Coraline. The man fell to his knees, coughing, while Coraline staggered about, swatting at the air, as though it was filled with stinging insects.

The cyst bursts, Jhi'kaara thought darkly as she tried to break her wild skid. Her hooves snagged on a hunk of debris and she fell, losing her grip on her rifle. Her flailing hand struck one of the corpses, cracking open a ribcage that felt like mouldering wood. Its head rolled over, spilling tarry blood from slack jaws. With a snarl of revulsion, Jhi'kaara tugged her hand free as the cloud rolled towards her. Shimmering motes swirled within it, their beauty belying the danger. *Spores.* Fi'draah's favoured curse. She'd faced such threats before, once in a hideously corrupting form, yet she sensed this was worse. The contamination these spores carried would run deeper than the flesh.

Spirit-deep.

Her eyes narrowed, trying to pierce the mist. Something was moving about inside the wheelhouse, just beyond the doorway – an immense, vaguely manlike shape. She couldn't make it out clearly through the spore cloud, but its flesh appeared to be *crawling,* as though it was formed from thousands of pale worms bound into a rancorous union. It drew closer, filling the doorway but unable to squeeze through, and she glimpsed the yawning, raw-edged wound that passed for its face. Remnants of a uniform clung to its bloated body like scraps of shed skin, identifying the monstrosity as something once human.

'Enemy contact!' Jhi'kaara yelled, longing for her lost rifle. 'Beware!'

With a gurgling roar the aberration rammed itself against the doorway, trying to batter its way out of the cabin. The metal frame buckled under the impact, but held. On its third attempt the beast's distended belly burst open, revealing a bone-rimmed maw. Another wave of spores erupted from the cavity, along with a swarm of tentacular entrails. The stricken janissary kneeling by the doorway shrieked as they coiled about him and wrenched him back into their nest. Mercifully Jhi'kaara lost sight of Thraft's fate in the deepening smog of spores. Fortified by the abomination's emissions they were floating towards her with renewed energy.

They smell me, she thought, scrabbling backwards. As the corruption reached her legs a hulking figure lumbered out of the cloud and yanked her up, lifting her above the contamination. A torn tentacle hung about Coraline's neck, still dripping ichor. Her face was purple and blotchy, yet she managed a grin.

'Rosa... stink...' the o'grinn gasped. She glanced over her shoulder as the beast howled and hurled itself against its cage again. The doorframe wouldn't hold much longer. 'Ugly mukka too,' Coraline judged, then hurled Jhi'kaara away. The throw carried the fire warrior across the deck, clear of the spores' reach, but she hit the ground hard, clanging her head against the metal. Darkness gathered in her eyes, clotting her vision like corpse blood.

'You won't... take me,' she breathed, fighting the nausea. 'Never.'

The whirring hum of a burst cannon roused her, followed by a bestial bellowing and a chain of explosions. Both subsided into a crackle of flames that sounded almost serene.

'Ta'liss,' Jhi'kaara groaned. She tried to sit up, but that only encouraged the darkness, so she lay still, lying flat on the deck. That was when she noticed the canopy of vines drifting past overhead. *The jungle.* She was *back.* Somehow the gunboat had slipped free of Rosa's coils, carrying her back onto the river.

We walk blindly along a knife edge, she thought hazily. *Slicing into oblivion.* They weren't her words. Whose then? Someone important surely, yet she couldn't recall a name or a face. Everything was slipping away.

A familiar figure loomed over her, made almost unfamiliar by its haggard state. How had her friend lost so much of herself so quickly?

'I burn it,' Coraline croaked, nodding towards the wheelhouse. 'Burn it all.'

'It needed burning,' Shea said, joining Coraline. The janissary looked unhurt, but there was a wild look in his eyes that spoke of subtler, yet perhaps still fatal wounds. 'Needed burning,' he repeated, nodding fiercely.

'For the Greater Good,' Jhi'kaara answered, knowing he was right, even if it meant they'd lost any chance of steering the gunboat. The convoy's survivors would have to save themselves, if they could.

'Sorry for head hurt.' Blood drooled from Coraline's lips when she spoke. 'Throw you too big.'

'You threw well, ta'liss,' Jhi'kaara whispered. 'I will recover.' Then she remembered the most important thing. 'We are back.'

'Yah... we...' Coraline's words broke into a hacking cough. When it subsided she was *weeping* blood. 'I done,' she said. 'You find... way out.' She jabbed a thumb towards the creeper-veiled sky and the stars beyond. 'All way out.'

'We will find it together, ta'liss,' Jhi'kaara answered, but it must have been in her head alone because her friend didn't reply. She tried again as Coraline lurched out of sight, but nobody answered except the darkness. This time she let it come.

You won't hold me, she vowed. The last thing she heard before her consciousness slipped away was Shea's fervent decree: 'It needed burning.'

v. Vigil

Tal'hanzo perched on a coral outcrop just off the island's coast, watching the lake, and as always, it watched him in return. The infestation of eyes was everywhere, extending into the misty horizon, leaving no patch of water untainted. He'd walked the island's perimeter many times since his arrival, searching for an opening in the blight, but it was always waiting. And yet its dominance wasn't complete. It clung to the rocks offshore, yet never quite touched the jagged coastline, always recoiling a few paces away, as though repelled by an invisible barrier. Therein lay the key to overcoming it. If he could find the source of the entity's aversion and turn it into a weapon then maybe he could defeat or even destroy it.

Destroy, he decided, yes that was what he wanted. Not evasion or escape. This abomination needed to be annihilated, for the sake of sanity and for all those it had devoured then debased. They were out there too, floating in the water or standing waist-deep in the shallows, facing the shore. Green fire flickered in their hollowed-out skulls as their liquid muscles rippled with the tide, but they were otherwise motionless. It was impossible to make an accurate count, but there were certainly over a hundred of them, scattered around the island in loose packs. Tal'hanzo had picked off the fallen t'au among them, then resolved to save his ammunition in case the gunboat returned. He hoped it would. He would welcome the chance to face its crew on land.

Does this beast serve you? he wondered, as he'd done many times before. *Or are you its slaves?*

'You're playing with fire, boss,' someone said behind him. 'Coming out this far.'

Tal'hanzo knew that was true. He usually confined his patrols to the shoreline, but this evening he'd leapt across several rocks to reach this vantage point, venturing deep into the abomination's territory. He couldn't have said why exactly, but he'd felt the need to test his foe. The ooze was clustered around the outcrop's base, yet it wasn't roused by his presence, as it would have been in the early days of their stalemate. It had learned patience.

'Our foe is a beast, Shar'kee,' he answered, 'but not a mindless one. A hunter must understand his prey.'

'You really think we're the hunters here?'

'I believe we must become so,' Tal'hanzo said, addressing his enemy as much as his comrade. Comrade? Yes, this strange gue'la had earned the appellation. Sharkey had led them to this refuge and navigated the fierce currents around it with skill, landing their barge safely. Afterwards he'd volunteered for the grim duty of culling the prisoners who'd been beguiled by the abomination.

'It's gotta be done by one of our own,' Sharkey had said. *'No officers left, so I guess I'm up.'*

The medicae had walked the boat's length, stopping beside each blankfaced prisoner to offer a swift prayer and a swifter end with Tal'hanzo's knife. The sober ones hadn't protested. They'd all seen what happened on the other barges. The mesmerised men couldn't be kept locked up, but they would have walked right into the embrace of the thing waiting in the water if they'd been set free. The knife was cleaner.

'We're a hard lot, us Brine Dogs,' Sharkey had said after it was done. *'Always 'ave been, even before the bloody Imperium turned up on Hook's Sink and shafted us.'* He'd offered the knife back, but Tal'hanzo let him keep it. He'd earned it.

Along with my trust, the veteran thought.

Fourteen prisoners had survived the cull, but two were lost in the days that followed. With Sharkey, the female janissary, who'd proved herself capable, and the last novice, who hadn't, they were all that remained of the convoy. There was one other – the missing Piranha rider, Dal'thyr, who they'd found on the shore, lying beside his wrecked vehicle. But his injuries were serious, perhaps fatal.

'Seventeen,' Tal'hanzo murmured. At best.

'Say again, chief?'

'How is Shas'la Dal'thyr?' Tal'hanzo asked in return.

'His fever's broken. Bones 'ave set clean, far as I can tell.' Sharkey shrugged. 'You lot ain't built the same as us, what with them hooves an' all, but close enough. I reckon he'll make it.' A pause. 'We oughta get back, chief. Gonna be dark soon.'

Day and night were unpredictable here, sometimes lingering interminably, sometimes passing before the rituals of work or sleep had even begun. Tal'hanzo had lost track of the days, but he'd learnt to read the transitions into night and Sharkey was correct. It would be dark soon.

'We will return to the ruin tomorrow,' Tal'hanzo said, coming to a decision he'd been avoiding for too long. 'We must search it again.'

Sharkey was silent. He feared the place, as did all the gue'la. Two of their number had disappeared when the survivors first descended into the caldera at the island's centre. The ruin was at its nadir, where sunlight somehow never fell. It was a vast coral spiral, like a petrified snake, its outer coils riddled with oval portals into a deeper darkness.

'It's an unholy place,' Sharkey finally said.

'It is the *only* place.' Tal'hanzo rose to face him. 'There is nowhere else left to go.' They both knew that was true. Their refuge was barren, as empty of features as it was of life, save for that shadow-drenched hollow. If there was an answer to be found on the island – a *weapon* – it lay there.

'Our supplies will last for many days yet,' Tal'hanzo said, holding the man's gaze, 'but not forever.'

'The lads won't like it.' Sharkey shook his head, then sighed. 'But I'll talk 'em round, shas'ui.' It was the first time he'd used the title.

'Return to the shore, Shar'kee. I shall follow soon.'

After the gue'vesa was gone the fire warrior returned his gaze to the lake.

'I shall die on this world,' he confided. 'But not here.' He spat into the ooze, mimicking a gue'la, as Jhi'kaara might have done. 'And not by your will.' He felt the fire in his blood rising again, eager to set his spirit ablaze, but this wasn't the time for that. He cooled it with a mantra of sobriety. The old disciplines of the Tau'va held strong, even if the philosophy itself had withered. He had been practising control since he'd arrived on the island, learning to temper his wrath. It must never become his master.

'You will burn,' Tal'hanzo promised his prey. 'For the Greater Good,' he added, testing the phrase and feeling nothing. Not even regret at its passing. That part of his life was over. Tomorrow the next would truly begin. Or perhaps end. Either way, he would face it with fire in his heart, as a warrior should.

VANGUARD

The pursuit of knowledge is absolution.
The conceit of absolute knowledge is merely hubris.

– Ordinance Mechanica Obscura #01010

The sky bled streamers of poisonous light over the grey-green morass of life below. Like the tentacles of some ethereal leviathan, the radiance touched and tested everything, questing for a foothold upon reality. The jungle shivered beneath its glare and the random chitter of numberless insects became a profane harmony. Like called to like and the tainted planet stirred towards wakefulness in the unclean dawn.

But Omnissiah willing, this world will sleep a while yet, Magos Caul reflected as he cancelled the blasphemous simulation conjured up by his cogitation engines. *I still have time...*

His carmine robes hung in loose folds about his skeletal frame as he floated above the concentric, whirling wheels of his data throne. His quartet of multi-jointed legs was furled up in arachnid repose and his myriad lenses had faded to dull green stains in the darkness of his cowl, disengaged while he gazed inwards at the infinitely malleable regions of the datasphere. The cogitator banks embedded in the wheels of his throne chattered as they saturated his nexus chamber with information from thousands of sensors across the planet.

<Canopus 30,> Caul clicked in binaric cant, switching his visual input to a defence servitor welded to the dome of his bastion. The position was optimised for the elimination of aerial predators and megaspores, and offered an unparalleled view of the contaminated sky. Through the servitor's eyes he saw the warp-spawned anomaly from his simulation as a numinous spiral behind the dirty clouds of Phaedra's troposphere. As night fell it would deepen into a multi-hued aurora that was vile, though only a ghost of the horror he predicted.

Ghostblight, whispered a voice. It came from the neural cage where the magos's instincts were interred alongside the rest of his humanity, smothered but not quite dead. He dismissed it as he dismissed every shadow of his former existence. His induction into the divine logarithms of the Omnissiah had elevated him above such emotionally charged nonsense.

Hypothesis: the anomaly encapsulates a binary reaction – a feedback loop of corruption, Caul speculated. *It draws current from the planet's taint and in turn galvanizes its host to greater virulence. Query: which is the host and which the parasite? Is this a symbiotic conjunction?*

The anomaly had first manifested in the sky twenty-seven days ago, invisible to the naked eye, but triggering dozens of Caul's sensor stations. He had failed to determine its origin, but it was growing stronger with every passing hour and building towards a Category Gamma warp storm. Could his fortress withstand a deathworld infused by the immaterium?

The magos redirected his focus to a servo-skull patrolling the perimeter of his base and trained its gaze upon the immense structure he had forged around his explorator ship nearly two centuries ago. The Iron Diadem was a tangle of manufactories and silos mounted upon a stalk of titanium pipes rising from a vast lake. Over the decades Phaedra had assailed the refinery with a tirade of spore tsunamis, silt quakes and hurricanes, yet its lamprey grip on the lakebed had never faltered.

Unfortunately the imminent catastrophe was not one of Phaedra's paroxysms.

Phaedra. Even the name sounded subtly poisonous to Caul. He had remained here only to dissect and codify the planet – *the enemy* – until leaving had ceased to be an option. During his sojourn he had crossed lines that some would call heretical.

But my purpose has always been pure, Caul reasoned. *This world exemplifies the degeneracy of the flesh. Its jungles are an inconstant, decaying riot of rage entwined with lust. Know thy enemy and decode it well.*

Yet his crusade might soon become untenable, and if he were lost then research of incalculable value it would be lost with him. That was unacceptable.

<Initiating inload enhancement protocol Kappa,> the magos intoned.

A swarm of delicate mechafilaments uncoiled from his cowl, swaying as they trawled the data-charged air like the feeding tendrils of a cuttlefish – filtering, filing and cross-referencing readings from across his territory, devouring parameters of light refraction, particle density, atmospheric pressure, gravitic arrhythmia and scores of other variables to fuel the ferocious engine of his mind. Caul tore through it all in seconds, slicing and splicing facts into possibilities, rejecting or promoting those possibilities to probabilities, then cycling back to hone the most promising towards a single categorical *certainty*.

It was a sublime effort, yet the answer eluded him like some slippery, chimerical prey.

<Inconclusive.>

Caul withdrew his mechafilaments and intoned the seventh mantra of Algebraic Concord to dispel the spectre of frustration. Every time he tried to determine when the storm would break, his conclusion was different. Sometimes he settled on months, sometimes weeks, but just as often it was days or even decades. The degree of inconsistency invalidated every answer. Even for a magos the variables were too byzantine – too *chaotic...*

I will not make the attempt again, Caul vowed, but it was an oath sworn only to himself, not the Omnissiah, for he knew he would break it as he had done countless times before. It was the same obstinacy that had chained him to Phaedra – an almost pathological refusal to accept imperfection.

<Timeframe irrelevant/apogee event inevitable.>

My research will be preserved. This time the oath *was* for the Omnissiah because Caul intended to honour it.

Submerging himself in the datasphere, the magos cast his consciousness further afield, leaping from one relay beacon to the next, riding the data-streams that shadowed Phaedra's labyrinthine waterways, seeking the holy warriors he had entrusted with his fate.

The convoy of skitarii war galleys sliced through the slime-encrusted rivers of the Coil in orderly procession, their massive steel watercogs labour-ing against the ooze while their chimneystacks wheezed black smoke. The five vessels were identical in size and unmistakable in intent, their blunt, cannon-crowned prows and crenellated gunwales giving them the appear-ance of floating fortresses. Each had set out from the Iron Diadem bearing a maniple of one hundred skitarii warriors and their sacred war machines, together with a support crew of engineers, bonded ratings and deck servi-tors. Still the voyage had taken its toll on their numbers. Some had been snared by Phaedra's lazy, lethal wiles – an incautious rating beheaded by overhanging razorvine; another snatched by a wyrmtree lurking on the riverbank, and an engine crew lost to an infestation of swarming skrabs. And more had fallen to the true enemy, whose stealthy hit-and-run attacks had grown more frequent as the convoy neared its destination. The losses were regrettable, but sure to happen. Most importantly, they had been planned for.

Standing on the elevated observation deck of the leading vessel, Alpha Phaestus-IR01 swept the riverbank with his long-barrelled rifle. The wooden stock of the antique weapon was wedged into the crook of his right arm in the age-old posture of a marksman as he scanned the jungle. Night had fallen, but his ocular omnispex transformed the bioluminescent snarl of fungi and petrified coral into a high contrast abstraction – the white heat of scurrying animals and the passive grey of vegetation. It was all irrelevant noise to the veteran skitarius. He was searching for the shrewd motion of sentient life. Enemy life.

His bonded war brethren were deployed around him at equal intervals, each covering a different watch vector. An ignorant observer might have mistaken the skitarii rangers of Squad Irridio for identical clones or stylised simulacra of men. All wore hooded crimson robes over interleaved segments of dark armour, hiding their features behind jutting rebreather masks and bulbous goggles that gave them a pitiless insect-like cast. They had appar-ently suffered the same catastrophic trauma to their lower limbs, for from the knees down every warrior's legs had been replaced with sculpted titanium augmetics. Only initiates of the Cult Mechanicus would have recognised this stigmata as the Red Planet's due, a hallowed rite of passage shared by all skitarii. They were holy warriors so it was only fitting that they strode the land with the purity of the Omnissiah to guide their path.

Especially a land as corrupt as Phaedra.

<Contact: 1 unit/unidentified. Coordinates follow...> Ixtchul-IR04 reported from his position in the ship's watchtower. To outsiders the ranger's signal would have sounded like a random burst of static, but to his fellow cyborgs it was a data-rich message. Three acknowledgments pinged back instantly, then seconds later a fourth – Brok-IR05, always the slowest of the squad. Alpha Phaestus-IR01 felt no rancour, for this wasn't a lapse on his subordinate's part; Brok-IR05 was simply the least of them, which was why he was designated the squad's '5.'

Every cog has its consecrated place in the machine, he reflected.

His vision flickered momentarily as he interfaced with the lookout's optics, then the dark riverbank was replaced by an eagle-eye view of the river ahead. Through Ixtchul-IR04's eyes he saw a thin figure waiting on a coral outcrop. It stood in a pool of light cast by a saucer-like construct hovering above its head like a diminutive spacecraft. A pulse of pious revulsion spiked the Alpha's brain at the sight of the alien machine, for though it was barely four handbreadths in circumference and appeared to be unarmed the drone's mere existence was an abomination.

It is a mockery of the Omnissiah's sacred engines...

With an almost physical effort Phaestus-IR01 switched his attention from the machine to its master. The alien was motionless save for a slight billowing of its frayed, ankle-length robe. Its arms were crossed from shoulder to shoulder as if in repose, but its black eyes were open wide and seemingly staring right back at him, inscrutable and aloof. There was no mistaking its cobalt skin and the flat wedge of its cadaverous face: *tau.*

The long war between the Imperium and the Tau Empire for Phaedra had bled out years ago, but the last of the aliens were still here, abandoned alongside their Imperial counterparts when the conflict drifted elsewhere. Bitter and desperate, neither side fought for anything beyond survival anymore. Only the holy warriors of the Iron Diadem still walked a true path.

Objective Skysight... The cohort's mission designation flashed across Phaestus-IR01's awareness with the insistence of pain. He neither knew nor cared what Objective Skysight actually *was*. It was enough to know that his magos demanded it and the xenos obstructed it. The rest would become clear in time.

<Initiate protocol Aegis,> Alpha Phaestus-IR01 transmitted to the bridge. Moments later the silent alarm was broadcast across the entire convoy, alerting sentries and rousing the dormant from their meditations. Engines fell silent and the war galleys drifted to a halt. The clatter of metal feet and the hum of activating weapons from the deck below told him that the skitarii vanguard had been summoned to their posts.

As he climbed the steps to the lead vessel's prow bulwark, Alpha Viharok-TH01 felt his mind recalibrating itself to battle mode. The abstract geometries spun by his meditation shift were fading beneath a flood of diagnostics from his squad and the strategic topography calculated by the cohort's Alpha Primus. The neural cogitator fused to his brain stem collated the data, and he frowned as Squad Thorium's tactical efficiency registered at 88.42 per cent. It was an acceptable performance, but acceptable was *unacceptable* to Viharok-THo1. The unit's tactical algorithms would require refinement.

My vanguard will demand perfection, he knew. *It is our duty to the Machine-God.*

'The Omnissiah purges!' Squad Thorium chorused as Viharok-THo1 joined them. Their bulky armour was painted black and striated with dirt and corrosion, their tabards stained with promethium and threaded with oxidised metal bolts and techno-fetishes. All wore sweeping sallet helms of dark iron inlaid with bronze and daubed with their squad rankings. Insects buzzed about them, drawn to the glow of their rad guns, only to pop or dissolve in the baleful energies that suffused the weapons.

Our presence alone brings death to the unclean, the Alpha vanguard observed with pride. *We wear the purifying fire of the Omnissiah like an invisible cloak.*

He frequently led his squad on absolution pilgrimages. They would march into the jungle chanting the Nine Canticles of Decontamination, leaving only stubborn death in their wake. The paths they walked became enduring scars across Phaedra's skin, for even her most tenacious fungi withered in their footprints. The vanguard bore a sombre blessing, yet they welcomed it despite the ravages it had wreaked upon their own flesh, for under their proud helmets the men of Thorium were cadaverous grotesques devoid of hair or teeth.

But they still had their strength. Nothing else mattered.

Catching sight of the waiting tau, Viharok-THo1 unslung his radium carbine and thumbed the power stud, offering its spirit his fealty. Like many skitarii, he revered his weapon as his master, believing his hands were merely tools to aid its will. In his case there was some truth to it, for his rifle was a priceless relic whose spirit had been stirred to permanent wakefulness by the magos. Such 'cognis' weapons hungered to fulfil their purpose, actively compensating for small flaws in a wielder's aim.

'By thy will I ignite thee and charge thee well,' Viharok-THo1 chanted in jagged lingua technis, leading his squad in the Seventh Litany of Liquidation.

<In thy light I smite with thee,> they reciprocated in reverent feedback.

'For thy spite I will slay or die for thee,' Thorium's Alpha concluded.

Neither fear nor doubt were functioning variables in the skitarii psyche. Where a common man might feel anxiety, the skitarii experienced only anticipation.

Phaestus-IRo1's vision glitched again as the cohort's Alpha Primus joined the sensory chain to the watchtower. All Alphas could access their squad members' optics at short range, but the Primus could interface with every warrior in the force, even across great distances. Phaestus-IRo1 held his breath reverently as he felt her icy assessment of the xenos.

<Positive identification: tau water caste,> the Primus relayed over the command band. <Threat level: indeterminate.>

'I bear no weapons,' the alien called, as if in answer. Its voice projected confidence, but Phaestus-IRo1 detected a tremor of tension. 'My designation

is Por'ui Ybolyan,' the tau continued. 'I am authorised to facilitate a concili-
ation with the respected warriors of the honoured Omnissiah.'

<Xenos morale broken,> Ptoltec-IR03 chittered from Phaestus-IR01's left.
The ancient cyborg's contempt saturated his code with static. <We will attain
their stronghold in 9.25 hours. Purgation imminent.>

'The enemy is most dangerous when it is cornered,' another ranger rasped
through the rebreather pipe wedged in his throat. While skitarii rebreathers didn't prohibit mundane speech they certainly *inhibited* it, making
flesh-speak a labour that many shunned; Rho-IR02 clung to it with obscure
stubbornness. It was rumoured that the former Guardsman hadn't embraced
the Omnissiah willingly, but his brothers knew that was irrelevant now, like
every echo of their past lives.

'The losses our respective forces have sustained in this conflict are without
purpose,' the tau envoy continued, extending open hands to the warships.
'The Wintertide Cadre and the Iron Diadem are the last significant forces
of order on this malignant world. For the Greater Good of both our factions
I urge you to cease this aggression.'

It was difficult to read the expressions of a tau, most of which lay in the
precise dilation of the mouth and nostril slits, but sickness was a universal
trait and Phaestus-IR01 had no doubt that Por'ui Ybolyan was *very* sick. Tau
didn't sweat, but the rash of boils and weeping lesions mottling this one's
face looked like splinterskin to him. He'd lost enough brothers to Phaedra's
blights to recognise the signs – xenos, human or post-human, the flesh was
always easy prey to her if left unsanctified.

'If you will communicate your grievance I shall endeavour to mediate an
accord,' Por'ui Ybolyan offered. 'However...' The alien's words exploded into
violent coughing and a perceptible shiver ran through its emaciated frame.

How is this creature still standing? Phaestus-IR01 wondered. *It isn't even
one of their warrior caste.* He expected the retching tau to topple from its
perch, but the coughing fit passed and when it spoke again its voice was
steady: 'However, be advised that further incursion into tau territory will
not be tolerated.'

<Contact: unidentified/west bank. Coordinates follow...> Rho-IR02 reported,
slipping into code when precision was required.

Phaestus-IR01 switched to his comrade's viewpoint and caught a hint of
movement on the riverbank. He crossed to Rho-IR02's position and squinted
with a lidless eye, triggering the magnification mode of his omnispex. Was
there a humanoid figure crouched in the pixelated skein of the jungle? His
rifle trained on the spot as if of its own accord, but he urged it to patience
as he relayed the sighting to the ship's nexus. Another alarm pulsed silently
through the cohort.

'They're watching us,' Rho-IR02 said.

There was a fanfare of encoded salutes from the vanguard as the Alpha
Primus stalked from the bridge, towering over the gathered skitarii like
a Space Marine amongst mortal men. Her silver carapace was devoid of
ornamentation save for a flanged cog embossed into her breastplate and

a vermilion tabard hanging from her waist. Both her arms terminated in broad, double-edged blades that swept over the digital eradication beamers moulded into her vambraces. In place of hands, a pair of mechadendrites sprouted from her hips, rising to sway like restive snakes over her sleek, backswept pauldrons. Every segment of her carapace had been polished to a sheen that matched the mirror finish of her visor, rendering her a gleaming, indecipherable blank.

With a hiss of servos the Primus bent her massive reverse-jointed legs and leapt to the prow rampart. Alpha Viharok-TH01 stepped aside as she took his place at the prow and faced the tau emissary. They regarded one another in silence, each taking the other's measure without the need for words. Finally Por'ui Ybolyan released a long, rattling breath.

'You will not negotiate.' It wasn't a question.

Silence.

'Then let there be an end to it,' the alien said with unmistakable weariness.

There was roar of thrusters from above and a volley of plasma fire surged from the sky to strike the Alpha Primus. She exploded with radiance as the conversion field woven into her armour twisted the heat into a halo of coruscating light. Viharok-TH01's auto-reactive lenses dimmed before the corona could dazzle him, but the furious code-blurts of his squad told him that others had been less fortunate. Their blindness would pass in minutes, but minutes were an eternity in battle. As if to prove this bitter truth, a plasma bolt punched through the visor of the skitarius beside him and crumpled the warrior's head into a molten slag of iron and bone. More fire streaked towards them from the riverbanks on either side and Viharok-TH01 realised his fallen comrade had been a collateral victim – the tau snipers were targeting the Alpha Primus.

<We are the teeth of the Omnissiah,> she declared in serene code as a barrage of plasma fire burst against her conversion field. <Initiate Purgation Sequence Decensus.'

Across the entire convoy skitarii warriors opened fire in perfect synchronicity, ranks of vanguard from the gunwales and smaller groups of rangers from the observation decks. Together they rained solid rounds and blistering arcs of electricity into the jungle, shredding vegetation and vermin in sweeping swaths of destruction as they chased down and obliterated the snipers. A bloated fungoid tower exploded into burning spore clouds that immolated a pair of lurking xenos. One of them staggered towards the river, but criss-crossing waves of electricity threw him back into the melting fungal pyre.

<War is our sacrament,> the Alpha Primus chanted, amplifying her codecast into a white noise hymnal that sent a current of fidelity through the cohort. She had been fashioned by Magos Caul personally, prised from death's grip and reassembled piece by broken piece into a perfect warrior. Many of the skitarii revered her as an avatar of the Machine-God, a belief the magos neither encouraged nor repressed. <In its absence we are but empty vessels awaiting the hallowed promethium of spite.>

The vanguard responded with a chorus of hoarse voices and serrated static, singing their praises to the Machine-God as they cleansed the xenos stain.

Something soared out of the sky and landed on the deck behind the Alpha Primus with a clang of metal. Viharok-TH01 swung round and saw a flickered silhouette outlined against the drizzle and flashes of gunfire. It was a looming, vaguely humanoid shape drawn in angular lines that rippled and tore as it moved. The invisibility that sheathed it was imperfect, oozing over its bulk in a patchy tide that revealed plates of dark, smoothly contoured armour. Bizarrely the stealth field had failed entirely around the blocky gun attached to the intruder's right arm, making it appear suspended in empty air like a phantom weapon. Viharok-TH01 threw himself from the ramparts as the nozzle of the ghostly gun spun up and spat a whirling torrent of plasma.

<Contact: tau battlesuit. Threat level: high,> he transmitted as he dived. <Coordinates follow...>

He rolled into a kneeling crouch behind the tau assassin and opened fire with his carbine. As the battlesuit turned towards him, Squad Thorium answered their Alpha's summons and hammered the intruder with radium rounds from the ramparts above. The sighted and the blind struck with equal precision, their aim guided by the firing vector Viharok-TH01 had relayed. The battlesuit's stealth field seethed erratically under the barrage and the Alpha saw its carapace buckling in the brief snapshots of visibility. He gritted his teeth around his rebreather in defiance as its burst cannon locked onto him.

My service will terminate here, he thought, *but this xenos filth will not long outlast me.*

'The Omnissiah condemns!' he spat aloud, drawing upon a primal well of hatred stemming from his former life.

A silver giant jumped from the ramparts, crashing down into a feral crouch beside the battlesuit. As she rose, the Alpha Primus sliced upwards with a humming, razor-edged blade. There was a screech of tortured metal and the tau's 'ghost' cannon clattered to the ground – along with the now visible arm that still wielded it. The damaged battlesuit leapt away with surprising grace as its jetpack flared into life, but the Primus lunged after its stuttering silhouette and rammed her blade into its breastplate, pinning the assassin as its feet rose from the deck. Struggling to break free, it clawed at her visor with its surviving arm, but found no purchase on the polished metal. The Primus thrust deep and the tip of her blade punched through the assassin's back, tearing open a wellspring of crackling electricity and steaming blood. A moment later the battlesuit was torn asunder as she fired her wrist-mounted eradication beamer within its chest cavity.

<Expurgation sequence complete,> the Alpha Primus transmitted. A ripple of electricity surged along her blade, oxidising the blood that stained it.

<Permission to land and pursue the xenos,> Viharok-TH01 chittered as he climbed to his feet.

<Negative. Irrelevant,> the Primus said. <Mission proceeds.>

Desultory volleys of gunfire could still be heard from the rear of the convoy, but there was no return fire. The attack was over. Por'ui Ybolyan had disappeared.

'It was *kauyon*,' the Alpha Primus reported later. 'Standard tau tactical methodology: draw out and ensnare your enemy.' She paused, considering. 'Sever its head.'

She dominated the data-rich nexus of the bridge like a resplendent statue, standing rigid on the command dais as she communed with her master.

'You are not the head of the cohort,' Magos Caul replied from his aerie in the Iron Diadem. While every skitarius was linked to the magos through its noospheric aura, only the Alpha Primus was blessed with fluid two-way communion. The neural data tether lacing her skull connected them intimately.

'The xenos underestimate our resolve,' Caul said. 'They underestimate *me*.'

'Conjecture: they did not anticipate success,' she said. 'Postulate: desperation.'

The magos never doubted the Primus's insights into the tau. The blue-skinned xenos were among the most subtle of the Imperium's enemies, yet they were transparent to her. She had studied his archives on the aliens obsessively, absorbing every facet of data, but he knew that wasn't the crux of her understanding. She had more reason to loathe the tau than most, even if she only remembered it at a blood-deep, visceral level.

She is my masterwork, Caul reflected with sober pride, *an exemplar of order forged from anarchy... and ignominy.*

There had been no victory for either side in the long war for Phaedra, only a sudden and inexplicable cessation of supplies and communication; simply surviving had required considerable flexibility from those caught up in the meat grinder. During the final years Caul had been obliged to cooperate with the tau, but he had done it in the Omnissiah's name, seizing the opportunity to study their technology. The depth of their heresy had appalled him, for their machines were diabolical contrivances imbued with thought, devoid of spirit. It was an affront to the Machine-God, yet it paled beside Phaedra's biological stain.

Compromise was a valid stratagem to secure my research, Caul reasoned. Nevertheless he would pay his penance when the last of his former associates were expunged. It was pleasing that their annihilation would fulfil a binary imperative, for the tau held the key to his escape from this doomed world.

Dawn. A code pulsed through the cohort and the skitarii galleys surged forward at full thrust. The Alpha Primus became her ship's figurehead, riding at the prow with her mirror-mask tilted into the spray and her blades hammered into the deck like monstrous pitons. Her bodyguards flanked her on either side, their legs splayed wide for balance as their silver-trimmed robes gusted in the wind. Both were female Alpha-level rangers who had been by her side since she was inducted into the skitarii. She remembered nothing before that time, not even her own face, though it must surely be a horror beyond endurance, for her helmet was a hermetically sealed puzzle box, its visor a rigid facade.

I have been reborn as the wrath of the Machine-God incarnate, she thought. *That is the only truth that matters.*

Abruptly the river yawned into a gaping estuary that disgorged the vessels into the open seas of Dolorosa Azure. Here the continent fragmented into scattered archipelagos that thinned out as the galleys reached deeper waters.

<Enemy base sighted,> the Alpha Primus codecast as the white walls of the tau enclave spilled from the horizon at precisely the coordinates the magos had predicted. Little escaped the web of men and machines that served as her master's intelligence network. She knew he had seeded informers among the humans serving the tau, nurturing traitors amongst traitors. Doubtless that was how he had identified their prize.

The Skysight... Even the Primus didn't know what their objective really was or why it was so important to her master.

As her ship hove closer, she noted the gargantuan, semi-sentient whirlpools surrounding the island and clicked her approval. The xenos had chosen well, for their base lay at the heart of a tidal minefield. The only safe approach was a narrow channel between parallel reefs that kept the whirlpools at bay.

That is where the tau will strike, she decided.

Suddenly the magos was with her, assessing the path ahead through her eyes, melding his intellect with her martial instincts to compute a strategy. A moment of hesitation, then previously concealed mission parameters were exloaded to her.

<Initiate formation Aversus: Maniple Epsilon advance to forward position,> they commanded in harmony. <Activate infiltration protocol Furtus.>

A skitarii speeder tore away from its mother ship, diverting sharply from the route the rest of the convoy was taking. Three more followed in its wake, each bearing a squad of rangers. The compact boats were absurdly vulnerable in the convulsing waters, but their spirits were as resolute as their pilots.

Rho-IR02 was hunched over the controls of the lead speeder. Piloting routines had been installed in every ranger's cortex, but the psych-simulators had deemed him the most capable mariner in Squad Irridio. It had been a question of latent instincts.

We will need every scrap of the Omnissiah's wisdom for this, he gauged as he sketched a path through the maze of whirlpools ahead, *but this is a good plan.*

The bulk of the cohort would pass through the sheltering reefs and strike directly at the tau enclave, forcing the aliens into open battle. Meanwhile a small unit of infiltrators would circle round to the far side of the island to secure Objective Skysight.

<Fact: Enemy force unlikely to exceed three hundred units,> the Alpha Primus had briefed them. <Postulate: minimal numbers will be reserved for sentry routines during battle.>

If the Primus is wrong we will die, Rho-IR02 thought. He was incapable of fear, but he was one of the few skitarii who could still conceive the idea of the Primus making an error. Then the first crosscurrents tugged at his speeder and his attention narrowed to more immediate matters.

The convoy of war galleys was half way through the reefs when the attack came.

A sleek hover tank burst from the concealing waters in the lead vessel's path, its thrusters roaring as it rose above the waves. The Hammerhead's slime-streaked carapace was battered and one of its engine nacelles was cracked, but it manoeuvred smoothly to bring its jutting railgun to bear on the intruders. Water shrieked into steam as it spat a shell wreathed in spirals of indigo light. The slug punched through the prow of the leading skitarii ship like an iron blade through flesh, virtually disintegrating the vanguard manning the forward turret. Simultaneously its flank cannons raked the galley's deck with a barrage of plasma bolts that sent the defenders ducking for cover.

Armoured figures rose from hiding atop the reefs on either side to rain more fire down on the invaders. The lenses set into their faceplates were arranged vertically, giving them a soulless, almost robotic, look, but their nimble movements belied it.

A warrior in lighter armour guided one group, coordinating his comrades' fire with a spectral beam that marked targets with pinpoint accuracy. The marker light itself was harmless, but the concentrated volleys of plasma that followed it were lethal. Keeping low, the tau spotter chose his victims with the judgement of a born hunter, singling out enemies that displayed notable authority or skill. The light fell upon the Alpha of Squad Kobaal as he directed his men at the starboard ramparts. A moment later a storm of plasma fire hammered into him, reducing him to a pair of smoking titanium legs.

The treacherous light drifted on.

Two rangers of Squad Uridion were marked and erased from the upper deck in quick succession. Recognising the danger, their squad brothers synchronised their targeting algorithms and hounded the spotter with a union of bullets and electricity, but the alien slipped between the deadly lattice with inhuman grace.

<Attention Uridion: aerial threat,> the magos signalled, catching sight of something through the faltering optical sensors of a dead ranger.

Uridion's Alpha, Exoss-UR01 ducked instinctively, but his surviving troops looked to the sky with weapons raised. A neutron beam struck Gelon-UR03 square in the chest, detonating his torso into a red mist of superheated viscera. Voxhul-UR05 was snagged by the shoulders and hauled into the air by a swooping insect-like monstrosity. Struggling to bring his weapon to bear, he glimpsed row upon row of multi-faceted eyes crowning a maw of thorny mandibles. He hesitated, momentarily mistaking the alien's chittering for code, then its talons let go and he was plunging towards the sea. Before Phaedra claimed him, Voxhul-UR05 saw his killer struck by an arc of avenging electricity from the ship. He chanted a mantra of praise as its smouldering carcass plummeted after him.

Kneeling, Alpha Exoss-UR01 switched his aim to another of the bipedal insects. There were at least twenty of them circling the convoy, like thorny scavenger birds out of nightmares. They rose and dived in alternate waves, striking in concert with the fire warriors attacking from the cliffs.

The Tau Empire is an unclean alloy of xenos filth and techno-heresy, Exoss-UR01 thought as he tried to lock on. His chosen target was flittering about to confuse his aim, but his targeting systems hunted it tenaciously. Twin diamond indicators were overlaid across his optics, spinning towards convergence as he tracked the creature. They blinked red as they melded into one, and then he fired. The lash of his arc rifle charred the flier's wings and it dropped like a stone.

Directly above...

Exoss-UR01 tried to duck away, but the unwieldy permacapacitor strapped to his back threw his balance and he stumbled, taking the full weight of the xenos across his chest. He crashed onto his back and a spike of hard chitin lanced into his abdomen, tearing through his lower spine.

<Designation: Vespid Stingwing,> the magos broadcast. <Xenos mercenary. Threat level: moderate.>

Exoss-UR01 heaved at the carcass pinning him, the carbonized chitin cracking open to reveal pallid flesh. As he thrust it aside a pulse round slammed into his left shoulder, almost tearing his arm from its socket. The pain inhibitor wired into his brain clamped down on his nervous system and flooded his senses with digital arias of fortitude.

I will endure and abjure the xenos!

Then the ship quaked as the Hammerhead tank struck again, this time punching through to the vessel's innards. A chain reaction of detonations ripped through the galley and the observation deck pitched violently, rolling Exoss-UR01 to the level below amongst a heap of the dead.

<Alpha UR01: proceed to forward observation vector,> the magos commanded.

<Acknowledged,> Exoss-UR01 confirmed as he struggled to escape the mound of corpses. The damage to his spine had turned his titanium legs into dead weights and he couldn't find any leverage–

Someone grabbed his wrists and hauled, tearing him free in an explosion of agony that brought an involuntary gasp to his lips. His eyes misted with blood and smoke leaked from his nostrils as the pain inhibitor increased its current, doing irreversible damage to keep him conscious.

<FoRtHeOmNisSiah...> his rescuer gibbered in broken code. The hulking vanguard was a dead man walking, his chest plate a mangled tangle of blood and iron. Only faith had kept the warrior on his feet, but this final effort finished him and he toppled over as Exoss-UR01 crawled past. The deck was ablaze and strewn with smouldering corpses.

I am the last of Maniple Epsilon, Exoss-UR01 realised.

The crossfire from the cliffs had moved on to target the second ship in the convoy, but Maniple Delta would prove a more formidable opponent. Exoss-UR01 felt no shame at the admission; it was simply a statistical *fact* that Delta's tactical rating was 4.27 per cent superior to Epsilon's. Nor did he resent the fact that Epsilon had been sacrificed to draw out the enemy.

The least capable are the most expendable, he thought as he crawled towards the ragged crater in the ship's prow. All the forward sensors had been destroyed so he would become the convoy's eyes. Hoisting himself up, he saw the Hammerhead backing away, matching its speed to the galley's lethargic drift. He sensed hesitation in the hover tank: its pilot knew it had killed its prey, but was uncertain how to put it down.

'Skitarii machines are forged to endure,' Exoss-URo1 croaked, unaware that he had lapsed into fleshspeak, 'even in death.'

Like the skitarii themselves...

Something tugged his attention towards the prow gun emplacement. The Hammerhead's opening attack had annihilated the gunner and dislodged the massive weapon from its mount, but the lascannon was still intact. Wheezing blood, the Alpha heaved himself over to the weapon, though with only one arm he'd be unable to adjust its firing arc more than a fraction. Reason told him it was hopeless, but faith said otherwise. As he put his eye to its cracked scope he felt the gun's spirit brush against his own and understood.

You are cognis... awake and thirsty for vengeance.

The Hammerhead was almost in his sights. He nudged the weapon and it moved with a fluidity that should have been impossible, as if his touch were merely the spur to its will. Together they locked onto the tank's cracked engine nacelle. Exoss-URo1 saw water hissing from the Hammerhead's railgun as it prepared to fire again.

He fired first.

For Epsilon and the Omnissiah!

The tank's engine housing ruptured, tearing a jagged wedge out of its carapace and spinning it out of control. Gushing flames, it careened into the reef and its railgun tore a scar through the living coral. The weapon detonated in a nova of light that stripped away the vehicle's canopy and incinerated its crew.

<Heavy armour purged,> Exoss-URo1 reported.

There was a reverberating clang as something rammed into his ship's stern – the second galley, shoving its dead brother further along the channel.

Turning Maniple Epsilon's tomb into a shield, Exoss-URo1 realised as his mind flickered out.

The Alpha Primus pounded across the upper deck of her vessel, her blades slicing the air in tandem with her strides as her quicksilver mind computed parameters of velocity, thrust and inertial drag a thousand times a second, honing her charge with every step.

Omnissiah guide my stride, she prayed.

She leapt at the last possible moment, launching herself across the gulf towards the coral escarpment on the galley's starboard side. Her twin blades lashed out to embed themselves in the lip of the cliff, and she hauled herself up and over like a silver mantis. She was moving again in seconds, racing along the narrow crest of the reef that paralleled her convoy, leaving her own vessel behind and drawing level with Maniple Beta.

There were no enemies this far back. The tau had concentrated their ambush at the centre of the channel, where the invaders were at their least manoeuvrable, exactly as she had predicted. They were neither numerous nor well equipped so they would wield their forces like a scalpel, not a sword.

The war for Phaedra was a sham on the part of the Tau Empire, Magos Caul had told her. *The xenos committed few of their own warriors to its prosecution and those they did were deemed mediocre or troubled. There were no ethereals or talented commanders to lead them and only a handful of battlesuits, yet impoverished as those forces were, these survivors will be their inferiors in every way. That is why they were discarded after the war.*

It was a logical deduction, but the Primus was not convinced. Her master's equations had omitted one crucial factor: desperation.

The tau are survivors, she had demurred with frigid conviction. *Hardship will harden them.* She occasionally wondered what torments the xenos had visited upon her to grant her such insights. *Was I their prisoner, or was I a traitor?* The insidious thought filled her with rage. *Was I a gue'vesa?*

Moments later she spotted the first squad of fire warriors. They were crouched low in a coral caldera, sniping at the ship in measured bursts. One wore a crimson-streaked helm that contrasted starkly with his white armour, marking him as a leader.

Shas'ui... the Primus remembered. *They call them shas'ui.*

The aliens didn't register her presence until she was among them. She beheaded the first and second with symmetrical slashes of her power blades, then cleaved the arms from their shas'ui as he turned. He fell to his knees, flailing about with his bloody stumps as she stalked past. The remaining xenos attempted an orderly retreat, loosing snap shots as she followed, but their long rifles were unwieldy at close range and her conversion field devoured the few shots that found their mark. She lunged and impaled the nearest warrior, then sliced up through his chest and helmet, bisecting him as she tore her blade free. The next panicked and lost his footing on the slick coral. Flailing wildly, he crashed into the one behind and they both plummeted from the cliff.

The purgation had taken seconds.

<For the Omnissiah,> the Alpha Primus offered, ignoring the impotent curses of the mutilated shas'ui bleeding out behind her. Then she was moving again, seeking the next group of xenos.

Seeking retribution.

'We are the last,' Rho-IRo2 said, turning his back on the empty expanse of water where the last of the skitarii speeders had disappeared. One by one, the other pilots had miscalculated and their boats had been swallowed by the whirlpools surrounding the island. 'Squad Irridio alone endures.'

<Confirmed,> Ptoltec-IRo3 clicked. <Contact with Squad Astatine terminated seven point five seconds ago.>

<Mission proceeds,> Alpha Phaestus-IRo1 commanded.

Rho-IRo2 assessed the beach where Irridio had landed. It stretched towards

the tau enclave in an unbroken swath of sand and seaweed. In the distance
he saw a string of bulbous watchtowers threaded by a high, white wall. There
were no sentries visible, but that didn't preclude sensors.

'There is no cover,' he said.

'The xenos will not expect an attack from this quarter,' the Alpha replied.
'They will trust the tides to ward this side of the island.'

'This is dead land,' Ixtchul-IR04 declared.

<Dead land: definition?> Phaestus-IR01 queried.

'Dead land... eats the soul,' the squat ranger slurred, as if he didn't understand the intuition himself. 'Nothing grows here.'

It's an echo, Rho-IR02 realised. Most skitarii experienced such shadows
of their past lives, but for the most part they made no sense and were best
ignored. Ixtchul-IR04 had been forged from local Saathlaa stock and the
planet still exerted a nebulous grip on him.

<Data logged,> the Alpha said. <Tactically irrelevant. Mission proceeds.>

Since stealth wasn't an option the squad advanced at a march, spreading
out in a wide arc with their rifles raised. The sediment of bloated seaweed
popped beneath their tread, disturbing swarms of scuttling skrabs that
gnawed at their metal legs. The air was leaden, but flashes of lightning
threaded the sky, teasing out rumbles of thunder.

The xenos were careless to leave this beach unguarded, Rho-IR02 decided.
Despite the whirlpools it seemed unforgivably lax... and unlike them. His
memories of the long war were buried under deep strata of reprogramming,
but he hadn't forgotten how fiercely the tau could fight. *No, this is not...*

There was a clang of metal on metal as he stepped down on something
hard. He froze and looked down. His right foot rested upon the seaweed-
smeared dome of something buried under the sand. *A mine.* The others had
halted, waiting for the inevitable killing blast, but it didn't come.

'Remain still,' Phaestus-IR01 commanded. His omnispex flashed to blue
diagnostic mode as he scanned the ground. 'The detonator may have failed.'

The mine emitted a low hum and pressed up against Rho-IR02's foot –
almost as if it were trying to *rise.*

'Alpha...' the rigid warrior began, then stopped as he saw a clump of seaweed stirring over the squad leader's shoulder.

Not mines...

<Drones,> Ptoltec-IR03 signalled as he opened fire.

Rho-IR02 yelled a warning as a saucer burst from the ground in a cascade
of sand and skrabs behind the Alpha. Like the Drone they'd encountered
on the river it was small, roughly the size and shape of a tank gunner's circular hatch, but the dual carbines jutting from its undercarriage marked
it as a killer. The Alpha swung round as it fired and his back erupted in
a rash of burning exit wounds as the machine carved twin trails of ruin
through his chest.

<Alpha down,> Rho-IR02 reported as he opened fire. His bullet drilled
through the dying Alpha's throat, ending him with merciful swiftness, and
punched into the drone behind. The saucer's electronic babbling rose to a
high-pitched twitter as the invading servitor bullet subverted its power cells

and *twisted*. Arcs of electricity raced across its shell as it span about on its own axis, whirling faster and faster until it tore itself apart.

More drones were rising from the sand around the squad, their domes shrouded in seaweed and barnacled with coral. Their movements were sluggish as they tracked the intruders with erratic bursts of plasma, but their chatter was growing more confident by the second, as if they were taking bearings from one another to sharpen their focus. The rangers didn't give them the chance to fully awaken. Working in data-linked communion, they designated and eliminated targets with glacial precision, always prioritising the most alert machines.

<Vector 213: Terminate... Vector 119: Terminate... Unit IR03: Evade...>

A bolt of plasma seared past Ptoltec-IR03, setting his robe alight, but the ancient cyborg ignored it, holding fast to his assigned firing vector.

How long have they been buried here? Rho-IR02 wondered as the last of the hovering machines exploded. He stamped down on the one trapped beneath him then stepped back, letting it surge up and into the squad's crossfire. It exploded with a screech of tortured electronics.

<Hostiles purged,> Ptoltec-IR03 confirmed, casting off his burning robe. The armour beneath was blackened, but the ranger's noospheric aura was radiant with battle lust. <The Omnissiah will not be mocked.>

Rho-IR02 turned to the tau base, expecting an alarm to sound, but there was nothing. He squinted, searching for movement, but he didn't have the Alpha's advanced optics. *The Alpha...* He glanced at the ruin that had been Phaestus-IR01, feeling nothing except concern that the squad's efficiency had been compromised. Yet he lingered, uncertain why.

<Squad succession protocol initiated,> Ptoltec-IR03 said. <Rho-IR02: designation incremented to status Alpha/acting.>

The elder cyborg knelt beside Phaestus-IR01's corpse and unsheathed a serrated blade. With brutal efficiency he hacked their fallen leader's ocular omispex free. The squad didn't have the means to install the augmetic, but it would have been wasteful to discard such a precious artefact.

<Your command?> Ptoltec-IR03 said, handing the bloody omispex to his new Alpha.

<All squad designations incremented,> Alpha Rho-IR01 answered. <Mission proceeds.>

Four ships had survived the gauntlet of the reefs, though Delta's had paid heavily to break the blockade. Riding low in the water and venting flames, it limped alongside its fellow vessels as they landed on the shores of the tau stronghold.

The aliens had fortified this vulnerable stretch of the island well, assembling the walls of their base from solid geodesic blocks buttressed with soaring, saucer-like watchtowers. Fire warriors manned the towers, while scores of lightly armoured human auxiliaries lined the parapets. The walls converged upon a forward-slanted bastion that housed a spiral portal whose maw could accommodate a heavy battle tank.

The fortifications were of incalculable value on a world where coral was the most durable material, but they were intended for an army of thousands and not the meagre hundreds that remained. The place dated back to the first years of the war, when the tau had staked a serious claim upon the planet, but those days were long past.

A binaric fanfare howled from the Mechanicus ships as their landing ramps crashed down and disgorged the skitarii cohort. Platoons of armoured vanguard led the attack, advancing up the beach in rigid formations. The front ranks unleashed contaminated volleys of radium rounds, alternating their fire to maintain a steady fusillade against the defenders. Smaller squads of rangers followed behind, shielded by their comrades' numbers and heavier armour as they sniped at the watchtowers.

'By cog and code we spite the xenos,' Alpha Viharok-THo1 chanted in lingua technis, his mind ablaze with euphoric war routines.

<Purge the stain,> Squad Thorium responded in pious code.

'With iron and radium we smite the xenos.'

<Purge their strain.>

The enemy gate coiled open like a metal heart valve and a squadron of sleek hover tanks glided from the fortress. They wove across the dunes in graceful, crisscrossing arcs, churning the sand into swirling dust devils beneath them. These Devilfish were lighter than the Hammerhead that had assailed the convoy earlier, but their burst cannons were devastating against infantry. They cut an arc of ruin through the invaders, scorching away iron and flesh with indiscriminate ease, but the vanguard were remorseless in their advance. As one warrior fell another stepped forward to take his place and soon the divine blight of their radium weapons began to take a toll on the xenos tanks. One of the Devilfish slipped out of its evasive dance to drift aimlessly over the dunes. Another's movements grew sluggish and its fire dropped to sporadic, uncertain stutters.

They have been anointed, Viharok-THo1 thought, recognising the signs. While the tanks were impervious to the vanguard's standard rad carbines, every seventh warrior wielded an antique jezzail rifle that could pierce weakened armour. The structural damage they inflicted was negligible, but every shell was blessed with a killing aura that lingered. A single serendipitous bullet could excise an entire tank crew if it penetrated their cabin.

The xenos will die in ignorance, the Alpha reflected, *never knowing that the Omnissiah's radiance has touched them.*

On the far side of the island the only sounds were the staccato splatter of rain and the low hum of Brok-IRo4's lascutter.

<Perimeter wall attained,> Alpha Rho-IRo1 reported. <No hostile contacts.>

The other members of the infiltration team kept watch while Brok-IRo4 worked at the tau barrier, slicing out a man-sized portal. The wall was a threadbare assemblage of interlocking hexagonal plates that had loosened in many places, leaving gaps in its surface. Peering through the cracks, the rangers had spotted insulated cables running from the palisade towards the compound beyond, but there was no current running through them. Either the generators were down or they'd been rerouted.

The xenos were dying long before we arrived, Rho-IR01 guessed. *If we hadn't come they would have been gone within a year.*

Brok-IR04 prised out the wedge of metal he'd loosened and the squad slipped into the enemy compound.

'Take a look,' the Alpha ordered Ixtchul-IR03, indicating the nearest watchtower. He was the most agile amongst them, capable of a swiftness that belied his iron legs. He nodded and loped towards the watchtower.

<Xenos defensive quotient sub-optimal,> Ptoltec-IR02 said, scanning the deserted expanse of the inner walls.

'This wasn't meant for us,' Rho-IR01 said, watching as the Saathlaa ascended the watchtower's winding ramp. 'This barrier was intended to keep Phaedra out.'

But she was already inside, he sensed.

Up in the tower Ixtchul-IR03 sliced the air in a *negative* gesture. The hand signal was another echo of the warrior's past, but it communicated his message as clearly as code: he'd seen no enemies.

<Received. Return,> Rho-IR01 sent.

It was beginning to rain in earnest now, turning the coral sand to sludge. Behind the gathering storm clouds he spotted a hint of dancing colours. He'd noticed the aberration before, but only ever at night.

What is that? He found he couldn't avert his gaze from the nebulous chaos. There was something in there... something...

<Alpha?> Brok-IR04 asked.

Rho-IR01 realised the others were gathered around him, Ixtchul-IR03 included. When had the scout returned from the tower?

How long was I staring at the sky like a broken servitor? Rho-IR01 thought. His head was throbbing with the afterimage of prismatic shadows.

He went rigid as new mission data poured into his mind from the magos. The brief communion cleansed him of confusion and he cast the tainted clouds from his mind.

'A prisoner,' he said. 'Objective Skysight is a prisoner.'

The beachhead was secure and the cohort was drawing closer to the xenos fortress, leaving a trail of the dead and the dying in its wake. Wounded vanguard limped, staggered or crawled behind their intact brethren, driven by the magos's will until they expired. Scarlet-robed rangers stalked past them, sometimes crushing their fallen comrades underfoot as they sniped single-mindedly at the enemy.

<Converging on perimeter wall,> Alpha Viharok-TH01 reported. His gaze was locked on the sealed spiral gate ahead. <Breach imminent.>

Twin whorls of light lanced a pair of vanguard to his right, sundering them into ragged sludge. He traced the missiles' contrails back to their source and saw a hulking battlesuit standing on the roof of the gatehouse. Massive cannons jutted from each of its shoulders, dwarfing the moulded block of sensors that served as its head. Its white carapace was striped with red and a black snowflake adorned its breastplate, marking it as a leader.

<Broadside battlesuit,> the magos identified remotely. <Threat level: high. Priority target.>

Sniper-rounds streaked towards the battlesuit as entire squads of rangers switched their focus, but the xenos giant was sheathed in an energy shield that blunted their strikes. The few bullets that punched through shattered against its carapace, discharging in ephemeral threads of electricity. As if angered by the assault, the Broadside turned on the snipers. Its twin cannons flared with indigo light and gouged a smoking crater out of the ground where Squad Lithios had been a moment before.

<Jezzail troopers, focus fire,> Alpha Viharok-TH01 commanded.

Throughout the vanguard every seventh warrior turned his sacred jezzail rifle upon the battlesuit, adding its wrath to the galvanic volleys of the rangers. The Broadside's shield began to pulse erratically under the sustained fire.

<Purgation imminent,> a score of skitarii predicted concurrently.

With a scream of thrusters two more battlesuits soared up to the bastion's ramparts to flank their beleaguered comrade. They were similar to the Broadside, but subtly sleeker and more compact, exchanging massive cannons for more manoeuvrable wrist-mounted guns.

<Crisis suits,> the Alpha Primus said, identifying the tau reinforcements through Viharok-TH01's eyes. Her body stood rigid and secure in her ship while her mind shunted from warrior to warrior on the battlefield. <We must commit the ballistarii.>

<Negative. They are primary assets,> the magos replied.

<Cohort attrition status stands at sixty-one point seven per cent and rising,> she computed.

<Acceptable.>

<The battlesuits are a destabilising variable,> she pressed. <They must be negated without delay.>

Silence. The Primus understood her master's reluctance. She knew how precious – *how irreplaceable* – the ballistarii were on this forsaken world, but ultimately even they were expendable.

<Magos?>

The cohort snapped to a halt as a signal pulsed through the warriors.

<Ballistarii deployed,> the magos relayed. <Initiate Protocol Equites Priori.>

In austere harmony the skitarii widened their formations, opening pathways through their ranks. A monstrous pounding sounded behind them, growing louder by the second until it became a thunder of pistons and venting steam. Moments later a towering bipedal engine strode past Viharok-TH01, bathing him in an exhaust of incense and voltaic code-psalms. A Skitarius was hunched in the machine's high saddle, manning its las cannon while a bonded mono-servitor steered in obedience to the gunner's will. Four more Ironstriders matched its step, charging past the vanguard lines in unison.

'On iron we stride! ' Viharok-TH01 bellowed after them.

Alpha Vhaal-FE01's skull was filled with thunder as he rode into battle – the tireless clockwork thunder of his Ironstrider's hooves and the eager red thunder of his own heart. Unlike his fellow riders, the Alpha was permanently bonded to his mount, the scorched husk of his body woven into its frame like a princeps at the heart of a Titan. Only three memories of his former life lingered: first, he had been a rider, though of what and when, he was clueless. Second, his final ride had ended in fire and pain. And third... Third was just a number that he cherished without understanding: 214. Somehow that triptych of shadows had conspired to make him the finest ballistarii rider in the cohort.

His machine swerved aside as an explosion tore through the ground ahead. He glanced up and saw the Broadside battlesuit's smoking railguns tracking him, angling for a killing shot. It had recognised him as a primary threat. The realisation sent a thrill of satisfaction through his cortex.

Fire... Pain... 214...

Both Crisis suits ignited their jetpacks and leapt from the bastion, soaring towards the ballistarii like humanoid spacecraft.

<Focus fire: Broadside battlesuit,> Vhaal-FE01 directed his squad.

The five ballistarii struck in concord, assaulting the massive battlesuit with a cannonade of heavy laser fire. Despite their headlong charge their aim was faultless and the lasbolts pounded the Broadside in rapid succession. Its shield collapsed and its carapace ruptured, spewing fire. The vanguard roared their approval in raw fleshspeak as the burning giant toppled from the bastion.

Then the Crisis suits were upon the ballistarii. One dived across Gyrax-FE04's path, angling to strike him with its claw-hammer feet as it landed. Its weight crushed the skitarius into pulp and tipped his mount over. The fallen Ironstrider's legs continued to pump mindlessly against the sand, whirling the construct around in circles like a broken toy as the Crisis suit stomped past it.

The second battlesuit unleashed a torrent of flames from its weapon as it came down, scorching Akosh-FE03 into oxidised bones. Encased in the Ironstrider's lower recess, his mono-servitor pilot survived to enact a pre-set emergency protocol. Spinning the machine around it raced for the ships, trampling a pair of advancing vanguard in its haste.

Prioritising the Broadside had been costly but necessary, Alpha Vhaal-FE01 decided, as he circled the second battlesuit. He swung his lascannon round to target it while his mount loped just ahead of its flamethrower's blazing arc. As he duelled with the xenos a tenebrous thought surfaced from the sludge of his past: *I have been here before.*

He opened fire, punishing the heavier war machine with a slow, but steady stream of las-bursts, allowing his cannon time to cool between every shot. There was plenty of time. His enemy had no shields, so every hit – and they were all hits – bit deep into its carapace. The xenos should have retreated, but the Vhaal-FE01 had it hooked, tantalizing it by *almost* slipping into its arc of...

Fire.

He nodded unconsciously as he struck again, knowing this would be the killing shot.

Pain.

The Crisis suit buckled and erupted into flames.

214.

The infiltration team fanned out as they entered the compound's outer precincts, weaving parallel paths through a hovel of ragged plasteel shacks that appeared to be Imperial in origin.

This is where their human allies are penned, Rho-IRo1 guessed.

Looming beyond the shantytown he saw the bulbous towers and cupolas of the tau enclave. They rose above the squalor of the human district like heretical monoliths, glimmering with a pearlescent sheen that was utterly alien.

<Contact: 1 unit/battlesuit,> Ptoltec-IRo2 transmitted from somewhere up ahead.

<Hold position,> Rho-IRo1 replied, speeding his pace.

As he pressed deeper into the compound the plasteel shacks gave way to windowless geodesic spheres and bulging ovoid towers. Like the perimeter walls, the xenos structures were assembled from hexagonal plates of white alloy that seemed to shrug off rain and dirt, but even here the decay was apparent, revealing itself in missing tiles and collapsed walls. And then there was the mould... Ixtchul-IRo3 hadn't been entirely correct about nothing growing on the island, for the grey blight was rampant. It mottled the smooth facade of the buildings and congealed into fuzzy slime between the tessellated plates. A heavy antiseptic stench hung about the place and there were signs of constant cleaning, but Rho-IRo1 sensed the tau were losing this battle. The sounds of distant gunfire made him wonder how they were faring in their other, more pressing battle against the cohort.

He found Ptoltec-IRo2 near an enormous, sensor-studded dome. The elder cyborg was crouched behind a Hammerhead that appeared to have been abandoned in mid-repair. Acknowledging his comrade's click of caution, the Alpha peered round the tank and spied a tall battlesuit standing beside a recessed hatch in the dome. The warrior's armour was dented and discoloured, but the weapons attached to its arms were clearly intact and its sensor lenses glowed softly.

This place is valuable to them, Rho-IRo1 guessed. *Even with the cohort at their gates they left a guard. This is where the prisoners will be.*

<I have circled the structure,> Ptoltec-IRo2 said. <There are no alternate entry points.>

'We have to attack together,' the Alpha whispered.

<Tactical proposition: we strike from multiple positions to diffuse our footprint,> Ptoltec-IRo2 suggested.

'Agreed.' Rho-IRo1 scanned the area, trying to formulate a plan. His thoughts were still occluded by the shadows he'd glimpsed in the sky.

<I have determined the optimal strike vectors,> Ptoltec-IRo2 offered. <Permission to transmit, Alpha?>

'Granted.'

Rho-IRo1 circled round to the coordinates his comrade had assigned him and took cover behind a stack of containers to the battlesuit's right.

Ptoltec-IR02 remained by the tank, staying close to their target to compensate for his arc rifle's shorter range. First Ixtchul-IR03, then Brok-IR04 appeared, each ranger stalking silently to his designated position. The Alpha offered a silent prayer to the Omnissiah and lined up the battlesuit in his gun sights.

<Purge,> he signalled.

Squad Irridio opened fire as one.

They all aimed true, but only Ixtchul-IR03's bullet pierced the sentry's carapace, lodging deep inside its left-hand weapon. Though Ptoltec-IR02's arc rifle couldn't inflict any structural damage, its electricity wreaked havoc on the battlesuit's sensor array and shattered both its lenses. The blinded guardian reacted instantly, its weapons jerking up to spew streams of superheated plasma in wide arcs that incinerated everything in their path. The ferocity of its response caught Brok-IR04 by surprise and a plasma burst hit him square in the chest. He staggered back with a smouldering crater in his breastplate and tried to fire again, but the arc swept back and scorched away his head and shoulders.

The others reacted more swiftly, ducking as the searing enfilade lashed towards them. The hab-sphere concealing Ixtchul-IR03 was shredded, burying him under a heap of molten debris. An instant later the servitor bullet he'd planted inside the battlesuit's weapon triggered a critical overload. Both the weapon and the arm bearing it were consumed in a white-hot eruption that splashed the sentry's chest with plasma.

'For the Omnissiah!' Rho-IR01 yelled, targeting the bubbling patch of armour.

<Purge the unclean,> Ptoltec-IR02 acknowledged, bathing the battlesuit's chest in electricity. He ducked behind the Hammerhead as return fire chased after him, but the volley tore through the damaged tank and its engine exploded, throwing him across the compound with bone-shattering force.

<IR02: Inactive...> the elder ranger reported.

This abomination is destroying us, Rho-IR01 realised as his comrade's biometric readings flatlined.

<Initiate Doctrina Omniscentia,> the magos signalled.

Rho-IR01 screamed as a hallowed war routine ignited in his brain and spread like cognitive wildfire, rewiring and quickening his neural pathways. His world liquefied into nonsense then crystallised into a vista of sudden absolutes.

I am His wrath made manifest.

His next bullet pierced the battlesuit's carapace with almost molecular precision and drilled through to the pilot's skull. An instant later reality collapsed back in on itself and Rho-IR01's mind began to shut down.

...

<... RhO... ach... I... rHoacH... I... I...>

...

An arc of bright pain lanced through Rho-IR01, jolting him back from oblivion.

<Proceed to objective,> the magos commanded.

The ranger realised his titanium legs had kept him standing while he'd blanked out. The battlesuit he'd fought was also standing, but its arms hung limply at its sides.

It's dead, Rho-IRo1 decided. *As dead as Squad Irridio...*

He flicked through his fellow rangers' biometrics. Ixtchul-IRo3's still showed activity, but he was trapped under a pile of fused metal. The others were gone.

I am the last. Inexplicably Rho-IRo1's eyes wandered towards the siren sky. <Proceed to objective.>

<Confirmed.> Rho-IRo1 strode past the lifeless battlesuit and slammed his hand against the dome's hatch sensor. He shivered as his master's will passed through him to wrestle with the xenos door mechanism. It was a swift, unequal struggle and the hatch spiralled open. Murky blue light spilled from the space within, pulsing softly. Raising his rifle, the Alpha stepped inside.

The chamber beyond was vast, yet smaller than its outward appearance had suggested. Its inner walls were composed of some kind of variegated, gnarly stone, not the smooth metal Rho-IRo1 had expected.

Coral, he realised. *The tau built a dome around one of Phaedra's ruins. Why...?* The thought process terminated abruptly as his programming cut in. Questions were irrelevant to his function. Only facts mattered. He appraised the chamber with clinical efficiency. The aliens had transformed the ancient temple with their techno-heresies, threading the coral with flanged pipes and glowing conductor strips that connected panels of softly humming machinery. And bodies.

Rho-IRo1 paused, trying to make sense of what he saw. The upper walls of the temple were lined with corpses – row upon row of them, neatly stacked and held in place by cocoons of translucent fabric. They were all human. Somewhere in Rho-IRo1's mutilated mind a voice kindled by the sky-blight raged at the *horror* of this place, but he had lost the capacity to listen. Dismissing the bodies, he scanned the ground level. A cluster of bulbous power generators occupied the centre of the chamber. Insulated conduits extended from the machines to a circular platform suspended from the vault of the temple. Whatever was up there, it was devouring enormous quantities of power.

Up there... Under the sky...

<Proceed to objective,> the magos pressed. <Ascend.>

There was a metal ramp fixed to the walls. It spiralled upwards, offering access to the gallery of corpses. Rho-IRo1 climbed, his tread filling the chamber with clattering reverberations.

They're not dead, he realised as he reached the first body. It was a woman, emaciated but still breathing. Intravenous tubes coiled about her form, insinuating themselves into her nostrils, mouth and wrists, feeding her just enough nutrients to withhold death.

<Negative identification,> the magos said. <Proceed.>

Rho-IRo1 moved on to the next captive, a shaven-headed, tattooed apparition who might once have been a giant.

<Negative identification. Proceed.>

A copper-skinned man... <Negative...> A scarred Saathlaa native ... <Negative...>

So it went until he stopped in front of a man with the sunken, brittle features of a living corpse. Even by the standards of the sleepers he was hideously atrophied, his skin stretched to parchment across an oddly distended skull. A metal circlet was clamped around his head, widening at the front to cover his high forehead.

<Positive identification. Secure Objective Skysight.>

The sleeper's eyes opened as Rho-IRO1 cut him free. They were feverish. *Enraged.*

'Give it back!' the prisoner hissed, clawing at his rescuer with palsied hands. His feeding tubes tore free as he lunged forward, spattering them both with dark blood. 'It's all I have...' He shrieked as Rho-IRO1 hauled him from his cocoon, then a spasm rippled through his body and his eyes fluttered white. The skitarius caught him before he could fall.

<Objective Skysight secured,> Rho-IRO1 reported. As he threw the sleeper across his shoulders he noticed a snapped cable trailing from the back of the man's skull. The other end protruded from the coral wall.

The xenos have wired them all into the temple, he realised. *Into Phaedra...*

There was a whisper-thin sigh from above, like the last breath of a living body as it became a corpse. Rho-IRO1 glanced up at the shadowed platform in the vault of the temple. Everything terminated there: the conduits from the plasma generators... The web of skull cables... The truth of this profane xenos experiment...

<Secure priority asset,> the magos commanded.

Incapable of disobeying his master, the Alpha turned his back on the mystery. Like questions, answers were irrelevant.

As he descended his thoughts turned to the sky.

The battle for the gates was over. Alpha Vhaal-IRO1's Ironstrider stepped over the smoking wreckage of the last Crisis suit. Its pilot had fought with skill, claiming another of his squadron before it died, but the sheer weight of the skitarii numbers had compromised it, allowing Vhaal-IRO1 to make the killing shot.

214... and counting... he thought fleetingly.

There was a roar of triumph from the vanguard gathered outside the fortress as the gates finally relented to the magos's will and spiralled open. The warriors surged inside and Vhaal-IRO1 heard gunfire from within, but it was sporadic – merely the dregs of a defence. This battle was done, but the xenos had not died easily. Five hundred skitarii had set out from the Iron Diadem, but fewer than a hundred would return.

<Alpha FEO1: proceed,> the magos commanded. <Secure extraction point.>

Vhaal-IRO1 rode forward, following his brethren through the gatehouse and into the hexagonal, multi-tiered expanse of the fortress beyond. The vanguard filled the cavernous chamber with jagged battle hymns as they exchanged fire with scattered bands of defenders. Most of the surviving

enemy were human traitors. All were extraneous to the ballistarii's current mission.

Responding to the neural lash of Vhaal-IRo1's will, his servitor quickened
their mount and they loped across the tessellated hall, ignoring the desultory fire that came their way. The inner gates of the fortress fell to the Alpha's
third shot and they burst through to the compound beyond. As they raced
through the abstract geometry of the tau enclave, passing pale clusters of
spheres and domes, the Alpha spun about in his saddle, alert for hidden
enemies. He expected none, but the vile xenos structures unsettled him
despite the dictates of his programming.

Fire... Pain... 214... It was Vhaal-IRo1's personal mantra to the Omnissiah and he chanted it over and over as he forged deeper into the unclean
territory.

He found the lone ranger standing beside a vast dome. A scrawny figure
was slumped beside his metal legs, evidently unconscious.

<Objective Skysight located,> Vhaal-IRo1 reported.

<Confirmed: extraction shuttle in transit,> the magos replied. <Estimated
arrival quotient: seven point two five hours.>

The ranger didn't acknowledge Vhaal-IRo1's coded salute. He was staring
at the sky and his noospheric aura had dimmed to a somnolent smog. The
ballistarii rider followed the silent warrior's gaze and caught sight of something swirling behind the clouds. *Something...* He averted his eyes sharply.
Nothing. There was nothing there. Evidently the ranger had been damaged
during the final phase of his mission.

Vhaal-IRo1 switched to sentry mode and waited for reinforcements.

The shuttle swept over the dome precisely seven point two six hours
later. The same journey had taken the cohort almost two weeks by river,
but there had been no alternative, for the craft could carry no more than a
dozen troops. Most of the skitarii would be returning to the Iron Diadem
as they had come.

<Objective Skysight secured,> Alpha Vhaal-IRo1 reported as their fragile
prize was carried aboard the shuttle.

By the magos's decree the cohort did not linger on the island. There was
a storm coming and the skitarii were required back at the Iron Diadem.
In the haste of their departure the shadow haunted dome at the heart of
the xenos enclave was forgotten, along with the broken ranger who stood
beside it with his eyes fixed upon the sky. Long after his brothers were gone,
Rho-IRo1 was still looking.

And in time the sky looked back.

<Shuttle circling for descent,> the Alpha Primus reported.

<Confirmed,> Magos Caul said. <Deliver the asset to the Nexus Chamber.>
He returned his attention to the diagnostics of his re-engineered bastion,
hunting for errors in the adaptations he had made. Since the warp anomaly's first appearance in the sky he had laboured to restore the Iron Diadem
to its original, space faring configuration. Its dormant engines had been

purged, sanctified and ignited many times and its machine-spirit had been unchained from the rituals of the refinery. It was as eager to be gone from this world as its master.

'Together we possess the heart and the mind,' Caul cajoled the ancient ship. 'Now we only await the eye.'

I was a fool to let myself be blinded to the stars, he admitted.

Losing his Navigator had been a grave error. He had guarded her from the planet's perils fastidiously, but she had simply worn out with the passage of time. Distracted by his research, Caul had forgotten that mortals were so vulnerable. Without a Navigator his ship would have been lost in the immaterium, so he had been trapped on this world, biding his time until a replacement could be found. But once again his work had consumed him and the urgency of escape had faded until the coming warp storm forced his hand.

It is a sign from the Omnissiah, he decided. *A push. It is time that I returned to the Mechanicus.*

With renewed focus he had directed his intelligence network to scour the planet for a replacement Navigator. Countless Imperial and rogue factions had spiralled down to Phaedra during the long war. Perhaps one of the precious mutants could be found among their detritus? And with perfect, almost ironic concordance, he had found his prize in the enclave of his former associates, obliging him to expunge his shame in order to escape.

Yes, the Machine-God's iron hand was undoubtedly at work here.

The Alpha Primus escorted the prisoner alone, for only she and the Diadem's consecrated cyborg guardians had access to the magos's sanctuary.

They are a wretched breed, she thought, regarding the wizened creature limping ahead of her, *yet the Imperium would collapse without their gift.*

Her prisoner hadn't spoken, but she could read the fury coiled up inside his puny frame, though its focus was unclear.

'If you attempt harm upon the magos you will suffer,' she warned in sibilant fleshspeak. Despite his fragility she knew her charge was potentially lethal, for it was certain death to gaze upon the thing locked away behind his metal circlet.

The xenos were wise to bind this creature's void eye, she thought.

<Approach,> Caul commanded as they entered the nexus chamber. He floated above his data throne in his customary spider-lotus position, flanked by a pair of heavily armoured cyborgs that had more in common with tanks then men. Their arms were fused into massive cannons that tracked the newcomers restlessly as they approached. To the Magos's bodyguards even the Primus was a barely tolerable intruder. She appeased them with a coded psalm of identification and thrust her captive to his knees before her master's throne.

'I have a ship,' the magos informed the withered mutant without preamble. 'You will guide it through the immaterium.'

The prisoner was silent.

'Repeat: I have a ship and I require a Navigator.'

A harsh laugh burst from the Navigator's lips. A moment later the sound became a low, almost feral whine. And then he was giggling. It was a wild, hopeless sound that had nothing whatsoever to do with humour.

He is dead to fear, the Alpha Primus realised. *Dead to everything...* With a flash of blood-deep insight she sensed the truth of things: their prize was quite insane.

'They stole it,' the mutant snickered. 'The tau... they stole my eye... you see...' He trailed off uncertainly and his gaze slithered to the Primus, fixing her with sudden calculation. 'Can you get it back, do you think?'

With a howl of white noise the magos lashed out with his mechadendrites, snaring the creature and hauling him into the air to hang suspended above his data throne. His noospheric aura blazed and delicate arcs of electricity played about his form as centuries of self-control fractured.

'You lie,' he said. His flesh voice was the rasp of a desiccated corpse. A swarm of mechafilaments surged from his cowl and wrapped around the prisoner's skull, insinuating needle-sharp points into his flesh.

'I'm blind,' his captive said solemnly. Delicate rivulets of blood were leaking from his torn scalp, but he was as dead to pain as he was to fear.

'You lie,' the magos repeated, but under his denial the Primus sensed a gnawing *dread*.

'They said my eye was too dangerous,' snickered the prisoner. 'They said it had to go... for the Greater Good.'

<Unacceptable,> Caul chittered. <I will not be denied.> His mechafilaments tightened in reflexive rage and the prisoner's circlet snapped apart.

<I wilL nOtTtT...> The magos's words distorted into a jagged howl of null-code as he gazed upon the terrible truth the mutant had been hiding. His noospheric aura flared into a brief, bright nova then imploded in nothingness.

Silence.

<Magos?> the Primus asked. There was no answer. Her master and the Navigator in his embrace had become a frozen tableau. Then she saw the scrawny mutant's form begin to tremble. At first she thought it was pain that wracked him, then she realised it was mirth.

'I lied,' he said. And then he was laughing again.

FIRE & ICE

War is not a binary condition. Despite superficial appearances to the contrary it does not begin or end with a single discrete event. There may be catalysts and culminations, but their antecedents and consequences – cultural, material and even metaphysical – extend through times past and future like ripples in a river that flows two ways. Accordingly, the war between the Imperium and the Tau Empire did not begin and end with the Damocles Gulf Crusade. That conflict was the first great blossoming of our enmity and it will not be the last, but we have now entered a subtler phase of the game. Fifty years have passed since the crusade. Nothing has changed. Everything has changed.

Here on the margins of the Damocles Gulf we are embroiled in a cold war, an intricate game of deceit, manipulation and coercion waged against a master player. It is a delicate struggle, but never make the mistake of thinking it any less inimical to the Imperium than the voracious depredations of the tyranids or the bleak pogrom waged by the necrons, for the tau are playing for the hearts and minds of mankind. If they triumph our species may survive, but its destiny will not.

– Aion Escher, Grand Master of the Damocles Conclave,
Ordo Xenos

SMOKE

Watch for the smoke of discord if you seek to light the flames of revolution.

– The Calavera

Eighty-one days before Unity, Kliest

Kreeger found his patron in the scorched hilltop temple he'd taken to haunting since they'd gone to ground on Kliest four months ago. It was a broken place on a broken world and it suited Haniel Mordaine's mood exquisitely. Of late, the disgraced interrogator had immersed himself in sketching the crumbling statue of Sanguinius Ascendant that loomed over the pulpit like a petrified angel, its wings spread wide to encircle the lost celebrants. It was primitive work, roughly hewn from the local granite, yet its brooding gravity drew Mordaine back day after day. Crumpled parchment litt ered the ground in testament to his increasingly frenzied attempts to capture the Angel's essence, and he would sometimes cajole or harangue the effigy as if it were actively opposing his efforts. Kreeger took it all in his stride. Mordaine was a noble and Kreeger had watched over enough of his kind to know they were *all* crazy. It was probably something in their blue blood.

'The conclave has our scent again,' he called, marching up the nave without reverence or reserve. 'It's time to move on, duke.'

'Again?' Mordaine turned reluctantly from his work. His eyes were like bloodshot sores in the shadow of a handsome face. 'Are you certain?'

It was an empty question because Kreeger was never less than certain of anything, but it was part of the ritual that had carried them from one failing world to another along the borders of the Damocles Gulf, always one step ahead of the Inquisition and ten more from hope. Perhaps half those worlds, Kliest among them, had been found wanting in their loyalty to the Imperium prior to the crusade, but all were paying the price in murderously increased tithes. Most would be stripped to the bone and abandoned within a scant few centuries.

It sends a message, Grand Master Escher had decreed. *If your neighbour falls, you fall. Nothing stimulates loyalty like judiciously applied fear.*

'We need to be off-world tonight,' Kreeger said, brandishing a sheaf of greasy identity papers. 'I've wangled us passage on a Gulf freighter. No questions asked.'

'Another cargo hold?' Mordaine guessed sourly.

'Fish tank,' Kreeger corrected. Seeing his employer's expression he pressed on quickly. 'Relax, we won't be sharing, duke. They'll be filling up at the *other* end.' He shrugged. 'Can't promise it'll smell of incense and amasec, but...'

'It will reek of a billion dead fish.' Mordaine grimaced. 'I despise fish, Kreeger.'

'Lots of fish on Oblazt.' The old soldier shrugged. 'Fish, promethium and ice are about all they've got.'

'Oblazt?' The grimace became a frown. 'The world with the floating hives?'

'They call them anchor hives. Build 'em on platforms spiked deep into the ice so they *don't* float. The Imperium's been sucking promethium and fish out from under the ice since forever. There's a whole ocean buried down there.' As always, Kreeger had done his groundwork fastidiously. To his mind it was the trick to staying alive.

'I'm not finished here.' Mordaine gestured vaguely at the stone angel. 'Anyway, perhaps it's time to stop running.' But there was no sincerity in his voice.

'Oblazt is the subsector's breadbasket and promethium wellspring in one,' Kreeger pressed. 'The kind of world the tau would make a play for.'

Mordaine hesitated, raking a hand through his lank, grey-streaked hair. 'Do you have something?'

'I've got a contact.' Kreeger shrugged again. 'He calls himself the Calavera.'

Thirty days before Unity Above the dome, Vyshodd Anchor Hive, Oblazt

The roof of the world was a convex plain of dark rockcrete, blizzard-scoured and barren save for a scattering of blocky maintenance outposts and comms towers. A tracery of thermal capillary pipes shone dully beneath the surface, hissing and steaming as they dissolved the rapacious ice before it could take root. The resulting slurry flowed down the dome into the perimeter recycling trenches, then on into the hive's reservoirs. Much of it would be superheated and pumped back into the canopy, a greatcoat against the cold. It was a crude but efficient system that maintained the ambient temperature of the city a few notches above freezing, but decades of neglect had taken their toll. Scattered mounds of hard-packed ice glazed the dome like glistening cancers where the hydrothermal network had failed, yet the outposts were dark and no servitors or icebreaker teams laboured across the surface to purge the blight. Such was the way of things on Oblazt in the wake of the Damocles Gulf Crusade.

Two figures surveyed this entropy-in-motion from the shelter of an antenna-spiked relay tower. Both were swathed in heavy grey thermal robes, yet they were otherwise unalike. One would have towered over a tall man, yet his shorter companion was the stranger of the two, for there was a subtle aberration in the set of his shoulders and posture that suggested an altogether inhuman heritage.

'Their world ends, yet they do not see it,' the alien observed. It spoke Gothic with the chilly precision of one who has mastered the language like a weapon. 'This blindness is the *lor'serra* of your kind. The *shadow truth* of your nature.'

'They are not my kind, traveller,' replied the giant. 'We parted company millennia before *your* kind possessed the wit to dream of touching the stars.'

'Nevertheless you were forged from their bloodline, Iho'nen. Such bonds endure even after they are broken, like the ghost pains of a lost limb.'

'You speak of your own wound,' the giant called Iho'nen judged.

'My wound is my purpose,' said the traveller with glacial passion.

'As is mine.' But in Iho'nen's voice there was no passion at all.

For a time they were silent, brooding on private shadows.

Finally the traveller spoke: 'I walk the *vash'yatol*, Iho'nen. I cannot linger on this failing world. When do we begin?'

'I have activated the Catalyst,' the giant answered. 'He is already here.'

Twenty-nine days before Unity The Iron Jungle

The locals called the inner skin of Vyshodd's dome the Iron Jungle. Climbing through the gloomy industrial labyrinth bolted to the perimeter wall of Sector Nineteen, Haniel Mordaine felt it was an eminently fitting name. His path spiralled upwards, shadowing the dome in a tangle of catwalks and girders that heaved and groaned like an iron man bloated with corrosion. It was an arduous ascent, but he'd resisted the lure of the intermittent pneumatic lifts, preferring the certainty of a long, hard climb to the possibility of a short, infinitely harder fall.

If this architectural heresy kills me I'll never know the truth of things, he thought grimly. *I'll never know the truth of* him. *Angel's Blood, is this Calavera even a man?*

For almost two months Mordaine had been lying low in a decrepit traders' hostel waiting for word from their contact while Kreeger salved his anxieties with cheap Oblazti lodka and narcotic glitterfish oils.

'The Calavera is in deep,' his lieutenant had explained. 'It's the way he operates. How he sniffs out the rot.'

'You make him sound like a dog, Kreeger,' Mordaine had taunted.

'A bloodhound,' Kreeger had corrected, 'the best the grand master had – and the only player in the conclave who buys your story. He's all you've got, duke.'

'And I'm grateful for his friendship, of course–'

'Friendship?' Kreeger had shaken his head. 'No, duke, you're *useful* to him. I've told you before, he thinks you're the key to the real enemy.'

'But I don't know a damn thing!'

A shrug. 'Maybe you don't need to.'

And then Mordaine had tried the Question, as he'd done countless times before: '*What* is he, Kreeger?'

And as always, Kreeger had offered the same hollow answer: 'Never met him. Nobody ever did except the grand master. All the rest of us ever had was a name.'

A name I never knew, Mordaine thought bitterly. *I was your protégé, Escher – your damned interrogator – but you never trusted me with the identity of your finest operative. And if you concealed that then what else did you hide from me?*

'How did you find him?' Mordaine had tried.

'I didn't,' Kreeger had answered. 'He found us.'

'Yet the entire Damocles Conclave failed?'

'Maybe because he's been covering our trail.'

Watching over me as I scurry from one dismal backwater world to another like a frightened rat! Tugging my strings...

Mordaine snatched at a guardrail as his boot punched through a rust-riddled plate and sent fragments clattering into the abyss below. Frozen rigid, he waited until the shuddering walkway had steadied before gingerly sliding his foot free. Once again he cursed the Calavera for sending him on this lethal errand.

Word had finally come two days ago.

'He's found them,' Kreeger had relayed. 'The tau are here.'

'On Oblazt?' Mordaine had slurred through a lodka-soaked daze.

'In this hive,' Kreeger had said. 'Whatever's coming, it starts here. It's time to step up and take control, interrogator.'

'Interrogator...' Mordaine had been ashamed of the sudden, gut-wrenching terror that seized him. 'I'll be exposed... The conclave will come for me.'

'And they'll find a man who's done his duty.' Kreeger had actually grinned then, but it was all teeth and no eyes. 'This is where you make things right.'

'I need to meet the Calavera.'

'What you need is muscle. An army. This is what he wants you to do...'

And once again I'm dancing to the Calavera's tune, Mordaine thought miserably as he resumed his ascent. *And the worst, most damnable thing about it is he's right! An army is precisely what I need.*

Two levels further up, his army found him. The sentries surged from the shadows overhead, leaping between the swaying gantries with the wild yet graceful assurance of natural acrobats. Watching them descend, Mordaine understood why they'd made the dome's canopy their eyrie. Oblazt might not be their home world, but up in this vertiginous web they were its masters.

Save for the quirks of fate, these warriors might have been enemies of the Imperium, Mordaine thought. *Savagery runs dangerously deep in the blood of the Iwujii Sharks. After all, they've been bred for it.*

The military harvested its recruits young on Iwujii Secundus, Kreeger had explained, fast-tracking children into soldiers through a state-sanctioned programme of internecine wars that culled the weak and brutalised the strong. It was a barbarous tradition that predated the planet's assimilation into the Imperium, but one the Departmento Munitorum had been rather taken with, for the practice offered a steady stream of hardened troops for the Imperial Guard.

'The Iwujii Sharks aren't what you'd call well-adjusted regiments,' Kreeger had warned, 'but they live, breathe and bleed the Imperial Creed. You've just got to handle them right.'

Offering neither threat nor submission, Mordaine studied the men who encircled him. They were all slight of build, with burnished copper skin and ebony hair that hung about their shoulders in elaborately braided dreadlocks. Their features were striking, with high cheekbones and sharply canted green eyes. Most didn't look a year past twenty and all exuded an energy that seemed to rage against stillness. They wore tight-fitting fatigues of viridian striped with crimson slashes like open wounds and a haphazard array of leather armour. The majority sported vambraces and greaves, one a pair of shoulder pads wrought with splayed claws, another a breastplate carved into the likeness of a snarling tree. These warriors were evidently Iwujii first and Imperial Guard second. They weren't the kind of troops Mordaine would have chosen, but they were the only regiment stationed on Oblazt.

Regiment? One company, Mordaine calculated soberly. *Just three hundred men to seize the reins of a hive and expose a xenos conspiracy...*

'My lieutenant sent word to your commanding officers,' Mordaine declared, hesitating only a moment before committing himself: 'I am Inquisitor Aion Escher, Grand Master of the Damocles Conclave. By authority of the Holy Orders of the Inquisition I am hereby sequestering all Imperial forces stationed on this planet to assist me in the prosecution of the Emperor's justice.'

Keeping his movements slow and steady, Mordaine drew a heavy seal from his coat and brandished it like a defensive ward. *The grand master's seal* – the seal he'd stolen after watching his mentor die.

I didn't know, Escher, Mordaine swore. *I didn't know that girl was an assassin...*

He quashed the guilt, drawing strength from the awe in the troopers' eyes as they recognised the stylised 'I' emblazoned on the seal. For a few brief weeks his every word would carry the sanction of the Imperium's most feared authority.

I can do this, Escher, Mordaine promised, though he didn't know if it was an apology or a curse.

Towards Unity Above the dome

Veiled by the emptiness at the roof of the world, the outsider called Iho'nen watched as the Catalyst moved his design towards its apogee. The remote outpost he'd claimed and upgraded with xenos tech was awash with a fluid cacophony of information – tapped vox-communications and vid-feeds... economic and social statistics rendered as filigree neon algorithms and charts... a constantly updating parade of psych profiles... Iho'nen drank it all in like a giant data-devouring spider, assimilating, correlating and assessing a thousand facts every minute.

Days passed, yet he stood motionless, waiting as rigorously calculated probabilities crystallised into absolutes. Occasionally minor errors would manifest, prompting him to intervene through a reagent element, but this did not trouble him. It was the errors, or more precisely their correction, that kept him from becoming irrelevant.

His fellow outsider, the xenos, did not watch with him, for he was travelling.

Three days before Unity Hösok Plaza, Vyshodd Anchor Hive

The first steps had gone smoothly enough, Mordaine reflected. Both the Iwujii Sharks and the hive's ruling oligarchy had acceded to his authority, albeit sullenly in the case of the Koroleva nobles. With his force swelled by the hive's Ironspine Hussars, he'd launched himself into the hunt with the fervour of a man racing death, which of course he was. If he didn't uncover something tangible before the conclave caught up with him, he would be finished. His life was almost certainly forfeit regardless, but there was still honour to fight for, and, somewhat to his surprise, he'd accepted that might be enough.

But everything hinged on finding the tau.

The spoor of the xenos permeated Vyshodd like a spreading disease. He'd discovered fragments of strange machinery in the manufactories – sleek, geodesic blasphemies that shrugged off dirt and sang with unholy life. Then there'd been the rogue tech-priest who peddled enhanced trinkets guaranteed to run for a lifetime without power-ups or prayer. Most unsettling of all had been the abominable xenos sculptures adorning a Koroleva pleasure mansion. The brash minimalism of those abstracts had been an affront to decent Imperial aesthetics! Individually they were petty heresies, but together they pointed to a systemic infiltration that had been eroding Vyshodd for years, possibly decades. And then there was Unity.

Unity – a simple, beautiful and perfectly ruinous lie.

Rumour had it that a common fishery worker had formulated the creed in her rest periods, scrawling her ideas on scraps of packaging then spreading them by word of mouth. The doctrine espoused such deviant notions as the right to free speech and the wholesale redistribution of wealth, wrapping them up in a muddled entreaty to embrace some kind of galactic fraternity. It was puerile nonsense, yet it had spread among the ignorant and the oppressed like wildfire, as insidious as any Chaos cult. Mordaine didn't doubt its true origins so he'd focused on rooting out the leaders, but all he'd found were followers – hundreds of them – who insisted that Unity had *no leaders*. How could it, when it was 'the Many of One'!

And throughout this dismal farrago there had been no word from the Calavera.

'Silence is good,' Kreeger would assure him. 'Silence means you're on track.'

'Then where are the warp-damned xenos?' Mordaine had railed. 'I've got nothing the conclave won't find themselves!'

With the hive's detention facilities overflowing and the population growing restive, Mordaine had tightened the screws, first with punitive rationing and curfews, then finally a string of executions, but nobody had come forward with anything he could use. Instead... *this...*

How can so many be so blind? Mordaine despaired as he weighed up the crowd gathering in the square below. He was crouched on a rooftop over-looking Hösok Plaza, a sprawling, statue-studded court dedicated to Oblazt's Imperial liberators. The symbolism of the venue was not lost on him, but it was the sheer numbers that appalled him. There were *thousands* of them, mostly scruffy manufactory bondsmen and icebreakers, but also a smattering of municipal clerks and free traders. All had daubed their foreheads with the concentric blue circles of Unity. Despite its simplicity, there was something inherently alien about the symbol that repelled him.

'I speak for the Many who walk as One!' someone called from the square – a tall woman with the gaunt, febrile features of a tormented artist. The crowd fell silent at her voice, as if at a prearranged signal. 'We offer you the open hand of friendship. Stand with us against the bloated tyranny that has betrayed this world!'

Mordaine could almost taste the seductive xenos heresy lacing her rhetoric. Yet despite her words the woman in the plaza appeared neither ignorant nor oppressed. Oblazt's ruling class was a race apart from the commoners and she had the look. Mordaine was unsurprised, for the most zealous prophets of change often rose from the ruling strata. Sometimes it was guilt that drove their heresy, sometimes merely ennui, but the Inquisition had long understood the perils of privilege.

'Cast off the shackles of your dead god and bear witness to a living unity that embraces all as One!' the demagogue implored.

'The heretics spit in the face of Father Terra,' someone hissed beside Mordaine. *Armande Uzochi.* Since Mordaine's journey into the canopy, the young Iwujii captain had become his second shadow, devoting himself to 'the great inquisitor' with an awe that bordered on reverence. Unfortunately there was a rancid, tightly coiled violence about the man that made Mordaine's skin crawl. He suspected Uzochi was quite probably insane.

The right man to have by my side today...

'Give the order,' Mordaine said, feeling disconnected – *disconnecting himself* – as Uzochi voxed the platoon leaders. Ranks of Iwujii Sharks rose along the rooftops like vengeful spirits, silent and watchful. There was a clatter of booted feet below, and white-uniformed Ironspine Hussars appeared at every egress from the square, lining up in neat formations. The crowd backed away, congealing at the centre of the square as if density might offer some safety, but the rebel speaker held her ground.

'Truth cannot be silenced!' she proclaimed, spreading her arms wide, palms open. 'Every martyr you burn will forge two stronger heroes!' Her eyes glittered a radiant azure, ignited by the passion of her belief.

Why did you choose me for this filthy work, Escher? Mordaine asked, as he'd done so many times before, but never of the grand master himself. *You knew I didn't have the conviction to stomach it.*

Impossibly, the rebel seemed to be looking directly at him now.

'An inquisitor must armour his soul in ice,' Escher answered from the crumbling mortuary of Mordaine's faith. *'The ordinary mass of mankind is irrelevant, as are even the most exceptional individuals. It is the divine*

thread *of our species that the Inquisition safeguards. All else is either expendable or inimical.'*

No. Mordaine strangled the dry, dead voice in his head. *You're wrong, Escher. Otherwise what's the point to any of it?*

'Captain...' he began.

'Purge the heretics!' Uzochi bellowed, misinterpreting him. 'For Father Terra!'

No! Mordaine tried to scream, but he had no voice and a heartbeat later there was a surfeit of screams as his army opened fire.

Kreeger was waiting for him in the stairwell, smoking a lho-stick.

'Tell the Calavera I'm done,' Mordaine said, stepping past him.

'He's going to come in,' Kreeger called after him. 'He has a few loose ends to tie up first, but–'

'Too late,' Mordaine said flatly.

'Only a couple more days, duke.'

'It was too late from the start, Kreeger.' Mordaine turned, letting the rage well up in his chest like purifying fire. 'We've been played – you, me and most especially your precious Calavera! Vyshodd was a trap. This slaughter... We've given the xenos exactly what they needed. We've proven the Imperium is a monster.'

'Always was.' Kreeger shrugged. 'Just like all the rest.'

Mordaine faltered, his fury leeched away by the other's indifference. Perplexed, he studied his lieutenant's deeply seamed yet oddly bland face, trying to make sense of the man who'd been saving his skin for more years than he cared to count. Everything about Franz Kreeger was grey, from his gaunt complexion and the dusting of stubble on his scalp through to the barren alchemy of his soul.

His story was fairly typical of his breed: twenty years a storm trooper in the Guard, including a stint at the Cadian Gate, then secondment to an Inquisition taskforce to Phaedra, a world somewhere on the fringes of the Damocles Gulf, where he'd impressed the presiding inquisitor enough to win a place on his retinue. Later that inquisitor had become the grand master of the Damocles Conclave and later still he'd assigned Kreeger to support a promising new interrogator.

'Keep him by your side, Mordaine,' Escher had advised, *'and he will keep you alive.'*

This was certainly true. Without Kreeger, Mordaine would have stopped running long ago. Angel's Blood, he wouldn't have run at all.

'This hive... This entire planet...' Mordaine whispered. 'It's going to welcome the tau with open arms.'

'We're still in the game, duke,' Kreeger said. 'The Calavera has taken a prisoner.' Then he offered a name.

Mordaine stared at him. And then he dared to hope.

FIRE

Once their hearts are ignited they will burn until hope itself has turned to ash.

– The Calavera

Unity, Vyshodd Anchor Hive

Liberation day dawned with a chain of synchronised explosions that levelled the nine Ironspine bastions, annihilating thousands of the Koroleva's Hussars with surgical precision. Simultaneously insurrectionists rose up in the hive's key facilities, fielding strange weaponry that outranged the archaic lasguns of the authorities. As the uprising spread its numbers grew exponentially, swelled by tens of thousands who knew they had nothing left to lose. After the atrocity in Hösok Plaza, few Oblazti harboured any illusions about Imperial mercy. Whatever hope they had lay in Unity.

But there was no hope.

The architects of the insurrection had made one fatal error, failing to consider the fragility of the anchor hive itself. The concurrent blasts that destroyed the Hussar bastions sent a shockwave of seismic proportions rippling through the hive's foundations, shattering dozens of anchorspikes and placing the remainder under intolerable strain. With each passing hour more disintegrated, causing the hive to buck and heave like a ship in a storm, tearing entire blocks apart. Whatever the outcome of the rebellion, Vyshodd had been mortally wounded.

At the roof of the world, the outsiders' hideout shuddered in sympathy with the hive's death agonies, but neither occupant appeared concerned.

'You did not foresee this instability, Iho'nen,' the traveller observed.

'It is irrelevant,' his giant companion replied, shutting down the outpost's power. This gesture was also irrelevant, but the centuries had made him fastidious. 'The deviation falls within tolerable parameters.'

'Unless the canopy collapses beneath us,' the traveller suggested with a trace of dry humour. 'Nevertheless, it pleases me.'

'The devastation?'

'Your fallibility,' the traveller said seriously.

'Then I will endeavour to disappoint you in future.' Iho'nen threw the hatch open and gauged the shuddering dome. 'It would be prudent to proceed swiftly.'

The hive was drowning in a swirling storm of smoke and snow, its harsh panorama of tenements and manufactories faded to coarse abstractions by the smog. Here and there angry reds and oranges bloomed among the dark blocks, marking the virulent spread of the fire. The streets were flooded with a deluge of citizenry, the dispossessed and the destroyers melded together into an amalgam mob by the impartial flames. They wailed and raged as they moved through the burning hive like trapped grubs, fighting and fleeing by turns.

High above the chaos, crouched on a girder like a bird of ill omen, Ujurakh, who his people called Sourblood, watched their terror and rejoiced. Although his perch swayed dangerously he was untroubled, for his blood was alight with the catastrophe. He had not felt so alive since the Empty One first brought him to this miserable world of ice and iron, many blood seasons ago.

A stir of movement on a rooftop below caught his attention. Curious, he craned his long neck sinuously, but the source eluded him. Clicking low in his throat with irritation he slipped beneath his perch, clinging on with his talons as he hung upside down, straining to pierce the snow-smog. Then he had them – a dozen prey beasts creeping across the flat roof, striving for swiftness and secrecy, but making a mockery of both. Half were dragging unwieldy cases while the rest flittered protectively around them with guns, and a taller creature hurried them along with a sabre. Ujurakh hissed with surprise, recognising one of the elusive high breeds of the city. Unlike the squat, pallid commoners he had been forced to hunt, this creature was tawny-skinned, with an arrogant bearing that spoke of easy command. Usually the high breeds kept to their fortified palaces, shielded from the squalor, but the fire had finally flushed them out. He guessed this one hoped to make its escape across the rooftops, never imagining that its path would carry it into Ujurakh's hunting grounds.

What secret twists turn such proud enshrouded meat? Ujurakh wondered raptly. *And what shifting, gifted shapes nest locked within?*

He snapped his beak shut to catch the saliva pooling in his maw and considered: the Empty One had summoned him, but fate had cast this mystery in his path when the hunger was upon him. That he had gorged himself mere hours ago mattered not, for the hunger ebbed and flowed with the inconstant contours of the fleshweave. *What to do?*

Then the fugitives were directly below him and the time for doubt was past. Ujurakh drew his twin carving blades and hurled himself into the air with an ululating squawk of bliss. The prey beasts looked up, their flat, dull faces made duller by bewilderment, the surprise dissolving to terror as they glimpsed his lethal symmetry. A couple of the guards raised their rifles, but their movements were sluggish to Ujurakh's fervent eyes. He twisted in midair, hooting as he danced around the languid flurry of their first las-rounds, knowing the first would be the last.

As the ground swept up to meet him, Sourblood flipped over, angling himself to strike one of the guards with his extended talons. The attack tore straight through his victim, sundering the man and splattering his comrades with blood. Ujurakh's powerful legs bent to absorb the impact and launched him back into the air, pitching him over the heads of the panicked gaggle. As they turned with pitiful slowness he dived among them with a blade in each hand, a slashing, slicing predator among indolent cattle. They flailed about and screamed and died until only the highborn remained.

'Please...' the creature whimpered, throwing aside its sabre and falling to its knees. 'It's yours!' It waved at the fallen cases that had burst open, scattering glimmering trinkets across the roof. Such baubles might have tempted Ujurakh once, but he was Sourblood now and beyond simple wealth. He had saved the high breed till last to test its mettle and found nothing but a snivelling hatchling. 'There's more...'

Disappointed, Ujurakh beheaded the beast with a scissoring, twin-bladed swipe and plunged his beak into the foaming neck. Though its spirit had been weak, its flesh was delightfully free of the fish and fire oils that tainted the common herd. The Sourblood croaked deep in his throat and fed.

The wind was a constant companion outside the dome, yet Sergeant Thierry Chizoba could still hear the hive's death screams. Then again, maybe it was the wind itself that carried the screams so far. It was certainly malicious enough.

Oblazt. Even the name is bitter, he mused. *It is no world for the Iwujii.*

The sergeant flicked his lho-stick away and continued his patrol, keeping close to the walls of the maglev terminus where it was a fraction warmer. Like every building on Oblazt, the station was a monolithic slab of crumbling rockcrete, but behind its derelict façade it had been kept in pristine condition by an army of tech-priests and servitors. Their true charge was the vehicle within, a Chain Engine big enough to whisk away every aristo in the city if things got too hot. Chizoba had once walked the length of the titanic train, counting over two thousand strides as he marvelled at its wrought-iron hide and brass-girdled portholes. There were nineteen carriages in total, suspended well above head height on a splayed skirt that shielded its magnetic suspensors. Wheels weren't good enough for this monster! It would soar over the ice on a tide of blistering energy while the gargoyles perched along its crenellated heights glared their contempt at the land below. Chizoba could almost taste the patina of spite that enamelled the train. It was an *old* engine that had borne witness to myriad sins, both sweet and sour. Their unquiet residue ran through its cogs like phantom blood.

It is a proud and vicious beast, Chizoba had sensed with a shudder. *Dangerous.*

How the bluebloods had raged when Inquisitor Escher had seized their secret engine for his headquarters, but they weren't going to argue with three hundred Sharks!

Except we're less than half that now... Chizoba cast a baleful glance at the storage shed where the bodies of his comrades had been stashed like frozen meat. *We knew something was coming, yet Grandfather Death took us like un-blooded fools!*

He'd been on the dawn watch when the hive had broken out in a rash of explosions, as if hit by an orbital bombardment. Moments later the station concourse had been awash with the pneumatic rhythm of gunfire and Chizoba had dived for cover as a hulking abomination forged from metal and bloodless flesh stalked from the terminus, spitting bullets from the barrels fused to its arms. More of the living dead machines had emerged from the hangar, bearing down on the nearest Sharks like Grandfather Death's heralds. Over a hundred men had been lost before the last of the combat servitors went down. Doubtless the attack had been the work of the cog priests who tended the train. There was no telling how many of the machine-worshipping scum had turned traitor – or why – because they'd all vanished by the time the fighting was done.

Another tremor shook the ice and Chizoba eyed the dome of the hive warily. An hour ago there'd been a thunderous splintering and a fissure had split the canopy wide open, ejecting torrents of black smoke into the roiling sky.

How long can we wait for the captain? Chizoba mused. *We bled to hold on to that damned train. It owes us a ride out of here.*

His eyes wandered guiltily to Lieutenant Omazet. She was kneeling outside the warehouse, chanting the death rites for the fallen, as was her sacred duty. She was an officer, but her authority ran deeper than any mundane rank could convey for she was also La Mal Kalfu, a priestess who had dedicated herself to Father Terra in his darkest aspect as the Midnight Judge. Her kind were rare and revered among the Iwujii and the Third Company was graced by her presence, but the troops feared her more than any commissar.

She is a blessed curse, Chizoba thought. He was reluctant to disturb her, but with the inquisitor and the captain absent she held authority here. She turned as he approached, breaking off the ritual to freeze him with her terrible, eyeless gaze. He knew the black pits of Adeola Omazet's eye sockets were just a contrivance of lens-grafts and paint, but when combined with the skull tattooed across her face the effect was uncanny. Besides, his *spirit* knew the truth of her.

'You have a question, Thierry?' she asked softly. He shivered at the sound of his name on her lips. It was customary for La Mal Kalfu to address their charges by their first names, lending their words an intimate threat.

'Do you think they still live, lieutenant?' he croaked.

'I believe they do,' Omazet said. 'And we will stand vigil until they return.'

He bowed his head, knowing she'd seen through to his true question: *When can we flee this place?*

'Faith is best served blind, Thierry.' She returned to her sacrament, dismissing him. There would be no flight.

His eyes raw with smoke, the hem of his scarlet greatcoat smouldering, Mordaine staggered through the burning streets, struggling to keep up with his surviving troops. The trio of Sharks dodged or leapt the debris in their path without breaking stride while he stumbled around it, wheezing hard. He'd lost sight of Kreeger and Uzochi a few blocks back, when they'd got tangled up in a skirmish between some desperate Hussars and what seemed like a whole sea of rebels. After that their orderly retreat had become a frantic race for the terminus.

'Back up!' the lead Shark yelled. 'That whole block's coming down!'

There was a rending screech as the upper storey of the building ahead sheared away and came tumbling down, ricocheting between the neighbouring tenements like a colossal, infernal die. Mordaine skidded to a halt, flailing wildly for balance.

'Down!' someone snarled, shoving him to the ground as blazing fragments sizzled overhead, decapitating one of the troopers and almost tearing another in half. The third lost a leg at the thigh and whirled about like a one-legged dancer until another shard ripped a tunnel through his chest.

'Up!' Mordaine's saviour rose beside him, looking like a wiry scarecrow in black flak armour. *Kreeger.*

'I told you this was a bad idea, duke,' the veteran said.

Yes, you did, Mordaine admitted. His lieutenant had argued sternly against re-entering the hive, urging him to sit tight and wait for their ally, warning that the Calavera had *insisted* on it. That had been the tipping point for Mordaine and *he'd* insisted on leading an expedition into Vyshodd to assess the uprising. It had been irrational but, after the string of humiliations he'd endured in the Calavera's name, the need to defy his shadowy benefactor had been irresistible – and disastrous. They'd turned back as soon as they'd run into the first mob, but it had already cost them dearly.

It was necessary, Mordaine thought furiously. *I am nobody's fool.*

'We should get moving, duke,' Kreeger said, watching him quizzically.

'I thought you'd fallen, Kreeger,' Mordaine said, but it was a lie. He couldn't imagine this grey man dying. He gestured at the rubble-choked avenue they'd been following. 'Is there another way to the terminus?'

'This is a hive.' Kreeger shrugged. 'There's always another way.'

Sourblood... The Empty One's call stirred inside Ujurakh's skull, a brittle but insistent whisper like the echo of something unforgettable forgotten. Lost in the rapture of his feeding he tried to ignore it, but the whisper became a whine, threatening the bright, obliterating pain that bound him to his master. Once he had mocked pain, as all great warriors did, but that was before he'd learnt what pain truly was. That did not lessen the rage and shame he felt at his bondage, though he doubted any of his blood kindred would have endured the torment any better. *Blood kindred?* He had none. They had named him Sourblood and cast him out!

Ujurakh realised his feast had grown quiet. The summons had numbed his palate to the delicate riddle of the flesh. Furious, he surged to his feet, letting the silent meat slip from his beak. Once again the Empty One had stolen his joy. With a squawk of disgust, he sheathed his blades in their leather harness and sprang into motion, sprinting for the parapet. He leapt at the last moment, soaring over the gulf to crash down onto the adjacent rooftop. Without pause he hurtled on, skittering over the frozen skin of the burning city, chasing the beacon that chained him.

'Sergeant,' a trooper called. 'You need to take a look at this.'

Keeping low, Thierry Chizoba crept over to the squad crouched by the gates of the terminus. They'd reinforced the position with the company's precious heavy bolter to cover the icebound expanse between their sanctuary and the great dome.

Chizoba squinted, trying to make out the figures approaching through the fluttering weave of snow. There were two of them, both clad in grey robes, their faces hidden in arched cowls. They were walking at a measured pace, seemingly untroubled by the soldiers watching them. One seemed impossibly tall, yet it was the other one that troubled him most deeply. There was something wrong with its gait, a subtle hop, almost as if its joints were deformed. Or built differently to those of a man...

There will be someone else coming,' the inquisitor had warned before he left. *'You'll know them when you see them.'*

'Go get the lieutenant,' Chizoba ordered, unsure why he was whispering.

Keeping low, Kreeger peered round the junction ahead. They'd almost reached the outer wall of the dome when a babble of voices had slowed them to a crawl and they'd found a throng of Oblazti gathered in the next street. Perhaps a desperate Koroleva captive had led the mob here or perhaps it had been blind chance.

'How many?' Mordaine whispered, already certain the answer was *too many.*

'It doesn't matter,' the veteran said. 'We're out of time. We have to go through them.'

'Kreeger...' Mordaine began uneasily.

'Surprise and shock,' his lieutenant interrupted. 'We hit them hard and push through to the terminus. Don't stop for anything.' He unclipped a strangely fluted grenade from his bandolier. 'When the numbers are against you...'

His words were drowned by a clamour of gunfire and shouts from the street behind them. Mordaine spun and saw a ragged band of Sharks charging towards them with Armande Uzochi at their head and what looked like half the hive on their tail. The Iwujii captain was laughing wildly as he snapped off shots at his pursuers.

'I guess we're done with surprise,' Kreeger muttered, twisting the casing of his grenade. 'Shock'll have to carry it.'

He hurled the explosive into the adjacent street and ducked back. There was a bright flare and a *whoosh* of heat and then he was moving again. 'Go!' Bolt pistol in one hand, shock maul in the other, he leapt round the corner before the concussion had faded. Mordaine drew his pistol and followed.

'Tears of Sanguinius...' He stopped in his tracks, appalled by the carnage in the next street. The grenade's blast had sounded insignificant beside the cataclysm tearing the hive apart, but it had exacted a terrible toll in the close-packed avenue. Through a haze of dust he saw bodies everywhere, charred and smoking. Those who could still stand were staggering about blindly, clutching at faces that had been scorched to the bone.

'Quit dreaming, duke!' Kreeger yelled from somewhere up ahead.

As the dust settled Mordaine saw the blast had only broken half the mob. Further along the street at least thirty still stood and Kreeger was already among them, swinging his maul like a madman. The survivors were sluggish with shock and armed with makeshift weapons, but their numbers would be telling once they rallied. All sported the concentric circles of Unity on their foreheads, marking them as wilful traitors rather than hapless folk caught up in the chaos. Suddenly that austere icon seemed to symbolise so much – lies within lies, encircling and constricting Mordaine's own fate into an unbroken and unbreakable spiral fall...

If I die here the Imperium will remember me *as a traitor,* he realised, *if it remembers me at all.* He wasn't sure which possibility troubled him more.

Filled with bleak rage, he set his antique laspistol to rapid fire and charged the mob. He was no marksman, but skill mattered little against such numbers, especially when a man was wielding an Argent Repeater. Kreeger had often mocked the baroque weapon as a vanity piece, but it was vindicating Mordaine's faith now.

Only the thread matters, Escher's words spun through Mordaine's head, over and over, like a mantra of exoneration for the lives he was ending. *Only the thread...*

Smoke billowed abruptly from his pistol's casing. As Mordaine fumbled with the setting a hulking rebel swung at him with a masonry-tipped pole. He flung himself backwards and the block whipped past his face with an inch to spare, then came arcing back like a pendulum. This time it whirled over his head as he slipped and crashed onto his back, mercifully holding on to the Repeater. As his attacker loomed over him he levelled the pistol with both hands and fired. The weapon whined and died. The rebel grinned as a bolt-round tore through his skull from behind.

'I told you to keep moving, duke!' Kreeger yelled, offering his hand. 'We–'

A spike erupted from his throat, spattering Mordaine with blood. Kreeger's eyes rolled down to peer at the tine jutting from his neck, then swivelled back to Mordaine like painted glass orbs. There was no fear in them, not even shock or pain, just a profound ambivalence. Stunned, Mordaine saw Kreeger try for a shrug. Then the spike was yanked free and the grey man toppled into oblivion.

Were you always dead inside? Mordaine wondered numbly. *Or did something make you that way?*

Mordaine rolled aside as Kreeger's killer, a one-eyed fishery worker, jabbed at him with the blood-slick harpoon. Desperately the interrogator feinted a roll, grabbed the spike and thrust back on it. Taken by surprise, his foe skidded over, losing his grip on the weapon. Screaming holy obscenities like a possessed man, Mordaine swung the harpoon about by its spike, striving to keep the traitors at bay.

With an ululating war cry Armande Uzochi leapt past him, whirling his heavy-bladed machete like a crazed dancer. A handful of Sharks followed, one stopping to haul Mordaine up as he passed. The interrogator glanced round and saw the pursuing horde was almost upon them. There was a mania driving that sea of wild, broken faces that had nothing to do with the ideals of Unity.

The tau will never understand us, Escher had once observed. *They cannot because they lack our infinite capacity for insanity.*

'Inquisitor!' Uzochi snapped. 'We must go!' The captain was radiant with violence, his sharpened teeth stained with blood.

At least Kreeger never enjoyed the killing, Mordaine thought vaguely.

Ujurakh vaulted over the wall of the station compound and flattened himself in the snow, listening for sentries. He could hear the prey beasts jabbering in the distance, but none were close. Predictably they had all flocked to the main gate, drawn only to the obvious threat.

Such blunt unthinking eyes with which they see with and seem to be like, the Sourblood mocked. *Their thoughts are as flat and feeble as their faces!*

After leaving the hive he'd set out across the ice and circled back, approaching his destination from behind, as the Empty One had instructed. For once he'd been grateful for his master's call, for without it he would have been swallowed by the white nothingness. Keeping low, he crept towards the building ahead, seeking the great engine his master had described.

Thierry Chizoba steeled himself as he returned to the gates where the robed giant waited, looming over the Sharks like a harbinger from the old tales. The stranger's face was shrouded inside his cowl, but he was obviously watching the road to the hive, indifferent to the shadow he cast. Only Lieutenant Omazet seemed unaffected, but then she was a shadow creature herself.

'I have secured the prisoner,' Chizoba reported, 'and Ironfingers has awakened the engine's machine-spirit.'

'They are coming,' the grey giant said. His voice resonated with a sibilant metallic harmony, doubtless due to a helmet of some kind, yet it was surprisingly soft. Not at all the kind of voice Chizoba would have expected from a Space Marine, for surely the stranger could not be anything else.

'I see nothing,' Omazet said.

'My eye sees truer than either of yours,' the giant answered.

Mordaine hurtled round another corner and suddenly he was past the canopy and racing straight into the biting teeth of the blizzard. He could see the dark smudge of the terminus ahead, just a few hundred metres away. Uzochi was still at his side, but the other Sharks were gone, devoured by the gestalt beast at their back.

It will follow us out onto the ice, Mordaine sensed, *and on into perdition.*

He heard Uzochi yell the watchword as the station's defenders came into sight. They were just vague sketches in the white maelstrom, and poor ones at that, for one of them seemed unfeasibly tall. As Mordaine tried to make sense of that deviant figure the rest opened fire. Las-bolts and solid rounds hissed past him, leaving steaming contrails in the flurry. He glanced round and saw the front ranks of the mob fall, but the rest surged on regardless – numberless – uncoiling from the hive like a serpent.

Even if we reach the train, the Dragon of Vyshodd will overtake us...

And then a small sun detonated behind him, washing the swarm with flames and beheading the serpent. The shockwave hurled Mordaine forwards and smashed him into the ice with a bone-crushing force then sent him tumbling towards darkness.

His back was on fire! Frantically he rolled over, screaming as his shattered ribs protested. Gasping breaths of jagged glass, he spat blood onto the ice. Blearily he saw Uzochi stagger past. The captain was howling with pain as he fought to cast off his blazing coat. Then Mordaine heard other, angrier howls as a pack of survivors lurched out of the smoke. Their flesh was blackened, but the murder in their eyes was undimmed.

You were right, Escher, Mordaine thought. *When we fall, we fall hard.*

An explosive mechanical roaring erupted over the wind and the damned were torn asunder. Dazed, Mordaine turned his head and saw a robed giant striding towards him. It was wielding the Sharks' heavy bolter as a mortal man would wield a rifle. The warrior spun about at the waist, scything down the traitors with blunt efficiency. Uzochi crashed down beside the reaper and caught sight of its hooded face.

'Grandfather Death comes for us!' he cried. Mordaine couldn't tell if it was terror or rapture that moved the captain, but in that scream he heard the last thread of the captain's frayed sanity snap.

Then the stranger was standing over Mordaine and he understood that Uzochi was right, for it *was* death incarnate. The wind had whipped away its cowl, revealing a stylised bronze skull whose eye sockets were melded into a single dark aperture. A crystal orb burned in the recess, embedded just above the bridge of its nasal cavity, lending the harbinger a cyclopean aspect.

'Calavera,' Mordaine whispered, knowing it must be so.

ASH

After the inferno has devoured itself, fall to your knees and scour the ashes, for that is where you will find Truth.

– The Calavera

Seven hours after Unity, Under the shadow

The broken man opens his eyes as he is carried into the hanger. He is almost overcome by terror when he sees the train squatting on the maglev track, for it looks like a titanic serpent – and wasn't a serpent hunting him just moments ago? But then he remembers that the vengeful serpent was made of flesh while this one shines bright silver. He even remembers that such serpents are called Chain Engines because they link the anchor hives of Oblazt. And then he also remembers that he cannot breathe and the terror returns twofold as he begins to choke on his own blood.

'Will he live?' a woman with the face of a skull asks as he slips away...

He joins Grand Master Escher in the brig of the *Enshrouded Eye*, the flagship of the Damocles Conclave. His mentor has brought him to see a tau prisoner captured at the tail end of the crusade. It is a tall, almost skeletally thin being that Escher calls an *ethereal*, one of the tau ruling caste. The creature regards him through the glass walls of its holding cell, assessing him as if he were the prisoner and it the captor. Its stillness runs blood deep, giving it the appearance of a surreal statue, a distended parody of a man forged to embody absolute serenity. Or superiority.

'Tell me, interrogator, what do you see?' Escher asks from the shadows. The question paralyses the broken man for he is both repelled and fascinated by the xenos prisoner. He understands that this is a test because *everything* Escher asks of him is a test, but even after years of service he has no idea what the ageless ancient wants of him. Perhaps it is Escher's blindness that makes him so impossible to read.

'Yes, what do you see, *gue'la?*' the ethereal echoes, its voice penetrating the glass with shocking clarity. Is it mocking him?

'I...' Pinned between the scrutiny of two inscrutable beings, the broken man hesitates. 'I see the unclean,' he says. 'I see a xenos monstrosity.' Though his answer is not false he knows it is inadequate and so it chokes him and there is...

Pain beyond endurance! He opens his eyes and sees that Death has sliced him open and is rummaging about inside his chest, searching for truth.

'You are killing him,' protests the skull-faced woman, but he cannot tell if there is concern in her rebuke.

'A rib has punctured his lungs, lieutenant,' whispers Death, whose face, naturally, is also a skull. 'He will drown in his own blood if I do not work it free.'

Another shadow lingers behind them both, little more than the transient impression of a dark man whose pale face is a geometric confluence of incandescent scars. He regards the patient with something that might be pity or contempt or perhaps nothing at all. One of his eyes burns with fever, the other, a corroded augmetic, with unholy fire.

'It's a lie,' the stranger tells him wordlessly.

Then something snaps inside the broken man's chest and he screams and the wraith is gone, banished to a deeper darkness where a daemon bell tolls.

Death looks up and appraises the broken man with a single eye of liquid glass. 'Pain is an illusion, Haniel Mordaine,' he says.

My name? Death knows my true name, Mordaine despairs as he falls into a memory of bright azure eyes and...

The hauntingly beautiful woman he has just introduced to Inquisitor Aion Escher blossoms with blades and strikes him down, unravelling his mentor into a meaningless spiral of blood and bone. She has murdered the grand master before Mordaine has even finished introducing her as his new data specialist. Then she turns to him with a smile like silver slaughter, but Kreeger puts her down with a bolt round before she can take a step.

'She was an assassin,' Mordaine says flatly. 'I brought an assassin aboard the *Enshrouded Eye.*'

'We have to go, duke,' Kreeger replies as he searches Escher's body.

'Go...?'

'Fast and far from here.' The mercenary nods in satisfaction as he finds the inquisitor's seal. 'These are gene-coded, but it won't hurt to have it.'

'I don't understand.'

'Like you said, you brought an assassin on board the grand master's ship,' Kreeger explains as if he is talking to a child. 'In the Inquisition's eyes that's going to make you a traitor or a fool.' Somewhere an alarm begins to wail. 'So, do you want to live?'

I can't die, Mordaine gasps at Death, even though he knows mercy is a mystery to such a being.

'No,' whispers the one-eyed harbinger. 'That would be wasteful.'

FROST

Truth is cold, yet it burns brighter than any delirium. Be wary, for it is the most pernicious of all vices.

– The Calavera

One day after Unity, The Ghostlands

The maglev train swooped through the white nothingness of the wilderness like a ghost engine haunting a phantom world, invisibly harnessed to the single track embossed into the ice. Despite its speed it moved in almost total silence, only the low-frequency hum of its propulsion drive and the soft crackle of magnetically charged particles exposing it as a contrivance of the material world. Flickering indigo fire played about the ribbed skirts of its undercarriage, illuminating the narrow gap between its grooved suspensor plates and the track. Few folk on Oblazt understood the technomancy that kept the train suspended an inch above the rail and none possessed the skill to repair it. It was old tech, dating back to the first colonisation of the planet.

Such things did not concern the Sourblood. It was the thrill of speed that had lured him out onto the hide of the machine. He crouched atop the rear carriage like a penitent gargoyle, his talons gripping the gabled hull and his arms thrown wide to embrace the screaming wind, exhorting it to scour away the filth of the hive.

The blood of the flat-faces runs thin, he rejoiced, *but their machine runs with fire in its belly!*

Ujurakh had already explored the length and breadth of the vehicle, travelling via the roof to evade the flat-faces as he mapped its narrow territories. There were nineteen carriages in total, trailing behind the sheared wedge of the drive cabin like a string of carved boxes. Each was linked to the next by a cantilevered platform that twisted and turned with the contortions of the track. The flat-faces would never linger at these exposed intersections and none had ventured onto the roof. They were not fools, Ujurakh had decided, but they were overly fearful of the cold. He would use that against them when the time came. And it could not come soon enough...

Twice already he'd almost surrendered to the urge to snatch a lone straggler as it passed between the carriages. Would they miss one flat-face among so many? But he already knew the answer that really mattered: his master would notice.

Wait, the Empty One had commanded, stamping the edict into Ujura-kh's skull with the promise of pain. *Wait.*

Two days after Unity

Slumped in a chair beside his cabin window, Haniel Mordaine stared gloomily at the frozen tundra of the Ghostlands. It was impossible to gauge the Chain Engine's velocity against that featureless limbo. He might as well be watching an endlessly looping vid-feed, yet despite the monotony he knew the train was devouring the distance to Yakov all too quickly. Yakov Hive, where the spaceport lay. Where the conclave would be waiting for him.

I'm not ready. I need more time.

'Two days,' he whispered. 'I lost almost two days.' He hadn't mustered the courage to examine his bandaged chest yet. The pain told him all he wanted to know.

'Your wound was most grievous, inquisitor,' Lieutenant Omazet said, hovering behind him like a sullen spectre. 'Without Captain Calavera's talents you would be a dead man.'

'*Captain* Calavera?' Despite his discomfort, the appellation amused Mordaine. Although it was by no means an unlikely title for a Space Marine, it didn't ring true for his tenebrous patron. It was too honest.

'I did not know your contact was an Astartes,' Omazet said. Was there a hint of accusation in her voice?

'An *Adeptus* Astartes,' Mordaine corrected. Abuses of High Gothic had always irked him. 'You didn't know because I chose not to tell you, lieutenant.' *And because I didn't know either, damn him!* 'How is Captain Uzochi doing?'

'He keeps to his cabin, chastising himself with shadows and solitude,' she said. 'An Iwujii officer bears a scar on his soul for every Shark he loses.' She paused, pointedly. *Reprovingly?* 'We lost many Sharks at Vyshodd, inquisitor.'

'Give me numbers, please,' he said, avoiding her gaze.

'All told, the Third Company now fields just eighty-two Sharks.'

They both knew what the numbers meant: the Third was no longer viable. If the survivors ever returned to their regiment they would be reassigned to other companies. For the Third it was the end, for its captain something more shameful.

'I regret your losses,' Mordaine said quietly. *Particularly the ones who died to satisfy my pride...* 'They were fine soldiers.' She said nothing and he pressed on swiftly. 'And this?' He said, indicating the comms report.

'Captain Calavera asked me to pass it on to you,' Omazet said. 'He communicated with the telepathica temple at Yakov privately.'

'I see. Well, I believe it's time I had words with the good captain.' Mordaine's ribs ground in protest as he rose from his chair. He grimaced as his head spun and Omazet's face divided into a pair of grinning skulls.

'Are you strong enough to walk, inquisitor?' the skulls asked. Coming from them, it sounded like an allegation.

'The Emperor's work... won't... wait on our pleasure,' he wheezed, fighting down the nausea. 'Duty is strength.' He picked up the laspistol she'd brought him. It was a poor replacement for his Argent Repeater, but needs must.

'Haniel,' she called as he turned to go.

'Yes, lieutenant,' he said.

Haniel? He froze. *How does she know my name? Damn those infernal lenses she wears! How can you read someone when you can't see their eyes?*

'Haniel Mordaine,' she murmured. 'That is what Captain Calavera called you when you lay at Grandfather Death's threshold.'

'A man in my position acquires many names,' he said dismissively. 'Surely this doesn't surprise you?'

She inclined her head. 'As you say, inquisitor.'

'Then don't presume to question me again.' As he stalked from the room he heard her tasting his name on her tongue, testing it for truth.

The Sourblood lay prone, wedged into a ventilation shaft above a softly lit chamber that occupied an entire carriage near the front of the train. His elongated head was pressed against a grille in the ceiling, twisted sideways so he could observe the space below with one baleful eye. It was a brazen hall, hung with obscene depictions of flat-face mating rituals and clotted with silk carpets and plump-cushioned chairs that begged to be shredded. It sang to him of cheap vanity and shallow hungers, conjuring up the grovelling lordling he'd gorged upon in the hive.

What thin, insignificant rhythms they entwine about themselves and think for a wonder, he sneered. *The fleeting feeder dreams of grubs!*

Intriguingly the throng of flat-faces gathered below appeared to agree, for they were treating the shameless carriage with open contempt, spitting and spilling their food with abandon as they feasted and caroused. Their leader, a short but powerfully muscled brute with a missing ear who the others called *Chee-zoba*, had named the place their 'mess hall' and his kindred had laughed and striven to make it so. Ujurakh had taken an instant liking to *Chee-zoba*. For a flat-face he had spirit and wit. When the time came he would make for good eating. Indeed, all the kine in this herd had a *vitality* that suggested they were not native to this flavourless waste world.

Unbidden, the hunger unwound itself in the hollows of his gut, urging him to tear aside the metal veil he lurked behind – *to tear it aside and tear into them!* A thick rope of drool slipped from his maw and splattered the shoulder pad of the flat-face directly under him. Ujurakh tensed, but neither the creature nor its comrades noticed the blunder. Furiously, he fought against the hunger, loath to abandon his spying. Curiosity was in his nature, as it should be for all his kind, for how else could a Shaper tease out the secret threads of the fleshweave and steer his people down a potent path? Already too many bloodlines had been doomed to stagnation by the apathy of timid Shapers. No, such as he could never be *too* curious, no matter what his kindred might say.

Never too curious, but perhaps incautious, he admitted.

The Empty One had commanded that he remain in hiding, and his master had a way of picking out every little transgression. No, these creatures' antics were not worth the price of his displeasure. Reluctantly Ujurakh slithered away.

'You are filthy, Akoto!' Sergeant Thierry Chizoba snapped. Startled, the trooper who'd invited his reprimand looked up from his cards and reached for the shoulder Chizoba was pointing at. He grimaced as his fingers found the slime coating his armour. His comrades sniggered and one of them called to a skinny figure perched by a window: 'Hey, you sneeze on Akoto again, Rémi?'

The accused trooper looked round, wiping guiltily at his wet nose. 'Not me,' he muttered with a lopsided grin.

'Go back to your stargazing, Rémi,' Chizoba said gruffly. No matter where he was, 'Krazi' Rémi Ngoro could always see the stars. The shiver fever had hit him hard after their arrival on Oblazt and it had messed up his head, but he was still the best cook in the company. Not that he had much competition any more...

So many lost, Chizoba mused as he regarded the men sprawled about the saloon carriage. His brothers had delighted in making the place their own and spitting in the face of the bluebloods who'd let the hive fall to heresy. Such decadence would have been unthinkable on Iwujii Secundus, where every infant entered the meat grinder of the Childe Wars as an equal and emerged a warrior, a slave or not at all.

'It wasn't me, sergeant,' Rémi insisted, tugging at Chizoba's sleeve. 'It was the rain.' He jabbed at the ceiling. 'I saw it in the window... like a mirror.'

Chizoba nodded vaguely. He had no idea what the man was talking about, but that was often the way with Krazi Rémi. 'Yes,' he agreed. 'It was the rain.'

Mordaine hesitated at the threshold of the Imperator suite. There was a musty, dust-wreathed odour permeating the gold-panelled cabin that unsettled him almost as much as its grim occupant. The Space Marine's bulk seemed to fill the space, though it was by no means cramped. The plush furnishings had been demolished and stacked neatly in the adjoining corridor, along with the door and much of its frame. The Koroleva oligarchs had not designed their luxury suites with giants in mind.

'You know who I am,' Mordaine said bluntly.

'I do,' answered the Calavera. He stood facing the doorway as if he had been expecting his visitor.

Which he probably was, Mordaine guessed. 'Are you a Chaplain?' he asked, indicating the giant's bronze death mask.

'I am not,' the Space Marine answered. 'Throughout the years I have served in many capacities, but never that.'

'But your mask... the skull?'

'It is my own emblem. Its significance is personal.'

'Then I'd be obliged if you'd remove it,' Mordaine said as he entered. 'I prefer to address a man face to face, especially when discussing matters of consequence.'

'I cannot.'

'Surely there's no need for secrecy between us?' Mordaine spread his hands expansively. 'You and I are allies and men of high standing in the conclave–'

'Your standing is that of a traitor and an assassin, Haniel Mordaine,' the Calavera said without rancour. 'In the conclave's eyes you are an outcast.'

'But as you are well aware, I am entirely innocent of the murder of Grand Master Escher.'

'Entirely?'

'I...' The words arrived stillborn in Mordaine's throat. It was as if the Calavera's crystal eye could see through to his soul.

And who's to say it can't? Mordaine thought uneasily.

'Your Chapter...' he hesitated. He could see nothing of the Space Marine's power armour beneath that ashen robe, but there was an undeniably magisterial quality about him, as though he'd been forged for judgement, not merely execution as most Space Marines were. Suddenly it all made sense. 'Are you of the Grey Knights, Calavera?'

Are you my judge?

The hatch of the saloon car swung open and a tall figure stepped inside. Its viridian greatcoat gusted in the wind as it regarded the mob of Sharks sprawled about the chamber. Warmth and sound leeched from the room as the men noticed the newcomer framed in the open doorway.

'Lieutenant...' Sergeant Chizoba began uncertainly, but she silenced him with a low hiss. The Sharks lowered their eyes as she approached – La Mal Kalfu, Father Terra's pitiless handmaiden incarnate.

'The spirits of our brothers still wail at Grandfather Death's gates, riven and raw with sacrifice,' Lieutenant Omazet said, passing through the men like a scythe of cold, condemning clarity, 'yet you cavort in this chamber of iniquity.' Her voice was little more than a whisper woven into the wind, yet every man in the carriage heard it. 'You dance like *ghuuls* on their unquiet graves.'

They needed this! Chizoba wanted to protest. *After the carnage and the betrayal, they needed something.* But he knew such excuses were rooted in false pride and her castigation was well deserved. 'The fault is mine,' he declared solemnly.

The lieutenant's bone-trimmed laspistol appeared to fly into her hand and Chizoba raised his chin, determined to die with honour, but her arm snapped out at a right angle as she fired. There was a hiss of molten glass as the las-bolt punched through a window. Without pause she swept her arm about in an arc, channelling her contempt into flashes of green fire that wove between the frozen Sharks, sometimes close enough to scald their flesh. When she was done, every window in the carriage had been punctured. Though the thick glass held, it was crazed with livid, melted craters.

'Purge this temple of vice,' Omazet commanded, holstering her weapon.

Without hesitation Chizoba lifted a heavy chair and hurled it through the nearest window. As the glass shattered and the snow rushed in his comrades surged to their feet, howling with righteous fury. Eager for redemption – eager to please *her* – the Sharks seized the degenerate baubles of the bluebloods and assaulted the windows as if they were the vile, corrupting eyes of the warp.

'Your questions are irrelevant,' the Calavera said. 'I am not your concern.'

'No?' Mordaine said, trying to cover the edge in his voice. 'Forgive me, but I find that difficult to accept.' He brandished the comms report Omazet had given him. 'You've summoned the Damocles Conclave to Oblazt. They will be waiting for me.'

'Yes.'

'*Yes.*' Mordaine was aghast. 'Is that all you have to say? You've betrayed me! I've crawled through fire and ice doing your dirty work...'

'Six days remain to you,' the Calavera interrupted.

'Six days to sweat blood and beg for your mercy, is that it?'

'Six days to find your answers and redeem your honour.'

Mordaine never saw the Calavera move, but suddenly the warrior was looming over him, so close he could make out the delicate strands of verdigris veining his bronze mask. So close that he realised his power armour was deathly silent.

'Your prisoner awaits,' the skull breathed.

'Prisoner...' Mordaine echoed blankly. He wanted to back away, but that merciless eye transfixed him. The cabin felt oppressively hot and he realised he was sweating heavily. It felt pathetic in front of this austere, desiccated being.

Prisoner... The word washed indolently into focus through the murk in his head.

'The prisoner,' Mordaine said, more forcefully this time. 'That wasn't a lie? You actually have the renegade?'

'That is for you to determine, *interrogator.*'

'None of this adds up...' Mordaine's words trailed off as the nausea flooded back, spurred on by a jagged tightness in his chest. That was when he noticed the rivets along the sides of the Calavera's mask. That grim visage was *nailed* to the giant's own skull.

'Who are you?' Mordaine whispered.

'A fellow seeker after truth,' said the warrior. Then with unsettling, untrustworthy concern: 'I regret that you are still weak, Haniel Mordaine. Sometimes I forget how fragile mortals are.'

That's a lie, Mordaine sensed in a flash of insight. *You never forget how vulnerable we are beside your kind. You relish the knowledge.* Suddenly the sense of crushing age radiating from the Space Marine was intolerable. It hung about him like an ethereal stench, a malaise of the spirit that stirred something to wakefulness inside Mordaine. *Something other.* For a fleeting moment he felt like a stranger inside his own head, hanging on to his body by a fraying cord of consciousness.

I cannot die... The thought wasn't his own.

Horrified, Mordaine turned his back on the Calavera and lurched into the corridor, clutching at the handrail running along the wall. The carriage tapered ahead of him, stretching out in a gently undulating river of windows and doors veined with throbbing gold and red velvet. He knew the train was gliding over the ice, frictionless and whisper smooth, yet he felt like a man caught in a storm-wracked sea. He retched, deep but dry, and threads of inky darkness crawled at the periphery of his vision.

'Do you require assistance?' the Calavera called after him.

'That... will not be necessary,' Mordaine rasped.

I want nothing from you. He shoved his forehead against a window, screwing his eyes shut as the frigid glass cooled his fever. *I won't give you the satisfaction.* Breathing deeply, he waited for the nausea to subside.

'I need to make preparations,' he lied, longing for the sanctuary of his cabin, where he could surrender to the darkness without shame. 'For the interrogation.'

'I understand.'

Of course you do, you smug...

'Tomorrow...' Mordaine said. 'I'll begin tomorrow.' He opened his eyes and saw a face gazing back at him through the frosted glass – an abstraction of grey flesh stretched taught over a serrated wedge of bone and deeply recessed black eyes. *And were those quills?* The phantasm was gone before he could decipher it, abandoning the glass to his own broken reflection. He stared at the gaunt relic, wondering what else was staring back at him through those shadow-crowded eyes.

'Do you see something?' the Calavera asked, and Mordaine realised the giant was standing beside him.

'Nothing,' Mordaine said. *But something sees me.*

Three days after Unity

Oblazt was a world of darkness, but its ice wastes shimmered with a dull, diffuse light, like the last flicker of a failing lumen bulb spun out eternally. The locals claimed it was reflected starlight, but Lieutenant Omazet didn't believe it. She could taste the hunger behind that anaemic radiance and she knew the Ghostlands were well named.

It is almost as if this debased engine has carried us into the twilight realm of Grandfather Death, she thought. *Perhaps we all fell at Vyshodd and never knew it.*

She dismissed the dark notion and focused on the gloomy corridor ahead. Someone, presumably the captain, had smashed every one of the glow-globes lining the passage, leaving only the pallid haze from the windows to illuminate her path. Uzochi had claimed this carriage when they boarded, refusing both succour and guidance, demanding only solitude. He'd looked like a man drowning in a poisoned dream.

He bleeds shadows as an untended wound bleeds pus, she mused with regret. Like all the Sharks she was fiercely loyal to her commander, but she had long suspected that Uzochi was like a tautly drawn bowstring – dangerous, yet also very brittle.

But is he beyond redemption? Omazet wondered as she arrived at the locked door of his cabin.

'Captain,' she said, tapping on the door. 'Armande... We must talk.' There was no response. She knocked again, harder this time. Something creaked above her head and she looked up sharply, squinting in the gloom. The ceiling was an ambiguous blur of grey panels and dark grilles, devoid of... She frowned. *Had something moved up there?* No, that made no sense.

There was a murmur from behind the locked door and Omazet put an ear to the enamelled wood. Someone was pacing about in there like a caged animal.

'Captain!' she called, rapping on the wood. The pacing stopped. Growing impatient, Omazet switched to the insidious, damning lilt of La Mal Kalfu: 'Armande, hear my breath and heed me, for I name you wayward, wordless and shaken-hearted. Craven-haunted, you'd spit on your oath...'

So it went until she heard a chuckle from within, rancid with anguish. A moment later the bolt was drawn back and a crack of shadow appeared in the doorframe, confining a bloodshot eye.

'Captain?' she asked. The eye blinked at her without recognition. 'Armande?'

'Is he with you?' It was the hoarse rattle of a man who hadn't slept in days.

'Is who with me?'

'*Grandfather Death,*' he whispered, as if fearing to say the name aloud. 'I know you are his disciple, woman. You paint your face in his image.'

'I serve Father Terra and no other.' She frowned. 'Armande, you have invited doubt into your heart...' As she reached for the door the eye widened in fury.

'I'll not parley with his lackeys!' he hissed. 'Tell him to come himself if he wants my soul.'

'Armande–'

'Tell him!' The door slammed in her face.

Omazet growled, a primal release of tension. She realised her pistol had slipped into her hand, as if demanding that she fulfil her most sacred duty.

He is no longer fit to lead us, she judged. *It would be a mercy.*

And yet some indistinct, malformed intuition held her back. She turned and stalked away, eager to be gone from this shadowy carriage.

The saloon car had been eviscerated and sacrificed as a penance for the sins of its patrons, yet the Ghostlands had transformed the gaudy chamber into a vision of almost ethereal beauty. Krazi Rémi stood at the entrance, bewildered by the frost-wreathed opulence. It looked as if the carriage had been frozen in time.

Like starlight made into stuff, he thought reverently.

He roused himself with a shake of the head. Such foolishness had earned the mockery of his brothers, but he was going to prove them wrong. He'd come back here to chase the rain. His thoughts were a raggedy jumble these days, but he was pretty sure rooms weren't meant to rain.

Nodding to himself, the scrawny Shark crept towards the place where he'd seen it happen, his boots crunching through the vitrified strands of carpeting. His breath hung about him like smoke, testifying to the cold that gripped the carriage. If he lingered here overlong he'd end up as another piece of frozen furniture.

Rémi grinned when he saw the suspect grille in the ceiling, delighted that his memory had clung on to it. Hunting about, he spied an overturned table. The ice had welded it to the fabric and there was an audible snap as he pulled it free. He froze, but nobody came so he pressed on with his quest. Grunting with effort, he dragged the table under the grille and climbed up. The panel's screws were frozen tight and his gloved hands were clumsy, but he worked at them with his knife until the grille came loose. Sliding it aside, he poked his head cautiously into the shaft above, shining his torch first left then right. Nothing. He sniffed. There was a heady stench lingering in the space, like the spoor of a wild beast. He hesitated, wondering if this would be enough for the others. Minutes passed as he tested the possibilities. No, it wouldn't be enough, he decided unhappily. Nobody would believe him. He needed more.

With a sigh, Rémi hauled himself up into the ventilation shaft.

He chose a direction at random, working his way along the shaft until it terminated at the carriage wall. *What? Oh...* There was a hatch above him. He squirmed onto his back and shoved, gasping as it came free and he was bathed in bright light. He was staring up at the sky and it was full of stars. *Real stars,* not the glittering lies that crowded his head like beggar's diamonds. He drank them in, marvelling that the blizzard had eased off and granted him this clear sky. Even so, it was bitterly cold and he knew he had to get moving before he froze up in the shaft.

I should go back, he thought, but the stars sang to him, urging him to race them across the top of the world. No... No, it wasn't the stars... It was the wind, a glacial whispering mistral plucked from the air by the speeding train. Rémi sat up, popping his head through the hatch to watch the tundra surging past on either side like a fleeting yet perpetual memory of whiteness. His breath froze, glazing his face with frost as he tried to remember who he'd been before the shiver fever had filled his head with smoke.

I should really *go back,* Rémi decided as he hauled himself out onto the roof of the carriage. The metal was frost rimed and slippery, but he felt no fear because he was a Shark and his balance was sharp, even if his mind wasn't. Anyway, the carriage was wide enough for a man to walk ten good paces to either side before reaching the edge. True, it slanted sharply after just *one* pace, but he'd be fine if he kept to the central spine.

His hunt forgotten, he picked his way cautiously across the ribbed hull, delighting in the iron gargoyles perched along his path. They were turned outwards to ward off evil so he couldn't see their faces, but he could imagine them, ugly orkoid brutes with sharp eyes and sharper fangs, angry at being stuck out here to freeze. They had a point about that because the cold was something terrible up here. He could feel it drinking his skin dry and sucking the breath right out of him, eager to carry his soul away...

He stumbled and yelped, almost slipping from the level spine of the roof. Those ten good paces to either side weren't looking so good any more. One misstep and he'd be sliding down the roof like a man caught in a waterfall. He froze up, wheezing hard and shivering uncontrollably as the Ghostlands flashed past on either side.

Got to get back inside, he realised, *out of this killing cold.*

He frowned, peering at the trail of carriages ahead. There was a dark shape moving at the far end and even at this distance it didn't look right. As he watched, it came rushing towards him like an insect, scuttling on all fours and leaping the gaps between the carriages in great hops, becoming more manlike with every step. And then it was close enough for Rémi to see that it was nothing like a man at all. It was a gargoyle come to life and its face was a lot worse than the ones he'd imagined.

His heart pounding like a caged animal, he remembered that he'd come out here to hunt. Whatever else he was or wasn't, Rémi Ngoro was a Shark.

Steeling himself, he reached for his laspistol. His fingers closed on empty air. Maybe the gun had slipped loose during his crawl or maybe he'd forgotten it. He hoped it was the first. It didn't really matter any more, but it was all he had left.

Closing his eyes, Krazi Rémi turned away from the horror and stepped onto the slippery, sloping surface to his right, proving he wasn't crazy at all.

'How long, Iho'nen?' the traveller, who had become a prisoner, demanded from the shadowed confines of his cell.

'Not long, but it is a fragile process,' the giant, who wore his many names like a shroud of half-truths, answered. 'I did not anticipate that his body would become so damaged. His final foray into the hive was unfortunate.'

'Is this error also within your *acceptable parameters*?' the prisoner asked.

'Not if he dies,' the Calavera admitted.

ICE

And after it has beguiled, tormented and betrayed you, Truth will reveal itself as nothing more than another lie.

– The Calavera

Four days after Unity

It is time, the Empty One's decree bled into Ujurakh's skull.

Unbound, the Sourblood surged from his lair in an empty promethium tank and scuttled into the ventilation system. Finally freed from the hateful shackles of meekness, his mind burned with the possibilities for wreaking ruin upon the flat-faces. It would have to be done with stealth and swiftness, for they were many and the Empty One's schemes prohibited open conflict. Ujurakh did not understand this stricture, but it did not trouble him unduly for he was a tangled creature himself, drawn to the craft rather than the brutality of slaughter. The hunger soared alongside him, seeking to deny him this dignity for it cared only for the feast, but he leashed it and made it his weapon rather than his conqueror.

Oh, we'll feed deep and well, springing loose the hidden spiral seeds of their flesh, Ujurakh promised, *but we'll weave our carnage with whisper-light perfection!*

He scurried from carriage to carriage, sometimes through vents, sometimes across roofs, peering through windows or grilles at his blind prey, assessing numbers and positions, measuring movements and distances, assembling the scattered pieces of the plan he'd devised during his concealment.

And finally, he was ready.

'A whole day!' Mordaine bellowed as he stormed into the Imperator Suite. 'You let me sleep through an entire day!'

'It was necessary, Haniel Mordaine,' the Calavera said. He was waiting at the centre of the chamber, exactly as he'd been waiting the first time. 'Without respite your body would have shut down catastrophically.' The Space Marine appraised him as a man might assess an insect with a broken wing. 'Even now your metabolic insignia indicate your condition is significantly impaired.'

Mordaine faltered, his fury diminished to bluster now that he was face to face with this eldritch being again. As always, the Calavera's logic was maddeningly irrefutable. He forced himself to stare into that cyclopean eye, wondering why he'd never challenged its nature before. Surely it couldn't be a conventional...

'It is an augmetic of rare and resplendent provenance,' the Calavera answered.

'What...?'

'Your eyes betray your thoughts as mine cannot, Haniel Mordaine.'

They were silent for a time, while Mordaine fumbled for the courage to press the challenge. *Do I really want to know this truth now?*

'I want to see the prisoner,' he demanded instead.

'As you will, interrogator.' The giant offered the ghost of a bow.

'You agree?' Mordaine couldn't conceal his surprise.

'Yes. It is time.'

At a grand thirty-one years, André 'Ironfingers' Pava was far and away the oldest man in the company, but maturity had only cemented his status as an outsider. Very few Sharks expected to see twenty-five, let alone their thirties. Indeed, surviving to such a ripe old age was regarded as vaguely scandalous among the Iwujii, but there was no getting round the fact that Pava was too useful to lose, so one commander after another had kept him out of harm's way – even Armande Uzochi, who was the craziest he'd ever served under. While this cosseting didn't endear him to his fellows, they weren't blind to his talents. Who else could they turn to when their guns or pict recorders played up? The Iwujii regiments had few tech-priests attached to their ranks, so a man with a knack for machinery was a precious if unloved commodity.

Pava hummed to himself as he monitored the control panel in front of him, delighting in the tangle of levers, wheels and intricately carved dials. While the deeper secrets of the Chain Engine's workings would always elude him, he had its *shape* now. It had taken some experimentation, but he'd eventually divined the right input mantras to awaken its machine-spirit and beseech it to soar across the ice. Afterwards he'd continued to refine his stewardship through trial and error, relying on his gift to win the engine over. It was an invigorating process and he realised he'd never been so happy in his life. Up front in the drive cabin he was a world away from the dirty looks and veiled insults of his so-called comrades.

Something thudded heavily onto the cabin's roof. Perplexed, Pava peered through the slanted viewport, trying to penetrate the white noise of hail and darkness. He heard a scrabbling overhead, then a clatter as the intruder slithered onto the access platform outside. Whoever was out there, they were now between Pava and the rest of the train. It suddenly struck him how isolated he was up front in the drive cabin.

He was fumbling for his laspistol when the hatch was flung open.

Sergeant Chizoba threaded his way through the silent throng of troopers packed into the barracks carriage, vigilant for any sign of laxity as he made another headcount. Some men knelt in prayer, while others sought wisdom in the scriptures of Father Terra, reading their spiritual primers with solemn frowns. Those who'd been inducted into the disciplines of the Jade Chord sat in contorted postures, their eyes closed as they meditated upon their transgressions. After the debacle in the saloon car they'd all woken up to the dissolution stalking them since they'd boarded.

Sometimes I feel the engine itself watches us like a fell spirit, Chizoba mused darkly, *testing and tempting us with a thousand glittering snares. A silver serpent...*

His former negligence still mortified him, but the seeds of corruption had been insidious and fertile, from the lascivious images adorning the staterooms to the fine spirits and exotic delicacies packed into the cargo carriages. But worst of all was the dazzling, hoarded wealth! Many of the Sharks had filled their pockets with loot in the first days, weighing themselves down like swine fattened on gilded muck, but Chizoba had put an end to it, standing watch as each thief cast his baubles overboard.

The serpent hates me for that, he decided, *but it fears me too.*

He'd reached the front of the carriage now, counting sixty-three Sharks in total. Taking into account the ones posted along the train there should have been sixty-four. Rémi was still missing. The fellow was probably sleeping off one of his shiver fits, but nobody recalled when they'd last seen him and Chizoba couldn't help worrying. He hesitated, unwilling to disturb his comrades' devotions.

I'll find him myself, he decided. *It's past time I did the rounds anyway.*

With a sigh he reached for his fur-trimmed greatcoat.

Hunched over the blood-spattered drive console, Ujurakh yanked a lever at the end of the sixth row, completing the pattern the Empty One had placed inside his head. Somewhere at the tail end of the vehicle magnetic clamps would be releasing, leaving the rearmost carriage hanging by a thread. That thread would require a personal touch to sever.

And so machines are unwoven and splayed wide open for the fools they are!

The sabotage delighted him, for the unravelling of things, be they fashioned from flesh, metal or mind, was the true calling of Sourblood. With a hoot of glee he leapt to the cabin door, lingering at the threshold to savour the sweet aroma of liberated flesh in the air. He had wrought fine work here.

'Sacred Throne!' a voice hissed behind him.

Ujurakh spun round and found himself face to flat-face with a kine beast standing on the access platform. He lunged before the patrolling sentry could reach for its weapon, his serrated beak ripping away the creature's face in a snap of crimson as his twin blades slammed into its shoulders, pinning it rigid. Ignoring its convulsive kicks, he lifted the pinioned ruin and cast it overboard with a squawk of rage.

The sentry's sudden appearance here infuriated him. He'd timed his attack to interweave *precisely* with the flat-face patrols, yet this fool – *this defiler!* – had surprised him, tarnishing the perfection of his plan! Riding the wave of his rage, the hunger heaved within him, urging him to linger and feed on the driver's carcass. Ujurakh slammed the hatch shut before the scent wafting from the cabin overpowered him.

One master already claims my shame. I'll be bound by no more!

He leapt for the roof of the next carriage, straight into the teeth of the gale. His anger had made him careless and the blizzard snatched him as he landed, spinning him towards the edge of the speeding train. His talons scrabbled for purchase on the icy hull as the maelstrom howled and tore at his quills. Desperate, he crouched and sprang forwards, crashing down at the centre of the carriage and hugging the roof like a spiny limpet.

Blood-blind fool! Ujurakh cursed himself. Then he was moving again, scurrying on all fours towards the rear of the train.

'I'm going to do the rounds,' Chizoba told the sentry standing beside the exit of the barracks car. 'I may be gone a while.' He swung the hatch open and the squall rushed in, dusting the interior with snow. A few hours ago the night had been quiet, but the blizzard had returned with a vengeance. The sergeant scowled, barely able to see the carriage ahead through the churning snow. Suddenly leaving this sanctuary seemed like the worst idea he'd ever had. But what if Rémi had hurt himself?

Reluctantly Chizoba stepped out onto the connecting gangway and slammed the hatch shut behind him, cutting himself off from the living. Alone in a swirling white void, he looked down and saw more whiteness rushing between the slats of the platform under his feet. The sense of unreality was oppressive. Though the Chain Engine was a goliath it sped through the maelstrom in almost total silence. Chizoba knew some kind of technomancy kept it floating above the track, but it didn't *feel* right. The engines he'd ridden back home were rickety contraptions, wedded to their tracks like a cranky old couple, but this one felt like a ghost train.

An infernal engine forged to ferry an army of the damned into the warp...

He yanked down on the lever of the door ahead. It didn't move.

A silver-clad snare for the wicked and the unwary...

Fear caressed his spine, feather-light and frigid. He imagined himself trapped between carriages, unable to go forwards or backwards as his blood froze and his flesh crystallised into a glass sculpture. Would his men laugh at his folly? He tugged again.

The sentry standing outside the prisoner's cell was obviously terrified. He was the youngest Shark Mordaine had seen, surely no more than sixteen. How long had he been alone in the holding carriage? Alone with the xenos behind that iron-shod door...

'Has the prisoner caused any trouble?' Mordaine asked him. The youth shook his head, unable to get a word out.

Is it me he's frightened of? Mordaine wondered. *Or is it the grey giant standing beside me?*

'The xenos is secure,' said the Space Marine. 'Fortunately the Koroleva equipped their transport with admirable incarceration facilities. One might say they had *foresight.*' There was a trace of humour in that deathly voice, but it only enhanced its inhumanity. In that moment Mordaine knew that he truly hated this ancient being.

'Then you may leave us,' he said curtly. He expected some argument, but the Calavera merely inclined his head and strode away. With a momentary howl of wind and a slam of metal he was gone from the carriage.

He wants me to do this, Mordaine realised. *That's what he's wanted all along.* He glanced at the Iwujii youth, seeking a last moment of human camaraderie. 'What's your name, boy?' he asked.

'Mifune, sir.' The guard wouldn't meet his gaze.

It is *me he's terrified of,* he realised. *Haniel Mordaine, the dread inquisitor!* Absurdly the boy's fear lent him courage.

'See that I am not disturbed, Trooper Mifune.'

Mordaine unlocked the cell door.

With an angry screech the stubborn lever gave way and Chizoba staggered into the next carriage. As he hauled the hatch shut behind him he heard something clatter across the roof above, as if in sympathy. He held his breath, listening with his back against the door, straining against the muted wail of the wind.

'I'll not let the unquiet spirits of this engine unman me,' Chizoba said, challenging the gloom. Maybe it was crazy, but sometimes a man needed to hear a human voice, even if it was only his own. 'There's nothing here that faith can't rout. In fact there's nothing here at all!'

Ashamed of the dread that had almost overwhelmed him, he advanced into the narrow aisle ahead. It passed through a warren of sealed storage vaults that bore the silver crown icon of the Koroleva. The bluebloods had situated this cargo carriage further upfront than the barracks, valuing their chattel over their troops. They wouldn't travel without an army of thugs to back them up, but they liked to keep them out of sight. Unfortunately this had obliged Chizoba's brothers to occupy the tail end of the train. He didn't know why that sat so badly with him, but...

There was a metallic groan behind him. He spun round, drawing his pistol in the same moment. The hatch he'd come through had swung open and snow was billowing into the carriage in languid, spiralling flurries. Chizoba crouched, levelling his weapon at the door, watching it rock back and forth in the wind like a beckoning hand. He waited, his hackles rising at its incessant creaking.

Nothing. It's nothing.

'Thierry, you're raising ghosts from the shadows!' he chastised himself. Once again the sound of his voice was like a flash of good sense in the darkness. Obviously he'd not shut the damned hatch properly.

'You a man or a boy?' he chanted. 'Predator or prey?' It was the first mantra of the Childe Wars and it spurred him into action. Holstering his pistol he marched back to the door and reached for the handle. 'Blade or blood?'

The wind lashed out and snatched away his hand. He stared at the gushing stump, frozen by superstitious terror. Then the wind surged into the carriage and he saw it was a predator.

* * *

As the Calavera had promised, the prisoner was secure. The tau sat rigidly on the floor, its back a few centimetres from the windowless outer wall of the padded cell. A bulky robe obscured the alien's form, but Mordaine could tell that its legs were knotted into a lotus position that would have defied human physiognomy. The alien's hands – only three fingers and a thumb to each – were clasped in its lap, bound by heavy manacles. A chain tethered these to a ring in the wall, restricting the captive's freedom to half a metre. It was a crudely effective device, yet Mordaine was not reassured. This was one of the most dangerous aliens known to the Imperium.

And I'm the one who'll bring him before the Emperor's justice, he thought. *Surely it will be enough to exonerate me. If this is really him...*

Mordaine lingered in the doorway, studying the xenos. It was quite unlike the ethereal his mentor had captured all those years ago. While that being had possessed an empyrean grace, this one was muscular and broad shouldered, with a warrior's bearing. However, the most striking differences were in the face. Whereas the ethereal's had been long and delicate, this creature's was square-jawed and severe, with cobalt skin tones that darkened to charcoal at its vertical nostril slit. A stylised white circle inscribed the right side of its face, framing its eye with geometric precision. He couldn't begin to guess at the alien's age, but he sensed it was in the prime of its life.

Can this really be the Scourge of Damocles? Surely he would be older...

Then the prisoner opened its eyes and Mordaine was no longer so certain.

'You may enter,' it said.

Crouched between carriages, Ujurakh wrenched on the lever controlling the last of the couplings securing the barracks car. With a hiss of servos the massive pin retracted, cutting the rear carriage loose from the train. Crowing with satisfaction, the Sourblood sat back on his haunches and watched as the snowstorm swallowed the receding box. The amputated car's forward momentum might carry it along the track for hours, perhaps even days before friction sapped its impetus. It was a waste of good meat, but it was necessary. Ujurakh wondered whether the stranded flat-faces inside would devour each other before the end came.

'You are the inquisitor,' said the xenos, playing the opening Escher had always favoured, making a statement out of a question and claiming the initiative.

Beginning the game without hesitation.

'I would stand to face you,' the prisoner continued, 'but it is impractical.' It lifted its manacles pointedly as Mordaine closed the cell door. 'You understand these hold me only because I tolerate it.'

The xenos spoke Gothic with patient, almost pained precision, as if constraining its thoughts to accommodate an inferior shape, but the authority in its voice was undeniable. It was an alloy of contradictions, alight with passion, yet aloof with calculation: the voice of a master player.

'I don't have time for games,' Mordaine said brusquely, trying to regain ground. 'You will answer my questions or you will suffer.'

'I am a warrior. Suffering runs in my blood like fire. I welcome it.' The prisoner was regarding him intently. *Sizing up the mettle of its opponent.* 'Do you not share such a bond with pain, gue'la?' *Are you not a warrior?*

'So you believe that pain is a virtue, xenos?'

'I believe the *conquest* of pain brings strength.'

'And I believe I have walked into the wrong cell,' Mordaine mocked. 'I expected to meet a fire warrior, not an ethereal.' It was a sly strike, but the prisoner didn't rise to it so he pressed on. 'I thought your craft was war, not philosophy.'

'If you believe the disciplines are distinct then you are ignorant,' the xenos said evenly. 'Or incompetent.'

I would certainly be a fool to think you a common warmonger, Mordaine conceded. To his disgust he was already tiring, as if the alien's mere presence was draining him. *I'm not ready for a drawn-out duel...*

'Come closer, inquisitor,' the xenos said. 'I offer you no imminent peril.' *The infernal thing is baiting me!* 'Let us talk as equals.'

Uncertain whether accepting the challenge would register as strength or weakness, Mordaine stepped forward... then hesitated. *Which is certainly weakness, damn it!* Angry, he forced himself to move, stopping a few paces from the prisoner. He should have appeared masterful, but his tension diminished him while the alien's tranquil repose elevated it. Wise to the power game, it didn't even raise its eyes, staring instead through his midriff.

'We are not equals,' Mordaine said without conviction. 'I am a servant of the God-Emperor of Mankind, cast in the mould of His... divine... aspect...' His hands were trembling uncontrollably so he clasped them behind his back – tightly – as if he were hanging on to himself. 'You are a xenos heretic, enslaved by the deliriums of a debased technology that will betray you. You are nothing.'

'Then why are you afraid of me, gue'la?'

The statement was so ripe with truth that it took Mordaine off-guard. As he floundered for a riposte he felt enervating tendrils unfurling inside his skull. The secret *other* buried inside him was stirring again.

No, Mordaine railed at the indifferent abyss. *Not here... not now.*

'I...' he breathed as breath failed him. The cell walls unfurled and swam away, as if seeking a more captivating configuration. His legs felt like hot wires sheathed in wax. Any moment now that inconstant flesh would melt, leaving his bones unable to bear their burden alone. Now the xenos *was* looking up at him, its black eyes drinking in his weakness dispassionately.

'I...' Mordaine gasped as his legs buckled.

The Sourblood tore another crimson strip from the carcass of the flat-face called *Chee-zoba* and crammed it into his beak, savouring the pungent flavour. After the poor fare this planet had served up, such flesh was intoxicating! Worlds shaped the taste of their meat and this creature had been spawned on a vibrant, full-blooded planet – one not unlike Ujurakh's own home world. As he chewed on the meat it rendered up fleeting impressions of wet green heat and red fury. He hadn't tasted the like for many seasons!

There had been a time when he had always fed well, travelling from one battleground to another with his kindred, trading their might for pay and flesh, but then the Empty One had come with false bargains and forbidden meat...

Warp-kissed flesh, tender, terrible and irresistible with promised displeasure!

Ujurakh shuddered at the memory of fragrant coral flesh and delicate, deadly pincers. *Possessed,* the Empty One had called the twisted, drooling captive he'd offered the Shaper. The sacrifice had shrieked in ecstasy when Ujurakh carved it open, then moaned in dissonant harmony while he glutted himself on its willing meat, enslaved by a hunger beyond anything he'd known before. Its essence had flooded his palate with myriad rival passions as he fought to unwind its truths and thread them into his own weave, but it was like trying to catch the lightning with his talons or extinguish the sun with his breath!

Too many possibilities entwined within infinite impossible tangles...

The Empty One had waited until Ujurakh collapsed, overwhelmed by the cacophony of sensations. Then he had summoned the kroot's kindred and denounced their Shaper as a Sourblood, a degenerate who would taint their bloodline to sate his base cravings. They had called for his life then, but the Empty One had bought it from them and taken Ujurakh as his slave, burying his voice deep inside the Shaper's skull and binding him to an invisible purpose that had carried them across countless worlds. Now, for the first time in so very long, Ujurakh could taste the joys of his old life.

Lost in his feasting, the Shaper didn't see the skull-faced female enter the dark cargo carriage. It was only when her torch beam lashed him that he awoke to the threat, but by then she was already firing. He sprang backwards and the las-bolt intended for his head took him in the abdomen, scalding him to the bone. Screeching in agony he retreated, flitting frantically from side to side in the narrow aisle as she stalked after him with her pistol levelled. A bolt caught him in the right shoulder... another in the left leg... a third burned away the quills of his crest. He hurled himself at the gaping doorway behind, flailing out to catch the guardrail of the gangway beyond, but his scorched arm was without strength. He yelped as his grip failed and he toppled over into nothingness.

Lieutenant Omazet approached the open hatch cautiously, keeping her pistol levelled, but the avian horror was gone.

So was the barracks carriage.

Hissing through her teeth, she stared at the void where sixty men had been. *We have been betrayed,* she thought bitterly. *I don't know how or by whom, but I don't doubt it for a moment.*

Biting down her rage, she approached the shredded wreck that had been Thierry Chizoba. The beast had dragged him to the centre of the carriage so it could feast away from the cold, leaving the hatch open for a quick flight if it was disturbed.

But its unholy appetite was its undoing, she realised as she knelt beside the sergeant. His face was contorted in a rictus of agony, eyes wide and staring with shock. His right hand was missing, along with most of his chest.

'We were already so few,' Omazet murmured as she closed Chizoba's eyes and traced the sacred aquila across his forehead. *Now we are nothing at all.*

But it wasn't true. There were at least a dozen troopers further along the train, along with Old Man Pava and the boy Mifune. And of course there was still Armande, if he could be roused from his madness. They weren't many, but they were still Sharks and together they would take vengeance. Determined, Omazet rose and hurried towards the next carriage. As she reached for the handle the hatch swung open and a vast shape was silhouetted against the snowstorm.

'Captain Calavera,' she said as the Space Marine entered the carriage, hunching to pass through the doorway. She backed away instinctively, not lowering her gun, though it was a stunted weapon against the armoured giant.

Why do I feel I might need it? Omazet wondered uneasily as the newcomer rose to fill the narrow space. *And why is his arrival so timely?*

'We have been betrayed,' she told him. 'We must reverse this engine without delay. If we are swift we may yet deliver my brothers from the winter's embrace.'

The Space Marine regarded her silently. His crystal eye was very bright in the gloom, yet it cast no light of its own. Omazet saw that it was a many-faceted orb, inset like a jewel in the dark recess of his visor. Beside his dread aspect, her own contrivance of tattoos and lenses seemed like cheap chicanery. How she envied him that face! Such a visage would make her one with Mother Kalfu herself...

Mesmerised, she stood rigid as the Calavera took a step towards her.

Mordaine's world melted back into focus, as sticky and seeping as the pool of blood congealing around his head. A drum was pounding between his ears, beating furiously against the wet gash in his forehead as if trying to hammer a way out.

I must have fallen on my face, he thought blurrily. *It's a miracle I didn't break my nose.* He hauled himself to his knees, groaning with the strain.

'I feared you dead, gue'la,' a voice said beside him. He turned and saw the xenos prisoner watching him. Angel's Tears, he'd fallen right by the creature!

Unable to suppress a moan of revulsion, Mordaine crawled away, feeling foolish – impossibly, unforgivably foolish – and collapsed with his back against the cell door, breathing hard. He reached for his holster, already knowing the weapon would be gone and – no, it was still there!

Why? Closing his eyes, he slowed his breathing, grasping for answers. *The xenos could have reached out and throttled me while I was senseless. Why am I still alive?*

Growling low in her throat, Omazet tore her gaze from the Calavera's siren eye. The giant halted and she heard something that might have been a sigh. The sound was like a sirocco fluting through a time-riven ruin. In that breath she knew he had come to her as Grandfather Death.

'Why?' she asked. She doubted her candour would surprise him, but it might earn her a measure of respect. 'Why turn on us?'

He stood motionless, contemplating her request.

'We are both warriors,' she urged. 'If I am to die here then grant me the dignity of truth. *Why?*'

'Because you would interfere, lieutenant.'

'In what?'

'In a matter that has been engineered with absolute rigour,' he said, betraying a hint of pride. 'Your company has served its purpose.' He made to advance.

'Wait!' she said quickly, hunting for something, *anything* to delay him. 'Do you truly see through that orb?'

'Not *through* it,' he said softly. 'The Aphelion is not a lens.'

'But you see with it?'

'More than you can possibly conceive.' Suddenly the pride was gone, leaving only an ineffable weariness. 'I have no surcease of sight, Adeola Omazet.'

'It is a curse then?'

'It is what it is. As am I.' He took a step forwards. Omazet took one back.

'What you *are* is a heretic,' she challenged.

'From a narrow viewpoint.' Another step forwards.

'You have turned your back on Father Terra's light!' Another step back.

'Light blinds, absolute light blinds absolutely.' Forwards.

'Is that how you lost your eyes?' Back.

'It is how I came to see.'

'How long was I out?' Mordaine asked hoarsely.

'Not long.' It was a vague answer yet an honest one, he sensed.

'Why didn't you kill me when you had the chance, xenos?'

'It would have served no purpose.'

'Vengeance doesn't interest you?'

'Against you?' The alien's nostril slit dilated with wintry humour. 'Enmity must be earned, gue'la. My people do not hate blindly, as yours do.'

'Your people?' Mordaine taunted, scrabbling for an attack. 'Who exactly are you speaking for? You're an outcast.'

'You presume much and understand nothing.'

'Then enlighten me,' Mordaine offered. 'Haven't you turned your back on the ethereals and built your own little empire in the Damocles Gulf?'

'In dark times empires arise around warriors of substance,' the xenos said without obvious pride. 'Fire purges the old and forges anew. So it goes.'

'And what exactly are you forging?'

'Such knowledge will not save you, *Haniel Mordaine.*'

The blood drained from Mordaine's face. Did everyone know his damned name? *How...? The Calavera? But why would he tell this xenos renegade anything? Where do the lies begin or end?*

'Name your Chapter,' Omazet said as she backed away from the giant, 'so I might curse its memory.'

'I have no Chapter,' answered the Calavera, advancing, 'for I am Legion.'

And so it went, their words slicing back and forth as their steps carried them inexorably towards the emptiness waiting at the other end of the carriage.

'What do you fight for?' Omazet asked finally, stepping out onto the connecting gangway that no longer connected to anything.

'Some might call it the Greater Good.'

'You have betrayed your blood to serve a xenos heresy?' Omazet had to shout over the wind, yet the Calavera's whispers slipped through it like serpents.

'Oh, a Greater Good than theirs...' The notion appeared to amuse him. 'Call it the *greater* Greater Good, if you will.' He raised a cautioning hand as her finger tightened on the trigger of her pistol. 'Do not imagine you can put my eye out as if I were some absurd monster of legend. The balance of the Aphelion exists outside the material sphere. You cannot touch it.'

'I can try.'

'Make the attempt and I will kill you.'

'And if I don't, you will spare me?' she challenged.

'I will offer you a choice. Die here... or take a leap of faith.' He swept an arm towards the white void behind her.

'We are both outcasts, gue'la,' the xenos said, 'but I have *chosen* my path. I know myself. What do you know?'

Nothing, Mordaine confessed. *I don't know why Escher elevated me to become his acolyte or why he was murdered or even what I want from you, xenos. And worst of all, I don't know what's happening to me.*

'You are an enemy of the Imperium of Man,' he declared, striking for safe ground, 'but to your own people you are immeasurably more repellent.' *I have to go on the attack!* 'Shas'O Vior'la Shovah Kais Mont'yr,' he said, pronouncing each meticulously memorised component like a curse, 'I name you traitor.'

'Make your choice, lieutenant,' said the Calavera.

'You offer me death either way!' Omazet snarled.

'Perhaps, yet my vassal beast endures.' The Calavera tilted his head attentively. 'I hear it still, failing and faint, but too hungry for life to accept death.' That cold jewel of an eye fixed on her again, weighing her up. 'Are you weaker than a xenos savage, Adeola Omazet?'

'Why take the chance that I might survive?' she demanded.

'Perhaps because you have impressed me,' the Calavera said, 'or perhaps because the improbability of it intrigues me.'

Omazet didn't believe either explanation for a moment. This monster had sloughed off such sentiments long ago. All of it – the pride, the dry humour, even the weariness – were merely after-echoes of emotion. Inside that bronze skull only austere purpose remained. A purpose he believed she would serve equally well through life or death.

'I will live, traitor,' she promised. 'And I will prove you wrong.'

Then she spat in his eye and jumped.

* * *

'Do you deny it?' Mordaine pressed. 'Or is the name too shameful for you to acknowledge?'

The prisoner made no answer. Its expression was unreadable.

'*Confess.*' Mordaine lashed out, trying not to let desperation seep into his voice. 'You are O'Shovah.'

You have to be, or this is all for nothing.

'You are–'

'I am,' the xenos said.

Mordaine closed his eyes and let the void take him once more.

VOID

Gaze into the Void and you will see yourself glaring back.

– The Calavera

There were voices in the darkness, prowling the silence like wolves, hounding Mordaine towards wakefulness though he sensed this was not their intent.

'... and what of the remaining gue'la troops?' one was asking.

'I have accounted for them all save their captain,' answered a resonant whisper. 'He was gone from his quarters when I purged the vessel.'

'Your plan bleeds errors as the aun breed lies, Iho'nen,' the first voice said.

'It is the nature of things,' the whisperer called Iho'nen replied. 'The Primordial Annihilator taints all endeavours with escalating imperfection, hence foresight is a potent but inconstant craft, traveller.'

'Yet it is your chosen craft, is it not?' the traveller observed dryly.

'As it is yours, but one must adapt to the changing tides of the maelstrom.'

'I am a hunter. To my mind a beast that cannot be mastered is best slain.'

'That has always been the way of warriors,' Iho'nen acknowledged, 'but you must become more than a warrior if you aspire to master fate.'

'Fate is an excuse for weakness,' declared the traveller. 'The strong forge their own paths.'

'Your path may yet forge a monster, *Mont'shasaar.*'

'That is not my name,' the other said coldly.

'Not yet and perhaps never,' Iho'nen conceded, 'but you acquired its shadow on Arthas Moloch when you took the Dawn Blade.'

'The Dawn Blade is a weapon like any other.'

'Like *no* other,' Iho'nen said intently.

'Then you advise me to discard the blade?' the traveller challenged.

'No, that time has passed and you must reap the storm you have sown.'

'As it should be, Space Marine.'

Space Marine? Mordaine thought hazily. *That whisper? Calavera...* As he tumbled back towards darkness he sensed one of the presences approach. His eyes opened fleetingly and he saw the xenos prisoner appraising him.

'I think you are wrong about this one, Iho'nen,' it said. 'He is broken.'

* * *

The ventilation shafts reeked of a sour animal stench but they were the safest paths through the narrow warzone of the train, so Armande Uzochi had claimed them without hesitation, just as another predator had done before him. The crawlspaces had kept him hidden and mobile even when Grandfather Death was dangerously close, as he was now.

Lying supinely above the prison carriage, Uzochi held his breath as the one-eyed Space Marine carried the inquisitor from the alien's cell. Slumped senseless in the giant's arms, Mordaine looked like a dead man and Uzochi wondered what torments he had endured in Father Terra's service. His eyes widened in horror as he saw the xenos captive emerge from the cell a moment later, stretching its limbs as if to shake out the indignity of confinement.

Horror turned to outrage as Uzochi remembered how these abominations had destroyed his company piece by piece, first in the hive through the uprising they had engineered and finally in the confines of this bedevilled machine, hunting down his men one by one. He had watched from above as Grandfather Death killed young Mifune, snapping the terror-stricken boy's neck with the indifference Uzochi would have shown a rat. Instinct alone had saved the captain, compelling him to hide before the cull had begun.

How did our La Mal Kalfu meet her fate? Uzochi wondered guiltily, remembering how he had rebuked her. *I was weak...*

The giant carried Mordaine into a cell further along the carriage, but the xenos lingered at a window. Fleetingly Uzochi considered slipping down behind it. With fortune and faith he might take the creature unawares then make his escape before its ally returned.

No, he decided, weighing up the alien with a shrewd hunter's eye. *There will be no surprising that one.*

He'd have just one chance at vengeance so he'd best make it count. This wasn't the moment. Besides, patience was a hunter's truest virtue and virtue would be his penance for failing Adeola Omazet. Uzochi let the tension slip from his muscles and waited.

... Days after Unity

Mordaine drifted towards wakefulness like a drowning man washed ashore, unsure whether the ocean had expelled him too late. Though the torment in his chest had subsided to a dull ache, his head was bloated with furtive, insistent voices. They whispered from a deep shadow stratum of memory, urging him to embrace an annihilating, irrefutable truth, like buzzing flies drawn to carrion dreams.

What's happening to me? Mordaine pleaded with them.

'Focus your thoughts, interrogator,' another, harsher whisper answered, silencing the shadow babble. 'Your prisoner awaits.'

Mordaine opened his eyes and saw the Calavera standing over him like a graven statue. *Has he been there all night?* The thought repelled him, but revulsion turned to confusion as his surroundings registered. *Why am I in a cell?*

'I have relocated you to the penal carriage for your own safety, interrogator,' the Calavera explained. 'Our enemies have infiltrated this transport.'

'The Iwujii...?' Mordaine asked through parched lips.

'Regrettably they have fallen,' the Space Marine said.

Fallen to invisible enemies on a speeding train in the middle of nowhere? Mordaine thought listlessly as he hauled himself from the bunk. *You don't even care if I believe you or not.*

'I will stand watch,' the Calavera said. 'You must attend to your duty, interrogator.'

Yes, I must, Mordaine agreed, *otherwise the voices in my head will begin to shout. And I don't want to hear what they have to say.*

As he shrugged on his jacket he noticed his laspistol was gone.

The young sentry was also gone and there was no replacement outside the prisoner's door. Mordaine didn't question it, but he knew he was alone with his enemies now.

'You grow weaker, Haniel Mordaine,' the alien said as he entered. 'Ask your questions before you expire.'

'And will you answer honestly, xenos?' *After all, what do you have to lose?* The prisoner considered the question. 'I will.'

He's admitted the name, Mordaine thought, *but that means nothing. I have to be certain it's him.*

'Farsight,' he murmured, testing the name as Lieutenant Omazet might have done. 'What's in a name, xenos?'

'To a tau, everything,' the alien replied. 'Bloodline and sept, caste and rank and conquest.'

'Conquest? Surely that's solely a matter for the fire caste?'

'You misunderstand *conquest*, gue'la. A diplomat of the water caste might earn the name Softsword for the gentle blade of her flattery, an artisan of the earth caste–'

'I understand the principle,' Mordaine said curtly, 'but I'd wager you don't hold all conquests in equal esteem.'

'Those of the fire caste have primacy,' the xenos agreed, 'for without our strength all others would be dust in the wind.'

'And what conquest does *Farsight* honour?'

'It exemplifies the first and finest precept of the Shas'va.' The alien's black eyes shone with icy pride. 'I know my enemy as I know myself, indeed *better*, for my foe is but a shallow shadow of myself. I see as he sees, think as he thinks – and act upon his actions before he knows them himself.'

'Is that what you're doing now?'

'You would be a fool to think otherwise, interrogator.'

'Then tell me, xenos, what action will I take now?' *Because I'm damned if I have any idea myself...*

'You will know when you find me waiting for you there, gue'la.'

So it began.

Inevitably they talked of the Arkunasha War, where Farsight's shrewd harrowing of the orks – *be'gel* he called them – had earned him his epithet.

Mordaine expected more pride, but instead the xenos grew sombre as it recalled the campaign.

'It was a long and bitter conflict,' the alien said. 'Many fire warriors were lost in the rifts of that blighted world, yet I cannot deny the beauty of it.'

'Beauty?' Mordaine asked. 'In a world of rust and killer sandstorms?'

'Not in the *world*, gue'la – in the war.' The alien's eyes dimmed with remembrance. 'The be'gel live for war, embracing it without question or justification. They fight for the joy of fighting alone.'

'And you admire them for this?' Despite himself, Mordaine was intrigued.

'No. They are beasts, but I respect their purity of purpose,' the prisoner said. 'After Arkunasha the water caste painted the be'gel as mindless primitives, diminishing them with words to salve the Empire's anxieties, yet this was only a half-truth. I have waged war against the be'gel many times, but even in that first war I recognised they were neither foolish nor predictable. They adapt and prosper by instinct alone, becoming stronger with every loss they suffer. On Arkunasha we exterminated generations in a handful of years, yet they spawned faster than we could cull them, each wave adapting more swiftly to the battlefield than the last.'

'The Imperium is eminently familiar with the orkoid threat–' Mordaine began, but the xenos ignored him, caught up in the tide of its memories.

'The veterans were the most dangerous,' it continued. 'Those who endured across many seasons borrowed Arkunasha's strength, growing skin of hardened oxide that shielded them from the rust devils and razor storms that scoured the deserts. We called them *be'kalsu*, the iron beasts. They stalked us from the heart of the storms, hidden from the sharpest eye or scanner, turning the hazards of the land against us. Many were torn apart as they rode the tempest, but this only made the survivors more reckless, more lethal.'

The xenos paused, steepling its fingers in contemplation.

'I remember watching from the sheltering ridge of Mak'lar when a monster cyclone spat out an army of spinning, flailing bodies, hurling them to the ground like the rocks the be'gel use to travel the stars. Most were killed instantly, but those that lived were still laughing when we finished them, broken yet unbroken. If the be'gel were capable of loving anything other than war, I believe it was Arkunasha.'

'And you?' Mordaine asked on impulse. 'Did you also love Arkunasha?'

'It was an honest war,' the xenos answered obliquely, 'until the end.'

'Surely the end was a great victory?'

'It was a *stolen* victory.'

'I don't understand. The Tau Empire defeated the orks decisively.'

'*I was not there, gue'la.*' For the first time Mordaine sensed the rage so tightly leashed within this glacial being. 'Towards the end there were… difficulties. We walked on a knife edge, but I could *see* the shape of victory, so close I could almost grasp it.' The xenos clasped its manacled hands, as if in supplication. 'With reinforcements I knew I could crush the be'gel within another season so I requested a fresh hunter cadre.' The prisoner's knuckles cracked with tension. 'The Empire sent an assassin.'

'They attempted to kill you?' Mordaine was stunned.

'They attempted to kill my *authority*,' the alien hissed. 'They believed I had grown arrogant and wilful, straying from my prescribed place in the Greater Good. Aun'Shi himself came to Arkunasha to censure me, though I was too trusting to recognise this at the time. He commanded me to withdraw before I won the war.'

'And then the Empire returned and won without you,' Mordaine guessed, beginning to understand. 'You were cheated?'

'I was *punished!*' The xenos lowered its hands, breathing deeply as it reasserted its iron discipline. 'The aun will not tolerate the ascension of another caste. They feared I would become a beacon of dissent for the fire caste.'

'Was that your intent?'

'It was not.' There was unmistakable pain in the alien's voice now. 'I believed in the aun. *Completely.* Every sacrifice I demanded of my cadre on Arkunasha, every drop of blood swallowed by the red sand and every death scream stolen by the red wind... It was all done for the Greater Good.'

This is the heart of his story, Mordaine sensed, suddenly eager. *I'll end the speculation and the theories. The Imperium will know the truth of this renegade from his own lips...*

'But surely the ethereals – the *aun* – they must have recognised your loyalty,' Mordaine speculated, sifting through the few facts known to the Inquisition. 'After the Damocles War they elevated you, made you first among the fireblades...'

'They fashioned me into a masterful slave,' the xenos hissed, 'a pliable figurehead to bind and blind the fire caste with fool's glory.'

'But you were the supreme commander of the tau military engine.'

'My authority extended no further than the will of the aun! I was a puppet saviour, my every word and gesture scrutinised and filtered by the water caste, my past rewritten and my future decided by committee!' The alien's expression contorted, becoming an abstraction of rage. 'But I was the fortunate one, gue'la. They caged my dying mentor's mind in a machine and cast my shadow sister and brother into stasis so their talents would never be lost to the Greater Good.' It lowered its head, as if drained – or shamed – by its fury. 'All of them obeyed without question, even Shaserra, who was the fiercest of us all.'

The Imperium has demanded such sacrifices of its servants for millennia, Mordaine reflected, *yet this xenos butcher is outraged by the notion. Does that make him naïve or magnificent?*

'Was that the turning point?' Mordaine pressed. 'The event that soured you to the Empire?'

'Among the tau loyalty is not so readily broken,' the alien said softly. 'There are no *turning points*, only fissures that multiply and swell until nothing remains of what was. I accepted my comrades' doom as I accepted my own, but in my heart I began to *question*.' The alien's eyes locked on Mordaine's own, unsettling in their intensity. 'And true questions invite annihilating, irrefutable truths.'

An annihilating, irrefutable truth...

Mordaine stared at the alien. Its words had echoed the whispering carrion choir that haunted his memories.

'Truth is a betrayer, is it not, Haniel Mordaine?' O'Shovah said.

Yes, Mordaine agreed, uncertain why.

'It is time,' the Calavera decreed.

Mordaine crawled from his bunk and spooned down the thin gruel his keeper had prepared, knowing it wouldn't begin to sate him.

'Our supplies were lost with the Guardsmen,' the Space Marine had explained. 'I can offer you nothing else.'

It was a lie, Mordaine knew. Another manipulation. The bastard wanted him half-starved and pliable, yet strong enough to continue the game.

But what are the rules? What's winning and what's losing here?

'I believe it's him,' he said listlessly. 'I believe it's O'Shovah.'

'With belief comes clarity and clarity forges purpose,' the Calavera instructed.

Perhaps that's so, Mordaine agreed uncertainly. The pandemonium of whispers haranguing him had certainly diminished. No... no, that wasn't quite right... They hadn't so much diminished as *contracted*, coalescing towards a single persistent voice that was at once utterly unknown, yet achingly familiar.

'Your prisoner awaits, interrogator,' the Calavera said.

Mordaine paced the confines of O'Shovah's cell, trying to quell his hunger with motion. It was the fourth day of the interrogation and he was intimately familiar with the hateful space now. He didn't have much time left. He had to raise the stakes.

'Tell me about the Dawn Blade, O'Shovah,' he said, almost casually. *The Imperium knows nothing of his notorious sword, yet it has come to symbolise our darkest fears about this renegade.*

'The Dawn Blade is a potent weapon,' O'Shovah said evenly.

'But a sword is a strange weapon of choice for a tau, is it not?'

'The be'gel taught me otherwise on Arkunasha.' The alien's lips curled sharply. The expression might have been a smile or something else entirely. 'I killed their leader in single combat with a blade.'

'So you embrace new tactics... new ideas...' Mordaine suggested reasonably. 'The gifts of the Ruinous Powers, perhaps?'

'I am not a fool, gue'la.'

'Chaos can make fools of the wisest men, O'Shovah.'

'I am *tau,*' the other said with dignity. 'I have gazed into the abyss of Vash'aun'an, which you call the warp, and faced its poisonous spawn. It holds no sway over me.'

'Are you quite certain of that, Mont'shasaar?' Mordaine goaded. He nodded at the alien's twisted expression, feeling a brief, blessed flicker of dominance. How splendid it was to be on the other side of a revelation for once.

'You talk in ignorance,' O'Shovah said, his nostril slit flaring with anger.

'And perhaps you choose your confidantes without caution,' Mordaine said. '*He* told me the name, you understand... the Calavera.' He turned his back as the alien searched his face, keeping the lie close to his chest. 'Mont'shasaar... I know the name, but not the meaning.'

The prisoner made no reply.

I've hit a nerve as raw as the sword, Mordaine sensed. *Perhaps more so...* 'Why are you so afraid of a name, xenos?'

'I fear nothing,' O'Shovah said frostily, 'but I have told you already – to the tau a name is everything. To be *misnamed* is a grievous insult.'

'Then tell me about Arthas Moloch instead,' Mordaine offered. 'That's where you stole your warp-tainted blade, isn't it?'

'The blade was *chosen*,' the xenos said, closing its eyes with finality. 'And I will not talk of that world.'

They spoke again the next day and the day after that, until day and night coiled into a single tangle of barbed debate and dreams of debate.

I fence with O'Shovah in waking and sleep, Mordaine thought or dreamt, *so perhaps it's all one and the same.*

Dimly he recalled the Calavera telling him he had only six days to find his answers, yet surely six days had passed long ago. The windows of the penal carriage were opaque with frost and he had seen nothing of the outside world since his trial began. Was the ghost engine even moving or had it stalled in limbo?

Are we damned to repeat this shadow play eternally? Mordaine mused, too weary for fear any more. Besides, the wise whisper seeping from his memories – *leeching his memories* – promised him this wasn't so.

Look a little deeper into the darkness and you will see the light...

And so I step onto the game board once again and I see that the alien's manacles are gone. He has grown indifferent to the ruse, as have I, for only our duel matters now, though why that should be I still don't understand.

'This Shas'va you keep alluding to...' Mordaine faltered, rubbing at his raw eyes. 'The Inquisition has no record of it. At least none that I've seen.'

'The Shas'va is the Path of Fire,' O'Shovah said. 'It is my own path.'

'You've invented your own philosophy?' Mordaine asked, intrigued despite his exhaustion.

'I have invented nothing. I seek truth and codify it as I find it.' O'Shovah paused, judging his next words carefully. 'My cadre is strong and my enclave is secure in the hands of my fireblades, so I have chosen to enter vash'yatol, the long walk between the spheres.'

'Walk to where?'

'I *travel*, Haniel Mordaine,' the xenos said passionately, 'between worlds and stars and stranger realms that I cannot yet name, passing among the hopes and fears of a thousand cultures like a shadow of smoke, gathering fragments of truth and meaning.'

'And the Calavera is your guide?'

'One cannot be *guided* on the vash'yatol,' the xenos said stiffly. 'Iho'nen is a fellow seeker of truth.'

'So he told me,' Mordaine said. Then on impulse: '*Iho'nen*... Why do you call him that?'

'It is the name he chose,' the alien said, then anticipating Mordaine's next question answered: 'It is without meaning.'

'How can that be? You claimed meaning was everything in a tau name.'

'He is not tau. The name has no referent.'

'I'll take a literal translation then.' Mordaine gave a sickly grin. 'Humour me.'

'There is no levity in it,' O'Shovah said, puzzled by the colloquialism. '*Iho* is simply *one who eats,* but *nen*...' It closed its eyes, considering. '*Nen* is the wound that scars both the body and the mind. A betrayal of oneself or a fall from one's path.'

'*Eater of Sins?*' Mordaine ventured, convinced by the taste of it. 'Not a name I'd put my faith in.'

'It is empty wordplay.'

'You don't believe that,' Mordaine said fervently. 'The Calavera does *nothing* spuriously. We both know it.' Impelled by an ambiguous fellowship he leant forwards. 'How did you meet him?'

The alien cocked its head, regarding him thoughtfully. 'I cannot deny that I was troubled by Arthas Moloch, interrogator.' O'Shovah paused, as if expecting a zealous attack, but Mordaine was silent. Satisfied, the xenos continued. 'Though I looked upon the abyss as an outsider, unmoved by its allures, the knowledge of its existence alone cast a hungry shadow. Old truths leave deep scars when they are revealed as lies,' he extended his hands, palms upwards, 'and the path to new truths is riven with deeper lies. I sought silence and solitude to rediscover my clarity of purpose.'

Sometimes I can hear the Calavera speaking right through you, O'Shovah, Mordaine realised. 'And you found a fellow traveller,' he prompted.

'Iho'nen came to me in the wilderness,' the xenos answered, 'and showed me that the wilderness was an entire galaxy.'

We're all puppets to that ancient monster, Mordaine despaired, *but who's pulling* his *strings?*

'Tell me, O'Shovah, what truths has he promised you?'

'Those that unite hearts and minds and worlds,' the xenos declared with dignified passion. 'I will not go to ground while the galaxy burns, Haniel Mordaine.'

'So you *united* Vyshodd Hive,' Mordaine scorned, letting the fleeting fellowship slip away. 'How noble of you, great Farsight!'

'It was the tyranny of your Imperium that seeded this world's revolution and made it such fertile ground for the aun. I merely quickened the seed.'

'So you could watch a city die?'

'So I could *know* its fall,' O'Shovah corrected, 'and to vex the intrigues of the aun. Despite their posturing they fear open war with your Imperium. They believe they are not ready. I know they will *never* be ready.'

'And you are?' Mordaine mocked.

'I am not. That is why I walk the vash'yatol.'

'So you can figure out how to win your great war?'

O'Shovah's expression clouded with an emotion the human couldn't decipher. 'Mont'shasaar,' the xenos said softly, 'it means the Terror That Burns Dark.'

'I don't follow you.'

'I do not walk the vash'yatol to learn how to win, Haniel Mordaine,' O'Sho-vah said. 'I walk to decide what I will do after I have won.'

'Your prisoner awaits,' intoned the Calavera.

And again... And...

'Inquisitor,' someone whispered in the darkness.

Drifting on the shallowest currents of sleep, Mordaine tried to make sense of this strangeness. His existence had narrowed to two voices and a whisper, yet this intruder was neither of these.

'Inquisitor, you must rouse yourself!' the anomaly insisted.

Mordaine opened his eyes and saw a vague shape in the gloom.

'Grandfather Death watches over you like a raptor,' the stranger said. 'I could not reach you before, but he converses with the xenos tonight.'

'Uzochi...?' Mordaine wheezed, dredging the name up from somewhere impossibly distant. 'Armande... Uzochi.'

'Rouse yourself, my brother,' the man said urgently, glancing at the door. 'We cannot linger here.'

'I thought he killed you all.' Mordaine clutched Uzochi's arm, testing his reality. 'I thought I was the last.'

'The last but one,' Uzochi confirmed, 'and our betrayer has stalled this daemon engine in the Ghostlands to finish his work.'

'I suspected as much.' *Six days trailing into forever...*

'Inquisitor, I have hungered to move against the heretics,' Uzochi said fervently, 'but I have nothing to touch Grandfather Death.'

'Nothing...' The presence of another soul in this nightmare, even a mad-man like Uzochi, energised Mordaine. It was proof that his enemy was not omniscient.

There must be a means of confounding him, he thought feverishly. *Escher would see it and Escher chose me to be his heir.* And with that realisation came sudden clarity.

'Captain Uzochi,' he said, 'I think there's a way...'

'Your prisoner awaits.'

Mordaine avoided the Calavera's gaze as he rose, taking care to keep Uzochi's laspistol hidden under his jacket. The weapon would be useless against the Space Marine, but it was an anchor to reality and he clung to it.

I've been fighting on his terms, but today I'll break the rules of the game.

'How long have we been travelling?' he asked on impulse.

'We are almost at journey's end, interrogator,' the Calavera said.

Yes, I believe we are, Mordaine agreed.

Peering round the doorway of an adjoining cabin, Armande Uzochi watched Grandfather Death lead Mordaine towards the alien's cell. Over the weeks Uzochi had mastered the constricted territory of the train, learning its secret paths and rhythms with deadly care, for his life had depended upon it.

Sometimes the grey giant would come looking for him, passing through the carriages one by one and scouring the shadows with his all-seeing eye, but each time Uzochi had slipped away and clung to the outer skin of the engine, shivering in the churning cold until the hunt was over.

But today I *am the hunter,* he thought.

The Space Marine reached for the cell door.

'Wait,' Mordaine said. 'I must gather my thoughts first.'

The Calavera turned and the interrogator took an involuntary step back. *Not backwards, you fool!* Mordaine chastised himself. *He needs to be looking the other way.* He walked past the giant, feigning deep contemplation.

'Your prisoner awaits,' the Calavera called to his back.

'Then let him wait a little longer,' Mordaine said lightly. Denying that dismal, eternal phrase made his heart soar. 'After all, he's only a prisoner.'

'A prisoner of singular importance.'

'Then why is he wasting time with me?' Mordaine swung round with Uzochi's laspistol in his hand. Doubtless Escher would have abhorred such melodrama, but Mordaine was drunk on defiance. As he expected, the Calavera was unperturbed.

You're so sure of yourself, aren't you? Mordaine thought with mounting anger. *How long have you been haunting the galaxy, spinning lies and pulling strings to bring down great men like Aion Escher?*

'Your weapon is ineffectual,' the Space Marine observed.

'Is it?' Mordaine asked, pressing the barrel against his own temple. 'I'm neither blind nor stupid.' *Though I've been both too many times before!* 'You want me alive or I'd be long dead.'

Over the giant's shoulder he saw Uzochi steal into the corridor.

Predator or prey? The exultant Iwujii mantra spun through Uzochi's head, cycling over and over as he crept towards Grandfather Death. *Blade or blood?* The weapon in his hands was heavy, abundant with sacred fury. *Man or boy?*

The inquisitor's advice had proven sound. Trawling through the nobles' storage berths, Uzochi had found real treasures among the empty relics of wealth – a cache of antique armaments that had probably seen little use in their masters' hands. Casting aside exquisite blades and pistols, he had finally stumbled upon a bulky object wrapped in velvet. His breath had caught when he tore aside the cloth and saw the meltagun. The weapon had been inscribed with gold filigree, but such frippery wouldn't diminish its wrath. Even an elder nightmare like Grandfather Death would succumb to its purifying fire.

Predator or prey...

'You used me to get to the grand master,' Mordaine accused, keeping his eyes locked on the Calavera – holding *his* gaze for once. 'I know Kreeger was your creature, along with the assassin that killed Escher, but I was the lynchpin, wasn't I?'

A sigh bled from the bronze skull, low and liquid. To Mordaine it sounded perversely like satisfaction.

'The assassin was not mine,' the ancient whispered. 'The grand master was mine.'

Mordaine stared at him, trying to make sense of the answer. 'That's a lie,' he denied. *It has to be, otherwise there's nothing left.*

'We infiltrated the Damocles Conclave almost two decades ago,' the ancient continued. 'Its remit is of interest to us.'

'We...?' Mordaine was still reeling. 'No... No, the grand master was an honourable man. He was nobody's pawn.'

'Indeed not,' the Calavera agreed. 'Aion Escher was a significant and valued piece. A cardinal at the very least.'

'You expect me to believe...' Mordaine faltered as he saw Uzochi halt a few paces behind the Calavera and level a massive-barrelled gun. 'Wait!' Mordaine cried urgently, hoping to stall them both while he rallied his thoughts.

The Shark hesitated, his gaunt face twitching as he glared at his ally.

By Sanguinius, the man has found a meltagun, Mordaine realised. It surpassed his best hopes. *He can send this devil's soul to the warp! But if he does I'll never know the truth...*

'Wait,' he repeated. 'If not you, then who? Who commanded Escher's murder?'

'The grand master acquired many enemies during his tenure,' the Calavera said. 'Perhaps agents of the Tau Empire or a rival faction within the Inquisition... Or perhaps someone opposed to his true loyalties.' His implacable eye seemed to fix directly upon Mordaine's soul. 'His loss would be regrettable.'

'Would...? Escher is dead. I saw him die myself.'

'Yet a mind may outlive its vessel if the eventuality has been prepared for,' the Calavera said, 'and if a psychically resonant host has been nurtured to fill the void.'

'What host?' Mordaine demanded. 'There was no...'

No!

'Tell me, Haniel Mordaine, did you ever wonder why the grand master chose a dilettante like yourself as his interrogator?' the Calavera asked. 'A man of modest talents compromised by many vices.'

Because he believed in me! Mordaine wanted to shout, teetering between hope and terror. *Because he recognised the honour beneath my shame!*

'Did you ever question why he kept you close above all others?' that insidious whisper slithered on, cultivating doubts that had always been there, waiting to be unearthed. 'Why he shared so many mysteries and revelations with an acolyte who lacked the wit to comprehend them?'

Because he saw greatness where others saw only mediocrity!

'Why he still haunts your thoughts like the imminent shadow of your true self? An annihilating, irrefutable truth,' the Calavera said, driving the blade home.

All the tests and the rituals and that ceaseless, soul-wracking assessment...

Uzochi was going to shoot! Mordaine saw it in the madman's glassy, hate-ravaged eyes. He fired first, his pistol surging up as if of its own accord. The Calavera made no move as the bolt seared past him and punched through Uzochi's forehead. The Shark's mouth gaped open, spilling smoke as his gun crashed to the ground. He stared at Mordaine, but his eyes were empty. There was nothing behind them any more. That vacant condemnation transfixed Mordaine long after the corpse had toppled, for it signified what he'd always been himself: a vessel devoid of substance.

But no longer... The pistol slipped from his grasp and hope followed it.

LIGHT

All roads end in ruin, yet not all ruination is equal. The fall may reap the Void or it may see the Light.

– The Calavera

'Will I die?' Mordaine asked some time later. He hadn't moved. Uzochi's sightless eyes still held him in thrall.

'You are not possessed,' the Calavera answered. 'Your mind has been imprinted with the template of another, but Aion Escher's spirit is gone. You will experience changes as the new pattern asserts itself, but your *self* will remain.'

'But will it still be me?'

'I cannot answer that, Haniel Mordaine.'

'I don't even know if it was me that shot Uzochi,' Mordaine said bleakly. 'Why would I do such a thing?'

'Because you want to live.'

Do I? Mordaine wondered. *Or is that the* other?

'All of this...' He gestured vaguely at everything and nothing. 'My exile with Kreeger, the fall of Vyshodd and that infernal interrogation... You engineered it all to awaken the sleeper inside me?'

'It was one of many synchronous, intertwined objectives,' the Calavera said. 'Each facilitated the other. As the revolution galvanised your quickening, so your presence sparked the revolution and both served to enlighten another significant piece. Farsight.'

'No.' Mordaine shook his head, appalled at the immensity of the ancient's conceit. 'I won't accept it. You couldn't possibly contrive such a thing. There are too many variables, too much scope for chance to play havoc.'

'Your prisoner awaits,' the Calavera declared. 'Is that not so?'

Hesitantly Mordaine opened the cell door. The room beyond was empty.

'The threads of fate will twist, fray and sometimes snap in the winds of Chaos,' the ancient warrior said. 'You are correct that nothing is certain, but much is *likely* for one who can see.'

'You knew...' Mordaine was aghast. 'You knew I would defy you today.'

'I knew nothing, but suspected much.'

And seeing changes what is seen, Mordaine thought, though he doubted the intuition was his own.

Later still, Mordaine asked about the xenos.

'He continues his journey,' the Calavera answered.

The interrogator didn't question how or where the alien had gone. The answer would prove a mundane revelation alongside the others. Instead he asked the question that really mattered: 'Was he truly O'Shovah?'

'Would you trust my answer?' the Calavera asked in turn.

'What would you gain by lying?'

'What would *you* gain by a truth you cannot recognise yourself?' the ancient countered.

Mordaine closed his eyes, seeking to sever himself from the cat-and-mouse ritual that bound him. He found refuge in pragmatism: 'What happens now?'

'The mechanisms of this transport are rudimentary,' the Calavera said with merciful directness. 'You will master them without difficulty.'

'To what purpose?' Mordaine asked, aloof and sightless.

'You will continue your journey to Yakov Hive, where the conclave's retribution force awaits your command, interrogator.'

'My command?' No emotion. No investment. 'I was under the impression the conclave had condemned me...' Mordaine stopped, quelling a flicker of anger. 'That was another lie, wasn't it? I was never implicated in the grand master's murder.'

'Indeed not. You were operating covertly to draw out his enemies.'

'You've been covering my tracks from the start,' Mordaine said levelly. 'There was no hunt.'

'Only *your* hunt,' the Calavera corrected. 'A hunt which has exposed a xenos conspiracy that extends to the heart of the Tau Empire. It was fine work. I envisage you will be elevated to the rank of inquisitor within two years.'

'And you'll have your cardinal back on the board.' Mordaine opened his eyes and confronted the warrior with detached hostility. 'What if I change sides, Calavera?'

'You will not. Once you recall the reasoning behind your allegiance you will make the same choice again.'

'You expect me to believe your intentions are benevolent?'

'I expect you to recognise that I offer the least of all probable evils.' The giant inclined his head. Perhaps there was genuine respect there. Then he turned and stalked towards the carriage door.

'Where are you going?' Mordaine called after him, feeling a stab of perverse terror at the prospect of his tormentor's departure.

Tormentor or mentor?

'I continue the war, Haniel Mordaine.' The Space Marine yanked the hatch open, awakening the storm outside. 'Do not linger alone in the Ghostlands,' he warned. 'There is danger here.'

The giant stepped into the bleached fury outside, becoming a shadow and then nothing at all.

All roads lead to ruin, but at the end of a very few there may be Light.

It was another stray intuition from the restive sediments of intellect embedded in Mordaine's mind, but the next impulse was entirely his own.

'O'Shovah,' he called into the wind and white darkness, 'wherever you are, xenos, may the God-Emperor watch over you.'

Smiling bleakly at his heresy, Haniel Mordaine turned his back on the void and went in search of his own annihilating, irrefutable light.

CAST A
HUNGRY SHADOW

'Faith is a ravenous beast that burns hotter than the fiercest fire.'

– Inquisitor Aion Aescher

As the three saviours climbed the mountain, the storm that had plagued their journey grew worse, congealing into a black blizzard that threatened to drag them from their narrow path. Soot storms were common on this scorched rock of a world, but there was a ferocity to this one that Ephras, who was Redemption born – and *reborn* – had never witnessed in his twenty-one years. A *rage*.

'We are being tested,' the young missionary murmured into his rebreather as he forged on, hunched into the wind. 'The Severed Spire rails at the Spiral Father's gospel and seeks to turn us from our calling!'

Spoken aloud, the thought energised him, renewing his oath to bring light to this unhallowed region. Since the coming of the great prophet, almost fifty years ago, the blood-deep blessing of the Sacred Spiral had spread across Redemption's single, fragmented continent, yet Spire Vigilans still remained apart, severed from its kindred mountains in both form and spirit. The seven spires of the Koronatus Ring jutted from the molten sea like titanic obsidian spikes, encircling the mesa at their centre with a symmetry that denied nature. Like the spokes of a wheel, vast suspension bridges linked the spires to the mesa, but the one serving – *or binding?* – Vigilans was riven with cracks and twisted out of shape. It was a path only the desperate or the deranged would choose.

Or the truly devout.

We crossed where so many others have faltered, Ephras thought fervently. *Neither wind nor fire shall turn us from our holy purpose. We –*

'Must shelter!' a harsh voice called behind him as a hand caught his arm. He turned and peered at the acolyte who'd spoken, unable to tell if it was Jujehk or Gurjah. Both his companions wore rough-spun brown robes and hid their faces in deep cowls, lest their blessings frighten the ignorant. There was no need for such measures in this wilderness, but caution was bred into their kind and they cleaved to it always. While Ephras was merely a man, the acolytes were true *spiralborn*, both exemplars of the Second Holy Paradigm of Form. One day their descendants would walk Redemption openly, but that rapture was decades, perhaps even centuries, distant.

'Look there!' the acolyte hissed, pointing at the rock face behind them. Ephras wiped at his soot-smeared goggles and squinted. There was a recess in the mountainside – angular and framed with tessellated blocks: *a shrine.* In almost two days of travel it was only the sixth they'd come across, which was another peculiarity of Vigilans, for the other spires were riddled with places of worship. The entire Koronatus Ring was a web of faith carved into the raw stone of the mountains, its origins rumoured to predate the Imperium of Man.

'Shelter!' the acolyte pressed. Like most of its kind, its jaws were not shaped for speech so it was frugal with words.

Ephras hesitated, reluctant to accede to the storm, but it would be folly to pass over this succour and risk falling. He smiled at his companion. 'Your eyes are sharper than mine, brother!'

And not just your eyes, he thought with a shudder of reverence.

The passage beyond the entrance was narrow and littered with the remnants of the bas-reliefs that had once graced its walls. Ephras frowned as his lumen lantern revealed the extent of the damage, for there was a completeness to it that surpassed natural dissolution. Someone had stripped these walls bare and crushed the carvings into fragments, expunging their meaning. This was *desecration.* Though he had no loyalty to the Imperial warrior gods that the people of Vigilans venerated, Ephras was repelled by the act itself.

Is it the Creed? he wondered uneasily. *Are they here?*

Such sacrilege was typical of the barbaric cult, but its disciples always left the mark of their messiah in their wake, and he could see no sign of the Scorched Hand on these walls.

'Breaking is old,' one of the acolytes said wetly. 'Many year.'

Ephras nodded. He had no idea how his brother knew this, but he trusted its instincts without question. While converts like himself bore the word of the Spiral Father, acolytes like Jujehk and Gurjah were His holy warriors. Without their protection Ephras would never have survived this far.

We could wait out the storm here, he thought, trying to assess the dark passageway ahead. The shriek of the storm was muted here, but the volcanic rumble of the mountain was much louder, echoing up from the depths like phantom blood rushing through the vessels of an ossified beast.

A beast that was still angry in death.

'Go deeper, Ephras,' his faith urged, for it had a voice, though it spoke rarely and only ever in a whisper. The missionary's heart soared with renewed conviction at the command. He had come to Vigilans to seek out those who had fled persecution during the dark days before the Spiral Father's rise, but his quest had no map. Faith alone was his guide, and it had spoken!

'Where there is darkness we must bring light, brothers!' Ephras decreed, striding into the depths.

She had forgotten her given name, but the lost ones had called her the Teller. It was a *true name,* for like the weight of the mountain, her words were undeniable, though she no longer spoke them aloud to make herself heard. The need for that had faded along with the lost ones' souls. She didn't recall when that had happened, or indeed how long she had been among them, but she had never forgotten the terror that had driven her here, for it was eternally sharp, preserved in a thousand flashes of burning brands and slicing blades and the castigations of the warrior women who had wielded them. Above all else, the Teller remembered her dead mother's warning: *If they find you, the Sororitas will cast you to the Black Ships.*

What the 'Black Ships' were or why they wanted her were secrets the Teller wanted no answers to, but if she thought of the future she saw the ships waiting there – eager predators, pregnant with pain. The future was nowhere she wanted to go, so she chose limbo, for herself and for those she ruled over. Broken beyond all desire save service, they tended to her needs while she brooded on nothingness. She reigned with one purpose only: to deny change and the horrors it harboured.

Yet change had come to her realm.

The Teller watched from the crowd of animated cadavers as three intruders entered her crumbling refuge, the light of their lanterns drowning the ruddy glow of the fire pit at its centre. She knew the strangers couldn't recognise her sovereignty, for she was as wasted and filthy as her subjects, so she took their measure with impunity as they hesitated at the threshold. Their leader was a tall, fair-faced youth who appraised her people with disgusted pity and an ignorant kindness that was somehow worse. She despised him instantly, but his comrades were... different. Though they were hunched and faceless under their robes, they radiated a cold, hard *hunger* that knew nothing of terror – that was beyond its touch. The realisation fascinated her for it offered hope, and repelled her because hope was surely a lie.

Evidently deciding the lost ones were no threat, the intruders approached, the youth offering platitudes as he passed among them. Incapable of curiosity or fear, the Teller's subjects fell back listlessly before the strangers, while she watched from beside the fire pit. She had already dismissed the youth, so she was shocked when he looked right at her – *into her.* There was something else behind his eyes, something as cold as his comrades, but much stronger – a mind that recognised what she was!

As the youth opened his mouth to speak, the Teller's coiled fear reared up into rage and she lashed out with her will, striking like an aetheric viper. The stranger screamed as his body was wrenched in a hundred opposing angles that snapped sinew, bone and sanity into a splintered abstraction of humanity. She held the twitching ruin suspended as the hooded ones slowly raised their arms, but she sensed a lie behind their surrender – something hidden.

'We offer–' one began, but she hurled it against the wall, high above the entrance, crushing it in a vice of will and rock until it ruptured. As if in recognition of their error, the survivor raised its *third* hand, revealing a barb-tipped claw sheathed in a hard blue plates, like an insect's shell.

'Peace,' the creature wheezed, straining to shape the sounds. 'We bring... peace.'

Peace? An end to dread? Through her rage, the Teller ached to believe it.

'Be strong,' the stranger urged.

Dimly the Teller sensed it was *the master* speaking now – the hidden mind she had seen behind the youth's eyes. It had slipped to another host. Perhaps something with such power could make good on its promise. She yearned to listen, but the rage would not be denied. It had been buried too long and it *thirsted*.

'Wait!' the creature hissed.

Her fury burst forth in a primal shriek and tore into the speaker. As its hood split open she glimpsed an elongated skull and a toothy maw, but an instant later they split in turn, obliterating the bestial visage in a spray of blood. But her rage was still not sated. A flick of her eyes shredded one of her followers, then another and another – her will tearing through the vacant crowd like a storm of razors.

Shuddering with effort, the Teller reeled the rage back in, binding it a heartbeat before it consumed her. She had kept it leashed since her escape and it had grown strong in the shadows of apathy. Exhausted, she slipped back towards nothingness, denying the lures of fury and peace alike. As her eyes glazed, she saw her subjects approach the bloody flowers that had erupted among them. Like their minds, their bellies were empty, but unlike ignorance, hunger knew its business well.

The Deadrock trembled and fine cracks tore through its glassy surface, rippling out from the man who knelt at its sheared pinnacle. The fissures glowed an angry crimson that he alone could see, though he had no eyes. Both had burst like overripe fruit when the taint of the Spiral had been seared from his flesh, along with all the lies he'd once lived by, old and new alike.

That had been over a decade ago and he'd come a long way since his purification. Unhindered by go-betweens, his sight had become *honest*, much like the man himself. He couldn't see through the eyes of others – that was his enemy's trick – but he could read this world like no other, for it was his god's canvas.

Someone just woke up, he deciphered. *Someone angry enough to break the chains. A woman? A girl?*

'Who are you?' he asked. His voice was like the murmur of a scorched corpse, but it carried through the gale raging around him. '*Where* are you?'

Along with the charred, heavy-duty coveralls he wore, his name was all that remained of his former life: *Gharth.* On a world defined – and damned – by names drowned in *meaning*, where every Spire was bound to a virtue it couldn't live up to, he cleaved to a name that meant nothing to anyone but himself. Inevitably the Scorched Creed had dreamt up other, darker titles for their messiah – the Blind Pilgrim... the Burning Man... the Fire Bearer – but they knew better than to use them to his face. To his mind the truth was stronger than any fable.

'Vigilans,' he whispered as the fissures darkened.

Gharth rose, his rubberised coveralls creaking as he straightened out.

He'd always been a big man, just shy of seven foot, with muscles swollen by forty years in Redemption's slab-mines, but his god had tempered him beyond natural vigour, hardening his bones and sheathing his skin in onyx scales that could turn a bullet. His hair had been seared away and his scalp branded with a splayed hand, its fingers linked by chains. Oily smoke leaked from his lips and the cauterized sockets in his face, hinting at the furnace within. An axe was strapped to his back, its double-headed blade hewn from the diamond-hard obsidian of the Deadrock.

'I'll set you free, friend,' he promised the lost girl.

Pulling down the bulbous goggles strapped to his forehead, Gharth leapt from the Deadrock, plummeting almost twenty metres to the plain below. He landed on his feet with his back unbent, barely registering the spine-jarring impact. His eighteen firesworn comrades, the Redeemed, stood vigil beside their war bikes, exactly as he'd left them when he'd climbed the sacred rock. A few were lesser giants drawn from the same industrial hell as their leader, but most were simply the lost who'd risen in damnation. Each had forged his – or, in the case of Kael, her – own armour, weaving their suits from industrial scraps and razorwire with solemn, clumsy devotion. They were a patchwork band, but they were tied by a bitterness more potent than blood.

We are those who were left behind.

'Vigilans,' Gharth told them as he mounted his bike. It was a massive coal-black monstrosity armoured with riveted plates that flared into a shield across the handlebars. Like its rider, it was favoured by their god and had many names, though Gharth alone knew its *true* name, an eight-syllabled tangle that hinted at a spirit more daemonic than mechanical.

'Will there be a burning?' the Redeemed growled in chorus.

'Until there's nothing left to burn.' Their messiah completed the litany. His bike roared as he gunned it into life, like a beast unleashed. Flames spewed from its exhaust as it surged into the maelstrom and the pack followed, eager for the hunt.

Standing in the gallery above the Hall of Rebirth, Aziah, the Chosen Claw of Spire Caritas, watched the throng of aspirants gathered below. Most had the haggard, soot-stained look of Redemption's serfs – refinery rats, magma scrapers or shrine thralls – but there were a few cleaner ones among them, probably city functionaries or wardens. More of their kind were turning to the Spiral Dawn every month, drawn by the promise of a cure for the black breath or driven by fear of the Scorched Creed. The lung rot was one of Redemption's perennial blights, but the fire-worshipping cult was a recent terror, its first atrocities dating back less than a decade.

'Make no mistake, the Creed's roots run deep,' Saint Etelka had cautioned the Chosen Claws. *'It draws its strength from the evil beneath the spires, which is older than the Imperium and infinitely more bitter.'*

And it is growing more confident, Aziah thought as he scanned the crowd for a threat. In recent years the Creed's raids and terror strikes had escalated, ranging beyond isolated shrines to the Spiral Dawn's heartlands. The murder cult was moving to a war footing.

'You smell danger, brother,' a voice growled at Aziah's shoulder. He glanced at the muscular acolyte that had crept alongside him. It was a creature of the Second Paradigm, its third arm terminating in a serrated blade of bone – an uncommon blessing that was revered among the kindred. Aziah couldn't recall a time when Bharbaz hadn't been with him, first as his protector, then his claw-brother and now, since his ascension to the Chosen Claws, as his lieutenant.

'The Creed,' Bharbaz said. It wasn't a question. The creature could *taste* its commander's mind, which troubled Aziah, for his thoughts were sometimes sour.

You are purer than I, brother, he reflected as he searched the sea of faces. Like all aspirants, their expressions straddled the gulf betwixt hope and desperation, awe and fear, sometimes heightened by the black breath's touch. Among the extremes were all the petty passions and indignities of the human condition that Aziah loathed.

I despise them because I recognise them, he admitted.

He thrust the shame aside and concentrated on his duty, hunting for the source of his disquiet. The aspirants had been searched when they entered the temple and issued with plain white tunics that offered scant opportunities for concealed weapons, yet his instincts were screaming. Something was wrong...

'The Sacred Spiral dawns eternal!' a voice rang out, resonant with warm authority. 'In its unfolding embrace we are reborn and raised beyond the taints and torments of this mortal gyre!'

Focused on the crowd, Aziah hadn't noticed Heliphos enter the chamber below. The high priest stood on a dais before the silver gates of the sanctum, his arms spread wide in welcome as he began the initiation ceremony. Despite his great age, Heliphos was straight-backed and muscular, his vitality preserved by the spiral blessing in his blood. A winding helix was tattooed across his shaven head, marking him as one of the Gyre Apostles, a convert embraced and elevated by the prophet Himself. The elder had fought beside the Spiral Father in the early days and been rewarded with stewardship of Spire Caritas, where new aspirants were received.

And I am entrusted with his safety, Aziah thought, his eyes narrowing.

'Our world is wracked by sickness and slaughter,' Heliphos pronounced, 'but you have taken the first steps from the cradle of despair into the light of the star gods, of whom the God-Emperor is but one.'

That was when Aziah found the assassin. The man was one of the higher caste aspirants, but he was stick-thin, his long face withered and blotched by lung rot. It was his eyes that gave him away, for while his fellows' were filled with eagerness, his shone with rage. Rage and something more...

Wildfire, Aziah realised, recognising the glitter of the Creed's unholy narcotic. The black crystal formed in the magma-drenched hell at the base of the spires, where only the damned would venture. It combusted when chewed, triggering a paroxysm of fury, along with a brief surge of strength and speed. Anything but the smallest dose was fatal, but that was a price the Creed's 'scorchers' willingly paid for a few minutes of divine slaughter.

It kicked in quickly so the infiltrator must have bitten down on a shard after Heliphos entered. The way his eyes were burning, it had been a big one.

'The Black Needle unweaves the world!' the fanatic bellowed in a savage rasp, cutting across Heliphos' sermon.

Then he was beyond words. Blood and smoke erupted from his mouth as his body jerked like a puppet dancing to an idiot god's whims. The woman in front of him turned and the scalding fumes caught her full in the face. As she convulsed and fell to her knees the assassin flung his arms wide, whip-lash fast. His nails – long and tempered to dagger-like sharpness – slashed open the throats of those to either side of him, spraying others with blood. Gurgling deep in his throat, he charged towards Heliphos, slashing a path through the terrified congregation.

'Scorcher!' Aziah shouted. Yanking his bonesword free, he vaulted from the gallery. The Spiral was muted in his blood so he had only two arms and neither sported a claw, but the weapon forged from the prophet's secretions was as much a part of him as Bharbaz's killing arm. It had been a gift to cel-ebrate the coming of the Third Paradigm, of which Aziah was the firstborn. They had made their first kill together when he was nine.

'For the Spiral!' the Chosen Claw snarled as the sword's hilt pulsed in his grip. He landed in a crouch and sprang forward, barrelling through the heaving, shrieking crowd. The aspirants were insignificant beside the *heresy* of this incursion and he thrust them aside in his eagerness to reach the assassin. One of the initiates leapt at him and lashed out in a frenzy of clenched fists and snapping teeth. Her wide, bleeding eyes were framed by a rictus snarl devoid of sanity. It was the woman who'd fallen to the scorcher's breath.

'We burn,' she croaked, oily smoke wafting from her seared lips.

Aziah rammed his blade between her jaws, but as he pulled it free a pair of tainted aspirants hurtled into him, one wrapping his arms around the Chosen Claw's waist, the other grabbing his sword arm. They chewed at his padded armour, drooling blood and fumes in their eagerness to reach his flesh. He saw others like them among the crowd, lashing about and leaping upon their fellows like wolves. True to its name, the wildfire was spread-ing swiftly through the crowd, its delirium carried by the smoke. The drug was dangerous, but Aziah had never seen such virulence. This was some-thing new. Something *darker*.

He yanked his sword arm free, hurling one attacker into the crowd and sinking his fangs into the head of the one embracing him. Though Aziah had no claws, his elongated jaws were filled with sharp teeth that made short work of the man's scalp and gnawed into the skull beneath. Seem-ingly oblivious to pain, his enemy didn't relent until Aziah's barbed tongue punched through to his brain. Noxious gas vented from the rupture, scalding Aziah's face and setting his hood alight. The stench of sulphur and burning flesh was appalling. With a snarl, he tore his blistered tongue free and stag-gered back, spitting rancid ichor as he slashed about in a wide arc to keep the tainted at bay. A red haze was falling over him. He couldn't tell the cor-rupt from the pure...

It doesn't matter. The revelation was exhilarating. Joyous! It drowned out the ceaseless psychic susurrations of the prophet that had shadowed Aziah's thoughts since birth. *None of it matters!*

As Aziah ripped off his smouldering hood he felt the wildfire rippling through him in agonising, ecstatic bursts, urging him to kill and kill again because *nothing* mattered. Nothing was real! Another madman charged him and Aziah roared, meeting him with a swing that almost tore him in two.

'I am risen!' Aziah bellowed, meeting his attacker with a swing that almost tore him in two.

'Remember yourself, Chosen Claw!' the Spiral Father hissed into his mind. The prophet's murmurs rarely coalesced into words for Aziah so they struck him like a physical force, dousing his fury in a wash of shame. He realised Bharbaz was fighting alongside him, its three arms whipping about in a whirlwind blur, the natural blade interweaving with claw and scimitar in lethal harmony. It was a perfect expression of the Sacred Spiral...

'I am *kindred*!' Aziah hissed. Gritting his fangs, he quelled the rage and appraised the scene.

It was mayhem. Over a hundred initiates and a score of human converts were crowded into the chamber, scrambling about and brawling and screaming. Many were clustered at the entrance, pounding at the massive doors that had been sealed when the ceremony began. Others were trying to climb to the galleries above, sometimes clambering over each other in their haste, but it was impossible to tell whether it was flight or fury that drove them. There was no sign of Heliphos, but the dais where he had stood was empty. Had he escaped to the sanctum?

'They are lost,' the Spiral Father decreed.

'Purge them all!' Aziah shouted to the acolytes manning the gallery, then turned to Bharbaz. 'We must find the apostle!'

Together they waded into the crowd, hacking down anyone in their path while the acolytes above sprayed the chamber with gunfire.

'Save us, brother!' a choking man begged, clutching at Aziah's robes. The Chosen Claw cut him down without hesitation; only the spiralborn could be trusted to withstand the taint that had come among them.

A ragged shape leapt from the crowd and slammed into the wall to his right, its hooked talons latching onto the stone. It was a tortured parody of a man, with arms tautened to twice the natural length, while its torso had shrivelled, as if one had nourished the other. The thing's head hung limply over its back, swinging like a pendulum from a long, stalk-like neck that looked broken or boneless. Its eyes had exploded and its jaws were slack, but it was unmistakably the assassin who had seeded this madness.

'The wall!' Aziah shouted to the acolytes above as the thing scuttled towards the gallery like a bipedal spider. 'Watch the wall!'

An acolyte leaned over the railings, but as he aimed his gun the abomination lashed out with one arm and tore his throat open. Its blind, swaying head screeched joyfully as fresh blood spattered it, then with a surge of speed the thing hauled itself onto the gallery. A riot of muzzle flares lit the shadows as the defenders turned their autoguns on the invader, but it was among them in seconds.

'Beware, brother!' Bharbaz yelled as a wailing madman leapt towards Aziah, reaching for him with blazing skeleton-claw hands. As the Chosen Claw swept his blade out he recognised his attacker: *Heliphos.* The apostle's hair was ablaze, his face a taut death mask splintering from the heat behind it.

'I have failed,' Aziah hissed and swept the apostle's head from his shoulders. It spun over the crowd, spewing smoke like a fleshy censer.

All around the chamber the burning damned were beginning to combust as the wildfire reached its zenith. In these final minutes they were more dangerous than ever. They needed no weapons when their touch alone was lethal. Fighting back to back, the two kindred held them at bay as smoke drowned the chamber.

This temple is forever desecrated, Aziah gauged bitterly. Then his world narrowed to a raw equation of hacks and parries, where a single miscalculation could be fatal. Even at arm's length, the heat coming off the damned was ferocious.

Finally there were no more. The chamber had fallen silent save for the pop and hiss of broiling flesh. Aziah realised the gunfire had also ceased. He squinted at the gallery, trying to penetrate the filthy swirl.

'Brothers?' he called. There was no reply. 'Brothers!'

A molten wheeze answered from somewhere above, slithering into a chuckle.

'The assassin still lives,' Aziah hissed as Bharbaz stepped beside him with its weapons levelled at the gallery.

'Show yourself!' Aziah challenged. 'In the name of the Sacred Spiral–'

The abomination burst from the gallery in a tangle of charred bones and claws, moving faster than Aziah would have imagined possible. The assassin's long face was still recognisable in the seething riot that his body had become, though its features were distended to monstrous proportions. Hellfire blazed in the warp-spawned thing's eye sockets as it plummeted towards him, its multitude of claws outstretched.

It is blind, yet it sees, Aziah realised.

An explosive chatter of gunfire sliced through the beast's roar and a volley of bolts punched into it mid-leap, shredding its torso and hurling it across the chamber. Aziah turned and saw a pale figure striding through the smoke, its rifle blazing as it tracked the scorcher's arc. The beast crashed down in a broken heap and tried to haul itself up, quaking as the mass-reactive rounds detonated inside it. Its head surged up on its wormlike neck, swaying about as it hunted for its tormentor, then fixed on Aziah once more. With a howl of hatred, the Chosen Claw charged the abomination with his sword raised.

'Betrayer,' it croaked an instant before he cleaved its skull.

Fresh rage flooded Aziah and he hacked at the carcass relentlessly, as if the blows could expunge that poisonous word.

Betrayer. Why did the accusation sting?

'Enough, Chosen Claw!' It was a woman's voice, cold and hard-edged.

Aziah swung round as the speaker approached. She was clad in ornate power armour that mirrored her slender frame, its ceramite plates polished to a white sheen that seemed to radiate light. A purple tabard embroidered with a silver spiral covered her breastplate and hung between her legs. It was a graceful rendition of the sect's symbol, quite distinct from the angular variant that Aziah and his acolytes bore. The woman's face was hidden behind the visor of her backswept helmet, but there was no mistaking her identity for she was the last of her kind on Redemption.

And I would know her among a thousand of her sisters, Aziah thought. *Ten thousand even.*

'The Sacred Spiral ward you, saint,' he greeted her, his voice tight.

'It appears *you* were the one in need of warding, Chosen Claw,' Etelka Arkanto observed. The Saint of Castitas stowed her storm bolter as a pair of First Paradigm acolytes strode up to flank her. They were massively built and gifted with four arms apiece, the upper pair flaring into curved rending blades, the lower terminating in long-fingered hands that looked almost delicate. Their hoods were thrown back, revealing crested skulls and noble, fang-filled faces tattooed with silver whorls. Both carried bulky plasma rifles and wore silver flak armour emblazoned with their mistress' heraldry. The Spiral Father had granted her the Shining Claws in honour of her service during the Reformation, which eclipsed even that of Heliphos.

Heliphos...

'The Apostle of Caritas is dead,' Aziah said, bowing his head.

'That is regrettable.' Etelka reached for her visor.

'The air is tainted!' Aziah cautioned, but she didn't hesitate.

'My blood is not yet so thin, Chosen Claw.'

There was a hiss as the airtight seal broke and her visor rose. The face beneath was pale and deeply seamed, but its high cheekbones and full lips had weathered the ravages of age remarkably well. Like Heliphos, she had been embraced by the Spiral Father and His blessing was potent. Fixing her violet eyes on Aziah, Etelka breathed deeply of the smoke.

She is not spiralborn! Aziah tightened his grip on his sword, yet he knew he wouldn't be able to use it. Not against her.

The saint released the fumes slowly and smiled. That grimace – frigid and vulpine – had always disturbed him. *The Spiral's song is stronger in my blood than yours,* it mocked. His anger stirred, the old and the new conjoined this time.

Betrayer...

'How did you know?' Aziah hissed. Every member of the sect was bound by the Spiral Father's omnipresence, but the scorcher had struck mere minutes ago. How had she made the long journey from Spire Castitas in time?

'I did *not* know,' Etelka said, 'but the Spiral connects.'

'The fault was mine–'

She silenced him with sharp gesture, dismissing his protests along with the dead priest. 'This outrage is not why I came to Caritas.'

'I don't understand.'

'These are dark times, but not without hope.' Etelka placed a hand on his shoulder and he suppressed a shudder. 'A divine vessel has been found to bear our first magus.'

Aziah's eyes narrowed at the wondrous news. 'A warp-weaver? Where?'

'There are complications.' The saint looked at him levelly. 'I am bound for the Severed Spire.'

She smiled again.

'I want you beside me, my son.'

A sullen wind lashed at Aziah as he approached the trailer at the back of Etelka's convoy. It was a windowless steel box mounted on six wheels. A sealed hatch was set into its rear, embossed with the silver spiral of Castitas. Reverently Aziah pressed a hand on the symbol and closed his eyes.

'It has been too long, my brother,' he murmured. A deep moan answered from within as the Cicatryx sensed its birth brother. The saint's second son was a holy aberration – a rare and revered divergence from the Four Paradigms. Such *misborn* were exalted in strength, but lacking in subtlety so they were kept hidden from outsiders, consigned to the darkest places until the sect required their might.

'Will it be war?' Aziah asked as Etelka joined him.

'Perhaps,' the saint replied, placing a slender hand beside his three-fingered paw. 'The Creed are pressing us hard and our veil wears thin. Without a magus to weave it anew the outsiders will soon turn upon us.'

'Then we will crush them!' There was a growl from the trailer as the Cicatryx echoed its younger brother's anger.

'And in turn the Imperium will crush *us*.' Etelka shook her head. 'No, it is too soon. The kindred are too few.'

'Then you will guide us on the narrow path,' Aziah said fiercely. 'As you have always done.'

'I am no magus, my son.' A note of bitterness had crept into her voice. 'And I am *old*.' Etelka stepped away from the carriage and regarded the roiling, soot-choked sky. 'A storm comes.'

'A bitter one,' Aziah agreed, following her gaze. Despite the planet's twin suns there was little to distinguish day and night on Redemption, but the storms were another matter – they decreed the cycle here. 'It would be wise to let it pass.'

'The Creed will not wait,' she said.

'They know of the weaver? How?'

'I have told you before – this *world* is a betrayer. They know.' She spat without decorum. 'We cannot wait.'

The Cicatryx growled again and scratched at its cell as its mother stalked towards her vehicle.

'Be still, my brother,' Aziah soothed it. But as he followed Etelka all he could think of was the word she'd used: *betrayer*.

As the convoy crossed the mesa, the storm mustered its strength, raising whirling soot devils from the plain and buffeting the vehicles, but withholding its full wrath.

It is biding its time, Etelka Arkanto judged, scanning the horizon. The jagged fang of the Severed Spire loomed ahead, a deeper darkness against the gloom, its bulk riddled with crimson veins. Unlike the other spires, Vigilans was volcanically active and prone to sudden violence.

'*It is spite given substance,*' Etelka's long-dead matriarch, Canoness Aveline had once proclaimed. '*Like a shard splintered from the warp.*'

Where else could a witch find sanctuary on this world? the saint mused. Her former sisterhood had governed Redemption for almost three centuries, standing vigil against the Scorched God and culling those who might become conduits for daemons. Ironically that purge had proved to be an unforeseen retribution upon the sect that overthrew them, for the Spiral Dawn could not breed its magus without a witch's warp-tuned blood.

'And without a magus we shall fall,' she whispered.

Etelka stood on the open deck of the lead war truck, gripping the guardrail of its wedge-like front. The *Silvergyre*'s industrial heritage had been muted with elegant white panels, but there was no masking its spiked wheels and the rack of buzz saws jutting from its fore. Those blades had been forged to chew through the stone warrens beneath the mesa and the vehicle's chassis could withstand a magma burst. Redemption's mining industry had been in decline for centuries, but its trucks were built to last so the sect had claimed and consecrated them.

Just as it claimed and consecrated me.

Recently Etelka's memories of the dark days of the Reformation had resurfaced, and with them, the guilt. It had been a constant companion in the early years of her rebirth, ripe with the threat of damnation, but with time and the prophet's guidance it had withered. She had not betrayed her sisterhood, but *liberated* them.

'I gave them peace!' Etelka told the wind, but her words sounded hollow, *faltering* – much like the prophet's psychic murmurs, which had weakened as the convoy neared the gorge.

The Scorched God is strong here, Etelka brooded.

'*I see the bridge,* Silvergyre,' a voice crackled from her helmet's vox bead.

'Confirmed,' she replied, squinting at the taillights of the two bikes leading the convoy. Though only twenty metres ahead, the scouts were almost lost in the churning gloom. She switched to the command channel. 'Prepare for the crossing,' she sent to the convoy. 'Slow, steady and vigilant.'

This is where we are most vulnerable.

Sensing their mistress' unease, the Shining Claws to either side of her activated their plasma rifles. She glanced round and saw the truck's stubber gun swinging back and forth in its open-topped turret, the head and shoulders of its operator visible. Another warrior manned the vehicle's servo-arm – a massive articulated claw fitted with a heavy laser and a searchlight. Both gunners were Third Paradigm neophytes like Aziah, their Spiral-touched heritage muted. Though their flesh was purple-tinged and hairless, their crests were subdued and they had only two arms, both unremarkable. Like all their generation, they were very young, but more dextrous with machines than their elder kin – seemingly closer to human.

Yet their serenity is flawless, Etelka reflected, thinking of the darkness in Aziah. Her darkness.

The convoy slowed to a crawl as it approached the bridge. Immense basalt pylons framed its cobbled ramp, each warded by a stone giant. The figures were too abstract and worn to identify, but their belligerent postures were unambiguous. Whatever they were, they revered war. Likewise, the pylons were carved into inverted swords, their hilts threaded with metal cables that connected them to the next pair along. The far side of the bridge, some two thousand metres distant, was shrouded in smoke and darkness

'This is a warrior's road,' Aziah said to Bharbaz, 'and a warrior's spire.'

His lieutenant said nothing, but its eyes were alert for danger as their vehicle mounted the stone ramp, hauling the Cicatryx's carriage behind it. They were at the rear of the convoy, their truck the last of three. Four lightly armoured Talon buggies supported the trucks, along with the scout bikes up front. All told, their expedition numbered almost sixty kindred.

'Some day we will go to war by the thousand, brother!' Aziah growled.

The bridge was wide enough to accommodate the trucks side by side, but the kindred were taking no chances. Vigilans had been abandoned centuries ago and its bridge was twisted out of shape, creating a sharp incline to the left, where the sidewall had collapsed into the gorge. Many of the pylons showed steel bones where their stone cladding had sloughed away, though the deck was clear of debris.

'Whatever falls here is swept into the abyss,' Aziah said, gazing at the red haze rising from the precipice. It seemed to promise a fate worse than a burning death.

As Etelka had feared, the storm broke when the convoy wasn't even halfway across. Howling crosswinds scoured *Silvergyre*'s deck and visibility dropped to a few metres, slowing the vehicles to a crawl.

'Say again, *Gyrerunner One?*' Etelka hissed into her vox bead. Once again, she was met by a snarl of static that *might* have been a voice. The storm was playing havoc with their comms and the scouts hadn't signed in for several minutes.

I let them slip too far ahead, she chided herself.

'I see them!' Bhezai, the neophyte manning the searchlight, yelled over the squall.

Etelka leaned forward, following his beam. Two lights were approaching, but she couldn't make out the shapes behind them.

'*Gyrerunner One?*' she voxed. 'Identify yourself!'

The shadows resolved into the compact form of bikes – then a *third* light blinked into life behind them. A fourth...

'I shall carve the penitent flesh on the bones of self-deception,' a voice rasped from Etelka's vox, so sharp and static-free the speaker might have been standing right beside her. *'For mistruth is its own unmaking.'*

'Creed!' Etelka shouted on the command channel. 'Scourge the heretics!'

As always, the Shining Claws had anticipated her will and their guns spewed superheated plasma before the words had left her mouth. The twin bursts intersected on the lead bike and it exploded into a fireball, shedding molten streamers as it spun away. Their engines roaring, the other bikes leapt forward, weaving about as they charged, seemingly untroubled by the darkness. Muzzle flare bloomed from their silhouettes as they opened fire, spraying *Silvergyre* with a hail of bullets.

Most of the barrage was blunted by the truck's frontal armour, but some swept onto the deck. Bhezai ducked as his searchlight shattered, showering him with glass. A lucky round slipped into the stubber turret, whipped past the gunner's head and ricocheted into the back of his skull. He slumped over the controls and his gun swung upwards, spitting bullets into the sky.

'Gyre Talons take point!' Etelka voxed the buggies. 'All units, forward full thrust!'

'But the storm –' the driver protested from the compartment below.

'Trust in the Spiral!' Etelka snapped, unslinging her storm bolter. 'We need to get off this bridge!'

As *Silvergyre* surged forward she returned fire, standing straight-backed with her legs braced for balance. Bullets whistled past, sometimes scraping her armour, but lacking the punch to penetrate its ceramite plates. She ignored them and savoured the release of battle.

I am a liberator!

Her bodyguards were crouched behind *Silvergyre*'s shielding, firing in alternate bursts to let their volatile plasma guns cool. Behind her, Bhezai swung the servo-arm about, punching fat las-bolts into the gloom as he hunted the raiders. There was a flare of intense light as he found a mark, virtually disintegrating both bike and rider.

'This is Aziah,' Etelka's vox announced. *'There are more behind us, saint!'*

She ignored him, her whole body reverberating with recoil as she tracked a bike until its light shattered and its casing ruptured. Belching fire, it flipped forward, hurling its armoured rider over the handlebars. He slammed into *Silvergyre*'s front and slid into its churning grinder. Etelka felt a rush of fierce joy as blood spattered her white armour.

'I give you mercy,' she breathed.

'They were waiting for us!' Aziah hissed. *'How did they–'*

'I see you, Sister,' another voice broke in as a hulking bike swept past *Silvergyre* in a blur of black iron and smoke. *'I see what you are.'*

'–trap!' Aziah finished.

There was a wail of tearing metal from somewhere behind Etelka and a buggy spun past where the bike had been moments before, its sundered chassis spewing flames. She ducked as the wreck careened in front of *Silvergyre* and crumpled under its blades. Blazing metal fragments showered the deck, burying themselves in the hull like powered daggers. A massive shard tore through the waist of an acolyte who'd just emerged from the truck's compartment. The warrior's legs tumbled back inside while its torso was thrown overboard in whirl of viscera. Another fragment buried itself in Bhezai's face, pinning him to an iron strut.

They are driven by the Scorched God's malice! Etelka raged. Keeping low, she gripped the guardrail as her truck rolled over the buggy, bucking violently. She cursed as she saw the Silver Claw on her right was dead, the top of its skull sheared away.

'*Beware, daughter!*' the Spiral Father urged with sudden clarity.

Etelka raised her head and saw a blunt-nosed colossus bearing down on her. It was a haulage tanker with bulbous wheels twice the size of *Silvergyre*'s own, its cab scorched with the splayed hand of the Creed. The open-topped cargo bay behind the cab was crowded with metal barrels...

'*All shall burn,*' her vox rasped.

'I...' Etelka began. Then her surviving bodyguard yanked her into an embrace and vaulted from the truck. They hit the ground seconds before the vehicles collided.

A thunderous explosion tore through the storm and a pillar of fire erupted on the road ahead. Aziah grabbed the guardrail as his truck lurched sharply to the right, hauling the Cicatryx's trailer in its wake and raking sparks from the bridge wall. The truck ahead veered to avoid the inferno, but it was already too close.

Kindred leapt from its deck as it plowed into the tangle of twisted metal and burning promethium. Their robes caught fire as they staggered about blindly, too devoted to accept death until a pair of heretic bikes cut them down as they swept past. A speeding Talon buggy swerved to the left, but its wheels burst as they touched the searing slick and the vehicle spun out of control. Its brakes screeching, it crashed into a bike and whirled into the gorge, carrying the entangled bike with it.

'*Silvergyre!*' Aziah shouted into his vox, already certain there would be no answer. The command truck was still recognisable in the conflagration, but its elegant façade was melting fast. As Aziah's vehicle drew level with the carnage, the second truck's hatch sprung open and an acolyte heaved itself out, only to combust in the intense heat.

'*Betrayal is honest,*' his vox hissed, somehow drawing his eyes to a hulking shape on the far side of the inferno. Though it was motionless, its outline rippled in the heat haze, flickering between a jagged-edged bike and a horned iron beast. The giant that sat astride the metal chimera was a changeless, indecipherable shadow, yet Aziah sensed it was watching him.

'*Burn the lie that binds, friend,*' the shadow told him.

'Beware!' Bharbaz yelled as a bullet raked Aziah's head. The Chosen Claw swung round and saw another bike storming towards his truck. Its rider sat high in her saddle with a pistol in each hand, her long hair streaming behind her as she sprayed bullets. She was an easy target, yet the truck's return fire was flying wide, slipping around her as if the wind itself was twisting the stubber rounds off course.

This world is a betrayer, Aziah remembered his mother saying.

The heretic leapt an instant before her bike slammed into the truck and exploded at her back, propelling her through the air like a human cannonball. She crashed onto the rear deck in a crouch, her back crawling with flames. As the kindred surged towards her she spun round, firing wildly and chanting in a guttural slur.

She is another giant, Aziah realised as the biker rose to her full height, her muscles straining against the loosely woven scraps of her armour. A riveted iron box encased her head, its front slashed open to frame blood-shot eyes. What he'd taken for hair was actually a plume of razorwire woven with obsidian fetishes.

'Heretic!' Bharbaz bellowed, lunging past Aziah, heedless of the bullets that thudded into its chest. The acolyte's scything claw lashed out and sliced off the berserker's left hand while its chitinous talon grabbed her other wrist. They were evenly matched in strength, but the woman had only two arms. She snarled as her enemy's third swept down and thrust its scimitar into her chest, its blade tearing through her patchwork breastplate. Aziah saw her eyes widen in ecstasy, their irises glowing as smoke gushed from her helmet.

'Wildfire!' he yelled, but it was too late. The heretic's visor exploded as she vomited a soul-deep spray of flames into Bharbaz's face, scorching the flesh from its skull.

'Chosen Claw,' Aziah's vox hissed, seeming to come from somewhere far away. *'Aziah...'*

Bharbaz's corpse toppled over, its charred skull snapping loose as it struck the deck. A moment later the biker's carbonized body disintegrated under the weight of its own armour. Through a red haze Aziah heard the Cicatryx battering at its cell – then the vox signal again, urgent and tight with pain.

'I need you, my son.'

Gharth slowed his bike as he reached the far side of the bridge, then swung round to a stop. The machine growled, eager to return to the slaughter, but he reined it in with a lash of contempt.

'Be still.'

His empty eye sockets fixed on the bridge, regarding the Spiral-tainted degenerates with deeper vision. They were consolidating what little they had left around their remaining truck, rallying with inhuman tenacity to repel another attack. There was no fear among them – no emotion at all save for the thorny, tormented reek of the fallen Sister and her spawn. Others might have found it ironic that the soulless were led by such lost souls, but Gharth was dead to such notions, just as he was dead to the exhilaration of his fellow Redeemed.

The riders were alight with the rapture of battle as they pulled up alongside him – and bristling against the cessation he had commanded. Only seven of them had survived, but he felt no sorrow for the lost; not even for Kael, who had stood beside him in vengeance since his awakening, and in love before that. Like the others, she had seized death with a joy he could not share. All that remained to him was a hate so immaculate it eclipsed all else.

'You shall awaken into cold ash,' his god's one-eyed herald had decreed, so long ago now, *'purged of the Spiral's taint and shriven of the vanities and delusions of the self.'*

'I want to remember,' Gharth had protested, gazing at the immolating wellspring the ancient had led him to. He could feel the xenos contagion of the Spiral Dawn spreading through his body, unravelling him with every

heartbeat, yet still he'd hesitated. *'I want to remember what they did to me – to all of us.'*

'You will not forget. Not that,' his guide had promised, *'but your hate shall become as ice. And from that ice you shall bring forth annihilating, irrefutable fire.'*

The first tongues of that promised fire had cleansed Gharth of taint, both xenos and human. The agony had been unspeakable, but he had embraced it with passion until passion itself had been scorched away.

'Not all ruination is equal.' Stepping from the flames, the burned man had not known if it was his god, the guide or himself who had spoken those words. Later he'd understood that the question made no sense.

Gharth swung his bike round to face the Severed Spire. To that brooding, dissident peak the Creed and the Spiralborn were one, both unworthy of anything but contempt.

'Do your worst, friend,' Gharth told it and kicked his bike into life.

The battered convoy completed the crossing at a crawl, with the two surviving buggies flanking Aziah's truck in close formation. Nothing came for them on the bridge. Nothing met them on the other side.

'Why did they break off the attack?' Aziah said to Bharbaz, squinting at the storm-wracked ridge above. 'They had us.'

The charred skull at his feet offered no reply. Neither did the surviving Silver Claw, Hezrakh, who had taken his lieutenant's place. One of the creature's arms had been torn off in the explosion, along with half its face, but First Paradigm kindred were almost as hardy as the star-born Purebloods that seeded them.

They make fine warriors, but poor lieutenants, Bharbaz, Aziah thought sadly. He quashed the emotion, ashamed of the weakness. His claw-brother had died serving the Sacred Spiral. Nothing else mattered.

'The heretics want us alive,' he mused aloud. 'Weakened, but alive.'

It was the only answer. Was the enemy taunting them?

Then Aziah's thoughts clouded as the Spiral Father's will washed over him, impelling him towards the mountain. The path to the warp-weaver's aerie unfurled before his eyes, the ruined temple shining like a beacon, reinforcing the *need* to get moving again, to follow–

Our enemy doesn't know the path, Aziah grasped with sudden conviction. Trembling with the effort, he slipped free of the prophet's compulsion. *No.*

Hezrakh growled and jabbed its claw towards the mountain.

'We go,' the two neophyte gunners behind Aziah chorused.

'No!' the Chosen Claw repeated, speaking aloud to brace his will against the psychic tide. 'The enemy needs us to lead them to the warp-weaver.' His skull was pounding with the affront of his denial. 'They don't know the way.'

The pressure relented and Aziah sensed the prophet turning the possibility over.

'The storm is their cloak,' Aziah pressed. 'It hides them, but does not blind them. We must wait until it passes.'

Hezrakh was staring at him with ferocious, empty eyes, as if its mind had become dislocated. Aziah knew every other member of the convoy shared that expression right now, just as Bharbaz would have done.

They are willing slaves. The thought was laced with revulsion. It was almost *heretical.* Then a wash of approval flooded Aziah's mind.

'*Lead as you see fit, Chosen Claw,*' the Spiral Father breathed in its wake. The prophet's presence faded, but His benediction lingered.

This is why you wanted me by your side, mother, Aziah thought. *You and I serve the Spiral, but not as slaves.*

'Be vigilant, brothers,' he ordered on the command channel. 'We depart when the storm wanes.'

Satisfied there was no immediate danger, Aziah climbed down to the compartment where the saint lay. Hezrakh had shielded her from the blast with its own body, but a long shard of metal had punched through its back and impaled them both. Her guardian had freed itself, but removing the fragment from Etelka had been too dangerous, especially with their healer lost in the skirmish. The shard jutted from her belly like a jag of frozen lightning, her armour cracked and blackened around the wound, looking almost diseased.

'Saint,' Aziah whispered, crouching beside her. 'Mother?'

Etelka's eyes were wide open, but their pupils were contracted to tiny points, exactly as they'd been when he'd found her.

'*I need you, my son.*' She must have voxed that last message moments before she slipped into oblivion.

'You shall be made whole,' he promised, running a hand over her brow. 'The Spiral connects.'

The saint hauled her broken body over a smooth stone surface. The sulphur-drenched air shivered with a deep rumbling that promised fire, yet the darkness was so complete it denied the possibility of light.

'You have no light, nor the sight to see it,' someone said, as if echoing Etelka's thoughts. 'You blinded yourself for lies. Only a madwoman would dream such blasphemies. Only a fool would listen to her ravings.' Then it struck like a lash. 'And only a heretic would murder for them.'

'You're long dead,' Etelka hissed, recognising the voice of her former superior. 'Go back to your corpse-god, Aveline!'

'I am with Him always,' Vetala Aveline, Canoness of the Thorn Eternal replied. 'Those who serve with faith, serve without end. What do you serve, sister?'

'We are not sisters.'

'We will always be sisters, heretic,' Aveline said without emotion. 'Why did you betray us?'

'You betrayed yourselves,' Etelka snarled, remembering the rituals of fasting and flagellation, and the ceaseless, senseless sermons and ceremonies, but most of all the burnings – the torment their order had inflicted upon those it claimed to protect. 'We served a lie!'

By the time the storm abated Redemption's twin suns had risen. They glowered through the wind-scoured sky, washing the mountain in a clash of ochre and violet as the kindred began their ascent. Like all the spires, Vigilans was girdled by a cobbled road that wound towards its summit, but the path soon narrowed, forcing the expedition to abandon the vehicles on the lower steppes.

Aziah left them in the care of his neophyte gunners, but he could spare no more to guard them. Other than the Silver Claw, the remaining eleven survivors were Second Paradigm acolytes armed with autoguns, scimitars and the blessings of their blood.

'They will be enough,' he whispered. 'They must be.'

While his followers gathered supplies, Aziah went to his birth brother's trailer and placed a hand on its hatch as he whispered his commands. When he was certain the Cicatryx understood, he opened the hatch and waited, but the divine aberration did not stir from the darkness.

'Your time comes soon, my brother,' he promised.

As Aziah joined the others Hezrakh lifted Etelka, cradling her limp form against its chest. Her condition was unchanged, but Aziah would not countenance leaving her behind. If the heretics attacked the vehicles he doubted the neophytes could repel them.

But they won't attack. They will follow us.

He appraised the road ahead. Even during the short climb they'd made so far it had spawned several tributary tracks, which would doubtless branch in turn, serving scattered shrines or monuments. Like all the spires save the austere pillar of Humilitas, Vigilans was a labyrinth that could swallow an unwary traveller.

Aziah closed his eyes and pictured the path revealed by the Spiral Father.

The darkness was endless, but not quite changeless. As she crawled, Etelka Arkanto sensed a sonorous pounding, so faint it was more a vibration than a sound. Even distant, it was threatening, like the heartbeat of a slumbering leviathan. Whatever it was, she wanted no part of it. Blindly she swerved to her right.

'Sacrifice is our only path through the maze of thorns,' Canoness Aveline observed. 'All others end in damnation. You understand this, sister. You always have.'

'That isn't true,' Etelka hissed, knowing it was.

'Without sacrifice there can be no salvation,' Aveline decreed. 'You are incapable of believing otherwise. Even in blasphemy, you are Adeptus Sororitas.'

'The Spiral Dawn set me free!'

'You allowed its corruption into your body and soul. Why?'

Etelka cried out to the Spiral Father, but even the whisper of his will was long gone.

'Why did you betray us, sister?'

As its brother had decreed, the Cicatryx waited until the purple sun had crawled behind the mountain before leaving its cage. Shunning the road, it crept towards the rock face, moving with an eerie grace that defied its bulk. The thin-blooded kindred standing watch from the truck didn't even glance its way as it began to climb, scythe-over-claw-over-scythe...

When it reached the ridge above, the Cicatryx crouched low and ran its long tongue through the air. *Nothing*. Nor on the next... But as it hauled itself towards a third the smell of seared flesh wafted down from above. The Cicatryx froze, clinging to the sheer rock as a pack of outsiders passed by. They were moving quietly, but their stench was like a scream to the Cicatryx.

It had its prey. It would not fail its brother.

Crouched in her sanctum, the Teller froze as she felt the intruders enter her realm, creeping through the temple gates as if they could hide from her. Most were like the hooded beasts that had come before, their souls cold and entirely at peace. But their leader was different, his serenity riddled with fractures that threatened to break him.

As the strangers pressed on into the tunnels she realised there was *another* among them – a woman whose thoughts were shrouded in darkness. When the Teller tried to look beneath that mantle it rose to engulf her, soaring on the vibrations of its own savage pulse. She wrenched herself free, her heart thudding in time with that dread beat.

Black Ships! Have they come for me?

Sensing their mistress' distress, the lost ones clustered around her moaned and scuttled around the chamber, some even stumbling into the fire pits.

'Fear can be turned, friend,' someone said. *'You can make it your own.'*

The Teller's gaze swept over her subjects, but she found no strangers among them. Her sanctum was still inviolate. With a surge of will she cast her mind back to the edge of her domain. While her attention had been on the dark woman, other intruders had arrived at the temple gates – eight of them, *following* the beasts. Seven were torches of eager, half-starved violence, but the eighth... Under his fire he was ice, infinitely colder than his quarry.

'Terror is the left hand of fury,' he said, his goggled eyes seeming to look right at her. *'It can be taken or it can be given.'*

Standing at the gates of the temple where he'd followed the degenerates, Gharth felt the witch's disembodied attention fall upon him, barbed with surprise and threat.

'Redemption is a lie, friend,' he told her, 'but you don't have to listen.' He raised his hands, proffering his smoking palms. 'I can show–'

There was a stentorian bellow behind him. Human instinct would have compelled most men to swing round, but whatever Gharth was, it wasn't remotely human anymore. He dived forward and the claw that should have decapitated him swept past overhead. Landing on his splayed hands, he vaulted aside as a massive three-toed foot stamped down where he'd been a heartbeat before. Then the Redeemed swarmed his attacker, shrieking with delight as they hurled themselves at it with blades and pistols.

The Spiralborn set a trap, Gharth judged, rising to his feet smoothly. *As we hunted, so we were hunted in turn.*

Unslinging his axe, he weighed up the beast that had climbed from the precipice opposite the temple. It was undoubtedly one of the xenos degenerates, but unlike any he had seen before. Despite its hunched posture the creature towered over his warriors, its chitin-sheathed bulk bloated with misshapen muscles. The ridged bulb of its skull framed a face that mocked humanity. Deep-set eyes leered above a gaping, fang-filled maw that spilled drool as the beast swung about with its three arms. The one on the right terminated in a three-fingered claw, while the pair on the left flared into curved scythes. And the giant was *fast*, slashing and punching in a frenzy that eclipsed the fury of the Redeemed. One of his warriors was already down and as Gharth watched, the beast's claw snagged another and yanked his head between its jaws. The man's legs flailed about as it chewed at his helmet.

'Watch and learn,' Gharth said to the invisible witch as he heard a footfall behind him. He swept his axe round in a wide arc, beheading the three-armed assassin that had crept from the temple. As he turned to face the gates more of the hooded xenos surged out, shrieking their poisonous mantras and spraying gunfire.

They waited inside to seal the trap, he realised as he strode to meet them, ignoring the bullets that tore through his coveralls. His hardened skin blunted most of them, while the rest lodged impotently in his flesh or bones. There wasn't much left of him that could be hurt by such weapons.

I'll prise them out later.

Moving in uncanny silence, Gharth whirled his axe about, wielding it with his right hand while his left traced smoking symbols through the air. The weapon's obsidian head shattered the scimitars or claws that met it, then swept on to cleave through metal, chitin and flesh with equal potency.

'Fire, walk within me,' he rasped. His focus blurred as his vision soared to encompass a 360-degree arc, then snapped back into sharpness as the world around him fell behind his warp-fired metabolism.

As his enemies slowed to a crawl he reached out with his empty hand and brushed a foe's head.

'Burn,' he said.

The creature's hood ignited as his fingers raked molten runnels through its skull. In the same moment his axe hacked down, hewing through the skull and torso of another degenerate. The cauterized halves drifted gently apart, the divided eyes blinking in confusion.

'For the Spiral!' one of the xenos bellowed, its voice distorted and deepened. It was their two-armed leader – the one Gharth must not kill. His god had decreed it.

'We're all heretics here, friend,' he said, blocking the creature's sluggish swipe and hurling it away. To his surprise its bone blade hadn't broken against his axe.

That weapon is alive, Gharth sensed.

He heard a rising hum as a beast with a scorched face stepped from the temple, the muzzle of its rifle glowing as it trained on him. Smoke gushed languidly from its vents as it vomited a gob of plasma. The blast glided towards him like liquefied light – slowed, but still too fast to evade.

'Truth burns cold,' Gharth told the Teller a moment before a miniature sun kissed his chest.

* * *

'You're lying!' Etelka shouted into the darkness. 'I freed myself!'

The primordial pounding was almost deafening now. She swerved again, then again, crawling anywhere but here... or there... or wherever that devouring heart lay, but every movement only drew her deeper into its gravity. She tried to stop moving and found her limbs wouldn't obey.

'Each of us is the crucible of our own becoming,' Canoness Aveline said. She spoke quietly, yet her voice cut through the cacophony. 'There is no escaping yourself.'

And in the final moments before she plunged into oblivion, Etelka Arkanto understood that was true – just as she understood that she hadn't turned from her sisters out of hope or hate.

'Why did you betray us, sister?' Aveline urged.

'Because I still could!' Etelka cursed, then shrieked as she fell and Redemption's shadow rushed to fill the void in her body, bearing not salvation, but damnation.

Impossibly, the Scorched Man was still standing. The plasma blast had seared through his chest and erupted from his back, leaving a smoking hole where most of his ribcage had been. Its edges still glowed, illuminating the intact spine within. To Aziah, that gnarled column looked like it had been carved from black crystal. Everything else, including the man's heart and lungs, had been incinerated, yet he stood unbowed, his axe held rigidly by his side.

How can he be alive? Aziah thought, stunned.

The heretic's goggled face turned toward him, ignoring the surviving acolytes and the victorious, blood-smeared Cicatryx.

'Betrayer,' the Scorched Man rasped, making it a promise. Then his gaze swept to the temple gates, where the Silver Claw stood, its plasma gun venting steam. Instinctively Aziah sensed he was looking *past* Hezrakh to the tunnel beyond.

'Embrace your truth, sister,' the heretic said to someone unseen. Suddenly crimson fracture-lines broke out across his black skin, spreading rapidly, like some tectonic pestilence of the flesh. With a crack, his charred spine splintered and his torso crumpled in upon itself. The axe slipped from his fingers and he toppled forward, exploding into dust when he hit the ground, as if he had been sculpted from ashes.

A harsh machine roar echoed up from the steppes far below, followed a moment later by the revving of an engine. Aziah froze, remembering the infernal bike the Scorched Man had ridden on the bridge. He could picture it circling the foothills like an iron predator, enraged by its master's fall. Was it madness to imagine such things?

'No, Chosen Claw, it is not,' the Spiral Father breathed into his mind. *'The insanity of the warp-tainted knows no surfeit.'*

As if to punctuate the prophet's words there was a scream from the temple, raw with despair.

'Saint!' Aziah hissed. The kindred had left Etelka in the entrance tunnel, watched over by an acolyte. 'Silver Claw, quickly!'

Hezrakh was stepping toward the gates when the shriek became a howl and an abomination erupted from the darkness. It hurled itself upon Hezrakh in a storm of barbed claws, tearing the warrior open before they hit the ground. The horror's gangling, crimson-scaled form rippled and flickered, as if it burned with a ferocious internal fire and it moved in jagged bursts that defied the eye – slipping and skipping between moments as it savaged Hezrakh. Through the blur of motion, Aziah made out a long skull framed by curved horns that swept over a hunched, spine-studded back. It looked like a perversion of the sacred Paradigms of Form.

'Daemon,' Aziah whispered, remembering the saint's warnings about the Dark Beneath the Spires. Redemption was riddled with gates for such warp-spawned vermin. The abomination's head jerked up at his words, though its tongue remained buried in Hezrakh's chest. Viscera slipped from its needle-rimmed maw as it regarded him with coal black eyes.

It knows me. Aziah moaned low in his throat as he noticed the scraps of armour snagged on the beast's hide. They were a pearlescent white.

With a wail of fury, the daemon vaulted towards him, its reverse-jointed legs thrusting it into the air like a locust. As it rose, he glimpsed the metal shard still jutting from its abdomen. *Her abdomen.*

'No!' Aziah snarled, raising his sword. He was shoved aside as the Cicatryx barrelled past him with an answering roar. His brother's bone scythes lashed out to meet the crimson blur, but the daemon jumped again in mid-air – seeming to dance between different worlds – and hurtled over the sweeping claws to land on the giant's shoulders. The Cicatryx bellowed and stamped about as the warp fiend raked and gnawed at its head, clinging to its back with barbed feet.

'Keep back!' Aziah yelled at the surviving acolytes as one was struck by a whirling scythe-claw. He could almost taste his brother's frustration – the Cicatryx's rigid scythes couldn't bend to strike its attacker, but its humanoid arm hung limply by its side, injured in the fight with the Redeemed. Yet under its frustration Aziah knew there was no fear, nor even true anger – *nothing* except the need to serve the Sacred Spiral. The Cicatryx was an aberration in form only.

I alone bear the saint's flaw, Aziah realised bitterly. *Her taint.*

With a hideous cracking the daemon's talons began to prise its victim's skull apart.

'Jump, brother!' Aziah yelled. *It is the only way.*

Without hesitation, the Cicatryx swung round and charged for the precipice, but as it flung itself over, the daemon leapt, then leapt again, somehow finding purchase in the empty air. Its eyes fixed on Aziah as it swept back towards the ledge.

'You can, my son!' it seemed to promise, offering an everything that meant nothing.

'NO!' another mind thundered and Aziah reeled as a wave of hatred surged past him and thrust the tempter away. Snarling and lashing about, it hung suspended over the drop, held in an invisible, unbreakable grip.

Black Ships, Aziah thought suddenly. He had no idea what it meant.

The air crackled with energy as the abomination was hurled away, cast with a force that would carry it beyond the spire's steppes to the molten sea beyond.

'Can it burn?' Aziah wondered numbly.

'No,' the destroying presence said again, but its thunder was distant now. *'No. No. No...'*

'No,' Aziah echoed. Then he stalked to the edge of the precipice and roared his own denial after the daemon: 'No!'

Shaking with anger, he turned and saw a woman standing behind him. She was naked save for the grime that encrusted her like a second skin, her form withered far beyond the point of natural starvation. Her limbs were like knobbly sticks and the sharp lines of her skull showed behind her face, giving it the aspect of a tormented corpse. For a moment he thought she was a crone, long past the age when she could fulfil the cult's most revered sacrament, but then he met her eyes – alight with rage and hope – and understood that he was wrong. She was not young, but neither was she old. Under her bone-deep mantle of deprivation she probably wasn't much past thirty. What suffering and terror had inflicted upon her, the ministrations of the Spiral Dawn would undo.

We shall restore you, Aziah thought reverently. *And in turn you shall make us whole.*

The Teller waited, watching the cold ones' leader as he watched her in turn. The cracks she had seen in his soul had deepened, yet he had somehow grown stronger – closer to the serenity of his thralls. Two of them had also survived the slaughter, but they meant nothing to her. Their harmony was like a chain – blood-borne and binding. It was worthless. But the leader was different. If he could find peace, then perhaps he could also offer it. If not, she would cast him after the dark one that had risen from the Under-spire. The Black Ships would not have her!

'No...' she croaked aloud.

'No,' the leader agreed, his fanged face sombre. 'I will never betray my kindred.' He stepped towards her slowly. 'The Sacred Spiral connects us, warp-weaver. Nothing is chance. You are fated to bear our magus.' He held out a three-fingered hand. 'Join us, sister.'

CULT OF THE
SPIRAL DAWN

'Their cults are numberless and diverse, yet beneath the veneer of sanctity, industry or vice that they cultivate, their true purpose remains singular and changeless. And all begin and end in darkness.'

– Inquisitor Haniel Mordaine, Ordo Xenos,
on the Cult of the Genestealer

PROLOGUE

REDEMPTION REBORN

Day and night on the scorched world were only different shades of darkness, a slow, shallow slide from grey to black across thirty-one cold hours. At their conjoined zenith the planet's twin suns were little more than pale smears in the sky, like candles behind a dirty veil.

Nevertheless the four hunters always moved by night, only emerging from their lair beneath the spaceport's fuel dump when the darkness was absolute. They had no memory of where they had come from, nor had they the capacity to care, but the imperative that drove them was clear.

Needing no light to see the warmth of their prey, they stalked the outer districts of the ragged city where they had awoken, targeting stragglers and binding them irrevocably to their bloodline with a swift, needle-sharp kiss.

Within three days the hunters had mastered the secret pathways of their new territory and taken a score of thralls. Despite the strangeness of this world it was just another hunting ground to them.

And yet, for one of the four – the first to claim a victim – that was no longer quite true. The shape of its hunt had changed, as indeed had the hunter itself. It understood this only dimly, but with every passing hour its thoughts grew sharper as the simple decrees of survival unfurled into new possibilities and the hunter became the Seeker. Its primal imperative remained undeniable, but the instinct was spiralling into a higher, *deeper* vision that allowed it a freedom to think and plan that had been impossible before.

Firstly, it recognised that its kindred hunters were not changing alongside it. Though they were bound by one purpose, the others remained creatures of pure instinct and always would. Now they followed where the Seeker led, accepting its primacy without hesitation. The apex predator felt no pride or privilege in its ascendancy. It simply was what it was, as were they.

From its thralls it learned much, drinking deep of their minds and seizing knowledge and concepts that would have been meaningless in its former, forgotten existence. This new world was ripe with prey, but they were scattered across a broken ring of spiny mountains beyond which there was only burning death. The Seeker's own territory was a vast mesa of basalt rock at the centre of the ring – it was like a mountain that had been sheared flat at its midriff by some unimaginably brutal yet precise force, leaving a blank slate for those who had come after. The thralls called this mesa *the Slab*, and their lone city, huddled in squalid senescence towards its northern edge, *Hope*.

The surrounding mountains were encrusted with temples whose vaults ran deep into the rock, extending into the bowels of the world below. Each of these *Spires* was a realm in its own right, but all were bound to the Slab by sweeping bridges of stone. A single authority ruled them all from atop the narrowest peak, revered and feared by the thralls in equal measure.

They called this authority *the Sororitas*.

On the fifth night of its awakening, the predator climbed to an escarpment at the edge of its domain and gazed at the Spire where the Sororitas laired. A red haze shimmered in the gorge below, where the planet's life-blood churned between the mountains. The haze of soot and smoke rising from the abyss would have been impenetrable to lesser creatures, but like darkness, it was no barrier to the Seeker's void-born eyes.

With an efficacy it neither understood nor questioned, the Seeker cast its awareness across the gorge to the congeries of domes and towers nestling at the mountain's peak. Like an intangible serpent it slipped through barriers of iron and stone in search of flesh and bone and mind. Lurking at the corners of perception, it stalked its quarry's thoughts, snatching stray emotions and scratching at convictions.

It found only a hard resolve that mirrored its own and understood that the Sororitas could only ever be an enemy. Given time, this foe would stir and hunt the hunters.

Watching from the rocks behind the Seeker, the trio of primal hunters flexed their claws restively, sensing their leader's growing aggression. Their empathy was ignorant, but they understood the only thing that mattered: *there would be killing soon.*

The dying woman's sanctum was in the abbey's central tower, directly beneath a glass cupola stained with a kaleidoscopic whorl of wings. It was the building's highest point, a spear of purity that lanced the mire of Vytarn's sky, just as the sisterhood of the Thorn Eternal had lanced the planet's spiritual mire for over three centuries. When a storm raged the wind would shred the smog-choked atmosphere, allowing listless rays of light through. In those moments the cupola would transmute the light into an iridescent spray that washed the sanctum clean of shadows and sorrows alike.

But tonight there was no wind and precious little light. The abbey's generator had failed again, and the candles the woman had lit at the start of her ceremony had burned down to nubs, leaving her in a tightening noose of darkness.

She knelt with her eyes raised to the bronze bas-relief of the God-Emperor that dominated the chamber. The Crucible Aeterna was an esoteric relic that placed Him at the centre of an orrery of stars bound by thorns. The barbs pierced His flesh and drew a silent scream from His distended jaws. His face was wizened with geometric lines and inset with lacquered eyes that burned with true sight. It was a harsh idol, but the woman felt it possessed a rare honesty.

The Imperium's deepest foundation is not glory, but sacrifice.

That credo had been her mentor's, but with time and suffering it had become her own, as her teacher had always known it would.

'But you were wrong about my death,' the woman whispered into the past.

'*You shall die well,*' Canoness Santanza had predicted, appraising the blood-spattered, fire-eyed girl who stood before her, battered but unbroken by her Confirmation Trials. '*But dying is not enough, no matter how well you do it, because then you can do no more.*' She had frozen the girl with a gaze long dead to kindness. '*The Imperium is forever at war and the duty of the Adepta Sororitas is without end. Do you understand, initiate?*'

'*I do, mistress,*' the girl had answered, but they had both known it wasn't – *couldn't* – be true. There had been too much fire in her thirteen-year-old heart.

Fifty-five years of service had dimmed that girl's fire, but never quite extinguished it. Despite the horrors she had endured and the righteous ones she had enacted in the name of her faith, Canoness Vetala Aveline had never become a creature of ice. Whether that made her more or less than her mentor was for the God-Emperor alone to judge.

I shall know soon enough, Aveline reflected as the slow killer in her lungs flexed its claws again. This time it drew a cough, but she strangled it into a brief, raw bark. The bronze Emperor's features danced between sympathy and mockery in the flickering candlelight.

Pitying or deriding a life of wasted piety...

As her trance receded, Aveline frowned at the gloomy chamber, irritated that the generator's faltering machine spirit hadn't been attended to during her long ritual. This was the third time in as many weeks that the power had failed, obliging the sisterhood to rely on the braziers and candles that decked the abbey, but if ever they had needed light it was now. The abbey's wardens had been sensing a dark presence for days – an oppression that was somehow *watchful.*

'It is not our old enemy,' Aveline declared, rising from her prayer mat with a grace that defied her pain. 'You can stand down from your vigil, celestian. I remain myself.'

A tall figure stepped from a curtained alcove behind her. In contrast to the canoness' plain robes, the celestian wore full battle armour, the elegantly wrought plates polished to a pearlescent sheen that was luminous in the gloom. Her face was hidden behind a sloped visor, but Aveline had no need for mundane clues to read her old comrade's disquiet.

'I know you disapproved of the ceremony, Phaesta, but it was a necessary risk,' Aveline said. 'I had to be certain the daemon had not broken free.'

'Another sister could have borne the burden, canoness.'

'But I am the strongest.'

At least in spirit, Aveline thought. *I left my soul unguarded for nine long hours. No daemon could have resisted such a lure, even one that recognised the trap...*

'You believe you have the least to lose,' Phaesta corrected. As always, the celestian had seen through to the heart of the matter. They had been sisters in battle for almost three decades and faced their sternest test together in the pits of this world, but sometimes Aveline found her First Sister's insight wearying.

'The Black Breath will take me within the month. This planet's air has killed me where all its daemons could not,' Aveline said without rancour, 'but I shall meet its poison with purification.'

'So the Convent Sanctorum has approved your request,' Phaesta guessed.

'I received the confirmation yesterday.' Aveline smiled coldly. 'Vytarn is no more. This planet has been reborn as Redemption.'

She was disinclined to mention that the name was officially appended with the number '219'. 'Redemption' was a regrettably common appellation across the Imperium, but Aveline felt certain that few worlds had a better claim to it than her own.

'You never told me the name you had chosen,' the celestian said quietly.

'You don't approve?' Aveline asked.

Phaesta hesitated before replying. 'It is a pious name, canoness.'

'A name that will make our *world* pious,' Aveline enthused. 'But there is more! The sanctity of the Spires has been recognised by the Convent. My application for reclassification has been accepted.' She laid a withered hand on her sister's shoulder. 'Vytarn – *Redemption* – has been sanctioned as a shrine world of the Imperium. That is the legacy I shall leave to the sisterhood.'

It is the legacy I shall leave to you, *my First Sister,* she added privately, *because you shall take my mantle soon.*

'For all its temples this is a dark world,' Phaesta said. 'A name changes nothing.'

It changes everything! Aveline wanted to say. *Names shape the truth of things.* But she knew the celestian would never accept such a notion. She might even call it heretical, though Aveline was certain the God-Emperor they both served would understand completely.

'The darkness under Redemption has been chained, sister,' Aveline pressed. 'We bound it with faith and fire two decades ago!'

'Yet evil shadows the Spires once more. Some taints run too deep to cleanse, canoness.'

'You are wrong,' Aveline decreed. Her lungs were on fire and she was eager to be done with this argument. 'We defeated the old foe and we shall defeat the new.'

By the sixth day of its inner journey the Seeker's mind had crystallised into true sentience. With self-awareness came a grasp of possibilities beyond the here and now, followed by a torrent of abstract ideas and imaginings. At the forefront of this was the insistent vision of an ever-turning, slowly unwinding spiral. The Seeker didn't understand the significance of the image until nightfall, when the truth sharpened into sudden clarity. The spiral represented the great imperative that drove its bloodline.

The Sororitas would call it a 'symbol'.

Gripped by a cold fervour, the Seeker sifted through the mental fragments it had stolen from the enemy during its incursion. Notions that had been nonsensical before now blazed with power, and from one moment to the next the great imperative became *holy*.

On the seventh night the Seeker bestowed this revelation upon its thralls, who carved the Sacred Spiral into reality, upon wood and stone and sometimes their own flesh. Their veneration elevated them from thralls to disciples, and in turn their worship exalted their master from Seeker to Prophet.

By the ninth night the Prophet's path was clear, but a shadow occluded the radiance of the Spiral: the warrior women who had inadvertently breathed life into it.

Armed with faith, the Prophet cast its mind across to its enemies' aerie once more to test them with new insight. This time it recognised the seams of madness running through their spiritual armour. In most cases the madness strengthened the alloy, but in a few it had become corrosive, and in none more so than the one called Sister Etelka, whose thoughts were riddled with dark doubts and darker regrets.

Night after night the Prophet gifted the warrior with whispered questions that she thought her own, insinuating itself behind her eyes until she *saw* the secret heresies of her sisters. Thus loyalty unravelled into loathing, then horror and finally hate as Sister Etelka was drawn into the Sacred Spiral and anointed as its first apostle.

On the nineteenth night, the Prophet assembled its congregation and pronounced judgement: *those that deny the Divine Imperative will be cleansed.*

That night Canoness Vetala Aveline clawed her way out of a writhing, thornwreathed fever dream and awoke to find herself in the abbey's sanctum, slumped before the Crucible Aeterna. The Emperor's tormented bronze visage was speckled with blood and the black detritus of Aveline's lungs.

'What's the truth of a name?' someone asked from nowhere.

That was when she heard the screams.

Gunfire and the whoosh of flames echoed through the vaulted corridors of the abbey, interwoven with a cacophony of snarls, guttural chants and a ceaseless, wordless whispering that seemed to bleed from the air itself.

The tapestries lining the walls of the grand nave were afire, bathing everything in hellish light as the celestian, Phaesta, and her three surviving sisters fought to hold the invaders back from the abbey's altar. The heretics' soot-stained skin and bloodshot eyes marked them out as the lost and the bland of Vytarn – the magma scrapers, refinery labourers and petty functionaries who kept the sickly promethium industry of the Slab running. Such grey spirits were the perennial fodder of the Archenemy, yet Phaesta felt their fall keenly.

'Your souls were in our care,' she whispered as she scythed them down with her storm bolter, 'but our eyes were turned to the past.'

There was no telling how many of the damned had invaded the abbey, but Phaesta feared it would be too many. Though their makeshift clubs and cleavers were no match for the sisters' blessed weapons, the heretics fought with the fearless ferocity of the possessed.

To her right, Phaesta saw a gaunt youth leap forward and grasp the barrel of Sister Galina's bolter, tugging it towards his chest as she fired. He was ripped apart, showering Galina with blood, but his sacrifice won his comrades precious seconds to close in and bring his executioner down by sheer weight of numbers. The celestian tried to cut a path through to her sister, but the press of the crowd was too great.

We are too few, Phaesta judged as she and her remaining sisters retreated towards the chancel. The Mission of the Thorn Eternal numbered less than fifty Battle Sisters, and many had died before the alarm was raised, most of them slaughtered in their sleep.

'*We were betrayed!*' Aveline hissed from the celestian's gorget vox. Phaesta knew the canoness was in the sanctum, watching through the eyes of the servo-skull hovering above the horde. '*Someone opened the gates for the heretics. One of our own.*'

'That is not possible,' Phaesta said as a cadaverous elder tried to embrace her. He was still smiling when she crushed his skull with the stock of her gun.

'*It is the only possibility.*' Aveline's voice was a tortured croak. '*Trust no one, sister.*'

Phaesta imagined the canoness hunched in the darkness while her sisters bled for the Thorn. She knew Aveline could barely walk, let alone fight, yet she found no pity in her heart. The canoness had invited this doom upon them.

This world was meant to be forgotten, Vetala, Phaesta thought bitterly.

As her squad drew level with the statue of Praxedes the Ascendant, an indefinable instinct compelled her to glance up, and she saw a dark shape squatting upon the saint's marble shoulders – a leering, malformed gargoyle that was all bones and teeth and far too many claws. Before Phaesta could shout a warning the creature lashed down with an improbably long arm and punched through Sister Arianne's breastplate with talons like powered scythes, wrenching her into the air in the same motion. Phaesta and her surviving sister swept the statue's shoulders with gunfire as the beast ducked away. Then the mob was upon them, snatching at their weapons and threatening to pull them down like poor lost Galina.

'Daemon!' Phaesta yelled as she swung about with her rifle, trying to clear a path through the throng while keeping the gargoyle in sight. It leapt to another statue, carrying Arianne like a broken doll in its claws. With a piercing howl it reared up and cast her aside, then leapt for the celestian.

Heedless of the heretics' weapons, Phaesta dived into the crowd, breaking through their ranks with her armoured strength as the gargoyle crashed down behind her. It slashed the head from a chanting madman and tore another in half as it came after her in a storm of claws. She yelled as its talons gouged deep rifts through her back-plate and into the flesh below. Thrown off balance, she hit the ground hard enough to dent her visor.

'Heretic!' a burly labourer snarled as he stepped between them and swung his cleaver down onto her helmet in a two-handed arc. The impact reverberated through her skull and ruptured her nose, but couldn't penetrate the sacred ceramite. Before he could swing again the gargoyle tore through him, mangling his torso into red tatters. The reprieve bought Phaesta time to level her gun and she met the beast with a volley of fire.

'Thorn take you!' she snarled as the rounds punched into its distended jaws, shattering the nest of fangs and throwing the thing backwards. A heart-beat later the explosive rounds detonated, vaporising its skull and spattering her with black ichor. Even in death the beast was dangerous, whirling about in a blind spasm as it fell. She lost sight of it as the mob closed in around her.

'They walk with daemons,' Phaesta breathed into her vox as the heretics' blows began to hammer down on her. They were nothing beside the pain in her lacerated back and the heady, sour-sweet odour of the abomination's blood. That stench was nauseating, yet strangely alluring. As if in sympathy, the whispering from the walls had taken on a sly, velvet resonance. Though it spoke without words its promise was unmistakable: an end to suffering if only she would surrender to that wondrous, wine-dark blood...

Phaesta denied it with a primal bellow that was something between a laugh and a cry.

'I am Adepta Sororitas!' she shouted as she forced herself to her feet, casting off the heretics with the armour's powered musculature. 'Suffering is my wine!'

She finished her attackers with precise, measured bursts before they could swarm her again and kept firing until she realised there were no more. Either the attack was over or the mob had retreated. Swaying on her feet, she surveyed the carnage in the nave as she loaded a fresh clip, her hands working of their own volition. Scores of broken bodies littered the space, among them Otokito, the last of her sisters, but darkness was rapidly claiming the fallen as the burning tapestries were consumed. Once again the abbey's power had failed, though this time Phaesta suspected it was by design.

'Celestian?' her vox crackled as the servo-skull descended to regard her with soulless, sensor-filled eye sockets.

Ignoring the canoness, Phaesta activated the lumen band affixed to her helmet and swept the chamber with its narrow beam. Something slipped between the columns to her right and she swung around, chasing it with a rapid-fire salvo, but its hunched, many-limbed scurry threw her aim and it disappeared into the shadows.

'There are more daemons,' she hissed into her vox, 'perhaps many more.'

'I saw them,' Aveline answered tightly, *'but I do not recognise them.'*

Phaesta pictured the canoness furiously poring through the order's for-bidden texts, trying to match the living gargoyles to the sketches in those malign tomes – hunting for a way to save her false Redemption.

You have already gazed too deeply into darkness, sister, Phaesta judged. Her beam caught another twisted shape, this time to her left, but it slipped away before she could take a shot. So there were two of them, advancing on her position from both sides.

'You must send a message,' she said urgently, already knowing how this encounter would end. 'The Convent Sanctorum must be warned of this incursion.' There was no reply from her vox. 'There is no other way, Vetala!'

'Celestian, I–'

Phaesta drowned Aveline's voice in a storm of gunfire as the beasts came for her. They charged from the darkness in perfect synchronicity, keeping low and angling between the columns to confuse her aim as she spun between them. Despite their bulk and strange gait they moved with terrible speed, their claws extended to claim her.

'Just the one then,' she whispered, dropping into a crouch and focussing on the attacker to her right. Aveline's servo-skull swooped down into her chosen target's path like a cybernetic wasp. The gargoyle barrelled through the fragile automaton, but the distraction slowed it fractionally and Phaesta locked on and shredded its chest. As it skidded into a tangled heap she tracked it and blew its skull apart.

'Warn them!' Phaesta shouted into her vox.

Already certain it was too late, she spun around to face the remaining gargoyle. Her wild fire tore through its left side, shearing away a pair of arms before it yanked her into its jagged embrace.

The hololithic transceiver chimed, confirming that Aveline's message had been received by the planet's orbital relay station. From there the encoded hololith would pass into the Convent's covert intelligence web. But Redemption was a remote world; even with the Diabolus Extremis priority she had invoked, it would be months before the message reached its destination.

Slumped in her chair, Aveline stared at the glowing runes on the transceiver's panel as if they might offer answers. Like the other ancient machines in the sanctum, it had its own power source. She supposed she should be grateful for that.

'Did I taunt fate?' she asked the machine.

Her question would have been better addressed to the Crucible Aeterna watching from the wall behind her, but she was not ready to face her god quite yet. Besides, she doubted she could rise from her chair. Her condition had worsened over the past week, whittling her breath into a rasp that barely sustained her.

'I should have passed command to Phaesta long ago,' she confessed to the patient transceiver. She had lost sight of the celestian after sacrificing the servo-skull, but Phaesta's silence told her all she needed to know.

'I am the last.'

'*And the least,*' a voice completed the thought, though whether it was her own or a judgement from the Crucible Aeterna she could not tell.

'*Does it matter, Vetala?*'

She laughed and the laugh became a coughing fit that almost finished her. The spasm subsided into a muted pounding and she realised something was attacking the sanctum's door. She dismissed it. Nothing short of Militarum-grade heavy weapons could get through that solid titanium portal, and she doubted the invaders had anything of the sort. Thankfully neither did the abbey, or it would be in the enemy's hands now. The sanctum's walls were reinforced and she had activated the cupola's shields, sheathing the glass in interlocking metal panels. Nothing could get in.

'*And nothing can get out, Vetala.*'

The vox set beside the transceiver hissed: '*Canoness, can you hear me?*'

CULT OF THE SPIRAL DAWN

With the supernal clarity of the dying, Aveline could taste the betrayal in the speaker's voice. *'The enemy has been purged,'* Sister Etelka reported, *'but many Sisters were slain. We have need of you, mistress.'*

Aveline ignored her. There was nothing she could do about the traitor and she didn't have the strength for empty recriminations. The Emperor would take his own retribution in time.

'Retribution...' she whispered. 'Yes, that would have been a more honest name.'

Etelka persisted, imploring, then wheedling, then threatening by turns, but finally she went away, leaving Aveline with the only voice that mattered.

'Look at me, Vetala,' it urged from the shadows within and without.

'Soon,' she promised.

The Prophet withdrew the tendrils of its awareness from the abbey and returned to the body waiting beyond the gorge. The old, primal part of its mind had yearned to fight alongside its followers, but its destiny had precluded the risk – and that was wise, for the peril had proved great. Most of its army had been lost in the attack, including two of its kindred hunters, yet the Prophet felt no regret at their loss. Their sacrifice had cleared the path for the Sacred Spiral and more would soon take their place. Many more.

All are one in the Sacred Spiral, the Prophet decreed unto the eager minds of its surviving thralls, *and the Spiral is All.*

PART ONE

REDEMPTION IN SHADOW

'Sow the first seeds of the Four-Armed God in darkness and nurture the star-blessed spawn in shadows, hidden from the prying eyes of the Outsider, lest he lay waste to the miracle before it can take root and prosper.'

– The Apotheosis of the Spiral Wyrm

CHAPTER ONE

The shadow had been alone in the cargo hold of the *Iron Calliope* for almost three months when the throng of white-garbed travellers came on board. Until their arrival the cavernous space had been his private kingdom – a realm of sealed crates, abandoned junk and the ghosts of lost crewmen. He'd paid for rations and passage on the freighter with the last of the blood money he'd made in the Tetraktys gang wars, quite certain he was being fleeced, but too weary to care. Interstellar travel was expensive, but many of the captains plying the trade routes of the Imperium were open to shady arrangements. This wasn't the first ship the shadow had haunted and it wouldn't be the last. Every one was just another step on the long road home.

Almost seven years, he thought bleakly, *and I'm not even halfway there.*

After the intruders' arrival he lay low for a few days, taking their measure as they erected tents among the storage racks and slowly colonised his domain. Stealth had become his craft over the past few years, so it was child's play to avoid the babbling, artless crowd. He estimated there were over four hundred of them, a roughly equal split of men and women, all young, but no children.

They were obviously religious types, but nothing like the Imperial zealots he'd occasionally had dealings with. A civilian sect then, probably a fairly standard variant of the Imperial Creed, though he didn't recognise the spiral symbol they venerated. The icon was everywhere – emblazoned on their white jumpsuits, etched into crystal pendants or tattooed onto the backs of their hands. The most devout wore robes and sported tonsures, their bare crowns stencilled with the spiral. To the shadow they looked ridiculous, but then he'd lost faith in faith long ago.

Pilgrims, he decided, *harmless and stupid.*

Unfortunately he couldn't evade them indefinitely unless he resigned himself to hiding until they were gone, which wouldn't be for another five months. From their talk he'd learnt they were heading for a minor shrine world further along the *Iron Calliope*'s route, and he'd be damned if he'd spend the next five months creeping around the fools.

No, it was time to stake out his territory.

'But it was so real,' Ophele said fearfully, 'not like a dream at all.'

'It's nothing,' Ariken advised. 'You're just missing home.'

'I hated home.' Ophele's long, delicate face was pinched and dark rings underscored her bloodshot eyes. Like many of the pilgrims, the girl had been sleeping badly for days.

Ever since the ship entered the warp, Ariken estimated.

Most of her companions were ignorant about such things, but the medicae had made it her business to learn about the dangers of space travel before embarking on this voyage. Though her knowledge was sketchy, she understood that their vessel was passing through a realm that was as inimical to the soul as the honest void of space was to the body. Ophele wasn't the only member of the congregation who sensed the leering *wrongness* pressing in on the ship.

'Change is always frightening,' Ariken said gently, 'even when you truly want it.' *Or need it.* She selected a vial from her supply case and passed it to the girl. Ophele wasn't much younger than her, yet she seemed like a child to Ariken. 'Take one before each sleep cycle. If things don't improve in a couple of days, come talk to me again.'

As she escorted Ophele from her tent, Ariken noticed that the chattering of the community had fallen to a murmur.

'What's going on?' she asked her nearest brother.

'A stranger,' the pilgrim said, pointing to the far side of the camp. 'Came out of nowhere.'

Nowhere... or a nightmare? Ariken wondered uneasily.

Her curiosity had carried her beyond the approved texts on space travel, leading her to dark stories that suggested the sacred shields protecting ships were not infallible. Sometimes *things* slipped past them from the outer darkness...

No, she decided grimly, *if that had happened I'd be hearing screams by now.*

Fighting down the dread, she pressed through the crowd and saw a man waiting at the edge of the camp. He stood motionless, regarding the pilgrims through a curtain of greying hair that had spilled loose from his headband. A patch covered his right eye and the lower part of his face was lost in a heavy beard that fell to his chest. It was difficult to tell his age through that tangle, but she guessed he was somewhere in his late forties.

He looks like he's been here for years, Ariken thought.

The stranger's khaki-grey fatigues were reinforced with flak plates at the shoulders and joints and a leather gauntlet encased his left hand. The patchwork uniform gave him a martial bearing, but he appeared to be unarmed save for the dagger tucked into his belt.

'Is he a ghost?' Ophele whispered to Ariken. The medicae hadn't noticed the girl following her.

'Only a man, sister,' a deep voice answered behind them. 'Be at ease.'

Ariken and Ophele made way as the congregation's shepherd stepped past them and approached the stranger.

'My name is Bharlo, friend,' the shepherd said, offering a warm smile. 'I am guide to the Forty-Second Congregation of the Unfolded.'

Though he wasn't much past thirty, Bharlo spoke with the easy authority of a man accustomed to being listened to. He was powerfully built and his bare arms were covered in faded tattoos that hinted at a darker past – a riot of burning skulls pierced by blades and the remnants of a dragon. His robes were cinched at the waist with a cord of purple silk and the spiral adorning his shaven head was gilded into his ebony skin. It looped down and around his cheeks, framing his face like a snake.

'Forgive us, friend,' Bharlo continued, 'but we didn't know we shared our ark with another traveller.' He raised his hands, palms open to reveal twin golden spirals. 'Will you break bread with us?'

The apparition's glare fell upon him, but Bharlo appeared unperturbed. After long seconds the stranger jabbed a finger at the far side of the hold and shook his head, then drew the finger pointedly across his own throat.

'I believe we understand you, friend,' Bharlo said, his smile never wavering, 'but know that we're here for you if you change your mind.'

As the stranger turned and walked away Ariken realised she had been holding her breath.

'He *is* a ghost,' Ophele said with conviction.

The shadow knew it would have been simpler to deliver his warning in words, but he thought the pilgrims would be more receptive to a sign.

Besides, I liked seeing the looks on their faces, he admitted. *They'd sooner jump off the ship than come near me now.*

Except for the leader – their *shepherd*... He might be a problem. Judging by his muscles and the skein of skulls and blades tattooed across his arms he'd been a ganger once, probably an enforcer, possibly even a minor clan boss. Perhaps such men could change, but there would always be a hard core to them. The shadow had killed enough of their kind to know it. Truthfully he hadn't been much of a fighter back in the days when fighting had been his duty, but he'd learned quickly on the long road home.

Over the next few weeks the shadow built his refuge, hauling crates and loose panels to his territory and assembling them into an improvised cabin. His retreat was in the remotest part of the hold, right up against the ship's hull. It was cold and most of the overhead lumen strips had died, obliging him to rely on the candles he'd filched from the cargo, but it was a price worth paying to keep the spiral-heads at arm's length.

At the start of each sleep cycle he would sit cross-legged in the darkness, trying to ignore their muffled prayers. He was quite certain nobody else was listening to them.

The shadow was returning from another salvage expedition, his arms laden with a teetering stack of food cartons, when someone spoke behind him.

'Hello, ghost.'

Surprised, he swung round and several boxes fell from the top of his haul. A girl was appraising him with frank curiosity. She wore the white jumpsuit of a common pilgrim, but the only spiral he could see was the one stitched to her breast pocket. Her brown hair was cropped short, though she wasn't tonsured.

'I didn't think ghosts scared so easily,' she said.

Ignoring his frown, she picked up the fallen cartons and returned them carefully to the top of the stack.

'Why?' she asked as he turned to go.

'What?' he answered reflexively. It was the first word he'd spoken in months and it sounded like an alien croak to his own ears.

'Why do you collect junk?'

'It's only junk if you don't use it.'

She nodded as if she were giving his answer serious consideration. He guessed she was in her mid-twenties and pretty in a quiet, trim way, but it was her watchful grey eyes that struck him. They lent her a stillness that belied her youth.

'I'm Ariken,' she offered.

'Cross,' he said, unsure why.

She nodded again, weighing this up with the same gravity as his previous answer, then appeared to come to a decision.

'Are you dangerous, Cross?' Seeing his frown she pressed on quickly. 'I ask because you're frightening people and most of them are frightened enough already.'

He began to walk away, but she stepped in front of him, her expression hardening.

'These are good people,' she said.

As good as dead then... He caught the thought before it slipped past his lips.

'I'm not your problem,' he answered instead.

'Thank you, that's what I needed to hear.' She smiled. 'I'll see you around, Cross.'

Cross bumped into Ariken a few days later and they spoke again, still brief and stilted, but over the weeks their chance talks grew surer, warmer, until it dawned on him that he was looking forward to seeing her. Reluctantly he realised he'd made a friend. He had no business with friendship, yet he found he couldn't walk away from it. Maybe he'd been a ghost too long.

Or not quite long enough.

By unspoken agreement, Ariken never intruded upon his refuge or too deeply into his past. He said he was travelling home and she left it at that, as if she knew anything else would break their trust.

In contrast she was unguarded about herself, both her past and her path. Like her fellow pilgrims, she was from Khostax-IV, a hive world suffocating under the weight of its own industry. A medicae by vocation, she wanted to see something beyond an artificial sky and a billion grey mirror images of herself, but most importantly, she yearned for *purpose*.

Cross recognised the story; it was as old as the human heart and it forked into infinite roads. In Ariken's case it had led to the Spiral Dawn.

'It sounds heretical to me,' Cross said when the subject of her sect came up. *When he brought it up.*

'Only because you haven't been listening,' Ariken said, exasperated. 'Anyway, what do you care about heresy? You don't believe in anything, ghost.'

'It doesn't matter what I believe.' He gave up on the stubborn panel he'd been trying to prise loose from the wall and looked at her sternly. 'It's what the rest of the Imperium believes that's going to matter.'

'The Spiral Dawn is a sanctioned sect of the Imperial Cult.' It sounded like she was citing an approved text. 'The God-Emperor is at the centre of the Sacred Spiral. He is the One in All from which all truth unfolds.'

'Then what are you looking for out here?'

'The Unfolding was revealed to the Spiral Father on Redemption,' Ariken quoted portentously. 'All true seekers are reborn into the Spiral upon the cradle world.'

'You don't believe half that nonsense do you?'

'Maybe half.' She grinned. 'The Emperor half, anyway.'

'It's not a game, girl. Who's paying for this holy jaunt of yours?'

She hesitated, pursing her lips.

'You don't know, do you, Ariken.'

'The shepherd made the arrangements,' she said guardedly.

'To ferry four hundred people across seven systems?' He shook his head. 'It doesn't add up.'

'Nor do *you*, Cross.' It was the closest she had come to questioning his past and they both looked away, suddenly awkward. His left hand was aching in its gauntlet, as it always did when he became angry.

'You can't trust them,' he said quietly.

'Who?'

Anybody!

'Priests!' he spat. 'And the higher up you go the worse they get.'

'Now *that's* heresy. I might have to set a witchfinder on you, ghost.'

He shook his head. 'You should have stayed at home, girl.'

'There was nothing there.'

'There's much worse than nothing out here.'

There are shadows like me, he realised.

Some days later Bharlo paid Ariken a visit. She had been expecting it.

'Do you believe our ghost is a good man?' He waited patiently while she considered his question.

'He doesn't think so,' Ariken said at last.

'Good men rarely do,' Bharlo observed, 'but good or bad, he *is* dangerous.' He placed a hand on her shoulder. 'You have fulfilled your duty of vigilance to the congregation, sister. You have no obligation to the stranger.'

She hesitated. 'And if he's a friend?'

The shepherd regarded her solemnly. 'Some men are past changing, Ariken.'

People change. You changed, she thought. But it was a banal, threadbare argument and she didn't believe it of Cross anyway.

'He and I recognised the truth of each other the moment we met,' Bharlo continued. 'Whatever path our ghost is on, he's gone too far to come back.'

Cross ended his friendship with Ariken shortly afterwards. At first he avoided her, then when that became impossible he answered her questions with harsh lies he called hard truths. He destroyed their rapport with the same calculation he exercised in battle, deriding her as an ignorant, deluded, *doomed* fool. She met it all with dignity, which made the betrayal harder than he had imagined.

'I hope you make it home, Cross,' she said at the end. 'Wherever it is.'

'I'm sorry,' he said after she was gone, unsure whether it was addressed to Ariken or himself.

His left hand felt like it was on fire. Wincing, he pulled off the gauntlet and examined the corpse-claw attached to his wrist. The bloodless skin was mottled with scabs, but he knew they were only the surface scars of much deeper wounds. The parasites that had burrowed into the flesh had almost claimed him for the grey, disease-ridden world that had swallowed his comrades seven years ago. Sometimes he was sure he'd died with them and this endless, pointless journey home was just a kind of purgatory.

I was a dead man crawling, he remembered. *I couldn't have survived.*

As the months passed he tried to absolve himself from self and become the shadow once more. But the void he had once inhabited was gone.

Redemption 219 was a sphere of striated greys scarred by patches of angry crimson where the clouds of ash had been swept away. Alongside that colossus the orbiting hulk of the *Iron Calliope* was only a white blemish, the smaller ship it disgorged a mere mote of bright dust.

The landing shuttle dipped towards the dark world, then levelled out as it brushed the hazy exosphere. For a few moments it glided over the curve of the planet, then its thrusters ignited and it hurtled forward, skimming high above the burning oceans in search of the anomaly that a lost visionary or madwoman had named the Koronatus Ring.

The planet's molten surface was spiked with obsidian islands that groped from the magma like charred skeletal fingers, offering no respite for the fragile creatures the shuttle carried. The only sanctuary to be found here was among the Seven Spires and the flattened mountain they encircled.

As it neared its destination the ship tilted sharply and tore through the outer mantle and into the roiling clouds below.

The descent to Redemption was infinitely worse than the ascent from Khostax had been. Ariken sat hunched on a moulded seat, gripping her safety harness as the landing shuttle shuddered and bucked, as if in the throes of a storm. Ophele was huddled to her left, her lips working in furious prayer, her right hand clutching Ariken's. The pale girl had become Ariken's second shadow during the voyage, following her about like a lost child until the medicae had given in and adopted her as an eager, but hopeless, assistant.

Maybe I've grown used to lost souls, Ariken thought. In the months following Cross' strange betrayal she had only seen him in wordless passing. Towards the end of the voyage she had considered attempting a farewell, but what was there to say really? The shepherd had been right: Cross was lost.

The shuttle shook violently and a collective tremor passed through the pilgrims crammed together in tight rows of twenty. The entire company was here, all four hundred and forty-four souls who had left Khostax in search of enlightenment, hope or simply change. She knew many of them weren't true believers of the Unfolding. She wasn't much of a believer herself, but that didn't stop her praying along with the rest of them as the vessel fought the turbulence. She had contrived to sit by one of the portholes, but there was nothing but blackness beyond the glass, as if the ship were diving into a void.

If we don't make it down I'll never know if the Unfolding is true, she realised.

Then again, if it *was* true she'd know after her death anyway. Surely her soul would simply spin into alignment with the God-Emperor's design and everything would make sense. In which case, what did it matter?

Oh, it matters, Ariken thought fiercely. Neither faith nor logic could deny the simple truth she felt with every fibre of her being: *I want to live.*

At first she whispered it, then, realising nobody could hear her above the roar of the engines, she shouted it – then again, louder.

'I want to live!'

Perhaps it was truest prayer of them all.

CHAPTER TWO

'You hear that?' Benedek said. His voice barely carried over the storm wailing and scratching at the outpost's walls.

'Can't hear anything in a blackout,' Corporal Anzio Cridd replied. 'Except your whining.' He didn't look up from the card tower he was building on top of the vox set.

'Sounded like a ship to me,' Benedek pressed.

'You've been hearing ships since that stubber went off by your head, Bartal.' Cridd held his breath as he slotted another card onto his tower's summit. He grinned as the edifice held. 'Doesn't mean the ships are there.'

'The lieutenant said there's one coming in tonight.'

'Then they sure picked a sorry night for it!' Cridd leaned back in his chair, unwilling to attempt another storey until his fellow Guardsman had shut up. 'Poor bastards.' He spun round and grinned. 'Welcome to Redemption, where you can freeze, burn and choke for the Throne, all in the same night!'

'We're on watch,' Benedek said seriously. The lanky trooper was standing by the window slit of their cramped bunker, staring out into the storm as if it made a difference.

'There's nothing to see out there, friend.' Cridd threw up his hands. 'You've just got to sit it out.'

Benedek wasn't a bad guy to share a shift with but he got twitchy during blackouts, and if he was honest Cridd couldn't exactly blame him. The soot storms were bad enough when you were behind the walls of the Locker with the whole regiment around you, but out on the Rim they could mess with your head. And out on the Rim in *Outpost Six...* Well, that was something else again.

Outpost Six. The Ghostwatch, the troops called it.

Officially this bunker was just another link in the chain of listening posts the regiment had erected along the perimeter of the Slab, but everyone knew it was unlucky. The outpost hunkered at the mouth of the crumbling bridge that led to Spire Castitas, where the old Adepta Sororitas abbey lay. Even the Spiral-lovers, who lorded it over the other mountains, avoided Castitas and its brooding ruin.

'You think the abbey's haunted?' Benedek asked, obviously thinking along the same lines.

'I think you talk too much, Bartal.'

'They say the Sisters lost their minds and turned on each other.'

'You *think*?' Cridd winked lasciviously at his comrade, who looked shocked and made the sign of the aquila. 'Relax, friend. I'm just messing with you.'

'Ain't right to joke about it, corporal,' Benedek said, suddenly formal.

Especially not with the abbey so close, Cridd guessed. Suddenly he was in no mood for jokes either. He thought of the men back at the Locker. Even the toughest bastards hated pulling watch on the Rim. Out here there was only wind and darkness – and that was without a blackout trying to drown you in soot.

'You ever wonder why we're here?' Benedek asked.

'You going Spiral on me?' Cridd mocked, but there was no venom in it.

The other trooper shook his head gravely. 'No, I mean what we're doing *here*? On this burnt rock of a world.'

'We go where they tell us to go.' Cridd shrugged. 'That's how it works in the Guard, friend.'

'But it's been six... nearly seven months,' Benedek protested. 'There's nothing here. Sergeant Grijalva, he says we're on the graveline.'

The graveline... Consigned to garrison duty until they dried up. It would be a shabby way for the regiment to end its service to the Throne, but after the meat grinder of their last campaign Cridd figured there were worse fates. Besides, he'd heard it all before – every trooper in the Eighth had a theory, but Cridd doubted even Command really knew why they'd been posted to Redemption. Things hadn't been right with the colonel since the Second Company got itself wiped out on Oblazt.

'Me, I think we're here for the Spirals,' Benedek said darkly. 'Something's off about them.'

'They're just priests, Bartal. More agreeable than most, I'd say.'

'Then why are the Spires off limits to Throne-fearing men?' Benedek inscribed the aquila again. 'They're hiding something. The preacher says–'

Something scraped the bunker's iron hatch – long and grating, like nails being dragged along the metal. The troopers froze. Benedek's eyes looked set to pop out of his skull. Cridd drew his laspistol and gestured at the window slit. His comrade stared at him and Cridd nodded sharply. Reluctantly, as if he were approaching a snake, Benedek peered outside.

'Don't see anything,' he said finally.

There are no ghosts here, Cridd told himself. *There's no such thing.*

But he knew that wasn't true. Every Guardsman of the Vassago Abyss knew it. Ghosts were in their blood.

Something slammed against the hatch.

'Maybe it was rock,' Benedek said hopefully. 'Wind's strong enough, right?'

The second blow was hard enough to shake the hatch in its frame. Cridd gripped his pistol as the pounding continued, though he doubted the gun had enough stopping power to worry whatever was hammering at their door.

Can any *gun stop a ghost?* he wondered numbly. *But if it's a ghost, why doesn't it just walk right through the walls?*

The assault ended as abruptly as it had begun. Cridd saw his tower had collapsed, scattering cards across the floor. He felt an absurd urge to pick them up, but Benedek moved first. Very carefully, the lanky trooper looked outside again.

It can't get in, Cridd decided, *so it's not a ghost.*

Was that better than the alternative? What *was* the alternative?

He glanced at the vox, but soot storms played havoc with the comms sets, cutting their range to a few thousand paces. No, they were on their own until the next Sentinel patrol came by. That wouldn't be for a couple of hours at least, but if they just stayed holed up...

'There's someone out there,' Benedek said. 'I... I think it's a woman.'

A moment later Cridd heard her voice. It was inside his head.

Ariken stepped out of the shuttle into a freezing black maelstrom. The gale tore at her clothes as she stumbled down the exit ramp, squinting to protect her eyes from the swirling dust. The rotten stench of sulphur was almost as crushing as the cold.

What...?

Her backpack almost unbalanced her, but she grabbed the swaying guide rope secured to the landing pad and clung to it like a lifeline, trying to find her bearings in this sudden midnight world. The pilgrim shuffling a few paces ahead was already a blur in the darkness. There was a wail of fear behind her.

Ariken turned and caught Ophele before the flailing girl was snatched away by the wind. Her friend opened her mouth to say something and swallowed a lungful of dust.

Why didn't they give us rebreathers? Ariken wondered furiously as she tried to calm the choking girl. *Or goggles at least?*

She forced her friend's hands onto the guide rope and pointed at a red haze up ahead. Ophele nodded and they pressed forward, following the rope over the shallow lip of the landing pad until the haze resolved into a marker light mounted on a tall piton. Ten paces further on there was another and Ariken realised they were spaced to offer a hint of light between each stretch of darkness.

Is that the best you could do? Ariken thought. *Why wasn't somebody here to meet us? To warn us!*

Glancing round she realised Ophele wasn't behind her anymore. Gritting her teeth, she fought her way back, pushing past one oncoming pilgrim after another until she saw her friend slumped beside the guide rope. Another man staggered past the fallen girl and Ariken lashed out at him, but he kept on going.

Cowards! Ariken raged as she knelt by her friend. Ophele's eyes were squeezed shut and she was shaking violently. Despite her frailty she felt like a dead weight when Ariken tried to lift her.

No, she thought, *it won't begin like this! I won't allow it!*

Abruptly the girl was pulled from her grasp. Ariken looked up and saw a robed pilgrim standing over her, holding Ophele in both arms. The newcomer's face was lost in a deep cowl, but from his height she guessed he must be Bharlo. She thought he'd been the first to leave the shuttle, but maybe he had returned to make sure everyone was safe. That would be just like their shepherd.

The pilgrim stepped past her and waited until she was back on her feet, then pressed on, bowing low into the wind with his burden. She followed, trying to ignore everything except the guide rope in her hands and the bobbing silhouette of the shepherd's back.

There is no darkness and no cold and no wind and no darkness and no...

The nightmare march ended as abruptly as it had begun. Suddenly a wall loomed in front of Ariken and in the wall a portal of blinding light. Then she was inside and out of the storm.

'We died,' Ophele croaked, 'all of us.' Her eyes were raw white wounds in her soot-smeared face. 'Our ship went down in the storm and...'

'I hurt too much to be dead,' Ariken interrupted. She didn't have the energy to be gentle right now. 'I'm sorry, Ophele, but this is real.'

They were slumped against the wall of a hangar, huddled among their fellow pilgrims for warmth. Everyone was shivering and wretched, their garments torn and stained almost black, their faces slack with shock. Even the shepherd looked broken. Ariken saw him a little further along, kneeling with his head bowed and eyes closed. His brow was caked in dried blood.

I never had a chance to thank him, she realised. By the time her eyes had adjusted to the light he'd gone, leaving Ophele lying by the entrance. Shortly afterwards the soldiers in black had appeared and herded them further into the hangar like cattle. One of them had slung her friend over his shoulder and then thrown her down at their destination. Another had struck Bharlo with the butt of his rifle when he'd demanded an explanation, then pushed Ariken away when she'd tried to tend him.

She eyed her captors warily, for surely that's what they were. Nothing about them said *saviours.*

There were at least thirty of them, spread across the hangar in groups of two or three. They were dressed in charcoal-black fatigues and angular breastplates that flared into crenelated shoulder guards. Their armour was painted a cast-iron black and hammered with rivets, giving it a rugged, industrial appearance. Most wore open-faced helmets, but a few had opted for caps or bandanas. Some went bare-armed, sporting warlike tattoos or iron armbands, while others had upgraded their armour to cover their limbs in interlocking plates. Their faces were mostly lean and unshaven, their eyes hard.

These are not good men, Ariken judged, recalling her conversation with Bharlo. It seemed like a lifetime ago now.

The noble two-headed aquila of the Imperium was embossed on their helmets and breastplates, but they also bore another symbol: a grinning skeleton in a wide-brimmed hat wielding crossed blades. The morbid icon was stencilled in bone white on their shoulder pads, looming over a stylised number '8', but it also served as the central motif for their tattoos.

That spectre is closer to their hearts than the Imperial Eagle, Ariken sensed.

The muted roar of the storm surged briefly as the hangar door was thrown open and two men entered. As they drew closer, she saw they could not be more unalike. One was squat and thickset, his baldpate fringed with a spiky halo of copper hair that matched his jutting beard. He wore a rough-spun cassock and a chainmail apron whose links were threaded with devotional icons. His eyes glowered beneath bristling eyebrows, their glare mirroring the energy of his stride.

The other man was much taller, his slim form swathed in a black great-coat that trailed to his boots. As he approached he swept a high-peaked cap onto his head and adjusted it with a smooth, practised motion. He was clean-shaven and blandly handsome, his pale eyes as expressionless as his features. She assumed he was an officer, though he appeared to have little in common with his charges.

'Are they here to help us, Ari?' Ophele murmured.

I don't think so, Ariken thought bleakly as the officers appraised the pilgrims. *I don't think there's any help for us here.*

'My name is Sándor Lazaro,' the short one announced. 'I bear the word of the divine God-Emperor.' He grinned ferociously, as if daring anyone to contradict him. 'Citizens of the Holy Imperium, you have been blessed today! Though you have strayed from the Emperor's true path your saviour is magnanimous.'

The preacher spoke in the baritone boom of a natural orator, yet Ariken detected a broken, anxious edge in his voice.

'You have been misled by false prophets, but I stand before you to say... that... it is not...' Lazaro's speech trailed into a raw wheeze. 'Not too late... to...' He gritted his teeth, trying to strangle a rising cough. 'To...'

He's sick, Ariken realised, appraising his flushed face. *Very sick.*

'To repent...' Lazaro almost choked on the words.

'Duty is its own redemption,' the man in the peaked cap intervened smoothly. He spoke more softly than his comrade, but with equal authority. 'And duty is what we offer you, citizens.'

'They seem nice,' Ophele whispered dully. Her eyes were glazed, her breathing shallow.

'This planet is at war,' the pale-eyed officer continued. 'We ask that you stand with us against the enemies of the Throne.'

At first the travellers met this with stunned silence, then a muttering began as his request sank in. Ariken saw the officer was unmoved by the discontent – almost as if he'd expected it. She felt a cold dread rising.

He's going to make an example of someone.

'We are loyal to the Throne,' a clear voice called out, cutting through the babble, 'but we are not fighters, sir.'

Ariken glanced round and saw a hooded pilgrim rise to his feet. As the soldiers trained their weapons on him he extended his arms slowly, showing he was unarmed. 'We knew nothing of a war on Redemption,' he continued.

'It is a cold war,' the pale-eyed officer replied. 'Our enemy is in the shadows.'

'Then I ask that you let us depart on the next ship.' Keeping his arms

raised, the hooded man stepped away from the crowd. 'I believe the Astra
Militarum has no mandate to draft honest Imperial citizens, sir.'

There was a murmur of support from the congregation, but it was hesi-
tant. Nobody wanted to be noticed. Ariken glanced at Bharlo: his head was
still bowed, as if in denial. It suddenly struck her that he hadn't been the
one who'd come to Ophele's aid outside.

It was you, Ariken decided, frowning at their enigmatic spokesman. He
had stopped a few paces from the officer.

'You have no jurisdiction over us, commissar,' he said.

'Except in extraordinary circumstances,' the officer countered, 'and this is
most definitely an extraordinary circumstance.' He raised an eyebrow. 'You
appear to be familiar with the Astra Militarum's code of conduct, pilgrim.'

'Not familiar enough, it seems.'

'Show me your face.'

Ariken knew who their spokesman was before he removed his hood.

They're both dangerous, Cross gauged as he faced the commissar, *but this
one is the greater threat.*

The preacher was transparent – a cornered animal enraged by its own weakness – but commissars were a breed apart from other men. Most of them were
incapable of the normal range of human emotions. It had been conditioned
out of them, leaving only martial traits like courage, contempt and cold wrath.
Cross had fought alongside enough of them to know their methods.

And yet there was something different about this man, something...

Nothing, he realised. That was all he saw in those pale eyes: an absence
of emotion altogether, perhaps even of conviction.

'These people are of no use to you, commissar,' he said carefully. 'They
aren't fighters.'

'But you are.'

Cross said nothing. There was no point in denying it. Commissars were
trained to recognise such things as other men recognised humour or beauty.

'Your wrist, *citizen,*' the commissar snapped.

Resigned, Cross raised his right hand and pulled back the sleeve. The
mark inscribed on his inner wrist hadn't faded. The identification tags were
made to last. He could have had it removed on Tetraktys, but that had felt
like one betrayal too many.

'Astra Militarum,' the commissar confirmed.

'And more than a common Guardsman, I suspect,' Lazaro added. His
voice was hoarse, but his coughing had subsided. 'Throne's Truth, I didn't
expect much from this rabble, but the Emperor provides.'

You're more than a blind fanatic, Cross thought as Lazaro weighed him
up shrewdly. *That grand speech was just for the crowd.*

'What was your rank, soldier?' Lazaro demanded.

'I was a captain,' Cross said quietly. 'Let the others go.'

'The choice will be theirs.' The preacher beamed. 'The Vassago Black Flags
only take the worthy.'

* * *

Lieutenant Kazimyr Senka had become a stranger to his brothers-in-arms. The regiment's armoured corps had always been a close-knit clan, as distinct from the common troops as the Third Company's veteran Gallows Dancers, but over the past few months Senka had grown distant from the tank crews and even his fellow Sentinel Sharks. Naturally he kept his disquiet hidden, for the warriors of the Vassago Abyss were not renowned for their tender hearts. He continued to drink hard and pray harder alongside his comrades, but he was dead to their revelry and reverence alike.

Murder destroyed my taste for lies, he reflected bleakly, *just as lies destroyed the shrines.*

He dismissed the dark train of thought and concentrated on steering his Sentinel between the boulders littering his path. The tall, bipedal vehicles were perfectly suited to traversing the badlands of the outer mesa. Their broad stride offered a fluidity of movement that wheels or treads couldn't hope to match, making them fine scout vehicles. To a veteran rider like Senka the machine's double-jointed legs felt like an extension of his own. When he was sealed up in the high cabin of his mount he became something more than a man.

Unlike the other pilots he looked forward to the patrols that freed him from the Locker. During the long, solitary circuits of the Slab's perimeter he could lose himself in the mastery of his machine. There were no answers to be found out here, but at least the questions were silenced. Recently however, his thoughts had begun to wander during the patrols, carrying him back to that fateful fourth shrine.

'I wasn't really part of it,' Senka said aloud, suddenly needing to hear a voice, even if it was only his own. Even if it was only another lie.

He leaned forward as his lights speared something in the gloom ahead. A few strides later a low-profiled bunker resolved itself out of the shadows: Outpost Six, his next port of call on the circuit.

The Ghostwatch, the common troopers called it.

He slowed his walker as he approached the outpost. This close to the precipice the terrain was treacherous, and the Black Flags had already lost one Sentinel to the gorge. He was damned if he'd be the second pilot to take the Fool's Fall. After the brutal attrition of Oblazt, the regiment had precious little armour left. It couldn't afford to squander machines on reckless pilots. Whatever else Senka might have lost, he still had his rider's pride.

'Shark Senka signing in,' he signalled the outpost. 'I have a clean sweep for perimeter patrol Delta. Your report, Six?'

He was met by a hiss of white noise.

'Outpost Six, do you read me?' he repeated. 'What's your status, Six?'

Finally a voice answered. *'Outpost Six.'*

Senka glanced at the rota taped to his drive panel. 'Cridd?' he asked. 'Is that you, corporal?'

A pause, as if the man on the other end were thinking about it, then: *'We waited for you, Lieutenant.'* He sounded sluggish. *Adrift.*

'Waited?' Senka frowned. Of course they'd waited. They were on watch duty.

'She told us to wait... so we could tell you.' There was a broken pause. *'They know.'*

'Say again, Six?' Senka queried.

'They know you, Senka.'

'I don't follow you–'

'Oh, you follow me,' the voice insisted, then it receded, as if addressing someone else: *'I'm done here, Benedek.'*

'Cridd?' Senka demanded. 'Corporal, what–'

He was cut off by a twinned report of las-fire – two shots, separated by a heartbeat.

'Cridd?' he called. 'Benedek?'

He switched frequencies, trying for the Locker, but he knew it was useless in a blackout. He was just putting off his next move. Reluctantly Senka shifted his vehicle into its stationary posture. While the Sentinel's legs bent to lower the cabin he strapped on his rebreather.

They know, Cridd had said.

Senka threw the cockpit release before he could change his mind and a farrago of wind and dust poured inside, eager to abrade and stain. Enginseer Tarcante would have stern words for him later, Senka guessed as he climbed out. The cabin was still almost six feet above the ground, but he knew the exit drill better than his own face.

I shouldn't be doing this, he thought as he lowered himself along the hull's handholds, then let go and landed in a low crouch. The bunker was about twenty paces away, still pinned in his Sentinel's beam. It looked pregnant with malice as he approached. The hatch was locked, but Senka had the override codes for all the outposts. He stopped with his hand outstretched, staring at the metal door. It was dented and scratched with deep, parallel furrows.

Get out of here now, Senka thought. *Run and don't stop running.*

Fighting down the rising fear, he punched the code into the access panel and raised his pistol. The locking clamps parted with a pneumatic hiss and the hatch swung open.

'Cridd!' he called over the wind. 'Benedek!'

He heard a wet, agonised moan from inside.

They know you.

'They don't know anything,' he hissed as he entered the bunker.

The two sentries were sprawled against the walls on opposite sides of the cramped space. There was a charred hole in Cridd's forehead and the laspistol he'd discharged was clutched in his left hand. Benedek was still alive, wheezing for breath as he groped spastically at the smoking ruin of his throat. As Senka knelt beside the dying man, Benedek's eyes locked on him, wide with terror.

'Why?' Senka asked. It was all he could think to say.

'*Tizheruk,*' Benedek hissed, forcing it out with his last breath.

Senka froze, trying to deny that ancient, baleful word.

Tizheruk... the Night Weavers...

On the back of his fear came the guilt, casting him back to the Spiral shrines he and his fellow puritans had razed across the Slab. The raids hadn't been officially sanctioned, but the order had come from a manifest authority. There hadn't been much violence at first – the hollow-eyed worshippers had just stood by as their spiral-tainted temples were *re-consecrated* with fire. Until the fourth shrine...

We murdered a priest, Senka thought wildly. *What if the Spiral isn't a heresy? Did we bring the Night Weavers down upon ourselves?*

'Kazimyr,' a voice whispered. 'Kazimyr Senka.'

He swung round and something vast and dark slipped away from his beam, disappearing into the storm.

'Who's there?' he yelled, levelling his pistol at the shadows beyond the hatch.

'Don't be afraid, Kazimyr,' the voice said, gentle and unmistakably female.

How can I hear her through the wind? Senka wondered, yet somehow the strangeness of it wouldn't harden into terror. Indeed his fear was melting away, like ice under a blazing sun.

But there is no sun, he thought blearily, *and no light.*

He realised there was a figure standing in the doorway. It was swathed in a long robe that blossomed around its head, shrouding its face. It was an enigma, yet he knew he had nothing to fear from it – *from her.* He tried to lower his weapon and discovered it was already by his side. She removed her cowl and he saw that her beauty transcended the promise of her voice.

'My name is Xithauli,' she said, 'and I know you, Kazimyr Senka.'

He realised it was the first time she had spoken aloud.

Whenever a soot storm raged, as it did tonight, the Retriever would climb to the highest tower of the Locker and seal himself in the chamber he had forbidden to all, even the preacher who had elevated him from a humble soldier to a holy crusader.

The regimental fortress had been erected around the spaceport, securing the planet's most vital facility, but more importantly it had been built in accordance with the Retriever's holy visions. Foremost among his specifications had been this high, stark tower. The circular chamber at its summit was empty of everything save his dreams, the tools he used to transcribe them – a crate of autoquills – and a ladder to reach its upper vaults. The walls had originally been painted a vacant white, but that emptiness had not lasted long.

Over the months the Retriever's great work had taken shape, extending across the walls in a delirious web of black scrawls. Countless icons were caught up in its strange geometry: angels and eagles, stars and skulls, cogs and consecrated blades – and myriad nameless things that ached to be.

He had laboured at the tangle with one autoquill after another, furiously rendering his visions into ink-bound reality before they could slip away, capturing their import even if he couldn't yet decipher it. Sometimes the ink ran dry and he would jab the nib into a wrist and continue in blood. Then the work would flow with greater fervour, but he would feel a shriek-ing, glacial rage welling up in his heart, as if he'd tapped too deeply into a seam of annihilating truth. In those moments he knew he would be able to see – *truly see* – the God-Emperor's design, but he always pulled back, fearful that the revelation would blind him.

'I'm not ready,' he confessed as he threw his quill aside yet again and fell to his knees, drained of everything save worship. He knew none of this was really his work. He was only a tool of the God-Emperor – a nomad soul in service to the highest of powers. That truth both humbled and exalted him.

He realised the soot storm was over and a trickle of grey light was seeping through the chamber's skylight. It was time to return to the squalid realities of the war for Redemption's soul.

'A lie is only as secure as the last man who embraced it,' he told the divine coil.

Then Colonel Kangre Talasca, commander of the Eighth Vassago Black Flags and Retriever of the Faith, rose and descended from the tower to re-join his regiment.

CHAPTER THREE

Cross didn't recognise the face staring back at him from the mirror. It was no more his own than the name he had adopted on the *Iron Calliope*. His hair was tied back and the beard was gone, revealing long, almost bookish features that suggested a scholar rather than a soldier. He recalled he had worn glasses once, clinging to the myopia of his youth despite the demands of his trainers at the academy to get his eyes corrected. It had been an absurd affectation for an Astra Militarum officer.

'You even wore glasses to a damn death world,' he mocked the stranger, who inevitably mocked him right back. 'You were a fool, Ambrose.'

He'd had his eyes fixed on Tetraktys, ironically just weeks before he lost one in an ambush. The surviving eye was still sharper than it had ever been in cooperation with its twin, yet it saw less that *meant* anything. He hadn't understood that until his friendship with Ariken.

'Don't forget again,' he warned his double.

He donned the black cap Preacher Lazaro had given him and left the cell assigned to him in the temple's cloisters. He was only mildly surprised to find there were no guards outside. After all, where could he run?

'There will be no more ships coming,' the commissar, Clavel, had told him when they left the hangar last night. *'We are alone with what's coming.'*

He had said it quietly, so quietly even the preacher hadn't heard his words. Cross wanted no confidences from that pale-eyed killer, yet he sensed the man hadn't been lying. The only way out of this – whatever *this* was – would be to see it through. He had accepted that from the moment he'd stolen a pilgrim's robe and boarded the shuttle to Redemption.

Redemption... It was that damned name, Ariken, Cross thought. *I didn't trust it with your life. It always sounded like a trap.*

Lazaro was waiting for him in the chancel. Like the rest of the temple, it was assembled from prefabricated panels, but its priest had adorned it with the paraphernalia of the Imperial Creed: prayer books, cheap tapestries and mass-produced icons masquerading as relics. Cross hadn't expected such shabby trinkets on a shrine world.

'Better,' Lazaro said, appraising his shaven face and black uniform. 'You look like a soldier now.'

'Where are my friends?' Cross asked. The pilgrims had still been huddled in the hangar when he left with the officers last night.

'I told you they won't be harmed. We may appear coarse, but we are an Astra Militarum regiment, not pirates or renegades, Mister Cross.' Lazaro was keeping his voice low, doubtless wary of triggering another coughing fit. 'Tell me, what are they to you? I don't believe for a moment that you're one of them.'

Cross hesitated, aware he had no real answers, even for himself. 'They're decent people,' he said.

'Innocents,' Lazaro confirmed, 'wayward souls lost in the wilderness!' His voice snagged and he continued more quietly: 'Innocence proves nothing, but *courage*... now that is something else entirely.' He regarded Cross keenly. 'You risked your life for fools. Either you have a hero's heart or you're a fool yourself, Cross. One of those could be useful to the Black Flags.' The preacher picked up the heavy, saw-toothed weapon resting beside the altar and strapped it onto his back. 'Come, it's time you saw the Locker!'

They stepped out into the dusty light of dawn. Seen from outside, the temple was just another block among the throng of rugged, soot-smeared buildings hunkered behind the walls of the fort. Only the symbol of the Adeptus Ministorum carved into its gates distinguished it from the rest: a stylised pillar bearing a haloed skull.

'You're wondering why our house of worship is so frugal?' Lazaro said, catching Cross' expression.

'I assumed Redemption was a shrine world,' Cross admitted.

'Like no other, but there are no temples here on the Slab. The shrines lie beyond the great gorge, carved into the mountains that encircle this mesa like the points of a crown.' Lazaro paused, bristling. 'And the mountains are not ours.'

Cross squinted, trying to see past the walls surrounding the compound, but the leaden air was impenetrable beyond a few hundred paces.

'Will it brighten up later?' he asked.

Lazaro snorted. 'The storm swept away much of the filth, but this is as bright as it gets on Redemption. And even this won't last long.'

Almost without conscious thought, Cross found himself assessing the fort's capabilities as they wove through the compound. The barracks, support structures and storage shacks were haphazardly arranged by the standards of his former regiment, but the outer wall was almost twenty feet high and built from sturdy rockrete slabs. Watchtowers buttressed it at regular intervals, all manned by Black Flags in riveted, faux-metal flak armour. The guards walking the walls were armed with lasguns, but Cross spotted heavier weapons on the towers. There was a sullen wariness about the men, as if they were caught between tedium and anxiety.

They don't know why they're here, Cross gauged, watching their haggard faces. For a professional soldier there was almost nothing worse.

The fort had only one gate, its massive twin portals forged from solid metal.

'Iron?' Cross asked.

'Steel,' Lazaro corrected.

'You don't have much armour,' Cross ventured, eyeing the ugly Hellhound tank facing the gates. Its hull was warped and crudely patched up. He had seen some light APCs, a few Sentinel walkers and the distinctive, brutal bulk of a Taurox outside the machine shop, but little else.

'We were grievously mauled in our prior deployment,' Lazaro conceded as they moved on. 'A frozen, xenos-tainted hell called Oblazt.' He almost spat the name. 'Our armour paid the highest price.'

'And your infantry?'

'Just under a thousand men remain. They will suffice.'

'To defend a planet?'

'To redeem the Koronatus Ring,' Lazaro said. 'The Ring *is* the planet.'

'I still don't understand what your mission is here.' *Or why you're showing me any of this,* Cross thought uneasily.

'Our orders were to fortify the Slab and hold it.'

'Against what?'

'Our enemy... remains in the shadows.' Lazaro's face was glistening with sweat and his breath was laboured. Though he hadn't slowed down, the tour was taxing him. 'It has been nearly seven months since we arrived.'

'Your last campaign...' Cross said carefully. 'It wasn't a victory, was it?'

'We were betrayed.' Lazaro's expression darkened. 'By a fellow Black Flag regiment.'

This is just a garrison duty, Cross realised. *You're too proud to admit it, but there is no war here.*

'I offer you a choice,' the skull-faced woman said, finally breaking the baleful silence she had adopted since entering the hangar.

Was that minutes or hours ago? Ariken wondered faintly. *How long have we been locked up in this miserable place?*

Nothing seemed certain anymore. She had been tending to Ophele when a sudden stillness had fallen over the pilgrims and her friend's glassy eyes had widened, focussing on something over Ariken's shoulder.

'I told you we were dead,' the girl had whispered.

Ariken had understood the moment she saw the malevolent skeletal figure that had crept into the hangar while her back was turned. In those first moments she thought the apparition was the Harbinger incarnate, but instead of death it had brought only silence, standing motionless as it studied the fearful crowd. Even the guards had fallen still, as if unwilling to draw the thing's eyeless gaze. It had taken all of Ariken's courage to see through the deception to the flesh and blood woman behind it. The stranger was sheathed in midnight black armour enamelled with white bones corresponding to limbs and a ribcage. The pale skull tattooed across her dark face completed the illusion of an intact skeleton.

'Your choice is simple,' the armoured woman continued, her accent strange and guttural. 'Serve under the Black Flag...' She smiled, as if at some private joke. 'Or go.'

Ariken waited for their shepherd to meet the challenge, for a challenge it surely was, but Bharlo didn't stir. She suspected he hadn't opened his eyes since the soldier had struck him.

He's broken, she thought sadly, *and this time we don't have Cross to speak up for us.*

'This isn't a game, girl,' her lost friend seemed to admonish as Ariken stood up. It was the hardest thing she had ever done.

The fortress had swallowed the spaceport whole. Judging by the troops sparring around the landing pads, Cross guessed the open space doubled up as the regiment's training grounds. A large, blunt-nosed ship sat on one of the pads. He sized it up furtively, trying not to let his interest show. It looked like a transport shuttle, probably intended for cargo, but he guessed it could handle passengers. He wasn't much of a pilot, but he'd made it his business to learn the basics during the Tetraktys sky raids.

I can get it into orbit, he gauged. *It won't go much further anyway. It's just a planetary shuttle so we'll need something else after that...*

But that was a problem for later. The ship could almost certainly serve as a piece in the escape puzzle he was trying to solve. He frowned as another detail on the field registered.

'You set us up, Lazaro,' he said coldly, 'like rats in a maze.'

The preacher sighed as he spotted the guide rope the pilgrims had followed through the storm last night. Rather than taking the most direct course to the hangar, it twisted back-and-forth around the field, at least tripling the distance.

'That was Omazet's idea,' Lazaro said. 'A test of sorts.'

'Then his idiocy almost got people killed.'

'*She.* Captain Omazet commands the Third Company. She is a very... *unique* officer.' Lazaro looked uncomfortable. 'She is overseeing the new recruits.'

Cross caught his arm. 'I want to see my friends.'

'I've already told you–'

'You've just told me their lives are in the hands of a sadist.'

'Their lives are in the hands of *the colonel.*' Lazaro's eyes blazed. 'As is yours.'

They glared at each other, then Cross sighed, weary of the game. 'What do you want from me?' he asked.

The preacher's fury faded as swiftly as it had come. Without it he looked almost frail.

'The Black Flags aren't short of fine fighters, Cross, but sharp minds...' Lazaro shook his head. 'We lost our best officers on Oblazt.'

'You want me to serve with you?' Cross couldn't hide his scepticism. 'A stranger?'

'You are not a man of faith are you, Cross?'

'I'm no heretic.'

'That isn't what I asked.' Lazaro held up an admonishing hand. 'You believe it's pure chance that brought you here – chance that put you on the same path as those blind fools and chance that forged your loyalty to them.' He grinned, recovering a measure of ferocity. 'I don't believe in chance, Cross. Come, we've kept the colonel waiting long enough!'

* * *

'You are a medicae,' the skull-faced woman said. It wasn't a question, yet Ariken knew she expected an answer.

'I...' Ariken swallowed, trying to revive her dry throat. The weakness angered her, driving her to face the apparition boldly. Up close, she could see the woman's empty eye sockets were only a contrivance of dark lenses. Everything about her was engineered to instil terror, but none of it was real.

'I know enough to tell you my people are exhausted,' Ariken said. 'We don't want any part of your army, but we need help – water, food and medicine.'

'That is not a choice I offer.'

'Then you're offering *nothing!*' Ariken snapped, seizing the anger that had been building in her since this ordeal began. 'You're just playing with us.'

'We look after our own,' the woman said, ignoring the outburst. 'Those who serve under the Black Flag shall receive succour.'

'Then we'll take our chances alone.' Ariken turned her back on the hateful creature and saw her fellow pilgrims staring at her, wide-eyed.

They won't follow me, she realised, *not one of them.*

'I will offer you a third choice, *Ariken,*' the woman whispered.

The fort's keep was an octagonal block reinforced with iron plates that ran the length of its central tower, giving the impression of a vast, outlandish battle-tank. Its doors were set into a jutting gatehouse crowned with a gun emplacement, but it was the pair of creatures standing before the portals that drew Cross' attention.

Abhumans, he realised uneasily. *Sanctioned mutants.*

The guards were muscle-bound giants with deep-set eyes and prognathous jaws that looked strong enough to chew through stone. Their thick torsos were girdled in white armour and their heads were encased in openfaced helms sprouting black crests. Both carried slab-like shields and massive mauls, yet despite their ferocity there was a gravitas about them that surprised Cross. They stood rigidly at attention, their expressions more stern than stupid, looking almost *noble.*

'The Silent Paladins,' Lazaro said proudly. 'The colonel's elite guard.' His hands inscribed an aquila and the abhumans rapped their weapons against their shields in acknowledgement.

'They are vowed to silence lest their coarse tongues offend the God-Emperor,' Lazaro explained, his expression almost beatific. 'They hail from Ctholl, the deepest of Vassago's Sunken Worlds. It is an accursed, primal place, yet its people are stalwart guardians of the faith.'

The doors of the gatehouse slid open and a young soldier emerged. Instead of flak armour he wore an iron-trimmed leather waistcoat over his fatigues.

'Shark Senka,' Lazaro greeted him. The man looked at him blankly. 'Lieutenant, are you well?'

'Forgive me, preacher,' Senka said, snapping back into the moment. 'I've just delivered my report. Yesterday's patrol... it was a bad business.' He glanced at Cross uncertainly. 'Cridd and Benedek... they killed each other.

I heard them arguing over the vox. A game of dice turned sour.' He shook his head. 'Forgive me, I must attend to my Sentinel.'

'Throne damn them!' Lazaro cursed as the young officer hurried away. 'We've lost too many men to such idiocy!'

Cross wasn't listening. Something about Senka's story had troubled him. *No, not his story,* he realised. *His eyes.*

That distant gaze hadn't been filled with horror. Under his exhaustion, Lieutenant Senka had looked almost *happy.*

'The soldiers have agreed to escort the congregation to our friends in the Spiral Dawn,' Ariken told the pilgrims. She raised her hands to quiet their ragged cheers. 'In return, Captain Omazet has asked that some of us remain. She wants volunteers.' Ariken faltered, sensing the skull-faced woman's gaze on her back. 'One hundred volunteers.'

I'm sorry, she thought, *it was the best I could do.*

'I've agreed to stay,' Ariken continued, 'but I'm not enough.'

Ophele struggled to rise, but she didn't have the strength. Ariken quashed a surge of affection – even if the girl made it to her feet she wouldn't last long among these black-uniformed monsters. Her only chance was with the Spiral Dawn.

'The captain won't accept the sick,' she said harshly, 'but if we can't meet her quota we're on our own.'

She told me I won't get one hundred, Ariken thought, watching the sea of pale faces. *Please don't prove the bitch right.*

Connant was the first to stand. He was an ex-PDF trooper, older and tougher than the others. Heike, the no-nonsense manufactorum forewoman was next, then dry, dull Jherem, an administratum scribe who'd barely spoken a word throughout their journey, then Jei, who was too young to be anything much yet... And so it went, until there were some thirty people standing. They weren't nearly enough.

Instinctively Ariken glanced at Bharlo. To her surprise he was looking right back at her. He nodded gravely and got up. As always, others followed the shepherd and the number rose to forty, then sixty before Ariken lost count. By the time the flow of volunteers had dried up there were well over a hundred pilgrims standing.

'You have your blood price,' Ariken told the captain with bitter pride.

'I will take only one hundred,' Omazet replied. 'Only the most worthy.'

'Leave us, my friend,' the colonel said.

Lazaro inclined his head and departed the conference room, leaving Cross alone with the regiment's commander.

'I am Kangre Talasca,' the colonel said as he paced the chamber, 'and you are Cross.'

He was dressed in a sable greatcoat woven with silver scales that shimmered as he moved. His olive skin was smooth and unblemished, but tautly strung across his shaven skull, like a freshly made-up corpse. He might have been anything between thirty and fifty years old.

'Cross...' Talasca mused. 'Is it your real name?'

It was spoken lightly, almost in passing, yet Cross doubted there was anything light about the slender man prowling the room.

'No,' Cross replied, 'it is not.'

'Our given names are unimportant,' Talasca approved. 'It is only the ones we choose that have meaning.'

'Then are you really Kangre Talasca?'

The colonel ceased his pacing and looked over his shoulder. He smiled, the expression somehow accentuating the cold silver of his eyes. They were elegant augmetic implants, far superior to the crude meat-work of Cross' own.

'If I am not Kangre Talasca, then who am I?'

'You are the colonel,' Cross ventured. 'Your duty to your men defines you.'

The smile widened, though it still couldn't warm the commander's eyes.

'A good answer,' Talasca said, 'but my duty runs much deeper than that. I am the Retriever, of faith and the faithful. I was not consigned to Redemption by chance. Do you understand?'

Not by chance, Cross thought. It was an echo of Lazaro's argument. More than an echo. Whatever the colonel was – or thought he was – the preacher had made him so.

'I asked if you understood?' Talasca pressed.

'I'm willing to learn.'

Moving with a predator's grace, the colonel strode over to him. 'Commissar Clavel told me you were an officer once. Are you a deserter now?'

Cross hesitated. The coiled violence in this man was palpable.

'I don't know,' he confessed with soul-deep weariness. 'I was wounded. Sick...' Following an obscure instinct, he removed his gauntlet and raised his left hand, suppressing a shudder at the corpse-claw reflected in Talasca's eyes. 'I thought I died, but perhaps *nothing* is chance... Retriever.'

If I've misread him I'm a dead man.

'I think the name you have chosen is a true one,' Talasca judged finally. Then he swung around and began to pace again. 'Tell me, what did you make of our armour?'

The test had only begun, yet Cross sensed he had passed the most crucial threshold.

After Captain Omazet had chosen her recruits they gathered at the gates to bid their fortunate brethren farewell. True to her promise, the captain had mustered a convoy of lightly armoured vehicles – she called them Chimeras – to carry the pilgrims to the Spire Caritas, where the Spiral Dawn would receive them.

'I want to stay, Ari,' Ophele wheezed, gripping Ariken's hands. Her eyes were raw and she was burning up. She had been too weak to walk so her comrades had lifted her into a transport.

'You'll be safe soon,' Ariken promised. She extricated herself gently and stepped away. 'They'll look after you in the Spires, Ophele.'

'No... no... That's not right... Wait–' The Chimera's hatch slammed shut, cutting off her frantic gaze.

'It's going to be okay,' Ariken whispered as the vehicle pulled away.

'I'm sorry, Ariken,' Bharlo said at her shoulder. His face was gaunt, as diminished as the man behind it.

'There was nothing you could do, shepherd,' she said.

'Perhaps, but a blind shepherd is no good to anyone.'

'What did she say to you?' Ariken asked. 'The captain?' After choosing her tithe, Omazet had taken Bharlo aside and spoken to him quietly.

'She saw the man I used to be, and advised me to find him again.'

'That man isn't someone you need anymore.'

'Perhaps.' Bharlo flashed his familiar, sad smile. Then he turned and climbed into the last vehicle. 'Good luck, my friend.'

Why didn't she choose him? Ariken wondered as the convoy departed. *If anyone among us can fight, it's him.*

Preacher Lazaro was waiting outside the conference room when Cross and Talasca finally emerged. Together they made their way to an austere dining room, where Commissar Clavel and three other officers joined them.

'Regrettably Captain Omazet won't be attending,' Clavel said. 'She sent word that she has been detained with the recruits.'

Talasca nodded curtly. Cross sensed the captain's absence was not unexpected.

'The Witch Captain thinks herself too fine for the company of Throne-fearing soldiers,' one of the officers remarked. His iron-grey hair and goatee were neatly trimmed, sharpening the lines of his hawkish face.

'She hates all men equally, comrade,' another of the officers said. He scowled, showing metal-shod teeth through a tangle of black beard. Piercings and tattoos fought for space on his shaven, bullet-like head. His fur-trimmed greatcoat bulged with his girth and he towered over the others.

'Major Shaval Kazán, our infantry commander,' Lazaro introduced the giant, then indicated the grey-haired officer, 'and Major Markel Rostyk, commander of our armoured corps.'

'Quezada,' the third officer said as the preacher turned to him. 'Captain, the Gallows Dancers.'

'The regiment's veteran platoon,' Lazaro explained. 'Quite exceptional men and women.'

'By the Emperor's Grace,' Quezada acknowledged. He was older than the others and wore a plain uniform distinguished only by a scarlet sash. His white hair was swept back from his seamed face and tied into a high topknot. While Rostyk and Kazán glowered at Cross, Quezada was merely watchful.

'Captain Cross will be serving with the Eighth in a support capacity,' Commissar Clavel said. 'I expect you to offer him every assistance, gentlemen.'

'Has he sworn the oath?' Major Rostyk demanded.

'I have, sir,' Cross said. He raised his right hand, revealing the sigil Colonel Talasca had inscribed upon his palm with needle and ink. 'I stand with you under the Black Flag.'

'It is the Vassago way, Cross,' the colonel had told him. *'Black Flag regiments are raised from the five Sunken Worlds of Vassago – Verzante, Lethe,*

Szilar, Cantico and Ctholl – but we always draw new blood from outsiders – the survivors of broken armies, warriors without hope or purpose, sometimes even renegades seeking a second chance. All are reborn beneath the Black Flag of Vassago.'

'It is a strange mark,' Rostyk said, scowling at the tattoo on Cross' palm. It was a stylised figure '8' with a watchful eye at its centre.

'But true to the man,' Quezada judged.

At a gesture from the colonel the company sat. Cross had expected the officers to quiz him about his past, but they ate in near silence, as if questions would transgress some tacit code of conduct.

Perhaps the mark is enough for them, Cross thought.

Talasca's table was as severe as the man himself. The meal consisted of water and standard rations spooned onto tin plates, but none of the officers protested and Cross' respect for the Black Flags rose a notch. This regiment might be eccentric, but its officers didn't exploit the privileges of rank – at least not in the presence of their colonel.

And there's a shadow hanging over them all, he sensed as they ate. *Oblazt left a deep wound, perhaps even a mortal one.* With a rush of shame he thought of his own lost regiment. *Am I the last of them?*

The three officers departed shortly after the meal and Cross realised the colonel hadn't spoken a word during the gathering. Talasca continued to brood after they were gone. Cross glanced at Lazaro and Clavel, but neither would meet his gaze.

'What did you make of them, Cross?' Talasca asked abruptly.

'Rostyk isn't as clever as he thinks he is,' Cross said, unsure if this was another test, 'but Kazán's sharper than he pretends to be. Quezada... I have no idea about Quezada.'

'I trust none of them,' Talasca declared. 'Other than the men in this room and my Silent Paladins, I trust no one.'

Mutiny? Cross wondered. It wasn't uncommon among demoralised regiments, especially those that had lost faith in their commanding officer.

'Tomorrow I shall meet with the Gyre Magus of the Spiral Dawn,' Talasca continued, changing the subject. 'He will protest our detention of the pilgrims.'

'I can't say I'm surprised. You've run roughshod over a sect of the Imperial Creed,' Cross said.

'You will attend,' Talasca told him, 'and observe.' He glanced at his advisors and an unspoken confirmation seemed to pass between them. 'But first there is something you must see.'

Night had fallen when they left the keep. The colonel led the small party across the compound in silence. Cross heard muffled coughing as they approached the infirmary, but the party veered off, heading for a smaller outbuilding. One of the Silent Paladins stood outside its heavy door.

'You'll need this,' Lazaro said, handing Cross a rebreather. 'They're standard issue on Redemption – for the blackouts – but you'll want it now.'

The others were already strapping on their masks so Cross followed suit, fumbling with the unfamiliar mechanism.

'Throne deliver us from darkness,' Lazaro muttered as they entered the outbuilding.

Cross faltered. Even through his mask the foetor of corruption in the enclosed space was almost overpowering.

'I removed the body from storage this morning,' Clavel said, indicating a tarpaulin-covered shape lying on a gurney at the far side of the room. 'It's almost three months old, but I believe it will suffice.'

Suffice for what? Cross wondered as he followed the others to the gurney.

'Show him,' Talasca ordered.

Clavel removed the tarpaulin in measured steps, trying not to damage the disintegrating corpse beneath. In places the putrefying flesh had stuck to the material and he had to peel it back slowly, yet he seemed unperturbed by the macabre work.

'It was found on a ledge just over the Rim,' Clavel said as the naked cadaver was revealed. 'Its neck was broken. We think it fell during a blackout.'

Fighting his revulsion, Cross forced himself to study the thing on the gurney. It was the general size and shape of a large man, but its frame was distended by bundles of fibrous muscles at the joints and neck. Its left leg was unremarkable, but the right terminated in a reverse-jointed, barbed talon. The left arm looked normal, but the right was sheathed in glistening blue chitin from the elbow down. Instead of a hand there was a bloated, four-fingered claw tipped with vicious bone spikes. The *third* arm was even worse. Fighting for space with the mundane left, it flared out into a serrated, scissoring hook that looked like it could tear through armour.

But it was the thing's face that made Cross' gorge rise.

Its vivid blue eyes were still intact in the sunken ruin of their sockets. They looked human, but a spiny ridge bisected them, running from the back of its elongated skull to the bridge of a flat, bestial snout. The lower half of its face was a nest of thorn-tipped tendrils that dangled limply over the edge of the gurney, dripping black ichor.

'It was only by the Emperor's Grace that we found it,' the preacher said, his voice heavy with loathing. He took something from a pouch on his belt and handed it to Cross. 'The beast was wearing this.'

It was a pendant, carved from obsidian and threaded with sinewy cord. The symbol it bore was a jagged spiral – a savage variant of the icon sported by the pilgrims.

'Have you reported this?' Cross asked, thinking of Ariken.

'As per standard protocol,' Clavel confirmed. 'We have received no answer. As I said, that was almost three months ago.' He paused, glancing at Talasca, who nodded. 'There's something else,' he continued. 'One of the Sentinel pilots brought me a report this morning...'

'Senka?' Lazaro said. 'The fools who killed each other over dice?'

'That is the story I instructed Senka to tell,' Clavel said. 'The guards killed each other, yes, but it wasn't over dice. We believe they were... influenced. Before they died they wrote something on the wall in their own blood. We believe it was intended as a warning... or a challenge perhaps.'

'*Tizheruk,*' Talasca said. His silver eyes glittered behind his mask.

'I don't understand...' Cross said. The word was like a spike in his mind and his nausea rose with renewed vigour. Instinctively he stepped away from the tainted corpse.

'The name dates back to the darkest age of the Sunken Worlds, Cross,' Lazaro said hoarsely. 'It predates the coming of the Imperium and our salvation. It means Night Weavers, the Stealers of Souls... daemons.'

CHAPTER FOUR

Kazimyr Senka loathed Hope. The planet's single, dismal city was an industrial stain on the Slab, dying, but not quite dead. It was a muddle of crooked tenements and narrow avenues that could quickly become a maze for the unwary. In the early days of the occupation, before Command had clamped down on things, several troopers had got themselves lost in its knotted streets.

They never found Blyre, Senka recalled as the mono-train approached the city. Through the dirty windows of his carriage Hope looked like something that had been broken at birth and reassembled over and over again, becoming more tangled with every iteration. It wasn't a place he wanted to be after dark, but he'd given the Spiral priestess his word.

And I need to see her again, he admitted.

The ancient mono-train creaked and shuddered as it slithered along the corroded rail. It had been built to ferry promethium to the spaceport at the mesa's southern reach, but these days it also carried supplies to the Locker or off-duty troopers to the city's Green Zone, the only district that had been approved for 'recreational activities.'

A black wave of refineries and storage depots rushed past Senka's window as the train entered the city's outskirts. Gloomily he imagined the throng of human grubs labouring in the plants as if nothing had changed. The Slab's promethium industry had been ailing long before the Black Flags' arrival, but trade had dried up completely after they'd blockaded the spaceport. Regardless, barrels of promethium had continued to pile up outside the Locker's walls every week, as if the citizens of Hope had no other purpose.

Which is probably close to the truth, Senka guessed.

For a man of Lethe, the most regimented of the Sunken Worlds, such apathy was unthinkable. Until recently he'd felt nothing but contempt for the grubs who wasted their lives here. Maybe that was why he'd been so ready to destroy their pitiful, spiral-branded temples. He hadn't thought it through, not even after the fourth shrine and the guilt its desecration had brought.

I never really thought anything *through,* he admitted, *not until she opened my eyes...*

'Wake up, Shark,' a voice said, rousing him from his introspection. A burly Guardsman was regarding him with disconcertingly skewed eyes. His heavy greatcoat bore a sergeant's stripes. 'We're in the Green.'

Senka realised the train had pulled into the terminal of the approved district and his fellow passengers, a band of off-duty infantrymen, were heading for the doors. Like most of the common troopers, they were Szilars – coarse, pragmatic men with more taste for drink than protocol.

'Go ahead,' Senka said. He was damned if he'd waste his breath concocting a cover story for a thug who'd probably be senseless within the hour.

The Szilar regarded him for a moment, his misaligned gaze impossible to read. Then the fingers of his left hand inscribed something in the air, keeping the motions hidden from his comrades. Before Senka could question him he was gone, following the others onto the platform.

His fingers had described a spiral.

You are not the first of your kind to embrace the Unfolding, the priestess had told him. *Truth is a potent weapon, Kazimyr.*

Night fell as the mono-train carried Senka deeper into Hope's tangle. He knew there would be little respite from the darkness until another storm cleared the air. Despite the lights lining the track the city's gloom was more oppressive than the darkness of the mesa.

More hungry...

Two stops later a group of grubs shuffled onto the carriage. Their gaunt, vacant faces were as grey as their filthy coveralls. They slumped onto the benches and sat in silence, staring into nothingness. Either they were too tired for camaraderie or they had forgotten what it was. None of them paid any heed to the stranger in their midst. In the flickering light of the carriage they looked like corpses on their final journey to the Black Trench that claimed everyone in the end.

If it took them now would they even notice, let alone care? Senka wondered.

Some instinct made him turn and he saw another pair of grubs sitting at the rear of the carriage. They wore the tough, rubberised jumpsuits and cowls of the magma scrapers who eked out an existence at the base of the Spires. Despite their hunched postures they were much bigger than their fellow workers, their long arms bulging with muscles. He couldn't shake the feeling that their jutting jaws were filled with sharp teeth – or that their shadowed eyes were watching him.

What am I doing here? Senka thought. But he already knew the answer.

As agreed, the priestess was waiting for him on the far side of the city. He held his breath as she entered the carriage, her robes seeming to glide above the ground like a ghost's mantle. Neither dirt nor darkness could dull their azure lustre, but their glamor paled beside her strange beauty when she threw back her hood. The grubs had departed somewhere along the way so he was alone with her, but that would have been true even in a crowd, for his world had narrowed to the sapphire glimmer of her eyes. They looked impossibly bright in the dreary carriage.

Like a serpent's eyes, a distant, drowning part of him shrieked. Suddenly he remembered the terrible thing she had asked of him last night. The thing he had written in a dead man's blood.

Tizheruk.

'Kazimyr Senka,' Xithauli murmured, tenderly smothering his screaming shadow. 'You haven't failed me.' She brushed his cheek and he shuddered at the delicate touch of her long, sharp nails. He tried to rise, but she pressed him back into his seat. 'Be still, we have some way to travel yet, my love.'

My love... Senka's heart soared like a lovesick youth's at her words, but he knew it was neither sickness nor youth, nor simply banal lust that energised him. He couldn't deny that lust was a *part* of it, but it was eclipsed by the resplendent *mystery* of her.

Finally, I'll understand. Even now, he couldn't quite grasp the *questions* he yearned to answer, for they slipped away as he tried to frame them, but that only drew him deeper into their orbit. *Her orbit.*

'It is the answers that frame the questions, Kazimyr,' Xithauli advised.

The old Senka would have scoffed at such talk, but now her words filled him with awe, not least because she had spoken directly to his mind, as she had done the night before. The priestess smiled and sat opposite him.

'Where are we going?' he whispered as the train left the city and picked up speed. His voice couldn't carry above the noise, but he knew that didn't matter.

'Veritas,' she answered. *'This track crosses the gorge to the Spire of Truth.'*

Veritas? It was the highest of the Seven Spires and the foremost enclave of the Spiral Dawn. *Truth...* A shard of memory lanced Senka and he glimpsed a hulking abomination following the priestess into the blackout.

'What was it?' Senka hissed, fighting to see clearly. 'Last night... the thing with you... the other...'

'There was no *other*, my love,' she soothed. 'Only you and I.' She smiled and he was lost. 'I will show you such wonders, Kazimyr Senka.'

The priests of the Spiral Dawn called him the Chrysaor. He was less than thirty years old, yet he was revered as a saint and had been since birth, for the blood-deep wisdom of the Spiral had moulded him into a champion that stood outside the Five Paradigms of Form that shaped most of its children. Like the cult magi, he was *born* to command, but while they ruled through subterfuge, his instincts lay in war. There had been no conflict on Redemption since the first days of the Spiral Father so the Chrysaor had waited without rancour, honing his mind and body for the day when he would lead his brethren to embrace new worlds. Patience ran deep in the children of the Spiral, but the arrival of the heretics had stirred something urgent in him – a cold wrath that drove him to *know his enemy.*

The Chrysaor's quest for knowledge often drew him to the mesa and the city, sometimes even to the walls of the heretics' bastion, where he would observe, learn and plan for the reckoning he hungered for. He had watched from the shadows as the heretics' sins grew from petty desecration to outrage. When they had destroyed the cult's temples across the Slab, he had almost succumbed to the urge for retribution, but some subtle, vital line had not yet been crossed.

Tonight his quest had led him back to the city.

He crept from shadow to shadow, keeping close to the walls as he followed three soldiers through the streets. The men had strayed beyond the usual haunts of their kind, perhaps seeking darker sport to sate their passions.

He had recognised their leader from the temple burnings – a scar-faced savage they called Hajnal – and latched onto them as they wandered away from the sullen bars of the Green Zone.

'We're going in circles,' one of the men grumbled.

'Only in the eyes of a blind man,' Hajnal snarled.

'There's nothing past the Green anyways.'

The Chrysaor hung back as the men squabbled. It looked like they might even start fighting. The outsiders' capacity for stupidity never failed to surprise him–

Where was the third man?

An arm wrapped itself around his throat and a blade pressed under his chin. 'Easy now, grub,' someone whispered behind him. 'See, the dark makes me twitchy. You move and I might jump.' The speaker raised his voice. 'I got him, comrades!'

Hajnal and the other man broke off their argument immediately and saun-tered over to the alley where the Chrysaor had been hiding. The third solider must have sneaked round while he was distracted by the fake squabble.

I underestimated them, the Chrysaor realised, *both their cunning and their shadow-craft. My contempt for their kind blinded me.* He felt no shame at the error, but he would not repeat it.

'Good work, Maklar,' Hajnal said to the knifeman. He glared at the pris-oner, trying to see beneath his hood. 'Why you been following us, grub?'

'You are mistaken.'

'Is that right?' All traces of Hajnal's brash stupidity were gone now, reveal-ing the stone-cold killer beneath. There was an aquila tattooed between his eyes, another hanging from a chain round his neck. Both were as crude as the zealot himself.

'I am unarmed,' the Chrysaor said, raising his hands slowly.

'I wouldn't say that, grub,' Hajnal growled, eyeing his barbed fingernails. 'Let's take a look at you. Man with nails like that must have a face worth seeing.' He reached forward and threw aside the captive's hood. 'What...'

The Chrysaor felt a thrill of release at the degenerate's shocked expres-sion. It was the first time an outsider had gazed upon his blessed visage.

'Veritas!' he hissed, spitting a gob of venom into Hajnal's face. In the same instant his third arm whipped out from beneath his robe, revealing a chitin-sheathed claw tipped with dagger-like talons. The claw ripped through the knifeman's arm below the elbow and he fell back, shrieking as his stump gushed blood. The third soldier moved with unexpected speed, drawing his laspistol and firing two-handed in one smooth motion, but the cultist spun aside and the bolts hit the injured man behind him square in the chest. The Chrysaor grabbed the corpse before it fell and thrust it towards his attacker. Though the gunman leapt aside, the distraction bought the cultist enough time to close in.

For the dead and the defiled, he thought as he grabbed the man's hands in his own and squeezed, crushing the fragile fingers and the gun they held into a mangled ruin. As the soldier began to scream the Chrysaor lashed out with his rending claw and tore off his face.

'Hee... ra... tak...' a voice gurgled behind him.

The Chrysaor threw aside the faceless corpse and turned to inspect Hajnal. The zealot was slumped against a wall, his body wracked by violent spasms as the venom turned his own blood against him. His face had swollen into a single shapeless bruise, haemorrhaging ichor as he choked. The chain of his pendant had snapped under the pressure of his bloated throat.

'Truth is beauty,' the Chrysaor decreed.

CHAPTER FIVE

Whenever Vyrunas ascended from the winding subterranean womb of the *Mandira Veritas* he felt a disconnection so profound he had to force himself to take the last few steps. The living god of the Spiral Dawn dwelt in the Gyre Sanctum below, where He had long ago retreated to meditate upon the Unfolding Path. All the Spiral Kindred were bonded by blood and spirit to their star-spawned progenitor, but Vyrunas' affinity ran deeper, for he had served as the cult's magus for over a century, weaving an invisible, but unbreakable, web of influence over the planet in his god's name.

I am old, Vyrunas reflected dispassionately as he climbed, *nearly as old as the Spiral Dawn itself.*

His progenitor's artifice had preserved a measure of his vitality, but both his mind and body were finally failing, exhausted by the rigours of his duty. Unlike the Spiral Father, Vyrunas was a hybrid creature, his exalted blood mingled with that of Redemption's mundane populace. For all his psychic puissance, he was not immortal.

'As within, so without,' he intoned. Above him the golden whorls of the Sleepless Gate spun open, revealing the soaring dome of the temple. In accordance with tradition he closed his eyes as he stepped out of the dark well and into the cavernous amphitheatre beyond. The *Mandira Veritas* was the sect's foremost temple, converted from an older, heathen structure in the early decades of the Spiral Father's reign. Every edge had been smoothed to a soft, organic curve, every surface polished to a dark mirror.

Our temple reflects the soul, not the body, Vyrunas thought as the gate whirled closed at his feet. The portal was set into the summit of a vast obsidian cone that rose from the amphitheatre in a corkscrew of ramps, like a coiled snake. The apex was precisely midway between the dome's oculus and the sanctum of the Spiral Father.

'Our lord is troubled,' Vyrunas told the priestess who awaited him. She acknowledged this with a shallow bow. Doubtless she had sensed the Spiral Father's disquiet. Like himself, she was a hybrid of the Fourth Paradigm, almost indistinguishable from the outsiders they shared their world with. More importantly she was a fellow magus, one of only three among Redemption's star-touched kindred.

'How long was I gone, Xithauli?' Vyrunas asked.

'Three days, Gyre Magus.'

Three, Vyrunas echoed. Each time he descended to commune with his god his inner voyage grew longer. The process had begun almost a year ago, but it was accelerating. Very soon now the tidal pull of the Spiral Father's dreams would swallow Vyrunas' ailing mind. The prospect did not sadden him, for it was the natural order of things, but the timing was unfortunate.

'You will be Gyre Magus soon, Xithauli,' he said.

'Yes,' his heir replied without emotion.

She is a youthful, female incarnation of myself, Vyrunas judged.

The magi shared the same direct bloodline, both descended from the esteemed Saint Etelka. They both radiated a glacial majesty, but in Xithauli it was amplified by an ethereal beauty that often left outsiders floundering. Her silken robes splayed up into a ribbed cowl around her head and silver bangles encircled her neck, lending it an elongated, almost serpentine aspect. In common with all the kindred she was completely hairless and her complexion was tinged a delicate violet. Outsiders mistook this colouration for make-up, assuming it was a contrivance to match her cobalt-stained lips and kohl-framed eyes. Likewise, the bony ridge running from her scalp to the bridge of her nose was decorated with crushed amethysts, creating the illusion of an ornament.

'Has the heretic commander answered my summons?' Vyrunas asked. He could have plucked the answer from his disciple's mind, but that would have been a discourtesy.

'He awaits you at the bridge, Gyre Magus,' Xithauli replied. 'He would come no further.' She hesitated. 'I tasted his thoughts again.'

'That was unwise.'

'The choice was not mine.' Xithauli's face twisted with revulsion. 'His mind reeks with spite, like a dark beacon. Being near him is like being buried alive with a corpse.'

'He is lost in his own darkness. The outsiders are often prey to such traps.'

'There was another with him,' Xithauli said. 'His mind was closed to me.'

'The pale-eyed one?' Vyrunas asked. 'The commissar?'

'No, this one is new. I think the scars in him run even deeper.'

It looks like a frozen shard of space, Cross mused, gazing at the obsidian splinter looming above him. The mountain was speckled with crimson lights that twinkled like stars against its dark mass. Preacher Lazaro had explained that they were ritual fires, each one marking a shrine along the path that wound up the mountainside.

'There must be over a hundred of them,' Cross breathed, awed despite his doubts.

'One-hundred-and-forty-four,' Lazaro said, 'and this is only one of the Seven Spires.'

They stood at the base of the mountain, waiting among the circle of standing stones that formed the first shrine along the Path of Truth. It lay just beyond the lip of the suspension bridge that connected Spire Veritas to the Slab. The Imperial delegation had crossed the gorge in a convoy of Chimeras supported by Sentinels, travelling in parallel with the monorail running through the centre of the bridge.

To Cross' mind the bridge was a monument in itself. Its towering stone railings were carved into a chain of open hands inscribed with the watchful eye of Truth. Lazaro had told him that every bridge was unique, though two had fallen into ruin for they led to abandoned Spires: Castitas, home of the shunned Adepta Sororitas abbey, and Vigilans, which had become an active volcano centuries ago.

'*Veritas is the highest spire,*' Lazaro had said, '*but I believe the roots of Vigilans run deepest.*'

After crossing the bridge, the vehicles had encircled the shrine of standing stones and several squads had disembarked. Cross didn't know if the colonel was being cautious or making a show of strength, but after the decomposing abomination he had seen yesterday he was glad of the numbers. The shrine's white-robed wardens had been evicted curtly, but they had acceded without protest, neither hostile nor cowed by the invaders. Cross had spotted no obvious signs of mutation among them; indeed they were markedly more comely than the scruffy Slab dwellers he'd seen labouring outside the fort.

'It's hard to believe...' he began uncertainly.

'That such folk would harbour monsters?' Lazaro suggested. 'I've fought more heretics than I care to remember, Cross. Some have been deranged fanatics, others devious beyond measure, but there was always something in their eyes that gave them away – an arrogance.' He shook his head. 'The Unfolded don't have it.'

'You think they're innocent?' Cross was surprised.

'I don't know what they are,' Lazaro said. 'Their Throne-damned Spiral makes my skin crawl, but they claim it's the God-Emperor's work. Besides, someone wiser than I sanctioned their sect.' He sighed. 'We need to be certain they're the real enemy before we move against them.'

'I've misjudged you, preacher. I assumed Clavel was the steady hand here.'

'Clavel? He's been pushing for war with the Unfolded since he arrived.'

'He wasn't with you from the start?' Cross glanced round and saw the commissar talking to Talasca by the shrine's hearthstone.

'Our old commissar was lost on Oblazt. Clavel turned up a few months ago.' Lazaro frowned. 'The colonel has taken to him.'

There was a buzzing drone from above and Cross saw a delicate rotor-bladed craft descending from the mountain. It flitted skilfully through the treacherous air currents like a winged insect, the whipped-air chattering of its blades becoming louder as it came in to land just beyond the shrine.

'It's the Gyre Magus,' Lazaro said. 'We should join the colonel.'

The Spiral Dawn's ambassador had come alone and unarmed save for a silver staff tipped with an obsidian helix. As he approached, Cross was struck by the resemblance between this man and the bewitching priestess who had first met them at the bridge. Though the ambassador was much older he had the same sharp cheekbones and piercing blue eyes, the same graceful walk and regal bearing. Were they father and daughter?

'Colonel Talasca,' the ambassador said, 'I am honoured that you hold my safety in such high regard that you have attended me with an army.' Like his presumed daughter, he spoke in a flowing, liquid lilt, almost chanting his words.

'This planet is under the protection of the Astra Militarum, Magus Vyrunas,' Talasca answered coolly. 'As is the Spiral Dawn.'

'Indeed, we are all servants of the God-Emperor's unfolding design, colonel,' Vyrunas acknowledged.

'You know Preacher Lazaro and Commissar Clavel,' Talasca said, 'but may I introduce Captain Cross.'

As the ambassador's gaze fell upon him, Cross felt something sweep delicately across his mind, like a phantom breath. He would have dismissed it were it not for a slight hardening of Vyrunas' expression.

He tried to look inside me...

'The Spiral embraces all,' Vyrunas said with a gentleness his eyes denied. 'May you find your truth on Redemption, Captain Cross.'

'I trust the pilgrims reached you safely, Gyre Magus?' Lazaro asked.

'Not *all* of them, preacher.'

'We offered them shelter during the blackout,' Clavel said. 'In return, some offered their services to the Astra Militarum.'

'They found their true calling,' the colonel added, flashing his dead smile.

'It would be regrettable if any harm befell them,' the magus said. 'And what of the other matter?'

'The Slab shrines?' Talasca shook his head. 'Nothing so far, but I assure you we are taking their desecration seriously.'

'Eleven people were butchered in the last attack, colonel,' Vyrunas pressed. 'You say you are here to protect us, yet the violations began with your arrival.'

Talasca's smile vanished. 'I will not stand by while you–'

'I am conducting the investigation personally, Gyre Magus,' Clavel interjected. 'If any of our troops are found responsible they will be disciplined.'

'There is another matter,' Talasca said, his eyes glittering. 'Three of my men failed to return from Hope yesterday.'

After that the duel began in earnest. Cross watched Vyrunas closely as they sparred. The ambassador's concern for the pilgrims appeared genuine, passionate even, yet there was an elusive detachment about his manner – almost as if something was missing.

Does he really feel *anything?* Cross found himself thinking.

The parley ended amicably, with assertions of respect and support from both sides, but to anyone with wits it was all a sham.

'Your thoughts, captain?' Talasca asked when the magus had departed.

Cross had been expecting the question. It was why he was here, possibly even why he was still alive.

'I don't know what he is or what his Spiral means,' Cross answered. That was true, but it didn't matter, for it was superseded by a greater truth, one he grasped without recourse to facts or even reason. It was rooted in the *instincts* that had kept him alive against all the odds.

'You believe Vyrunas is dangerous,' Talasca finished for him.

Cross looked at Lazaro and Clavel. One was cautious, perhaps even noble, while the other wanted a war...

Do I want to be the man who tips the scales?

He thought of Ariken and the other pilgrims who had been lured here. Yes, that was the right word. The Black Flags had never been the planet's real trap.

'I think he's more than dangerous,' Cross said. 'I think he's lethal.'

Xithauli was waiting beside the spire-copter when the ambassador returned from the meeting.

'Will they release the other pilgrims?' the disciple asked.

'No,' Vyrunas replied, 'they seek to provoke us. They covet the Spires.'

'Then let them come!' Xithauli said, showing a flash of sharp teeth.

'Do you want war?'

'I seek only to serve the Unfolding, Gyre Magus,' Xithauli answered. She seemed confused by the question.

It was *an unnatural question,* Vyrunas admitted. The kindred had always been unified in their purpose. Indeed it was almost inconceivable for them to be otherwise, but these were unsettled times. The intruders had made them so. Naturally the cult had reached out to the soldiers and secured some converts, but there was a deep-rooted hostility about the regiment that had proved remarkably resistant to the Spiral Gospel. Unravelling so many twisted souls could require years of patient work.

And I don't have years, Vyrunas understood, thinking of the Chrysaor. He was still a creature of potential rather than true power, but Vyrunas could feel his *imminence* in the growing aggression of the kindred. The Chrysaor had killed again recently and three dead Guardsmen would be difficult to disguise as accidents.

If I don't act soon his rise is inevitable, Vyrunas realised, *and that would endanger everything we have built here.*

There was no rivalry between the Gyre Magus and the Chrysaor, for they were two facets of one purpose, yet their natures were obliquely contradictory. Where Vyrunas saw disorder, the Chrysaor foresaw war. One wove with shadows, the other with fire. Events alone would determine which aspect of the Spiral was in the ascendant. For now shadows prevailed, but perhaps that was no longer enough...

The outsiders have left me no choice, Vyrunas decided. *I have held back too long already.*

'Did you find a fitting nightmare among the Misborn of Spire Castitas?' he asked. The Misborn were blessed aberrations, their bodies deviating wildly from the Five Holy Paradigms. They were enormously strong, but also feral, so Vyrunas had kept them hidden in the old Sororitas abbey for the day when the cult would have need of them.

'I have found a champion like no other, Gyre Magus,' Xithauli said. 'It has been touched by the Dark Beneath the Spires.' She extended her hands, palms open. 'We shall give the heretics their *Tizheruk.*'

It disturbed Vyrunas to hear that twisted word on his disciple's lips. Such poison had no place in the Unfolding, but Xithauli was strong enough to withstand its allure. Indeed, she had studied the dark tomes the cult had

found in the bowels of Spire Veritas without coming to harm. The tranquillity of the kindred made them impervious to such corruption. It was surely
the truest measure of their bloodline's superiority.

'Then let it be done,' Vyrunas decreed. 'We will turn our enemies' fears
against them.'

Ariken's first day in the Astra Militarum had been a study in misery. She
and her fellow recruits had been issued with fatigues, padded brown jackets and rebreathers, then lined up to receive the regimental mark from the
captain herself. The skull-faced woman had stared into each recruit's eyes
and whispered something before inscribing the icon onto the palm of their
right hand. Omazet had worked swiftly and skilfully with her needle, but
she had spared them no pain.

After receiving 'the Black Mark', the recruits had been placed under the
auspices of a compact, softly spoken madman called Nyulaszi. He had
informed them, almost cordially, that he was their Shank Sergeant and
incidentally their worst nightmare – then proceeded to make good on his
word, subjecting them to a string of exercises, tests and humiliations that
would doubtless continue for weeks or even months.

Driftwood, Nyulaszi had christened them. Ariken didn't know if it was
a broad term for all Black Flag recruits or something he had coined especially for the pilgrims, but she couldn't deny it fitted. They were lost souls
going nowhere.

The needle alone would have finished you, Ophele, Ariken thought as she
studied the mark on her palm. Each of the recruits had received a slightly
different one, as if the captain had been guided by some obscure whim or
insight. In Ariken's case the core symbol '8' had been rendered as an angular
helix with unfolded wings, transforming it into the symbol of healing.

I like it, she admitted reluctantly.

She was sitting on the steps of the shabby billet assigned to the recruits.
The cold and the darkness outside were better than the needful stares of
her comrades.

'So you're a soldier now,' a familiar voice said. Ariken looked up and saw
someone standing at the foot of the steps.

'I wouldn't have recognised you, ghost,' she said, 'except for...' She tapped
her right eye, indicating his patch.

'I share the feeling.' Cross rubbed his shaven chin ruefully. 'It seemed
like a good idea at the time...'

'I'm glad they didn't shoot you.'

'I think they came close.'

She shook her head. 'Well, you were right about Redemption.'

'I wish I'd been wrong, Ariken.'

'At least Ophele made it,' she said, 'and most of the others. That's something.'

He looked uncomfortable.

'Cross, what aren't you telling me?'

He held up a hand. 'Please, I don't have much time, Ariken. They don't really
trust me. Not yet.' He looked at her intently. 'I came to tell you to be ready.'

'For what?' she asked cautiously.

'For when I find a way out.' He was rubbing his gloved hand. 'Until then stay watchful and trust nobody. Can you do that?'

She bit down on the questions that came flooding up. 'Yes.'

'You'll make a fine soldier, Ariken Skarth.' He turned to go, then hesitated. 'One more thing – learn to fight.'

She showed him her inked palm and smiled thinly. 'I'm a Black Flag now, remember?'

'No,' he said. 'I don't think you'll ever be that.'

PART TWO

REDEMPTION IN BLOOD

'Cloak thyself in signs and wonders so that you may walk beside the Outsider as his saviour, but if he should raise his hand against you then cast aside the veil of kindness and become his terror. Let loose his own darkness upon him, for the Outsider's fears are many and beyond endurance.'

– The Apotheosis of the Spiral Wyrm

CHAPTER SIX

'You are marked for divine wrath, child,' the priestess had sung. 'Follow in my footsteps and unfold yourself into the Sacred Spiral.'

The Misborn had not understood her words, for its mind was as malformed as its body, but the *feelings* she had imparted alongside the words had blazed with a clarity it had never known before: it had been *chosen* – singled out to become a terror upon those who threatened its kindred.

Until the priestess had come for it the Misborn had been a vague shadow creature, bound by blood to its brothers, yet also a thing apart from them. After its tortured birth it had been cast into a dark maze where it had fought with others like itself, the strong culling the weak, as their instincts demanded. The Misborn understood dimly that its kind were aberrations to the natural cycle of the Spiral, yet they were also blessed – and none more so than itself, for it had been chosen for vengeance.

The priestess had led her charge out of the maze and guided it across the crumbling bridge beyond, revealing the secret paths only the cult's initiates knew. On the far side of the abyss the Misborn had strayed, driven into a rampage by the stench of the creatures hiding in a hard shell overlooking the bridge. It had hammered at their lair until its mistress had reined in its rage and destroyed their shared enemy with gentle words where strength had failed. That was when it learned that she was called *Zee-thaali*.

For many days and many nights thereafter, the Misborn's saviour had prayed with it in her temple, weaving new patterns into its body and soul. Zee-thaali had incised its flesh with spirals and darker, stranger symbols that twisted its muscles into new shapes, granting them a flexibility that matched their strength. Its mind had also quickened, rising from dull savagery into predatory cunning. Finally it was ready to receive its name.

'Tizheruk,' Zee-thaali decreed, imprinting the word upon the Misborn's primal spirit, 'that is your name and nature now, child.'

Tizheruk... the Reborn echoed, embracing the thorny word.

'Terror runs deeper than simple killing,' the Priestess continued, 'you must become a nightmare of blood and shadow to the outsiders.'

Then the acolytes of the Spiral brought a metal cylinder that stank of dead fire and Tizheruk's saviour instructed it to get inside. Tizheruk had to dislocate its limbs and contort its muscles to squeeze its bulk into the container, but pain was alien to it so it did not hesitate. After the cylinder was sealed the Reborn waited in darkness while it was carried from one unknowable place to another. As the darkness stretched Tizheruk slipped into torpid hibernation, dreaming of the terror it would wreak in the name of the Sacred Spiral...

It's going to be a bad one, Sergeant Alonzo Grijalva judged, watching the turbulent sky. The wind had picked up and flecks of soot were already blowing under the watchtower's roof, spattering him like dirty rain as the storm gathered strength. The Locker's walls offered scant shelter during a blackout, but Grijalva would take that over being out on the Rim, especially with the stories doing the rounds these days.

'Fall over the edge and it's not just your body that'll burn,' Ibolya, the cook who doubled as the regimental bone-teller, had said darkly. 'It's warpfire down there, drifters.'

'OK, let's get the old lady covered up,' Grijalva said to Jei. 'Then you can get some recaff going. And put your rebreather on, idiot!'

Jei fumbled with his mask and Grijalva shook his head. His fellow watchman was one of the Driftwood recruits and as green as they came, but he worked hard and brewed decent recaff. He wasn't a bad lad.

'You breathe it, you bleed it,' the sergeant chided, quoting their new medicae. She had advised the Guardsmen to wear their masks whenever they were outside, blackout or not, but nobody was up for that.

Should have sent the bloody Death Korps here, Grijalva thought. *They're born for a filthy sinkhole like this.*

Together the watchmen hauled a tarpaulin sheet over the tower's tripod-mounted stubber gun. If soot clogged up the weapon's guts Enginseer Tarcante would have their hides.

'How long do you think the dark'll last?' Jei asked in his spiky, lo-hive accent.

'Maybe the night, maybe days,' Grijalva said. 'Worst I've known lasted over a week.'

They heard an engine rumbling below and a Chimera rolled past, following the curve of the inner wall.

'Where they goin' in a blackout, chief?' Jei wondered.

'Not our problem, son,' Grijalva said. 'Just thank the Drowned Star you're not going with them.'

The windows of Lazaro's chamber rattled as the first wave of the storm reached the fort's temple.

'I need to go,' Cross said, watching as specks of soot swarmed across the glass. 'We'll be heading out as soon as the blackout falls.' He appraised the Regicide board on the table between them. 'The game was yours anyway.'

'It's still a poor way to end it, Ambrose.' Lazaro's voice was a pained rasp and his hand trembled with the weight of the marble cardinal it held. He cursed as the piece slipped and toppled several others.

'Let me,' Cross said, reaching for the board, but the preacher slapped his hand away irritably.

'I'm not dead yet, damn you!'

Cross regarded his friend as he tidied the pieces. Lazaro was a shadow of the doughty evangelist he'd clashed with only three months before. His robes sagged on his frame and his eyes were stained yellow. The Black Breath had its claws deep inside him now.

'I've failed you, Ambrose,' Lazaro said as he worked. 'I thought I'd rekindle some faith in you before I went into the Trench.'

'I'm not sure it was ever there, Sándor. Besides, I'll take friendship over faith every time.'

'Then tell me your story, man,' Lazaro urged. 'Maybe I can give you some Throne-damned absolution before I'm done, whether you believe in it or not!'

'Or have me burned as a heretic, preacher?'

They were silent for a moment, then Lazaro steepled his fingers and looked at him intently. 'What do you think you'll find at the abbey, Ambrose?'

'I honestly don't know. The records of Redemption's past are riddled with inconsistencies. There's even a tale that Space Marines watched over the Spires once,' Cross sighed. 'But all the scraps I found suggest the Spiral Dawn rose when the Thorn Eternal fell. Perhaps the cult just filled the void left by the Adepta Sororitas...'

'But you don't think so,' Lazaro finished. 'There's something else – something I didn't want to say in front of Clavel. I don't trust the man, but the colonel didn't want me to pass this on either...'

Cross waited, letting his friend make up his own mind.

'All my requests to High Command for off-world records have gone unanswered,' Lazaro said, 'along with the colonel's demands for new orders. We've received *nothing* since we deployed here. Sometimes I wonder if our messages ever got through.'

'There will be no more ships,' Cross said, frowning.

'What?'

'It's something Clavel said on that first night. He told me we were on our own. I didn't know what to make of it.'

'Watch him, Ambrose.'

'I intend to.' The commissar was the last person Cross wanted at his back on the imminent expedition to the abbey, but Clavel had insisted on being included. 'Before I go there's something I need to ask you, Sándor. The attacks on the Spiral shrines...'

'I didn't order them,' Lazaro said flatly, 'and I don't believe the colonel did either.'

'Thank you, my friend.' Cross rose. 'For what it's worth, I'll tell you my story when I get back.' *What I remember of it anyway.*

'Then I'll be sure to cling on to life for your tale,' Lazaro said sourly.

Jherem's breathing was a tortured, phlegm-choked rattle.

He won't survive the night, Ariken judged sadly as she swabbed his brow. The shy scribe had been one of the first pilgrims to volunteer alongside her for Captain Omazet's tithe. He would be the seventh to die. Two recruits had been killed in accidents during the early weeks of their training, but the others had succumbed to the disease carried in the planet's air. Sometimes the sick wasted away within weeks, sometimes they lasted for months, but there was no cure.

This is the real enemy, Ariken thought, gazing along the row of cots lining the infirmary. There were seventeen dying troopers here and scores more were showing symptoms. At this rate the Eighth would be a regiment of corpses within a year.

'I'm looking for the medicae,' someone said behind her. Startled, she turned and saw a young man standing a few paces away. He was dressed in the uniform of a Sentinel officer, but it was his face that drew her gaze. His finely chiselled features shone with vitality and his eyes sparkled.

'I didn't hear you come in,' she said, hoping the muted light would hide her blush. 'Sir,' she added. Obscurely she realised she was alone with the dying and this stranger.

'Forgive me, I didn't mean to frighten you.' He smiled and Ariken's blush deepened. 'I'm Lieutenant Senka. Kazimyr, if you will.'

'Skarth,' she said stiffly, unnerved by his easy charm. 'I'm the medicae, sir.'

'I understood Lieutenant Kopra was the medicae?'

'The Breath took him three weeks ago,' she replied. 'I assumed his duties after I finished basic training.'

'You're one of the pilgrims!' he said brightly, his smile widening. '*Ariken!* Yes, I've heard of you. The girl who stood up to the Witch Captain!'

Ariken had heard the nickname before, though never spoken so brazenly. 'I don't think Captain Omazet would approve of that title, sir.'

'Oh, don't be so sure, Ariken,' Senka said conspiratorially. 'Your commander is a strange one. We found her on Oblazt, you know – the last of her regiment. She was half-dead with frostbite, but still fighting a guerrilla war against the rebels. They called her the Snow Witch.' He grinned. 'Like something out of a child's tale, but with teeth!'

'You wanted to see the medicae, sir. Are you unwell?'

'Do I *look* unwell, corporal?' Senka came closer, trapping her between the beds. She could hear the wind scratching at the windows. What was he doing here with a blackout on its way?

'Then why...' she began, but he held up a hand for silence.

'I came to offer a *suggestion*. I've heard rumours of talented healers among the Spiral Dawn. Given the gravity of our situation here...' He swept a hand across the infirmary. 'I thought it might be worth seeking their advice.'

'The Unfolded are barred from the Locker, sir.'

'That's why the suggestion should come from our medicae, don't you think?' He leaned closer. 'Besides, you still believe in the Sacred Spiral, don't you, Ariken?'

His gaze was intense, almost predatory, and yet she sensed that somewhere deep inside, Kazimyr Senka was *screaming.* Her hand slid to the bone-handled knife Omazet had given her after she'd completed her training.

If you touch me I'll kill you where you stand, she thought, *and to the warp with what comes after.*

But Senka stepped away, still beaming. 'Please consider my suggestion, Ariken. I'm sure we'll talk again.'

When he left the infirmary Ariken realised her fists were clenched so tightly her nails had drawn blood.

A harsh scraping sound stirred the sleeper into wakefulness. Moments later the lid of its prison was lifted away and a beam of light shone inside.

'As within, so without,' a rough voice intoned over the wind. The man peering into the canister with misaligned eyes was an outsider by birth, but Tizheruk could smell the Spiral in his blood. He had been blessed. He was kindred now.

The man backed away as Tizheruk surged out of the container that had held it for so long. The Terror swayed, its form twisting violently as muscles writhed and bones cracked, knitting back into their natural alignment. With awakening came a gnawing, insistent hunger.

'We have prepared a sanctuary for you, holy one,' the cultist said reverently. Another man stood beside the speaker, his face aghast at the sight of Tizheruk's glory. He also carried the blessing, but its hold upon him was weak beside his fear.

The Terror reared up and the fleshhooks coiled inside its cavernous ribcage whipped out and punched through the unsteady convert's breastplate. Before he could utter a sound they yanked him forward and Tizheruk's feeder tendrils smothered his face, piercing his eyes and forcing their way down his throat, stretching deep into his chest cavity. His comrade watched in rapt silence as the Terror drank. When it was finished nothing remained of the coward's head. Sated for the moment, Tizheruk slung the carcass over its shoulders and regarded the remaining cultist.

'I am Trazgo,' the man with the malformed eyes said. He threw back his head, offering his neck. 'I will serve you with strength or sacrifice.' When Tizheruk made no move he nodded solemnly. 'This part of the fort is quiet, but it's unwise to linger here. Will you follow me, holy one?'

Though his words were nonsense, Tizheruk understood his intent. Moving with surprising grace, the Terror lifted a claw and inscribed a spiral.

This is the worst storm I've seen, Cross thought as he hurried through the churning darkness. If anything would cover their expedition from prying eyes this was it. They'd waited weeks for a blackout to fall, but this one was almost too much.

The Chimera assigned to the mission was waiting by the gates when he arrived, its engine already running. A lone trooper in a rebreather mask stood by the vehicle. He hammered on the closed hatch as Cross approached.

'You're late,' the masked man called, and Cross realised it was Clavel. The commissar had sensibly opted to exchange his greatcoat and cap for standard kit for this mission.

'Logistics,' Cross yelled over the wind. It was a vague answer, but he didn't give a damn what Clavel made of it.

The hatch swung open and they climbed inside.

'Clear to go,' a trooper in a crimson bandana called as he yanked the door shut behind them. His eyes had been replaced with jutting optics and the cog symbol of the Adeptus Mechanicus was tattooed on his bare biceps.

Not an enginseer, Cross gauged, *but perhaps an assistant.*

He pulled off his rebreather and wiped away the sweat. Eight soldiers were crammed into the cabin. Even by the loose standards of the Black Flags this squad was eccentric. No two were dressed exactly alike and their equipment was adorned with charms and fetishes whose meaning he could only guess at. The augmented trooper was the strangest of them, but they were all individuals.

'Gatekeeper, this is Chimera Seven,' the driver said into the vehicle's vox. 'I have passcode Risen Sea for you. Repeat, Risen Sea. Open the gates, friend.'

'Acknowledged, Chimera Seven,' the receiver squawked back.

'You're late, Cross,' the white-haired officer sitting beside the driver said.

'Logistics,' Cross said, repeating the excuse. 'My apologies, Captain Quezada.'

'It will be several hours before we reach the bridge,' Quezada said dryly. 'I suggest you rest while you can, Mister Cross.' The insult was thinly veiled.

'Don't want you falling asleep in my line of fire, sir,' the woman sitting opposite Cross said. Her dirty blonde dreadlocks hung about her scarred, square-jawed face and her arms bulged with muscles. She was cradling a bulky plasma rifle, its casing engraved with row upon row of kill marks.

'You saying you've got a *line* of fire, Rahel?' the hatchet-faced man beside her drawled. He nodded at Cross. 'You're the man who closed down the Green Zone, right?'

'The colonel acted on my advice,' Cross said levelly. 'Six troopers have disappeared there since the regiment arrived on Redemption.' *And there's something* wrong *with that city,* he thought, recalling his occasional fact-finding visits with distaste. *Something that runs deeper than mundane dissolution and vice.*

'He made the right call, Trujilo,' the dreadlocked woman said. 'That place was off.'

'Didn't like the competition, eh, Rahel?' Trujilo goaded.

After that Cross ignored their talk. He'd served alongside enough veteran squads to recognise the ritual banter for what it was. They would bait each other between missions, but there was nothing frivolous about these fighters. The moment things turned serious so would they. Every one of the eight, from their aloof officer to the softly spoken driver would be a proven killer. The prospect of sharing a transport with such troops would have unnerved him once, but now he just found them tedious.

'Gates are open. You're clear to go,' the gatekeeper voxed. *'Throne ward you, Gallows Dancers.'*

The engine's rumble rose to a throaty roar and it surged forward. Cross saw the commissar had taken Quezada's advice to heart: his eyes were shut and he appeared to be dozing.

Nothing about you adds up, Cross decided, *but right now I think you have it right, Clavel.*

He closed his remaining eye.

By the time Ariken's shift ended the blackout held sway over the fort, transforming its narrow paths into wind tunnels, but she knew it wouldn't deter her mentor and therefore it mustn't deter her either. Besides, she was still angry with Senka. Sleep was the last thing on her mind.

'Teach me to fight,' Ariken had asked Omazet on her second night as a Black Flag. *'I won't be Driftwood.'*

At the time she'd been exhausted by a day's training, yet she had sensed that a hundred such days wouldn't prepare her for the danger Cross had hinted at. Omazet had recognised her challenge and their 'blood trysts' had begun that same night. The rites of their training sessions were far more brutal than the regime Sergeant Nyulaszi put the recruits through, and Ariken understood the captain wouldn't hesitate to kill her if she slackened. Those were the terms of the challenge.

Three months later Ariken had more scars than all the other recruits put together, but she could hold her own against opponents twice her size in unarmed combat and fire a lasrifle like a veteran. After the Driftwood Hundred had finished their training her promotion to Corporal had been inevitable, as was the nickname Nyulaszi had awarded her: 'Black Shepherd'.

But it still wasn't enough and so the blood trysts had continued.

Ariken threw open the door of the hangar where the Witch Captain was waiting and bowed as Omazet strode forward, bearing blades.

'They never come here, holy one,' the cultist called Trazgo said. 'This wreck was already here when we built the fort. We think it came down during a blackout over a century ago.'

Ignoring the man's babble, Tizheruk inspected the misshapen steel cave. It was deep inside an enormous metal beast that lay half-buried at the heart of the outsiders' territory. Though it only had one entrance it was filled with winding paths and many hiding places. Despite its strangeness it was somehow familiar, as if Tizheruk had been here before, long ago, though that couldn't be. Odd symbols were inscribed across its cold walls, repeated many times.

'It is called the *Obariyon,*' Trazgo said eagerly, following his lord's gaze.

Tizheruk's curiosity passed quickly. Its mind was not built for mysteries. The lair was good, but the Terror could not go to ground yet. Its hunger was too strong – for blood and for wrath.

Mustering the entirety of its limited intellect, Tizheruk regarded the cultist and made the second sign that its mistress had taught it.

'I understand, holy one,' Trazgo said, recognising the slashed spiral of retribution. 'I will take you to the heretic preacher.'

Ariken's weapons clattered to the ground again and she froze, conceding defeat.

'Your anger ruled you,' Omazet chastised, drawing the blade of her weapon across Ariken's throat, the touch so light it didn't quite break the skin. She danced away and dropped into a low stance, one curved machete arcing over her head like a scorpion's stinger, the other sweeping before her defensively.

'I made myself a slave,' Ariken conceded as she retrieved her weapons.

Rage enchained is an asset, but rage unbound is a traitor. It was the first truth that Omazet had taught her.

Ariken focussed her anger into a frozen spike and leapt towards her mentor again. They met in a whirl of twinned blades, dancing around each other in the circle of light that delineated their arena. The art of the dance lay in keeping both weapons in constant play, each opening a path for the other. Every attack was a defence, every defence an opportunity for another strike.

'We'll talk again,' Senka had intimated. Or threatened?

Riding her rage, Ariken hacked and parried in a concatenating rhythm of violence and serenity, becoming one with her weapons. The captain wore a light tunic, but her limbs were tattooed with the same skeletal pattern as her armour, so fighting her felt like duelling with death itself.

'You still believe in the Sacred Spiral, don't you?' Senka mocked.

This time Ariken lasted almost a minute before her machetes were twisted from her grasp and Omazet's were at her throat again. The end had never been in doubt, yet Ariken had almost seen her victory. Rationally she understood she would never defeat Omazet, but doubting herself would dishonour her mentor.

'The rage empowered you this time,' the captain approved as she stepped away. 'Where does it stem from, Ariken?' There was no warmth in her use of the forename. Omazet addressed all her troops that way, subtly turning the informality into an intimate threat.

This woman isn't my friend, Ariken understood, *but friendship isn't what I need to survive.*

She told the captain about her experience with Senka, surprised by her revulsion when she recounted it. Omazet was silent for a long time, but when she spoke, her answer was unexpected.

'If I offered you the chance, would you go to the Spires, Ariken?'

'I don't understand...'

'The Unfolded are our enemy. While the colonel dances around this truth I know it as I know the rhythm of my own blood. And I believe you have also come to know it.'

'Then why would I go to them?' Ariken asked, thinking of Ophele and Bharlo and the rest of the pilgrims who had been delivered to the sect.

'Indeed, why would you?'

Is she making me into a monster? Ariken wondered – and on the back of that: *Do I want to be like her?*

The old, terrible nightmare had him in its jaws again, dragging him back through the ravishing cavalcade of sins that had ruled his youth, taunting him with everything he had renounced in service to the Throne. For a nobleman of Verzante, the dark jewel of the Sunken Worlds, life offered limitless opportunities for pleasure – often petty, occasionally unspeakable. Were it not for the whims of chance that trap would have become his grave. Chance...

There's no such thing! Sándor Lazaro protested.

'There is only *chance,'* the haunter of his dreams mocked. *'Everything the missionary told you was a–'*

'Deceiver!' Lazaro hissed as his tormentor shrieked and he tore free.

'Deceiver...' he repeated into the darkness as he awoke. The sheets of his bed were twisted and drenched with sweat. His throat was on fire. Grimacing, Lazaro reached for the water jug by his bed–

A second shriek sliced through the wind moaning at the windows. It was muffled, but the agony and terror behind it were unmistakable.

It wasn't the nightmare that screamed, Lazaro realised feverishly, *it was the scream that woke me.*

A cold hand pressed down against his chest, crushing faith and fire and life from his wasted carcass.

'The Emperor protects!' he rasped, defying the killing fear.

Fighting for breath, he hauled himself up and clasped the hilt of the eviscerator sword propped beside his bed. His wasted biceps trembled as he lifted it, but he felt a surge of faith as his fingers found the activation stud. The weapon's serrated blade had spilled the blood of countless traitors on Oblazt and the memory of their sacred cleansing filled him with renewed vigour. The urge to rouse the blade was almost overpowering, but he held back.

'Not yet, my friend,' he breathed.

The corridor outside his chamber was dimly lit, but there was nowhere to hide except for the sleeping cells and all the doors were closed. At this time of night only the temple's wardens should be here.

I fear Vladislav and Lohmati have gone to the Black Trench, Lazaro thought grimly. He offered a prayer to his studious assistants as he crept along the corridor. The staircase beyond was empty and he saw the lumen globes in the hall below were still lit. As he descended his foreboding grew, as if he were submerging himself in an invisible, enervating miasma, but a fierce joy shone through.

I'll die tonight, Lazaro sensed, *but it will be on my feet with a blade in my hand.*

The evil was waiting for him in the chancel, as he knew it would be. The candles had been lit and smoke wafted from the incense burners, but they couldn't mask the stench pervading the chamber. It was a sour-sweet musk, inviting and repellent by turns.

There was a congregation of four tonight. Three of the celebrants were propped up on the pews, facing the altar, though they had no heads. Two of the headless wore the robes of his assistants, the white fabric stained dark by blood, while the third wore regular fatigues. The last worshipper turned as the preacher entered. Lazaro couldn't read the focus of his skewed eyes, but the man looked as if he had been crying.

'What happened here?' Lazaro demanded, strangling his revulsion.

'Redemption, priest.' The celebrant smiled like a sly child.

He's either mad or possessed, Lazaro judged. As he strode forward the thing that had been crouching behind the altar unfolded itself.

'Sacred Throne...' Lazaro breathed as he tried to make sense of the aberration towering over him. The daemon, for it could surely be nothing else, was a hulking, misshapen parody of a man, naked save for a filthy tabard hanging from its waist. Patches of blue chitin blotched its livid flesh, thickening into hard plates around its shoulders and neck. Its right arm split at the elbow, one branch ending in a three-fingered claw, the other in a perfectly formed human hand. The left arm hung low and tapered into a long, curved hook. Its head was a hairless bulb with recessed eyes and gaping jaws that trailed thorn-tipped tentacles.

'*Tizz-ah-rukk,*' the daemon moaned, slobbering with the effort of speech. Somehow Lazaro felt sure it was *grinning* at him. He thumbed the activation stud of his eviscerator and its blade roared into life. The weapon bucked in his hands like a living thing, eager for retribution.

Nothing is chance, Lazaro decided, *this was always my fate.*

'For the Emperor!' he yelled as he charged forward.

He swung his eviscerator in a wide arc as the aberration's chest tendrils lashed out at him. The blade cut through two of them cleanly, but the others whipped away and retracted. With a wet roar the beast swept out with its curved claw, slicing through the air like a scythe. Lazaro parried and the impact almost threw him from his feet. The eviscerator's rumble became a howl as its belt-driven teeth gnawed against the bony appendage. Smoke erupted from its casing as the sacred machine raged against the profane.

'Tizz-ah-rukk!' the beast moaned again, spattering Lazaro with filth.

The preacher gritted his teeth, driving the blade deeper as his body quaked in the grip of the vibrations. With a tortured shriek the sword's belt snapped and tore free. It ripped through Lazaro's left arm just below the shoulder and whirled away like a razor-edged lasso. His neutered weapon slipped from his remaining hand and clattered to the ground, its engine still whining. The scything claw swept back then plunged forward and punched into his chest, driving through until the tip exploded from his back. Lazaro retched blood as the abomination yanked him from his feet and drew him in. It tilted its head to regard him and he sensed something *other* assessing him through its idiot eyes – an implacable, utterly inhuman intelligence.

It is true, the secret mind sent, *nothing is chance.*

Then the beast's feeder tendrils lashed out.

The coil is without a beginning or an end, Colonel Kangre Talasca thought fervently, *for everything is entwined – enshrined in a single tangled moment.*

The black tempest was raging outside the keep, its fury raising visions from the wounds that Oblazt had left in Talasca's soul. The horrors of that frozen world had almost destroyed his faith, but Redemption had unveiled the blessing behind the curse. From torment came revelation.

'I am not to be disturbed,' he instructed the leader of his Silent Paladins. 'The God-Emperor calls to me, Karolus.'

The abhuman warrior inclined its head gravely and the colonel placed a hand on its armoured chest.

'You and I are destined for glory, my friend,' Talasca promised. He turned away, heading for the tower to continue his great work.

CHAPTER SEVEN

Through the delirium blossoming from his infected hand, the shadow heard something whispering, beckoning him towards the spectral ruin that waited in the jungle – and beyond that, the veiled paths between the stars.

I'll be gone for some time, he thought.

'Cross,' someone was saying insistently. 'Cross!'

Who...?

'We've reached the bridge.' A hand shook him.

'Clavel?' Cross mumbled, stumbling back into wakefulness.

'You were out cold,' the commissar said. 'Though you started to talk towards the end...'

'Sleep well, sir?' the scarred woman sitting opposite Cross asked. Her hands were busy running last-minute checks on her plasma gun. All the veterans in the cabin were performing the same ritual, attending to their weapons with a care that bordered on reverence.

'Very well, thank you,' Cross replied mildly. 'I should be able to keep out of your line of fire now, Trooper Rahel.'

The woman threw him a broken-toothed grin, clearly surprised that he'd remembered her name.

The Chimera lurched to a halt and the driver cut the engine. 'Can't risk taking us closer to the Rim,' he said. 'Not in a blackout.'

'Understood, Virgilio,' Captain Quezada replied, clapping him on the shoulder. He turned to the others. 'Masks up, Gallows Dancers! We walk from here.'

Outpost Six had been abandoned since the deaths of its last watchmen. Though their bodies had been removed, the word scrawled across the wall in their blood was still there:

TIZHERUK

Cross had to force himself to study the faded, rust-coloured text. It was *jagged*, both in its execution and in the feelings it evoked. *Unclean.*

'What am I leading my troops into?' Quezada asked, stepping beside him.

'I've already briefed you, captain,' Clavel answered. 'We believe Redemption may be harbouring a heretical cult.'

'You didn't tell me about *this*, commissar.' Quezada gestured at the blasphemous word. The three officers were alone in the bunker, waiting while the squad's scout reconnoitred the bridge.

'What purpose would it have served?' Clavel asked.

'We don't know what it really means,' Cross said, meeting Quezada's gaze, 'but the Gallows Dancers weren't chosen for this expedition by chance. We need the regiment's best.'

The captain's helmet vox crackled. 'Quezada,' he acknowledged.

'Galantai,' a clipped, heavily accented voice replied. *'The bridge, it is a wreck, captain. Much of it has fallen into the gorge and what remains is treacherous.'*

'Can you get us across?'

'We will have to tread lightly, but it can be done.'

'Confirmed, we're on our way.' The captain switched channels to the Chimera: 'Virgilio, pull back two kilometres and await my signal.'

'Aye, captain,' the driver confirmed.

Quezada regarded his fellow officers coldly. 'If my squad suffers because you have been holding something back...'

'Understood, captain,' Clavel retorted. 'Let's get on with it.'

The rest of the squad was waiting at the mouth of the bridge, the beams of their helmet lights zigzagging through the swirling soot. This close to the gorge the wind was ferocious.

'Stay close and don't stray from the path I mark!' the scout, Galantai, warned over the squad-wide channel, shouting to make himself heard. 'And watch your step in the wind. It's worse on the bridge!'

He was a short, lean man who appeared to favour a permanent crouch. In place of regular flak plate he wore leather armour and a fur-trimmed skullcap. The lasgun slung over his shoulder had an unusually long barrel, suggesting he was a sniper as well as a scout.

'Stick with me, old man,' Trooper Rahel yelled to Cross. 'I'll catch you if you fall!'

The bridge to Spire Castitas was carved with stylised flowers – a bloom with a sweeping frond on either side. Cross recalled it was an ancient symbol for chastity, but there was nothing pure about this crumbling monument. It was a twisted twin of the one he had crossed to Veritas.

Chastity is no longer welcome on Redemption, Cross thought, unsure where the intuition came from.

The party of nine walked in single file, maintaining a tight formation behind the scout. Galantai hadn't been exaggerating – things were *much* worse on the bridge. Most of its walls had collapsed, leaving the party dangerously exposed to the gale from both sides. In places the ramparts had fallen inwards and shattered across their path, forcing them to divert around boulder-sized chunks of debris. The deck was riddled with cracks that sometimes split into gaping chasms through which the abyss shone like hellfire. A deep, primordial rumble reverberated up from the gorge and the rotten-egg stench of sulphur seeped through their masks.

'It's like we're passing into the Third Hell,' Cross whispered, recalling a myth of his home world.

'Down!' Galantai signalled, dropping to his knees. Everyone obeyed without question, waiting as the scout eased his rifle free and peered through its glowing scope.

'Hostiles,' he reported. 'Two... no, three.'

Hostiles? Cross thought uneasily. *Are we ready to assume that?*

'Armed?' Quezada asked.

'Nothing visible.'

'Can we slip past them?'

'No, they are camped in our path. Lookouts probably.'

'Bleed them.'

Wait–

A sharp snap of las-fire pierced the wind. Seconds later another followed.

'Two kills confirmed. Third mark has gone to ground,' Galantai reported. 'He will run...' They waited. 'I have him.' He fired. 'Clear.'

They reached the bodies a few minutes later. There were two males and a female. All wore rubberised black jumpsuits under rough-spun white tabards decorated with spirals. Each corpse had a cauterised crater in its hairless head where the scout had found his mark. Galantai knelt beside the woman and stripped off her mask, revealing a brutish, almost bestial face.

'Ugly bitch,' Rahel opined as the scout ran a finger over the corpse's brow, tracing a pronounced sub-dermal crest.

'I have seen this before,' he said, 'in the city... but never up close. They try to hide it.'

'Is she armed?' Cross asked, joining him.

Galantai pulled a stubby gun from the woman's utility belt. 'Auto pistol.' It was a common, low-cost weapon, but its grip was inlaid with elegantly carved bone. 'Quality work,' Galantai approved, slipping the weapon into his own belt.

Quezada addressed Clavel. 'Thoughts?'

'It confirms there's something on Castitas they don't want us to see.'

'Are we going to start a war tonight, commissar?'

'We may not have a choice, Captain Quezada,' Cross murmured, staring at the crest on the dead woman's forehead and thinking of the elaborate make-up worn by the ambassador, Vyrunas.

Is this what he was trying to hide?

The cultist's features were like a caricature of the elegant priest's own and her eyes – wide with the shock of sudden death – were the same startling sapphire.

Are they mutants? Cross wondered.

'Throw them over the side,' Clavel ordered. 'We need to get moving.'

Cross wasn't listening. Something else had just struck him: the decomposing three-armed abomination had also had a crest.

They encountered no one else on the bridge or on the long, winding path to the Spire's summit where the abbey lay. Up on the mountain there was less detritus for the wind to galvanise so the blackout eased as they climbed.

Dawn broke as they crested the peak and Redemption's twin suns, Salvation and Damnation, glowered through the clouds. The bastion of the Thorn Eternal loomed ahead, crowning the Spire in a cruciform wedge of crenelated walls and steepled towers. No guards appeared as the squad crept towards its iron gates.

'This looks new,' Galantai said, indicating the access panel beside the portals.

'Regev,' Quezada called, 'can you crack it?'

The trooper in the crimson bandana inspected the panel, his augmetic lenses glowing green behind his mask. 'Looks like a standard data-seal.' He pulled a compact device from his backpack and touched it to the panel. As he tweaked dials on the instrument digits scrolled across its display.

'Specialist Regev has worked alongside our enginseer since Oblazt,' Quezada explained to Cross with a hint of pride. 'The soldiers of Vassago adapt to the tides of chance.' He turned to the scout. 'Galantai, watch the mountain path. I don't want any surprises at our back.'

The scout nodded and crept away.

There was a chime from Regev's device and the gates vibrated as their internal bolts retracted. The specialist muttered a prayer to the Machine God and pressed a hand against each portal. They swung inward smoothly, revealing a long atrium with an avenue of columns running through its centre.

'Breach and secure,' Quezada ordered.

The six veterans fanned out as they swept inside, falling into the well-worn patterns of the squad while the outsiders, Cross and Clavel, followed behind.

'Clear,' the troopers reported one by one.

'Air is clean,' Regev added, consulting his auspex.

'Masks off,' Quezada said.

The squad's relief turned to expressions of disgust as the stench permeating the place hit them.

'You said it was *clean*, cog-lover!' Rahel said, throwing Regev a dirty look.

'Of toxins, yes.'

'Gybzan, take point,' Quezada ordered. 'I want your fire up front.'

'Aye, sir.' A squat, heavyset man brandishing a flamer stalked forward. His helmet and armour were painted with crudely rendered holy sigils and snippets of prayer. The fuel cylinder strapped to his back bore a clumsy, flame-winged aquila.

He's a devout pyromaniac, Cross gauged, *like so many flame troopers.*

As he followed the squad along the columned avenue he saw the stonework was mottled with scorch marks, bullet holes and deep scratches.

'There was a fight here,' Gybzan said sombrely, as if he was imparting a profound secret. 'A big one.'

'The Battle Sisters wouldn't have died any other way,' Rahel growled.

'Story goes they went mad,' the hatchet-faced trooper said. 'Grubs in town say their canoness fell for a daemon.'

'Grubs know crap, Trujilo,' Rahel hissed. 'The Adepta Sororitas are *untouchable*. That's why somebody took them down.'

A doorway lay ahead, but the door itself had been ripped from its frame and hurled across the atrium.

'Sacred Throne,' the flame trooper said when he reached the opening. He stepped aside, making room for the three officers.

The doorway opened onto the great nave of the abbey. Its stained-glass windows were intact and its foundation pillars still stood, but the floor was gone, leaving a sheer drop beyond the threshold. Cross looked down and saw the ground had collapsed onto the level below, crushing its chambers into a rubble-strewn wasteland. Light trickled down from the windows, illuminating the broken statues that jutted from the debris like fallen angels. But it was the sea of bones that shocked him. They were everywhere – the harvest of many thousands of corpses. This sacred space had been turned into a vast charnel pit.

'We are fortunate,' Clavel judged. 'The sunlight will facilitate our passage.' He appeared unmoved by the devastation.

'You want me to take my squad down into that graveyard?' Quezada asked stonily.

'There is no alternative, captain.'

'What exactly are we looking for here?'

'Evidence... records perhaps.' Clavel shook his head. 'If anything survived the attack it will be in the abbey's sanctum. We have to get across.'

Quezada was silent for a while, surveying the pit. 'They used shaped charges to blow the floor,' he said finally. 'What I don't understand is why.'

'Desecration,' Gybzan spat. The flame trooper's face was dark with fury.

'But they left the windows intact... and the frescoes,' Cross said, frowning. 'No... I think this was something else.'

'Indeed,' Quezada said, 'that is what worries me.' He turned to his comrades. 'Masks on, Gallows Dancers. It is time to earn our name.'

The pit was over thirty feet deep. A metal ladder had been installed, presumably by whoever had destroyed the floor, but the bolts fixing it to the wall were badly corroded.

'It's unsound,' Regev said after a cursory check. 'Probably hasn't been used in years.'

'Ropes,' Quezada ordered, pulling a grappling hook from his backpack.

The veterans abseiled down expertly, slipping into watch duties the moment they landed. Rahel and Gybzan lowered their bulky weapons before descending, then dropped down after them. Both seemed more concerned about the guns than their own safety.

Only Cross struggled, losing his grip towards the end and falling into a pile of bones. He discovered they were coated in slime and what looked like dung. Some of the veterans shook their heads as he got up, but nobody mocked his fall. There was no room for levity in this graveyard.

They pressed forward, weaving between piles of rubble and sections of wall that still stood. Vast cracks yawned along both sides of the pit, opening into raw tunnels that descended into darkness. They looked like animal burrows, but Cross didn't want to dwell on the kind of creature that could have dug them. By unspoken consent the squad kept away from them. Wherever they led was nowhere anyone wanted to go.

'All these bones are old,' Trujilo murmured as they crept over a mound of the forgotten dead. 'The reek ain't from them.'

He's right, Cross thought, *the flesh that bound these bones is long gone. These people died decades ago at least.*

'It's not just rot,' Rahel said. 'There's something else...'

'Hold up!' Gybzan called from somewhere up front. 'We got a problem.'

There was a long stretch of surviving wall up ahead, cutting directly across their path.

'Can't risk climbing it,' the specialist, Regev, said. 'It could collapse under us.'

'Then let's punch a hole through.' Rahel aimed a kick at the barrier.

'This whole level could be unstable,' Regev protested. 'We should avoid...' He trailed off as a deep, liquescent moan oozed from the burrows on either side and reverberated around the pit. It sounded like the catacombs were breathing. A distant clattering followed, then fell silent. The squad waited, but there was nothing more.

'Spread out,' Quezada ordered. 'Look for a way through.'

'Perhaps the tunnels–' Regev began.

'Not the tunnels,' the captain said firmly.

The eight intruders fanned out along the wall, searching for a break in the barrier, but their eyes kept straying to the tunnel mouths.

We're not alone down here, Cross thought with dismal certainty. He saw something gleaming among a pile of dirty bones and knelt to brush them aside. Lying among the detritus was an elegant helmet with a sloped visor. It shone a pearlescent white, as if the filth couldn't touch it.

'Looks like an Adepta Sororitas battle helm,' Rahel whispered beside him. There was a melancholy note in her voice.

'Over here!' Trujilo hissed from further along the wall. He indicated a narrow fissure as the others approached. 'Might be a way through.' He crouched, peering inside. 'Full of bones though...'

'Can we clear it?' Quezada asked.

'Faster to crawl over them, captain.'

'Not going in there,' Gybzan said as if that concluded the matter.

Something moved at the periphery of Cross' vision. He turned and regarded the tunnel entrance to his left, squinting into the darkness. Where did these passages go? To the abbey's crypts or somewhere much deeper? Almost reluctantly, he shone his light into the space.

A hulking, malformed figure stood in the recess, watching him.

'Captain...' Cross started to say.

Trujilo yelled and leapt away as a claw lashed out from the fissure he was examining. As he fell on his back he opened fire, pouring las bolts into the crack. There was a hiss of rage from within and another claw appeared, followed by a third. They gripped the edges of the crevice and hauled a contorted shape towards the light.

'Flamer!' Quezada shouted as he activated his power sword.

Gybzan stepped forward, adjusting the nozzle of his weapon as he came. With a whoosh of heat a torrent of fire flooded the fissure. The thing within thrashed about and howled as its refuge became an inferno.

'The tunnels!' Cross shouted as the figure he had spotted lurched towards them. It was a three-armed blasphemy with bloated muscles and a bulbous, elongated cranium. The face was a lumpen mockery of humanity, devoid of anything save dim fury. Its jaws yawned wide, spilling drool across its barrel chest as it trampled through the bones.

Mutants, Cross thought. *They have to be.*

He opened fire, gripping his bolt pistol with both hands to steady his aim. The bullets punched into the giant's torso, the entry wounds erupting into raw craters as the mass-reactive rounds detonated, but they didn't even slow its advance.

'Vassago burns!' Rahel shouted, stepping alongside him. She braced her legs as she pulled the trigger of her plasma gun. There was a momentary delay as the weapon powered up, then a barrage of plasma bolts struck the abomination, incinerating its right shoulder and tearing a smouldering rift across its chest. It crashed to the ground as its spine melted, but continued to drag itself along with its remaining arms.

'Finish it!' Rahel snarled as her gun vented steam. It would be several seconds before she could risk another salvo. Cross advanced on the dying monstrosity, punching bullets into its skull as he stared into its eyes.

They're blue, he realised a moment before its cranium exploded.

With a thunder of riven masonry a section of the barrier wall collapsed, covering Regev in rubble, and another of the aberrant giants lurched through the rift. Hissing like a gargantuan snake, it reached for the trapped specialist with an oversized arm.

'For the Emperor!' Clavel shouted as he stepped between them and parried its claw with his chainsword. The whirling blade spat black ichor as it chewed into the creature's flesh. Struggling against its strength, Clavel dropped his right hand to his holster and pulled his plasma pistol free. As the beast swung at him with its other arms he thrust the gun between its jaws and fired. The blast scorched away its face and burned through the back of its head. Clavel dodged aside as the giant toppled forward and fell across the specialist, who was still struggling to free himself. Congealing plasma oozed from its skull and spilled across Regev's breastplate, eating through the armour in seconds. He shrieked as his chest dissolved into a smoking crater.

'This way!' the commissar called to the others, gesturing towards the fallen wall.

The savage bellowing of the abominations was coming from all sides now and more were emerging from the tunnels, while smaller beasts – presumably juveniles – crawled from mounds of rubble or cracks in the ground. There was no telling how many of them inhabited the charnel pit.

They were hiding from the sunlight, Cross thought wildly. *They don't like it, but they're not afraid of it.*

'Down!' Rahel shouted as another of the giants loomed over him, its sinewy, razor-tipped arms swinging towards his head. He threw himself to the ground and its talons whipped across the crown of his helmet, tearing it loose. Dazed, he rolled aside as the claws slashed down, rending the stone like bladed piledrivers behind him. A hail of plasma screamed overhead, followed by a rush of fire as Gybzan strode towards his attacker. The flame trooper was singing a martial hymn as he drove the monstrosity back.

Cross staggered to his feet and crashed into another veteran. The man's arms had been torn off at the shoulders, leaving only splintered, bloody nubs of bone. His mask was gone and his eyes were wide with shock. He was trying to say something.

I don't know his name, Cross thought absurdly. He saw Quezada stalking towards them with his bolt pistol raised.

'I think–' Cross began.

His words were cut off as the nameless trooper's head jerked violently and sprayed blood. Quezada thrust the corpse towards a pair of smaller abominations that were crawling towards them. His gun was still smoking from the mercy killing.

'Gallows grace you, brother,' the captain intoned, then jabbed his sword towards the section of fallen wall by Clavel. 'Through there!'

Gybzan fell in with them as they pressed forward, sweeping his fire in a wide arc behind him to deter their pursuers.

'I'm running low!' the flame trooper warned.

Trujilo and Rahel had flanked Clavel on either side of the gap. The three of them were spraying shots into the beasts, Rahel and the commissar alternating their plasma volleys to let their weapons cool. Regev lay nearby, half-buried by the carcass of the giant that had brought down the wall. The dead specialist's augmetic lenses still glowed behind his mask.

'They're strong but slow!' Quezada said. 'If we keep–'

A juvenile mutant burst from the bones beside him, mewling and spitting. The creature was a squat tangle of muscles, its lumpy head barely reaching the captain's waist, but one of its arms flared into a scythe-like claw twice its height. As Quezada cleaved the mutant's skull it lashed out with the claw, slicing clean through his left thigh. The veteran yelled as the leg gave way and he toppled. Cross caught him and lowered him against the wall while the others offered covering fire. Blood was pumping furiously from the captain's stump.

'Go,' Quezada said. None of his troops argued.

They know their craft too well, Cross thought. *If we slow down we're dead. They'll honour their fallen later.*

'Do you want the Emperor's Mercy, captain?' Clavel asked, his eyes never leaving the battle.

'Gallows Dancers make their own mercy, commissar,' Quezada said, pulling a grenade from his belt. 'Take the sword, Cross.' He indicated the power weapon beside him. 'It's too good for this graveyard...' His face was white with blood loss. 'Go!'

Quezada seized his mercy scant seconds after they were through the wall.

The blast reverberated around them, sending concussive tremors through the ground as they hurried across the charnel pit. If the whole place came down then so be it.

'The other side's just ahead!' Rahel shouted.

A man-sized mutant lurched into her path and she dodged aside, saving her precious gun for a greater threat. Cross swung at the beast with Quezada's blade. He was no great swordsman, but he'd learned the basics at the academy and a power weapon such as this would have been lethal even in the hands of a novice. The curved blade carved through his foe's midriff as if it had a mind of its own, almost tearing the beast in half.

'My thanks, captain,' Cross said.

There was a stentorian bellow from the right and a statue hurtled through the air towards the survivors. It slammed down a few paces from Rahel, showering her with fragments of stone and bone. She swung round, cursing vividly as she saw the thing that had thrown the missile.

'Seven Hells...' Cross hissed.

Even among these giants this beast was a colossus. Its brutish head was squeezed between swollen, chitin-plated shoulders. Both of its arms split into multiple appendages at the elbows, each branch swelling into a three-fingered claw tipped with talons. With a roar, the monstrosity stomped towards them, hunched almost double, with its long arms trailing behind it.

'Keep moving!' Clavel shouted.

They raced on, all caution abandoned now. As they reached the far side of the pit, Trujilo cast his grapple at the wall, trying to snag the threshold of the chamber above, but the hook clattered back down.

'Too high!' he yelled.

'Regev had the powered grapple,' Rahel snarled, shaking her head furiously.

'Look for another ladder!' Cross ordered. He doubted he could haul himself up thirty feet of rope anyway.

'It's coming,' Clavel warned as the colossus caught up with them.

We have to kill it, Cross realised. He holstered his pistol and gripped the power sword two-handed. 'Gallows Dancers-' he began, but the flame trooper was already moving.

'Burning Throne!' Gybzan yelled as he strode towards their pursuer. Focussing the last of his fuel into a tight stream, he met the beast's lumbering charge. It barrelled into his inferno, howling with fury as it was set alight. Burning and blinded, it pressed on until it crashed into its tormentor and dragged him into a savage embrace. Gybzan's fuel tank ruptured explosively, immolating them both in fresh flames. The blast killed him instantly and shredded the beast's arms and chest.

The others circled the blazing abomination as it whirled about with its charred victim fused to its torso. Roaring its defiance, it flailed at them with its mutilated arms as plasma bolts tore craters into its hide, burning hotter than any natural fire could. Cross closed in as it weakened, slashing at its trunk-like legs with his coruscating blade until they gave way and the behemoth fell.

'Gallows take you!' he snarled and plunged the blade into its melting face.

The beast thrashed about, but he kept it pinned, embracing the emptiness blossoming inside him. Dimly he realised he'd missed it.

'It's done!' someone was shouting. 'Cross, it's over!' He stared at the masked woman. 'There are more of them down here,' she urged. 'We need to move, Cross!'

They found the ladder soon afterwards. It was wet with slime and the bolts securing it to the wall were loose. Clavel tugged at the frame cautiously, frowning as it shifted in his grip.

'We'll have to take it one by one,' he said.

Trujilo went first. While he climbed, the others crouched behind the statue of a brooding cardinal, listening to the pit dwellers lumbering through the maze of rubble. It sounded like they were brawling among themselves now.

Fighting over the dead, Cross guessed. *Ours and theirs.*

'Clear,' Trujilo voxed. *'It's in bad shape. You got to take it slowly.'*

Clavel opted to go second. Trujilo had tested the ladder and now its condition would only worsen with each ascent. The second place was the safest.

What kind of commissar are you, Clavel? Cross mused, as he had many times before.

'So what's walking on your grave?' Rahel asked him when they were alone. She kept her voice low and her eyes on the maze.

'My grave?'

'It's something we say in the Sunken Worlds.' She shook her head. 'I meant *what's the ghost on your back?* Because you surely have one, Cross.'

'My ghost?' he thought about it. 'I think that would be *me.*'

'That one goes with the job,' Rahel snorted. 'No, I saw how you fought back there. You've got *another* ghost, my friend.' She indicated his eye patch. 'Something to do with that maybe?'

He shook his head. 'The eye is nothing, Rahel.' His gauntleted hand was itching furiously. It felt like the parasites had returned to finish their work. 'I–'

'Clear,' Clavel voxed, *'Captain Cross next.'*

'Confirmed,' Rahel sent. 'You're up, Cross.'

He considered arguing, but it would only waste time and the sunlight trickling down from above was fading fast. It was still morning, but that meant little on Redemption. The sky was already congealing into its perennial gloom.

'You owe me a story,' Cross said as he got up. 'It takes a ghost to know one, trooper.'

It was a long climb. The rungs were treacherous with slime and he paused every time the ladder wobbled. He was breathing hard by the time Trujilo helped him over the edge. The pit below was completely dark now.

'Clear,' Cross sent. 'Get out of there, Rahel.'

'Confirmed. On my way.'

She was a couple of yards from the top when the ladder groaned and lurched violently. She froze. Leaning over the lip, Cross and Trujilo stretched out their arms to her.

'Move yourself, trooper!' Cross urged.

'It'll hold,' she said. 'I just got to take–'

With a shriek of tortured metal the ladder tore away from the wall and tilted backwards. It held for a moment, swaying, then arced gently away into the darkness with its burden. Long moments later they heard it crash down among the rubble, along with the answering clamour of the abominations.

'Rahel!' Cross shouted. He expected no answer and none came.

The last of the sunlight was gone by the time the three survivors pressed on. Clavel appeared to have a working knowledge of the abbey, so they followed his lead in silence. Cross assumed the commissar had studied a floor plan prior to the mission, but if so, he had never offered to share it. The path he chose led resolutely upwards, taking them into the abbey's heights. Beyond the pit the building was largely intact and seemingly deserted, yet the miasma of oppression never diminished.

'It's here,' Clavel said as they reached the end of a pillared corridor. A circular metal hatch was set into the wall ahead, its facade embossed with the symbol of the abbey's order: a dagger-like thorn encircled by chains. The surface was scuffed and scorched, but the damage was obviously superficial. Most of the wall around the hatch had been torn away, revealing more metal beneath.

'They couldn't get in,' Trujilo observed, 'and that made them mad.'

'I don't see how we'll do any better,' Cross said, slapping the hatch. 'It feels like solid steel.' He looked around. 'I can't see an access panel.'

'The mechanisms of a Sanctus Haven are subtle,' Clavel said, 'and their portals are forged from titanium. Step aside, captain.'

You're not even bothering to pretend anymore, Cross thought as he made room for the commissar. *Is that because it doesn't matter now that we're here?*

Clavel placed his palm on the crown of the thorn, paused for several seconds, then traced the length of its spike, paused again then swiped to the left and followed the curve of the chains towards their apex. He hesitated, then removed his hand and began the sequence again.

'What's he doing?' Trujilo asked, frowning.

'I'd guess there's some kind of haptic sensor embedded in the hatch.' Cross was intrigued despite his suspicions. He'd been a scholar before he became a soldier and the old curiosity was still strong. 'It's probably coded to recognise a specific tactile pattern.' Trujilo looked at him blankly. 'You open it with gestures,' Cross clarified. 'Though I'm not convinced *he* knows them,' he added as Clavel started over yet again.

Many attempts later there was a sonorous chime and the hatch began to rotate clockwise, corkscrewing slowly inwards as it spun. When it was nearly three feet deep it veered sharply into a recess to the right.

'Touch nothing,' Clavel instructed before stepping through.

The chamber beyond was small, its domed vault less than fifteen feet overhead. A stone table occupied the far side of the chamber, its surface inset with panels of machinery whose dials and readouts glowed softly, evidently still powered despite the passing of a century. A high-backed chair had been overturned near the table; it lay among a jumble of books and loose scrolls, suggesting they had been scattered in the same moment. To the left was a recessed alcove containing an empty bunk and basic subsistence facilities. To the right was a shrine.

'Seven Hells,' Cross breathed as he studied the relic at the shrine's heart. It was a circular bas-relief forged from dark bronze and nailed to the wall with massive spikes. The subject was a skein of stars entangled by thorns, at the centre of which was a huge, geometrically scarred face. Its eyes were screwed tightly shut and its jaws clenched against the agony of the barbs that pierced it. The effigy was resplendent with terror and torment, yet that aquiline face was unmistakable. Cross had seen it depicted a thousand times over on his travels.

It was the God-Emperor of mankind.

'There's nobody here,' Trujilo murmured. 'How does that add up?'

It doesn't, Cross thought uneasily. *Someone locked themselves up in here. Where did they go?*

There was a mechanical grinding sound from above as the shutters covering the dome retracted. The sky beyond the stained glass offered little reprieve from the darkness, though it was still only midday.

'The power core is still running,' Clavel said from the control table. 'They're built to last for centuries, but I couldn't be sure until we were inside.' He pulled a hololith crystal from a slot on the panel and stowed it in his backpack, along with several data cubes, then knelt and began to sort through the fallen books.

'You're not a commissar,' Cross said, joining him at the console.

'I served in that capacity for many years,' Clavel replied as he searched, 'but the Imperium required a higher duty of me.' He nodded as he found a tome bound in azure-hued leather. Stowing the book in his pack, he returned to the console.

'There's nobody in here,' Cross said. 'Doesn't that strike you as strange?'

'It is irrelevant to our objective.' Clavel fiddled with some dials and the vox caster embedded in the panel crackled into life. It looked like a powerful set, probably capable of broadcasting across the entire Koronatus Ring, perhaps even into orbit.

'Our objective...' Cross began, but Clavel silenced him with a sharp gesture.

'War is not a binary condition,' he said into the speaker grille, keeping his tone precise and formal.

'Nothing has changed,' a flat voice replied almost immediately, as if it had been awaiting his transmission.

'Everything has changed.'

It's a code phrase, Cross realised.

'Authorisation approved, Calavera Five,' the stranger said. *'What is your status?'*

'Primary and ancillary objectives are secure,' Clavel replied, 'but my incursion in the abbey may have ignited the Wildfire event.'

There was a pause. *'That is acceptable. All Imperial assets are in place for strategic assessment. Delaying Wildfire is unlikely to yield further significant data.'*

'I require an extraction.'

'Confirmed, we are acquiring your position now.' The vox fell silent.

'Who are you?' Cross demanded, levelling his pistol at the pale-eyed man. Without hesitation Trujilo followed suit with his rifle.

Clavel arched an eyebrow at the guns, but his composure didn't waver. 'I am someone who can offer you a chance to live.'

'That didn't work out so well for the Gallows Dancers,' Trujilo said sourly.

'They died in the God-Emperor's service, trooper.' Clavel reached slowly for his collar. 'I am not going for a weapon,' he cautioned as he tugged a plain silver amulet from under his jacket. At a press of his thumb it flicked open, revealing a small ruby rosette. Set into its heart was a stylised silver column inscribed with a cyclopean skull.

'Operative Clavel of the Calavera Conclave,' said the commissar-who-was-not. 'Ordo Xenos.'

'The Cradle of the Misborn has been desecrated, Gyre Magus,' Xithauli reported, her eyes closed. 'Many of the Blessed Ones have been slaughtered.'

Vyrunas regarded his disciple keenly: psychic energy coiled about her slender frame, tracing flickering mandalas in sympathy with her displeasure. She had become a fiery beacon at the summit of the *Mandira Veritas* as she communed with the gestalt spirit of the Spiral Dawn.

'I did not see it,' Vyrunas admitted. In truth he saw very little anymore. His vigour was fading fast, and with it his perception.

'I have dispatched a coterie of Acolytes to the abbey,' Xithauli said, opening her eyes. 'The heretics will never leave Spire Castitas.'

'I concur.'

'Even if they are silenced, war will come, Gyre Magus.'

And you hunger for it, Vyrunas recognised, *along with all our kind.*

The Ravening was pounding in the hearts of the kindred now, stirring their blood into righteous violence as the Chrysaor's influence waxed. Even Vyrunas felt the call to war, though it was a muted echo for him.

It is time for Xithauli to take my mantle, he decided. *She is a magus and more than ready to lead us alongside the Chrysaor.*

'I will go to the outsiders' bastion,' Vyrunas said. 'The heretic priest is dead and their terror walks among them. I shall offer them salvation.'

'It is too late.'

'Perhaps, but I must try.' Vyrunas tilted his staff horizontally across his chest and offered it to her. 'I await your blessing, Gyre Magus,' he said.

Xithauli regarded him in silence for a long moment, hesitating out of respect rather than uncertainty. She knew it was her time.

'So the Spiral flows,' she intoned finally and took the staff. 'You have my blessing, Vyrunas.'

CHAPTER EIGHT

Though it was past midday the blackout hadn't let up, but it was a pale shadow of the deeper darkness that oppressed the Locker. The troopers went about their duties as if nothing had changed, losing themselves in the counterfeit comforts of routine in silence. Talk was too dangerous. Talk risked straying onto the horror in the temple. Under other circumstances Command might have covered up the savage desecration, but too many men had seen it – an entire congregation turning up for morning prayers. No, there had been no silencing the whispers, not until dread itself had done what Command couldn't, because once everyone knew the story nobody wanted to talk about it, at least not until the blackout had run its course. For now the Black Flags just had to hold steady and stay sharp.

Sergeant Alonzo Grijalva understood all this, but the Driftwood recruit posted with him in the watchtower didn't have the instincts for it yet. All the boy wanted to do was *talk*.

'Nine men, chief,' Jei was saying as he poured fresh recaff, 'how could someone kill nine men without nobody seeing nothing?' He handed Grijalva a steaming mug. 'All in one night...' The youth shook his head, trying to look sombre.

He can't see himself as one of the nine, Grijalva realised. *Dying's still impossible for him – something that happens to other people.*

They were in the watchtower's small guardroom. The hatch to the upper level was closed, as were the doors leading onto the bastion walls. There was no point standing outside in a blackout. Besides, one of the murdered men had been snatched from a tower top and Grijalva wasn't going to tempt fates without good reason.

'Connant said their heads was gone,' Jei was jabbering, 'torn right off, even the preacher...'

There was a hammering at the western door and Grijalva almost spilled his recaff. The next patrol wasn't due for another fifteen minutes.

'Watchword!' he snapped as Jei started to throw the bolt. The youth threw him a salute and spoke a challenge into the door grille.

'Skyshadows,' a rough voice replied.

Grijalva nodded and Jei opened the door. A burly Guardsman shuffled in with the wind. He pulled off his rebreather as the youth slammed the hatch shut behind him. His greatcoat was filthy and he reeked of something worse than sulphur.

'Bad out there,' the newcomer said. 'Word is it'll last days yet.' His accent was so thick it slurred his voice.

'I've seen worse,' Grijalva said, frowning as he recognised the Szilar sergeant's walleyes. The man had always been a troublemaker. 'What's your business here, Trazgo? You're not on the wall rota.'

'Off-duty.' Trazgo shrugged. 'You got any recaff to spare, comrade?'

'Our recaff's for the patrols.'

'No matter, can't stay long anyway. I'm walking the whole fort.'

'You said you were off-duty?'

'Different kind of duty,' Trazgo said gravely. '*Sacred* kind.'

'Well ours is just the regular kind, so...'

'I'm spreading the word. Last night was a *sign* – a warning to the faithless.'

Grijalva frowned. 'You saying you know something about the slaughter?'

'I know there's worse to come,' Trazgo said. 'The Eighth is tainted, comrade. Been that way since Oblazt. The colonel isn't right in the head – or the soul.'

'I've heard he paints,' Jei piped in, 'but never lets nobody see.'

'You ever wonder *why*, boy?' Trazgo said darkly. 'Him and his puppet preacher put us all on the road to the damnation.' He hawked and spat. 'Emperor's justice caught up to Lazaro last night and it's coming for the rest of us.'

'You've said your piece,' Grijalva said. 'I'll be sure to pass your thoughts on to Major Kazán. Now get out of my tower.'

'Easy, comrade.' Trazgo raised his hands. 'Just doing my duty to the God Emperor... trying to save some souls.' He nodded at Jei. 'You still got your spiral aquila, Driftwood?'

'I...'

'I'd wear it, boy.' Trazgo headed for the opposite door and paused. 'Think it over, comrades. And remember, justice walks by night.'

'What was that about, chief?' Jei asked when the Szilar was gone.

'Nothing good, lad,' Grijalva said. It was going to be a long day.

And a longer night, he thought warily. A man's eyes couldn't tell the difference between day and night during a blackout, but his soul was sharper.

One of the colonel's abhuman bodyguards stood in a pool of light outside the temple door, an oversized rebreather covering its face. It raised its maul as two figures approached from the darkness.

'The colonel sent for me,' Captain Omazet said, meeting the armoured guard's gaze sternly. It jabbed its maul questioningly at the shorter figure. 'The medicae,' Omazet answered. 'She is with me. Let us past, paladin.'

Ariken imagined the guard's sluggish mind testing this puzzle: it had expected one person and received two. Finally it decided the first qualified the second and stepped aside.

'Steel yourself,' Omazet warned as they entered.

Colonel Talasca was waiting in the chancel, his back to the door as he studied the altar. He was alone save for the dead, who were many.

No... Ariken froze at the threshold. Redemption had hardened her to

suffering and death, but nothing had prepared her for the atrocity perpe-
trated here. Eight corpses lolled in the pews, headless and encrusted with
old blood. Another hung above the altar, dangling from the rafters by its feet
so its lifeblood had gushed onto the sacred stone. Ariken moaned as she
recognised the brown cassock of the hanging cadaver. Talasca spun round
at the sound, his hand whipping to the hilt of his sword.

'You requested my presence, Retriever,' Omazet said. Ariken knew her
captain had already seen this carnage – all the senior officers had. Even
so, her composure was admirable. Nothing could have compelled Ariken
to *return* to this slaughterhouse.

'I asked you to attend me alone, captain,' Talasca said.

'Ariken is my aide,' Omazet replied. 'Her blade is my own. And she has
a sharp mind.'

Talasca regarded Ariken, his eyes narrowing to silver slits in the gloom.
'Then tell me, girl, how did the preacher die?'

'With the Retriever everything is a test,' Omazet had warned Ariken many
times. *'When he tests you – and one day he will – look to the essence of his
question.'*

Ariken indicated the broken eviscerator sword lying near the altar. 'He
died a warrior,' she answered with a ferocity she didn't feel, 'with fire in his
heart and a blade in his hand.'

'Spoken like a Black Flag,' Talasca approved. He returned his attention
to the hanging corpse. 'Enginseer Tarcante believes the butcher returned
here many times during the night, bearing a new... *offering* on each occasion. I do not know when the preacher died, but I am certain his killer
tasted his contempt.'

'He was a great warrior,' Omazet agreed.

'He was the *soul* of the Eighth, captain! This desecration strikes at the regiment itself. It mocks everything we are!' He stepped away from the altar
and Ariken saw the scars gouged into its facade. It took her a moment to
recognise the spiky lines as a word. Blood had run into the fissures, illuminating it against the white stone, yet she couldn't quite read it...

'Don't,' Omazet hissed, as if reading her thoughts. 'It is a scar upon the
soul.'

'But *you* are familiar with the name are you not, captain?' Talasca asked.

'I am a Black Flag officer. I studied the Lays of Vassago when I took the
oath of command.' Omazet paused, then hissed through her teeth. 'Is this
an *accusation*, Retriever?'

'No, Captain Omazet, it is a sacred commission. I believe there is a Night
Weaver among us.' Talasca smiled, betraying his madness. 'And I want you
to find it.'

'Shark Senka requesting egress,' Kazimyr Senka voxed the gatehouse. 'Watchword is "icefire". Let me through please.'

'Confirmed,' a voice replied. *'I don't envy you, Senka. It's like the Trench
out there today.'*

'I've seen worse, friend.'

The gates opened and Senka sped out onto the mesa, pushing his Sentinel hard despite the darkness. It had been too long since he'd last escaped the Locker's confines, and he relished the speed. After the deaths at Outpost Six many of the perimeter bunkers had been abandoned and there were fewer patrols. Though Command had tried to cover up what had happened to Benedek and Cridd, rumours had leaked, as they always did in a Black Flag regiment.

Of course I helped them along this time, Senka thought, smiling.

He veered off from his allotted course and headed for Hope. The detour would take a couple of hours, but with so many outposts deserted he had plenty of time. Nobody would notice the deviation.

'We're free now,' he whispered to his Sentinel as they strode across the mesa.

It appalled him that he had been a slave for so long – or that he had seen his fellow Sharks as *brothers*. Every one of them was cut from the same austere mould. They were all minor Lethean aristocrats, sober, unimaginative men who loved their Sentinels more than the wives and children they had left behind when they joined the Astra Militarum. And Kazimyr Senka had been one of them, following obediently in that same banal tradition – marrying at eighteen and siring twin sons before abandoning them to serve the Throne, secure in the knowledge that his family's wealth would provide for them in his absence.

I was blind, but now I see, he thought with fierce joy. *My Xithauli gave me sight!*

Senka hadn't seen the priestess for months now, but they would be together after Redemption was liberated and that day was coming soon. He wondered if tonight's summons was from her. As always, the message had come via Trazgo, telling him to stop off at the city on tonight's patrol. The Szilar sergeant had also given him a small satchel to deliver.

'Be careful,' Trazgo had cautioned. 'If you're caught with it Command will have your skin.'

'What is it?'

'Refractor field generator.' Trazgo had grinned. 'The colonel's own.'

'How...?'

'A brother in the keep.'

Senka saw twin lights burgeoning in the darkness ahead. Wary of a collision, he slowed and veered aside, though the approaching vehicle wasn't moving fast. Moments later a mesa buggy appeared. Its sleek carriage was framed between big, spiked wheels and a silver spiral adorned its bonnet.

It's coming from Hope, Senka gauged as they passed each other, *and heading for the Locker.*

'Spiral ward you, brothers,' he said automatically. Then he sped forward again, eager for the lights of the city and the beautiful woman who surely waited there.

Searchlights pinned the buggy as it approached the fort's gates.

'Who goes there?' a voice demanded from the vehicle's vox.

'I bear the revered Gyre Magus,' the hooded cultist behind the wheel said as he slowed to a stop. 'Your commander is expecting him.'

'Hold position and await instructions.'

'My magus?' the driver asked the passenger sitting behind him.

'Comply,' Vyrunas answered. 'They will admit us.'

'Understood, Gyre Magus.'

Gyre Magus, Vyrunas thought. Though Xithauli had allowed him to retain the title for this final undertaking it felt like a sham. They were both irrevocably magi by blood, but there could only be one Gyre Magus.

I shall not see the Spiral Father again, Vyrunas reflected as he waited. *Whatever happens here tonight, my service to Him will be complete.*

When Vyrunas had last descended to the Gyre Sanctum the prophet's will had almost consumed him, dragging him into a whirlpool of waking dreams he couldn't begin to grasp. He had risen five days later, his body wracked with pain and his mind twisted out of shape. The heretics had made his lord's visions savage, yet when Vyrunas had looked into His eyes there had been only wisdom and an infinite tenderness.

'The kindred of Redemption are part of something greater,' the Spiral Father had whispered into his mind. *'Truth flows through our blood like a silver cord, connecting us to our transcendent kin between the stars. Someday they will come for us and we shall be made whole again.'*

'I will not see it,' Vyrunas whispered, looking within himself for the sadness that so often afflicted outsiders, but finding only serenity. He knew Xithauli disdained such introspection, but Vyrunas believed it deepened his understanding of the outsiders, sharpening his ability to draw them into the Spiral.

We are both magi, yet we are not the same, he decided. *I was born to work in shadows, she in blood. Perhaps that is why my time is truly over.*

Kangre Talasca was perched on a pew among the headless dead, his eyes fixed on the hanging body of the preacher, as if by becoming one with the congregation he might see what they had seen. Major Rostyk had wanted the bodies removed and decently buried, but the colonel had forbidden it.

'You have too much to tell me yet,' Talasca whispered to the dead.

It was said that madmen could not doubt their own sanity, therefore to suspect madness in oneself was a proof of sanity, but Talasca knew that was nonsense. He had never doubted his madness, but he recognised its *divinity* and embraced it, for it was the kind that bore insights.

One such insight had led him to set the Witch Captain on the trail of the daemon that stalked the Locker. She was an enigma within the regiment – a clever tactician and a skilled fighter, but in place of a soul she had only a shadow. Without her guidance the Eighth would have been lost on the ice fields of Oblazt. Every man in the regiment knew it and hated her for it, but the Black Flags honoured their blood debts. Sometimes Talasca feared her madness might be holier than his own.

The Night Weaver will be her test, he decided. *If she is truly blessed by the God-Emperor she will prevail.*

His vox crackled. *'The ambassador is here, sir.'*

'Bring him to the temple,' Talasca said. Another of his insights had moved him to receive the Gyre Magus in this slaughterhouse. He wanted to see Vyrunas' face when he entered. That would tell him more than a thousand words ever could.

'You're cleared for entry to the Locker, Gyre Magus,' the gatekeeper voxed. *'The colonel will send someone for you.'*

'Proceed,' Vyrunas told the driver as the steel doors parted.

A squad of soldiers were waiting for the vehicle in the courtyard beyond.

'Shall I accompany you, Gyre Magus?' the driver asked, glancing at Vyrunas in the mirror. The weariness in that desiccated face went far beyond natural exhaustion...

The driver snapped the chain of thought quickly. His passenger might sense it as *doubt*.

'No, remain here,' Vyrunas said, pulling up his cowl. 'Fulfil your duty to the Spiral, brother.'

The driver felt the breath of the ancient's will, but it was only a cursory, disinterested touch. After all, he was nothing but a common human cultist.

'Spiral ward you, Gyre Magus,' he said as Vyrunas climbed out of the vehicle. He waited until the soldiers had escorted their charge away before letting the veneer of his faith fall away. Then his hands began to shake, the tremors spreading swiftly through his body until he had to grit his teeth to stop them chattering. Keeping the mental facade intact throughout the journey had almost broken him. He'd learned to guard his thoughts closely in the Spires, but this was the *Gyre Magus*.

I wouldn't have lasted a moment if the bastard had looked directly at me, the driver realised. He was still amazed he'd managed to secure this duty, but it had been a huge gamble getting this close to a magus. He'd counted on his passenger's arrogance, but it was probably Vyrunas' exhaustion that had saved him.

The old man is dying, he thought. *No! Not a man,* he corrected himself angrily. *Never make that mistake!*

Steeling himself, the driver got out of the buggy and raised his arms as guards surrounded him.

'I need to see Captain Omazet,' he said.

The Witch Captain sat on a prayer mat with her back straight and her legs crossed in a rigid lotus position. Her eyes were fixed on the Imperial mandala that hung on the wall of her chamber. It had always helped her find clarity.

In her old regiment Adeola Omazet had been called 'Le Mal Kalfu'. She had been an officer, but also a preacher of sorts, though her gospel had focussed entirely on the Emperor's most ruthless aspect, as the arbiter of His species. Like her god, she showed those who strayed little mercy. Her former charges had feared her more than any commissar, for she could read the slightest doubt in a face or a voice, but they had also venerated her as a dark saint.

The Black Flags were no different.

Yet for all her talents, Omazet was not a psyker. She had no innate ability to track the spoor of a daemon. Then again, she wasn't convinced it *was* a daemon that walked among them. The atrocity at the temple seemed too contrived. *Too convenient almost...*

There was a tapping at her door.

'Enter,' Omazet said. She expected Ariken, but it was Nyulaszi. The Shank Sergeant hesitated at the threshold. None of her company would trespass into her chamber, even those few she favoured.

'We have a visitor, captain,' Nyulaszi said. 'One of the spiralheads. He says he's cut loose from the cult. Says you know him.'

'Bharlo,' Omazet guessed, staring into the mandala.

Ariken's squad took Trazgo just before nightfall, encircling him as he shuffled into the infirmary. He had visited just about everywhere else in the fort so she'd been expecting her turn. The Szilar sergeant sized up the troopers and shook his head, dismissing the guns levelled at him.

'You going to murder a Throne-loving man in cold blood?' he asked.

'I'll ask the questions,' Ariken said, facing him squarely.

'Did the skull-faced bitch put you up to this?' Trazgo asked, eying her company insignia.

'You approached my squad today – others too, all over the fort,' Ariken challenged. 'We asked around.'

'Just doing my rounds. I'm a sergeant, *corporal*.'

'Off-duty, you told us,' Heike, a stocky, shaven-headed woman said. The former manufactorum overseer was tougher than the rest of the squad combined.

'A real soldier, he's *never* off-duty, Driftwood,' Trazgo mocked.

'You know something about the murders,' Ariken said.

'Do I, girl?'

'You said it was the Emperor's judgement,' Heike hissed, jabbing her shotgun at him. 'As good as threatened the rest of us!'

Ariken could feel things slipping out of control. Her friends – *her troops* – were frightened. Almost everyone in the fort was, but these people were only a hairsbreadth away from being civilians. Any moment now someone was going to shoot this degenerate.

'We don't want to die,' Ariken said more gently. 'You know something, sergeant. We just want to be a part of it.' She stepped closer to him, trying and failing to connect with those ambivalent eyes. The reek from his greatcoat was nauseating. 'We were sworn to the Unfolding once.'

She held something up. His right eye flicked to the metal spiral in her hand while the left remained fixed on her forehead.

'Can you save us, sergeant?' Ariken urged.

'I can show you a miracle.' Trazgo smiled, revealing yellow teeth.

The Gyre Magus regarded the carnage in silence. Waiting beside the violated altar, Talasca searched the ancient priest's face, evaluating every nuance of expression with his augmented vision. He saw neither horror nor revulsion there. *Distaste* perhaps, but even that didn't run deep. He sensed it was the *messiness* of the scene that troubled Vyrunas. The carnage offended the magus' instinct for order. It was precisely the sterile, soulless response Talasca had expected, but when Vyrunas finally spoke his words were unexpected.

'Our time runs short, Retriever. The daemon is growing stronger.'

'You believe this incursion was daemonic, Gyre Magus?' Talasca couldn't hide his surprise.

'As do you,' Vyrunas said. 'We have both stood against corruption long enough to recognise its stain. That is why I have come to you, Retriever.'

'I admit your request for a meeting was unexpected.'

'When I heard of this outrage...' Vyrunas swept a hand across the scene, 'I knew I could hesitate no longer.' He walked along the aisle towards Talasca, the hem of his robes trailing through runnels of dried blood. 'The Spiral Dawn has also suffered such atrocities. Many of our temples have been despoiled and our priests slaughtered. It grieves me that the evil has found you. We endeavoured to shield you from its thirst.'

'Shield us?' Talasca asked blearily, trying to make sense of the elder's words. His thoughts felt sluggish and crowded with shadows.

'This world is both sacred and profane, Retriever. The Koronatus Ring is a divine *weapon* – the Spires are its seven-pronged blade and the shrines its beating heart. We who watch over them are bound to the God-Emperor by a sacrament aeons old.'

Vyrunas' eyes glittered as he drew closer, dimming everything around him and deepening the shadows in Talasca's mind.

'Before the Spiral Dawn, the Sacred Thorn carried the burden,' Vyrunas continued, 'and before them, the Resplendent Angels. Countless others have stood against the darkness that shrieks and weeps and hungers beneath this world.' He stopped before the colonel and extended his hands, palms upwards. 'Now I call upon you, Kangre Talasca. Stand with us in the God-Emperor's name!'

Talasca stared at the magus, his mind ablaze with the tormented *glory* of the words.

I want to believe, he realised. *It is all I have ever wanted.*

'You'll find what you're looking for inside,' Trazgo said, pointing at a hazy silver shape ahead. The wrecked ship lay at the eastern edge of the landing field, where it had crashed over a century ago. Most of its vast bulk was buried, but the tail section jutted from the ground. There was a dark fissure in its silver shell.

'I don't understand,' Ariken said.

'That's why you've come to learn.' Trazgo smirked. 'Don't worry, I know the way.' He stepped towards the wreck, but Heike blocked him.

'I don't like it,' she said. There was a chorus of agreement from the rest of the squad. 'I ain't going in there. Not at night anyways.'

Ariken checked her chrono. Her friend was right. True night had fallen.

'What's in there?' she pressed Trazgo.

'Truth,' he said. 'If you want it.'

'Embrace the Sacred Spiral of the God-Emperor,' Vyrunas entreated. 'Seize your destiny, Retriever!'

The magus' whole body was trembling under the strain of the psychic web he was weaving over Talasca – and by the madness he was *un-weaving* inside the man. The colonel was weeping now, his tears stained red by revelation and the weight of Vyrunas' will as he was dragged towards the Spiral. The process was infinitesimally delicate, but it was the man himself that harrowed Vyrunas. Talasca's soul was a barbed tangle of self-loathing and rage. Walking his thoughts was like navigating a polluted, eternally coiling river that led nowhere. The magus' own sanity was dissolving in its black waters as doubts and deliriums he couldn't comprehend assaulted him.

The outsider's mind is poisonous, Vyrunas recognised. *He has been touched by the Dark Beneath the Spires. He–*

Something thudded into Vyrunas' back. The magus looked down and saw the tip of a blade jutting from his ribs. Before his eyes it jerked forward, trailing bright agony through his chest and splashing Talasca with blood. There was more pain as the blade was yanked free. Choking, Vyrunas staggered around to face his attacker and saw a woman with the face of a skull. Before she could strike again, the magus lashed out with a whip of psychic force and threw her across the hall.

'Spiral flay you!' Vyrunas hissed.

Coughing blood and streamers of psychic energy, the magus turned to Talasca as the colonel's blade arced towards him. There was a moment of bright agony before the world was swept out from under him and he was spinning wildly through the air, his perspective whirling about too swiftly to comprehend. Mustering the last of his will, he slowed his perception of time and saw a robed corpse standing before Talasca. Blood was bursting from the raw wound of its neck in a sluggish fountain. As the headless man crumpled, Vyrunas understood that he had failed.

Let the Ravening come then, he conceded.

Then he let go and dropped into nothingness.

A savage bellow echoed from the fissure in the wrecked ship. It was utterly inhuman, but there was no mistaking the fury and pain behind it. Ariken's comrades stared at each other, their eyes wide behind their masks. There was another roar, closer this time.

'Form up!' Ariken ordered, levelling her laspistol at the rift. 'This is why we're here.'

Her squad obeyed hesitantly, those with rifles kneeling as they covered the dark entrance. Trazgo chuckled softy as he watched them.

Ariken tried her vox bead: 'Bridge, this is Squad Three-One. Over.' The answering voice was drenched in static. Even at this range the blackout was killing their comms. 'Bridge, we have a situation at the landing field.'

'You could run,' Trazgo suggested.

'Shut up, scum!' Heike snapped.

'Truth can't be silenced.'

'I said–' A third roar cut her off as something vast and dark burst from the fissure.

'Blessed One!' Trazgo called. 'I come bearing penitents.'

The twisted giant whirled towards his voice and strode forward on massive reverse-jointed legs. To their credit the troopers held their ground and opened fire. A hail of las bolts lanced through the darkness, scorching the beast's hide in a hundred places, but it kept coming, wading into the barrage with two of its claws warding its face.

Sacred Throne save us, Ariken prayed as she glimpsed the nest of tentacles behind its shielding claws.

As the abomination drew closer Heike opened up with her shotgun, carving deep cavities into its flesh. With a shriek of rage, Trazgo leapt at her, grappling for the weapon as the beast loomed over them.

'Scatter!' Ariken yelled, diving aside as a serrated hook arced towards her. It swept past and raked through the chest of the trooper beside her, hurling him into the air in a welter of blood. A grasping claw snatched another man by the head and swung him about like a crude meat whip. Heike threw Trazgo off and rolled aside as the giant trampled through them, crushing the traitor underfoot. Moments later it was gone.

It wasn't after us, Ariken realised as she watched it disappear into the main compound. *We were just in the way.*

But even distracted, the abomination had left carnage in its wake. Broken bodies were scattered around her, at least three of them dead. Others were moaning from deep slashes or shattered bones. Among them was Trazgo, though Ariken could tell at a glance that he was finished. His abdomen was a pulped red ruin and his limbs were contorted into unnatural angles. He glanced up as she stepped towards him.

'They lied to us all,' Ariken told him.

His lips tried to coax words from his ruptured throat, but only blood came. As he began to retch she shot him between his crooked eyes.

'Should've let the bastard choke,' Heike said, limping over to her. She was one of the few who'd escaped serious injury.

'That's not who we are,' Ariken said, throwing her spiral pendant onto the traitor's corpse. 'We need to sound the alarm.'

The Terror stormed through the fortress, seeking the heretics who had defiled the Sacred Spiral. The hidden god watching from behind its eyes had unshackled Tizheruk from its restraints. Freed from the imperatives of stealth, the beast rampaged, roaring as it raked its claws along the heretics' walls. Sometimes enemies appeared from their boxy lairs and scurried about, striking at its hide with their pitiful weapons until they were crushed.

'*Tizz-ah-rukk!*' the behemoth bellowed as a tall metal beast on spindly legs stomped towards it from the darkness. The strider answered Tizheruk's challenge with a grinding machine roar and vomited a hail of sharp lights from its single stubby arm. It was like the fiery spittle of the small heretics, but faster and much hotter. Tizheruk reeled and staggered back from the assault, shielding its eyes as the burning lights chewed into its flesh. The metal beast followed, but its attack wavered, as if it was catching its breath.

Without hesitation the Terror hurled itself forward and clasped one of the strider's legs with its split right arm, while hacking at its iron sinews with the hooked claw of its left. The strider trampled about, trying to dislodge its tormentor, but Tizheruk clung on, worrying at its leg until something vital gave way and it buckled. The Terror leapt away as its foe teetered and keeled over, spewing flames. A heretic crawled from its body, but the beast grabbed him and shook him violently until he fell apart.

The fight had slowed Tizheruk and there was a harsh wailing coming from all sides now, drawing more of the heretics. Dimly it felt strength leaching from its battered body. Its hook had snapped in half and one of its legs trailed weakly, but its god urged it onwards. Growling low in its throat, the Terror lurched on, surrendering to its master's guiding hand as they hunted the true prey together.

'How did you know?' Talasca asked as he searched among the pews.

'I set a spy among them,' Omazet said, 'though truthfully I never expected him to return.' She was still slumped against the wall where the psychic blast had thrown her. Her carapace armour had absorbed most of the impact, but her body felt like one big bruise. 'He told me the magus had come to see you. That troubled me.'

'I am in your debt once more, captain.' Talasca bent and picked something up. Omazet saw it was the charred husk of Vyrunas' head, scorched by his final psychic exertion.

'The heretic tried to *turn* me,' Talasca hissed, holding up the head with both hands and peering into its cauterised eye sockets. 'I felt him in my mind, twisting my honour against me with half-truths.'

'We need to hear my spy's story, colonel.' Omazet rose painfully. 'He said something is happening in the city.'

'Can he be trusted?'

Something rammed into the wall behind the altar, cracking its bas-relief aquila and scattering dust across the chamber. Talasca dropped Vyrunas' head and drew his sword and bolt pistol.

'Karolus, to me,' he said into his collar vox, alerting the paladin that stood watch outside the temple.

As the chamber shook under another assault, Omazet joined Talasca, her twin power machetes already unsheathed. The next attack sent deep fractures racing through the wall.

'It would be prudent to withdraw, colonel,' she said.

'Yes,' he agreed, but he remained motionless. Omazet saw he was smiling – eager for retribution after the violation of his mind. She understood completely.

The wall collapsed in a shower of debris that buried the altar and set the hanging body of the preacher swinging like a morbid pendulum. A blasphemous aberration heaved itself over the rubble, trailing the dead weight of its ruined right leg behind it. The beast's hide was a riot of gashes and burns, many of them still smoking, but its blue eyes were sharp.

'*Tizz-ah-rukk,*' it hissed wetly.

As the giant lumbered towards them the officers stepped to either side, hoping to confuse it, but it fixed on Talasca immediately, as if he had always been its target. He danced backward, firing wildly and parrying with his sword as the beast barged through the pews after him, scattering corpses in its wake. Omazet followed behind, slashing and stabbing at its chitin-plated back until she reached softer flesh. With a hiss it swung round and lashed out with its distended, twin-clawed arm. The talons raked deep grooves in her breastplate and sent her staggering away, but barbed tendrils whipped out from its ribcage and hooked into her armour, catching her before she could fall. Hissing eagerly, the beast reeled her towards its tentacle-fringed maw.

This is not how I die, Omazet thought calmly.

The tendril hooks were torn away as a hulking abhuman barrelled into her attacker with a slab-like shield. The impetus of the charge propelled both giants into the rubble-strewn altar, but the beast took the brunt of the impact. Crushed between steel and stone, it snarled and tried to lash past the shield, but its remaining arm was trapped. Grunting with strain, Talasca's bodyguard ground his foe against the stone until he was rewarded with a staccato chorus of shattering carapace. He backed off, then renewed his assault with his crackling power maul, battering the spasm-wracked abomination. With a cry of fury, Omazet staggered alongside him and added her machetes to the attack. A moment later Talasca joined them, hacking with his power sword.

It took the abomination a long time to die.

True night had fallen over the abbey by the time Clavel's extraction vessel arrived. Cross heard a sudden roar of engines from above and a shadow fell across the sanctum's dome.

'*Valkyrie Alpha in position,*' a voice hissed from the vox-set on the table. '*Breaching dome in sixty seconds. Confirm, Calavera Five?*'

'Confirmed,' Clavel responded. He turned to Cross and Trujilo. 'We need to evacuate the sanctum.' Neither of them argued.

The gunship opened fire shortly after they reached the corridor outside. Remarkably, the reinforced glass held for several seconds before surrendering with a cataclysmic crash.

'Why drag us through that hellhole?' Cross demanded. 'Why didn't you just blast through the damned dome from the start?'

'Breaching the haven forcibly would have triggered a data-wipe,' Clavel said. 'That was not an option.'

Nothing remained of the dome when they returned. The sanctum was covered in broken glass and most of its contents were shredded. The control console was a ruin, but Cross saw the malevolent bas-relief shrine had escaped unscathed. Somehow that didn't surprise him.

Cross stared at the giant face. It was staring right back at him with wide-open, painted eyes.

They were closed before, he thought, his blood running cold.

A rope dropped from the gunship hovering above and he glimpsed armoured figures moving about in its open hatch. Without a word, Clavel grabbed the line and they began to winch him up.

'What's our play, captain?' Trujilo asked.

'I think we're out of choices,' Cross said, his attention returning to the bronze idol. 'We can't go back and I'll be damned if I stay here.'

As he was hauled out of the sanctum someone whispered to him from below, her voice so faint it was little more than a memory of sound: *'Look at me, Ambrose Templeton...'*

It was a woman's voice, withered with age and sickness, yet the mind behind it had seen his true name. If he obeyed her request, Cross feared he would see *her* eyes staring back from the bronze face.

He didn't look back.

CHAPTER NINE

Kazimyr Senka loved Hope. True to its name, the city was a bastion of freedom in the shadow of Imperial oppression. It hid its true face behind a mask of misery, but that would soon change.

We won't have to hide much longer! Senka thought fiercely.

As he approached the city's outskirts a large truck raced forward to meet him, its wheels bouncing across the dirt road. Its carriage was reinforced with riveted iron plates and the flat wedge of its front was fitted with massive cylinders lined with buzz-saw teeth.

Those look strong enough to grind through stone, he gauged.

The servo-arm jutting from the truck's deck carried a bulky laser weapon that Senka didn't recognise. He guessed it was designed for industrial work rather than combat, much like the vehicle itself, but he didn't doubt its lethality.

'Identify yourself!' a voice demanded from his vox as the big gun swivelled to track him.

'Spiral Strider,' he replied. 'The watch phrase is *Risen Truth.'*

'Welcome, brother!'

The truck swung alongside him and the bald Neophyte operating the servo-arm flashed him the sign of the Spiral. The hallowed symbol was daubed across the truck's bodywork, though it was unlike any rendition Senka had seen before, its form jagged and lined with ridges. It was nothing like the flowing symbol Xithauli had tattooed between Senka's shoulder blades.

It's more like a spiny worm... He quashed a pang of apprehension. It was fitting that the sect would go to war under a harsher icon and leave the Sacred Spiral untarnished.

'The reckoning is coming,' he crooned to his Sentinel.

His hopes were confirmed as he reached Openhand Plaza, where his meeting was scheduled. Powerful floodlights lit the square and he saw it had become the staging field for an army. Three more of the armoured trucks were parked along the perimeter, along with several buggies whose hoods had been fitted with guns. Music boomed from the vehicles, filling the square with discordant beats interlaced with swirling, organic harmonies. A throng of citizens in grey coveralls shuffled among the vehicles, hauling fuel drums and ammunition crates, while hairless, pale-skinned Neophyte cultists directed them. The cultists wore rubberised jumpsuits emblazoned with the Spiral Wyrm, though some had upgraded their garb with scraps of armour. All were armed, most with autoguns, but here and there Senka saw more dangerous weapons – lasrifles, shotguns, flamers, even a plasma gun. One pair was carrying a massive, pronged cannon between them. He didn't recognise the gun, but like the trucks, he suspected its origins lay in Redemption's promethium industry.

'Everything can become a weapon in the hands of the righteous,' Xithauli had told him. *'Nothing is wasted!'*

White-robed Spiralfire Acolytes walked openly among the crowd, their hoods thrown back to reveal bulbous, bone-crested skulls and purple flesh. They moved in a loping crouch, as if they were stalking some unseen prey. Most sported deviant, chitin-covered arms in addition to the natural two, and their jutting jaws were filled with fangs. They were *hybrid* creatures, their kinship to the feral four-armed monsters Senka had occasionally glimpsed all too apparent.

'Their kind are truly blessed by the Spiral,' Xithauli had explained when Senka first encountered the Acolytes. *'They are drawn from the First and Second Paradigms of the kindred – champions born for holy war! Revere them, for the Spiral runs strong in their blood.'*

Despite her assurances, Senka found the Acolytes disturbing. There was a barely restrained violence about them that made his hackles rise. He understood that they were his brothers, but whenever they looked at him he sensed a cold hunger, as if *he* were the prey they hunted.

Four of the hybrids met him as he climbed from his vehicle. Their leader wore a Vassago breastplate, the black iron repainted a lurid magenta and embossed with the Spiral Wyrm. The Acolyte's third arm terminated in a single scythe-like talon, but he also carried a fleshy, barb-tipped whip that writhed in his grip, as if with a life of its own.

'Brother!' the leader said wetly, his long tongue flitting between his fangs. 'I am Iaoguai, Iconward of the Spiralfire coterie. The Primus awaits you.'

'The Primus?' Senka asked, trying to hide his unease.

'You knew him as the Chrysaor, but our lord's apotheosis is now complete.'

Senka's fear hardened. He had only encountered the cult's secretive warlord once before, but that had been enough to last a lifetime. The man had questioned him doggedly about the regiment's capabilities, his gaze unwavering and his voice laden with threat. Talking to him had been like navigating a maze of blades.

Xithauli, Senka thought over and over, using her name as a mantra to steady himself as the Acolytes led him to a tent at the centre of the square. He faltered as he saw the banner mounted outside. It was a swathe of flowing velvet, taller than a man and ribbed with silver spines to hold the material steady. A Spiral Wyrm adorned it in gold, set against a field of deep violet. Whorls of sharp obsidian hung from its hem and it was crowned with a long, crested skull inlaid with amethysts. The overall effect was utterly *alien*.

'The sacred banner of the Spiral Wyrm,' Iaoguai said proudly. 'It shall be my honour to bear it into holy war.' He ushered the dazed Sentinel pilot into the tent.

Primus Chrysaor stood behind a trestle table draped with a map that

Senka immediately recognised as a plan of the Locker – after all, he had provided most of the details. The warlord had exchanged his robes for a leather trench coat with a high, gold-trimmed collar that flared behind his hairless head. It hung open, revealing a breastplate that appeared to be woven from melted bones. His human arms were folded, but the segmented third swept about restlessly, its three-fingered claw slicing the air.

He's worse than the Acolytes, Senka thought with a stab of terror.

The warlord looked up from the map, almost as if he had smelt Senka's fear. His visage was bestial, but it possessed an uncanny dignity that elevated him above the hybrids as a Space Marine stood above a common man.

'Spiral Strider,' the Primus greeted him, his voice sibilant, yet deep. 'Did you bring the shield?'

'I did, my lord.' Senka held up the satchel Trazgo had given him.

The Primus smiled. It was monstrous. *And wondrous...*

His eyes are like Xithauli's, Senka realised. Why hadn't he noticed that before? Under that implacable, imperious gaze his doubts withered.

'We have much to discuss, brother,' the warlord said.

'I am yours to command, my Primus!'

As Xithauli descended towards her lord's sanctum she chanted an elegy of cessation for her dead predecessor. It was a mark of respect, but it was utterly devoid of sentiment, for Xithauli was no more capable of sorrow than she was of pride in her ascendance. Vyrunas had urged her to study the emotions that plagued the outsiders, but Xithauli had never seen the need. In her experience manipulating their flaws was absurdly simple, and she had never shared her fellow magus' inquisitive streak.

Perhaps his great age corroded his judgement towards the end, she reflected.

She reached the conical antechamber at the foot of the steps and waited as its guardian unfolded from the gnarled walls. The creature's gangling, chitin-sheathed bulk loomed over her, its head tilted inquisitively to the side. Its indigo carapace was inscribed with gold spirals, all rendered in the aggressive, angular aspect of war.

'As within, so without,' Xithauli intoned, bowing her head to the ancient apostle.

The Riven Hunter was the last of the Purestrains that had stalked alongside the Spiral Father in the First Days. Both its left arms had been lost in the purgation of the Sororitas abbey, yet no Purestrains of the later cycles could match its cunning or speed. The creature stood second only to the Spiral Father Himself in the cult's reverence.

'Attend me, my Gyre Magus,' a voice murmured soundlessly from the pit in the chamber's centre. *'The Ravening comes and I would share my dreams with you.'*

Xithauli closed her eyes as the ritual demanded and stepped over the lip of the pit. Flexing her will to slow her fall, she descended towards the sunken cavern below. By the traditions of the Spiral Dawn the sanctum was forbidden to all save the Gyre Magus, so this was the first time Xithauli would gaze upon her four-armed god.

'*The long age of shadow and secret war draws to a close...*' the Spiral Father mused. His thoughts were sluggish, as if He was straining to form the insights. '*The Unfolded have woven with unquiet words... and quiet claws... for over a century... but as the Spiral flows... so the path unwinds into new rites.*'

It is the Ravening, Xithauli sensed as her bare feet touched warm water. *War calls to His blood as strongly as it calls to my own. His thoughts are clouded by divine wrath.*

She froze her descent, holding herself on the surface of the shallow pool that filled the sanctum.

'*Look upon me, Gyre Magus.*'

Xithauli opened her eyes and saw He was a god of war.

PART THREE

REDEMPTION IN FIRE

'Should the sacred bloodline become imperilled beyond the salves of shadow or terror, then rise up against the Outsider and cast him down with tooth and claw and purifying fire!'

– Apotheosis of the Spiral Wyrm

CHAPTER TEN

It's coming, Ariken thought as she followed Captain Omazet into the war room. *Whatever Cross was afraid of, it's beginning.*

The regiment's senior officers were gathered around the long table with the colonel at their head, but it was the robed man to Talasca's left that drew Ariken's attention. He nodded a solemn greeting when he saw her.

Bharlo.

Major Rostyk frowned as Ariken sat beside Omazet, doubtless wondering what a lowly corporal was doing here, but the others paid her no heed. Truthfully she didn't give a damn what any of them thought. Less than an hour had passed since the horror outside the wrecked ship, and her place was with her squad – what was left of it anyway – but Omazet had insisted on her attendance.

'You are my shadow,' her captain had said. *'I want you at my back.'*

When everyone was seated they turned expectantly to the colonel. Talasca was hunched over the table, his hands clasped before his face as if in prayer, his eyes closed.

'Captain Omazet,' he said quietly.

'We are at war,' Omazet began without preamble. 'Our enemy is the Spiral Dawn.' She nodded to Bharlo. 'Say your piece, pilgrim.'

'They're massing in the city,' the former shepherd said. 'Raising an army.' His face was lean to the point of starvation, his eyes bloodshot and haunted.

'How many?' Omazet asked.

'Thousands,' Bharlo said. 'Mostly city grubs and Neophytes, but others too... the *Blessed Ones* – Acolytes and worse.'

'Are they daemon-worshippers?' the bearded giant, Major Kazán, asked intently. He appeared unsurprised by the news.

He's been expecting it, Ariken sensed. *Looking forward to it even.*

'I don't know *what* they are,' Bharlo said. 'Something worse maybe...'

'Gentlemen, we cannot trust this civilian's word,' Rostyk protested. 'If there has been a misunderstanding with the sect we should request a parley.'

'There's *nothing* to talk about,' Bharlo hissed. 'They're done talking.'

'The Spiral Dawn is unorthodox,' Rostyk urged, 'but it reveres the Emperor.'

'A four-armed emperor,' Talasca said, finally opening his eyes. 'Their magus looked into my mind and I looked back. *I saw what he was inside.* They are an abomination.'

'I have always known it,' Kazán said, nodding.

Talasca's silver gaze fell upon him. 'The attacks on their temples,' he said, 'that was your hand, Kazán?'

'And I stand by them, colonel.' The giant scowled, showing his metal-shod teeth. 'An honest Szilar warrior can *smell* corruption.'

Except among his own men, Ariken thought sourly, remembering Trazgo.

'We're wasting time,' Bharlo pressed. 'They're coming for us. We have to hit them first.'

'What are you suggesting?' Omazet said, watching him closely.

'I can lead you straight to them,' he said eagerly. 'I know the secret paths and the watchwords.'

'What about Ophele?' Ariken asked suddenly. She ignored the looks the officers threw her way, some puzzled, others angered by her presumption. 'What happened to her, shepherd? And all the others?'

Bharlo sighed. 'The last time I saw Ophele she was two months pregnant, though it looked closer to six. Their spawn grow fast.' He shook his head. 'She was overjoyed because she'd been honoured by the cult Iconward.'

'And the others?'

'They're *all* gone, Ariken. They were embraced... *infected* within days of our arrival. Were it not for the captain's warning, and my old talents, I'd be lost too.' He turned to Talasca. 'I'll lead you right to them, but let me fight alongside you.'

A pistol slid across the table towards him. 'Take it, shepherd,' Ariken said. 'You've earned it.'

Bharlo flashed his old, sad smile. 'Thank you, sister.' He picked up the weapon and the smile vanished, along with the light in his eyes.

'So the Spiral burns!' he shouted as he whipped the gun towards Talasca's head. The trigger clicked, but there was no discharge. In the same instant Ariken's machete thudded into his chest. Bharlo stared at her dully.

'I ejected the power cell,' she said.

The pistol slipped from Bharlo's fingers and he slumped into death, pinned to his chair by the blade.

'I don't think he knew he was theirs,' Ariken said. 'Not until the end. But it was in his eyes.'

The soldiers manning the gunship were manifestly elite troops, but they were nothing like the spirited veterans who had accompanied Cross to the abbey. All wore black carapace armour and helmets fitted with metal masks, the lenses so dark it was impossible to see the eyes behind them. Their lasrifles were bulkier than the standard model and cables coiled from their stocks to the soldiers' backpacks. Their leader had swapped a helmet for a crimson beret, but was otherwise as faceless as his subordinates. The entire squad sat in silence, so still it was easy to imagine they were automatons.

Or simply hollow men like Clavel, Cross decided. He turned to the pale-eyed Inquisition operative sitting beside him. 'Where are we going?'

'Spire Vigilans,' Clavel said, 'the conclave maintains a base there.'

'I heard Vigilans was volcanically active.'

'It is. That's why the Brood avoid it.'

'The Brood?'

'That is our designation for the degenerates of the Spiral Dawn,' Clavel said. 'They are a xenos strain. A particularly dangerous one.'

'And you're here to destroy them?'

'We are Ordo Xenos.'

That's not what I asked, Cross thought warily. 'How long have you known about them?' he asked.

'They have been under observation for some time.'

'But you didn't warn us. Not even when we went into that damned pit.' Something else struck Cross. 'You have no intention of warning anyone now, do you?'

Clavel regarded him coolly. 'Your combat proficiency is mediocre at best, captain, but you have proved yourself tenacious and resourceful. You may be useful to the conclave, but if you compromise my mission I will remove you.'

Cross didn't doubt it. He noticed Trujilo was watching them closely. The surviving veteran had heard every word. A glance passed between them, confirming the unspoken alliance that had begun in the abbey's sanctum.

We're the strangers here, Cross thought, *and the betrayed.*

'There are others like Bharlo,' Ariken said to Talasca, 'Black Flags they've turned.' The eyes of the man pinned to the chair beside the colonel were still open, accusing her in death. 'I've seen them.'

'Traitors and heretics,' Kazán growled.

'I think it's something deeper than that,' Ariken said, frowning. 'More like a disease...'

'A daemonic plague of corruption!' Kazán nodded sagely. 'I have heard of such things.' He grinned at Ariken. 'You did well to draw the assassin out, corporal.'

'He was a victim,' she said sadly. 'They all are.' *And I was almost one of them,* she thought. *I'm sorry, Ophele.*

'We need names if you have them,' Omazet said.

'Senka,' Ariken answered without hesitation.

'No, my Sentinel Sharks are Throne-fearing men,' Rostyk protested, but without conviction. He looked baffled and very old, as if the speed of events had drained him. Under other circumstances Ariken might have felt sorry for him. 'They're all good men.'

'So was Bharlo!' Ariken snapped. 'Maybe even at the end... The Unfolded use our faith against us, major.'

'Rouse the Locker to full alert,' Talasca said, rising from his chair. 'The assassin told at least one truth – they are coming for us.'

The flight lasted a little over an hour. Towards the end the Valkyrie tilted sharply, evidently climbing, then set down with a roar of thrusters. As he disembarked, Cross saw the gunship had landed on a narrow escarpment near the summit of another Spire, presumably Vigilans.

'Tempestor Aickman, with me,' Clavel said to the squad commander.

The party of four crossed the ledge to the rock face beyond, leaving the troops with the gunship. Their destination was a monolithic building whose facade was carved in the likeness of an ornate broadsword.

This is a warrior's temple, Cross judged as they passed through the entrance in the blade's tip. The tunnel beyond was dark, but their lights revealed armoured giants carved into the obsidian. Perhaps the myths of the Koronatus Ring were not entirely fanciful, for these statues certainly depicted the Adeptus Astartes. The transhuman warriors were wrought in their true scale, dwarfing the mortals who walked among them, but they were subtly stylised rather than slavishly lifelike. Their postures were stern and regimented, yet they exuded a dignified elegance, as if they were warrior artisans.

Did they carve this themselves? Cross wondered, marvelling at the work.

Their path ended at a plain steel hatch that looked incongruous in the ancient temple. Clavel placed his palm upon the surface and it slid aside, revealing another of the masked soldiers.

'Unquiet dust,' Clavel said and the sentry lowered his weapon, allowing them past. There was a shabby, well-worn look to the facility beyond that suggested it had been running for years, if not decades. The walls were sheathed in corrugated metal and flickering lumen strips lined the ceilings, illuminating a network of corridors and doors. Though the base looked big enough to house an army, they encountered nobody as Clavel led them deeper.

'You're shutting this place down,' Cross ventured.

'Vigilans is an ancillary base,' Clavel said. 'Our primary facility has always been orbital.'

'But you're pulling out. Abandoning the Black Flags.'

Clavel met this with silence.

Shortly afterwards they reached another sealed door and another sentry. The hexagonal chamber beyond was gloomy, most of its light coming from the vid-screens tessellating its walls. Banks of machinery lined five of the room's six facets, each monitored by a red-robed tech adept. The operators stood stiffly at their posts, connected to their consoles by silvery mechadendrites extruded from their cowls. Optic sensors glowed green under their hoods and a soft, almost subliminal electronic chatter burbled between them as they worked.

At the centre of the chamber was a dais fitted with a high-backed command throne whose arms bristled with controls. The chair rotated to face the newcomers as they entered, revealing a man in an elegant scarlet jacket trimmed with gold. His long, grey-streaked hair was swept back to frame handsome features with an unmistakably aristocratic cast. He looked about forty, but Cross knew there were no certainties with the Imperium's ruling echelons. Such men and women had access to countless juvenat therapies. For all he knew, this man might be over a century old.

'Inquisitor,' Clavel said, making the sign of the aquila.

'You have secured the assets, Calavera Five?' the seated man asked. His voice was refined and soberly authoritative, exactly as Cross had imagined it would be.

'Primary and ancillary,' Clavel confirmed, removing his backpack. 'Shall I resume operations at the Locker?'

'No, you will lead the Excision Team.'

'I assumed Calavera Two–'

'Calavera Two and his team have not returned from their expedition to the Underspire,' the inquisitor said. 'We must assume they are lost.'

'Understood,' Clavel said. 'I advise you to evacuate the planet without delay, inquisitor. Once the Wildfire begins Vigilans may be compromised.'

Cross could contain himself no longer. 'Please, whatever this *Wildfire* is, we have to warn the regiment it's coming.'

'Wildfire is *war*, Captain Cross,' the inquisitor replied mildly, 'and it has already begun.'

The Locker had been on high alert for hours. Command had finally killed the klaxons, but spotlights blazed atop the towers and barracks, lancing the darkness with powerful beams. Everyone had been mustered for duty, summoned to the walls or assigned to extra patrols, though few knew why.

Trooper Oriss was different. He knew *exactly* why.

The secret blessing in his blood had roused him from sleep before the alarms sounded, its call igniting a righteous fire in his veins. He had jerked upright on his bunk and seen his spiral brother, Palmar, watching him from across the dormitory. Without a word they had taken up their daggers and walked the length of the long room, Oriss taking the right and Palmar the left, swiftly and silently sending their former comrades into a deeper sleep.

Oriss had felt no guilt, for the men were heretics.

Afterwards they had hurried to the compound's primary ammunition depot, picking up three more Spiralyte cultists along the way. The building was sturdy, its single door too solid to breach without heavy explosives. One of the colonel's abhuman slaves stood outside, and there would be more guards inside, doubtless trusted veterans of the butcher, Kazán.

There the five cultists waited, lurking behind a nearby storage shack.

Eventually a sergeant appeared, marching towards the depot with his squad behind him. As the man gave the watchword and the door opened, Palmar dashed joyfully among the heretics, bearing an unpinned grenade in each hand. The blast lacked the punch to damage the door, but it wreaked havoc on the men and threw the abhuman from its feet.

'Spiralfire!' the four remaining cultists yelled as they raced forward.

The abhuman was trying to get up, but one of its arms had been torn off at the elbow and it couldn't get the leverage. It raised its bloody stump as the cultists encircled it, evidently hoping for assistance.

'For the Four-Armed Saviour,' Oriss intoned as he rammed the barrel of his shotgun into the creature's eye and fired.

The depot's door was swinging about on its hinges, intact, but wide open. Two Spiralytes raced for the entrance and a hail of gunfire cut them down. Oriss gestured to his surviving brother and they flanked the doorway from either side. Moving in perfect synchronicity they pulled pins from their grenades and hurled them inside – then followed up with another pair as the defenders began yelling. Oriss was reaching for his third grenade when the first detonated, triggering a wave of explosions inside the depot. A moment later the entire building quaked and erupted, obliterating everything around it.

Spiralyte Oriss died a happy man.

An explosion thundered through the storm, sending shockwaves up the length of the comms tower. Standing by the window, Captain Ignacio Gharis saw a plume of fire rising from the other side of the compound.

'Sacred Throne, what was that?' Trooper Vyndos said from his post by the master vox caster. His scrawny, bearded face was pale. Even at the best of times he seemed to flutter on the edge of anxiety. To a veteran officer like Gharis the man was a disgrace, but his knack for the vox was undeniable.

'Just do your job,' Gharis said, trying to work out what had gone up in smoke. *Throne help them all if it was the ammo dump.* 'You heard Command. We need to warn the outposts.'

'Blackout's killing the signal–'

'So boost it!'

'I'm already running too much juice through her,' the operator protested as he fiddled with the hissing set. 'I push her any harder and she'll melt!' He murmured a prayer of solace to the machine's ailing spirit, as if to apologise for the disrespect.

Gharis turned as the door opened and Edvaro entered.

It's not his shift yet, he thought.

His instincts registered the gun in the newcomer's hand before his conscious mind caught up. Gharis pulled his sidearm free as Edvaro fired. The las bolt lanced through the captain's stomach, but he shot back from the hip, hitting the traitor squarely between the eyes. As Edvaro slumped to his knees and toppled, Gharis saw there was someone else behind him. Without hesitation he pumped las bolts through the door and the second intruder tumbled back down the stairs.

'Lock... door!' Gharis gasped at the stunned vox operator. 'Warn... Command.' His strength gave out and he slid to the floor.

The Bridge was a compact hub of comms stations and monitor banks situated at the heart of the Locker's keep. All the regiment's vox bands could be tapped into from this nexus, theoretically enabling Command to coordinate every trooper in the fort individually, even during a blackout. It was the most secure room in the Locker and the last place Omazet wanted to be right now.

'*We're under attack,*' someone was wailing from one of the vox banks. '*Gharis is down!*' There was a battering sound behind the panicked speaker's voice. '*They're right outside the door–*'

'This one is yours,' Omazet said to Ariken. 'Go!' Her aide nodded and hurried from the room.

'Reinforcements are on the way, Vyndos,' Lieutenant Mellier voxed from her station. She turned to Omazet, clearly shaken. 'We despatched a squad to the comms tower twenty minutes ago.'

'Perhaps they are the ones attacking it,' Omazet said bleakly.

'I don't understand...' Mellier's pale, pretty features were drawn. She looked too young to be coordinating the Bridge.

Which is why I am here, Omazet admitted. Kazán and Rostyk had been despatched to their respective forces and Talasca had vanished to his tower, ignoring her protests. The urge to rejoin her own troops was strong, but she trusted her lieutenants and someone had to run the Bridge in the colonel's absence.

The vox hissed as another transmission came through: *'This is Squad Nyulaszi. We are at G-Barracks.'*

'Copy Sergeant Nyulaszi,' Mellier replied. 'Have you made contact with Platoon Eighteen? They still haven't signed in.'

'That's because they're all dead in their bunks,' Nyulaszi said, his voice tight with anger. *'Looks like a sleep reap.'*

Mellier glanced at Omazet, confused.

'They were killed in their sleep,' the captain explained. She leaned into the vox. 'Nyulaszi, head for the comms tower. Ariken may need support.'

'Confirmed, my captain.'

How deep does this treachery run? Omazet wondered.

That was when the music started, bursting from every comms station at once and reverberating around the room. It was a nauseating symphony of dissonant beats and oozing textures that had no place in a sane person's ears. A deep, gurgling voice began to chant across the sludge, like a drowned corpse praising its fate.

'Kill it!' Omazet snapped.

Mellier cut the volume and studied her monitors. 'It's on every channel, broadcasting across the whole fort.' She looked at Omazet. 'It's coming from the comms tower, sir.'

Major Markel Rostyk marched his Sentinel through the inky blizzard, his searchlights scouring the ground ahead. Antonov and Brodski flanked him on either side, keeping their vehicles within twenty paces of his own so they could maintain unbroken vox contact. They were about twenty miles out from the Locker, patrolling the road to Hope and the monorail running parallel to it. Rostyk knew it was folly to endanger himself out on the mesa, but after the madness in the conference room he needed to be in his Sentinel again – *needed to be doing something he understood.*

Rostyk rarely allowed himself the indulgence of introspection, but the folly of Oblazt had shaken something loose in him and Redemption looked set to break it. On Oblazt, Black Flag regiments had turned on each other; here one regiment – *his regiment* – was turning upon itself. A plague of treachery, the girl had said. Something that could seduce even Throne-fearing men. It made no sense to him...

'I see lights on the track, major,' Brodski reported. *'It looks like the train.'* His position on the right flank was closest to the monorail.

'Antonov, stay on the road,' Rostyk ordered as he veered towards Brodski and crossed the track. They halted their Sentinels on either side and waited as the train rattled towards them. Soon the operator was visible in the brightly lit drive cabin. She was female but bald, like most of the city's grubs. When she spotted the Sentinels she started signalling urgently with her hands, clearly distressed.

'*She is in trouble, sir,*' Brodski said, stating the obvious as always.

'Trust nothing,' Rostyk cautioned. *That is the only certainty anymore,* he thought sourly.

Both Sentinels turned to face the monotrain as it passed between them. The first carriage was packed with grubs – a drab swarm of hairless heads, pale faces and grey jumpsuits. Like the driver, they waved frantically at the Sentinels, mouthing soundless pleas, as if urging them to run. The next carriage was the same, and the one after...

'*They are fleeing the city,*' Brodski guessed.

Rostyk didn't answer. Something about the grey throng was nagging at him.

There are no children, he realised. *No elders either.*

'They are not running,' he hissed. 'This is an army.' And the train would carry it right to the Locker's walls.

'Antonov,' Rostyk sent urgently, 'fall back and destroy the track.'

'*Confirmed, major.*' The third pilot's voice was already distorted by static, though he couldn't be more than fifty yards away.

'*They are unarmed, major,*' Brodski protested.

How can I be sure? Rostyk hesitated. *I was wrong before...*

Then the last carriage slipped into view and he saw it was full of monsters. Their faces were leering, bestial parodies of humanity, all sharp teeth and ridged crests, like gargoyles carved from flesh and bone. When they spotted the Sentinels they snarled and shattered the carriage windows with over-sized claws.

'Fire!' Rostyk shouted, squeezing down on the trigger of his multi-laser. A fusillade of las bolts raked the carriage, tearing through its flimsy walls and cauterising the unclean host within. The abominations surged towards the rear of the carriage as the train carried them into his killing stream. A few fired back from the windows, but their weapons couldn't penetrate his Sentinel's armour.

'For the Sunken Throne!' Rostyk roared, filled with loathing at the sight of the gibbous, scuttling hybrid things. They exemplified the pandemonium that his world had become.

I should have remained on Lethe, he thought with sudden clarity. *My daughter will be twenty-two, my son eighteen...*

Something punched into his cabin, triggering warning lights. Rostyk pivoted round and saw a hybrid tracking him with a bulky, pronged gun from the rearmost window.

'The Trench take you!' Rostyk snarled and obliterated the gunner before it could fire again. Scant seconds later the train had rolled past him.

'*What were they?*' Brodski voxed from the Sentinel opposite. He sounded dazed – as if his mind couldn't process the horror his eyes had sent its way.

'We have to cleanse the rest of them,' Rostyk said.

'I–' Brodski's voice splintered into white noise as an armoured truck hurtled into his Sentinel, smashing it from its feet. There was a howl of tearing metal as the walker was ground apart by the spinning blades on the truck's front. As the vehicle chewed through the Sentinel a servo-arm jutting from its deck swung a cannon towards Rostyk.

'Throne flay you!' Rostyk yelled, as he opened fire on the goggled operator hunched behind the arm. The man ducked away and answered with a lance of searing light. Rostyk jerked his Sentinel aside, but the blast grazed his canopy, tearing a molten rift through the plating.

A direct hit would have atomised me, he gauged.

As the truck picked up speed again Rostyk darted forward and swung behind it, weaving about as he gave chase. The operator swung the cannon towards him again, trying to get a mark.

'Too slow, scum,' Rostyk whispered as he hunted the goggled figure.

Bullets spattered the side of his canopy. Still racing forward, he pivoted his cabin and saw a sleek buggy had pulled up alongside him. The stubber fixed to its roof was juddering as it sprayed bullets at him on full auto. Rostyk returned fire, punching through the vehicle's light armour in seconds. It spun away into the darkness, gushing flames. He swung back to the truck as another bolt of energy lanced past him. There was no telling how many more vehicles were out here.

It is time to run, Rostyk decided. *The Locker must be warned.*

But he couldn't leave Brodski's death unanswered. Pushing his Sentinel's engine to the limit, he accelerated and flanked the truck. As the cannon swivelled to meet him he fell back abruptly, catching the operator by surprise. Before the man could duck again Rostyk opened fire and the degenerate was scoured from the vehicle. Keeping his finger on the trigger, Rostyk tilted smoothly to target the cannon, battering its casing until it erupted into a bright nova that tore through the truck's deck, incinerating the men crammed into its hold. The vehicle careened out of control and flipped over, skidding on its side until it exploded.

'Antonov?' Rostyk voxed as he raced on. 'Shark Antonov, do you copy?' There was no answer from the squadron's third member. Fearing the worst, Rostyk headed for the monorail and saw the tail lights of the train in the distance. It was still moving, carrying its malevolent payload to the Locker.

I have to get in front of it.

A Sentinel stalked out of the gloom ahead, coming straight for him. Instinct made Rostyk veer sharply away, carrying him out of the killing stream it suddenly unleashed. The other walker tracked him as he raced forward, the barrel of its gun blazing as it spun.

That's an autocannon, Rostyk realised as he zigzagged towards the enemy Sentinel. It was still recognisably a Black Flag machine, but its canopy had been sprayed purple and emblazoned with a jagged spiral. More importantly, its antipersonnel gun had been replaced with a heavier weapon, turning it into a vehicle killer.

Senka. Despite the changes, Rostyk recognised the Sentinel. Every Shark's Sentinel had its quirks and he knew them all.

'Traitor,' Rostyk voxed on an open channel as he sped past.

'Liberator!' Senka threw back as he gave chase.

Rostyk cursed as he saw the wreckage of Antonov's Sentinel ahead. The man had been a sharp pilot, but his instincts had always been blunt.

And I didn't warn him about Senka, Rostyk admitted. *I didn't want to believe it, let alone voice it.*

It was irrelevant now. All that mattered was destroying the train. Weaving about to evade Senka's fire, he followed the monorail, fixing his attention on the train ahead. He was gaining on it rapidly.

'You are serving a lie!' Senka shouted. *'You are all slaves–'*

Rostyk killed the vox. There was nobody left alive out here worth talking to. He caught up with the train less than a minute later. Gunfire poured from the windows as he raced alongside the packed carriages. Most of the grey throng was poorly armed, but occasionally heavier ordinance streaked his way. He ignored it all, intent on the drive cabin ahead.

I can't stop them all, but I can slow them down.

As he reached the second carriage he saw a hunched figure scuttling along the tram's roof towards him, its four arms outstretched as if for balance. It was sheathed in a spiny blue carapace that glistened in his lights and its jaws gaped wide open, showing dagger-like teeth. He tilted his laser, raking the roof with bolts, but the beast leapt across the gap and crashed down onto his Sentinel's canopy. Rostyk swerved about wildly, trying to dislodge it as it scrabbled about above him, then a claw punched through the roof, narrowly missing his head. It gripped the ruptured metal and began to prise it back as a man would open a can with his knife.

I'm dead, Rostyk thought calmly.

'Lethe endures!' he roared and jammed the accelerator down. His Sentinel hurtled forward, its legs pounding the ground like sledgehammers as they carried it towards the head of the tram. Warning lights flashed across his drive panel and the machine juddered violently, its engine screaming in the throes of a meltdown. As its canopy was wrenched away and the beast reached for him Rostyk hurled his vehicle in front of the tram.

'Can't see nothing, chief!' Jei shouted over the wind as he played the watchtower's searchlight over the ground beyond the wall.

'Pray it stays that way!' Grijalva called back, spinning their tripod-mounted heavy stubber in the light's wake. All along the Locker's walls the other towers were mirroring their own, fulfilling the last orders they had received. That had been over an hour ago. Since then there'd been nothing on the vox except the damned music. Grijalva tried his comms bead again and grimaced as the clamour assaulted his ears. Everything about that sound was plain wrong.

It's hungry, he thought with a shudder.

He looked around and saw that the beacon light of the comms tower was still shining. It was the highest point in the base, built to act as a relay point and booster for their vox. If it fell, their comms fell with it.

'It's not ours anymore,' he muttered.

* * *

'Arise with the Spiral!' Ariken shouted up into the tower's stairwell. There was no reply. Hesitating only a moment, she entered, stepping gingerly over the body lying at the bottom of stairs. 'Trazgo sent me to help, brothers!'

As she mounted the winding staircase she chanted the Mantra of Helical Concord, keeping her hands raised. It was a gamble, but they needed the tower back and this was the only plan she had. If anger was making her reckless then so be it.

I sent you to them, Ophele, she thought, *and they destroyed you.*

There was another body halfway up, straddling the steps like a broken doll. She pulled the spiral pendant from the dead man's neck and placed it around her own, clenching her teeth as she did so.

There's no shame in turning their tricks against them, she told herself, but it didn't erase the revulsion the obsidian spiral evoked in her. Her rage hardening with every step, she continued her ascent.

A trooper stood in the doorway at the top of the steps, covering her with a lasgun. Her heart sank as she recognised him. *Connant.* He was a former pilgrim and the first who had stood alongside her to fulfil Omazet's tithe. The ex-PDF man had quickly proven himself capable and risen to command a Driftwood squad of his own.

He's my friend, she thought. *One of the last I have.*

'Ariken,' he said, surprised. 'You're with us?'

'Where else would I be, brother?' she said fiercely. 'The heretics stole our lives, but they can't murder the truth!'

'Trazgo never told me...'

'He does like his secrets,' she said, throwing him a wry smile.

'That he does!' Connant's face lit up, as if her words had lifted a burden from his shoulders. 'I shouldn't have doubted you, sister. You were always the best of us.' He gestured urgently. 'Come inside! I have to seal the door again.'

There were two more armed troopers inside the room, a man and a woman, both former pilgrims. They smiled as they saw Ariken, their joy infectious. Another soldier was huddled beside the master vox set, his scalp bleeding from a head wound.

'Who's he?' Ariken asked.

'Vox operator,' Connant said, 'too useful to waste. Besides, I think we can talk him round when this is over.' He shook his head wearily. 'Too many dead already.'

'You're a good man, Connant,' Ariken said, surprising him with an embrace. 'You always were.'

I can't do this, she thought as she slipped her pistol free. *It's too much.*

But the instincts Omazet had forged in her brooked neither doubt nor sentiment. Ariken shot Connant in the back of the neck and thrust him towards the others, diving to the floor as he crashed into them. Before they understood what was happening she was firing again. Her first shot hit the man in the chest, the second drilled through the woman's cheek. The man's breastplate absorbed the blast and he stared at the scorch mark in shock.

'Ariken, what...'

'I'm sorry,' Ariken said and shot him in the head. She turned to the cowering operator. 'Kill that music and get the vox back online.'

You were wrong, Cross, she thought. *I am a Black Flag now. There's nothing else left of me.*

Senka roved the length of the wrecked monotrain, watching his brethren clamber from the overturned carriages. His old commander's sacrifice had paid off catastrophically. The train had hit the Sentinel like a bullet, obliterating both the walker and the drive compartment in a ferocious blast. Senka had watched in horror as the carriages behind had derailed and skidded across the rock, spitting sparks then flames before capsizing. The first carriage had torn free of the rest, rolled onto its roof and exploded as something inside – a grenade or a heavy weapon – had detonated, triggering a chain reaction. Nobody had climbed out of that inferno.

There must be hundreds dead, Senka estimated, his heart heavy.

Goliath trucks and mesa buggies were pulling up alongside the carriages then speeding on towards the fortress, their decks and cabins crowded with survivors. Senka felt a visceral thrill as the truck bearing the Primus appeared. The vehicle's purple bodywork was adorned with savage spirals and a cult banner rose from its deck. A pair of chitinous beasts crouched on either side of the banner, gripping the floor with a multitude of claws, their elongated heads flitting about like snakes. The Primus himself stood behind the wedge-like front, his expression dark as he surveyed the devastation.

'We shall have a reckoning!' Senka thought aloud. He saw another of the four-armed beasts scuttle from a nearby carriage and race towards him. Its carapace was lacquered with gold spirals and its left pair of arms had been sheared off.

The Riven Hunter, he realised, recognising the hallowed creature from Xithauli's parables. Pride welled inside him as it vaulted onto his Sentinel and clambered up to the canopy. It had chosen him to bear it into battle!

'I have been blessed,' he said solemnly.

Singing the Razorcanto of the Spiral Wyrm, Senka got under way again, eager to bring ruin upon the heretics.

Ensconced in the sanctuary of his tower, Colonel Kangre Talasca painted feverishly, obscuring the dark coil he had earlier wrought. The Spiral heretic had come within a whisper of turning him from the God-Emperor's light and Talasca burned with shame, but his rage burned brighter still, driving him to examine the web the deceiver had woven across his soul. It was incomplete and frayed, but its strands were everywhere and he forced himself to follow them. When Vyrunas had invaded his thoughts the magus had left his own unguarded, and there were seeds of truth scattered among his lies.

'My god sleeps... waking...' Talasca muttered, scrawling a spiral-bound eye, 'bound by flesh... buried in truth. *Truth...*'

Veritas! Talasca saw. *Their god is under the Spire Veritas and it is a creature of flesh and blood. A beast that can be killed by blade and fire...*

His hands were whirling now, working in synchronicity to weave new patterns betwixt the old. To saner eyes their creation would have been sense-less, but to the Retriever there was order in the chaos, splendour amidst the squalor. A face emerged in the crucible of ink, noble and malevolent, both elevated and tormented by the sea of thorns it ruled and rued. Talasca closed his eyes, though his hands continued their frantic dance.

'Look upon me, Retriever,' the splintered shadow urged, speaking in a swirl of borrowed voices. *'Look and learn the lies.'*

'Stand with us in the God-Emperor's name,' Talasca echoed the half-lie Vyrunas had offered.

He opened his eyes and looked into the dark coil.

And in time he understood what he had to do.

CHAPTER ELEVEN

- INPUT: RUN HOLOLITH -
- OUTPUT: ACCESS DENIED - SANCTION DIABOLUS EXTREMIS -
- *INPUT: QUERY SANCTION DIABOLUS EXTREMIS? -*
- OUTPUT: ACCESS RESTRICTED TO CONVENT
SANCTORUM SUPERIOR -
- *INPUT: ABSOLVE SANCTION EXTREMIS -*
CLEARANCE LEVEL CARMINE -
- *INPUT: GENECODE CARMINE FOLLOWS -*
- OUTPUT: PROCESSING - PROCESSING - PROCESSING -
- OUTPUT: GENECODE VALIDATED -
- OUTPUT: SANCTION DIABOLUS EXTREMIS ABSOLVED -

The senior tech-priest ceased its electronic babble and addressed the man sitting on the command throne: 'Sanction Extremis absolved, Inquisitor Mordaine.'

'Run the hololith, Logis Cheopz.'

'Confirmed.'

The air in front of the throne shimmered and a spectral image materialised. It was a seated woman, seemingly floating above the ground in a globe of blue light. Her emaciated face was framed in a severe bob of white hair and her posture was hunched. It was impossible to tell whether it was age or illness that had ravaged her, but for a moment Cross thought he was looking at a corpse. Then her eyes opened and she began to talk, her voice desiccated, yet commanding.

'I am Vetala Persis Aveline, Canoness of the Third Mission of the Thorn Eternal. It has been my honour to preside over the planet Redemption 219, formerly designated Vytarn, in the Ikiryu Sector, for almost thirty years. My identification ciphers are embedded in the encryption frame of this missive, so I won't waste my breath speaking them. I am unlikely to retain transmission capability for long so my words must be brief, but I have appended them with holo-pict recordings that will attest to their gravity.

'As you will be aware, Redemption has recently been classified as a shrine world of the Imperium. This is a status it eminently warrants, not least because of the eldritch malediction that its holy spires cage. The temples of Redemption are not hollow monuments, but living exemplars of faith and

fire – weapons against the Long Night. But like all weapons, they must be wielded. Our Mission has stood watch against the evil beneath the Koronatus Ring for over three centuries, fulfilling our sacred covenant with the Angels Resplendent, but our service ends tonight.

'The abbey has been overrun and my sisters have fallen, most in battle, one in shame. I am the last and I shall not outlive them long.

'Our doom was inevitable from the moment we pledged ourselves to this world, for that has been the fate of all its wardens throughout the millennia. We embraced that sacrifice willingly, yet I do not believe our undoing is the work of our oath-bound nemesis.

'Another evil has arisen on Redemption – something new and strange. Its aspect is foul beyond measure and the influence it exerts over irresolute souls surely marks it as malefic in nature, yet I can find no mention of its four-armed, indigo-hued daemons in the Apocrypha Daemonica of our Order. I must pass the burden of identification on to you, my revered sisters, along with the stewardship of this blessed, benighted world.

'Study the images I have encoded alongside this missive and name this new foe, but do not delay your retribution long, for though the Mission is lost the dark vigil remains. Redemption must be watched, sisters!

'In service to the Throne of Thorns, eternally.'

The image froze, rippled then winked out. For some time the witnesses in the control room were silent.

'Her warning never got through,' Cross said eventually.

'Oh, it got through,' the inquisitor, Mordaine, demurred, 'though admittedly not to her intended recipients. My predecessor intercepted the transmission and identified the canoness' *daemons* as alien organisms. The Ordo Xenos has experience with this species. It was not a matter for the Convent Sanctorum.'

'I don't understand…' Cross frowned. 'If you already had the message then why send us after the crystal?'

Mordaine waved a dismissive hand. 'The hololith crystal was a secondary objective… a loose end. It would be regrettable if it fell into the wrong hands.'

You've crossed a line somewhere. Probably several of them, Cross guessed. 'How old is that message?' he asked, following his intuition through.

'It was recorded over a century ago, captain.'

'You've known about this abomination from the start,' Cross said, appalled. 'You've been on Redemption all along.'

The cult was waging war on two fronts that night. As Primus Chrysaor descended upon the heretics, so Magus Xithauli ascended the coiled cone of the *Mandira Veritas* to aid the Spiral Father in battle against an older, darker foe.

'As within, so without,' she intoned, taking her place at the apex of the towering edifice. She raised her arms to the dome high above and energy crackled between her hands as she chanted the Mantra of Binding. Seven psychically gifted Neophytes encircled her on the tier below, pooling their energies with her own. Below them was a coven of the temple's most favoured Spiralfire Acolytes, who could offer only faith.

Below them all, crouched in the Gyre Sanctum and poised at the eye of the gathering psychic maelstrom, was the Spiral Father. His mind burned with the Ravening, but He resisted its call. To do otherwise risked everything, for He had another duty to fulfil this night – a compact He had unwittingly entered into when He overthrew the Spires' former wardens.

For deep below the Spiral Father, nailed at the metaphysical core of the Koronatus Ring, was *the Other*, and it could also taste the Ravening. While slaughter was a means to an end for the kindred, it was the end itself for the Dark Beneath the Spires. Stirred by the bloodshed on the mesa, the prisoner raged and strained against its cage, but the Spiral Father kept it pinned with an iron will. One of the Neophytes in the temple fell, drained to a withered husk to aid his lord's struggle.

The galaxy is rife with horrors, Xithauli reflected as she watched the cultist die. *Only unity in the Spiral can preserve the light.*

'This xenos strain poses a uniquely insidious threat to the Imperium,' Inquisitor Mordaine said. 'Its most potent weapon is deception, both of the mind and the body – and its patience is limitless. An infestation can span many generations before revealing itself.'

'You make it sound like a disease,' Cross said.

'*It is a disease*, albeit one with claws.' Mordaine pressed a button on his throne and a hologram appeared, depicting a hunched, four-armed monstrosity. 'The canoness' daemons,' he said. 'Logis Cheopz, if you please...'

'The Ordo Xenos has designated this organism a *Purestrain*,' the tech-priest said in his electronic monotone. 'They are apex predators, capable of tremendous feats of strength and stealth, but their primary function appears to be infiltration and infection. When they encounter other life forms they will seek to implant them with a xeno-seed that rapidly subverts the host's body.'

'The cult calls it *the embrace*,' Mordaine said with a hint of distaste. 'The victims appear unchanged, but deep in their blood they are no longer entirely human. Their offspring will be monstrous hybrids of man and alien.'

'The deception is refined with each succeeding generation,' Cheopz said. 'Our observations suggest the hybrids are superficially equivalent to the standard human template by the fourth generation.'

Hairless and crested and sapphire-eyed... Cross' mind reeled as the truth he had only glimpsed before was drawn into pitiless focus.

'It doesn't end, does it,' he said quietly, 'after the fourth generation.'

'No, it begins again,' Mordaine said. 'Our observations suggest the fifth generation are always Purestrains.'

It's been over a century, Cross thought. *How often has the cycle repeated? How many of them are there?*

The vid-screens flickered as a tremor ran through the chamber.

'What in Throne's name was that?' Trujilo asked uneasily.

'The Koronatus Ring is currently experiencing a high level of seismic instability,' Cheopz replied as if he were commenting on a mild rainfall. 'Such spikes are rare, but not unprecedented. Anxiety is not required.'

'We're sitting on top of a volcano here, cog-priest!'

'The probability that a substantive eruption will be induced is minimal.'

The *Mandira Veritas* shook, gripped by a subterranean seizure as the Other lashed about in its cage. Xithauli felt the Spiral Father's mind tense as He tightened His grip on the prisoner, using the Spires to focus His will into a weapon. Another of the Neophytes encircling her fell, his mind snuffed out to vitalise their lord's psychic riposte. Only five of the disciples remained, yet Xithauli sensed this battle would last the night, echoing the eruption of blood and fire out on the mesa.

Our lord is also caged, she realised, *ensnared by the burden of vigilance and salvation.*

'That is the fate of all true gods and emperors,' a distant, nameless voice whispered from the torrent of conflicting hungers, *'four-armed or otherwise.'*

'How did these xenos get to Redemption?' Cross asked.

'The Purestrains possess no technology,' the tech-priest answered. 'Their most common mode of proliferation is concealment aboard Imperial vessels.'

'*We* carry them between worlds,' Mordaine said. 'In Redemption's case we believe it was freighter called the *Obariyon*. It was almost certainly pure chance.'

Nothing is chance, Cross thought impulsively.

'The canoness' warning presented us with an unparalleled opportunity to study the pathology of the contagion from its inception,' Logis Cheopz droned. 'Moreover, this planet's isolation was conducive to a rigorous, yet covert quarantine.'

'But its promethium trade–'

'Was with us, captain,' Mordaine said. 'Our operatives bought whatever Redemption had to sell and destroyed it.'

'The conclave has observed exacting security protocols throughout,' Cheopz added, somehow managing to sound prim, 'however the imperative of this xenos strain is *propagation*, therefore sporadic breaches were tolerated and cult missionaries were permitted passage off-world. Naturally all were excised in orbit.'

'So how did they get their damned message out?' Cross challenged.

'They did not.'

'You're wrong, cog-priest! The pilgrims kept coming to this Throne forsaken...' Cross trailed off as he saw the truth. 'It was your conclave. You lured the pilgrims here.'

'Supplementary subjects were required to sustain the integrity of the experiment,' Cheopz confirmed. 'Significant data pertaining to the xenos lifecycle accrued from their assimilation into the Brood.'

'You dropped civilians into the web and watched the xenos eat them alive.'

'On a genetic level that is technically correct, however–'

'What about the Black Flags?' Trujilo cut in. 'Are we here to feed your spiders too?'

'No, trooper,' the inquisitor said, 'your regiment was selected for its belligerence and tendency towards paranoia. Admirable traits under the circumstances.' He looked at Cross. 'Don't you agree, captain?'

'What's he talking about?' Trujilo demanded, confused.

'They knew the Black Flags would antagonise the cult,' Cross said. 'You were sent here to fight the spiders, corporal.' Then he asked the most important question. 'Why are we still alive, inquisitor?'

CHAPTER TWELVE

Ariken's squad was waiting for her in the infirmary. Five of them had survived Trazgo's trap, but two were in no shape to fight.

'I did my best,' Heike told her, 'but I'm no medicae and Saul bled out on the way here.' Her craggy face was still streaked with blood and grime.

'The beast tore off his arm,' Ariken said. 'There was nothing you could do.' She looked at the bunks lining the infirmary. Some were occupied by recently wounded troopers, but most held men and women in the last stages of the Black Breath. The strongest had a few weeks left at best, but she suspected the Locker itself had much less.

Tonight will decide it, Ariken thought. *We need everybody.*

'Round up weapons for everyone,' she said, heading for the medical supply cabinet.

'Everyone?' Heike called after her, confused.

'I'm going to get them on their feet.'

If nothing else, it will be a cleaner way to die.

'The ammo depot is gone,' Kazán shouted over the wind.

'Can we salvage anything, major?' Omazet replied from his vox bead.

Kazán glared at the rubble where the building had stood. 'If we have many hours to spare!'

'I think that is unlikely.'

'Has there been any word from Rostyk?'

'Nothing since his patrol left.'

'He cannot be trusted,' Kazán cautioned. 'He defended the heretics.'

'Major Rostyk dislikes change. He... Hold please, major.' Kazán scowled, waiting. When Omazet spoke again there was a new urgency in her voice: *'Something is happening at the gates. A crowd from the city.'*

'On my way,' Kazán growled.

'Major Kazán is en route,' Omazet said into her vox set. 'Await his arrival.'

'Acknowledged, captain. Gatehouse out.'

With the comms tower recaptured, the fort's vox had been restored and the Bridge was buzzing with incoming reports.

'Tower Twelve has fallen silent,' Lieutenant Mellier reported from her post. 'Thirteen has supplied an old watchword.'

'Twelve *and* Thirteen,' Omazet hissed. 'That leaves a blind stretch of wall to the east.'

'I have despatched Squad Terziu to investigate,' the young lieutenant said.

Mellier is efficient, Omazet decided, *and she can think for herself, but unfortunately Corporal Terziu cannot. I want one of my own on this.* 'Send Squad Karcel in support.'

'Karcel is engaging traitors at the supply depot, captain,' Mellier said briskly. Then, as if reading Omazet's mind: 'Nyulaszi has the comms tower and Ariken is securing the infirmary.'

And I trust nobody else, Omazet thought, impressed by the coordinator's astuteness. The girl had a talent for this work.

'What do we have at Twelve-Thirteen?' Omazet asked, frowning.

'It's where the old monorail cuts off, sir,' Mellier answered immediately. 'The terminus is about fifty feet outside the wall.'

'Can you handle comms, lieutenant?'

Mellier hesitated just long enough for her answer to carry weight. 'I can, sir.'

'Then the Bridge is yours.' Omazet rose. 'Tell Terziu I'm on the way.'

'Light in Twelve's gone!' Jei shouted.

Sergeant Grijalva squinted through the soot storm and saw he was right. The watchtower to their right was dark.

'Get the light on it!' he called back.

Jei swept their searchlight over to the neighbouring tower and something slipped away from the beam, ducking under the battlements before Grijalva could get a clear look at it. His instincts were jangling, and when that happened Alonzo Grijalva always listened.

'Show me the wall!' he yelled, swinging his stubber to cover the intersecting ramparts as Jei obeyed.

'Dretch!' the boy hissed, resorting to a hive curse in his alarm.

A monstrosity was charging along the wall towards them from the other tower. It was stooped in a feral crouch, scuttling on six limbs like an insect wired on combat stimms. The beast's serpentine head darted up and snarled into the light as Grijalva opened fire. His salvo battered its blue carapace, but it kept on coming. Fighting for calm, Grijalva tracked the creature, trying to aim the bucking weapon at its head. Scant feet from their tower it fell in a tangle of kicking limbs.

'Bridge, this is Tower Eleven,' Grijalva said into his vox bead. 'We have–' He ducked as bullets whistled past him from the dark watchtower. 'Light it up!' he barked at Jei, 'and keep your head down!'

To his credit, Jei didn't hesitate despite the barrage coming their way. Grijalva was already returning fire blindly when their searchlight picked out the hairless, hunched figure manning Twelve's stubber. It was operating the gun two-handed, while a malformed third arm handled the trailing ammo belt.

'That a man?' Jei yelled, then yelped as his searchlight shattered.

'Bridge, this is Eleven,' Grijalva voxed. 'We're under attack from Twelve!'

* * *

'They say they've escaped from Hope, sir,' the lieutenant commanding the gatehouse walls said, offering his magnoculars.

'The Locker opens for no one,' Kazán said. He took the lenses and peered down from the battlements. There was a crowd of city grubs clustered about sixty feet from the gates. Multiple searchlights played over them, illuminating a swathe of grey jumpsuits and bald heads. He saw no weapons, but there were at least a thousand of them, so anything could be hiding behind the front ranks.

Kazán grabbed the gatehouse's loudhailer. 'Citizens,' he announced, 'there is no place for you here!'

'Please, lord!' a man shouted from the crowd. 'Hope has fallen to daemons! They are not far behind us!'

'Leave this area now!'

Omazet heard gunfire as she neared the fort's eastern wall. Two of the towers ahead were blazing with muzzle flare as they battered each other.

'Grijalva in Tower Eleven reports hostile action from Twelve, sir,' Mellier voxed.

'I see it, lieutenant.'

Omazet raced past a storage shack and crashed into a burly man. He spun round and she saw he was no man at all. The creature's face was a bestial travesty of humanity and its right arm bifurcated into a pair of curved hooks. As the monstrosity swung at her she leapt back, drawing her twin machetes in the same fluid movement.

'Heera-taahk!' the hybrid thing hissed, raising the autopistol in its left hand. Omazet lashed out and lopped the limb off at the wrist, then dodged away from a retaliatory swipe. The beast came after her, chanting a slurred prayer as it swung the hooks in alternating blows. She saw other figures clashing in the gloom beyond, the flash of las-fire dancing between them.

Squad Terziu, Omazet thought, *what's left of them anyway.*

A trooper staggered towards them from the fray. Omazet's opponent lashed out at him reflexively, impaling him with a reverse swing. With an ululating war cry Omazet leapt forward, spinning both her machetes into a stabbing arc as she attacked. As the hybrid wrenched its hooks free she plunged her blades into its chest and yanked down, tearing it open to the abdomen. The dying invader howled, lashing out with its long tongue as she thrust it away.

What manner of beasts are they? Omazet wondered as she stalked forward and cleaved the skull of another infiltrator from behind. As its comrade turned she rammed her second machete through its jaws and twisted. The creature fell among the bodies littering the area, both human and hybrid. The surviving Guardsmen rallied at the sight of her and charged from cover to engage the intruders.

'Bridge, I need reinforcements at Twelve-Thirteen now!' Omazet voxed.

'Confirmed, captain. Squad Karcel is en-route to your position.'

Shrieking a subhuman prayer, a cultist loped towards her with an industrial tool that ended in a massive circular saw blade. Realising that whirling, blood-streaked wheel would chew through her machetes in seconds, Omazet backed away. The hybrid grinned, running its tongue over snaggleteeth.

'The Spiral Wyrm has turned, heretic!' it sang it in a shockingly human and *feminine* voice.

Then it charged, coming at Omazet with surprising speed. She leapt back and the spinning blade scraped her right pauldron, shearing off a layer of ceramite. Almost unbalanced, she lurched away and crashed against a building. As the hybrid swung again she dived aside and the blade punched into the wall where her head had been a moment before. With a shower of sparks the saw chewed through the metal panel and its teeth caught for vital seconds. As the hybrid tried to tug it free, Omazet rammed a machete through its temple. Still gripping its weapon, the creature slid to its knees, carving a fissure down the wall as it fell.

It was the last of the intruders.

'We need to secure the watchtowers!' Omazet yelled to the remaining troopers. 'I think–'

There was an ear-splitting boom as the wall between towers Twelve and Thirteen shattered.

Major Kazán ignored the explosion. It had come from somewhere in the eastern sector – too far away for him to make a difference. He had to assume the Witch Captain had it covered. Besides, he had his own problems right now. The crowd of grubs gathered outside the gates had begun to wail, their voices blurring into a cacophony of abject terror.

'This is your final warning!' Kazán shouted as they advanced, moving as one. He pushed aside the trooper manning the gatehouse turret and seized the controls of its autocannon.

'Sir, they are civilians...' the lieutenant said, stepping towards him. There was a sharp gunshot and a bullet erased his face in a splash of blood.

'Snipers!' Kazán cursed, ducking behind the cannon's blast shield.

As if some secret switch had been thrown, the mob's terror flipped into fury and they broke into a charge, closing on the gates in a frenzied tangle. As Kazán had suspected, the ranks behind were armed, but weapons weren't the only things the crowd had been concealing: gangling, four-armed horrors bounded from the throng and sprung over their vassals like locusts.

'Gates are under attack!' Kazán snarled into his vox as he opened fire. 'Daemons!'

Gunfire blazed from the watchtowers abutting the gatehouse, their heavy bolters supporting his spinning autocannon. Las-fire rained down from the troopers along the walls, lancing through the night like darts of light. The blistering fusillade tore through the civilians, obliterating them in droves, but the chitinous beasts were much harder to kill. They wove through the barrage in a whirlwind frenzy and withstood anything less than sustained fire. As they drew closer they veered away from the gates and launched themselves at the walls on either side. Kazán saw one of them punch its talons into the rockrete of the western tower and begin to clamber up, claw over claw.

'Focus on the daemons!' he shouted. The arc of his mounted weapon couldn't reach the climber so he wrenched it free. With a roar of defiance, he swung round and shredded the beast. A sniper round whipped past his head, chewing off his right ear.

'Cowards!' Kazán raged. He knew there was no way to strike back at the snipers. They would be entrenched somewhere in the darkness, free to do their dirty work with impunity. He had always loathed their kind. To his mind they were the thieves of war, stealing lives without risk to their own.

'Reload me!' Kazán yelled as his cannon spun down. He cursed as he realised everyone else on the gatehouse walls was either dead or wounded, already picked off by the snipers. His muscles straining, he bent at the knees, grabbed another drum and rammed its belt into the gun's ammo slot.

'I need more men up here!' he shouted into the courtyard below.

He heard the throaty roar of engines and a pair of trucks appeared from the darkness, bucking on their bulbous wheels as they sped toward the gates. A bolt of energy lanced from the lead vehicle and punched a hole in the western tower, incinerating one of the heavy bolter teams. As the trucks drew closer their turrets opened fire, raking the walls with bullets.

They have better armour than us, Kazán thought bitterly. He rose to his feet and slammed the cannon's barrel down onto the battlements. Crooning to its machine spirit, he tracked the lead truck, sweeping its deck until the gunner in the open-topped turret was thrown back in his seat, almost decapitated. Moments later the one manning the energy cannon was flung from his post. Kazán stayed focussed on the battered vehicle until something inside it ruptured and smoke poured from its deck. Losing control, it careened about wildly and crashed into the walls.

'Vassago endures!' the captain bellowed as his kill exploded.

Grijalva watched as a plume of fire bloomed behind the hostile watchtower. The infiltrator who'd been firing at him roared in ecstasy as its tower collapsed under it. Grijalva ceased fire, aghast at the ruin that lay beyond the fallen tower.

We've lost the whole stretch of wall between Twelve and Thirteen, he realised. *The Locker is wide open.*

Burning liquid drenched the debris, casting a hellish glow across the compound and adding smoke to the soot storm.

'Reckon they blew the promethium dump,' Jei said.

The boy was right. Sector Twelve-Thirteen was where the city grubs had been delivering their promethium barrels since the Locker was built. The fuel had been stacked up along the wall over ten barrels deep, but nobody had questioned it. If the grubs were stupid enough to keep supplying the regiment with free fuel who was going to argue?

Except they were never stupid, Grijalva understood. *That was just us.*

'They're coming, chief,' Jei warned, pointing beyond the wall.

'Sacred Sunken Throne,' Grijalva hissed as he saw the army advancing on the breach. Its vanguard was a shovel-fronted truck with iron-shod wheels that churned through the liquid fire. Its deck was crowded with crouching monsters, but one stood boldly on a raised platform at the back, its scarlet trench coat flapping in the wind.

That's their leader, Grijalva guessed immediately, *and the bastard's as full of itself as any damn officer I've ever seen.*

A pair of hulking, malformed brutes wielding industrial hammers lumbered behind the truck on trunk-like legs, and behind them came a swarm of hunched, demi-human horrors in white robes. Though they were all equal in their ugliness no two were exactly alike. Grijalva saw a riot of hooks and claws and twisted appendages he couldn't even begin to guess at. Most of the hybrid things had three arms, but a few had four or even five, sometimes split at the shoulders, sometimes at the elbows. Bony crests were set into their foreheads and their faces were hideously serpentine, elongated and filled with fangs, yet still disturbingly expressive.

The spinning blades jutting from the front of the truck spun up as the invaders reached the shattered wall. Spitting sparks and rockrete, they began to grind through the rubble, rapidly clearing a path for the horde behind.

'Reckon we're fragged, chief,' Jei said.

'Reckon you're likely right, lad,' Grijalva agreed.

'Bridge, we have a breach at Twelve-Thirteen,' Omazet voxed as she watched the enemy truck chew its way into the compound. She and the survivors of Terziu's squad were crouched behind a pile of storage crates near the rubble. 'I need everything you have.'

'But the gates–'

'That is a distraction, Mellier,' Omazet hissed. 'This is the real push. Get me some armour or the Locker is finished!'

We are winning this, Kazán gauged. The assault on the gatehouse was floundering. No reinforcements had arrived to replenish the attackers' thinning ranks and most of the four-armed beasts were dead. It was just as well because he was down to his last ammo drum.

'Major Kazán,' his vox hissed. *'There's been a breach at Twelve-Thirteen. I'm redirecting your armour.'*

'Take it,' he said. 'It's doing no good behind the walls.'

Fresh troops surged onto the gatehouse from the courtyard below. As they fanned out along the wall a purple Sentinel raced past, strafing the battlements with bullets. Three men were hurled back into the courtyard as the others dived for cover. Ignoring the bullets whipping around him, Kazán stood his ground and chased the vehicle with his own fire.

'Spawn of Tizheruk!' he yelled after it.

As the Sentinel reached the far side of the gatehouse a beast vaulted from its canopy and landed beside a crouching trooper. Its elongated skull was crested with spines and its black eyes gleamed with cunning. Before the trooper could react, it reached out with an oversized claw and crushed his skull, killing him almost casually. Kazán levelled his cannon as the beast darted towards him in a lopsided scuttle, barrelling through everyone in its path. Only ragged stumps remained of its left arms, but he sensed this creature was no maimed, hamstrung thing.

Its wounds have made it stronger, he judged as he opened fire, paying no heed to the troopers between them. They were already doomed so the bullets were a mercy beside the thing's claws. His volley tore them apart, but the beast wove through the gunfire with terrifying agility. Bullets slipped away from its hide as it leapt back-and-forth between the battlements and the platform, its speed almost defying the eye.

'Unholy vermin!' Kazán raged as he hunted it, his whole body quaking with the cannon's recoil.

And then the beast was upon him, diving from above with its claws outstretched. Kazán lurched back as its blade-like talons sheared through the spinning barrel of his gun, scattering misfiring bullets. He swung at it with the broken weapon, but the beast wrenched it from his grasp and slung it away. With a creak of stretching bones it unfolded itself and rose to its full height. Though Kazán was a giant among men, the abomination was over a head taller than him. Up close he saw that its blue hide was inscribed with foul icons and a fragment of white armour hung from its neck.

A trophy, he guessed. The blasphemy renewed his fury and he flung himself forward, surprising his enemy. Wrapping his arms around its waist, he hurled himself over the platform, carrying the beast with him.

They crashed into the courtyard below in a tangle, with Kazán on top. The beast's arms were trapped under his chest, straining against him like coiled steel. Knowing he couldn't hold it, he yanked his dagger free, but as he thrust the blade towards its face he met its gaze and froze.

Beauty is a many-toothed wyrm unwound between shivering stars, he saw, *and truth sings bright unto the fruiting worlds that hang ripe and empty...* The stream of alien impressions flowing from the beast numbed him with inviolate nonsense.

'No...' he moaned as he struggled against the glamour.

There was a wet hiss and a rigid appendage extruded from the creature's jaws. It took Kazán a moment to recognise the dripping, thorn-tipped thing as a *tongue*. Like a spring-loaded dart the organ lashed out and embedded its stinger under his jaw.

'Kill...' Kazán choked at the shocked Guardsmen circling him. 'Kill...'

Something cold was pumping into his face, spreading a terrible numbness through his body. With it came a sour-sweet taste that turned his thoughts to sludge, dissolving rage into regret, hate into hope.

'It's like a disease,' the medicae girl had said.

Then the beast surged up and Kazán was flung aside. He slumped with his back against the gates like a broken doll. Paralysed, he watched the Guardsmen open fire on the horror. Its carapace broke out in scorched pits, but it shrugged off the attacks and leapt among the troopers in a frenzy of fangs and claws.

Sacred Throne, help me, Kazán prayed, fighting the apathy creeping through him, body and soul. Making his hand move was like climbing a sheer cliff – a

half-remembered talent from some other life, but inch by inch he forced his
hand to draw his bolt pistol.

By the time he raised it he had forgotten why.

Crouched among a riot of mangled bodies, his chitinous saviour turned
and regarded him. Its carapace was blackened and spattered with blood,
but to Shaval Kazán's awakened eyes it was beautiful.

The heretic truck was almost through the rubble of the fallen wall. It had
taken its blades scant minutes to clear a path.

'Bridge, where's my armour?' Omazet hissed into her vox. Karcel's squad
had reinforced her, but that still left her with less than twenty troops and
only a couple of weapons with any real punch. The stubber team in Tower
Eleven was still alive, but without support none of them would last long
against the horde coming through the breach.

'Armour is imminent, captain,' Mellier replied.

With a final shove the truck pushed into the compound. The pair of giants
looming behind it followed, swinging their hammers as they strode forward.

We can wait no longer, Omazet decided. 'Tower Eleven?' she voxed.

'I hear you, captain,' a gruff voice replied.

'The mob is yours, Grijalva,' she said. 'You have to slow them down.'

'We'll fill the Trench with 'em,' he promised. The revulsion in his voice
told her he would be as good as his word.

Omazet raised her lasgun and lined up its sights on the scarlet-coated
cultist standing on the vehicle's deck. Every one of her team would be following suit.

'We can't stop their army,' she had told her troops, *'but we can cut off
its head.'*

'Bleed him!' she shouted.

Her troops opened fire from behind storage crates and mounds of rubble,
all of them targeting the regal figure standing on the truck's rear deck. He
erupted with coruscating radiance as the barrage struck him from multiple angles. His shape was thrown into stark silhouette at the centre of the
aura, but he didn't fall.

He has a refractor shield of some kind, Omazet gauged. Such equipment
was rare and expensive. How had this heretic acquired one? She dismissed
the question as irrelevant. All that mattered now was punching through
the shield; they weren't infallible and this one was taking a lot of punishment. Despite the hail of fire, the warlord stood unbowed, as if he were
truly untouchable.

Is it real courage, Omazet wondered, *or just blind faith?*

The silhouette raised its sword and the truck surged forward, roaring
towards Omazet's position. Its gun turret blazed, sending a fusillade of
bullets ahead of it. She ducked behind cover, but the man beside her was
thrown back in a groaning, bleeding heap. A second volley finished him
before she could pull him into shelter.

'Stay on the mark!' she voxed her team as she rose and resumed firing.
'We have to crack the heretic open!'

Sergeant Karcel's gun spat from the roof of a shack, battering the warlord with molten plasma. The refractor shield flared up and winked out, finally overloaded. Omazet's next shot hit the heretic squarely in the chest, but didn't penetrate his ribbed breastplate. She raised her sights and saw he was looking directly at her, his expression mirroring her own loathing.

The Spiral isn't just a sham to them, she realised. *This is a holy war.*

Then the truck rammed into her barricade, its blades chewing through the metal crates in a torrent of sparks. Omazet dived aside and rolled as the truck spun about, raking the ground around her with stubber fire. She scrambled to her feet and ran for fresh cover as the gunner tracked her. Trusting to her instincts, she wove about wildly and threw herself behind a mound of rubble.

There was a throaty chatter of gunfire from the watchtower as Grijalva joined the fray, transforming the breach into a killing ground, but the monstrosities were breaking into the compound regardless. For every one Grijalva mowed down another two slipped through. Guardsmen were racing to engage them from all sides, either drawn by the clamour or directed to sector Twelve-Thirteen by the Bridge. They found whatever cover they could and opened fire, trying to keep their distance from the bestial invaders.

'Captain, I've been informed the colonel has left the keep,' Mellier reported. 'He's not responding to my–'

'Not now, lieutenant,' Omazet snapped, cutting the signal off.

She rose to a crouch, trying to get a bead on the warlord again. The truck had flattened the crates and was wheeling round towards her. A Guardsman darted past it and threw a grenade, but the warlord snatched it from the air and hurled it away before it detonated. A burst of plasma streaked past him and Omazet saw Karcel on the roof above the truck, his gun venting steam.

With almost feline grace one of the four-armed beasts riding the vehicle pounced onto the roof beside the sergeant. Karcel fired again without hesitation, searing away the creature's head before it could attack. As he turned back to the truck a long needle slammed into his cheek. Evidently guessing he was as good as dead, Karcel risked a third shot and the overheated weapon exploded in his hands, immolating him in plasma.

It was a mercy, Omazet guessed, seeing the bulbous needle pistol in the warlord's hand. *Whatever poison that heretic has will be vile.*

There was a clatter of metal as a trio of Sentinels strode past her, two of them heading for the truck, the last veering towards the breach. Trailing behind them came the ugly bulk of *Old Scorch,* the regiment's only surviving tank. The battered Hellhound's turret was swivelling about as it trundled towards the wall.

Father Terra be praised, Omazet thought. *Finally!*

Up in the watchtower Grijalva swung his chattering gun about in a tight arc, focussing on the inner mouth of the breach. As the invaders broke through he mowed them down, paying no heed to their sporadic return fire. The hybrids were clambering over their own dead now, but it scarcely slowed them.

Dying doesn't much matter to them, he guessed. *Might even be what they want...*

The blackout had finally let up and burning promethium illuminated the terrain below, giving Grijalva an eagle-eye view of the battle. He grinned as he saw the regiment's armour appear. It wasn't much, but right now it looked pretty damned good to Alonzo Grijalva!

One of the Sentinels raced towards the breach, its multi-laser blazing at the giant aberrations that lumbered into its path. The two brutes swung their hammers about in wide arcs, but the walker backed away as they advanced, staying out of their range as it harassed them. Hybrids charged towards it from cover, firing their autoguns wildly as they came. One of them hurled an improvised grenade, but it bounced off the vehicle's casing and spun away.

Moments later *Old Scorch* rolled into sight, crushing a pincer-clawed savage under its treads as it passed the Sentinel. The fat barrel of its inferno cannon shook and it belched a torrent of fire, its turret rotating back-and-forth to bathe the invaders in a wide arc. Cultists died in droves under the searing wash, charred to misshapen skeletons in seconds, but the giants pressed on, becoming mountains of melted muscle and bone as they drew closer.

'Back off!' Grijalva muttered, already knowing it was too late.

One of the brutes hurled itself forward and slammed down onto the Hellhound's cannon in a molten heap. Squeezing three arms around the barrel, it expired, clogging the weapon's nozzle. The turret swivelled about turgidly under the carcass fused to its gun.

The Sentinel darted forward to intercept the second giant with a concentrated hail of fire, focussing on the charred stub of its head. Heretics leapt onto the walker's legs, clinging on with their hands and hacking at it with claws and scythe-like talons. Grijalva swept them away with his stubber until it clicked impotently.

'Reload me!' he yelled.

'We're out, chief,' Jei said with a helpless shrug.

Grijalva cursed. Even if the ammo dump still stood they were in no position to resupply. 'Grab my rifle from below, lad,' he growled. 'The one with the long barrel.'

A missile streaked over the rubble and exploded against the Sentinel's left leg. The walker unbalanced on the shattered limb and toppled over. Grijalva hunted about and saw a goggled cultist crouched among the ruins of Tower Twelve. He was stooped under the weight of a rocket launcher and he was already reloading.

That gun's Astra Militarum issue, Grijalva realised, *one of ours!* His fingers squeezed the trigger of his empty gun furiously, sending phantom bullets at the thief.

The surviving giant reached the fallen Sentinel and raised its hammer in a three-handed grip. Grijalva flinched as it brought the head down in a crushing blow that cracked the walker's canopy open. A grenade exploded beside the beast and it staggered backwards, swinging its hammer about blindly, obviously confused by the attack. Its chest exploded in a boil of craters as rapid fire spattered it and a Chimera swept by, its heavy bolter blazing. The vehicle's rear hatch flew open as it passed and a squad of troopers leapt out. They rolled into a crouch as they landed and opened fire immediately. Moments later their transport took a direct hit from a missile and erupted in flames.

It's mayhem down there, Grijalva thought, then turned as he heard a pounding from the room below.

'They're breaking into the tower!' Jei yowled as he clambered up the ladder and slammed the hatch shut behind him.

'Hatchway is yours, lad,' Grijalva said. 'Kill anything that tries to get up here.' He took the sniper rifle from the boy and flicked the safety off.

'With what, chief?' Jei asked, jabbing his laspistol pointedly. 'They're dretchin' monsters!'

'Go for their eyes. You can do a lot with a torch if you point it just right.' Grijalva balanced his rifle on the wall and put his eye to the scope, searching for the thief with the missile launcher. 'It's everything or nothing now.'

'We will take the war to the enemy,' Talasca said, addressing the abhuman paladins standing before him in the machine shop. 'That is our divine mission, my brothers.'

The four giants rapped their power mauls against their white breastplates, their brutish faces rapt.

'As the heretics defile our gates, so we in turn shall slip through theirs, unseen and unopposed until we fall upon their false prophet. Tonight we are the Emperor's executioners!'

A squat, red-robed figure emerged from the armoured vehicle behind his squad and approached, its metal-shod feet clanking. The newcomer's face was hidden behind a black iron mask split by a horizontal visor, and angular armour bulged under its robes.

'I have completed the Nine Benedictions of Ignition, Retriever,' the enginseer said, 'and awoken the engine of your war carriage.' His voice was a deep, abrasive croak.

'You have wrought well, Tarcante,' Talasca said, eyeing the enlarged hatch of the Taurox.

'The machine's spirit welcomes such noble warriors, Retriever,' Tarcante said, indicating the ogryns, 'but the adjustments were the work of many weeks.'

How did I know I would have need of this? Talasca wondered. But in his heart he had *always* known it, hadn't he? Like everything else, it had been in the Dark Coil. Nothing was chance.

'It is time, brothers,' he said to the paladins. As they clambered aboard he watched for any sign of doubt. Ogryns were infamously fearful of enclosed spaces, but not one of the four hesitated. His heart soared with pride.

'Colonel,' Tarcante cautioned, 'the Spire Veritas is nearly five hundred miles distant. Even at maximum velocity the journey will take many hours. Are you certain you do not require my presence?'

'My thanks, enginseer, but this is a voyage we must undertake alone.' He smiled enigmatically. 'And the Spires shall guide our path.'

'He's gone,' Ariken said quietly. She closed the dead man's staring eyes, but it was an empty gesture. There was no disguising the agony he had died in. His body was twisted in the throes of the seizure that had killed him.

The seizure I induced, she thought as she turned away. He was the last of the patients in the infirmary. Eleven of the sick had responded well to the stimms she'd given them – well enough to get on their feet anyway. Three had thrashed about and fallen into a deeper stupor, and this man – Marc Hildago his name was – had died. Badly.

They were dead anyway. That was the logic of the Black Flags, the kind of thinking men like Talasca or Kazán – or her own mentor for that matter – would have embraced without hesitation.

Ariken turned to the ragtag force she had assembled. There were eighteen of them: the remains of her squad alongside the walking wounded and the risen dying. They were all revenants in a way, perhaps herself most of all.

'The regiment needs us,' she said. 'If we don't fight we'll die.' It wasn't much of a speech, but it was all she had for them.

'Spoken like an honest soldier, corporal,' an officer with cropped grey hair said. His name was Gharis, she remembered. She'd found him slumped against the wall in the comms tower with a las wound to the gut. It had cauterised itself so he hadn't bled out, but he was in bad shape. Though his eyes were bright with stimm-induced vigour he was deathly pale. Walking about was the last thing he should be doing.

'You'll lead us, of course, captain,' Ariken offered.

'We both know I'm just one wrong breath away from the Trench, corporal.' He smiled thinly. 'Besides, this ghost is yours to carry.'

She nodded, knowing he was right.

'Bridge,' she said into her vox bead. 'This is Squad Ariken. Where do you need us?'

This is wrong, Sheval Kazán thought, his hand hesitating on the last lever. Yes, it was wrong, yet it felt utterly *right*.

He looked around blearily. The gatehouse was full of bodies, their heads and chests ruptured by bolt rounds. How had that happened? Then he remembered: *they were all heretics.* He smiled. *Weren't they?* He frowned.

'Major!' someone called behind him. 'We've lost contact with...' The voice trailed off.

Kazán turned and saw a Guardsman standing in the gatehouse doorway, his face aghast at the carnage.

'They were heretics,' Kazán said.

'Heretics, sir?'

'They are everywhere, trooper.' Kazán shot him and pulled the lever.

Senka smiled as the Locker's gates began to part. Fitful gunfire was still coming from the walls ahead, but all the big guns had been silenced and the path was now open. The Spiral had turned once more, as he had always known it would.

A Goliath truck pulled up beside him. The cult banner soared above its deck, gripped by the Iconward Iaoguai. The First Acolyte turned and saluted Senka with his scything claw, his noble face grave. Senka saluted back, though he knew his brother couldn't see it. Their kin littered the ground outside the walls, slaughtered in their thousands by the Imperial heretics, but their sacrifice would be avenged.

Iaoguai signalled sharply and his truck sped forward. His heart soaring, Senka followed.

Tonight the shadow over Redemption will be lifted, he thought fervently.

As he loped through the gates a blazing light dazzled him and something rammed into his Sentinel with the force of a wrecking ball. His cabin pivoted crazily as his walker toppled over, then crumpled as the oncoming vehicle rolled over it. Senka shrieked as his legs were crushed under the drive panel.

When the collision came the Riven Hunter was crouched on the gatehouse walls, awaiting the Iconward. As its kindred entered the fort an armoured vehicle sped from the opposite direction and barrelled into the walker. Barely slowed by its kill, the enemy machine raced through the gates towards the mesa.

Without hesitation the Hunter hurled itself from the wall and slammed down onto the vehicle's roof. Grasping the ridged surface with its humanoid hand, it gouged deep furrows into the plating with its rending claw. The squat turret mounted on the roof swivelled towards it, but the Hunter thrust its legs against the gun barrel and halted its arc. As the cannon spat impotent bullets across the mesa, the Purestrain renewed its attack.

Senka's canopy had cracked open, but he couldn't pull his legs free of the wreckage. As he struggled, he saw Iaoguai's truck reverse alongside him.

'Brother!' Senka shouted. 'Help me!'

The Iconward spared Senka no more than a glance. As his truck turned towards the gates a shaven-headed giant ran forward and clambered onto its deck. *Kazán.*

'Please...' Senka begged as the truck surged away in pursuit of the vehicle that had crushed him. He choked as smoke filled his lungs then screamed as fire followed. The canopy was burning around him.

Xithauli! Senka clasped his beloved's image to his heart, but in those last honest moments he found no succour.

The armoured roof of its prey finally gave way and the Riven Hunter's claw punched through to the cabin beneath. Gripping the torn metal, it ripped away a chunk of plating to create a fissure. Eager for slaughter, the beast squeezed its torso into the gap like a lizard. As it pressed forward slab-like hands seized it and heaved it inside. Surprised, the Purestrain struggled in their grip and whipped over onto its back.

'Purge the unclean!' someone shouted.

The Hunter saw the glint of silver eyes from somewhere up front. Then the hulking brutes crammed into the cabin were upon it, cudgelling its carapace with crackling mauls that sent waves of pain through its body. There were four of them, all clad in white armour and open-faced helmets. Though their blunt features were contorted with rage they attacked in absolute silence.

Trapped between the savages, the Riven Hunter lashed out and writhed about to avoid their blows, but in its battle-wise heart it knew there could be no escape. After one-hundred-and-thirty years on Redemption and untold more adrift in the void between the stars, the ancient beast's journey finally ended.

Kazán stood at the fore of the truck, his hands gripping its frontal armour as he squinted into the horizon, seeking their quarry. Dawn was finally breaking. The blackout had cleared and pallid light wept across the mesa, unveiling the flat basalt plain.

'A new dawn for a new truth,' Kazán muttered, but his thoughts were as muddy as the sunlight, slipping between doubt and certainty with every heartbeat.

Finally he spotted the dark bulk of the Taurox ahead. The armoured vehicle was heading for Spire Veritas, exactly as the holy Iconward had suspected. Kazán glanced at the hybrid champion who bore the banner of the Spiral Wyrm and frowned. For a moment he had seen a monster.

The chatter of gunfire from the truck's turret roused him and he ducked as the Taurox's cannon fired back. As they closed on their quarry Kazán's eyes were drawn to the silver eagle emblazoned on its rear hatch. The symbol shone with purity, burning through the slurry of lies in his skull.

They are like a disease, Kazán remembered. *An unholy plague...*

He looked at the Iconward again. This time the monster remained.

'I am tainted,' Kazán whispered. He embraced the horror, using it to hold back the lies. They were already rising in him again, oozing into his mind from his unclean blood. He knew he would be irrevocably lost in a few hours.

I killed my comrades...

Staying low, Kazán crawled to the gun turret and rose behind its operator. Fixing the silver eagle in his mind, he clamped his hands around the cultist's head and twisted sharply.

'For the Emperor!' he bellowed.

There was a howl of rage behind him as he hauled the limp body from its chair and seized the controls of the stubber. Squeezing down on the trigger, Kazán spun the bucking gun round, meeting the Iconward's lunge with a storm of bullets. The sharpened haft of the banner plunged into his chest as his volley hammered into the champion, obliterating its torso. Coughing blood, Kazán kept firing, propelling the dying Iconward backwards until it was thrown from the truck. Then he angled the gun towards the banner jutting from his chest...

He froze, held rigid by the razor-clawed spiral hanging before him.

All are One in the Spiral, his blood sang. *Arise in the wake of the Four-Armed God!*

He shuddered as his punctured lungs gave out. The spasm broke the banner's hold and he opened fire, shredding the unclean standard into tatters. As his vision darkened he staggered round, longing for a last glimpse of the silver eagle that had redeemed him.

The horizon ahead was empty.

It's gone, Kazán realised dully. *How...*

He died before he could complete the thought.

'Way is clear,' Uchzhaf the Four-Clawed growled sibilantly as it scanned the deserted expanse of the landing field. 'Guards is gone.'

Uchzhaf was a hybrid of the Second Paradigm, blessed with four arms and a face that had more in common with a Purestrain than a man. The Acolyte leader's naked torso was covered in chitinous plates, and a whorled horn jutted from its forehead. Speech was as arduous for Uchzhaf as walking was for the old man who cowered beside it.

To Matias, who was neither truly kindred nor a warrior, Uchzhaf was a terrifying and magnificent figure – everything that he himself longed to be. And yet, despite his frail body, Matias knew he was more valuable than the Four-Clawed, for the cult's future beyond Redemption lay in *his* hands – his and the three Purestrains that accompanied them.

'Won't the sound of the engines draw them back?' he asked anxiously, eyeing the cargo freighter on the central landing pad. 'The vessel has not stirred in years. It will take time to rouse its spirit.'

'Outsiders busy, brother,' Uchzhaf hissed. The Acolyte surged from their hiding place behind a stack of crates and loped towards the ship. 'Follow.'

Matias obeyed, his legs protesting as he rose. One of the Purestrains lifted him gently in its long-fingered claws and carried him, as it had done since their party had infiltrated the fortress during the chaos of the battle. Without the creature's help Matias wouldn't have lasted ten minutes. He had been well into his middle years when the cult had embraced him – over thirty years ago now – and only the Blessing in his blood had kept him alive. He had come to Redemption among the Nineteenth Congregation – just another pilgrim seeking answers the Imperium couldn't offer – but the Gyre Magus had singled him out as *special*, for in his former life he had been a pilot.

What if the access codes Trazgo stole don't work? Matias agonised as they neared the vessel. *Or what if the craft's machine spirit denies my imprecations? What if I've lost the knack?*

He crushed the doubts. They were the lingering stain of his old life, but he had transcended such things. The Spiral had brought him this far and he would not fail it.

'I will carry the Blessing to the stars!' he vowed.

The Valkyrie rose with a clamour of thrusters and surged forward. Fighting his nausea, Cross weighed up the soldiers crowded into the cabin with him. Clavel had called them Tempestus Scions. He claimed they were fearless killing machines who lived only to serve the Emperor and Cross saw no

PETER FEHERVARI

reason to doubt it. Once again, the troops sat in rigid silence, as if this was a routine patrol rather than the suicide mission Cross suspected.

'Why are we still alive?' he had asked the inquisitor.

'If you can't answer that question yourself then I fear I've overestimated you, captain,' Mordaine had replied seriously.

'You think we might be useful.'

It had been the only possible answer, but given where their ship was heading their usefulness probably wouldn't last long. The *Mandira Veritas* was the Spiral Dawn's foremost temple and the nerve centre of the entire organisation. Even with the mass of the cult's forces drawn to the Locker, it would be heavily guarded.

'Consider it a rite of passage,' Mordaine had said as the Excision Team prepared itself for the mission. *'If you're the man I think you are, you will survive.'*

'I always wanted to try the heavier gear,' Trujilo said beside Cross, tapping his carapace armour, 'but this chafes like the Trenchrot. This on the other hand...' he hefted his rifle, *'this* I like. They say hellguns pack twice the heat of a regular torch.'

'The weapon is called a hot-shot lasgun,' one of the soldiers opposite said, his voice sounding synthetic through his mask.

'Always be a hellgun to me, brother,' Trujilo growled.

Like the carapace armour Clavel had issued them, hellguns were reserved for the Astra Militarum's finest, but Cross had declined one himself, favouring his old bolt pistol and Quezada's power sword.

Quezada... Gybzan... Regev... Rahel... The names of the lost veterans spooled through his mind again, all of them sacrificed for Mordaine's experiment. And likely as not, the rest of the regiment would follow them tonight.

'Why didn't you warn them?' Cross had demanded at the end. *'If you wanted to shut down the cult then why not send the regiment in with its eyes open?'*

'Ignorance was part *of the computation,'* Mordaine had answered. *'This contagion is not an isolated incident, Cross. I believe the Brood have spread throughout the Imperium, devouring entire societies from within.'* For the first time, Cross had detected a trace of emotion, though he was still unsure if that cold, rational enmity really counted. *'They prey on ignorance. The question is whether ignorance can ever endure against them.'*

'So just end the lies,' Cross had urged. *'Warn everyone!'*

Mordaine had stared at him as if he were a madman.

Talasca... Lazaro... Ariken...

'Did you have any loyalty to them?' Cross asked the pale-eyed man sitting on his other side. 'To the Black Flags?'

Clavel answered without hesitation: 'My loyalty is to the Imperium.'

'So you snooped on us and strung us along,' Trujilo accused. 'What else? You seed the Locker with spy-tech so your cog-boys could watch us dance?'

Clavel didn't answer. He closed his eyes and began to breathe deeply.

'Remind me again why we're fighting for these bastards, Cross?' Trujilo asked.

'Because the other ones are much worse, my friend.'
And that's the whole sorry story of the Imperium, Cross decided.

CHAPTER THIRTEEN

The skull-faced woman crossed the frozen plain, numb to misery and pain alike. Betrayal and broken bones were insignificant beside the simple imperative of survival. All that mattered was taking one more step, and after that *just one more*, on and on, deceiving herself with small victories so she wouldn't abandon the endless, hopeless march.

Sometimes a shadow walked beside her, though there was no light on the tundra to sustain it. She never looked at it directly, fearful that it would fade beneath her gaze, or worse yet, harden into reality, but occasionally she glimpsed the harrowed geometry of its visage.

It is a dark companion, she judged, *as am I.*

'What do you want from me?' she asked eventually.

'You are walking an old battlefield, *Le Mal Kalfu,*' the shadow said, addressing her by her true name, 'but it can kill you all the same.'

Oblazt, she remembered, *a world of cold wastes and colder betrayal.*

'I endured,' she said fiercely. 'I endure...'

The blizzard darkened into swirling soot and the ice became obsidian. *Redemption, a world ablaze with new betrayals...*

Adeola Omazet awoke to the new battlefield.

She saw the cult's truck accelerate towards her once more, its grinders chewing through the reckless Sentinel it had just destroyed. The scarlet-coated warlord on its deck was looking straight at her again. Omazet had no idea how he had identified her as his nemesis on the battlefield, but his perception didn't surprise her; he was a creature forged for war, his combat instincts tuned to a razor's edge. If she ran from cover the truck's stubber would tear her apart, but if she remained where she was its buzz-saw blades would do the same job seconds later.

A choice that's no choice at all, Omazet thought bitterly. *It's time.*

Her tongue prised free the tablet she'd wedged between her upper lip and gum before leaving the keep. It was a custom of her old regiment to prep a stimm before battle, but the blessings of the black pills came at a price, so she'd rarely used one. Now she bit down without hesitation, breathing deeply as fire surged through her blood.

This is not how I die!

As the truck bore down on her time seemed to flex into an elastic, ambivalent blur. Her muscles swelling with the flow, she leapt onto the rubble she'd been hiding behind – then leapt again as the truck's grinders rammed into her perch. Howling with defiance she pulled her legs up high and soared over its frontal plates. For a distended instant a storm of bullets battered her armour in slow motion, then she crashed down onto the stubber's barrel. It buckled under her weight and she tumbled to the deck as the weapon exploded in the gunner's face.

Pain wracked her as she rolled onto her knees and drew her machetes. Her armour was riddled with dents and she suspected half her ribs were fractured, but the stimm kept her muscles working.

Until it stops my heart.

Rising to her feet, Omazet swept past the turret and charged the warlord who stood on the rear deck. He opened fire with his needle pistol and metal darts pinged against her blades as she whipped them about protectively before her face. His bestial features tautened into a snarl as she closed with him.

'Heretic!' the warriors bellowed in mirrored fury.

He met her machetes with a long sword of gnarled bone and the chitin-plated claw of his third arm. His agility matched her chemically induced swiftness, and his multiple limbs wove about in an alien rhythm that would have overwhelmed a lesser opponent in seconds. Honed to new sharpness by the stimm, the rhythm of her decades-old razordance drowned out pain and doubt as they clashed.

I am risen!

The warriors struck and parried in an immaculate storm of blade and bone, each of them vying for an advantage, but every opening closed the moment it was glimpsed. Sometimes the warlord took sly shots with his needler, but she always saw them coming and blocked the darts. For all his skill, he hadn't yet mastered the *stealth* of close combat.

That is his only weakness, Omazet sensed.

She was seeking a way to turn the insight against him when a missile hit the truck at just the right angle and the deck heaved beneath her. With a screech of sundered metal the vehicle flipped onto its flat nose, catapulting her into the air. As it exploded she hurtled through the wall of a storage shack and crashed into a pile of crates with bone-breaking force.

The memory of the impact jarred her awake and Omazet realised she'd been walking another old battlefield.

How long was I out? she wondered, staring up at the shack's ceiling. Had her duel with the warlord happened seconds or minutes or even hours ago? She could still hear the clamour of battle outside, but it was fading fast, drowned by a rising hiss of white noise.

Did he survive? She tried to rise, but her body wouldn't heed her will. Wracked by wounds and chemicals, her muscles twitched impotently under her cracked armour.

'I have to finish him!'

She could *see* the white noise now – it was swirling around her in a blizzard, like hungry snow. It *was* snow, she realised as she recognised the tundra. She was back in the frozen limbo of Oblazt's Ghostlands, walking the empty plain once more.

Empty? No, not quite...

'This is not how I die,' she hissed at the shadow walking beside her.

In the sickly light of dawn the Locker looked like an unclean graveyard that had spilled its burden into hell. The dead and the dying were scattered across the compound, men and beasts alike torn, crushed and charred in endless disorder. Wrecked vehicles lay among them, some still belching smoke and fire, others long since burned out.

The unclean horde pouring through the breach had slowed to a trickle shortly before dawn. Now even that flow dried up, finally exhausted by the attrition. Likewise, the defenders' sporadic reinforcements had dwindled to occasional stragglers.

Enginseer Tarcante was the last of the Black Flags to heed the call. He strode into the mayhem flanked by a pair of massive combat servitors. The squat, red-robed enginseer swung about with his axe while his guardians decimated the invaders with the heavy bolters fused to their arms. Desperate Guardsmen fell in behind the cybernetic trio as they pressed on to a building opposite the breach and entrenched themselves. The servitors took up positions to the east and west, while the troopers fanned out along the walls or found positions on the roof.

Old Scorch trundled to support them, crushing invaders under its treads and laying down fire with its pintle-mounted stubber. Though its cannon was still hopelessly clogged, the machine's tempestuous spirit was undaunted. It had not endured the carnage of Oblazt by chance.

The surviving Sentinels and Chimeras also rallied to Tarcante's position, the armoured transports forming a loose circle around the building while the tall walkers prowled behind them. The makeshift bastion drew the horde like a magnet and fierce fighting raged around it, but the enginseer's defence was as robust as it was unimaginative.

Now there's a commander I have time for, Grijalva decided. He was offering Tarcante's forces whatever support he could from his watchtower, sniping at the most heavily armed or monstrous invaders. He had long ago slipped into a detached, perfectly focussed state, repeating the same killing cycle over and over – *seek, shoot, load... seek, shoot, load...*

The pattern drowned out the angry battering sounds behind him until the tower's trapdoor crashed open. Grijalva spun round and saw a hybrid hauling itself up through the hatchway. Jei jammed his laspistol into its eye and fired. The invader shrieked and dropped back into the room below, but another surged up in its place almost immediately. Firing on full auto and yelling curses like a madman, Jei spattered its face with las bolts. As it fell he stood astride the hole, shooting two-handed into the darkness below.

'Watch your power!' Grijalva warned moments before his comrade's weapon stuttered into silence. As Jei fumbled to change the power cell a whip of what looked like woven sinew lashed up and caught his ankle. He looked at Grijalva, shocked.

'Chief...'

The whip jerked the boy through the hatchway as Grijalva leapt forward. He flung himself prone and caught Jei's arm, bracing himself against the ground.

'Hold on!' Grijalva shouted, heaving with all his strength.

Jei's eyes were wide with terror as he hung suspended over the chanting, screeching things clustered around the ladder. The whip holding him snapped free suddenly and Grijalva hauled him upwards. He was almost out when a spine-backed monstrosity leapt up and caught his dangling legs in pincer claws. With a final shriek he was yanked down into the eager swarm.

Grijalva rolled away and snatched up his fallen rifle as the screaming started then ended with merciful swiftness. He spun and fired on sheer instinct as a hybrid emerged. The hot-shot bolt punched through its cranium and it dropped like a stone.

I'd murder a commissar for a grenade right now, Grijalva thought as he pulled his laspistol free. If he kept firing the long-las he'd wipe out the power cell in no time. His only chance was to alternate the weapons and make every shot count. If he could take down all the bastards who'd taken a bite out of Jei he'd call it just about even.

Emptying his mind of everything else, he sat with his back against the tower wall and killed vermin.

With a final heave the band of Acolytes hauled the twisted metal chassis of the truck aside and their Primus scrambled free from the wreckage. The Chrysaor's left eye was swollen shut and one of his human arms hung limply, broken in at least three places. His needler was ruined, but his hallowed bonesword was mercifully intact. The *Spiral Fang* was an artefact forged from his lord's secretions, and losing it would have been close to sacrilege. He felt the living weapon's hilt pulsing in his grip, urging him to finish the duel he and the heretic woman had begun.

We are bonded in holy war, the Chrysaor thought as he scoured the rubble-strewn area for his enemy.

'Primus, your wounds...' one of the Acolytes began. Almost of its own accord, the *Spiral Fang* lashed out and impaled him. The Acolyte's expression was blissful as the bonesword sucked him dry of vitality, transferring a measure of its harvest to its wielder. The Chrysaor shivered as the holy infusion rushed through his body.

'Take them down!' someone unseen shouted.

A grenade landed at the feet of the Primus. He leapt back as an Acolyte threw itself upon the explosive and erupted in a red geyser. Guardsmen appeared from the wreckage around his kindred, their lasguns blazing. He whirled aside as a stocky female soldier fired a shotgun at him. The shell tore a crater in the chest of the Acolyte behind him and spattered the Primus with blood.

'Dretch eater!' the woman yelled as she racked her gun.

The Chrysaor's jaws distended and he spat a gob of venom in her face. She fired convulsively as she fell and the blast punched through his chitin-clad left shoulder, but he scarcely felt the pain.

'For the Spiral Wyrm!' the Primus bellowed as he charged the would-be assassins.

Rage welled up inside Ariken as she saw Heike drop to her knees. Her friend's face was already swollen with the warlord's venom and her body was quaking violently.

'No!' Ariken cried. It was a pointless, empty denial, but she couldn't have suppressed it if her life depended on it.

This ghost is yours to carry...

Her squad had been advancing towards the breached wall when the heretic vehicle had sped past them. Recognising the woman skirmishing with the warlord, they'd given chase, but by the time they caught up with the truck it was a burned-out wreck. Then the abominations had turned up, wailing as they heaved at the twisted metal chassis. Ariken's squad had waited in hiding, letting them finish in case their captain was under the wreckage, but only the warlord had emerged.

You've killed her, you bastard! The force of her fury surprised her.

Ariken and her comrades opened fire as the bestial commander swept towards them with the last of his white-robed vassals at his heels. Las bolts poured into the charging hybrids, mowing down the underlings and tearing holes through their master's coat, but his darting movements cheated the eye and nobody landed a clean shot on him.

'Rage unbound is a traitor,' Ariken hissed, reaching for calm as she aimed, but it was far too late.

'The Spiral burns!' the warlord snarled as he leapt among them.

There are nineteen of us, but it's not nearly enough, Ariken realised.

The beast in scarlet swung his sword about in wide, sweeping arcs and slashed with his three-fingered claw, cutting a swathe of death through his foes. Ariken blocked with her rifle as he hacked at her and it snapped in half. She staggered back and drew her machete, hunting for an opening – for some weakness she could exploit.

Omazet would see it! Ariken thought frantically. *He can't be perfect.*

But she was not her mentor and she saw nothing except the torment of the men and women she had led to this slaughter.

'Run girl!' Captain Gharis yelled. The warlord's claw slashed his chest open in a welter of blood. As Gharis fell he fired a burst at close range, catching the creature in the side of the neck. The heretic swayed and stumbled, smoke pouring from his charred throat.

This is the moment, Ariken judged.

She leapt at the wounded monster, already seeing his death with perfect clarity as her machete swept towards his neck.

'For the–'

His claw whipped out and caught her blade before it found its mark. She pressed against the hard chitin and found she had no strength left in her.

Agony bloomed in her belly, but it was swiftly leeched away by a numbness that was somehow worse.

'So the Spiral turns,' the warlord snarled. He twisted the machete from her grip and it clattered to the ground.

There was a roar of gunfire from somewhere nearby and his gaze whipped away, seeking the source. Then he stepped back, yanking his serrated blade from her stomach in the same motion. As she fell she saw him slipping away behind the wreck.

There are much worse things out here, Ariken, Cross had warned her.

'What happened to you, ghost?' she wondered as darkness gathered at the edges of her vision.

'Do you want to live?' someone asked her. It sounded like an old woman, but there was an echo of another voice behind her, and behind that echo another...

'Do you want to live?' the trail of voices urged.

'Yes,' Ariken said faintly.

'Then look at me, Ariken Skarth.'

'Who are you?'

'Redemption.'

CHAPTER FOURTEEN

The rumble of the Valkyrie's engines changed pitch as the craft slowed and began to hover. Green lights flashed along the cabin and the rear hatch swung down with a hydraulic hiss. Cold wind rushed inside as the squad advanced in rows of three, the metal loops of their harnesses sliding along the guide bars overhead as they approached their assigned drop points.

Standing in the fourth and final row, Cross glimpsed the sweeping curve of the temple's dome. It was a colossal structure, its soot-encrusted glass reinforced with iron ribs that looked almost organic. A monolithic obsidian helix rose from its apex and smaller spines dotted the ribs, arranged in a spiral.

Did the cult build this? Cross wondered. *Or did they corrupt something that was already here?*

There was a whoosh as the Valkyrie launched its twin missiles. They streaked towards the temple, leaving white contrails in the dirty sky. A moment later an inferno erupted from the dome, cracking its centre wide open and disintegrating the helix.

'Initiating insertion,' the pilot announced.

The cabin lights turned red as the Valkyrie swooped towards the wound it had torn in the temple like an eager predator. The first wave of Tempestus Scions leapt from the craft before the burning plume had even faded.

Xithauli looked up as a thunderous blast reverberated around the temple. Fire blossomed overhead, raining shards of fused glass and metal onto the coiled pyramid below. Ripped from the psychic embrace of the Spiral Father, the magus reeled at the devastation.

'The *Helika Veritas* is gone,' she moaned.

A fragment struck her cheek, slicing and burning in the same instant. The pain roused her and she threw up a telekinetic shield, warding herself from the razor-sharp debris. Her eyes blazed as the Spiral Father gazed through them upon the ruination.

'The heretics have come for me!' her lord roared through her throat.

Dark figures dropped through the riven dome on ropes, spitting bolts of laser fire as they descended. Xithauli's heart pounded like a war drum as she tried to contain the Spiral Father's seething presence. Then He was gone, but his blessing remained, fuelling her psychic might.

'So the Spiral Burns!' Xithauli sang as she levitated above the pyramid's summit with her arms spread wide and her staff raised. Abandoning her faltering shield, she muttered a mantra of deception and spun her form into a cascade of mirror images, shrouding herself in illusions as searing bolts darted around her.

She whispered a blessing, focussing her attention on a band of Acolytes surging up from the tiers below. Her whisper rose to a shriek and the Acolytes wailed with ecstasy as their muscles swelled with unnatural vigour under her benediction. Their eyes glowing with violet light, they opened fire as they scuttled towards the summit, but neither their faith nor their weapons could match the invaders' lethality. Though the soldiers were moving fast and wielding their guns one-handed they fired in precise bursts that tore a swathe of death through the cultists.

Xithauli snarled and lashed out with her mind as the invaders neared her. A spasm seized her chosen target and he thrashed about on his rope like a tormented puppet. Moments later his goggles shattered as his skull erupted behind his mask.

The surviving pair dropped to the pyramid's summit and snapped free of their ropes. In smooth synchronicity they threw grenades into the throng below, then swung round to target Xithauli, sweeping her myriad images with las-fire. A bolt scorched her thigh and another drilled through her hip, sounding bright chords of agony through her body.

'As within, so without,' she chanted, embracing the pain and using it to strike back. She clawed at the nearest soldier's mind with her own, hunting for flaws. His psyche was like a block of iron, devoid of any doubt or vice to latch onto, so she wrenched at his motor functions instead, jerking him round so his gunfire punched into the third soldier. As his comrade fell, her victim snapped free and looked directly at her. Appalled, she realised she had stretched herself too thin and her illusion had fallen. She quickly hissed a new mantra, swinging her staff across her body and picturing a shield blossoming from its centre. The effort almost finished her, but the soldier's volley burst against the barrier in an impotent spray. Xithauli screamed silently as the silver staff grew red hot.

'Pain is a delusion of the flesh,' she chanted as her hands burned.

Screeching with wrath, the last of the Acolytes she had blessed surged onto the summit and leapt upon her tormentor. As they pulled him down with claw and blade Xithauli dropped from the air and collapsed beside them. Hanging onto consciousness by a thread, she rolled onto her back and saw three more of the baneful soldiers descending.

'Forgive me, Father,' Xithauli murmured as they picked off her Acolytes.

She turned as she heard the golden whorls of the Sleepless Gate swirl open, revealing the dark portal at the summit's centre. Her heart was pounding furiously again, accelerating to match the rhythm of her god's wrath as He drew closer.

He has abandoned the Ritual of Binding, Xithauli realised. *If the prisoner under the Spires breaks free then so be it.*

'This one's still alive, sir,' a masked solider said, looking down at her.

Another man appeared beside him and regarded her with pale eyes. He pointed his plasma pistol at her head.

'Where is your master, degenerate?' he asked, his voice as empty as his gaze.

'I come, outsider,' the Spiral Father promised with Xithauli's voice. *'I shall devour your soul.'*

A blast of searing plasma silenced them both.

Cross was the last to reach the pyramid. By the time he freed himself from his harness Trujilo and the surviving soldiers had formed a defensive circle around the summit. They were firing their hellguns in alternating bursts at the cultists charging up the corkscrewing ramp of the structure. Clavel stood over the body of a robed woman whose head and shoulders had been scorched away.

The priestess, Cross guessed, remembering the eerily beautiful woman he had seen on his first visit to Veritas. A woman who had never been human...

'No sign of Vyrunas?' he asked.

'Vyrunas died at the Locker some time ago,' Clavel answered. 'This was their new Gyre Magus.'

Cross didn't bother asking how he knew this. Doubtless Trujilo had been right about spy-tech being seeded throughout the Locker, otherwise there would be little point in the inquisitor's experiment. For all he knew, the conclave might even have surveillance in the Spires. He wondered if Mordaine was watching the Black Flags remotely right now, taking notes as they made their last stand.

I'm sorry, Ariken, he thought. He hadn't said farewell to her when he'd left for the abbey – hadn't thought he'd have to.

'So what now?' Cross asked. 'Their leader is dead.'

'The Gyre Magus was not their leader,' Clavel said. He walked over to the aperture yawning at the centre of the tier. Cross saw steps descending into darkness from its lip. 'We must locate the vector organism.'

'The hostiles are fighting on two fronts, sir,' the Scion officer reported. He was scanning the temple's distant floor with a pair of magnoculars. 'Someone else is attacking them from below.'

'Interesting, but currently irrelevant,' Clavel said. 'Our primary objective–'

Something vast burst from the portal in a tangle of chitin and engorged muscles, snatching up Clavel in its long-fingered claws as it surged onto the pyramid. The creature's elongated skull was crested with spines that ran the length of its hunched back and curved tail. A second pair of arms sprang from its shoulders, multi-jointed and tipped with immense serrated blades. Most of its body was sheathed in interlocking plates of blue chitin, but its bulbous head looked almost gelatinous, the mauve, deeply wrinkled flesh pulsating softly. Its void-black eyes glittered with a ravenous alien intelligence under the golden spiral etched into its sloping forehead.

What hope do we have in a galaxy that spawns such blasphemy? Cross thought, his sanity fraying as he gazed upon the Spiral Father. *The void between the stars is a cesspit.*

With a deep hiss the abomination thrust Clavel's head into its gaping, fang-filled maw. His legs kicked about as it gnawed at his skull, killing him almost playfully as it regarded the intruders.

Someone shrieked, lost and broken. For a moment Cross thought the madness was his own, but then he saw Trujilo hurl himself from the pyramid. As if the scream had snapped them free, the Tempestus Scions opened fire, their hellguns scorching pits into the thing's carapace. It ignored them for a contemptuous moment, its eyes locked on Cross.

'I can show you the truth you have forgotten,' the Spiral Father promised him, speaking directly into his mind, *'if you have the courage to see it, Ambrose.'*

The next instant it was moving, twisting about and lashing out with all four arms in a dizzying blur. Clavel's body swung limply in its distended jaws as it fought, dead but not forgiven.

I died, Cross remembered, *but I didn't believe it.*

He stood rigid, paralysed with despair as the skirmish raged around him. The six Scions fought with a tightly focussed ferocity that would have been impossible for lesser men – ducking and rolling and diving and firing as the eldritch nightmare hunted them across the tier. Their hellguns left scores of wounds, but none deep enough to slow their foe, and with terrible inevitability the men began to die.

The first was impaled as he dodged a whiplash strike from a serrated blade a fraction too late. The second skidded in a pool of blood, slowing him just enough for a hand to seize him and hurl him from the pyramid. The third was torn in half by a scything slash when his hellgun jammed and his attention wavered for a critical second.

The fourth to die was the officer, but he chose his own death, hurling himself at his foe as he detonated a melta grenade. The fireball carbonised the star god's ribcage and incinerated Clavel's corpse. With an abyssal screech, the beast flung the charred cadaver aside and rose up on its haunches, its body flickering with traceries of psychic energy.

Muscle and claw are the least of its strengths, Cross realised with horror. *The magi were only this creature's disciples.*

The beast lunged for one of the soldiers. He slipped between its claws, but this time its *gaze* was the true weapon and he couldn't evade that. His entire body convulsed and he slipped to his knees. The star god was upon him in a second, swiping off his head with a flick of its claws.

The last soldier didn't falter for a second. Though he surely recognised his doom, he continued the cat-and-mouse duel as if every second of survival might snatch victory from defeat. Watching the undaunted Scion, Cross finally remembered the impunity that emptiness offered.

Everything else is just a lie or a wound waiting to happen.

Without hesitation he embraced the void and the despair that had paralysed him evaporated. He activated Quezada's power sword and raised the humming blade. That was when he saw the newcomers. They were spread out in a silent circle along the edge of the tier – four giants with crudely noble faces and the shaven-headed, silver-eyed madman who led them. The ogryn paladins' white armour was pitted and spattered with blood.

They fought their way up the pyramid, Cross realised. *They were the other attackers the Tempestor saw.*

'*Reality is merely the illusion that prevails,*' the voice of the Coil had told Kangre Talasca when he'd gazed into its depths and awoken to the truth. His newfound sight had unveiled previously unseen – *unimagined* – perspectives, opening up the secret paths that riddled the ambivalent territory of the Koronatus Ring.

'*Mind, not matter, is the firmament of existence. Will, not body, the most primal force.*'

Driving the Taurox along a knife-edge between madness and revelation, Talasca had brought his squad right to the gates of the enemy, cheating not only time and space, but also the wardens his quarry had left in his path. Now all that remained was to fulfil his destiny – to slay the xenos god-beast that had tainted this sacred world.

'Nothing is chance,' he decreed as he weighed up the abomination at the pyramid's summit. 'We were born for this, my brothers!'

The false prophet saw the paladins and hissed. It stunned the remaining Scion with a cursory mental whiplash and turned in a slow circle, assessing each of the newcomers before moving on to the next. Talasca was the last.

'*Your revelation is just another lie,*' the Spiral Father whispered to him.

Then it lunged out with the full force of its will, its black eyes streaming vermilion fire as it sought to prise his soul apart. Talasca reeled under the onslaught, but his faith warded him for precious seconds and his brothers did not hesitate. Moving as one, the four paladins stormed forward with their Slab shields raised and slammed into the beast with crushing force, then began to batter its carapace with their mauls. Cross followed them without hesitation and Talasca understood that he was part of their holy circle now. Wielding his sword two-handed, the captain hacked and stabbed between the ogryns, tearing deep wounds into the beast's flesh.

Assaulted from all sides, the Spiral Father released its grip on Talasca and fought back, thrashing against the wall of shields that trapped it. Freed, the colonel yelled a wordless war cry and charged to join his brothers. He lashed out with his slender power sabre in intricate, twisting strikes that wove through to the sinews between its carapace, always finding a worthy mark, as if the blade itself was hungry for justice.

In turn the star god raked the barrier with its talons as its jaws gnashed at the paladins' helmets. One helm was torn loose and the beast's barbed tongue punched into the skull of the unfortunate warrior, seeking the soft meat within. The abhuman paladin held his position in stoic silence, hammering at his foe until the questing organ shredded his brain and he collapsed in a twitching heap.

'Tighten the circle!' Talasca shouted and the surviving paladins pressed closer, allowing their prisoner no avenue of escape. 'Scourge the unclean!'

They killed the god-beast piecemeal, the paladins slowly cracking open its carapace while Talasca and Cross weakened its limbs.

'For Redemption!' the Retriever bellowed as one of its scything claws finally gave way, hacked off at its elbow joint.

A second ogryn died when the beast finally tore through his shield and yanked him into its grasp. Another fell when the star god's barbed tail slid beneath his shield and stabbed up into his groin, punching through to his abdomen. But by the time the circle was broken, the Spiral Father was too weakened to escape. As it lurched brokenly towards the portal the surviving ogryn blocked its path, pressing the beast back with his shield while his comrades continued to harry it.

Finally one of the abomination's legs splintered and it fell in a knot of broken limbs and smoking chitin. It writhed about and lashed out at its foes until they hacked off its remaining arm. As Talasca raised his sword for the killing blow it fixed him with its black eyes.

'You are deceived,' it breathed into his mind.

'For the Throne of Thorns!' the Retriever shouted as he plunged his glowing blade through the spiral icon on its forehead.

Nothing else crawled through the trapdoor. Grijalva waited with his pistol levelled, wary of the silence. His entire world had narrowed to this grim vigil atop Tower Eleven, an eternity with his back against the wall, killing monsters. He'd long ago lost count of the number he'd taken down, but whatever it came to it *still* wasn't enough to pay for Jei's death.

The lad made the best damn recaff I've known since the Verzante piazzas, Grijalva thought absurdly.

Minutes passed, but the trapdoor remained empty. Eventually it dawned on him that he couldn't hear the beasts mewling and chanting in the room below anymore. In fact he couldn't hear much at all.

The shooting has stopped, he realised. *Has the Locker fallen? Are the bastards playing with me?*

Suddenly weary of it all, he hauled himself up and looked over the wall. In the thin light he saw that the fighting was over. What remained of the horde was retreating through the breached wall in disarray. He caught sight of the warlord among them, its trench coat tattered and smoking. Instinctively Grijalva reached for his long-las, then remembered its charge had died long ago. There was nothing he could do to the vermin so his attention switched to Tarcante's position.

The makeshift redoubt still stood.

'Throne bless you, cog-priest,' Grijalva breathed.

He heard a thunderous rumbling as a vast, angular shape rose from the centre of the compound. It took him a moment to recognise the old cargo vessel the regiment had inherited when they annexed the spaceport. Like most of the troops, the sergeant had assumed it was just a relic, its service days long over.

Who's flying the damn thing? Grijalva wondered as the vessel climbed. As it was swallowed by the roiling, lightning-flecked clouds he let the question slip away. Whatever the vessel meant, he was in no position to do anything about it.

* * *

'Clear,' Cross voxed the Valkyrie. He stepped back as it began to winch up the Scion slumped unconscious in the harness. There was blood trickling from the man's nose, but he was still breathing. Cross couldn't tell how much damage the Spiral Father's glancing psychic attack had done, but if anyone could pull through the trauma it would be a man like this.

He'll probably try to kill me for taking his mask off, he thought. *Or for freezing up while his comrades were slaughtered.*

Trujilo had also survived, though it might have been kinder if he hadn't. Cross had heard him moaning after the battle and found him curled up a few tiers below, both his legs and his mind broken. The veteran stared ahead with vacant eyes as Cross tightened his safety harness.

A seismic rumble reverberated through the temple as another tremor shook the walls. The quakes had begun during the skirmish and worsened steadily over the past few minutes.

It feels like the whole temple's going to come down, Cross thought uneasily.

'Clear,' he voxed. As Trujilo was winched up, Cross joined Talasca and his surviving paladin at the edge of the tier. They were watching for cultists, but so far the lower levels had remained empty.

The xenos are in shock, Cross guessed. *When we killed their god we hurt every damn one of them, but it won't last.*

'The Valkyrie can't carry the ogryn,' he warned the colonel. 'We'll have to fight our way out.'

'You are mistaken, Cross,' Talasca said. 'Karolus and I cannot accompany you.'

'That's insane, man. This place will be crawling with xenos soon.' *If it doesn't collapse before that...*

'We will not be here.' Talasca indicated the portal the Spiral Father had erupted from. 'We are going deeper into the Spire.'

That's insane, Cross wanted to say, but the expression on the colonel's face stopped him. Mundane measurements like sanity no longer applied to this man. The path he walked now ruled him completely. It probably always had. Whether that proved to be for good or ill, Cross was in no position to obstruct it.

Who am I to judge anyway?

The pyramid surged in the throes of another tremor, fiercer than any that had come before.

'The Emperor walk with you, Retriever,' Cross said.

'He does, Cross.' Talasca smiled and for the first time the expression appeared genuine. 'Come, Karolus.'

As the pair entered the dark aperture Cross pulled on the last of the harnesses. 'Clear,' he voxed. Ascending as they descended, he stared down at the desecrated temple – a temple that had almost certainly been built on the foundations of something much older.

Lie upon lie, within and without. Damned if you do or don't, he thought, slipping back into the lyrical patterns that had defined his former life. *Die if you will or won't. All's one...*

'Cross,' his vox buzzed. 'This is Mordaine.' The inquisitor's voice was badly distorted.

'Your vector organism is dead,' Cross replied flatly. 'So is Clavel, along with most of the others.'

There was only the briefest pause. *'Acceptable.'*

'What about the Black Flags?'

'We have a problem, Cross.'

'I asked about my regiment, inquisitor.'

'They survived.' Mordaine hesitated again. *'I regret to say their casualties were significant.'*

No. You don't regret it, Cross thought, *not any of it.* But he was too tired for real bitterness. Doubtless that would come later.

'I am relaying this signal via the Valkyrie,' Mordaine continued. *'The disturbance we are experiencing across the Ring is worse outside the planet's exosphere. Much worse.'*

'That doesn't make sense.'

'Redemption is not a natural world, Cross. Things here are… fluid. We've lost the orbital station. And my ships.'

'Lost contact you mean?'

'No… we still have contact, but the operatives on board have been compromised.' Another pause, this time much longer. *'I am not certain they're even human anymore.'*

'The Brood got to them?' Cross was shocked. 'How in the Seven Hells–'

'Not the Brood,' Mordaine cut in. 'Redemption.'

'The Black Needle unweaves the world amidst the fervour dreams of sinners become blind saints!' the voice shrieked across the flight deck, alight with madness. *'In fire and ice and poisoned water and with every breath of tainted air, the Word shall beget the Void and–'*

His hands shaking, Matias killed the vox, but he couldn't silence the *message* that fuelled the voice. As he stared at the ship's controls the twisted parable scratched at his thoughts, like a malignant seed that had taken root in his skull.

It's in the fabric of space itself, the pilot realised, *shrouding the planet like another layer of atmosphere. A polluted layer…*

The voice had exploded from the vox when the cargo ship had broken through Redemption's storm-wracked stratosphere. Matias had identified the source as a massive orbital station, and even a cursory scan had revealed that the place was bristling with weapons. That had been the first shock.

The second had been the insidious message itself.

'And a perfect geometry of mistruths shall unmake the prevalent horizon of sense and sanctity,' Matias mumbled, 'and carve stranger flesh upon the bones of self-deception–'

A clawed hand grasped his shoulder, cutting off the nonsense spilling from his mouth. The pilot glanced fearfully at the Acolyte hunched in the chair beside him, but he saw only camaraderie on its savage face.

'Take strength in Spiral, brother!' Uchzhaf urged.

'You don't hear it…' Matias moaned.

'I hear, but is empty words.' Uchzhaf squeezed harder. 'Is nothing!'

Nothing, Matias thought. Rather than distress, the pain of the Acolyte's grip brought a clarity that eclipsed the dark parable. 'Nothing!' he confirmed fiercely.

As he returned to his task the Sacred Spiral seemed to revolve before his eyes, spinning tranquillity through his soul. With a smile, Matias coaxed the ship away from the daemon-haunted world, steering his precious cargo towards saner stars.

CHAPTER FIFTEEN

The Spiral Father was dead. The Primus had known it the moment his god's perpetual psychic murmuring had ceased, yet he had clung to the hope that the silence might be temporary – that some unknowable event had disrupted the kindred's communion with their progenitor. That the blessed contact would eventually resume...

But there could be no doubt anymore.

His god lay sprawled at the summit of the *Mandira Veritas*, its hallowed carapace scorched black and its limbs hacked off. To compound the blasphemy, the Spiral Father's head was missing, either cast from the pyramid or carried away by a heretic. None of the kindred save the Gyre Magus had gazed upon the star god before, but even desecrated and ruined, His sacred form was unmistakable. The Acolytes who had accompanied the Primus to the summit were moaning deep in their throats, their eyes wide as they stared at the corpse. He knew it was not grief that harrowed them, but *confusion* – confusion at the impossible murder of their god and confusion at the silence his death had wrought. A silence that would never end.

'It is unwise to linger here, Primus,' a high, lilting voice said beside him. 'This Spire is no longer ours.'

The Primus turned to the robed youth who stood beside him. Gualichu was the last of Redemption's magi. He was not yet sixteen, but he already had the gravitas and bearing of a leader. Born among the kindred of Spire Caritas, he had been held in reserve during the Ravening, along with the rest of the Caritas Cabal. They were now the most numerous of the kindred, their Spire the cult's strongest bastion.

'What happened here, magus?' the Chrysaor asked.

Thousands had died during his attack on the heretics' fortress, including many of the cult's finest warriors, yet he sensed a worse fate had befallen the kindred left to guard Spire Veritas. When the remnants of his army had returned to the mountain they had found the bridge and the long road to the pinnacle abandoned. Inside the *Mandira Veritas* itself there had been hundreds of bodies, their bloody tangle standing testament to a fierce battle. Most of the dead were kindred, but they were far too few to account for the thousands that had remained on Veritas.

'Where did they go?' the Chrysaor pressed, his attention falling on the dark portal yawning at the centre of the summit.

'Nowhere we should follow, Primus,' Gualichu answered pointedly, following the warlord's gaze. He closed his eyes as he cast his mind into the contaminated aether of the temple. 'The Gyre Sanctum has been violated. The Ritual of Binding was not completed.'

'Then the Dark Beneath the Spires is unbound?'

'No...' The magus hesitated. 'Not unbound, but uncoiled.' An angry rumble rippled through the temple. Gualichu's eyes flicked open. 'We must leave this Spire now,' he hissed.

'We shall reclaim the *Mandira Veritas*,' the Chrysaor vowed, glaring at the portal as if it were his nemesis. 'The Spiral Wyrm will rise once more!'

But our truest hope lies with those who have escaped this baleful world, he admitted.

Three days had passed since the attack and Lieutenant Mellier was still in command of the Locker. There had been no word from the colonel and all the senior staff were either dead or presumed so.

Two captains had survived, but neither was in any shape to take over from her. Captain Gharis had lost an arm and far too much blood, but Enginseer Tarcante, who was the closest thing they had to a medicae now, thought the veteran officer would pull through.

Captain Omazet was another matter entirely. The salvage crews had found her lying in a wrecked shack, battered and comatose. Tarcante had done what he could to keep her alive, but he couldn't say whether she would ever awaken. The injuries to her body were superficial, but he suspected she was lost in some deeper trauma of the mind or spirit. Such things were unpredictable.

Three lieutenants remained, but Mellier's peers had deferred to her immediately. She still wasn't sure how she felt about that, but she had too much on her mind to worry about it. Right now she just had to do her job and keep the regiment running.

It's what Captain Omazet would demand of me, she had decided firmly.

Eighty-two Black Flags had survived the assault, including the armour crews, though over half were wounded, some seriously. Another nineteen had been out on the perimeter during the blackout, blithely unaware of the darker storm raging back at base. And yesterday a Chimera had drifted in carrying a pair of veterans, apparently the only survivors of an ill-fated expedition that had cost them two officers and the commissar.

'Captain Quezada's signal cut out,' the exhausted scout, Galantai, had reported in his heavy Szilar accent. 'And then the spiral-heads came for us – scores of them. I had to cut and run – to warn the Locker.' He'd shaken his head ruefully. 'I see that didn't work out so well.'

Old Scorch had endured, along with three Sentinels and a couple of Chimeras, but they weren't nearly enough to defend the Locker, so Mellier had pulled everyone back to the keep and dug in for a siege. It wasn't much of a plan, but it was the best she could come up with until she received fresh orders, which probably wouldn't be any time soon.

The planet's orbital relay station had fallen silent, but *something* was transmitting from up there, spewing out an endless stream of gibberish with the passion of divine revelation. As Mellier had listened to that frenzied voice the shadows in the room had begun to crawl, as if roused to sedition. She'd cut the signal off quickly and discovered her nose was bleeding.

There's no help for us there, she had concluded with a shudder.

The master vox pinged, startling her. She frowned as she saw the signal was coming from somewhere beyond the mesa. It had to be the enemy.

'Locker,' she answered, expecting an ultimatum or a threat.

'This is Cross.' His voice was barely audible. *'Captain Ambrose Cross.'* He reeled off an identification code. *'Who am I speaking to?'*

'Lieutenant Mellier.' She hesitated. 'Sir.'

'What about Rostyk or Kazán?'

'I am currently the regiment's most senior officer, captain.'

'Let me speak to Preacher Lazaro then.'

'Preacher Lazaro is dead, sir.' There was silence on the other end. 'Captain Cross, I said that–'

'I heard you.' When he spoke again there was fresh urgency in his voice. *'Listen to me, Mellier – you have to pull out of the Locker. Take what you can, but get out of there fast.'*

'Forgive me, sir, but–'

'The cult will be coming for you, Mellier. You don't have much time.'

'I have secured the keep.'

'It's a death trap and if you're any kind of Black Flag you already know it.'

Mellier sighed, wishing this decision would fall to someone – *anyone* – but her. 'And where exactly would we go, Captain Cross?'

'Come to Vigilans. We have a base here.'

'We?'

'An ally… I'll explain when you get here.'

'How do I know this isn't a trap?'

'It doesn't matter,' he urged. *'It's the only chance you have, Mellier.'*

'I will consider your proposal, captain.'

'Don't think about it too long.' He hesitated. *'One more thing… The medicae, Ariken… Skarth. Did she make it?'*

'We never found a body,' Mellier said, 'but no, she isn't among us, captain.'

'I understand. Thank you, lieutenant.' It sounded like he had expected the answer. *'Come to Vigilans.'*

The signal cut off.

Cross slumped back in his chair, rubbing unconsciously at his gloved hand.

'You should meet them at the bridge,' Inquisitor Mordaine said over his shoulder.

'I'm not sure she believed me.'

'As you said, it doesn't matter. Mellier is intelligent. They will come.'

You probably have psych-profiles on all their officers, Cross guessed. *Did you know I was coming to this forsaken planet?* He dismissed the paranoid notion. Even a calculating creature like the inquisitor couldn't predict such things.

Nothing is chance...

With a sigh he faced Mordaine. 'What happened to your men up there?' The orbital station remained lost to them. It continued to transmit its incomprehensible message in a ceaseless tirade, while the ships that had accompanied the station had simply vanished. 'What's happening to Redemption?'

'I don't know,' Mordaine said. It was probably the most honest thing Cross had heard him say. 'There may be more to Aveline's story than I anticipated.'

That part is a lie, Cross judged. *You never doubted her.*

There was a shadow in the inquisitor's expression that might have been unease, but it was impossible to be sure. He sensed that Mordaine had excised such emotions in a more profound way than Clavel or the Scions had done, or ever could. Everything about the man confirmed Cross' original suspicion that he was older than he looked. Probably *much* older...

You understand the void better than I do, inquisitor.

'How long before the Ordo Xenos sends reinforcements?' Cross asked, already suspecting the answer.

'This study is of an extremely sensitive nature.' Mordaine looked at him levelly. 'It began and ended with the Calavera Conclave.'

'So we're on our own.'

'Not quite... I have other operatives, but they are committed elsewhere. It will be some time before they respond.' That *some time* was loaded with enough ambiguity to stretch into years.

I won't be going home, Cross realised. He was surprised at his relief. Nothing but regrets awaited him there and he already carried more than his share of those.

'The Brood are our priority,' Mordaine decreed. 'It is imperative that we consolidate Vigilans.'

'And then?'

'Then we watch the Spires and see what comes for us, Captain Cross.'

Ariken awoke into a darkness more absolute than any she had known before. The air shivered with a low, molten drone, like the breath of a slumbering volcano. That ceaseless exhalation was hot and reeked of sulphur, yet the smooth stone she lay upon was cold.

'Where am I?' she whispered.

'Under the Spires,' the darkness answered, speaking with the voice of an old woman.

'Which one?'

'There is only one Underspire.'

'How did I get here?' Ariken demanded, recognising the withered croak.

'You slipped through a crack in the firmament. Redemption is riddled with them.'

'A crack in the ground?'

'In the *soul*, girl.'

'I don't understand.' Ariken tried to rise, but her body wouldn't obey. 'Am I dead?' she demanded.

'That is entirely a matter of perspective. Open your eyes.'

CULT OF THE SPIRAL DAWN

'They are open!' Ariken protested, staring into nothingness.

'They are not. Try again, Black Flag.'

'I...' Ariken floundered, opening and closing her eyes repeatedly, but open or closed, she saw only blackness. 'There's nothing!'

'Look *inside!*'

Ariken shut her eyes again and slowed her breathing, reaching for the serenity she had sometimes – rarely – attained in her duels with Omazet; a state where her body had been in motion, yet her mind had been perfectly still. *The candle at the heart of the storm,* her mentor had called it.

Motes of grey shadow began to bloom in the darkness like ashen flowers. As they blossomed they gyrated languidly and coalesced into the *impression* of a woman. The phantom was devoid of definition, yet there was an aura of terrible severity and age about it. Somehow it was *precisely* as Ariken had imagined it would be – a perfect counterpart to the voice in the darkness. Other figures flowed behind it in a spectral trail, their souls receding into oblivion.

The first was a giant resplendent with nobility, yet strangled by sorrow...

The second was a man who reeked of hungry dreams turned sour...

The third... the third was inscrutable and utterly alien...

A plangent mechanical ticking rose through the igneous rumble of the Underspire, like the pulse of a monolithic clock. It was punctuated by the grind and whirl of some impossibly vast engine.

'Arise in the Crucible Aeterna, Ariken Skarth,' the phantom woman said. 'We who watch over Redemption do not watch alone.'

Matias was slumped in his chair, the beatific smile he had worn since their escape frozen into his face. Uchzhaf the Four-Clawed could not remember exactly when the pilot had expired, but it had been many hours ago. Their stolen vessel was old and its systems had begun to fail a few days into their voyage. The air was now bitterly cold and so stale that Uchzhaf struggled for breath. Hybrids of the First and Second Paradigms were strong, but their human heritage was a flaw and Uchzhaf would soon follow Matias into the Spiral's embrace. That did not matter; like the pilot, the Acolyte had served its purpose.

Only the blessed ones are important, Uchzhaf thought, turning to regard the three Purestrains that crouched behind it. The creatures had no need of air or warmth. They could even endure the void of space if necessary, but Uchzhaf did not believe it would come to that. The ship was adrift now and its cogitator would only expend fuel to steer it clear of danger. Its blind voyage might last for years or even decades, but Uchzhaf had faith that the Spiral would guide its children to a new hunting ground.

'Sleep, brothers,' the Acolyte hissed. 'Sleep until the Outsiders come.'

Even to Uchzhaf, the Purestrains' black eyes were inscrutable. Moving as one, their heads tilted to regard the hybrid for a long moment. Then they crept from the room to seek a hiding place. When they were gone Uchzhaf followed, but its destination was quite different. Breathing heavily, the hybrid loped along the corridor until it reached an airlock.

When the Outsiders arrived they must not find the corpse of a *monster* on board.

Uchzhaf the Four-Clawed had one last duty to perform for the Spiral Wyrm.

EPILOGUE

There was no day or night, no sense of time passing or distance travelled, only an absence of awareness that ended as abruptly as it had begun.

The Sleeper awoke, roused by an almost preternatural certainty that things had *changed* – that the outsiders were here.

It slipped from the snarl of pipes where it had secreted itself and unwound its gangling form into a stooped crouch. The metal maze was lightless and cold, but a residue of air remained, probably because nobody had survived to breathe it.

As the creature crept along the corridor it ceased to be the Sleeper and became the *Survivor*, for the minds of its fellow hunters remained silent. They had not awoken.

Instinct had compelled the three hunters to disperse across their new territory, each one choosing a different region for its slumber, lest some localised catastrophe claim them all. That had been wise, for the Survivor sensed that the others were gone. Maybe something had breached their enclosed world or perhaps parts of its structure had simply collapsed. Either way the Survivor was alone.

By the time it reached the end of the corridor it had forgotten the others, its mind narrowed to a single, all-consuming purpose: *the Blessing had to be shared.*

It didn't take the Survivor long to find its prey, for the intruders moved about in a riot of noise and bright beams. There were many of them, all wearing bulky suits and masks, but few had helmets. Despite their lights they were blind to their stalker, for the Survivor had mastered every trick of the corroded labyrinth before entering its sleep.

As the intruders pressed deeper they grew more confident and began to split into smaller groups, until six split into four and eventually two. But as their numbers diminished so the intruders' caution began to grow once more. The hunter sensed that the pair it stalked would remain together until they re-joined their kin.

It was time.

The Survivor surged from a shaft above its quarry and scuttled along the ceiling, seizing and abandoning handholds with all six limbs. The persistent groans and creaks of the maze camouflaged its charge so it was almost upon the intruders before they registered the disturbance. As the one in the rear began to turn the Survivor snatched it up and cracked its head against the wall, rendering the creature senseless. Its companion swung round, its torch beam flitting about wildly before finding the thing on the ceiling. The prey's eyes widened above its mask... then dulled as they met the hunter's gaze.

Still clasping its first victim in one claw, the Survivor dropped to the ground and rose above its frozen prey. With a wet hiss its tongue extruded, dripping mucus.

Very soon the outsider would be kindred.

ABOUT THE AUTHOR

Peter Fehervari is the author of the Warhammer 40,000 novels *Requiem Infernal, Cult of the Spiral Dawn* and *Fire Caste,* as well as the novella *Fire and Ice* from the *Shas'o* anthology. He has also written the Warhammer Horror novel *The Reverie,* as well as many short stories for Black Library, including 'A Sanctuary of Wyrms', which appeared in the anthology *Deathwatch: Xenos Hunters,* and 'Nightfall', which appeared in *Heroes of the Space Marines.* His more recent works include the stories 'Aria Arcana' and 'Blindsight'. He lives and works in London.

YOUR
NEXT READ

THE LION: SON OF THE FOREST
by Mike Brooks

The Lion. Son of the Emperor, brother of demigods and primarch of the Dark Angels.
Awakened. Returned. And yet… lost.

An extract from
The Lion: Son of the Forest
by Mike Brooks

I

The river sings silver notes: a perpetual, chaotic babble in which a fantastically complex melody seems to hang, tantalising, just out of reach of the listener. He could spend eternity here trying to find the heart of it, without ever succeeding, yet still not consider the time wasted. The sound of water over stone, the interplay of energy and matter, creates a quiet symphony that is both unremarkable and unique. He does not know how long he has been here, just listening.

Nor, he realises, does he know where *here* is.

The listener becomes aware of himself in stages, like a sleeper passing from the deepest, darkest depths of slumber, through the shallows of semi-consciousness where thought swirls in confusing eddies, and then into the light. First comes the realisation that he is not the song of the river; that he is in fact separate from it, and listening to it. Then sensation dawns, and he realises he is sitting on the river's bank. If there is a sun, or suns, then he cannot see them through the branches of the trees overhead and the mist that hangs heavily in the air, but there is still light enough for him to make out his surroundings.

The trees are massive, and mighty, with great trunks that could not be fully encircled by one, two, perhaps even half a dozen people's outstretched arms. Their rough, cracked bark pockmarks them with shadows, as though the trees themselves are camouflaged. The ground beneath their branches is fought over by tough shrubs: sturdy, twisted, thorny things strangling each other in the contest for space and light, like children unheeded at the feet of adults. The earth in which they grow is dark and rich, and when the listener digs his fingers into it, it smells of life, and death, and other things besides. It is a familiar smell, although he cannot say from where, or why.

His fingers, he realises as they penetrate the ground, are armoured. His whole body is armoured, in fact, encased in a great suit of black plates with the faintest hint of dark green. This is a familiar sensation, too. The armour feels like a part of him – an extension, as natural as the shell of any crustacean that might lurk in the nooks and crannies of the river in front of him. He leans forward and peers down into the still water next to the bank, sheltered from the main flow by an outcropping just upstream. It becomes an almost perfect mirror surface, as smooth as a dream.

The listener does not recognise the face that looks back at him. It is deeply lined, as though a world of cares and worries has washed over it like the river water, scoring the marks of their passage into the skin. His hair is pale, streaked with blond here and there, but otherwise fading into grey and white. The lower part of his face is obscured by a thick, full beard and moustache, leaving only the lips bare; it is a distrustful mouth, one more likely to turn downwards in disapproval than quirk upwards in a smile.

He raises one hand, the fingers still smeared with dirt, before his face. The reflection does the same. This is surely his face, but the sight sparks no memory. He does not know who he is, and he does not know where he is, for all that it feels familiar.

That being the case, there seems little point in remaining here.

The listener gets to his feet, then hesitates. He cannot explain to himself why he should move, given the song of the river is so beautiful. However, the realisation of his lack of knowledge has opened something inside him, a hunger which was not there before. He will not be satisfied until he has answers.

Still, the river's song calls to him. He decides to walk along the bank, following the flow of the water and listening to it as he goes, and since he does not know where he is, one direction is as good as the other. There is a helmet on the bank, next to where he was sitting. It is the same colour as his armour, with vertical slits across the mouth, like firing slits in a wall. He picks it up, and clamps it to his waist with a movement that feels instinctual.

He does not know for how long he walks. Time is surely passing, in that one moment slips into another, and he can remember ones that came before and consider the concept of ones yet to come, but there is nothing to mark it. The light neither increases nor decreases, instead remaining an almost spectral presence which illuminates without revealing its source. Shadows lurk, but there is no indication as to what casts them. The walker is unperturbed. His eyes can pierce those shadows, just as he can smell foliage, and he can hear the river. There is no soughing of wind in the branches, for the air is still, but the moist air carries the faint hooting, hollering calls of animals of some kind, somewhere in the distance.

The river's course begins to flatten and widen. The walker follows it around a bend, then comes to a halt in shock.

On the far bank stands a building.

It is built of cut and dressed stone, a dark blue-grey rock in which brighter specks glitter. It is not immense – the surrounding trees tower over it – but it is solid. It is a castle of some kind, a fortress, intended to keep the unwanted out and whatever people and treasures lie within safe from harm. It is neither new and pristine, nor ancient and weathered. It looks as though it has always stood here, and always shall. And on the wide, calm water in front of it sits a boat.

It is small, wooden, and unpainted. It is large enough for one person, and indeed one person is sitting in it. The walker's eyes can make him out, even at distance. He is old, and not old in the same way as the walker's face is. Time has not lined his features, it has ravaged them. His cheeks are sunken, his limbs are wasted; skin that was once clearly a rich chestnut now has an ashen patina, and his long hair is lifeless, dull grey, and matted. However, that grey head supports a crown: little more than a circlet of gold, but a crown nonetheless.

In his hands, swollen of knuckle and weak of grip, he holds a rod. The line is already cast into the water. Now he sits, hunched over as though in pain, a small, ancient figure in a small, simple boat.

The walker does not stop to wonder why a king would be fishing in such a manner. He is aware of the context of such things, but he does not know from where, and they do not matter to him. Here is someone who might have some answers for him.

'Greetings!' he calls. His voice is strong, rich and deep, although rough around the edges from age or disuse, or both. It carries across the water. The old king in the boat blinks, and when his eyes open again, they are looking at the walker.

'What is this place?' the walker demands.

The old king blinks again. When his eyes open this time, they are focused on the water once more. It is as though the walker is not there at all, a dismissal of minimal effort.

The walker discovers that he is not used to being ignored, and nor does he appreciate it. He steps into the water, intending to wade across the river so the king cannot so easily dismiss him. He is unconcerned about the current: he is strong of limb, and knows without knowing that his armour is waterproof, and that should he don his helmet he will be able to breathe even if he is submerged.

He has only gone a few steps, in up to his knees, when he realises there are shadows in the water: large shadows that circle the small boat, around and around. They do not bite on the line, and nor do they capsize the craft in which the fisher sits, but either could be disastrous.

Moreover, the walker realises, the king is wounded. The walker cannot see the wound, but he can smell the blood. A rich, copperish tang tickles his nose. It is not a smell that delights him, but neither does he find it repulsive. It is simply a scent, one that he is able to parse and understand. The king is bleeding into the water, drip by drip. Perhaps that is what has drawn the shadows to this place. Perhaps they would have been here anyway.

Some of the shadows start to peel away, and head towards the walker.

The walker is not a being to whom fear comes naturally, but nor is he unfamiliar with the concept of danger. The shadows in the water are unknown to him, and move like predators.

+Come back to the bank.+

The walker whirls. A small figure stands on the land, swathed in robes of dark green, so that it nearly blends into the background against which it stands. It is the size of a child, perhaps, but the walker knows it to be something else.

It is a Watcher in the Dark.

+Come back to the bank,+ the Watcher repeats. Although its communication can hardly be called a voice – there is no sound, merely a sensation inside the walker's head that imparts meaning – it feels increasingly urgent nonetheless. The walker realises that he is not normally one to turn away from a challenge, but nor is he willing to ignore a Watcher in the Dark. It feels like a link, a connection to what came before, to what he should be able to remember.

He wades back, and steps up onto the bank. The approaching shadows hesitate for a moment, then circle away towards the king in his boat.

+They would destroy you,+ the Watcher says. The walker understands that it is talking about the shadows. There are layers to the feelings in his head now, feelings that are the mental aftertaste of the Watcher's communication. Disgust lurks there, but also fear.

'Where is this place?' the walker asks.

+Home.+

The walker waits, but nothing else is forthcoming. Moreover, he understands that there will not be. So far as the Watcher is concerned, that is not simply all the information that is required, but all that is available to give.

He looks out over the water, towards the king. The old man still sits hunched over, rod in his hands, blood leaking from his wounds one drip at a time.

'Why does he ignore me?'

+You did not ask the correct question.+

The walker looks around. The shadows in the water are still there, so it seems foolish to try to cross. However, he has seen no bridge over the river, nor another boat. He has no tools with which to build such a craft from the trees around him, and the knowledge of how to do so does not come easily to his mind. He is not like some of his brothers, for whom creation is natural...

His brothers. Who are his brothers?

Shapes flit through his mind, as ephemeral as smoke in a storm. He cannot get a grip, cannot wrestle them into anything that makes sense, or anything onto which his reaching mind can latch. The peace brought about by the song of the river is gone, and in its place is uncertainty and frustration. Nonetheless, the walker would not return to his former state. To knowingly welcome ignorance is not his way.

He catches a glimpse of something pale, a long way off through the trees, but on his side of the river. He begins to walk towards it, leaving the river behind him – he can always find it again, he knows its song – and making his way through the undergrowth. The plants are thick and verdant, but he is strong and sure. He ducks under spines, slaps aside strangling tendrils reaching out for anything that passes, and avoids breaking the twigs, which would leak sap so corrosive it might damage even his armour.

He does not wonder how he knows these things. The Watcher said that this was home.

The Watcher itself has been left behind, but it keeps reappearing, stepping out of the edge of shadows. It says nothing; not until the walker passes through a thicket of thorns and finally gets a clearer view of what he had seen.

It is a building, or at least the roof of one; that is all he can see from here. It is a dome of beautiful pale stone, supported by pillars. Whereas before he had been finding his own route through the forest, now there is a clear path ahead, a route of short grass hemmed in on either side by bushes and tree trunks. It curves away, rather than arrowing straight towards the pale building, but the walker knows that is where it leads.

+Do not take that path,+ the Watcher cautions him. +You are not yet strong enough.+

The walker looks down at this tiny creature, barely knee-high to him, then breathes deeply and rolls his shoulders within his armour. He presumes he had a youth, given he now looks old. Perhaps he was stronger then. Nonetheless, his body does not feel feeble.

+That is not the strength you will need.+

The walker narrows his eyes. 'You caution me against anything that might help me make sense of my situation. What would you have me do instead?'

+Follow your nature.+

The walker breathes in again, ready to snap an answer, for he finds he is just as ill-disposed towards being denied as he is to being ignored. However, he pauses, then sniffs.

He sniffs again.

Something is amiss.

He is surrounded by the deep, rich scent of the forest, which smells of both life and death. However, now his nose detects something else: a rancid undercurrent, something that is not merely rot or decay – for these are natural odours – but far worse, far more jarring.

Corruption.

This is something wrong, something twisted. It is something that should not be here: something that should not, in fact, exist at all.

The walker knows what he must do. He must follow his nature.

The hunter steps forward, and starts to run in pursuit of his quarry.

II

He flows over the ground, each step sure and certain and placed to perfection. Walking is second nature and not something about which he has to think, but running awakens something within him. This sense of urgency, this sense of a goal towards which he is striving; it provides focus and clarity, and makes him not only more aware, but also more aware of his own awareness. He realises that he perceives the forest in a new way: not as a homogenous landscape, but as terrain. The ground on which tracks will be left, the plants that will show the signs of a body passing, the thickets where a predator might wait in ambush and those in which lurking would lead only to becoming a meal for the plant itself: these things are as clear to him as words upon a page.

This *is* his home, and nothing can hide from him here.

The scent leads him onwards, as distinct as a wrong note in a symphony, and strengthening as he closes on it. The Watcher is forgotten, as are the king in the boat and the shadows in the water. He is hunting beasts through the trees, just as he used to long ago, back before...

Back before what?

The hunter slows, his focus disrupted for a moment by another flash of something that is not even memory, but perhaps the shadow of one. He does not remember what came before, but he remembers that there was something to remember, which is both welcome and infuriating. All he knows is that he hunted like this in the past.

He shakes himself. Memory will return when it returns, *if* it returns. For now, he still has a quarry to chase down. He presses on, still following the scent of corruption.

The hunter is not certain when the forest begins to change character, for there was never before any way with which to mark the time except by counting his own breaths or heartbeats. However, at some point he becomes aware that the mist is thinning. The light around him has a source now, high up and to his left, and he can feel the heat of this sun upon his scalp; it is a thick heat, a wet heat, the type that reaches into the throat and threatens to clog the airways. The trees are different, as well: they are still tall, still towering, but this is no longer a world of massive, low-hanging branches. Now their crowns splay out far above him, and their trunks are bare apart from the climbing plants that seek to scale their neighbours to snatch a glimpse of light for themselves. The air is alive with the chittering of insects, and the hunter can no longer hear the song of the river. He pauses and reaches down into the ground once more, this time coming up with a fistful of mouldering leaves. They carpet the ground, thick and brown, and do not easily give up the prints of those who have passed over them before; not like soft earth does, the tracker's friend.

The hunter does not know where he is now, any more than he truly knew where he was before, but he knows that this is somewhere else. He is no longer home.

The scent of corruption is still strong, though. Stronger, even. The hunter is drawn forwards, pressing on through this new undergrowth: purplish ferns, pale roots trailing down from above, hanging vines, and plants he does not know with broad, glossy leaves edged with spikes. He does not feel the same connection to this forest, but he is closing on his quarry and he will not lose it once he is this near, no matter his surroundings.

There is movement up ahead. The hunter can hear the faint creaking of stems, as his quarry passes through the brush. He begins to build a picture of what he is following. It is large, certainly, for it cannot avoid making some noise as it moves. It feels like a predator, too; its movements sound like his own, designed not to alert prey to its approach, rather than something going about its own business. He can smell the faint tang of offal and rotting meat, such as might be caught between a hunter's jaws, or smeared across its snout where it has fed on a carcass.

A large, dangerous predator. The hunter removes his helmet from where it is clamped to his belt and, with a strange familiarity of movement despite being unable to remember having ever done it before, lowers it over his head.

The helmet clicks into place, making an airtight seal. Displays power up instantly, and the hunter finds himself looking at read-outs detailing his armour's power reserves, the external temperature, humidity levels and atmospheric composition, and even the day length of the world he is on – eighteen point five-four hours – as estimated from the infinitesimal movement of the local star in the sky above him. Without knowing how he knows what to do, he blinks through the vision options available to him: standard, polarised, infra-red, thermal-imaging, and on and on.

He settles on the standard vision. Everything has its place, but he will have no need of enhancements for this. He sets the air intakes to open, allowing himself to still experience the scents of this world, and moves back into the hunt. Even clad in his armour, thick though it is, he has no problem moving stealthily. The suit responds intuitively to him, as though it is a second skin. He does not pause to ponder this. It feels as natural as breathing.

He inhales, and detects the odour of his prey. There is no wind in this dense understorey, so he has little concern about his own scent giving him away.

He inhales again, double-checking. His armour, feverishly analysing his surroundings, offers up a breakdown of molecular concentrations and pheromone trails which overlays his vision like ghostly fluorescent trails. He is not mistaken.

There is more than one predator, and they have split up, to the left and right as he looks at it.

The hunter scans the ground, but the leaf litter is as obstinate as before and refuses to divulge its secrets. Is he following two predators, or more? Even his senses, sharp though they are, have limits. Still, hesitation is not his way. He follows the trail that leads to his left, balancing speed with stealth. If he slays this corrupted beast, whatever it may turn out to be, he will need to do it quickly enough to then retrace his steps and pick up the scent of its pack mates. He blinks a command and the audio receptors on his helmet increase in sensitivity, ready to warn him if anything chooses to hunt him while he is on the trail of his quarry.

He does not hear clawed feet or muscled bodies converging on him through the undergrowth, but he does detect something else from up ahead: voices. Human voices. Not the eerie sensation of the Watcher in the Dark's communication, where meaning suddenly arrived in his head, but true voices like his own – not quiet, not stealthy, but broadcasting their position to all with ears to hear them. If the hunter is certain of anything, it is that his quarry has both the ears to hear them, and the intention of doing harm.

He breaks into a sprint, all his own stealth forgotten as he smashes through tangling underbrush. He hurdles the giant trunk of a fallen tree just in time to hear a scream, and see a monstrous shape sheathed in scales of iridescent green spring towards a huddle of humans.

The hunter launches himself into a leap, a black-armoured arrow powered by superhuman muscle and sinew. He strikes the beast in the flank with his knee, and feels rib bones the width of his wrist crack from the force of the impact. The beast sprawls onto its side with a roaring scream, its pounce cut short, but the hunter has no time to finish the job before the undergrowth rustles and two more creatures emerge on the far side of the humans.

There are three humans: two adults, and a child. All three are unkempt, dressed in ragged clothes, and the two adults sport growths of facial hair which appear to owe more to lack of grooming opportunity than to cultural significance or personal choice. The child is prepubescent, of an as-yet indeterminable gender, with long straggly hair, and eyes wide and white in a dirty face. The hunter sees this within the space of a moment as he glances past them. The humans are weak, tired, and scared, of little value as allies in this struggle, and as likely to freeze in fear as they are to respond to instruction. He dismisses them, and springs over their heads.

The predators are a different matter altogether. They each stand taller than a human at the shoulder, but the similarities between them taper off at that point. The one the hunter struck down to begin with had a scaled hide, but one of these others has purplish-green fur interspersed with patches of scales, and the third's skin appears to have hardened into chitinous carapace in many places. They all have long jaws lined with sharp teeth, but one has additional tusks that protrude below its chin, and another has large, ridged horns that curl back from above its eyes.

The hunter comes down from his leap with his hands clasped together to form one giant fist, and lands them in a titanic blow directly between those horns.

The predator's head is driven down into the forest floor so fast that the rest of its body does not have time to keep up, and its rump is still standing as the hunter rolls away and turns towards the third creature. This one faces him and opens its mouth, but no roar of rage or aggression emerges. Instead a long, thickly muscled tongue lashes out to cover the space between them, some thirty feet or more, and the tip of it engulfs the hunter's right hand with a hideous sucking noise.

Strength means little without leverage. The hunter does not have time to set his feet before he is hauled off them by the tongue, and wrenched through the air towards the creature who has snared him. He draws back his free fist, determined to turn his headlong flight into an attack, but he is smashed out of the air by a massive, clawed paw a moment before he can strike his blow.

He is pinned face down on the ground, and he automatically shuts his helmet's air intakes to prevent himself from inhaling dust or dirt. Then his concerns become more immediate, as the creature draws his hand into its mouth with its ensnaring tongue and bites down on his arm at the elbow.

The force is tremendous, and could have easily snapped a regular human in two at the waist. The hunter's armour withstands it, although red warning icons flash up into his vision to let him know how close it is to giving way. The beast shakes its head to and fro, trying to achieve through wrenching and tearing what it could not manage through direct force alone, and nearly tears the hunter's shoulder out of its socket in the process. He grits his teeth, waits for half a second to get his timing right, and hauls his arm back out of the beast's jaws in the moment that it starts to shake its head back the other way, and its grip on his limb slackens ever so slightly.

The hunter's arm scrapes free. The predator's teeth leave grooves in the smooth surface of his vambrace, then snap shut as the resistance disappears. In doing so, they sever the creature's own tongue, which still envelops the hunter's fist.

The beast screams in self-inflicted pain, and lifts its paw from the hunter's back to claw at its own mouth, from which dark blood is leaking between its teeth. The hunter springs up, shaking the tongue tip loose. Without the muscle contractions to hold it in place, it is no more than a fleshy cylinder which flops wetly onto the forest floor.

The beast lunges for him, at least two tons of flesh driving behind a fanged maw, which opens to engulf the hunter. This time, however, he has the chance to set himself. He spreads his arms wide and his fingers close for a moment on the tips of its jaws, just as he shifts his weight and twists his torso. His muscles tense, and the servos in his armour spring into action to support them.

The hunter pivots, and uses the beast's own momentum to send it spinning through the air into its horned companion, which is only now rising to its feet after being stunned by the hunter's blow. The two predators collide and collapse into a thrashing, howling pile of limbs and tails.

All of this has taken perhaps ten seconds since the hunter first leaped over the terrified humans. He has been aware of their shrieks and gasps as he struggled with the predators, but only now does he turn back to them. They are still where he left them, their arms full of sticks: not weapons, but firewood they have collected. They are small, and weak, and unable to defend themselves against threats such as this. The hunter supposes that he might easily consider them pathetic. Perhaps he did, once, in whatever existence he had before, if he had dwelled too long on the differences between him and them.

Now, he sees only lives that need his protection. He is strong and they are weak, and therefore he will lend them his strength until they no longer need it.

The animal whose ribs he cracked is struggling back to its feet with the resilience of the wild. The hunter sees the hunger in its eyes. Its desire for flesh to eat is no more malicious than the mutations that have turned its tail into a scorpion's stinger, or the vines that constrict the trees around which they grow so tightly that the tree dies, or the fungi that grow into their victims' brains and kill them by bursting out through their skulls. It is the nature of humanity to see the fate the wild has in store for them, and cheat it. Here and now, the hunter is that cheat.

'Stay out of my way!' he shouts, the first words he has directed at the humans. He does not intend them as hostile – they are supposed to be a warning for the humans to keep their distance from the struggle – but they shrink away from him anyway with a new, sharper fear. He dismisses their reaction. There will be time enough to clarify things when he has dealt with the predators, and his primary purpose is to make them stay clear. He does not, at this point, particularly care what their rationale is for obeying him.

He sprints at the wounded beast, which snarls and lashes out at him with its stinger. The hunter catches it behind the venom bulb with one hand, and rips the weapon off with his other. The predator howls again and wrenches backwards, and blood spurts from the severed trunk to spray across the hunter's faceplate, clogging and obscuring his eye-lenses. He wipes at them, but hard, shiny armour can only smear fluids ineffectually. He can still hear the beasts around him, but hearing alone will not be sufficient to win him this fight.

He drops the stinger and reaches up, pops the neck seal expertly, and removes his helmet. He throws it towards the humans and shouts, 'Clean that!' He does not have time to see whether they scramble to obey his order or shrink from the helmet as though it is a grenade, because the now stingless beast is coming at him again.

He steps slightly to the side, and punches upwards. The uppercut crashes into its lower jaw, and is powerful enough to knock the beast off its feet and flip it over, causing its onrushing mass to miss him and come to a slumped halt in the leaf litter. The hunter pounces on it, seizes its head, and wrenches, pitting his strength against the resistance of its neck muscles and spine. It is a brief struggle: the predator's neck snaps, and when the hunter releases its head it drops limply to the ground.

That leaves two.

He picks up the severed stinger and moves to attack. The other beasts have disentangled themselves, not without a couple of snaps at each other, and spread out to flank him. The one with the severed tongue roars at him, which is its last mistake. The hunter hurls the stinger into its mouth, and the barb pierces the roof of it. The venom bulb discharges automatically, pumping toxins into its bloodstream. The creature stiffens, falls to the ground and begins to thrash, no more immune to its pack mate's venom than their prey would be.

That leaves one.

The final predator charges the hunter, faster than even he is prepared for. It ducks its horned head low and swipes upwards at the last moment, hammering its weapons into his chest. He is lifted off his feet and sent flying gracelessly through the air, the ground and the sky rapidly swapping places as he tumbles. Perhaps he would have recovered his equilibrium sufficiently to land on his feet, or perhaps not, but the sudden intervention of a tree trunk renders it a moot point. He strikes hard enough to splinter the wood, and falls to the ground.

His armour has held, but it will not stand up to many more impacts of such force. He clambers back to his feet, a little short of breath, a little shaken, and with his hearts pounding. This too is a familiar sensation, but familiarity with mortal peril does not bring any guarantee of survival. Lessons can be learned, and adjustments made, but each struggle is contested on its own merits.

The predator has forgotten about the humans. Now it only has eyes for the hunter, this thing that has stepped into its territory and challenged it. Whether it considers him to be a rival seeking to claim its food for himself, or some sort of alpha prey animal which can attack and hurt it, is of little consequence. The outcome will be the same.

Only one of them can live.